"I am concerned with only one thing," says Joyce Carol Oates, *"the moral and social conditions of my generation."* These are spelled out with exquisite compassion and compelling detail in her novels and stories.

●   ●   ●

Miss Oates, born in 1938, teaches English at the University of Windsor in Ontario. In 1970, *THEM* won the National Book Award for fiction; she was awarded a Guggenheim fellowship in 1967. She has also won several O. Henry prizes for her short stories.

Fawcett Books
by Joyce Carol Oates:

THE ASSASINS   23000 $2.25

CROSSING THE BORDER   23751 $2.50

DO WITH ME WHAT YOU WILL   23610 $2.95

EXPENSIVE PEOPLE   23705 $1.95

NEW HEAVEN, NEW EARTH   23662 $2.50

NIGHT-SIDE   24206 $2.50

THE SEDUCTION AND OTHER STORIES   24204 $2.75

SON OF THE MORNING   24073 $2.75

THEM   23944 $2.95

THE TRIUMPH OF THE SPIDER
   MONKEY   23817 $2.25

UPON THE SWEEPING FLOOD   23294 $1.75

WHEEL OF LOVE   C2923 $1.95

WHERE ARE YOU GOING, WHERE
   HAVE YOU BEEN?   30795 $1.75

WITH SHUDDERING FALL   X2930 $1.75

Joyce
Carol
Oates

them

FAWCETT CREST • NEW YORK

them was written partly with the help
of a grant generously given by the
John Simon Guggenheim Memorial Foundation.

THEM

THIS BOOK CONTAINS THE COMPLETE TEXT OF THE
ORIGINAL HARDCOVER EDITION.

Published by Fawcett Crest Books, a unit of CBS Publications, the
Consumer Publishing Division of CBS Inc., by arrangement with
Vanguard Press, Inc.

ISBN: 0-449-23944-6

Chapters 2 and 3 of Book 3 were originally published in different
form as a short story, "Adultery," in *The Critic,* April–May 1968.

Special alternate of the Book of the Month Club, April 1970

Printed in the United States of America

35   34   33   32   31   30   29   28

For my husband, Raymond

. . . because we are poor
Shall we be vicious?
     —*The White Devil*
— JOHN WEBSTER

Author's Note

This is a work of history in fictional form—that is, in personal perspective, which is the only kind of history that exists. In the years 1962–1967 I taught English at the University of Detroit, which is a school run by Jesuits and attended by several thousand students, many of them commuting students. It was during this period that I met the "Maureen Wendall" of this narrative. She had been a student of mine in a night course, and a few years later she wrote to me and we became acquainted. Her various problems and complexities overwhelmed me, and I became aware of her life story, her life as the possibility for a story, perhaps drawn to her by certain similarities between her and me—as she remarks in one of her letters. My initial feeling about her life was, "This must be fiction, this can't all be real!" My more permanent feeling was, "This is the only kind of fiction that is real." And so the novel *them,* which is truly about a specific "them" and not just a literary technique of pointing to us all, is based mainly upon Maureen's numerous recollections. Her remarks, where possible, have been incorporated into the narrative verbatim, and it is to her terrible obsession with her personal history that I owe the voluminous details of this novel. For Maureen, this "confession" had the effect of a kind of psychological therapy, of probably temporary benefit; for me, as a witness, so much material had the effect of temporarily blocking out my own reality, my personal life, and substituting for it the various nightmare adventures of the Wendalls. Their lives pressed upon mine eerily, so that I began to dream about them instead of about myself, dreaming and redreaming their lives. Because their world was so remote from me it entered me with tremendous power, and in a sense the novel wrote itself. Certain episodes, however, have been revised after careful research indicated that their context was confused. Nothing in the novel has been exaggerated in order to increase the possibility of drama—indeed, the various sordid and shocking events of slum life, detailed in other naturalistic works, have been understated here, mainly because of my fear that too much reality would become unbearable.

Since then we have all left Detroit—Maureen is now a housewife in Dearborn, Michigan; I am teaching in another university; and Jules Wendall, that strange young man, is probably still in California. One day he will probably be writing his own version of this novel, to which he will not give the rather disdainful and timorous title *them*.

1

Children
of Silence

1

One warm evening in August 1937 a girl in love stood before a mirror.

Her name was Loretta. It was her reflection in the mirror she loved, and out of this dreamy, pleasing love there arose a sense of excitement that was restless and blind—which way would it move, what would happen? Her name was Loretta; she was pleased with that name too, though Loretta Botsford pleased her less. Her last name dragged down on her, it had no melody. She stood squinting into the plastic-rimmed mirror on her bureau, trying to get the best of the light, seeing inside her rather high-colored, healthy, ordinary prettiness a hint of something daring and dangerous. Looking into the mirror was like looking into the future; everything was there, waiting. It was not just that face she loved. She loved other things. During the week she worked at Ajax Laundry and Dry Cleaners, and she was very lucky to have that job, and during the week the steamy, rushed languor of her work built up in her a sense of excitement. What was going to happen? Today was Saturday.

Her face was rather full, and there was a slight mischievous puffiness about her cheeks that made her look younger than she was—she was sixteen—and her eyes were blue, a mindless, bland blue, not very sharp. Her lips were painted a deep scarlet, exactly the style of the day. Her eyebrows were plucked in exactly the style of the day. Did she not dream over the Sunday supplement features, and did she not linger on her way to work before the Trinity Theater in order to stare at the pictures? She wore a navy-blue dress pulled in tight at the waist. Her waist was surprisingly narrow, her shoulders a little broad, almost masculine; she was a strong girl. Upon her competent shoulders sat this fluttery, dreamy head, blond hair puffed out and falling down in coquettish curls past her ears, past her collar, down onto her back, so that when she ran along the sidewalk it blew out behind her and men stopped to stare at her; never did she bother to glance back at these men—they were like men in

9

movies who do not appear in the foreground but only focus interest, show which way interest should be directed. She was in love with the thought of this. Behind her good clear skin was a universe of skin, all of it healthy. She loved this, she was in love with the fact of girls like her having come into existence, though she could not have expressed her feelings exactly. She said to her friend Rita, "Sometimes I feel so happy over nothing I must be crazy." Dragging around in the morning, trying to get her father up and trying to get her brother Brock fed and out before somebody started a fight, still she felt a peculiar sense of joy, of prickly excitement, that nothing could beat down. What was going to happen? "Oh, you're not crazy," Rita said thoughtfully, "you just haven't been through it yet."

She combed her hair with a heavy pink brush. It worried her to see her curls so listless—that was because of the heat. From the apartment across the way, through the open window, she could hear a radio playing music that meant Saturday night, and her heart began to pound with anticipation of the long hours ahead during which anything might happen. Her father, who had been out of work for almost ten years and who couldn't do a thing, liked to lie in bed and drink and smoke, not caring that so many hours rushed by he'd never be able to get back—but Loretta felt that time was passing too quickly. It made her nervous. She scratched at her bare arm with the brush in a gentle, unconscious, caressing gesture, and felt the dreaminess of the late summer afternoon rise in her. In the kitchen someone sat down heavily, as if answering her, in response to her wondering.

"Hey, Loretta!" Brock called.

"Yeah, I'm coming." Her voice came out harsh and sounded of the dry cleaners and the street, but it was not her true voice; her true voice was husky and feminine.

She went out to get supper for Brock. The kitchen was narrow, and he had to sit right in her way, so that she made a face and said, "Excuse *me*," ironically, squeezing past. Brock was dressed for Saturday night too. He wore a blue suit and a yellow necktie. He had just turned twenty a few weeks before, which seemed to Loretta very old, and on his face a permanent expression of nervous cunning had settled. Like Loretta, he had blond hair, but it had darkened; it was dishwater blond, and he didn't wash it more than once a month—it was stiff with grease. He had a strong, angular face with prominent cheekbones. This had been their mother's face. Since their mother's death some years before, Loretta had begun to notice her in Brock's face. And in his sudden, impulsive bursts of rage—he was always after the *old man* and certain neighbors—she could see her mother's restless spitefulness; it was frightening.

"Jesus Christ, is that perfume? That stuff that stinks?" Brock said.

"Go to hell. You're not funny."

She took a bowl of potatoes out of the icebox and put them into a frying pan; she had peeled them earlier. The grease sizzled and spat up at her. Brock, sitting so importantly at the table, right at the end so that she had trouble getting back and forth, was like the malicious spitting of grease: she had only to glance at his amused eyes to see how hateful he was.

"Look, what the hell is eating you?" Loretta said.

"Is the old man in yet?"

"You know he isn't. He went out this morning with that Cole to look at some vacant lot. Oh, I know it's crazy—don't look at me. It isn't my fault."

"What vacant lot? He's going to *buy* a vacant lot?"

"He isn't going to buy anything."

"With what? Where's the money? What's he going to buy it with?"

"Forget it. He isn't hurting anyone. What difference does it make?"

"He's sick. He should be carted away."

"Carted away where?"

"He should be locked up."

Brock leaned forward on his elbows and spoke in his rapid, vague, somehow uninterested voice, and yet there was a peculiar nervous malice behind it. Loretta really disliked him. He was her brother, and in the years of their childhood he had done well by her—he'd fought with kids who teased her, following the rule of the street, but that was maybe for his own honor, and at one time no one could tell that Brock Botsford, the lanky, stooping kid with the blue-eyed stare, would grow apart from the other boys into this strange, mock-serious man. But now he frightened her; she didn't want her girl friends to talk to him because surely they'd walk off and say, "Isn't he *queer?*" in that marveling, quiet way girls do, summing up a lifetime with unfailing skill.

"Oh, you talk too much. Go get a job yourself, get a

good job, if you think you're better than he is," Loretta said nastily.

She sat at the other end of the table. Brock's arm lay almost across the whole table, and with his restless fingers he could have taken hold of her own arm and squeezed it. She stared at his hand. He worked in a factory now. It wasn't clear to Loretta what the factory made. It didn't make cars like factories in Detroit and Flint; instead it made parts . . . parts of cars? parts of trains? Brock worked in what was called the machine shop, and his hands were always dirty, the nails always ridged with grease, and beneath the grime his skin was dead white the way their mother's had been. For such flabby, calculating skin Loretta had no love, only pity; it worried her because it seemed to her *not right*. Brock went from job to job, along with two or three of his old school friends who were dumber than he though just as loud, and they liked to stand with their hands in their jacket pockets and snicker at Brock's wild jokes and glance at Loretta to see if she caught on. She thought they were all hopeless bastards. The world was pulling into two parts, those who were hopeless bastards and weren't worth spitting on and those who were going to get somewhere. There were boys like her cousin Frank Benyas who had been in Children's Court five times, no less, and who'd made their mothers' lives miserable, and yet there was a certain honest seriousness about them that meant they would do well. Frank was now a printer's apprentice and he would do all right. There were other boys, like Joe Krajenke and Floyd Sloan and Bernie Malin, who had all been in trouble, even in jail, but their eyes didn't glint with the pointless, uneasy malice of Brock's—especially Bernie Malin, whom Loretta liked and whom she thought about often, for long, dreamy minutes. Bernie was all right. He lost his temper and knocked people around and then the next day he was sorry, and he had a job, and whatever it was that kept people from falling through the bottom of the world the way her brother had fallen, Bernie had it, it was a mystery.

"You are such an aggravating bastard, sometimes you make me sick," Loretta said. She spoke fast and hard, the way a sister speaks to a brother, hiding nothing. In his presence she sat with her shoulders slouched and her arms resting on her stomach, which slumped out a little when she was careless. "That whole business last night was stupid. Why are you always picking on him? Then you don't even bother to hide that stupid gun of yours. What's wrong with you? Are you trying to give him a stroke or something?"

Brock laughed. "That'd be the day!"

"A heart attack or something?"

"Why not, after what he did to Ma?"

"Oh, he didn't do anything to her. What the hell! It wasn't his fault he got fired. Everybody got fired. She was crazy to blame him for that, she always had to blame somebody, that was the way she saw things—"

"Look, don't call her crazy."

"Well, look," Loretta said, drawing her lips into an exaggerated smile, "I'm not defending either one of them because I'm fed up with this whole business. I'm fed up with home. So he's afraid to work; well, so is Rita's father—he never went back either. They're afraid of breaking things or fainting or puking on the job, I don't know. It's crazy all right, but I don't blame them. Why do you always want to blame people for things they can't help? Ma believed in God, but you, you don't, so why do you always want to blame people?"

"What's that got to do with it?"

"I just don't give a damn about it. I don't look back on it, that's all."

"Well, I do."

"What are you going to do with that gun?"

Brock tapped at his forehead with his fingers and pretended to think. "I'm going to kill somebody with it," he said seriously.

Loretta said "Tsk," to show her disgust, and stood up to stir the potatoes. She showered them with pepper. Let him burn his mouth out, the miserable bastard . . . She glanced over at him and saw how bent his shoulders were, even inside the new suit. Twenty years old! It had taken him two weeks' pay to buy that suit, and as soon as he'd bought it he'd turned sneering about it, ashamed of it; she had no idea why. That was Brock. Wanting something for a year, wanting something all his life, as soon as he got it it would turn to garbage in his hands and he'd be left sneering down at it, puzzled. She felt sorry for him. She said, "Are you keeping it for somebody, is that it?"

"Who wants to know?"

"You're keeping it for Harry Honigan." Harry Honigan was a neighborhood character who had gone on to better things, so he said, and had an apartment farther uptown and a good car; unfortunately he had been sentenced to ten years in prison just the other day. Brock had always hung around him like a puppy. When Honigan was in trouble he drifted back to the neighborhood, where his mother took him in and fed him well and wept over him, and his grandmother and aunts crowded around him, protecting him, and at such times Brock might get to see him. When things were good no one heard of Harry for months. "It's got something to do with Harry," Loretta said.

"Aren't you smart."

"Are you keeping the gun for him? When does he think he's getting out?"

"No, it has nothing to do with Honigan. He's finished."

"Oh, he'll get out again, won't he?"

"He's finished."

Loretta stirred some hash in with the potatoes. She stirred it slowly round and round, thinking of Harry Honigan, who was finished. "Well, that's too bad," she said.

"Might be that I feel like killing somebody," Brock said slyly, as if she'd forgotten what they were talking about.

"Sure."

Brock had gone through spurts in his childhood, through "phases," as their mother kept saying. For a while he had been thought simple-minded because he was slow to hit other kids back and slow to respond at school. And he'd been very small for his age. Then, in fifth grade at the nuns' school, he had begun to grow and get smarter, and then he had the reputation of being a little crazy. It was Brock who crawled on the school roof one day, just for fun, and across the railroad tracks that went over the canal, and it was Brock who ran yodeling and flailing his arms when a policeman was after all the boys. Brock had done it to make fun of his own terror, to make fun of running itself—that was the kind of strange thing about him that people didn't understand. When a drunken cop had beaten him up one night, mistaking him for somebody else, Brock had lain in an alley, bleeding, and when somebody found him his first remark had been, "I landed without my parachute!" So he was peculiar. He wasn't crazy exactly. You couldn't decide what was what and forget him, though of course he was a hopeless bastard in general and would never accomplish anything, he was too wild; but there was no joy in his wildness, she saw that. From the time he was thirteen until his eighteenth birthday he'd been secretive and edgy, miserable to

have around the house; like his mother, he could go for
weeks without smiling. Now that he was twenty, now that he
was out on his own and had a little money, he was more
gentlemanly to Loretta in an ironic, overdone way. She
couldn't figure him out. She couldn't take him seriously.

While he ate, she scraped the frying pan noisily and ran
water in the sink. Their father hadn't come home all day;
no supper for him. She'd have to put supper in the oven. She
stood on her toes and tried to look out the window, but all
she could see was a fire escape on the building across the
way. A German family lived there, four mean kids and a
mean old man and a woman who spoke only German. They
had to be taken seriously. Downstairs in this building was an
old, soiled woman whose name Loretta did not know. She
saw her all the time. And down the way, out on the street,
people were already beginning to drift into the city heat,
not really minding the heat but oddly pleased with it, its
fluidity, as if they were creatures in a sea who were all kin,
bound by the same element, which touches them on every
pore and draws them helplessly together.

"Where are you going tonight?" Brock said suddenly.

"Out."

"With who?"

"Who wants to know?"

"I do. I want to know."

Loretta folded her arms. She felt like a heroine in a movie,
confronted by a jealous husband in a kitchen while outside
the camera is aching to draw back and show a wonderland
of adventures waiting for her—long, frantic rides on trains,
landscapes of wounded soldiers, a lovely white desert across
which a camel caravan draped voluptuously in veils moves
slowly with a kind of mincing melancholy, the steamy jungles
of India opening before British officers in white, young officers, the mysteries of English drawing-rooms cracking before
the quick, humorless smirk of a wise young woman from
America. . . .

Brock was staring at her. She watched as his jaws ground
the food she'd made for him, and she had the idea that he
wasn't tasting it. That was Brock's problem—he never tasted
anything.

"If it's any of your business," she said, "I'm going to see
Sissy."

"Sissy?" Brock said. Sissy was an old friend of Loretta's
who was not pretty like Loretta, whose waist was thick, who

went about in embroidered blouses her grandmother made—
a half-blind old woman who never left her room—and who
therefore had an outdated European peasant look, a blunt,
innocent look, very dull. Sissy herself was a nice girl. About
her Brock could never say anything bad, his mind simply
stopped. So he stared at Loretta.

"We're going to cut out patterns for a dress. She's going
to help me," Loretta said.

"You're lying."

"I am not lying!"

Brock lifted the food to his mouth with the natural fas-
tidiousness of someone who dislikes eating. He grinned at
her suddenly. "You know, I been hearing some things about
you, sweetheart."

"What things?"

"You know."

"I don't give a damn. It's all lies."

"Bernie Malin, is that a lie?"

Loretta felt her face get hot. "What about him? Did you
talk to him?"

"I wouldn't talk with a punk like that! What is he, sixteen
years old? A punk like that? Somebody said you and him
were fooling around not too long ago."

"Let them talk."

"Don't you go bringing him up here."

"I don't bring anybody up here, not to this dump."

"Well, don't."

"Maybe I already have—what then? Maybe I already did
bring him!"

"Did you?"

"What business is it of yours? I live here, I come and go
by myself, on my own, I work and make my own money. I
don't have to take any shit from you. If you don't like it
you can move out! A twenty-year-old punk yourself! Why
don't you move out anyway?"

"So Bernie can move in?"

"Oh, the hell with that!" Loretta was flushed and beneath
her anger, rather pleased. "Bernie's all right," she said. "I
like him. But he's nothing special. I told you I was just going
to see Sissy. I don't fool around with kids like him and get a
bad reputation. When I get married it won't be to any kid
like that."

Brock had finished eating. He pushed his plate away, in
the manner of his father and other men they knew; there

was something about the gesture that both irritated Loretta and made her want to laugh. They were so predictable!

"Seems to me you're pretty interested in my business," Loretta said. "Don't you have any business of your own to worry about?"

"No."

"Why don't you take some girl out yourself? Why don't you spend a little money? All you do is play pinball and stand around with those ass-hole friends of yours that even you can see are dopes. What's wrong with you anyway?"

"I am a mystery to myself," Brock said, smiling coldly.

"Oh, if you're going to talk crazy!"

She took his plate from him and put it in the sink. Stacked in the sink were a half-dozen dishes, some of them still crusted with food; silverware lay in a heap. One of the forks was caught under a plate and made the whole pile uneven. The very slowness of Loretta's movements, the very fact of the cramped little kitchen built up a pressure in her, in her bones. She was uneasy. She did not really mind. She did not even mind Brock's stupid teasing, which she was used to anyway and which never came to anything. All her life she had been teased. Children were teased, especially girls; it was inescapable. Before her father had gotten bad he had teased her and made her cry, without meaning to, and she remembered her grandfather, too, bothering her, pulling her hair, a mean-smelling old man with uneven whiskers who fought with her grandmother, shouting and shrieking in another language. That past was connected with another city, a slummy two-family house across from a coal yard where all the kids played, and with a different kind of work—optimistic work, like the kind her grandfather had had. He had made thousands of dollars in a single month with his construction crew and then lost it all in a way Loretta could never figure out and didn't care much about—because to her and to the other women in the family it was lost and that was that—an incontestable and somehow respectable fact! That old man had teased her lovingly, and she'd had enough sense to know that he loved her, so when he died she had not pulled away like Brock from the bed where he had been pleading for them—she'd been right there. And her own father had teased her in that curious way, showing love, while her mother had scraped pans angrily and dropped things in the sink to let them break, showing what *she* thought of fooling around and of love when there was so much work to be done, always. Then the whole family had picked up and moved themselves to this city in a hired truck, and in the very room next to this kitchen Loretta's mother had died five years ago. Now the old man slept there alone. Had it ever really been a death-room? Nobody could tell, nobody could really remember except Brock. He liked to say, "The old man killed her," and Loretta was sure to shout back, "Like hell he did! *She's* the one who killed *him*," as if it were important to get things straight, to get at the truth. What was the truth?

Lying around the house were old snapshots of her father: a dark-haired man with a smiling, quizzical look. The man who stumbled around this miserable apartment and was sick in the bathroom and in bed and who whined for Loretta all the time (what had he done with that money he'd saved, for example?), was not the same man, sorry to say. Two different men, two different times. Once he had worked with a construction crew, building houses, dozens and dozens of houses, tacking up siding and building garages with yellow trim, and he had had his own car, and when things had started caving in, all the relatives had told him enviously, "Well, people will always need houses to live in!"—which turned out not to be true. Houses were not built, half-built houses stayed half built, until kids pillaged them or the weather itself beat them down. It was 1930. It was 1931. Loretta's father went to work as a night watchman but he lost that job in a few months to someone's brother-in-law— "Likely story," his wife said—and after that he worked wherever he could get a job, even selling papers. Loretta remembered all those years. And then, when younger people began getting jobs again, back from government projects and optimistic from the government checks that became as regular and permanent as the cycle of the seasons itself, her father had gone back to building. But the times weren't quite right yet and so he waited a few years, and the times never got quite right for him. He was terrified and couldn't make sense of his terror, so he had started drinking. The young men who had jobs didn't keep them either, because the times backed up and shook people off, but Loretta's father kept drinking and finally he was a kind of aged youngish man of the type Loretta often saw on Sunday mornings, sleeping in the doorways of churches or closed shops. That was that. A change, a different man. A new man. When he got a job with a warehouse, unloading trucks, he'd come back home at noon on the first day, explaining that he had dropped a carton of glassware and then admitting that he hadn't dropped anything because he had been afraid to try, afraid of dropping it and getting into debt for it. And so he kept on until the present, coming and going and not really getting in Loretta's way unless he was sick to his stomach or made a mess of some kind.

"Well, don't you get in any trouble tonight," Brock said.

"Don't *you.*"

She followed him into his room, the "parlor," because there was something not finished yet between them. She didn't know what. In her blue dress, with her hair shining and wavy, she felt that she had a right to get things clear with him. Brock took a comb out of his pocket and flicked it through his hair quickly, returning it to his pocket in almost the same gesture. His hair, long unwashed, was never mussed and kept the same shape for weeks. He put some kind of hair lotion on it that made Loretta think of bicycle wheels, the grease that gets on your fingers from them. Impulsively she touched his coat pocket. She felt the weight of the gun inside.

"So you've still got that gun!"

Brock pushed her away.

"Really, what's going on?" Loretta said.

"Nothing."

"Where did you get it?"

"Nowhere."

"But what are you going to do?" She stared at him. For the first time she wondered if he was serious.

"I don't know yet."

The cheekbones of his pale, lean face looked particularly sharp; it was as if the bones of his face were thinking for him.

"You're going to get in some trouble," Loretta said. She spoke in the fatal, final, partly satisfied singsong her mother and other women in the family had used, as if they'd already come to the end of all the worst possibilities and were waiting there for the men to catch up.

"No, I'm not. I don't know what I'm going to do," Brock said. He took out the gun and held it in the palm of his hand. It was an ordinary pistol, a revolver. Loretta had seen pistols like it many times; people were always pulling out guns like this to show off.

"If you give it to me I'll hide it for you," Loretta said.

He pulled away.

"What if Pa finds it and shoots himself? You know how he gets."

"He won't find it."

"What if you get in a fight with Pa? Look, this isn't funny —why are you grinning like that?"

"I'm not grinning."

"You're grinning like a stupid bastard!"

"I am not—I'm not," Brock said viciously. But the corners of his mouth still jerked up rigidly; the muscles of his face were in two tight bunches on each cheek. He was very pale.

"Are you going to wait for Pa and start a fight with him, is that it?" Loretta said.

"No. I'm going out."

"When he comes in drunk are you going to start a fight? What for?"

"I don't start those fights, he does."

"Is that what you're up to?"

"I got better things to do."

"He won't be home all night," Loretta said. "He'll be back in the morning, a mess. Look, you're not going to hurt him, are you?"

"I said no."

"Why are you acting so crazy then?"

He laughed and put the gun back in his pocket. He was ready to leave.

"Well, go on, go out! Get out of here!" Loretta cried.

When he left she wandered back to her room to check her appearance. Perspiration had gathered in little beads on her forehead—she hated that. She dabbed them off with a handkerchief. Thinking about Brock got no one anywhere, she knew that; he'd been in and out of Children's Court years ago and he'd been picked up and kept overnight in jail many times; it had no effect on him either to make him wiser or shrewder, and other people's thinking about him had no effect either. What he liked best was to sit and read newspapers and let the papers fall to the floor when he was finished with them. But he never talked about what he read, never said anything. He had secrets. With his stupid friends he could bellow and snicker like any idiot of twenty, but that was a disguise too, they didn't know him and nobody knew him, and consequently nobody exactly trusted him. Loretta pushed him out of her mind and leaned closer to the mirror, so close that her breath made a fine film on it, and the image that stared back at her with watchful, expectant eyes was the only subject of interest to her soul.

Was her face beautiful?

It was getting late. She began to hurry. All the wonders of the street crowded to her mind, which was already a little wild from the nonsense with her brother, and she caressed her freckled arm slowly, fondly, not thinking. She simply stood in the dim little bedroom as if she were taking a confused, final leave of it, not thinking. She was Loretta. It did not make her envious that other girls like herself popped up everywhere, healthy and ready for a laugh, ready for a good time after a week of work; she liked the fact that there were so many Lorettas, that she'd seen two girls in one week with a sailor outfit like her own, and a hundred girls with curly hair flung back over their shoulders! Her girl friend Sissy was the only girl who wore those heavy embroidered blouses, beautiful blouses with scarlet and green and yellow threads woven silkily into designs of peacocks and windmills, and Sissy would never meet herself coming and going, but Loretta was not Sissy, Loretta was Loretta. She put some more lipstick on and went out.

Walking down the street, she felt her very heels buoyed by the tense gaiety of Saturday night. Everyone was out! She half expected to see Brock skulking about at the corner, where he and his friends sometimes stood, and she wouldn't have been surprised to see her father sitting on someone's front stoop with his arms hanging down between his thin knees, given up, a wreck, asleep with his eyes open. She didn't see them but she saw everyone else. The calves of her legs took strength from the hard, hot flatness of the sidewalk, everyone's sidewalk, and she smiled and shot greetings out to people airing themselves after supper—she knew everyone and everyone knew her. It wasn't such a bad neighborhood. Her mother had hated it, but the neighborhood wasn't bad; people just liked to walk around a little and relax after a long week, and sometimes they got into trouble, but it didn't last. There was nothing wrong with that.

From Monday until Saturday noon Loretta's back and shoulders and arms ached from her work, and her hair had to be pulled back in a miserable frazzled knot, and she knew she was nothing much to look at, but on Saturday night everything was changed. The men took off their dirty workclothes and put on suits stiff and new like Brock's,

shined their shoes, manipulated their hair into place; the unmarried girls did over their faces with tweezers and eyebrow
pencils and rouge and anything else on hand, and put ribbons
in their hair in imitation of a movie star or let their hair
slide over one eye in imitation of another movie star—and
all this was marvelous, all this was wonderful! Loretta believed that the very universe opened up on Saturday night,
that the tight little secretive cells burst into lovely buds. Who
would want to be a wet blanket? What kind of idiots (girls
from Loretta's parish school, which she had quit last spring)
would go around at this time trying to sell salve in transparent blue jars with religious pictures thrown in free, or
trying to sell tickets for a church raffle?

This was a fair-sized city on a Midwestern canal, and it
had grown up jaggedly around the canal, spreading out in
two irregular half-moons, with bumps and hollows of still
vacant land and other stretches of crowded and devastated
tenement areas. The main business was a "little steel" plant
that employed men in a quarter of the city's families, and
factories of other types and railroad yards and big warehouses were within range of Loretta's eyes, had she cared to
climb to the top of her building and stare out over the warm
haze of that evening. The air was hazy, yes, but melodic
also, and rich with mysterious odors—a giant bakery down
the street gave off a continuous smell of ferment that slightly
tainted every one's taste, but still there were odors of
flowers that were invisible and rich home-baking from open
street-level windows and, by the Dwight Corner Tavern, a
pleasant stale smell of beer and roast beef. Even across the
street and down by the first of the bridges there was a carnival sense of abandon in the air, slightly stirred by the colorless waters beneath and the steady harsh falling of water
from the locks. Had Loretta more time, or had there been
fewer men hanging around, she would certainly have leaned
dreamily on the bridge railing to watch the water pour
through the locks—she'd done this hundreds of times—for
everyone was eager, in the monotonous, fascinated way of
people who live in cities built around canals, to see what
kind of boat was coming through and whether anyone would
dare toss a bottle or a piece of junk down onto it. But she
passed across the curving bridge with hardly a glance down
at the troubled waters far below—this bridge was very high
above the canal, dizzingly high—and she passed by the
playground of the Catholic school she had gone to for years,

marked off with high wire fences on which the kids had climbed all the time, and she passed the school itself, toward which she hardly glanced—really, Loretta no longer saw it—and on past the small group of men hanging around the firehouse in their shirt sleeves, some of them friends of her father's, and she paused to talk with them, laughing shyly and lowering her glance, stepping back in the brief pause of a conversation to let them know she had somewhere to go, she didn't really have time to spend with *them*. Loretta Botsford, and how she was growing up! In their eyes she was nearly grown up, which was a matter of lipstick and a certain self-conscious swing of her shoulders and hips, exactly in the style of the day—they acknowledged her, they let her go.

Sissy's mother had a flat just above a drugstore on Main Street, which was no better than where Loretta herself lived. It was about five minutes away. So she had five minutes of a kind of wild, open freedom during which anything might happen. On the street men were driving by and might have been glancing at her, but she didn't look at them, and anyway most of them would be with girls at this time on Saturday night; she looked ahead at the front of the clinic, to which she and Brock had taken their father ten or twelve times at least—a nightmare, that place, with small cubicles whose walls didn't even reach to the ceiling, and tired ugly nurses, and doctors her friend Rita called crooks since the time one of her babies had died of an ear infection. They were butchers, bastards, crooks. All of them had money; such people had money because each patient was two dollars, and two dollars a head added up. It made you dizzy to think of all that money. And dentists were just as bad, or maybe they were worse. She never thought about her teeth, which were bad; she didn't dare let herself think about those dull, relentless aches that paralyzed her some nights, going right to the bottom of her jaw, and her gums sometimes bled when she brushed her teeth—no, better not think of that, better forget it. She sucked ice when the pain got bad. When it got too bad she had the tooth yanked and paid three or four dollars and that was that.

A streetcar clambered by, heavy with grillwork, and Loretta carefully did not look up to see who might be watching her—this gloomy thunder took the hill ahead of her and drew her up slowly behind it, Loretta now beginning to wonder if maybe her five minutes were running out without anyone knowing about it or caring. Buildings of gray-green, buildings with store fronts soaped and abandoned, and above them in a raucous confusion of radios people leaning out windows on their elbows, the expanse of their arms like the white expanse of curtains on either side of them, framing them. Someone called "Loretta!" It was a girl from school. Loretta waved but hurried on past.

When they'd first moved to this city—her father piling up all their junk in the back of a truck and driving the truck himself, coming to the city with a slow, dreary crowd of other country people (but people from farms, not "business" people like themselves), all of them making the rounds of apartment buildings, asking timidly for rooms, for help, for directions to the nearest government buildings—she had first thought the city was terrifying. Now she loved it. When they had moved here she had been a child, and in that world of childhood each day had been a skirmish. Sometimes she had done well, sometimes she had failed, sometimes it had been pretty bad and she'd run with a bleeding face through alleys, prowling with horror amid the debris of vacant lots she could not recognize. af aid of angry mothers as well as strange kids—that hadn't been so nice, better to forget it. Brock, so dreamy and slow for years, had been bloodied up more than once and called a *hillbilly*, which he wasn't, when all he had to do was open his mouth to let them hear that he hadn't a Kentucky accent—and Loretta, a curly-haired little girl with confused impulses of tenderness and viciousness, had made her way painfully by courting the important kids in her class, knowing by instinct which girls were important, which girls had older brothers to protect them and were therefore valuable. But all that was past and indeed she rarely thought about it. She rose up out of childhood, and the terrors of its valleys and mountains sank to a monotonous landscape beneath her eyes, forgiving or indifferent or both, and though she knew the very same kids now who had tormented her as a child she did not really recognize them as those kids, and they did not recognize her, as each year drew them farther into adulthood.

On her way to Sissy's she ran into Bernie Malin, who was with some friends of his, and in that slow clumsy ballet of boys they edged away while he came to walk with her, smoking a cigarette and talking eagerly. "What do you mean," he said, "going to make a dress! Sew a dress! Spend all that time sewing a dress? Don't tell me nobody sewed that one you're wearing, that's a real *store*-bought dress, that's got style!"

"Oh, what do you know?"

He was in front of her, blocking her way, and so she had to stop, and behind them at the corner his friends stood around, probably watching—she was upset when she should have been pleased, and she didn't understand this, but Bernie was the cause of it all and so she said coldly to him, "Sissy and I made this date last week." The word "date" was a strange word to use to him.

Bernie shrugged his shoulders and grinned at her. He was a smallish, slender boy, hardly taller than Loretta, but rather handsome in a doll-like way. Mechanical too were his mannerisms, which were centered mainly on his cigarette— bringing it to his pursed lips, taking it thoughtfully away —and Loretta felt a little dazed by this, unprepared, wondering what there was about him that so upset her.

She said, "Why don't you go fool around with your boy friends," and he said, "Those dopes don't exist for me." The very expulsion of his breath excited her.

They walked up the hill side by side. This was the better part of downtown, a single, long block of stores. Bernie's arm occasionally brushed against hers but neither seemed to notice it. He asked her about Brock. He asked her about certain friends of hers, boys they knew in common. He asked her about her father. *His* father had once worked with her father, and that connection seemed important to them both.

They wandered over toward the canal, and at a break in the line of buildings they stood and leaned against the railing. It was getting dark. Down by the locks there was a building in which certain lock officials worked. Bernie said that he'd once sneaked down there, past the No Trespassing signs, and looked in the windows of their little building. Loretta said sarcastically that that must have taken some courage. Bernie asked her how she'd like to go swimming in the canal, right with all her clothes on. Loretta asked if he thought he could do that all by himself. Bernie said that a friend of his brother's was having some people over to his house for a party, and it would be nice if she could come. Loretta remembered and forgot Sissy in the same instant, frowning down at the lights bobbing on the water. Her attention was focused on finding out who this friend was. They explored their mutual acquaintances and the relationships among them, trying to find a link, some way of breaking through. He knew her brother and was a little afraid of him. She knew his brother and was a little afraid of him. Bernie leaned against the railing, as if it were a familiar place for him, facing her, and the way he laughed with his mouth hardly showing a smile and the way he brought his eyes up to hers in a certain harsh movement made her give in. Loretta lived in an eternity of flesh: all week she knew the resistance of muscle, she knew its sad limits, and left to herself she explored her toenails as earnestly as her face, summing everything up, judging and hoping. Her arms, her legs, her stomach and hips, the dipping line of her spine, the rather thick set of her ankles—it was all she had, she trusted it; like a sack of flesh filled with precious organs and eager blood she leaned a little toward Bernie, waiting.

"Look, please, will you come with me?" he said.

"Why should I?"

"Don't you want to?"

"You could have asked me before tonight."

He shook his head mysteriously.

"You know my name all right," Loretta said. "You know where I live."

"I was working till after six tonight."

"Working where?"

"Unloading stuff."

"Where?"

"With my father."

He was boyish and sweetly nervous, leaning toward her. She began to smile. Between them there rose a heady excitement that was punctuated by honking horns in the Saturday-night parade of restless cars. He seemed to her prematurely wise, this boy small in his bones and small in the handsome, cocky slant of his eyes, and he put her in mind—she didn't know why—of the feature-paper heroes of only the other day, Baby Face Nelson and Dillinger, who were dead now but still very important. An aunt of one of her friends, come to visit, told them about Dillinger in Chicago and how she had seen with her own eyes the hem of a dress of a friend of a friend, stained with Dillinger's blood from where she'd squatted down to soak it up in an alley—Jesus Christ, someone had said, why would anyone do that? But Loretta understood and wished violently that she had been there too, to kneel in the blood and bring it back home in triumph, because there wasn't much else to remember a man by except something raw and ugly, and that blood had been real enough in him, warm and coursing through his veins until some policeman's bullet let it loose.

"Will you come with me?" Bernie said earnestly, a real seriousness pushing against the movieland style of his voice, and Loretta knew that she had to give in. Everything was mortal. She and Bernie were alike locked in flesh.

She walked with him back across the bridge, the arch of the cobblestone surface prickly beneath her sensitive feet, and the few lights down on the canal painful to her eyes, while Bernie talked on and on about something he and his brother were planning, revenge on a store that had cheated them or hadn't given them jobs, and Loretta had no feeling of alarm as he spoke of setting fire to all the straw and crap in its basement, tossing some gasoline around and getting the hell out, and letting it all go up in a big ten-alarm blaze —that would show those bastards!

She and Bernie went to a house not far from Loretta's own apartment building. Out on the street they could already hear the noise, lots of people yelling, so she let herself be cajoled into the front room where a crowd of people older than she and Bernie were drinking and dancing clumsily to music from a radio. She guessed that it was a safe party at the moment, though she was always a little edgy and alert for danger. The women wore their hair like Loretta's, hanging down past their shoulders, or curled and frizzed up around their faces, and the men were stylish older versions of Bernie. She felt a sudden infatuation for the precocious adulthood in Bernie, which had nothing to do with his having quit school and his running around but everything to do with his shoes and trousers and the knowing smirk with which he caught some guy's wisecrack but did not bother to return it.

He walked with her outside into the back yard and then into an old garage so filled with junk that there would have been no room for a car in it, and the two of them drank beer and pressed close together in the dark. She put her arms around his neck. A swift, keen sensation of helplessness rose in her; she thought of being lifted into the air in a balloon, carried crazily and helplessly up into the sky, and she thought of grabbing onto the last car of a train and being snatched away along the gleaming rails, never to be seen again . . .

Back at the house someone was yelling. She thought she saw a police car pulled up in front. So the two of them got out the back way, climbing over a fence, weak with laughter and very affectionate, quick to fall into each other's arms. Up at her door, in the dingy hallway, she stood with him for half an hour, for forty-five minutes, until finally she said, "You can come in with me if you want to."

Bernie, shaken and not quite himself, drew back from her and said, "You mean it? Do you mean it?"

She said, "If my pa is home he'll be passed out, don't worry, he just falls in bed and that's that, and my brother won't be back till morning. Anyway, nobody comes in my room, it's my room and my business, my own life, nobody dares to come in there!"

He kissed her and wrapped her in his eager arms. She gave herself up to him but thought of one thing: her mother's old dresses in a closet, the arms stiff as if bent permanently into the shape of the arms that had gone inside them.

2

Sick and exhausted, so exhausted that even the ache had gone out of her, she slept . . . and seemed to be stumbling around in rooms she'd never seen before, taking hold of the helpful arms of people, staring into their eyes but finding no center to them, no iris to the eye. But it was not a dream of terror: she felt only exhausted and wet with sweat, overcome. A heavy, leaden warmth lay upon her, like clouds of dusty smoke, stroking her body. Then there was a loud sharp noise. She woke.

She woke at once, already screaming, the scream mangled and inaudible. It was stuck back in her sleep, deep in her mind. She woke at once. Through the door of her room, in the faint light, someone ran and stumbled against a chair in the kitchen—she knew just which chair it was, on that chair were dish towels drying from last night—and so, suddenly, she was awake for good.

In her bed, beside her, was a boy. She knew him but for a moment could not remember his name or why he was here. With the sheet twisted around her she began to draw slowly away from him. A thought came to her as suddenly and as sharply as that cracking noise: *He's dead.* Her mind seemed to pause after this. She stared down at him. Then, slowly, a painful sweat broke upon her, breaking over the stale film of sweat that had been so soothing and so sweet. She was able to think clearly enough, *He's dead, that bastard killed him,* and these words passed through her mind as if they were someone else's words, someone looking in the window. The boy lay very still. The sheet had been yanked partly off him. She wanted to grab hold of him, wake him up. Bernie Malin! Why didn't he wake up? What did he want from her, lying there so heavily, unmoving? Her terror made no impression on him; he seemed to sleep a man's stubborn sleep, oblivious of her. One of his arms lay curled upon his bare chest and the other hung down over the edge of the bed. He had dark silky hair. Loretta got out of bed very quietly. She backed up, staring at him, until she felt the wall against her back, and so she stopped, very still. She stared at the boy to see if he was or was not breathing. Minutes passed. She would try again; she would stare very hard at him to see if he was or was not breathing.

It must have been very early, before dawn. Why hadn't the shot awakened everyone, got them going, running up the stairs, ringing alarms, peering in her window? She felt the wall hard against her back and wondered why it had not collapsed, fallen, to let everyone look in at her? She believed she could already feel the vibrations and thuds of footsteps out in the street, an army of gawkers and accusers, and what wouldn't they think up to yell in her face! *What are you going to do now, you little whore, how are you going to get rid of him?* Minutes passed. She stood crouched and sweating in the dim light, staring at the bed.

Gradually she began to see the blood on him. It was moving. Across the side of his head, shyly turned from her, a stream of blood was moving and soaking into the pillow. That pillow was twisted in two; he must have liked to sleep with a pillow bunched up like that. She did not move. She could smell his blood. Words came to her again, like an incantation, *My brother is to blame, him, that bastard . . .* If she could throw it all in his lap, take all this trouble and toss it like garbage at him, if she could get rid of it somehow, then she would be free—this choking pressure inside her chest and throat, this crazy sensation of terror that she wasn't sure could be her own, it was so strong, she'd be free of it and her brother loaded down with it, they would run up to him and grab him and yell into his face, *his* ugly face, *You murderer! You bastard!*

But nothing happened. She waited, sniffing at the odor of blood and bodies, the odor of damp sheets, her brain reeling and her body very still, waiting, but nothing happened. Was nothing going to happen? Maybe a gunshot in the middle of the night wasn't much of a surprise after all. Maybe no one heard it, no one would raise a shade angrily, no one would jump out onto a fire escape to see what was what. This was not the movies. Nothing followed fast upon anything else; nothing was connected with anything else.

She groped around for something to cover herself with. She could not see very well. Her fingers closed upon something, a cotton dress she wore around the house. Bending, she did not lower her eyes but kept them sharp upon the boy's head, fearful of a change if she looked away. Blood was moving, blossoming on the side of his head. It was not going to stop. She was afraid that a sudden movement of hers would knock something over and disturb that flow of blood, get it going faster, so that it would gush out of his head and onto the floor and soak through the floor onto the ceiling beneath, running warm and sticky over everything. She moved very slowly. What she saw was real enough, but part of her mind kept pushing it away, nudging it aside, it wasn't *hers;* if only she could get hold of Brock and scream for everyone to come see what he had done: just look at this! How she would scream it out for the whole city to hear! How she would run up the street, accusing that bastard! She slipped into the dress and saw that her hands were trembling; she couldn't control them, and yet they somehow obeyed her, sliding buttons through buttonholes as always, going through the same routine as always. A person has to get dressed, she thought wildly. The boy did not look at her getting dressed. She waited again for him to stir, to wake up with an embarrassed little joke and make everything right again . . .

Terrible, how still Bernie lay, how stubborn that lithe little body had become! One shot had done it, like magic. Suddenly Loretta hated him; her hatred burst upon her, and it was enough practically to set her screaming in rage, for men always disappointed you, there was no hope to them, nothing. There was no center to men: their eyes, smiling or serious, had no center to them, nothing. Loretta stood in a hazy, vivid hatred, watching the boy. It was the heaviness of his body she hated too. All his flesh had turned to poison. What had been so hot and sweet earlier that night was now heavy with death, and the fact that death had come so fast and without any struggle showed how little you could trust the body, even the body of a man, arms and legs and chest and belly, all of it useless. She put her knuckles against her mouth and began to whimper as the realization of what had happened came into her mind, and came into it again, fast and fierce as Bernie's love had been, pounding against her. "My God," she said in a whisper, "did it really happen? Did *he* really do it?" Brock had run out and left her, and what was she going to do? What could she do with that body? Where was she going to hide? The gun had gone off right beside her, a few inches away from her head. An explosion in her ear. Her brother must have leaned right over the bed and put the barrel of the gun against Bernie's skull and pulled the trigger, that bastard, and the noise had yanked her right out of sleep and she would never sleep again. Somewhere in Bernie's brain was the bullet that had done everything. So much power packed into a little bit of metal, a power greater than the man behind it, far greater. So it had been fired. So Bernie was dead. Loretta forced herself to look carefully around the room, her room. She had to figure out exactly where she was. This room was a puzzle.

. . . And what if she went crazy? Her mother had gone crazy, screaming her hopeless, mad scream, weeping for hours, for days, lying in her soiled bed, crying that her head was splitting in two. Loretta had seen other crazy people, had seen how fast they changed into being crazy. No one could tell how fast that change might come. That bastard with his gun had made all this happen, set everything going, and none of it could be stopped, not even if Brock himself were to run back up the stairs and stumble back past the door again and lean into her room—that was it, Loretta thought in horror, that was it, what made it so terrible, that it couldn't be stopped, nobody could stop what was happening. She looked around. To get out of this room she had to pass by the end of the bed, right by Bernie's feet. In the dim light he looked as if he might still be sleeping; if she hadn't heard the gunshot maybe she wouldn't have guessed . . . but the blood kept soaking into the pillow, yes, that couldn't be stopped. He was dead now and could not move. How could she move so heavy a body?

She was sixteen years old. She wondered if she would ever live past that age. Time seemed to have stopped. She needed something to help her, something to grab hold of, she didn't know what. An object fell off her bureau, a bottle of fingernail polish; she let it go, forgetting it. Inside the top drawer of the bureau was a tangle of clothes. They were hers. She stared at them and a choked scream rose in her throat, a cry for her father. She actually said "Pa!" out loud, as if the word had come from her by its own strength. She pulled at a bureau drawer, and it made a rasping, protesting sound of wood against wood. This released her; she ran around the end of the bed and out into the kitchen, bumping into a chair and sending it halfway across the room. "Oh, Jesus! Look what he did in there!" she cried. She pushed the door of her father's room open. Though she could see the room was empty she said softly, timidly, "Pa?" The bed was unmade, just as it had been the day before. Her father hadn't come home. For a moment she couldn't remember whether he had been home at all that week or in the hospital again. No, he was home, he was just out somewhere sleeping it off, better for him to be out of this mess anyway. He couldn't take it. It would drive him crazy. For the first time since the shot she felt a sense of satisfaction—better for her father to be free of this mess.

The clock on the icebox said five-thirty. This was Sunday morning. Everyone was sleeping except Loretta and Brock, who was running somewhere down an alley. People asleep nearby would maybe hear the thud of his footsteps outside their windows but nobody could care enough to lean out and shout after him, "Hey, why are you running? What are you running away from?" Police in all-night diners would be drinking coffee and reading newspapers, and if they bothered to glance out to see Brock they wouldn't bother catching him—let him go, who gives a damn about a murderer? Too much trouble to run after him. Out loose like that, Brock had all the world to roam in, but she, Loretta, was stuck in this apartment: the kitchen, which was very still except for the clock ticking, with its bare-topped table and its slightly uneven sink with two gawky faucets and a soap dish in which a thin piece of pink soap remained, and its pile of dishes, dishes nobody would ever wash except Loretta herself!— this trivial fact angered her—and above the sink a small window, not very clean, and on either side, looming up to the ceiling, cupboards without doors, in which plates and glasses were piled in a dreary way, so very familiar, and the window at her right hand—the window Bernie was going to climb out of if there was trouble and someone came home early. He had been going to climb out that window, that had been their plan. It had been thought up in another dimension, one that hadn't come off. And to one side there was that room she would never go in again, never. She would never walk through that doorway again, never go near that blood-soaked bed and that dead boy who had brought her so much evil. On the other side of the kitchen was her father's room, where things lay scattered around on the floor and on the bed, a smelly mess that she wouldn't straighten up be-cause he didn't like anyone touching his private things—his "secret" things, clippings in a cigar box and other papers, old receipts, which no one cared about anyway; his room was narrow as a box, just the same size as hers. The two rooms framed the kitchen between them, and until now Loretta had never thought about this. The space in which she and her father and Brock lived was the space of a few boxes, ruled out and walled in, and all the unconscious living that had gone on in it!—all those years, unconscious! It was strange that it should end like this. Just past the kitchen was Brock's room, really a kind of parlor, where he slept on a daybed and kept his things hidden in a trunk, everything pushed back against the wall, out of sight, so that it never looked as if anyone really lived there: an anonymous room, the way he wanted it. Loretta looked into his room. The door to the hall was partly open—as he had left it in his haste. She went to this door and touched it; it was a surprise to her that the apartment was open like this, anyone could have strolled in, even a kid could have walked in. She did not seem to know what to do. Around the shabby edges of the drawn shade a faint light shone, and this light would get stronger as the day opened and expose everything, but do no harm to Brock's half-vacant room—no one would be coming back to this room, it would never expose or accuse him, it was an innocent room, and even the worn brown carpet on the floor had the innocence of something forgotten.

She ran out of the apartment and down the hall. It was early; no one was awake to help her. The shabby, familiar look of the hall brought back to her all the times she had walked out here without knowing who she was or how dan-gerous her life was. A dead boy lay in her bed, still bleeding. She would have screamed except it was morning and too quiet. No one, nothing, was in the hall; she was alone and breathing very hard. Her eyes were like stone in her face, hard and tight, and on the top step of the stairs her toes twitched to get her out of here. She went down the stairs cautiously. Down one flight, around on the landing past someone's garbage can, down another flight, and then she was in the vestibule. Someone had dropped a penny there, right in the middle of the floor, and her eye seized upon it out of habit, and she picked it up and thought, *That's good luck!* Outside, the morning was hazy. She felt her toes and muscles itch with the desire to run like hell.

She did not run. She turned into a side alley, hurrying. She was barefoot, in her house dress, drenched with sweat; probably wild-eyed and wild-haired. She touched her hair like a blind girl, patting it, smoothing it down. If anyone saw her, what would they guess? Barefoot out on the street like a hillbilly or a nigger! A cruising police car would pull right over to the curb and a policeman—maybe even someone she knew—would grab her wrist and that would be that. There was a dead boy in her room, in her bed. She began to sob, hurrying up the alley. "God, you have got to help me out. This one time," she said. Her strong legs carried her on, and her breath came in strong jags. At the end of the alley she paused, her eyes darting around but settling on nothing. It seemed to her that God would probably help her out. Maybe He would give her some kind of answer. If someone raised a shade in the building nearby, let it shoot up, that would be a sign. Or if a horn blew somewhere. But nothing. Loretta turned and ran down the alley behind her building and came out to a narrow street, a lane. Everywhere there were boxes and piles of junk, a clutter she half knew by heart but had never really looked at until now, but now she was afraid of rats—with her bare feet—and if Bernie's people were out already looking for him, she could maybe hide in that junk somehow. She could hide there until dark. Bernie's brother would be out looking for him, and everyone would tell him about *her,* and so he would show up at her place, looking for *her.* Bernie's brother was no taller than Bernie had been, but dark and swarthy and ugly, mean-faced, kind of crazy, not much interested in girls. He played with knives. He had a gun.

What she had to do, Loretta thought, was get a gun herself. Get a gun first. Then she could figure out what to do next. First she needed a gun, but to get the gun she needed money. Back in her room she had three dollars saved, which was nothing, and anyway she wasn't going back up to that room. She would get a gun, she thought, and then she would be safe. It came to her that girls had their faces slashed for all kinds of small mistakes—she'd seen a woman running

down the street once with the side of her face streaming
blood, all that blood erupting from the slash of a man's
razor; and she already felt the slash like lightning from her
jaw to her temple. And she thought of a girl beaten half to
death, found out in this alley one morning. She thought, *I
have to get a gun,* and every part of her body strained forward at this certainty, focused on it. She could understand
now why her brother had a gun. Everyone needed a gun; it
was crazy not to have one. Now she had to run half-naked
out into the street looking for one. She felt grit under her
feet and looked down just in time to miss stepping on a
chunk of heavy glass, but she didn't slow down. The hazy
warm air was filled with the urgency of getting a gun. She
could almost hear the words . . . *a gun, a gun* . . . in the air
about her. Once she had a gun, then, then she could take
care of herself.

In her yellow-flowered cotton dress she ran past a cigar
store that was closed and dark. She ventured out onto a wide
street—a car was some distance away, no danger—and
started across it, running across the cool cobblestones in her
bare feet, panting like a cow. First she had to get some
money from somewhere and then she had to buy a gun—
she strained her mind on this problem. And it seemed to
her that her entire life had risen up to this moment, like a
road rising ignorantly along a slow incline; all her good in-
tentions and hopes and her pretty face would come to flower
this Sunday morning and save her, or lead her to mutilation
and death. One or the other, no way out.

She was in someone's back yard. Panting, a sharp pain in
her side, she paused to lean against a fence and tried to
think . . . tried to think about a gun, about Bernie and
Brock, Brock's gun . . . about Bernie's brother, whom she
had seen only a few times but about whom she'd heard so
much . . . yes, he was crazy, he was a killer and only needed
someone to kill. Brock had been a killer and had needed
someone to kill, but she hadn't known that. She had understood it too late. He had killed for no reason but because he
had been ready to kill, the time had come. And Bernie's
brother, rested after a few hours' sleep, would gather himself
together and start out after her, grim and satisfied with his
duty. Or maybe he would let her go, he'd only frighten her?
Maybe he would let her go?

She went to Rita Moreines's place. The screen door clattered under her pounding. She opened the screen door and

pounded on the inside door. She was bathed in sweat. She called out, "Rita! Rita, let me in!" Let all the neighbors hear, she didn't give a damn but wanted only to get inside. Her skull seemed to be getting tighter and wilder. What dripped down her face was either tears or sweat, she didn't know which, and she yelled "Rita!" and tore at the door with her fingernails. Just now it came to her, mysteriously, lightly, that this was the second time Bernie had been shot! When he'd been fourteen, an old man had shot him with his rifle. The old man had been hiding in his store after dark, all set to blow out the brains of the kids who kept breaking into his place at night, he hadn't blown Bernie's brains out but only shot him in the shoulder. Bernie had been in the hospital for a while but didn't die, and later everyone kidded him about it. But no one was going to kid him about anything now. He had been a boy of maybe seventeen, wiry and quick, but now his brains were ruined and nothing was left of him, nothing except that body up in Loretta's room.

"My God," Rita said, opening the door. She was fastening a green robe around her. "Loretta, what the hell's wrong?"

Loretta pushed past her and got inside; she closed the door.

Rita said, "Is somebody after you? Is your father out there?"

"No. It's all right," Loretta said. She leaned against the kitchen table, pressing her wet palms flat against the top and leaning forward, her head drooping. She felt very dizzy.

Two of Rita's kids came into the room. "Go back to bed," Rita said. "Get out of here."

Rita sat in a chair at the table and waited for Loretta to get hold of herself. She said in a deliberate, level voice, not showing much surprise, "If it's your old man gone nuts again, you can stay here. Relax. You know, you're running around half naked? Look, kid, you better do something about your old man. There are four or five guys just like him—I mean, that I know personally; they got something not working right in their heads and drinking sets them loose. They all been out of work too long. Is it your father or what?"

Loretta shook her head. "Can I borrow some shoes?" she said.

"Sure. Where are you going?"

"I want . . . I need to . . ." She tried to straighten up. When she brushed hair back from her forehead she was startled to feel how wet her face was. She said, "I need some money. I'm in bad trouble."

"What kind of trouble?"

"In trouble. Awful bad trouble."

Rita was staring at her. Her black hair, dyed, was as mussed and wild as Loretta's, but her expression was very still; she was trying to figure out what Loretta meant. Finally she said, "With the police, honey?"

"No."

"Not your father?"

"No. But my father will be home in a while. Maybe he might be on his way home." Loretta looked around in a daze. "What time is it?"

"Take a look."

The clock was on the icebox, just like her clock at home. It said six. "It's so early, that's why I can't think right," Loretta said. "My father isn't home yet but he might come home . . . or maybe he won't, I don't know. Sometimes they bring him or somebody calls the cops. They found him lying outside the Ticonderoga Bar that time. It was awful cold and he might have frozen to death. But I don't know when he's coming home."

"Why is it so important when he comes home? What happened?"

Loretta waved her off. "Can I borrow some shoes? A dress?"

"Where are you going?"

"Maybe out of town. But first I have to see somebody."

"Who?"

"I can't tell you."

"What do you mean, you can't tell me? Why not?"

"Well, I need some money for a gun."

"A gun?"

"I'm in trouble, I need a gun," Loretta said.

"You better stay away from a gun if you're in trouble or not."

Loretta wiped her face again. Rita was lighting a cigarette. She seemed to be staring around the room, leaving Loretta to herself. This kitchen was cluttered and dirty; a pile of old newspapers lay on one of the chairs. That pile had been there for weeks. Loretta could see a comic-strip page on the top of the pile, and in spite of the hazy, dazzling air about her she read through "Gasoline Alley" and part of "Dick

Tracy," wondering if she'd read them before; she probably had, they seemed familiar.

She made herself look up at Rita again. "So can I borrow some clothes?" she said.

"Sure," Rita said.

There was so much maternal heaviness in her, so much strictness and half-begrudged affection, that Loretta was pained to think of how much less a mother her own mother had been, less suited for dealing with the surprises of life. Rita was in her mid-twenties but already she had two husbands behind her and many men, in various cities. She wore a green silkish robe, not silk, and the healthy pink skin of her throat and chest made Loretta know that here was a woman like herself, made of the same kind of flesh and predictable in the same way.

"I got some stuff in here you can have," Rita said. "But are you going to tell me about this? When it's all over?"

"When it's all over, yes," Loretta said.

They walked past Rita's children. Rita brushed them aside, muttering, "You little pests! Get out of the way, get lost!" They closed the door to a back bedroom. "Here, here's a dress. Take that thing off and put it on before you get arrested," Rita said. She pulled something out of a pile of clothes. "There's some shoes over there. I only got fourteen dollars. But you can get something with that if you really need it."

"I don't want to take all your money."

"Go ahead."

"Then what about you?"

"I can get something from Harry Kaiserkof, you know . . ."

Loretta pulled the dress over her head fast, embarrassed to have Rita see her. A flush of shame descended from her face to her chest and belly. Was she crazy, doing this? What was she doing in Rita's place at six o'clock on a Sunday morning? She thought, *Anyway, this can't last long.* She got her head free of the dress, breathing in panicked snatches of air. The first thing that caught her eye was a framed picture on the wall of the little Dionne quintuplets, hardly more than babies. She said, strangely, pointing toward the picture, "I don't think I want to have a baby. . . ."

"What?"

Rita was looking at her as if she were crazy. She said, "Oh nothing, no, forget it. I'm sort of nervous."

"You want some coffee or something?"

"No, thanks."

"If you want to stay here you can."

"No."

"Is all this something to do with Brock?"

"Well, yes. With Brock," Loretta said. She buttoned the dress. She looked down at her trembling hands. "Yes, Brock. It was Brock. Brock did it," she said.

Rita walked with her to the door. Loretta looked out into the street, saw nothing, got ready to step outside. She wondered if her body would keep working long enough to get her through this morning.

She left. She had in mind a pawnshop two blocks away, with guns in the window, but at the end of the street, standing there and watching her, was a cop.

So it was coming to an end already: there was a cop.

It was Howard Wendall, dressed up as a cop and so he must be a cop though she hadn't heard. He began to grin at her, and his lazy, sullen eyes traveled up from Rita's shoes to Loretta's frozen face, as if he already knew everything and was waiting for her to confess.

"Where're you coming home from this time of the day?" he said.

Loretta could not answer.

After a moment he said, "Hey, guess what!"

She stared at him.

"Guess where your old man is!"

"Where?"

"He's sleeping it off downtown. Got picked up."

Loretta nodded slowly.

"Him and a few other old guys, they got picked up. Sleeping it off right now," Howard said.

He was a large young man, in his early twenties but with the premature middle-aged look of certain sullen, crafty, but stupid men who mix their suspicions and their enthusiasms. Loretta had known him for years and had talked to him often in that singsong, mock-sweet style in which she talked to certain men, but he had never exactly been interested in her, and now he stood at the end of the block, on the same sidewalk she was on, waiting for her to confess. The uniform had transformed him. He looked taller and stronger. Fox-faced but not thin, with a slight flush spreading along his cheeks, he tried to grin, but the grin faded at her silence.

"He's all right, just sleeping it off. He ain't sick or anything," Howard mumbled.

His dark brown hair was parted on the right, an exact part. The policeman's uniform, like the pink dress of Rita's that Loretta now wore, gave notice that a new life had been started; a big change had taken place. Loretta remembered this Howard Wendall as an older kid who was not the most dangerous or the loudest of the kids but who hung around with them, a kind of second lieutenant, an enthusiastic participant in trouble: in short, a familiar kind of boy. His sly, bold face could work its way from looking vicious to looking empty, and what might be behind it, in his brain, was anybody's guess. She remembered that he and some other boys had dangled Floyd Sloan over the edge of a roof some years ago, and Floyd Sloan himself was a tough kid.

"I'm in awful bad trouble!" Loretta cried.

And so she brought him back to the apartment, up the stairs and into the kitchen, in silence; and there, there was her room, where she would never go. She began to cry. Howard went to the door of her room and looked inside, then he went inside. He was gone only a few minutes. Then he came back and looked at her, embarrassed and sullen. "You better sit down," he said. Loretta wept. Her fingers were spread out on Rita's dress, clutching the material and releasing it in jerky spasms. Howard walked around the kitchen. In his uniform he seemed to take up all the room; he bumped into the table, into the stove. "Damn it," he said. He was bearish in his silence, sullen and red-faced. After a while he opened the door of the icebox. He pushed a milk bottle aside, he stooped over to lift a plate from a bowl, to see what was inside. Finally he said, letting the door swing shut, giving it an angry push, "Jesus, you really got yourself in it now!"

Loretta sat very still. She could hardly see, she was crying so hard.

He walked around the room. He brushed against her, and his touch was a surprise, almost painful. She could hear him breathing hard. "That goddam dirty little punk, him, he got what he deserved! Good for him!" Howard muttered. His breathing got louder; he was looking from one part of the kitchen to another, not seeing anything, very angry. A kind of rage seemed to rise in him, driving him around and around the table. Loretta wiped her face and watched him. "What the hell," Howard said violently, looking sideways at her as he passed, "he was a goddam punk. *He* was asking for it one of these days." His dark, suspicious eyebrows began to work; thoughts rose in his mind with a terrible angry energy. "All the Malins are no goddam good! The old guy beats the mother even, and everybody knows it. If *he* fell off a roof or was found out on the street, shot up or run over by a trolley, nobody would give a good goddam anyway. His father wouldn't. I mean, if he was found up in your room or out back in the alley he's dead as a doornail, the little bastard, he's every bit as dead either place! The little bastard!" Howard paused and stared at Loretta. His face was quite red. She could see his chest rise and fall with the effort of his breathing. "Well, you got yourself into it now! You're really in trouble now!" he said. He bumped against the table and, with his leg, knocked one of the chairs aside. He stared at her, his face working. "You made a mistake, huh? You really made a mistake bringing him up here. Jesus, you made a mistake, you really . . ."

He stared at her as if fascinated; she had never seen anyone look at her like that. She herself was very still, no longer thinking, only waiting. Howard scratched his head. His hair seemed to come apart—it looked wild right away. The part was jagged.

"Your brother took off and you're the one who's left, huh? Well, Jesus, you're really in trouble now!" He made a whooping sound, mirthless and brief. He grinned at her. "It's going to be a big joke, and people are going to get a big laugh out of it. That little bastard got what he deserved, good for him, good for your brother! But your brother better stay out of town. You're the one that's left, huh? You're left with that bastard in your bed and, Jesus, what a joke—there ain't anybody in this town that won't know about it by noon today, I can guarantee you that."

He gave an abrupt start forward, coming to her. He took hold of her hair and gave her a shake. "Yes, you made a mistake, you got yourself in number-one trouble, kid, you and him thought you were so smart. And don't you cry either, I don't like to see people crying."

She did not try to get away from him. She sat frozen, still, waiting.

"You made a mistake bringing that dirty little punk up here. Why him, what's so hot about *him?*" Howard cried. "Don't you cry, cut it out. I don't want to see no goddam crying. It makes me nervous to see people cry, and anyway

I ain't said what has to be done. He could just as soon be found out in the alley as up here, he's dead as a doornail, huh? What's the difference, huh? Look, what's the difference?"

He was agitated, red-faced, very strange. Loretta stared up at him. Their eyes were locked together. "Don't feel bad," he said.

They stared at each other for a long moment. Loretta felt nothing at all; her skull was hollow, burned out. Then she heard him unzipping his pants. She half rose, maybe to run out of the place or maybe to make it easier for him, and he grabbed hold of her and the two of them stumbled back against the table. He had begun to moan, clumsily and softly, as if in pain. Loretta saw the dishes still piled in the sink. She saw the clock on the icebox but didn't have time to see what it said.

"Don't you worry about it, not that little bastard," Howard said, clutching at her, pulling up her dress, "don't you think about him, not about *him,* the hell with *him!*"

And then, struggling with Howard, struggling to make it easier for him, she did think of Bernie for the first time: he was dead. She had loved him and he was dead and she would never see him again. Never would he come to her the way Howard was trying to come to her. He was dead, it was over, finished, that was the end of her youth. She tried not to think of it again.

3

Pregnant and married, she went to live with him on the south side of town. In boxes and bags, she packed up the few things she had and moved to an apartment his mother had found for them, not far from Mama Wendall's own house. It was an imposing street to her, with lines of elms blocking the upper windows of old brick homes, and tattered front yards marked off with lengths of string fixed to sticks stuck in the ground. The yards were marked off precisely. Though kids ran through them and knocked the string and the sticks down, still the yards were marked off, and Loretta liked this touch of privacy. She felt that she was entering a new life. She was finished with her old life—taking care of her father and Brock, living in that dump, working in that dump, unmarried, on the loose. She was going to forget everything about it. She was going to have a baby. She was a different person.

Here, when she was finished cleaning up the apartment, she could walk up and down the street, balloonlike in her maternity dresses, and talk with other young wives like herself, crooning over their babies or fixing her face into a look of sympathetic anger if they spoke of whatever it was they spoke of—things that worried them, the uncertainty of their husband's jobs, or the uncertainty of the country or of Europe—so she screwed up her face into a look of sorrow, like an apple withering in a flash and unwithering again by magic.

She was fond of saying to her friends, "Well, people are really good, I found that out. I had a bad problem but somebody helped me out and I can't complain about the world," thinking of Howard and how he had saved her, how he had fallen in love with her and married her and changed her life entirely, Howard Wendall appearing out of nowhere early on a Sunday morning, dressed in a policeman's uniform and come to help her. "Yes, people are really good, deep inside their hearts," she would say, almost crying, thinking of what her life would have been if Howard had not come along.

Three stories and an attic high, their house was imposing to her too, because, apart from the house her father had had many years before, she'd never really lived in a house. She faced it with a pointed solemnity, gazing up at the peak of the roof so mountainous above her as she turned up the short front walk. Flushed with excitement in the early autumn air, excited by gossip from her new friends and the prospect of this *baby* she was going to have, she stared up at the very top—the roof of dark green shingles, edged with moss in delicate patches, the great brick chimney soot-darkened and amazingly high, set off against the autumn air. The house itself was made of brick, darkened by time, but very sturdy and like a fortress, and its windows, set in their frames of painted wood, were enormous. The house had been trimmed not long before: window frames and door frames and miscellaneous trimming done in dark green. The house faced another house across the street, not quite identical, the two of them set in opposition like seasoned soldiers wary of each other but withdrawn from action—the kids who played about the front yards and front porches, stirring up noise and splattering mud, made the houses seem all the more gigantic and silent. Their look was silent. Loretta had dreams about this house, about her living alone in it, owning it, being able to lock all the doors and windows and owning everything: her own house!

From the front porch to the sidewalk stretched perhaps ten feet of ground given over to a kind of lawn, its barriers of string and sticks long since broken down but its grass flourishing in odd patches, and in other patches sunk with footprints and the ruts of small wheels; in the spring grass seed had been scattered out here by Mr. St. Onge himself, the landlord, but rain had pushed all the seeds into the deepest gullies and only there did bright green grass thrive. St. Onge liked to catch Loretta going in or out and tell her about his troubles. He was a slight man with worried blue eyes and an inquisitive mouth, and though Howard told her to keep the hell away from him—St. Onge was a trouble-maker, always calling the police to report people trying to break into his house or kids fooling around outside—still Loretta hadn't the heart to avoid him. She let him whine into her polite, glistening face; she let him talk to her about his married daughter, his dead wife, the other roomers in the house, about the people next door and across the street, and about people who had once lived in the house but were now gone, even dead. St. Onge was suspicious about all change. He had his ideas about why the bus routes had been changed. He had his ideas about the Mayor, the Governor, the President. Listening to him, or not quite listening to him, Loretta thought of an advertisement for some kind of insurance—a man and his shadow, *that warning shadow*, that was a sign maybe of death or old age or trouble to come, an advertisement she saw all the time and that discomforted her.

Out walking with her new friends, she saw how much alike the houses were—big brick houses with heavy upper stories, with narrow driveways and rickety garages in back—and it pleased her and her friends to see how uniform everything was. They were anxious for everything to be uniform. They wanted to sink into the neighborhood, just as their flesh wanted to take seed in it and stretch itself to a more prodigious health, anxious to memorize the façade of each house they passed, comparing, accepting, recognizing by the pattern of a pillow out on someone's porch swing the very same pattern of the curtains in their parents' front room or their grandparents' front room—so everything flowed together, warm and jumbled and sweet.

Loretta's closest friend, Janette, was a trim little girl with two children already and flashing wicked eyes, who had enticed Loretta into taking part in a worldwide chain letter that promised Loretta $1,000 in cash exactly one year and a day after she paid her dollar—this was done without Howard's knowing, of course. The girl knew everything, more than St. Onge. Her information was shrewder and crueler than his. She knew about miscarriages women on the block had had, beatings from drunken husbands; she knew about arguments with in-laws, and whose car was being repossessed, and whose younger sister was in trouble. But her main theme was how good this neighborhood was, how clean it was, how much better than the place she had come from that had wops practically around the corner and *colored* just on the other side of a block of warehouses—and the essence of it was that they had all come very close to the edge of something, their parents especially, and some of the older people had breathed this in and turned terrified and helpless for life, but they, the young, they with their new babies and their new husbands, were on their way up and never would the bottom fall out again. The government in Washington was like a net set up not ten feet below them, to save them.

Janette's husband drove a truck, which was common; but Howard, a patrolman, took on the stature of a dangerous man, better kept at a distance, but admired and feared. Loretta's little friend prodded and teased her to talk about him. What kind of a man was he? Was he very brave? Did he use his gun much on the job? Had he ever killed anybody? Was he very *loving* to Loretta? Was he happy about her being pregnant? Shyly Loretta drew back from discussing him; not that she wasn't puzzled at times by his silence or the sudden eruption of his words and anger or his beery, abrupt love-making, but she was demure enough to keep such things to herself, away even from Howard and Howard's mother, who urged her to come over all the time—she was a good girl, she knew enough not to tell secrets, she knew that there were certain things you must never say out loud.

Janette had crazy ideas: on their walks she would look up at the houses they passed, and if it happened somehow that all the shades in the front windows formed a straight line, even and neat, she would grab hold of Loretta's arm and say, "Now, that means good luck. Lucky for us." Or, seeing an aged, mean-looking woman, the same woman it seemed they were always seeing, she would grab hold of Loretta's arm and say, "I bet that old hag is fixing a curse on us. Because she's old and we're young." It worried Loretta to think that maybe the future might be decided that way; she knew that such things were wrong, the Church said they were wrong, but still they worried her. She said nothing about Janette to Howard. He didn't like Janette, just as he didn't like St. Onge or the men he worked with, though nothing in his life suggested he would get anything better, so Loretta kept quiet about Janette, and when Howard came home at night she talked to him about things they needed for the apartment, things she had seen downtown, or she talked about her father and his troubles or what Mama Wendall had said that day.

She had come to the end of her life, Loretta thought, and it was a solid, good feeling to think that she would probably live here forever, watching the kids in the neighborhood growing up, sharing complaints and good news with all her friends, managing gradually for her husband to get to playing pinochle with their husbands, bringing up her own children. Everything was fixed and settled, good. There would be a time, even, when Mama Wendall would not be around. She liked Howard's mother well enough but imagined surprise deaths for her, accidents. But really she liked his mother. Janette said, "I don't see how you can stand that old bitch," but Loretta never answered. The two of them played Chinese checkers a lot, out on the porch, and leafed through romance comic books with pages softened by dirt.

The veranda of the house was furnished with several wicker chairs and a wicker sofa, painted black but now chipped a little, and cushions that had to be taken in at night, and on the broad railing there were plants with flat thin leaves. The veranda was partly shaded. During the day someone kept a radio on nearby and Loretta could hear it, a soft murmur of music and words, a kind of lullaby; most of the songs were about love. She herself did not think about love any longer, but she liked the music and she went around singing the words. Life had stopped for her and she could relax, sleep. She liked to go to the movies with Janette once or twice a week—Ginger Rogers dancing, Errol Flynn fighting—and the movies passed before her eyes and left her a little more content, as if her life were somehow becoming more settled. It was like the odor that pervaded the house, something you couldn't figure out. It was not just a smell of food—it seemed to have coal dust mixed up in it; it

was not really unpleasant. On humid days it was heavy.
There was a slightly sulphurous, oniony tinge to the air, so
different from the stale, sickish odor of the apartment where
her father still lived. And she liked Howard's cigars, the
smoke that somehow cleared a certain territory in their own
apartment, pushing other odors away. Everything was taken
in, absorbed, woven into the sweet, slumbrous density of her
married life, for which she had even been given a new body.

One day she went to take a few dollars over to her father.
But the old man was gone, the apartment empty, and she
had to ask around the building to find out what had happened. Someone told her he'd been taken to the hospital.
Which hospital? Loretta asked, but the woman didn't know.
So she went to the main hospital, but he wasn't there; the
receptionist told her he must be at the *State* hospital. "The
State Hospital is for crazy people," Loretta said, stunned.
She hurried away to get out of that woman's sight. State
hospital! Her father was committed! She took a trolley back
to the old neighborhood, perspiring in the early October heat,
and anxious to see a familiar face, and she finally went
over to the place where Rita worked and asked her if she
knew anything.

"Honey, how would I know?" Rita said. "Didn't they ask
you to sign a paper or anything? I thought you had to sign
a paper."

Loretta felt panicked, confused. She pretended to be looking at dress material. Great bundles of cloth lay on the
counters, all kinds of colors and patterns. She kept unwind-
ing and rewinding some cotton cloth with bluebells on it;
Rita chattered. It seemed to Loretta, half listening, that all
the girls she knew, all the women, had rivers of words to
deliver into her, and she too felt buoyed up by a great
pressure of words, language, talk, excited gestures, like a
gigantic heartbeat somehow drawing them all closer together
—all the women; the men were forever silent.

Rita said, "It's a damn shame about your father, but maybe
it's better that way. Maybe he got in trouble."

"He sort of liked to fight," Loretta said. She thought of
him as dead.

"It's funny that Howard doesn't know anything about it."

Loretta wound the cloth back onto its big heavy roll. She
appeared to be thinking about this. Her mind dropped back
from her father at the State Hospital for the Insane to her
father coming up the stairs, drunk and dirty, or waking in a

nightmare, yelling, and all the trouble she'd had with him after her mother's death. What was it worth, all that? Having a father or being a daughter? What did it mean? She woke slowly to the present, to Rita's question. "Oh, if it's a boy we're going to call it Jules. Howard's grandfather was named that. If it's a girl we're going to call it Antoinette."

"They're both nice names," Rita said.

Loretta couldn't stand around the store any longer, so she drifted away, wondering what to do, a little ashamed of having a father who was put away and wondering if everyone knew about it. Did being crazy run in the family? Her mother had gone crazy too. She felt shaky. For a while she stood on the sidewalk, letting people pass by her, blank and silent. Then she had an idea: she would go up to see her aunt, her mother's sister, whose oldest boy was a policeman and so the family always knew what was going on. The aunt greeted her without much enthusiasm. Loretta came in, sat down in the parlor, stared at a smart brown-tinted photograph of this cousin-cop in his uniform, uncomfortable at the resemblance to Howard. She let her eyes wander to the big ivory crucifix hanging over the sofa. She said, "I guess you heard they took my pa away to Danby?"

"Well, I heard something about it," her aunt said.

There was a mustardy odor in this house. Loretta plunged ahead. "How bad is he, do you know?"

"No."

"Did Billy say anything about it?"

"A little."

"I feel bad that they took him away. I mean, he wasn't a bad guy but just drank too much. He was sort of mixed up sometimes but not crazy. Did Billy see him? I mean, was he arrested or what?"

"Billy didn't actually see him," her aunt said a little coldly, "but he heard about it. Howard probably heard about it too. Why don't you ask him?"

"I don't think Howard knows anything about it."

Loretta's aunt said nothing but her mouth moved primly.

"Was he arrested in a fight or something? Did he break some windows? Hit somebody?"

"I don't know really."

"They wouldn't just take him away without him doing something?"

"I'm afraid I just don't know."

"How long do they keep them locked up?"

"How long? Until they get well, I guess."

She was surprised at her aunt saying this, at her saying it so generously. The woman's hands lay limp in her lap; she'd always been so cold, distant.

"He didn't go crazy, did he?" Loretta said, sweating.

"Go up and see him," said her aunt.

"I don't want to go see him! I'm afraid to see him," Loretta said.

On the trolley going home she sat with her hands resting on her stomach, her thoughts turned in a panic inward and down to her stomach, wondering if the baby was decided yet—a boy or a girl. She hoped it would be a boy, *Jules*. She thought about having a baby. She thought about a baby of her own. But, getting off the trolley, she started to cry suddenly because it was not fair that her father had been arrested and taken off to that place, like a crazy man, just to be put out of the way. She imagined him in a straitjacket. She imagined someone coming into his room and knocking over that cigar box full of papers, kicking the papers around . . .

When Howard came home that night she was sitting in the bedroom with the shades drawn. "You home?" he called out. She answered faintly. This must have been enough for him because he said nothing further. He went into the bathroom. She heard him in there, hearing the sounds without any special distaste, because she'd been hearing them all her life and at least Howard closed the door after himself. Then he came into the bedroom and stripped off his dark shirt. "There was something I heard today, real crazy, about Eleanor Roosevelt and a nigger, but I don't remember how it went. You heard it?"

"No."

"What's wrong with you?"

"I feel bad about my father."

He was silent, undressing. He tossed his clothes onto the bed. When he came back from working Howard seemed to age, his beard pushing out with the energy of his worries, and it took many hours of deep sleep to renew the fat health of his face. He glanced at Loretta sideways.

"You know about it, don't you?" Loretta said.

"He's sent up for thirty days' observation."

"What's that?"

"Thirty days' observation."

"But why?"

"He was acting funny."

"Acting funny how?" Loretta cried.

"Like he was crazy."

"Who tells who's crazy? Why didn't you say anything about it to me?"

"He's better off up there."

"Why is he better off?"

"Look, he almost got run over by a car. He's drunk all the time. He said in the station they might as well shoot him, he didn't want to live. He's always been a little crazy and he's better off up at Danby, so forget about it."

"When can we go see him?"

"Not for thirty days."

"That isn't true!"

"Who told you it isn't true?"

"But thirty days is a month. He'll be all alone up there, and it might make him worse. I heard what that place is like."

"Anyway we're rid of him," Howard said.

In his stubborn silence he stood apart from her, waiting. She saw that he had turned into a man, a man like her father or her friends' fathers or any father anywhere, any man, silent and angry, hungry but impatient with food, pushing it around on a plate, stuck with a terrible burden of flesh and needing someone like Loretta to ease it. She cried for her father and for Howard, feeling her body turn bitter. "What if he dies up there? They kick them around, I know that! They beat them up!"

Howard made a grunting sound of contempt.

"And you, what if they get you up there sometime? You think you're so smart it can't happen to you?"

"It won't happen to me," Howard said.

"And did he really say he wanted to die? Did he really say that?"

Howard walked out of the room.

"Did he say they might as well shoot him?" Loretta cried. Howard didn't answer.

So much for Jules's grandfather.

4

Jules was born in a mild month, bringing in a new season with his energy and fretfulness. Now Mama Wendall came over all the time, every day, and every day the staircase shuddered beneath her ponderous footsteps. But Loretta stared at the baby and everything else fell away from her, as in a movie the background will sometimes shift out of focus. She bumped into things. She left the radio on when the station had shifted and there was only static, something that annoyed Mama Wendall, who had sharp ears and sharp eyes.

She was always bringing the baby things. One day she brought him a Dopey doll, in rubber.

Then on another day, when Jules was almost a year old, Howard came home early one afternoon, his legs wobbly, and told her in the doorway that he had been *suspended from the force*—words she had never heard spoken before, the kind of words that belonged in a newspaper. His drunken gravity by itself terrified her.

"Suspended—what does that mean?" she cried.

"Like on probation."

"But what does it mean?"

He sat at the kitchen table and let his chin sag. In that instant he reminded Loretta of her brother, though Howard was not as smart as Brock: it was the posture of hopelessness. She put her hand over the baby's soft warm skull, over his silky hair, and thought in terror, *Then things are not settled in my life.* Howard poked at the Dopey doll with his forefinger. His face had no expression.

After a while he said, "There are these guys that have something to do with restaurants. Cocktail lounges. Like in the Lenox Hotel, that place. The Lenox Hotel."

He paused. Loretta stared at him.

"They have something to do with the union. I don't know."

"What are you talking about?"

"There is some money being kicked back."

"From who?"

"From the hotels."

"Kicked back why? Did you take money?"

Howard shifted in his chair. He had a bearish, rumpled look, yet there was something strangely tender about him. In this defeat the very hairs of his sizable wrists and hands looked gentler; Loretta felt a jolting in her blood, wanting to comfort him. Her father, during his quiet, bad times, sitting like this at the kitchen table, had looked tender too. It was the only time men looked tender—in defeat.

"Did you take money?" Loretta said.

"No."

"Then why are you fired?"

"I'm not fired exactly."

"Then why . . . why did it happen?"

"Fifteen guys got it. I was one of them."

"But if you're innocent—"

"That isn't so easy to prove," Howard said, not looking at her.

After a while Loretta said, "Those sons of bitches are trying to drag you down! They're not going to get away with it!"

Howard sighed with the sigh of Loretta's lost father.

"We better go see your mother to tell her," Loretta said.

They changed into good clothes as if for Sunday. Howard was morose and serene, Loretta was powdered, angry, in a flurry. She carried the baby and chattered about how they wouldn't get away with it, those bastards, trying to put the blame on him when he hadn't done anything. Her own cousin Billy had been busted also, Howard said. Good, said Loretta. Was Billy guilty? Howard thought he was, he didn't know too much about the whole mess, he was on the outside and nobody ever told him anything. . . . Good for Billy and Billy's mother, Loretta thought, imagining her cousin in his fancy uniform brought low at last, hounded out of the squad car he was so proud of (Howard was only a patrolman) and forced to turn in his gun and his badge. Good, let them all be dragged down. And the people at the top? she asked. They were all crooks, Howard said sullenly but without enthusiasm. Loretta was fluent in her bitterness: the way the world was! How crazy!

"My father always got fired from his jobs," she said angrily. "Somebody always came along to push him out! Somebody's nephew or son-in-law, any old bastard popping out of the woodwork, and they'd kick my pa out and give the new guy the job. He kept falling off the bottom. Nobody ever gave him a chance. If he went crazy that was why."

"Yeah, he never had a chance," Howard said.

The Wendalls' small frame house looked ominous to Loretta's eye; she didn't know exactly what was wrong. Then she figured it out—the shades were all drawn. Howard noticed it too. He showed the same sullen, caged satisfied look he had been showing all afternoon, as if the worst had finally caught up with him and it was finished; but his eyes were alert. His eyes with their queer centerlessness, in his large face, were jumpy though the rest of him was heavy, pulled down. His policeman's tough walk, his drawing up of his shoulders, had been abandoned along with the uniform, and now he walked like any man out of a job—that posture of familiar failure, the stomach sagging, the chest shapeless, the shoulders hunched forward as if it were easier to walk that way, leaning forward into a future of pure gravity.

Mama Wendall was waiting in the doorway. Loretta felt Howard pull back a little, seeing her. But his mother shoved the door open and came out, a broom in her big hands. She began shouting, "You stupid fool! You, you dumbhead!" She swiped at Howard with the broom. He tried to push it away, whining, "Mama, watch out, that hurts," but she paid no attention and rushed at him, bringing the broom down hard on his shoulders.

The baby began screaming. Loretta, terrified, backed into some junk by the steps—plywood crates—and into some mud.

Howard stood with his arms in front of his face while his mother struck him. "You disgraced us, you!" his mother yelled. "Stupid ass-hole, you great big dumb baby!" Her hair was in a gray mess, her wide face gleaming with a film of sweat. Now that Howard was cornered against the porch, she gave up in disgust and threw the broom at him. "Mixed up with whores! Taking money from whores! You want to break your mother's heart? You want to kill your father? Huh? Want to give your father a stroke? Want to see him laying there in the coffin dead and have it all your fault, you little snot-nose, you smart-aleck! Taking dollar bills from those whores, those dirty bags, them with their diseases! Probably you brought home a disease too, huh, and come over to visit us and use our toilet, huh! Didn't you? Didn't you?"

"Mama, no!" Howard cried.

"Get inside, you dumbhead! You want all the neighbors to hear?"

She herded them both inside. Her heavy body seemed to be shuddering behind them, blocking the doorway, panting with outrage. Loretta bumped right into the kitchen table, feeling faint, and Mama Wendall snatched the baby out of her arms and began rocking it angrily. Big tears ran down her gray, rough face. "The baby of such a father! Such a father! My own son turned out such a stupid dumbhead!"

Papa Wendall sat in the darkened parlor, listening to a

radio. They were herded into that room. Howard sat miserably on the end of the sofa and hid his face in his hands.

"Yes, cry, go on and cry now it's too late, you big dumb cow!" his mother cried. She rocked the baby against her chest and glared from one face to the other.

Loretta stood in perfect silence. She felt she was a guest no one had noticed. She felt that a sudden movement of hers would turn all of Mama Wendall's wrath onto her. Papa Wendall, a man with glasses and a slow, grunting manner, did not look at anyone. Behind his elbow, from a radio slunk partly into the darkness of the room and mixed up with the thick crocheted doily that covered it, came the news of the day's sports.

"And there's trouble back home too, back there too," Mama Wendall said grimly, meaning the Old Country. Looming gigantic in the half-light, rocking the baby against her breasts, she seemed to be mooning over the world and over her grandson, considering him; with her big strong fingers she had seized this baby, and from such fingers no one could ever take him away. "You, poor baby, the son of such a father!" she crooned.

"But he didn't do anything," Loretta whispered.

Mama Wendall did not even look at her.

"He got blamed but he wasn't one of them. It was something different, it was something to do with a hotel."

After a long furious moment Mama Wendall said, "Like hell he didn't do anything."

She was larger than her husband, about Howard's size, a slightly brute-nosed woman in her fifties, hefty and large-boned, with a rather pleasant high color that was now grayish, a washerwoman's coloring, enormous ears that looked as if they'd been tugged at all her life in frustration, and a heavy, corseted bottom. She was shrewd and calculating and never let herself get angry except to rush along the right track, never making a mistake. So Loretta knew in despair that Mama Wendall was right and that Howard was guilty and that he'd even been mixed up somehow with prostitutes. Yes, it all made sense. Mama Wendall never made a mistake.

"Now, what we are going to do is *this*," Mama Wendall said angrily.

5

"Spring is a good time to move," Mama Wendall said.

Howard was driving the truck, his mother was riding with him, and the rest of them were following in Papa Wendall's car. They were on their way out to the country. They were going to move in with an uncle of Howard's, an old man who had stayed back on the farm when everyone else had left. Howard already had a job at a gypsum mine—not as good as his police job, but good enough. Loretta sat in the back seat of the old Ford, crushed in between some boxes and her sister-in-law Connie, a fat girl of fourteen. Connie was always in a dense, sullen silence, her lips slightly parted. The baby was already wet, Loretta noticed, but it was too late to fix him; he lay miserably on her lap, twisting and whimpering. "This baby is just so lively," Loretta complained brightly to the air.

Papa Wendall was driving, following the truck at a safe distance. His arms moved stiffly, and he rarely gave any indication of hearing Loretta. Still, Loretta fixed her concentration on the wrinkled back of his neck and tried to make talk; out of her husband's family she had picked Papa to "like." He was older than his wife by ten years.

The drive was long and bumpy, and along the way Howard had a flat, so they stood around in the dusk while he and his father toiled at fixing it. Mama Wendall fussed over the baby and cast her shrewd eyes to the horizon as if she might see there what was coming next. So tall, she seemed able to see farther than most people. "No rest for the wicked," she said with a strange, pleased sigh, jiggling Jules in her arms.

Connie did not get out of the car. "With a fat bottom like that you should get out, get some exercise for a change," her mother said, but not unkindly. Now that they had left the city and were on their way to a new life—her idea of a new life—she was rather pleased.

Loretta stood near her because of the baby. If Mama Wendall should drop him—if anything should happen to that baby, Loretta thought, she'd stick a scissors into that old bitch's throat. She hated Mama Wendall. But Loretta put on a good show in front of everyone, trying to get Howard to cheer up and Connie to be friends and the old man to talk once in a while; after all, they were going to live together from now on, and shouldn't they all be friends? But out of the whole bunch only Mama Wendall was chatty, and her chattiness somehow went around Loretta, excluding her. It was peculiar.

Sometimes she said to Loretta, with a sharp smile, "Is this baby in a fever?" or "Is this baby wet *again?*" And Loretta was annoyed to see how very shrewd, how very knowing, were the old woman's eyes, fixed upon what was young and therefore helpless in Loretta, knowing how to seek it out.

There was a forlorn sensation in her, rising often, out of melancholy and weary joy, that everyone who was born must be a person—one person only—and that this personal, private, nameless kernel of the self could neither be broken down nor escaped from; so she smiled vaguely back at Mama Wendall's evil smile, thinking, *Well, I'm young enough, I can take it;* or thinking, *He saved me from something terrible, Howard did, and after that doesn't my life belong to him and his family?*

In that family there were odd people, far-flung and secretive. The most interesting was Howard's older brother Samson, who was a tool-and-die maker in Detroit, at Ford's, evidently doing well but reluctant to send money home. They spoke often of Samson, sometimes bitterly, sometimes with pride, sometimes to put down Howard, who had been fired, after all, from a lousy job and was on his way to a lousier one. Howard never spoke of his brother, never. There was an aunt of fifty who was a nun, who'd left her order and returned to it again, and of her everyone said, "She's crazy but harmless." And there was this uncle of Howard's to whose house they were going. His name was Fritz and he was over seventy. He was a hermit, they said, and needed "bringing out" into the world again. Mama Wendall said he needed a woman around the place to get it clean and to feed him right. The farm was on the outskirts of a small town. Everywhere around this town the farmland was deserted, because farmers had sold their land and moved out years ago, escaping the Midwestern dust and drought and on their way to the cities, headed for government buildings, for welfare, for unemployment. But Fritz hadn't enough sense to sell, they said, and so he had stayed, and the town was recovering slowly, the gypsum plant had reopened, and they were on their way with a truck full of furniture and crates and boxes, to settle down forever. As Mama Wendall said, "America is really the country, not the city. People should live in the country. The country is a better place than that smelly city for a baby. Look what the city did to Howard."

That first month out in the country Loretta lay awake many nights and wept, hearing the old house creak, feeling the darkness stir with soft-winged insects around her, everything mysterious and damp. She thought of the lovely dirty city with its municipal buildings of fake marble and its department stores and elevators and its scrubby open parks where anyone might meet. She cast her mind back to the look of the muddy canal and its high, built-up banks, that frightening look of a canal with steep sides into which you might fall to drown helplessly; she lay with her back against Howard's back, sore-eyed, beaten-down, the words of Mama Wendall dinning in her ears just as the oppressive, heaped plates of Mama Wendall's kitchen table taunted her, now that she was pregnant again and inclined to nausea—everything was too much, too much. Out here in the country—out here, in this mysterious cricket-filled country, where anything might happen and yet nothing at all ever happened, where Howard went to and from his unexciting work and ran into no old friends, got into no particular trouble, was spiritless, dull, fat—out here there was good clean fresh air for the baby but nothing else. Loretta wept for her lost city and its dirty air.

Overcome by Mama Wendall, she and Howard had little to say when they were finally alone. It was as if his mother were still in the room with them, considering them with her ponderous lined brow, judging them. She had a head like a statue's head, a marvelous ugly brow, sharp green eyes. If her body was cowlike or bearish, like her son's, still her eyes were cruelly wise and let nothing get by. Howard was slowing down, getting fat, and him not yet thirty, Loretta thought in a panic, letting himself go already! She twisted in her bed, thinking of this monster of a woman and her son, the two of them arm in arm, and she, Loretta, standing bitter and helpless on the outside: the wife, the mother, the pregnant girl left outside. Her heart filled with bitterness.

The house in which they lived was like an old barn, and behind it were old rotted barns, one of them partly burned down from a fire that had been caused by lightning. Many of the trees around the house had been struck by lightning and scarred. Loretta took that for a sign of bad luck; nothing was ever struck by lightning in the city, but out here, out in the open, lightning could sweep in anywhere. Everything was too open. They lived on a dirt road, on the top of a small hill. Torrents of rain rushed down that hill in a rainstorm and gathered into pools that stood around for days, down in the apple orchard; and there was a real stream, not far away, fed by smaller streams and ditches, where Loretta took Jules to play, half-hearted herself while the child laughed with delight. If Jules had not been with her to keep her vision focused up short she would have gone crazy, but Jules was enough; his very energy and querulousness were enough to keep her occupied. In the kitchen Mama Wendall was boss, and she herded both Loretta and Connie around, giving them orders, teasing them, getting them to stand straight with a sudden poke of her elbow; and outside during thunderstorms the flashes of lightning came dangerously close, terrifying Loretta; and the old house was infested with cockroaches and mice, and even rats might come in freely to have a look at the new tenants. But still she had Jules and she was pregnant again; that kept her sane.

Summer passed. Another winter passed; they were snowed in for a week, gathering together out of frustration and hatred, all but Mama Wendall—she seemed to enjoy it. She enjoyed "emergencies." She strode through the house giving orders, stuffing newspaper into the cracks around windows, putting on her husband's overshoes and coat and going out to fool around with a shovel in that impossible snow. Before spring came Loretta had another baby to take care of, and her life had settled down into a dull hypnotized routine of housework and babywork under the dominion of her mother-in-law. The men of the house were usually silent. Howard's silence expanded weekly, daily; he seemed to be sinking into middle age, and whatever life he had by himself on those occasional days when he didn't come right home from the mine Loretta knew nothing about and couldn't ask him. She didn't dare ask him. Howard was a father now, one of the fathers of the world, preoccupied with work he hated and sullen with the daily effort of his own body, so sluggish and stubborn. He was stirred to an uneasy awakening by Jules's liveliness—Howard would say, "Get that kid off my back"—but pleased somehow by the new baby, Maureen, who slept most of the time and caused no trouble. Howard would sit staring into the baby's crib for long

stretches of time. Jules didn't seem to notice his father's indifference but was all over the place with his enthusiasm—a
boy with dark brown, slightly curly hair, dark eyes, long
dark eyelashes. When he got too noisy sometimes Loretta
gave him a few swallows of beer, in exasperation, to quiet
him down. She drank beer herself now, to quiet her nerves.
Between the baby Maureen and the child Jules, Loretta supposed she had to prefer Maureen, who, after all, was a female
but she had the idea that Jules was the sharpest one: Mama
Wendall believed that the first-born was always the sharpest.
She had a positive faith in brains. Though Jules sometimes
stammered, this was just his hurry to get things said, she
thought; it meant that he was faster than anyone else. People who got ahead, people on the radio—H. V. Kalten-
born was her particular favorite, for some reason—were
cited for their *brains,* which meant their slyness, a kind of
mild criminal facility that put them ahead of all the nameless people of the world, like the Wendalls. For certainly
her people were anonymous, backward, exasperating, Howard
in his silence and Papa Wendall with his radio (he had hurt
his back that winter and could no longer work), not to mention poor fat Connie with her daydreams, waiting for a man,
and the owner of this big drafty house, Fritz, a man who
sat down to supper in dirty overalls, smelling of sweat and
dirt, a faceless silent man no one noticed.

The seasons passed in all this masculine silence, and only
Jules broke the spell with his cries and complaints and laughter. Sometimes amazed at the son she had borne, Loretta
blossomed in spurts, singing out in the back yard as she
hung up the heavy wash, or smiling to herself, as if she
had done something very clever, not knowing how she had
done it. Just before Howard left for the war she became
pregnant again, for the third time. With a kind of idle curiosity she considered that this was maybe her third child by
Howard and maybe only her second. She could never make
up her mind whether Jules looked like Howard or like Bernie
Malin; sometimes she thought one way, sometimes the other.
But all that energy! that charm! She lay awake beside her
sleeping husband and dreamed of Bernie, imagining him
alive, smiling pleasantly into the dark and imagining him in
her arms. Jules had Bernie's energy and charm, that was
certain.

Like other people in the area, they took to listening closely to newscasts and reading newspapers; they talked to peo-

ple in town, comparing news of sons and husbands and
nephews. Everyone was drawn together, worried and angry.
Loretta listened to all the talk she could get. She liked to
listen to talk, the talk of women, being drawn to them and
soothed by them, even by their baffled anger. She thought
of Howard "over in Europe" and tried to imagine what his
life was like. But she could not feel it; she could not imagine that Howard himself felt it, that it got into his bones and
made any difference to him. She imagined him sitting somewhere, his gaze fixed on something close to him, with a look
of being half-asleep though he was wide-awake and sullen.
But when any of the women asked her about him she answered quickly and brightly, "I just got a letter!" or, if she
hadn't heard for a while, she would answer sadly, her eyes
searching their eyes for sympathy, "There hasn't been any
news." When Howard came home, she thought, all this
sympathy would end. No one would ask her about him again.
And in the midst of thinking about Howard she would
find herself thinking about Bernie again, imagining him in a
soldier's uniform. It was easier to imagine Bernie than to
imagine Howard. One came to the eye faster than the other,
that was all.

Meanwhile Jules grew fast, eating everything Mama Wendall gave him, cleaning the plates set before him heaped with
potatoes and noodles and rice and vegetables, with a few
chunks of fatty meat, his slight frame burning everything
up. He was a noisy, joyful child and Loretta could not help
loving him best. He followed her everywhere; he followed
his grandmother everywhere; he disappeared and turned up
at neighboring farms; he played with children older than
himself, not afraid of them. He was not afraid of anyone.
Loretta, cautious in the way of a city girl, wondered at all
the nerve this kid had and the distance he could travel—
sometimes, riding with Papa Wendall on her way home from
town, she saw the little boy playing in a ditch with some
other children or walking along the road in a grownup's
hurry, only a child and so strangely independent. If they
slowed down for him to get in he'd say, "No, don't want
to," and wave them on, or jump across the ditch and run
off into a field. He was like a wild animal, running off
when they called him; then he turned up later, surprised at
their anger. He was perverse and wilful, a mysterious child,
and Loretta began to think he must be a little strange in
the head to sit as he did on the stone steps of the district

schoolhouse, waiting for recess or noon hour; he was only five years old, too young for school, but the building itself drew him. He hung around it all day and went back after supper sometimes, just to hang around.

There were times when he came home smudged and bloody, his clothes ripped, and it was Mama Wendall who bathed him and gave him advice. Loretta angrily tried to get between them, almost stammering herself, saying, "That's the last time you play with that little bastard!" But Mama Wendall ignored her and said to Jules, with the solemnity of a horse, "You just keep fighting back. You got to make your own way." Jules escaped her too, a sly child, and went wherever he wanted to go, unmoved by stones thrown at him or taunts about his great-uncle, that crazy hermit.

Loretta would scream at him that if he wasn't good his father would never come back home. His father, she said, would bring back another little boy and kick Jules out—how would he like that? "I'll go sleep in the Bentons' barn," Jules said, being practical. He showed no anxiety. Loretta, giving in, wondered why she had thought he would show anxiety. What was the use of it? It did no one any good. So she gave him beer to drink to quiet him down when he was unmanageable, and sometimes she spanked him when he kept climbing out of bed. She went out of her way to be loving to the little girls, excluding Jules, but he seemed to know he was her favorite, the only real man in this tomb of a house of silent men; Howard, gone off to the war, was no more silent in his absence than he had been at home. Jules made the house shake with his running. They glanced at each other, Loretta and Mama Wendall, and shared a sly secret pride at having produced this boy at least—the rest was nothing much.

One Saturday everyone except Fritz went to town to see something spectacular that had happened—a two-passenger plane had crashed somewhere. The volunteer firetruck was pulled up off the road, firemen were working in the midst of flaming rubble and junk, and around them was a ring of people drawn in great excitement to the billowing black smoke from a fuel fire. The air was vibrating in spasms from the heat. It looked as if it were shivering, in violent anticipation of seeing something awful. The firemen were all old or middle-aged, and the men who watched were either old or middle-aged, or they were boys, so it seemed to Loretta that this crash was an event through which she might stare vacantly, her gaze caught by no man's body and her own body not involved in anything. She was quite free, protected. She was slightly heavy now herself from Mama Wendall's starchy meals, and she never bothered with makeup or fixing her hair. She was a solid-footed peasant girl with a tan from the sun, and with the newest baby, Betty, in her arms, and Maureen toddling alongside her, and Jules running ahead, she made her way over to all the excitement, drawn by the noise. In just such a catastrophe Howard might be lying at this moment, burning, exploded out of his bones' sluggishness, but that thought was really not believable. It was said that the men in this crash were officials of some kind, from the state government, men unlike Howard and fated to die a sudden, flaming death—unlike Howard, who would probably come home looking just the way he did when he left.

Loretta paused at the edge of the crowd, staring. She did not really want to see anything much. The fire was enough for her. She had never known the air could shrivel like that, shuddering with heat; and she'd never seen or heard such a fire! So this was what those photographs of burning planes were all about—the billowing, gulping noise of a gasoline and oil fire, a queer sound that put her in mind of sheets flapping on a clothesline. Grass burned around the plane. Weeds caught on fire and shriveled in a second, flame illuminating their dark kernels and then blinding them and, in another second, wasting them away to nothing. She stood transfixed, not wanting to see anything more. Everyone else was pushing forward, chattering. Kids were running loose. Jules had pushed through to the very front, slipping out of her grasp. She saw a woman shove him backward, but he caught his balance at once and edged forward again. Loretta called out, "Jules! You get back here!" Then she lost sight of him. The crowd trampled field grass and strained inward, looking to see the very center of that flaming wreck, not content with seeing less than everything. Someone cried out. There was a chorus of exclamations—surprise, amazement, a kind of despair. Loretta turned away, not wanting to see, but not very upset and vaguely annoyed only by the heat and all these people and Jules getting away—why was everything such a bother, she thought, why was she always unhappy?

She strolled back to town. She came across Connie in the drugstore, talking with a boy with a sunken chest who worked there, and she asked Connie if she'd seen Jules. Jules had got away. No, Connie hadn't seen him, so Loretta walked around with Betty in her arms and Maureen fooling around alongside her, feeling lopsided without Jules tugging at her other side. People were coming back from the fire. They were still chattering about the bodies. Loretta didn't quite want to hear what people were saying, but she could make out that one of the men had had the top of his skull sheared right off—"like with an ax." Hearing this, Loretta looked away primly. Her face shifted into a grimace of horror and then shifted back, untouched.

They couldn't find Jules. Mama Wendall went around asking for him while Loretta sat, exhausted, in the truck. They went to the sheriff's office and reported a boy missing. Then they drove home. Loretta felt her head ache with an unreal, unclear sense of loss: a husband gone, a son gone, was this possible?

She did not sleep all that night. Mama Wendall made coffee and clucked around, keeping watch in her bedroom slippers and housedress. "Don't worry, kids come back. They always come back," Mama Wendall said. Loretta was too tired to listen. Near morning the old woman finally went to bed and Loretta wandered outside. She walked around the cleared-off part of the farm, testing her body by touching her hips and thighs and stomach, asking herself who she was and how she had come to be so exhausted and old when nothing permanent had really happened to her. She had thought certain things were permanent, fixing her, but she had been mistaken. Nothing was permanent yet. Nothing had fixed her yet. She happened to look in one of the barns, and there she saw someone—it was Jules. He was sitting with his back to her, in the hay, a small child, very still, just sitting. It was frightening that he should sit like that, so still. She could hear him saying something, talking to himself. A rapid, frightening mumble . . . a kind of breathy argument. Probably he was stammering, which she hated, the beginnings of words stumbling over themselves and piling up so that nothing could get loose, as if he were choking, so small a boy, suffocating with the urgency to speak. She had come upon him often in the past and heard him talking to himself. If she caught his attention he would get up and walk away with dignity. But now she was a little frightened to come upon him like this, alone and not needing her. And there was something dark and strange about the place he was hiding in. Why hadn't he come up to the house? He was hiding from them. He was hiding from them and talking to himself, arguing out something. He seemed both angry and scared. She froze. She did not call him. He might have been some- one else's child, a stranger's child. She leaned against the rotted doorway and felt a giddiness rise in her, cut off from Jules by his aloneness, his being so unchildlike. Some days later, helping him wake out of a nightmare, she thought she knew what had frightened him so: that man's head split in two, the top part sliced off. Jules had evidently pushed up close and seen it. She comforted him but could not under- stand how that sad fact had fixed itself so seriously into a child's brain when it had already faded out of her own.

6

The countryside with its distant hills and aimless dirt roads formed him. All his life he would close his eyes upon a land- scape of absolute distance, luring him forward as if he were tottering on the brink of a perpetual delirium, a child still trapped inside his adult's bones. He ran away for the first time when he was six and was found fifteen miles away, by a farmer's wife. "Little boy," the woman said to him, her voice questioning and kindly, "who do you belong to?" He had stared in silence at this woman as if he did not think she was real. To talk like that, in such words, in such a melodious voice! To him there was something musical and distant about her—an ordinary farm woman in a dress and a man's sweater, shivering in the early-morning air, her face mature and lined with thought the way his mother's never was—and he stammered out his name, ashamed and per- plexed. She drove him home herself, back to the high, gaunt, ugly Wendall house that was an eyesore even among the eye- sores of the Huron Road, and there presented him to his mother and grandmother, and so the adventure had ended. When his mother wept angrily over him, he said, "I'm sorry, Ma, I'm sorry," and it fell upon him like a blow that he had made her unhappy and that the two of them were bound together, irreparably. He loved his mother but he kept think- ing of the woman who had driven him home, an older, frown- ing, serious woman, a real country woman. His mother had a pale plump face in which tears sometimes gathered without effort, creasing in the lines around her mouth, and Jules hated to see that. He hated to see his mother unhappy because she was so helpless at it, so weak.

He dreamed about running away again, back to that farmhouse or to another like it. In the evenings he listened to "The Lone Ranger" and at school he leafed through piles of old books left in a back room, anxious to learn whatever he could; he borrowed comic books from the other kids, wanting to memorize everything. The next time he ran away he would run clear across the country and send his mother a postcard so she wouldn't worry. But which direction should he run in? He dreamed about being The Lone Ranger. He played at being a horse, then at being the man who rode the horse, and at school he got constant practice in running because older kids chased him for long, breathless, speechless minutes. They gave up in sullen admiration, never catching him. They said, "He runs like a deer!" Sometimes he turned back upon them with his fierce eyes, and they caught up to him and laughed from their superior height, sometimes letting him go, not hurting him. He had a breathless, jagged laugh. Angry or excited, he began to stammer. They said to him, "How's the old hermit? You his little boy, or what?" The right taunts could drive him wild and he would rush at them, kicking and punching. They began to say of him, marveling, "Jules Wendall is a crazy little kid."

When he was quiet, though, he could pass for an ordinary child. At school he worked in his coloring book (this was the main instruction for first grade), coloring in outlines of people and animals and trees with the same dutiful neatness as the other children, though he sometimes colored things the "wrong color"—he learned that there were wrong colors and right colors and that it was important he didn't mix them up. And he was fascinated by maps—the old ripped maps in the classroom that could be pulled down over the blackboard, or maps of the war in newspapers, those tiny, flattened-out replicas of a terrain he might someday actually see. The war interested him though he did not know what it was. He could watch on the maps the advancing and retreating armies, and imagine himself with them, crossing mountains and rivers, flowing along in great numbers, adding up all the distances of the world. Sometimes Loretta let him play with the deck of cards—she herself was always playing solitaire—and he imagined a loose, complicated game in which a turn of a card meant a victory for one army, a defeat for the other, and in his mind's eye the newspaper map would be amended. The turn of cards was not something he had power over, though he turned the cards. He could not help what the cards might be and, in a sense, he could not help turning them. In a kind of daze, very quiet, obsessed, he would sit at the old dining-room table for hours, flipping cards, looking from the cards to the map in that night's newspaper, squinting, worried over what he was doing. Somewhere on that map his father, his actual father, was marching.

But when Loretta talked about his father, a *soldier*, carrying a gun and sent God knows where, he tried hard to believe it but couldn't. He tried to think of his father as a soldier, but he kept seeing a slack-bellied man in the front room, drinking beer, waiting. What had his father been waiting for? His father hadn't even played with the deck of cards, as Loretta and Jules did. What was being played out for him, which cards were being turned over, he hadn't even interest enough to find out—it was being done for him, no matter. And so his father had waited. And his mother now walked in a half-sullen, half-content dream around the house, waiting, barefoot or wearing old run-over moccasins like the kind his Aunt Connie wore, and his grandfather went out to work a few mornings a week (he was a janitor for the high school), and his Uncle Fritz, that embarrassing, mumbling old man, slept in a kind of perpetual sleep in his back room—all of them waiting, but waiting for what?

Only Jules and his grandmother, that noisy old woman, were awake. They were first to see a car or a truck come in sight along the road; they were first to get to the door if someone turned in the driveway. The two of them woke early in the morning, anxious to get up—Grandma Wendall to begin the day's cooking, for the canning of fruit maybe, or to begin the wash, and Jules to check the traps he kept down by the creek—because it seemed to them that time went by feverishly, and that there was never enough of it. At times, so restless he could not sit still, he clowned his exasperation at having to wait for other people—he was always waiting for his sisters, waiting for his mother, who had all the time in the world. "Sit still, Jules!" Loretta would snap, made clumsy by his impatience. But he could spend hours lying in the front room reading a book or looking through maps, things he sometimes stole from school; he had the intense, quiet look of a child plotting something. In general he could pass for an ordinary child. His bones, his face, his intelligent eyes, his nicked and scabbed knees—all were signs of ordinary life. But a certain feverishness set upon him often, especially at bedtime, and when people scolded him he could not help imitating them, his little face peaked and daring and insolent. Even his grandmother would cry out, "Jesus Christ! You're going to get all that snottiness whipped out of you!"

One day he was playing in one of the barns, a barn that had been partly burned down years before, and his sister Maureen came out to watch him. Sometimes he ignored her, pretending she was not there, sometimes he drew her right into his games, grateful for her. He did not know, himself, whether he liked her or was embarrassed by her. He was a little jealous of the slow, stubborn, passive power she had—she got her way by looking sad and defiant, not by whining and jumping around the way he did; he sensed that she was not so interesting to older people as he was but that these people loved her better. Maureen came out to watch him play magic. He was a magician; he could create things with his hands, in the air, outlining them again and again in swift, skilful strokes. Maureen, sitting and watching him, could create nothing. She watched. He was so insistent that he could almost make her believe she saw something. "Now do you see it, a rabbit hut? Look at it, dummy, it's right here!" He was squatting in the hay. Maureen stared down at him with her mild, rather empty green eyes, a not very clean child in a very short cotton dress, barefoot, with a long dotted scab on her leg ready to be picked off. Jules, suddenly irritated, took a box of matches out of his pocket, which he had stolen from the kitchen. With the box held high in one hand and the other hand moving in magic circles around it, he called out a complicated vocabulary, mainly having to do with kings, queens, jacks—the cards that were for him mysterious and powerful—and Maureen leaned closer, watching him in fascination.

He took out a match and lit it.

"That's bad," Maureen said.

"Why is it bad?" Jules said.

"You're bad."

"I'm burning the rabbit hutch myself—it's mine to burn up!"

It seemed to him that the flame of the match belonged to him, that it had something to do with the words he had uttered. No one else knew those words. He stared at the match, and when the flame stung his fingers it seemed somehow a mistake, an insult. He shook out the match and lit another one at once. A few yards away, scratching one foot with the toenails of the other, his sister stared at him, smiling. He felt that he had her now. She could not look away from him if she wanted to.

He let the match drop into the hay. "I can do this too. I can do anything," he said.

He squatted in front of the little fire, lost in a sudden reverence for its power. He tried to cup it and hold it down small between his hands. But it took hold, growing. It made a crackling sound. He remained there, staring at it, before it occurred to him that he had made a mistake. Then he jumped to his feet and tried to stamp the fire out. The hay was dry, and the fire took hold with energy, moving backward out of his command. His skin stung with the sharp heat that was so suddenly on its own and had nothing to do with him or his words.

"We better get out of here!" he said, but he was still a little transfixed by this magic, slowed down. He and Maureen stared at the flames. A pile of hay caught fire in a small soft explosion, a puff, which amazed Jules. He had never seen anything like it. The other fire he had seen, the other big fire, was the airplane fire, and that had been boiling and vicious, flames rising as high as a house, out of control. The memory of that other fire stirred him.

He said to Maureen, sharply, "You better get out of here."

She remained staring, transfixed. It might have been that she was waiting for him to touch her, to release her. "Did you do all that?" she asked slowly.

"I said you better get out."

"Could you burn down everything by yourself? Like that?"

The fire began to spread in several directions now, still skirting him as if aware of his power, but at the edge of his vision it was leaping and taking on an energy the match's thin flame had never hinted at. Hayseeds and dust on a rafter caught fire in a quick liquid-like spreading, running up toward the cobwebbed roof like lightning in reverse, striking Jules with its beauty. He backed up. He took hold of Maureen, but she pushed his hand away, staring at the fire.

"Could you stop it now?" she said.

"You goddam dumb baby, how dumb can you be! You want to burn up?" he said. He dragged her to her feet. They crawled out through a back window and hid.

The barn seemed suddenly to explode into flames. Jules and Maureen hid by a stone wall not far away, watching in silence. People ran out of the house, Grandma Wendall was yelling, Connie was amazed, Loretta, always taken by surprise, was buttoning a housedress around her. Jules whispered to Maureen, "We can say it was a thunderstorm. We can say it was hunters."

The firetruck arrived too late. The barn was finished. When the excitement was over and everyone had gone home, Jules came out to be whipped. His grandmother did the whipping. It was a silent, sweaty event, with no one else around. Grandma Wendall had said to Loretta, "I don't want you bawling too. Go in the house!" Jules did not cry for a while, resisting the terrible pain of the stick his grandmother was using. She yelled at him, "Come on and cry, you little bastard!" He could hear the stick moving through the air, its sinewy sound. He seemed to hear it strike him an instant before it actually struck. From his buttocks, down his thighs and down his legs, blood began to run, quickly, and only when he knew what it was did he start to cry. He was very frightened. Grandma Wendall gave up and threw the stick at him in disgust, and the whipping was over.

She yelled, "You'll wind up in the electric chair and I'll pull the switch!"

7

Loretta often walked with the children to town, having nothing to do and wanting to get away from Grandma Wendall. She went to the drugstore and bought Cokes for all of them, and, once there, settled, she would glance around as if prepared to see someone she knew—but not surprised at seeing no one—and take out the letters that she carried in her purse. She would spread them out on the sticky table top of the booth. They had been folded and unfolded so often that they were about to fall into pieces. They were from *home*, she said. She read to them, her face serious and fixed for reading:

Dear Loretta,

How are you? Long time no see. How is Howard? This place is getting next to me here, how is the country? Please write. Did you know that Sissy E. is in the convent? There's nobody much around this place now. My heart could break, it's so slow.

And another letter, which Jules knew wearily by heart and could have recited:

Dear Loretta,
Guess what I am in Detroit! Did you wonder who was writing you from Detroit? There is this man Leonard who I have gotten to know and who is a Detroit boy from way back. Come and see me sometime. There's a lot going on here. Youd be surprised at all the niggers here. Come see me Loretta and the hell with his mother.

She puzzled over these letters, which were scrawled on thin blue stationery in pencil, and looked up at Jules as if to see what he thought of them. Jules finished one Coke and waited for another. Sometimes she bought him another, if she felt right about the letter and what it might mean. And they all wanted to stay away from home as long as possible, though it was hard with a baby fretting and Jules impatient at having to sit in one place. Loretta didn't want him to run free in town since the time he had gotten lost, though she knew well enough that he had run away on purpose, avoiding them. "Anyway you might get hit by a car," she said. She looked through her letters. She licked her lips, thinking. And one day, in the same booth in which she always sat, she spread the letters out before her and, reading them, her lips moving slightly, she drew herself up straight and Jules saw a change come over her, over her face. She frowned, her eyes darted around the table just once, her hands pressed themselves palm downward on the table top. She must have decided something.

That night, after supper, she told Mama Wendall she was leaving. "I and the kids are going to Detroit," she said.

And thereafter followed a long, noisy evening, a fight of whining words and threats—Loretta reckless and shrill, Mama Wendall belligerent though she remained seated, her face contorted with anger. Jules went at once to look up Detroit on the map. He was a little disappointed that it wasn't farther away. Loretta kept backing up, a smile pulling her face slightly out of shape, as if it were someone else's smile, not hers. "Oh, you big old horse!" she cried finally, "you let me alone! I'm free to go where I want!"

"You were a whore once and now you're going back to be one again!"

"You shut up! Don't you talk about me like that in front of these kids—and it isn't true, none of that is true!" Loretta screamed. She was very pale, backed against the kitchen wall, screaming. The children looked on in silence. They looked from their mother to their grandmother and back again, trying to calculate who would win. Loretta cried, "You and your big mouth—all these years I had to take it! Now you and your mouth can shut up, goddam old bitch of a horse, a cow! Bitch, bitch, bitch!" She started to sob. She ran out of the room.

"You can see that your mother is crazy," Grandma Wendall said quietly to Jules.

But Jules's heart was pounding with excitement; he knew he wouldn't sleep that night. He got up around five and got dressed to wait for the others. Grandma Wendall made breakfast for him, silently, ponderously, and when she heard someone waking upstairs she said to him, "You could always stay here, not go with her. You could stay here with me."

"No," said Jules.

"You don't have to go where *she* takes you. You're your father's son too."

"No," said Jules sadly.

To save shame, Papa Wendall drove them to the nearest bus depot instead of letting them walk, as Loretta had threatened. So they dressed up as if for church and looked at one another with nervous smirks, Loretta like one of the children herself. Papa Wendall had nothing to say to them. He let them out at the bus depot and drove away.

"Shit on you, you old bastard!" Loretta cried out happily. "So, kids, that's that with *them*. Now we are entirely on our own."

When they neared Detroit it was late in the day. Jules had a headache, the baby was feverish, people sitting near them kept glancing around in irritation—one of the kids was always whining or kicking a seat; they couldn't help it. Jules couldn't help it. Loretta lay back in her seat with the baby on her lap, exhausted from the ride, her hair in a mess and her face flushed. She kept saying, "Rita will treat us real well when we get there." But getting to Detroit was not easy. They began entering a city and kept entering it, going in deeper and deeper but not coming to any center.

Jules stared out the window. He had never seen anything like this. No map had prepared him for all these streets, these wide boulevards, these buildings and cars and trucks and people, both white and colored, women with painted-on lips and eyebrows of thick dark lines pausing to cross streets, in shoes with high heels, and young men with hair sprawling out pointed behind their ears, looking very dangerous. His head ached violently.

In a daze, Loretta kept muttering, "Soon as we get in we'll call Rita . . . the number is right here . . . she'll be so glad to see us and'll treat us real well . . ." But the bus kept crossing intersections, stopping and starting, until Jules thought he would go crazy. He couldn't take this. He wanted the still, empty space of the country even if it was punctuated by his grandmother's thumping footsteps and his grandfather's snoring and the dim, oppressive memory of his father, a man in a soldier's uniform. Maureen began to cry. She cried wearily, like a child who feels the need to cry too often. Loretta said, giving her a pinch, "Don't you go bawling, because this is a wonderful city and a wonderful opportunity, and Rita will take real good care of us."

After some hours in a great bus station, hanging around to make the same telephone call again and again, and after what seemed to Jules a nightmare space of time during which he believed that the police would come and arrest them all, send them back to the farm, Loretta finally got hold of her mysterious friend. She jumped up and down in the pay booth like a teen-ager, overjoyed. "Rita! It's me! *Me*, Loretta!" Jules tried not to listen to her, because their lives depended upon this, but he had to stay near his mother in case something terrible happened. Over on the bench the baby had finally fallen asleep, flush-faced, and Maureen sat with her pale, serious, defeated eyes on her mother. Loretta cried out for joy. Some magic was being worked, Jules thought. Certain words. Incantations. Some woman at the other end of the line, a woman who had written exactly five letters on blue paper, and now this—the end of the bus trip, this. His head was seized by a sudden bluish pain as if a stranger's hand had enclosed it tightly.

They got to Rita's place, which was on a jumbled busy street, and the baby was changed at last and the kids fed hamburger, and Jules lay pretending to sleep while he listened to the women talk, one of whom was his mother.

"No, look, I ain't kidding you," the strange woman said,

"he won't take no mess and won't laugh anything off, not *anything*. Sometimes I'm scared to death, that's the truth. But he's a real man at least. How many of them left around here are real men?"

"I have thirty-four dollars and a few cents. Let me check—"

"No, honey, sit still. Jesus!"

From a radio somewhere came a muffled whine of music, a popular song about love. *If you love me and I love you . . .* Jules fixed his mind upon Rita's voice, canceling out his mother's. This woman was saying two things, one in words and the other beneath the words, and he was afraid his mother was hearing only the words. "No, sure, he won't care. He's out of town anyway until Friday. No, I don't know exactly, that's his way, he won't talk much or explain anything. Men who talk a lot are no good anyway. Look, Loretta, didn't I tell you to come visit, and you know me, I never lie . . ."

So they spent the night there, and Jules thought mournfully of the big house out in the country and his bed there and the country itself, where space was everywhere and there were no airless boxed-in streets. And when morning came they were up and on their way out, Loretta fussy and lightheaded, talking too much. Rita kept saying, "But, honey, you could stay at least until Friday, really," and Loretta kept saying with a nervous giggle, "It's time I made my own way. I'm old enough." Jules winced at her foolish, almost hysterical laugh. She said, "Jesus Christ, I'm almost twenty-five years *old*," and finally they were out, trailing along the street, their mother in high-heeled shoes and a yellow dress rumpled from the bus ride, her hair pulled back into a sloppy knot, her lips dabbed with lipstick that had begun to crack.

She found them a room above a funeral parlor. It was the first place she looked at, the first place she saw a sign— ROOM FOR RENT—and she went for it breathlessly, as if fearful it would be taken before she got inside. The room was furnished, with one bed. She put all the kids in it. No cover, but that was all right; Jules put his mother's sweater over Maureen and the baby.

"This is a nice room, isn't it?" Loretta said.

Jules said, "Yeah," and sat on the edge of the bed, a thoughtful and stricken child of nearly eight who wondered how long they were going to last. "Now what are you gonna do?" he said.

Loretta was looking at herself in a compact mirror. Turning away from Jules, moving so deliberately, she seemed to solidify the form of her body, bringing out the thick slow curve of her hips. She had changed into a flowered print dress, all golds and oranges and pinks, and her fingers tapped busily around her hair—she'd combed it out onto her shoulders, hair streaked blond and brown. She seemed to be getting instructions from her reflection in the little mirror.

"You guys all go to sleep now. You didn't get enough sleep last night."

"Sleep *now?*" Jules said.

"You watch them girls then."

She left. She went out into the street. All that night she had been thinking about Rita and Rita's man, her mind turning dizzily upon them; she had forgotten Howard entirely. She did not even think to take the wedding ring off her finger.

It was now early afternoon. She walked down the street, alert and yet not alert, in a kind of bright, vivacious daze, her eyes not quite taking in all the people around her—so many people, cars, high buildings, so much to see!—and she turned off onto a side street, swaying in her high heels, already exhausted. Time passed. She was lost but didn't think about it. She felt vaguely that some invisible thread would get her back to the kids, and anyway Jules had sense enough to watch out for the girls. Finally she saw a man walking alongside her who glanced over sideways at her, in a certain way. Her heart pounded. She looked ahead, she looked back at him. The man was about her height, in a brown suit that might have been an expensive one, she couldn't tell— she hadn't even seen a man in a suit for years!—and he stared at her with a serious, quizzical look, in silence, even a little shy, until she said, "Hello!" That did it. He slowed down, he circled around to confront her. She said again, "Hello . . . this is a nice day . . ." She was grinning. The man said cautiously, "What were you thinking of?" For a moment she stared at him. Then she went blank; she could not think of anything. Then she came to and said, "Ten dollars . . . ten . . ." And he said again, stooping a little as if to hear better, *"What* were you thinking of?" She said, "Ten dollars . . . ?" and her voice ended in a humiliating quaver, a question.

The man took hold of her wrist. "All right, you're busted," he said.

"What?"

"The patrol car is just up ahead, around the corner. Come on."

She could not move. She wasn't fighting him, her body was just stunned, heavy. He began shaking her hard. He was no longer cautious. He didn't care who heard them, passing by on the sidewalk. He said in a nasty voice, "Come on! Around the corner! You're busted!"

She managed to say, "Let me go and I'll walk by myself—people are watching!"

Around the corner was a patrol car, as he had promised, with the words DETROIT POLICE in white on its side. Loretta was led up to it to be introduced officially to the City of Detroit.

8

When Jules was twelve he fell in love for the first time. His feelings settled sharply upon a young nun who taught fifth grade at school—a tall, quick, surprised-looking woman who played piano at assemblies; she was his sister Maureen's teacher. It was the piano that had drawn him to her. Marching into the auditorium for assemblies on Thursday mornings, Jules had noticed her, admiring the rapid runs and rushes of her pale fingers. He was entranced by the fluttering of her black sleeves and the flash of white at her slender wrists. Left to himself in class, pretending to be working on an assignment, he let his mind drift onto her and onto the intricate melodious passages of her music, which seemed to him exotic, amazing, beyond anything he or the people he knew could ever attain. There was something magical in her, in her very being. She seemed a part of the music she made.

Every evening Maureen had something to say about Sister Mary Jerome. She was a quick-tempered young nun in spite of that fragile look. "Today Sister cried again," Maureen would report, interested and curious. Why did the nuns sometimes burst into tears? Why did they sometimes slap the wrong students, running down to the aisle and picking out the wrong students?

"You kids are something, making the nuns cry," Loretta would say. "The whole bunch of you need a licking."

"But I don't know why she cried. She just did," Maureen said.

After school Jules ran half a mile to a five-and-ten-cent store where he worked. Though he was legally too young for a job, he was hired for a quarter or half a dollar an hour if he showed up early enough, to help unpack and unwrap. He dealt with crates of dishware and toys and various junk. Rattling around in his head were the lessons of that day and the shouted threats and news of the playground, the fluttered passing of Sister Mary Jerome in the corridor and any news about her he might have heard. "How's your teacher, did she cry again?" he would ask scornfully of one of Maureen's classmates.

His mother no longer bothered to cry. For years she had cried; now she had stopped. His father was like a great wall leaning inward, about to collapse on top of them, but since he had never quite collapsed they gave up fearing him and crying about him. At least Loretta had given up. Jules associated Sister Mary Jerome's tears—he had to imagine them, having never seen them himself—with an exoticism that his mother had never had. And the women in movies cried often. They cried beautifully. At the piano Sister's clever, violent hands controlled the keyboard, and each note was struck beautifully inside Jules's skull, to be replayed while he struggled with crates, unloading them, digging through baskets of shredded paper and cardboard. Occasionally he cut his hands. Once he stepped on a nail and it went through his shoe and sock, but nothing happened, only a little blood. Sometimes, at home, he discovered large mysterious bruises on his legs. But while he worked, a strange excitement controlled him. The other kids fooled around and snatched things when no one was looking, but in a daze Jules strained muscles to do the job right. When Sister Mary Jerome was in his head he was always a good boy.

"Here, Jules, have one of these—try this," one of the salesgirls said. She was sixteen or seventeen and liked to come out to tease him. She gave him cigarettes. Jules, who had been smoking for two years but could not afford cigarettes, pretended shyness and accepted them. The girl struck a match and held it up for him, staring with a peculiar smile into his face. "Well, how's your mother these days, kid?" she said.

"Okay," said Jules.

"How's your father?"

"Okay."

"I seen you guys in church. Is your mother going to have a baby again?"

It was a question Jules thought should not be asked. He nodded his head, embarrassed.

The girl smiled at him broadly, as if he himself had achieved something.

"You guys hoping for a boy or a girl?"

"I guess a boy."

"You know all about it, huh? All about that stuff?" said the girl.

She had a sharp, dented, almost pretty face, with long black hair that fell past her shoulders. Around her wrist was an identification bracelet her boy friend had given her. On her forearm was a small tattoo of a heart with an arrow through it and the initials R.J. drawn about it in a design resembling lace; she had shown it to Jules one day, but most of the time it was covered up. She said that the five-and-ten manager, an old bitch, didn't like it. "One of these days I'll tattoo you," she told Jules.

The alley behind the store was always filthy. Big boxes, busted crates, overturned garbage pails, everything was in a mess; dogs seemed to seek out this stretch of alley and Jules was always stepping into something. With him worked a few other boys, differing from day to day, the biggest being Ramie Malone, a friend. Ramie had a reputation at school. He stole things from cars, sometimes even radios; that was his specialty. He was thirteen. Late at night he wandered up and down the neighborhood a few blocks from home, where there were many cars parked outside taverns. He worked alone and sold his merchandise with no trouble to a friend of his brother's. All Jules's devotion to Sister Mary Jerome was threatened by Ramie's enticing tales. "If this deal I got going works out, you won't see me back here for a long time," Ramie would promise. He would show Jules switchblade knives someone had given him. He would talk excitedly of the latest news, news not put in the paper, of men found in the trunks of cars only a few blocks from Jules's house, tied with "bobwire," shot dead, and kids their own age pushed off roofs by niggers. He would tell Jules of a nigger given a beating at one of the precincts, all the men pounding on him with their clubs, all over his body and on his face, "until that bastard's eye popped right out of his head and onto his cheek, the real thing. Ain't that something?" Ramie had a cousin, or a friend of his had a cousin, who was a policeman. He knew everything.

He told Jules all about the niggers. "What they want most is to get some kid like you or me, white kids, and scalp us. They do that. A man was found with his scalp half ripped off, and he said niggers did it. You got to watch out for those dirty bastards." Jules felt a prick of terror at the promise of trouble; he looked about, awaiting it. When he saw a Negro on the street he stared cautiously, wondering when the trouble would come. What secret did niggers have? Where was the mystery? A few years ago there had been a riot on the Belle Isle bridge and people were still talking about it, still angry. Jules wished he could have seen that riot.

At work he couldn't help hanging around Ramie. He kept asking him, "Who was it that got scalped, *who?*" or "But *which* kids got pushed off a roof?" He trembled, waiting for Ramie's answer, which was usually evasive and insulting. And sometimes, relying desperately on Ramie's superior knowledge, he asked him, "Why does my sister's teacher cry at school? It's Sister Mary Jerome. Do you know her? She nuts or something?"

"They're all nuts," Ramie said.

"But what about her—why does she cry?"

"How should I know? All those bitches only need one thing."

At home Jules nosed around his mother when she was in a good mood, when she was alone, listening to the radio; he wanted to understand the way women were. Loretta liked to listen to "The Hit Parade." He wondered if Sister Mary Jerome would like it, if she were allowed to listen to it. He hung around his mother, and occasionally he asked, "You got anything you want me to do?" She was always flattered when he or Maureen asked her this. Much of the time she lay on the sofa, drinking beer and resting the bottle on her stomach, peeling the label from it with her fingernails, listening to the radio. Alone during the day, she was lazy and bland. She listened to songs on the radio or "Ma Perkins" and "One Man's Family" and "Dr. Malone." Jules liked her this way, stretched out and lazy, within his reach. On certain days she didn't bother to make supper, she didn't feel well, she didn't feel up to it, and Maureen and Jules would go out into the kitchen and make something, playing with food. They made supper with an eye to pleasing their father.

On those evenings when he didn't show up they kept the plate warm in the oven without even being asked to; Jules did a lot around the house without being asked to. He hated to be made to do anything, and he had learned that it was less trouble to do things himself. It kept his mother quiet, lying still and content; it kept his father quiet. But his father's bulk loomed up in his mind, dark and threatening as any Negro, and he thought idly, *One of these days he's going to die.*

He liked his home and he liked school. But he was always tired at home and always tired at school. After that spring morning in 1950 when he first fell in love with Sister Jerome during an assembly, his exhaustion was complex; he was up much of the night and after school he had to work, but still he was lively and enthusiastic, and only when the drill of catechism and history and grammar began did his mind begin to go. He thought of the nun's fluttering sleeves and her fingers on the keyboard. He thought of her pale, serious face, her eyes that glanced up in a kind of timid alarm when he saw her in the corridor or at Mass. He helped to serve Mass on Monday and Wednesday mornings at the convent. A few hours later, at his desk, he would think back on that eerie dawn in church (the oldest church in Detroit!), a red-brick church of enormous proportions, very dark, shadowy, musty, with an old Irishman saying Mass, crotchety and unpredictable, sometimes giving the altar boys a poke to hurry them up, and the silent, fluttering file of nuns coming up the aisle to the communion rail, among them his beloved Sister Mary Jerome. He slept maybe three or four hours a night, and his mind boggled a little during the day, particularly when motes of dust whirled about his head in the sunlight. *I love her, I love her,* he thought, sounding in his imagination the dull, sonorous notes of a church bell, planning to run across the building to the fifth-graders' room when school was out, under the pretext of meeting his sister. He was a fairly tall boy for his age, a little nervous, high-pitched, and with a high, sometimes irritating voice; he had clear skin and clear, serious eyes, though he could not always keep them focused on what he was looking at.

They were studying American history in seventh grade.

Drill began at the front of the room, the far right row, and continued around the room to the back of the far left row, then to the front again. It went on forever; it never stopped. When the day was over it simply began again, the next day. If there was a weekend or a holiday, it simply began again at the next desk, the next day. Each child seemed to take a long time with his answer. Jules tried to listen, but after a while his mind began to disintegrate, shattering slowly into lovely erotic fragments. He did not want to put together Sister Mary Jerome and what Ramie said, the two thoughts, the two realities, but they came together of their own accord and left him baffled and trembling. The nun who taught seventh grade was old, or looked old. She had a voice like Jules's father. "Who was Abraham Lincoln?" she asked, her coarse, downy face turned toward the student who was to answer next. A child responded slowly, as if dull-witted, "Abraham Lincoln was a President. Of the United States."

On to the next student: "Which President was he?"

"He was the . . . the sixteenth President of the United States."

And on to the next: "When is Abraham Lincoln's birthday?"

"Abraham Lincoln's birthday is February twelfth."

And around the drill went, around the room, relentlessly up and down the rows, while Jules kept his head up and tried to listen. They all had their battered old books open; they glanced down to find out the answers to Sister's questions, sometimes running their fingers slowly along the lines of smudged print. They were all frightened when it was their turn to recite. Jules dreamed of Sister Mary Jerome and her tears and her music, and sometimes when his turn came he was unprepared, startled, and had actually to look down at his book to find out the answer. That was not quite the way Sister wanted the drill done: she wanted everyone to know the answers and to recite sitting up straight, looking at her. So she would frown at him, sour and suspicious and motionless at her desk, and after a few panicked seconds Jules would repeat the answer, not looking down at his book, coming out with the answer that was the only right answer, the words that were the only words to be spoken at this particular moment: "Abraham Lincoln was assassinated in office. In eighteen sixty-five." Then he returned to his dreaming again.

At noon hour they were herded into a "lunchroom" where they ate their lunch out of paper bags brought from home, and fifteen minutes later they were herded out to the "playground." Beyond the fence, out on Howard Street, trucks bound for the bridge to Canada rumbled by, and Jules felt a sharp envy for adults who could drive back and forth across the continent and even into a foreign country. They need never return to any particular home. In their trucks they were elegant, free, the distance they covered was godly and magical. But he fooled around with the other kids, letting their jokes and fighting drive such things out of his mind, and when he was feeling especially good he plotted strategies for them. He thought of himself as a commander of some sort. A general, an admiral, a minister of war. He got his friends to ambush other kids or to sneak back into the school building, which was forbidden. He made plans for them; sometimes he drew diagrams for them to follow. "Now you got to take this route, the side route," he would say sternly, poking one of the boys, "and you, you got to take the other route. I won't stand for no mess. Deserters will be shot." He happened to be taller than most of his friends, and some accident of voice or energy kept him ahead of them; he bullied them until they could no longer take it and ganged up on him, then scattered and came back in a day or two, unable to resist him, drawn by his ideas and his daring. He led them into the basement of the school, chanting, "On to the Tigris! On to the Euphrates! The Mississippi! The Hanging Gardens of Babylon!" His magic words drove them on, frightened and giggling. If they were caught, it was always Jules who was blamed.

"You have the Devil in you," the Mother Superior told him one day.

He sat in her dour office, a captive. She was a large woman like his grandmother, and in her own way just as coarse and strong; he had to respect her. She was not quite a woman, like his mother and Sister Mary Jerome, but he respected her. With three careful, hard blows she struck his extended hands, his shoulder, and the side of his head.

"Why are you always getting into trouble? Why can't you sit still right now? Why are you so bad?" she asked him angrily.

"I'm sorry, Sister," said Jules.

He had been caught smoking in the boys' room. The janitor had walked in on him.

"Who taught you to smoke?"

"Nobody, Sister."

"Who gave you cigarettes?"

"Nobody, Sister."

"Did you steal them?"

"No, Sister."

"Where did you get them from?"

Silence. Jules sat in the hard-backed chair, wondering how he looked and whether his face was red, whether the other kids would be able to see the marks of Sister's fingers on his face. Sister leaned across her desk, grunting, and struck him again on the side of the head. He fell back against the chair. His nose began to bleed.

"Don't you have a handkerchief?"

"Yes."

"Then use it! Are you that much of a pig?"

He held his handkerchief to his nose, glad for something to hide behind, frightened and miserable and yet a little excited by this attention. Why did he feel so excited whenever anyone looked at him, even if it was a glance that preceded a blow?

"Do you want to wind up in the electric chair?"

"No, Sister."

"Yes, I think you do. I think that's what the Devil in you is planning."

She spoke seriously, even a little flatly. It was clear to Jules that she was not making anything up, not figuring anything out; she was recalling something. His future was known to her, like the past. She knew everything. Jules sniffed the blood back into his head, not wanting to make a mess. It got into the back of his mouth somehow and he had to swallow it. Giddy, the taste of this bad blood. He would get drunk.

Sister was talking about a boy who had been bad in this school ten years before. He was now at the state penitentiary for life; he should really have been sent to the electric chair. But he would go to Hell when he died. "Do you want to wind up like that?"

"No, Sister."

"A certain number of boys must grow up to die in the electric chair," Sister said distantly.

He thought suddenly of the lovely flash of electricity that would kill him: he'd seen preparations for many electrocutions, in the movies and in comic books. Hangings, firing squads, gas—these were promised as well, and in other countries you could be garroted, but the electric chair, with its clumsy, homely similarity to ordinary chairs, fascinated him.

She was staring over Jules's head. Then she looked at him again with her distant, cold gaze.

"Your sister Maureen is in Sister Mary Jerome's room, isn't she?"

"Yes, Sister."

"Your sister is a very good girl. A good student."

"Yes, Sister."

"And your other sister, Betty, tries hard."

"Yes, Sister."

"Why are you different?"

She was silent for a while, contemplating him. Women contemplated and judged, he had found that out; men did the hitting, but without thinking about it. Their blows were senseless, had to be avoided, that was all. But women were always thinking, sifting, judging, preparing. Jules sat very straight, his handkerchief to his nose. He waited. Into his mind came a sudden weird thought—maybe Sister Mary Jerome would get fed up with all of this, all this crap, the ugly building and the ugly nuns, the noisy, bratty kids, the snot-nosed kids, the early Mass, the stink from the lavatories; maybe one day he would see her out on the street, strolling the way certain other young women strolled, watchful and without a destination, their eyes alert for passing cars. Sister Jerome's pale nervous face would do well in such a setting: there were too many overdone faces. Jules had gathered from innumerable arguments between his mother and father and between his parents and his father's relatives that his mother had been "out on the street" once and hadn't even been able to succeed at that. "What a cow, what a stupid cow! Ain't that the last straw!" His father had laughed about this many times; his father brought out this old story whenever he was drunk. It seemed to please him. So Jules imagined Sister Jerome in an outfit like her nun's outfit, with long black skirts and sleeves and a kind of hood, making her way toward the hazy downtown streets, timid and a little arrogant, and he, Jules, coming up beside her and saying, "My ma would love for you to come home with me. You can have supper with us right now . . ." And she would come to live with them: that would straighten everything out.

After school, if he couldn't get a job at the five-and-ten, he drifted around with a few other boys, in and out of alleys, on the lookout for whatever they could find. Because the streets here were heavy with traffic and because trucks were parked everywhere, their territory was broken up; they couldn't see very far ahead of them. They played in vacant lots and down toward the bridge, where the river lapped up dead fish and great floating streams of oil. They fooled around in warehouses, in parked trucks, explored the railroad yard, the Trans-American Cartage Company, the Greyhound garage, anything. They collected pop bottles and kicked through gutters looking for crumpled popsicle wrappers that could be saved up for prizes. When their mood was more restless they drifted into small grocery stores, and the smallest of the boys played chickie for them up front while Jules himself, smooth and blind with daring, would march right out with a ten-cent pie stuck in his pocket. A few times he was caught and knocked around, but most of the time he got out safely. When he escaped he felt curiously deflated, disappointed. The territory he wandered in stretched from about 21st Street to about 10th Street.

When he was loose on the street, though, his heart was still with Sister Mary Jerome: when he was bad he felt guilty. But he couldn't help being bad. He couldn't help feeling guilty. He went to confession and said breathlessly to the old priest on the other side of the confessional, "I was inattentive during Mass. I was disobedient to my mother and father. I neglected my morning and night prayers . . ." One by one the sentences came from him, exactly the same every week, and he kept in the back of his mind his sinful fascination with Sister Mary Jerome and his occasional thefts and his slapping around of certain kids who wouldn't obey him. Of God he had no thoughts at all. He had no belief in God, no interest. He pressed his fingertips against his eyeballs and tried to imagine, deep in the interior of his own brain, a being not quite himself who watched him, angry and hateful and loving of him, but he could not imagine it, not really; who beside Jules could love or hate Jules? When he turned quickly on the street it was usually to see no one—nothing. There was nothing behind him. Nothing followed him. At night, when he woke suddenly, there was nothing close to him, breathing over him, watching. He was only himself, free. But it was still possible that he had a devil in him; a devil was to his imagination a kind of persistent failing, a dragging over to one side, as when a car's tires begin to go on one side and drag everything over that way, relentlessly. If he had a devil, the devil's name was Jules also. This devil might draw him to the electric chair. Ramie Malone said that if you killed somebody in Chicago you would go to the chair because they didn't fool around. Chicago seemed attractive to Jules.

On Thursdays he was impatient to get into the assembly room, wanting to hear Sister Jerome's music. He was angry with the thumping footsteps of the other students. All those stupid kids! Those snot-nosed little bastards! Jules sat hunched forward in his seat, drowned with love for Sister's deft fingers and arms. During the assembly Sister Jerome sat off to one side on the stage, primly and quietly. Jules's eyes burned upon her. He did not think she was a beautiful woman but he had no interest in beauty; he needed something fierce and pure, lips without lipstick, a pale, grave brow, a face ready to burst into tears.

One day, after the assembly, he made his way up toward the stage. He said to Sister, "That piano playing is so nice . . ."

She looked around at him in alarm.

"I like to listen to piano music," Jules said, nearly stammering.

She tried to smile. "Do you have a piano at home?"

She was putting together sheets of music; the knuckles of her hands were white and prominent. "No, not at home," he mumbled.

She bowed her head, silent, as if his words puzzled her, then turned and disappeared behind the heavy velvet curtain. Jules wanted to call after her but could not speak, could not think of anything to say. She did not return. He wandered out into the sunlight, making fists, staring at his own knuckles, and wondering if he could learn to play the piano.

After that he hung around her homeroom from time to time, standing with his arms folded, waiting for her or for something. Nothing happened. If she noticed him she gave no sign. She hurried by, her head ducked, her face very pale, and in her arms books and papers. His very soul shivered at the rattling of her long black loose rosary.

Maureen came up to him in the hall and said curiously, "What are you doing here?"

"Go to hell,'" he said.

Sister Jerome gave piano lessons in the auditorium to certain girls on certain days. Jules managed to find out these days. He crouched in the darkness at the rear of the room, staring at the half-lit stage, at Sister's grave bent head and her pale, humorless, precise lips as she said sternly, "One-two, one-two, one-two—what are you doing?" The piano's pedals thumped, the notes were hollow and too loud. Jules crouched in the darkness and dreamed of certain tender things, his fantasies stroked by her one-*two*, one-*two*, the relentless rhythm of her half-angry voice. Why was she so angry, what was it that kept her pale and held back, so timid? He imagined her tears flowing to violence as brutal, brutal music broke from her, all that was held back by that one-*two*, one-*two* of her music lessons. He believed that he loved her.

Then came the hours after school, a reluctant freedom. Maureen and Betty would straggle home and Jules would be out for a few hours running loose, until, exhausted and sometimes bloody, he showed up at the house (they lived now in a two-family house) around six. By then his mother's first round of anger would have quieted down, and Betty or maybe even Maureen would be shut up in the clothes closet to "cool off." So Jules could make his appearance safely. He would say, eying his mother's loose, soiled bathrobe and a certain arrogant puffiness about her face, "You want me to do anything around here before *he* comes home?" This put the two of them together, as if on a raft, against *him*. He wanted her to feel that. And, softened by his gentlemanly tone, his mother might hug him and tell him there was garbage, yes, he could take outside. Or he could run and let Betty or Maureen out of the clothes closet.

Loretta was not always drunk. Sometimes she came home from shopping, wearing a pretty dress and high heels, her hair coming loose but not yet a mess, and she would put out on the kitchen table all the things she'd bought, for Jules and his sisters to look through. Most of it was food. He was fascinated by cans and cellophane packages being produced out of a big brown bag by his mother's fingers, and Loretta herself enjoyed taking these things out, all these unsurprising surprises. She said to them, "Oh, you stupid dopes! You're crazy, there's nothing in here! What do you expect, huh? You're pests! Julie, you're a big dope! You think it's Christmas or maybe your birthday?"

But she was pleased herself. She gave them stamps of green or yellow and the three kids haggled over which of them should paste them in the stamp book. They were supposed to take turns, but in his enthusiasm Jules could never quite remember whose turn it was; he kept insisting it was his. "Give them to Jules, he does the best job," his mother would always say finally, and that shut up the girls. She was wobbly and warm, his mother, and if she gave in it was usually to him; Maureen was the good girl but something about her quiet face put Loretta off. "She's always looking at me, that one. Watching," Loretta complained. Betty, who was a short, tough, noisy kid, had none of Maureen's looks and none of Jules's brains; she made her way by shouting and nudging. Jules and Maureen tended to ignore her. She had no dignity; she did not count.

When their father came home there was not always trouble. Sometimes he came home for supper on time, and he sat at the table with them and ate, and after supper he sat in the living-room and dozed over a newspaper. He had a hairy, large head with prominent ears that gave the appearance of hearing everything, though he was really getting deaf, Jules thought, or getting too lazy to hear. He couldn't believe that his father had ever been a cop. What a laugh! How could that fat bastard reach for a gun—how could he get it out in time to use? Jules was secretive and polite around his father, fearing his father's quick temper and his cruelty, but he was open with his mother and the girls: "That old bastard gets next to me, I tell you. One of these days . . ."

Sometimes there was trouble when his father came home drunk. On these nights there was nothing to do but get out. Loretta went across the way to a girl friend's house, where the two of them played cards most of the night and sucked Royal Crown Cola or beer, and Jules and the girls went outside if the weather was good enough. They wandered down the alley, free, on their own. Most of the time they climbed to the roof of an apartment building where some of their friends lived, and some of these kids spent the night out—some sneaked out, some had to get out because things were too rough. Maureen sat with her back against the ledge and slept, her arms on her knees, her head drooping onto her arms; Betty fooled around; Jules would look restlessly out over what he could see of the neighborhood and of Detroit, making plans—the next morning he would ask Sister Jerome if he could take piano lessons from her; the next afternoon he would steal something large and salable, maybe a radio; the next evening he would split his father's skull in two with an ax, then take off across the country, following a map. Why not? Why not across the country, why not across the world? He yearned for the freedom of trucks and trains and planes. Why not split his father's stupid solid head?

Why not seize Sister Jerome's pale thin hand and bring it to his lips?

Sometimes, after a few hours, they could sneak back home. By then their father was unconscious and no trouble. Sometimes, if Maureen was sound asleep, they would spend the night out—"camping out"—and Jules would sit drowsily on guard. He would drop off to sleep, then wake again, startled, his heart miserable, his mouth tasting of something foul. Very early, before dawn, he would wake Maureen and Betty. They would climb down to the alley and return to the house.

"Jesus, that bastard gets next to me," Jules went around saying.

At confession he recited, "I was disobedient to my mother and father . . ."

He was to recall his childhood in flickers and flashes, as if it were a movie made before his time, one of those old halting, comic films in which foolishly dressed people could have felt no pain, no anguish. How could such out-of-date people be human? Had he, Jules Wendall, ever been a child? Really a child? In the sense in which other people have been children? And what did it mean, to have been a child? Did it mean that the child Jules was still with him, encased within his bones, an alert, nervous, hollow-eyed kid with a love of maps and music and pale, fierce women? Was he always to be half carrying the groggy Maureen back to her bed? Was he always to be dreaming of crushing his father's skull, even after his father was dead?

One day, his thoughts half on Sister Mary Jerome, he allowed himself to be taken to her home by his friend from the five-and-ten. She wore her hair pulled back in a ponytail. She was very excited, talking about a murder in the neighborhood. "Oh, I'm not gonna tell you what they found! Not all of it! It wasn't in the papers either!" Twin girls, under twelve, had been stabbed to death in the hours before dawn. One had been stabbed in her room and the other out on the street, where she'd run, chased by the murderer for nearly a block, so that bloodstains led from her room right out onto the sidewalk. Everyone was talking about it; the girl could not stop talking about it. She kept poking Jules. She kept saying, "They can't put everything in the paper!" No one was home. She let him in the house. She turned on the radio. She said to Jules, who was very frightened, "I'm gonna cut my initials into you, kid." Jules had thought that girls got hurt doing this or having it done to them; but he discovered that there was no pain between them. There was only a sudden sweet layer of perspiration between them. The girl's little cries fluttered about the four walls of the room, driving Jules into a swoon half of terror, sucking his strength out of him. He was always aware of himself, *Jules*. He could not force his eyes shut, as the girl did: they kept popping back open, alarmed and dry. But he was very weak. He had no strength. He wanted to weep but everything in him was dry, empty.

"Now you love me," the girl said lightly. She pinched his cheek. She was like a girl in the movies, light and bouncy in her bare feet, patting her hair into place.

Jules stared open-eyed at her.

"Yes, you love me, you're gonna think about me all the time," she said. "When you hear that song on the radio, you're gonna think about me. I was the one who turned you out, kid. You remember that."

"Yes," said Jules.

"All your life—"

"Yes," said Jules.

9

It was a misty gray day, the kind of day Jules loved, with that faint metallic sheen to the sky that touched the edges of buildings and cars; he was cutting school for a good cause, taking his grandmother down to the clinic. So he whistled under his breath and sucked in the smudged air like a good boy, fifteen years old and dressed well in a silkish shirt and dark, slightly pegged pants, with his dark hair long and combed back in harsh wings to form a wavy mass at the back of his head. He kept seeing himself from a distance, flashes of himself—Jules Wendall—and could not help being pleased. He put his arm out cavalierly for Grandma Wendall to take. The old woman seized it with a muttered complaint that dampened him a little. "You'd think one of *them*, those two, could drive me there themselves."

It was 1953 now, and Grandma Wendall was in Detroit living with them, a widow, her thick lardlike legs a mess of splotched and broken veins, her gray hair frizzled and thin at the very top of her head, her face lined with angry, contemplative lines that gave her the appearance of being an ancient man, soured on life but not ready to leave it. She poured into Jules's patient, miserable ear all the ugly news of her widowhood and her decline into a mother-in-law, pushed into a back room in a dump of a house on Twentieth Street, a dump of a street, bossed around by a frowzy dump of a woman who drank too much. "But God bless her, she's your mother and that's that," Grandma Wendall said, twisting her mouth, leaning on Jules heavily, "but anyway it's to your credit you take after our family—not after your father but after *me*. You and I have the same brains."

"I'm not anywhere near as sharp as you," Jules said, playing to her the same banter he'd played for years, but a little distracted; he wondered where the hell the bus was. Why was there always such a wait? His grandmother was tough in her bones and brains, that was true, but she was wearing down as the months went by, and just this walk from home to Fort Street left her out of breath. She panted like a horse, like a cow, baffled at the failure of her body to keep up with her assessment of herself. They waited in the fog on Fort Street, Jules conscious of his handsome (though slightly blemished) young face, his duck-tail haircut, his neatly flashy clothes that put him in a certain high-school crowd—at the very top of that crowd, he liked to think, being clever and mobile enough. He was spending his adolescence in the faint shadows of actual gangsters, or the friends of gangsters; something in him yearned for the doomed, derelict, glamorous style of their living. He took some of his language from them or from their imitators or from movies, and his clothes and even his walk had a slightly retarded, lounging, lethargic, contemptuous, self-conscious air about them, a pimp's style; he was very pleased with all this.

He said to his grandmother, "Pa couldn't take off from work. He had two sick days last month."

"What about *her?*"

"I can take you as well as her, can't I? You said you liked to ride the bus. You want a cigarette or something?"

Her husband had died of cancer of the throat, and during this lingering death of all times she had begun to smoke. She astonished everyone. She carried on with Jules a man-to-man, boy-to-boy, brotherly, childish camaraderie, conspiratorial and pointless to Jules but, he supposed, a means for her to take revenge on that middle generation she believed had wronged her, her son and his wife. So, with a smirk, as if they were both putting something over on Loretta, she accepted a cigarette. Jules was saddened to see his grandmother such a lumpy woman in her dark, long, shapeless coat and her pushed-down hat of some indecipherable style, with a torn veil and dark brown wings of feathers. What an old woman she'd become! Better for her to have been transformed into an old man! She complained about that bastard, the Mayor, and that other bastard, the Governor, and most of all that bastard who was President of the United States. Taxes, too many taxes. Social Security was a racket, a joke. They were playing a joke on her. If she wasn't an old woman she would fight. The United States was crazy, she could tell from the newspaper, and Europe was crazy, a loss. "All of the world is a garbage dump," she said.

On Fort Street a steady stream of cars and trucks passed. The river was not far away. Jules looked about and his eyes took in the heavy, unbeautiful span of the Ambassador Bridge, the bridge to Canada, a sight he'd lived under for many years. He wondered what was the way out, which direction he should take. Though his grandmother mouthed sourly these complaints, it was too late for her: she could never escape.

"All my life I lived around men," the old woman was saying angrily. "I know men. Women I don't know. Women I don't talk to. You're better letting them alone. You are a man yourself, at your age, you got common sense, I can talk to you. Right? But your mother . . ."

So it was about his mother again. Jules said evasively, "Oh, let Ma alone."

"Does she let me alone? Does she ever let me forget whose house I'm living in? I just ask you that, I put it to your common sense. Tell the truth. Does she let me alone?"

"I don't know."

"A crazy house, wide open like that. People coming and going, those friends of hers, them, those women got nothing better to do than drag their asses around in a bathrobe and drink beer all afternoon, playing rummy all the time. It's no wonder Howard stays out late, I don't blame him. And your sister Betty is going to go bad—"

"That's her business."

"Your sister Maureen is too skinny."

"She's okay."

The old woman sucked at her cigarette. Jules observed

from the corners of his eyes that she did not know how to smoke with any grace. "My boy Samson has sure turned against me," she said, latching onto another favorite topic. When Jules did not reply she said confidentially, "He's the one with the brains. He's got them. Poor Howard was standing behind a door or something when the brains were handed out. When Samson was just a little kid, I forget how old, he'd been fooling around with fixing things. Like the car, the toaster, stuff like that, the oven, wires and stuff. Now he's got in good at Ford's, and it's a big celebration for me to come over, his wife thinks I should kiss her big feet or something, but I sit there in the chair and look around and I don't say much. I'm thinking plenty though. She can tell what I'm thinking about *her*. But I never ask them for anything—they can wait till hell freezes over before I ask them for a dime, them with all their money. Any day they wanted to they could take me in. They have a room in the upstairs. I'm no trouble, I can cook for myself, but no, nothing. Let me stay with Howard, let me stay with your parents who got troubles of their own and a dump on Twentieth Street thrown in. No, I'm just talking, Jules, don't get me wrong. Don't get me wrong . . ." And on and on in her jocular, angry, whining monologue, while Jules held himself protected against her bitter insults, his eyes fixed upon the smoggy distance. She said, "That kid of theirs born with the bad ear—that serves them right, *her* with her snotty face and those cut-glass plates and crap she thinks so much of!"

Loretta had had a baby with a bad heart a few years before; it had been a boy, had died at eighteen months.

"All right, Grandma," Jules said.

"People get what they deserve. You'll see."

"All right, please."

"Well, I'm not doing it! I'm not the one! God will take vengeance in His own time. I'm not passing judgment or waiting for anything," she said hatefully.

Jules saw the bus on its way. Relief. Gratitude. He guided the old woman up the steps and down the aisle, fearful of her falling—she had fallen more than once already, hard, and it had been Jules's task to get her home again. No light-boned old woman was his grandmother, but a leaden, lumpy old man whose very muscles seemed to work spasmodically against her. The bus smelled of exhaust and sweat. Jules sat beside his grandmother, but half out in the aisle to give her room, and gave himself up to the ride. *Someday I will change all this,* he thought with a flash of joy.

He thought of a wilderness, land out West; a golden sky, or perhaps a golden field of wheat . . . mountains . . . rivers . . . something unmapped.

The bus went slowly. Stops and starts. Jules's eyes took in the other passengers and saw no one interesting; he'd seen them all before. He fixed his attention finally upon one woman, a fairly pretty woman. He liked women. He felt his pulse quicken at the sight of a woman of some charm, and he could find charm in almost anyone, in a nervous flicker of the eyes, a tugging of a skirt. Having lived so close to his mother for so many years, yet at a certain intelligent distance from her, he understood the bewilderment of women in Detroit. They were bewildered, confused, fearful. He dreamed of offering his brains to them, putting himself in their service, helping them through a bus ride or across a street or when their husbands came home drunk. A woman in a laundromat in Detroit only appears to be in control of the machines! A woman in a car only appears to be in control! Inside, her machinery is as wobbly and nervous as the machinery of her car, which may have been slammed together by someone as mutely angry as Jules's father, now on the assembly line at Chrysler. Jules began to smile, thinking of women. Through his mother's pale puffiness he could see a pretty face—he didn't need to be reminded by the snapshots she loved to pass around—and though her legs were clumsy he could imagine some grace to them in the years before her mother-in-law and the baby with the bad heart and Howard's nightly snoring, which kept Jules awake many hours and raised his hatred to a passionate height. His sister Maureen had a delicate, intelligent beauty that pleased him; she was *his sister,* and on the street he took pride in defending her. In Betty he had less interest. She was tough and quick and could take care of herself.

"Why do you think Betty will go bad?" he asked his grandmother.

When he was least prepared for it he gave in to her: there was something in him, as there was in his mother, that leaned toward the old woman with pained and fearful expectation.

The clinic was a new, cheap building, only one story high, with a parking lot surrounded by a fence that seemed to be made of bright brown cardboard but was probably made of wood. Jules guided his grandmother inside. Already exhausted, she sank into a chair spitefully; Jules had to stand. The bus passengers were here already. More of the same. Detroit people—Polish mothers, Polish children, old men out of work, middle-aged men out of work, welfare slobs, the sick, the dying, the prematurely gray and the prematurely wasted, all of them sitting staring at one another with gaunt, suspicious eyes. The whites stared at the whites and at the Negroes; the Negroes stared at other Negroes and at the whites.

Whenever someone came in the front door everyone looked at him with a kind of hope and then registered disappointment; it was mysterious, this ritual. A few patients came out of the inner part of the building and seemed to be finished for the day. They put on their coats in that humble, resigned way of people on charity, halfway out the door as the left sleeve is conquered, head bowed, eyes spiteful and apprehensive.

Jules nearly fell asleep standing, the fluorescent lighting was so hypnotic, the odor of unwashed bodies so oppressive and yet so narcotic; he thought dreamily of the girl in his class whom he now adored, and he thought of the life he would break into when he got out of school and was on his own, finally, a man, leading a life that involved raising his family and then getting out from under them. First he would raise them to be like other people. Then he would get out from under them. *I will change my life in the end,* he thought. He would go to California.

They waited. The first hour passed slowly. Some skinny children played in the waiting-room. They knocked over an ashtray. Their mother, a very thin, angry woman, slapped their faces and forgot them. The receptionist leaned over her counter and said in a courteous but sharp voice, "Please keep those children quiet." They were quiet for a while, sullen and weary, then their legs began to twitch and they were up again, fooling around. A man with a trembling head said suddenly, loudly, "I been waiting here since nine o'clock! They told me come at nine o'clock. I was here before the doors was unlocked!" The receptionist stared at him. She was a youngish woman with a severe, lined face. "What is your name, please? Come up to the desk, please," she said. The man did not seem to hear. He had a beery red face and an enlarged nose, all pores and blackheads. He said to Jules's grandmother, seeing some kinship in her impatient scowl,

"They give you pills with flour in them here. This place, they give you air bubbles in the blood so you die. It's free."

Jules's grandmother, always unpredictable, snubbed the man.

The second hour passed into the third hour. Jules was still standing, too weary to try for a seat. The children were still playing, wandering from one side of the room to the other; other children had joined them. A Negro boy of about five cringed behind his mother's thigh, watching the white children. He sucked noisily at his thumb.

At last Jules's grandmother was called. She stood; he helped her into the consulting room, embarrassed at her clumsiness. He never knew whether she was exaggerating pain or suppressing it. When he got back, her seat had been taken by a fat woman, so he remained standing. A strange, cool patience entered him. He picked up a copy of the *Saturday Evening Post* and read an article on football. He read it carefully, as if he were reading about something from another planet: but to know anything was valuable. He had no interest in sports. All that energy expended among boys, for a trivial goal with no profit, seemed to him foolish, but still some people took it seriously—why did they take it seriously? He picked up an issue of the *National Geographic* with thumbprints of blood on its cover. Its photographs fascinated him, tugging at his eyes as if to exclaim, *Look, look at this, look at this skyline, look at this formation of rock, look at this African chieftain, look, why are you here, who are you?* He put the magazine back and leafed through a copy of *Time*. He read about the Negroes of America—"A Decade of Prosperity"—the achievement of equality, of justice, affluence in Harlem; he read the cover story, about a man from India named Vinoba Bhave. "I have come to loot you with love," said this man. Jules read, fascinated: "We are all members of a single human family." Vinoba Bhave read only three books, Euclid's *Elements*, Aesop's *Fables*, the *Bhagavad Gita*. Jules grew excited; he too would read these books. He would get hold of them the next day. Vinoba Bhave said, "My object is to transform the whole of society. Fire merely burns . . . Fire burns and does its duty. It is for others to do theirs."

These words stayed in his mind, in spite of the fat lady's sniffing. "Fire burns and does its duty."

What he would like, Jules thought suddenly, was not to be a saint exactly but to live a secular life parallel to a sacred life—a modern life, at all costs—to expand Jules out to the limits of his skin and the range of his eyesight. He could do it. He needed only time and some space to move around in. *Fire burns and does its duty* . . . He could believe in fire and in himself. He too would do his duty. In the United States of America complicated maps are given away at any filling station, just ask for one, all that valuable information given away for nothing—about this world there is much information, mountains of facts and wonders, but about the other world there is nothing, and so Jules detached himself from it without regret. He believed in himself. He did not trust anyone else. Expelled from the nuns' school for beating up some little Italian bastard, he'd also been kicked out of the routine of helping to serve Mass during the week. All that was ended. Anyway, he liked the public school better. The teachers did not cry. They got angry but they did not cry. He missed only the long dark skirts and sleeves and nervous rosaries of the nuns, those sexless but very female females, dour and goodhearted but easily stirred to white-eyed violence . . . every one of them a mother to him, ready to be adored like the Virgin Mary, no matter if her breath was a little sour and some dark hairs jutted out of her jaw, no matter. He did miss them. But he did not miss the church, the early Mass, the pictures of Jesus as an adult and as a baby, glorified, bleeding, dying, dead, or risen again, in an ecstasy of power. He had not liked Jesus. He had resented the nuns' interest in Him. He, Jules, would be a better man, or at least a cleverer man—why not all the kingdoms of the earth? Why not? The kingdoms of the earth would only go to someone else; that was history.

Another hour passed. His grandmother was still gone. New people had come in, standing back against the wall; they did not even think to unbutton their coats. Jules tried not to think of his grandmother struggling in some back room, fighting a losing battle with some nurse. What terror in the grime of his grandmother's underclothing and the secrets of her once-female life! Every time she came to the clinic there was a battle. They lost her records, or couldn't find them; her doctor was out having coffee; there was a draft from a window; an impatient nurse snapped that most patients washed themselves before coming to the clinic . . . The old woman would come out swearing. Too loud, bustling and clumsy and loud in the waiting-room, letting everyone know that *she, she* was not going to stand for this treatment.

After another long hour she appeared. A nurse was beside her, helping her along. Jules went to her at once and extracted the prescription slips from her fingers. He saw by her face that the news was bad. He helped her on with her coat, got her outside and down to the corner and waiting for another bus. Another bus. Detroit. Afternoon. He was spending too much of his life, Jules thought, waiting for buses. His grandmother was silent. Her big, doughy, ugly face was turned away.

Jules said lightly, "They sure make you wait in that goddam place!"

His grandmother nodded.

"Which doctor did you get this time?"

"I don't know."

"Don't know? Was it the same one, the guy with the glasses?"

She shrugged her shoulders.

"I thought you liked him. Don't you know who took care of you?"

"How do I know?" she snapped. "I should know, me? I should know anything that goes on? I'm an old woman, the world is shit to me, shut up about it! You with your pointed shoes and tight pants, shut up!"

Suddenly he wanted to cry.

It was late afternoon by the time he got her back home again. They lived in a two-family house on a sleazy, comfortable little street, with a lot of dogs and children in the neighborhood. Mexicans lived not three blocks away, but they were not like Negroes. No one was home but Loretta, who was taking pins out of her hair at the kitchen table. She looked guiltily and cheerfully at Grandma Wendall.

She said, "Well?"

"Well what?" said Grandma Wendall. She took off her ugly hat and stood with it in her hand.

"How are you? What did they say?"

"*He's* got the thing for the pills."

"What did they say?"

"Who knows what they said?"

"Did you tell them about the blood?"

The old woman smiled at Loretta contemptuously. "You don't need to ask what I tell them, what I don't tell them. Whose business? I tell them what comes to mind. I talk to the doctor face to face. Who else's business is it?"

Loretta rubbed her hands across her face. "All right. When do you have to go back?"

"Four days."

"Four days!"

Grandma Wendall went into her room. Loretta took her hands away from her eyes like a little girl and looked at Jules. Jules tried to smile, then smiled.

"She passes blood," Loretta said. "I bet she didn't tell them. She always keeps something back. She has secrets nobody gives a damn about."

"Why wouldn't she tell them?" said Jules. "She wants to get well."

"Dying people don't want to get well," Loretta said.

Jules got away from her. He went to the bathroom and slicked his hair back and went out to his job, which was at a liquor store. He helped load up the delivery truck and rode along in it; he was aching for the day when he could drive the truck himself. Today he kept thinking of his grandmother bleeding, bleeding into the toilet bowl, her face shut up with secrets and pain, and he kept thinking of that Indian, whose name he could not quite remember. *We are all members of a single human family*. He wondered if that was true. His mind kept turning and turning upon it, fascinated.

The liquor store was down on Fort Street. Deliveries were made all the way out to Grosse Pointe, and though he wasn't paid much he liked the expensive look of the bottles and their fancy titles; he liked being around success; he liked riding in the truck and unloading liquor at the service entrances of big houses. He tried to put the thought of his grandmother out of his mind—that old woman with seeping, leaking insides and a heart spiced with poison—but it was no better to think of the next day, school the next day, homework due he wouldn't have time for. Instead he thought of an older Jules, a successful Jules. Grown out of this boy and into a successful man. He wondered about the form in which success would come to him—nothing as obvious as liquor, owning a liquor store, nothing so common.

He worked until after six, then cut off for home through back alleys. He was exhausted. But a kind of rapture came to him in the darkening, wet, foggy air that concealed him so well and gave to him only vaguely the forms of automobiles and trucks and other people. At such times it occurred to him that he might pass unseen through the city, knowing its back alleys and knowing how to turn invisible; he thought of himself as a character in a book being written by himself, a fictional fifteen-year-old with the capacity to become anything, because he was fiction. What couldn't he make out of himself? Every night his mother whined about money, every night his father sat silent and smoldering, a man without money, every night Grandma Wendall spoke in sour jabs about someone with brains who had made it to the top—that is, someone who had money. His friend Ramie Malone talked constantly about money, making money, doing somebody out of money; he talked about his brother who had a used-car lot and sold junkers to people who didn't know any better and who couldn't read at all, let alone read about interest rates—Polacks, niggers, spics, Mexicans, all of them there for the taking, to be taken. Again and again, taken. But Jules could not keep his mind fixed on money. If he was a character in a book of his own making, why should money hold him back? He would get it and would float upon it. First he would buoy up his family and slide out from under them, agile and shrewd, and float out and away upon the ocean of America, all the way across the Midwestern prairies and the Rockies to the West Coast, where the future of America lay, waiting for people like him. He could change his name. He could change his looks in five minutes. He could change himself to fit into anything.

The day had exhausted him. He gave in to such fantasies as if physical weakness opened doors in his mind, and in the drab, dangerous minutes after his father came home and before supper was put on the table he sat loafing by the radio, lost in a dream, pale and slouching. Wasn't he half Alan Ladd in *Shane*, wasn't he half Marlon Brando? But he mixed up with the people in the clinic, the fat lady and the man with the trembling head and the noisy kids. He'd been there. He was one of them. He heard the news about Korea —"hope for truce." Well, good. Doors kept opening and closing in his mind. He got the second section of the newspaper and skimmed through it. One item caught his attention: a nineteen-year-old Texan who had been given $19,000 by a rancher. Given $19,000. The two of them had become friends in a Texas jail, where the rancher was serving a life sentence for killing his wife. He'd given the boy $19,000 to go straight. The boy had married a ninth-grade girl and bought an expensive car and was on his way, going straight . . .

He didn't want $19,000, Jules thought bitterly. He wanted

a wilderness, a clearing in the wilderness, something like that old farm of his childhood where another Grandma Wendall had lived.

Nearby, his father sat drinking ale from the bottle. His father's blue shirt was stained with perspiration. His hair had become thin, but irregularly thin; his forehead was lined; he seemed to be turning into a version of his own mother. This man shut every door in Jules's mind. He could remember nothing, not even the newspaper story.

Seeing Jules look at him, his father said suddenly, "You still hang around with that Malone kid?"

"Why?"

"What about that other one, what's his name, that little bastard with the pop-eyes, that little bastard?" his father said.

Jules pretended to be thinking.

"You mean Roszak. He's in jail," Betty said, coming into the parlor from the kitchen. She sat down on the arm of the sofa, wriggling her dirty toes, leaning over toward Jules.

"In jail where?" said Jules, though he knew this was true.

"A wonder you're not in with him," Betty said.

"I'm no friend of his," said Jules. He felt his scalp prickle, knowing he was close to trouble, but for some reason his father let this pass.

Betty grinned at Jules. "Ramie Malone is going to be busted too. That smart-ass!"

"What do you know about it?" Jules said.

"I know plenty."

She was a dumpy little girl, eleven years old. There was something toughly precocious about her as if she were really not eleven but twenty, or thirty, or forty, dwarfed but pleased with herself. Jules frequently saw such people in Detroit—usually men, with small quick steps, a darting manner, self-conscious, gawky, the kind of body you wanted to kick. Loretta's looks were half submerged in Betty's face, features that should have been pretty but were blunted, the lips too thick, the nose too thick, as if Loretta and Howard had gotten together in drunken fun and fashioned a face out of clay, each fighting to get his own looks represented. She led a gang of kids, girls her own age and a few younger boys, who fooled around on the street and made trouble in a small way.

Their father sat across from them, silent again. He must have been thinking of something else, not hearing them. What did their father think of? Of his job? Of his sick, stinking mother? Of her Social Security pension? Of the car breaking down again? Of the rent on this dump of a house? Of the niggers moving in a few blocks away? Of his wife's sullen padding in bedroom slippers out in the kitchen? Of supper, pork chops frying in a pan? What did he think about? Jules was sure that he was not thinking about the hope for a truce in Korea, and if the UAW wanted more sick-pay benefits and retirement benefits he was not thinking about that, because why should he? Nor was he thinking of his daughter egging him on to give his son a good slap across the face, which the son deserved; nor was he thinking of the bell-bottomed green lamp on the table beside him, nor of the *Detroit News* half read on the floor, nor of the radiator with its fake wood top and its row of little glass birds, nor of the silhouette picture on the wall of a gracious lady with a superior nose, one of Loretta's touches, nor of the grimy, ripped red slipcover on the sofa, nor of Jules's rotting sneakers and Betty's rotting teeth . . . Under the glass of the coffee table were snapshots of the family. Everyone was there. Jules was there as a baby, as a pouty young kid, as a skinny twelve-year-old; Betty and Maureen were there, Betty as a baby, Maureen as a skinny twelve-year-old; Loretta was there in one bright hectic color snapshot, dressed in yellow, a canary-colored hat on her head, holding a baby in her arms, maybe the one who had died; and Grandma Wendall was there, sure enough, looking like a self-righteous tank in a navy-blue dress, decked out for Sunday; even Howard was there, minus his paunch, in a dim photograph, in disguise as a soldier. Jules felt his mind mist over. What were all these people and things doing together, what were they doing to him?

A few weeks before, cruising around the neighborhood with Ramie and some other kids, Jules had seen his father and mother leaving a grill that had a bowling alley attached to it, and in the beery neon light the two of them had looked very . . . very married, very much together, deep in a conversation interrupted by Howard's barking laugh and Loretta's girlish wrist-shaking, a gesture that said, *Hey, isn't that something?* It shocked Jules to think that his father and mother did get along at times. They themselves were not aware of it, and it was a shame he couldn't draw Loretta aside and say to her, "Well, it must not be too bad, why the hell are you always complaining about him? I mean, I saw the two of you laughing together one night out on the street, the two of you . . ."

Maureen came to get them for supper.

He was hungry but he went out with dread. Anything might happen out here in the kitchen. What he must do is concentrate on getting through it and out to his night-time job. Right. He sat between Maureen and his father, his usual place. Shakily he thought of the future: that night, and the next day, and the real future. The future was important, not the present. These minutes spent around the supper table, these ten or fifteen minutes he had to get through, were not important except as they were part of a process leading to the future, a future that would be a good surprise, he felt sure. He began to dish out food for himself. His father leaned over his plate and cut a piece of meat with the edge of his fork. Betty jiggled the table. Maureen let one hand fall sadly on the edge of the table, just for a moment. Loretta leaned against the table so that her heavy breasts inside her dress were outlined.

It was irritating and painful for them to have to think of Grandma Wendall, because she hadn't come out.

"Where's the old lady?" said Howard.

"Laying down," said Loretta.

"She sick again?"

"Oh, something hurts. Her gall bladder."

Betty reached for a piece of bread. Her left arm was scarred faintly from the wrist to the elbow; some drunken mother of a friend of hers had thrown a hot iron at her, claiming that Betty was beating up her daughter, but Betty had claimed that they were all crazy there and that the old lady had been ironing clothes one minute and the next minute had thrown the iron right at her. Jules stopped thinking about Betty. He thought of the night-time streets, which excited him, and of the girl he loved in school, a daytime girl who had no eyes for him and was faintly embarrassed by his attention. He himself had a girl, a girl with thick black hair who tagged along with him in school . . .

"Did you find that punchboard?" Maureen said to Betty.

"I lost it."

"How'd you lose it?"

"At school."

"Is that something I have to pay for?" Loretta said.

"I'm gonna tell Sister I lost it."

"Maybe somebody stole it," said Maureen.

"Sure somebody stole it."

"You probably stole it yourself, you," Loretta said knowingly but without interest.

The subject passed.

Maureen looked around the table with her hazy green eyes, a quiet girl with slender arms and a slender neck; there were melancholy shadows around her eyes. She was thirteen years old and in eighth grade at the nuns' school. She looked back at Betty. "Did you steal it?" she said.

Betty made a face.

"How sick is Grandma?" Maureen said.

"She's okay."

"She gonna die?" said Betty.

"Shut up," said Loretta.

"Yeah, you tell me to shut up, you tell me I stole that punchboard that cost forty cents," Betty cried. "I'm spost to sit here and shut up?"

"Shut your mouth, I mean it," Loretta said.

"Shut your own mouth!" Betty said.

They ate. Jules looked at the center of the table where the salt and pepper shakers were parted. His fingers ached to bring them side by side, together.

Was something going to happen? Would tonight be the night he'd grab the butcher knife and let his old man have it? Right in that fat gut?

But if he did that, Jules thought, his forehead lightly coated with sweat, if he did that, then he'd be ending everything too soon. Too soon. Fifteen years old, that was too soon to end it. Hadn't the nuns and his mother and grandmother and even a few cops promised him he wouldn't live past twenty, which meant he would live at least until he was twenty? Twenty years of age was a distant, monstrous goal; he'd never make it. A vast, wild, undesired desert, twenty years of age, and he would feel no grief at dying. But fifteen was young.

"Ethel is going to work in a beauty parlor," Loretta said.

Howard said nothing.

"We went to a movie today. She won a free plate—she's got all the luck. I got nothing."

"I didn't steal that punchboard," Betty said. "Somebody stole it from *me*."

"I said shut up about that."

"Well, nobody can prove I stole it."

Jules caught Betty's rodent-like, frightened look and he

figured that she had stolen it, whatever it was; she'd been caught stealing things in the past and she always denied it. Denied everything. That was her style, stupid and flat-footed, denying what was obvious.

"A lot of kids take things at school," Maureen said. "Sister Mary Margaret went in the cloakroom today and said she found something in somebody's coat pocket that wasn't supposed to be there, and those people had better return the things, but she wouldn't say who it was. She was real mad. Nobody did anything. She went around the room asking who took her calendar, it was a little calendar up on her desk, and she asked everybody one by one but they said they didn't know. I was scared when she came to me. She said, 'Maureen, *you* know, don't you?' I said no. I had my fingers crossed and my toes crossed."

"Who took it?" Betty said.

"Oh, that Floyd or maybe Anna Cruise, I don't know. I don't hang around with those dopes."

"What'd they do with it?"

"Threw it out, somebody said."

Loretta looked up suddenly. "Is that her making that noise? The old woman?"

No one had heard anything.

Maureen said, "I'll go look."

"You sit still," said Howard. "This is supper."

Jules stared at the table for a few seconds and then brought the salt and pepper shakers together. They made sense together.

"She needs more pills," Loretta said.

Howard, eating, didn't look up.

"I said she needs more *pills*."

"All right."

"Well, your brother Samson said he'd give her twenty dollars a week, and she told him to go to hell, now what do you expect? We got to buy all them pills."

Howard didn't answer.

"Those pills cost three dollars every goddam time! Last year it was something else, then they took all the goddam tests over again and it was something new . . ."

Howard pushed his plate away from him toward the center of the table. He had big beefy hands. Jules looked at those hands and saw the pale half-moons of the nails, a surprising sight.

Loretta said angrily, "When she drops dead your brother

and his wife will send flowers. Have some Masses said. Connie will come up here by Greyhound and have another baby right in the front room. She'll want to stay here so I can wait on her. Your goddam family will all move in sooner or later. Let them."

Howard looked at her. "What are you talking about?" he said.

"If Connie comes up to Detroit—"

"Is she coming?"

"Your mother says maybe."

Howard appeared to be listening but said nothing.

Loretta said, leaning forward against the table, "Well, I don't want her! I don't! I got Maureen moping around here. I don't want two of them moping around!"

"I'm not moping around," Maureen said, surprised.

"I'm not taking anybody else in! I take care of her now and for what? For nothing! She told your goddam brother to go to hell with his money and now what? Now what? I can clean up after her! Sure! And she said herself that your brother said he wouldn't give that hundred dollars to you that time because you'd spend it on yourself—that's what your brother thinks of you!"

"She made that up."

"No. *No*, absolutely *no*, your mother does not make anything up but always tells the truth, just ask her. Everything she says is absolutely the *truth*, that's why we keep her around here."

"All right," Howard said.

"All right yourself."

"How sick is she?" Betty said, jiggling the table.

"You shut up!" Loretta cried.

Howard stood suddenly. He stared down at his hands. "You want your face pushed in?" he said in a strangled, quiet voice.

Loretta jumped back from the table. "You try it! You, you goddam big sow, you pig, you stinking mama's baby pig!" she screamed.

Maureen put her hands over her head. Betty cringed away. Jules got ready to escape. Their father headed for the back door, stumbling. He had a quiet, dense, obscure look to him, even to his back; they could hear him muttering to himself.

Betty put her fist into her mouth to keep from laughing.

"Good-by! Good night! Sleep tight out in the alley with

the rats! You know where you belong! Bastard! Mama's baby bastard!" Loretta cried.

She had a dazzled, alert look about her. Her jaw seemed to flash toughly, and then she moved about the kitchen, flowing about it, very strong in her bare legs. She had won again. "It's true and he knows it, everybody knows it, when that old sow dies he'll squeal like a little pig, everybody knows it, am I telling some news? Jesus Christ, but I'm sick of this!" She picked up his bottle of ale and took a drink from it.

"Grandma can hear you," Maureen said.

"She has ears, let her hear." Loretta sat down in Howard's chair. "So he has a tool-and-die thing of his own, a factory, he's setting himself up in business. Your uncle. Uncle Samson. So he's going to make money and his wife can spit in my eye, and your father will stand for it all because he's a goddam stupid ass-hole and all he can do is push me around but he can't make any money himself because he's a goddam stupid ass-hole. Am I telling news? This is such old goddam stale news it's not even on the radio any more, everybody knows about it."

"You're really something," Jules said.

"Watch your mouth. Who got kicked out of the nuns' school for fooling around, huh? You'll end up like your father, you think you're so smart."

"I'm not ending up like him or anybody else."

"Down in the morgue before you're twenty!" She pushed Howard's plate a little farther away from her. She took out a pack of cigarettes and lit one. Her face was smooth and high-colored.

Jules went back to eating, feeling somehow pleased.

After a moment Betty said, "What movie did you see today, Ma?"

"Oh, it was real nice, I liked it fine," Loretta said. She always began this way when talking about movies.

"What was it about?"

"It was real nice. It had a kind of complicated plot, you didn't know at first what was going on. You want me to tell you? There was a real big house, and a party going on, and the butler and the maids are working hard. The butler is real handsome, he's making sure everything is just right, he puts out a fire some stupid rich old guy sets by mistake with his cigar, and a rich old bitch gets locked in the bathroom and he unscrews the door to let her out—that was real funny. Well, the story is about this butler and the maids, they're real cute, and the chauffeur and the gardener and some other people that work here—it takes place in Philadelphia, the family is very wealthy but they're really bankrupt but don't know it yet. The old man is in the stock market. He has a daughter and a son and a crazy wife, a real funny old rich gal with wigs and stuff—she does card tricks and plays the harp, she's just great, she loans her wigs to the maids and everything. Well, the butler gets the *Wall Street Journal* every morning before the old guy comes downstairs, to see what is going on in the stock market, and he finds out in a headline that the family is bankrupt. But he doesn't want to tell them because the old guy has a heart condition, and also the daughter is going to get married to some French banker. And the movie is about how the butler gets the other servants to fool the family. They have a big ball for the daughter's engagement and everything, and all the stuff is borrowed or stolen from different places, like florists and diamond stores and restaurants and stuff. *Funny, it was so funny!*"

"What happened in the end?" Jules said patiently.

"Oh, the stock market goes back up. The daughter gets married. The butler marries one of the maids, there are two of them after him throughout the whole show. It ends all right," Loretta said.

"I wish I could see it," said Betty.

"Find that punchboard, kid, and you're on your way!"

"I *told* you, Ma—"

"Forget it. Forget it." Loretta crushed out her cigarette in a plateful of mashed potatoes. "Look, kid, I got a headache from your lazy bastard of a father. And that old woman gets next to me, I mean she gives me a pain where a pill won't reach. You little pests think you're so special but you don't know nothing! You, Jules, you look so goddam smart-aleck but you don't know nothing! I wasn't always this low. The two of them bring me down low. I could lay on the sidewalk out front and croak, that's how low they get me, but I wasn't always like this. There was a man who got killed because of me, shot right in the head, shot dead, and it happened because of *me,* and nobody's ever going to get shot in the head for you, Reeny kid, with your sour puss and your gawky neck, and you, Betty, you look like a pigeon or something that's going to have babies. I wasn't always like this, and when I get rid of that old bitch I'm going back to work again, with Ethel. I'm getting out from under all of you and your smart-aleck mouths and all the food you eat up. Christ! I'm sick of all this. I want to be like people in that movie, I want to know what I'm doing, I don't want to be shoved this way then that way. Now, if we got to move out of this house like somebody was saying, if they want to fix the street—now, now that's what drives me crazy. Listen, Jules, it drives me crazy the way I always have to move from one place to another. You remember out in the country? Then we came to Detroit? Then all them dumps, them bus rides? I can't stand always moving around! I want my own place, my own house. I want to be like somebody in a movie, I want to get dressed up and walk down the street and know something important will happen, like this man who was killed because of me—like that—and on my death-bed, Jules kid, I'll tell you a secret about him and shake you up, just wait. I wasn't meant to be like this—I mean, stuck here. Really I wasn't. I don't look like this. I mean, my hair, and I'm too fat. I don't really look like *this*, I look a different way. And the toilet is bad again, there's water on the floor, well, I can't give a goddam about that, I wasn't born to mop up every toilet in the city or take care of some old bat that should have dropped dead twenty years ago. Or have him climb on top of me, that fat bastard! No, listen, I really wasn't and I'm not drunk now and you know it. I'm telling you the truth. Face to face. I'm saying what I feel. You think you're all special, all people who are born think they're special, but you're no more special than me. I know who I am—I got a lot of things to do and places to see and this isn't all there is in the world! Not this! Not for me!"

Jules had momentum enough to get him all the way to Tenth Street before he tried for a ride. He walked backward in the street, his thumb in the air. Cars passed close to him, very close, but the drivers did not appear to see him; Jules, with a look of cool anxiety, appeared not to see them either. Car after car passed him. His eyes began to water in the early spring wind that swept off the river. There was an odor of metal and smoke in the air, a wet taste to it. In the middle of a scrubby block of buildings and vacant lots he was lucky enough to get a ride; the driver took him all the way downtown, to the parking lot where he worked.

He worked for fifty cents an hour, helping out the at-tendant in the busy hours between seven and two in the morning, when people in marvelous cars came to entrust them to Jules or to the sunken-necked attendant, a man named Rich who was maybe thirty or forty. The smell of such cars' insides stirred Jules's lust in a mystical way, and the smell of ladies' perfume, sometimes lingering with the cold leather or borne lightly on the air as they passed in their furs and immaculate hairdos, made his brain burst into fragments of wild hope. Such cars! Such women! Such men, in their excellent coats and gloves, their shoes excellent, their faces cleanly shaved and their hair newly cut, everything perfect. These people were headed for two or three good restaurants nearby, or across the way to the Sheraton-Cadillac, where things were going on not just on Saturday nights but forever, endlessly. Jules, shivering in his jacket, dressed skimpily on purpose, backed cars into place with great reverence for their beauty and never nicked a bumper or a fender; he believed he had a magic touch with beautiful and expensive things, while the moronic Rich had no touch at all but banged cars into place, trusting to luck. Rich sat in the attendant's little shack, playing with a plastic game in which numbered squares of about twenty digits could be slid from place to place, the object being to line up the numbers in correct order; and while magnificent people drifted by him and the Sheraton-Cadillac Hotel sent its lovely lights out into the night in a spangled pattern someone as gifted as Jules might interpret, Rich saw nothing except the little flat rectangle of plastic in his hand, as if the mysteries and secrets of the world were present in this and had already shown themselves too difficult for him. "Hey, look how close I came to getting them in this time," Rich would say to Jules, who was dreaming and brooding at his elbow, and he would shove the game into Jules's face—Jules, who had no use for games and was slightly puzzled by them, by the energy people shot into them and lost forever. Rich had a short neck and a small, round head upon which a gray woolen cap seemed to have been pulled permanently; his manner was that of a studious but slow child, more childish than Jules's sister Betty, and his frequent appreciative smiles were not comforting.

When the lot was filled up, which often happened as early as nine o'clock on a weekend night or on a Wednesday, and a period of quiet lasted until about midnight, Jules sat sunk in his own thoughts, smoking a cigarette, estimating how far it really was across the street and over to that hotel. The distance between the hotel and the parking lot was nothing, but the distance between the parking lot and the hotel was everything; many times he had helped a man who had had too much to drink, putting his hands gingerly on the stranger's good coat or stooping to retrieve his gloves from the sidewalk, and he was shrewd enough to see how the steps they took together, while appearing to be the same steps, were in reality far different. They were not walking together, not really. The tips of a dollar or more he sometimes got were a sign of this difference and that it existed powerfully and irreparably. He always said, "Thank you, sir," brightly, mechanically; but he could not summon up in his heart any real hatred for the rich. He felt that his true essence was of great value and would someday be expressed in ordinary signs of cars and women, and in that sense he was already one of them, though disguised from them in a windbreaker with soiled cuffs and collar and in a punk's slightly blemished face.

It was lively tonight and even Rich was hurried, mumbling words of greeting and gratitude into faces that seemed not to hear them, and Jules felt his energy strain upward to its highest pitch at about eleven o'clock, then begin to subside alarmingly as if he were turning into an old man. In a giant black Lincoln he peered at himself anxiously in a mirror, glad to see that he still looked all right, and for a long moment he sat there, trying to relax, to collect his thoughts. His grandmother . . . the clinic. All right. He had got through that. Her slow bleeding insides . . . if she wanted to bleed she would bleed. She would die to spite them. The fight at the supper table had come and gone. It might have happened days ago. It was over, forgotten. What did he care about their fights? Sometimes his father banged out the back door, sometimes he slapped Loretta's face, sometimes he slapped someone else's face, sometimes he broke a chair or a plate—it hardly mattered. Jules was too old to run away. It was shameful to be always running away. Until a few years ago he had run away from home every few months, curious about the city or bitter about home, and he had always ended up in the Children's Shelter—worse than home, though anonymous, a confusion of homes. Whimpering, sniveling kids, black and white, too many of them. Everyone was tired. Bones stuck out angrily. Yellowish teeth were prominent. Too much. Running away was a mistake. He was too old now to run away but too young to move out. His father wasn't going to run *him* out of the house. He adjusted the rear-view mirror in the Lincoln and looked at himself again, seriously. Did he have the looks to get him out of this Lincoln and into one of his own? Did he have the brains? Or would something in him give out before he was old enough to collect all the rewards his imagination promised him?

The lot closed at two and he drifted off toward home, cold but dully excited. He was always in a state of excitement, of queer, formless tension. There was little traffic on Fort Street. He crossed through an alley beside a garage, his hands stuck in his pockets. He felt that he was invisible. Above, the sky was misted over with cloud or smog, and he felt that he could make his way without being seen into any building or house in the city. A pang of excitement seized him, almost a pang of lust. He wondered if he could break into a building tonight, alone, on his own, why not? With Ramie and other boys he had made his way into darkened stores and had lugged out merchandise, nothing too heavy or expensive or personal, and they had never been caught. With his friends he was visible, just as they were, and a clumsy chain linked them all together no matter how fast they ran; by himself he was light as air, with all possibilities open before him, just as they were open to the enviable heroes of books and movies. He paused at the end of the alley and looked up and down the street. On his own, now; he was entirely on his own. The block was a block of commercial buildings, all dark. *Bruce Kmetz & Associates, Reinert Resale, Olsen Construction Co.* Nothing here.

He walked on. He approached a bar and grill, George's, closed for the night. In George's would there be some cash lying around? Could he break into a cigarette machine or wasn't that worth the risk? What about a burglar alarm? All the money he'd made this evening he had to turn over to his mother or risk her hysteria, and only the tips, which he kept quiet about, were his own. But anything he stole was entirely his own. No one else had anything to do with it. The money he got here and there, secretly, would pile up out of sight and help him transform his life.

He headed for George's, which was one of those taverns on a corner that are made of concrete and look like a great concrete block, with narrow slits of windows. The neon lighting was turned off. Jules supposed that there was a back entrance, an easy way in; maybe he could locate a crowbar or a board or something to break open the door. He stood out front, waiting. He missed his friend Ramie, who would have known exactly what to do.

He walked around the side of the building. Some junk lay in back. A back door, a mess of garbage pails, boxes. He walked all the way around the building, beginning to be nervous. It was too dark. Too quiet. Out in front again, by a street light, he stood for a few minutes to give himself time to think. He lit a cigarette.

A squad car turned the corner, cruising slowly.

Jules made a mistake—he took a guilty step backward. He turned and began to walk. He walked slowly, bringing his elbows closer to his body; he did not look around at the car. But it was too late—he had made a mistake. The car braked to a stop in the middle of the street, the door flew open, and a cop yelled, "Hey, you! Just a minute, kid!" Jules threw his cigarette away. His brain went blank and he turned to run. He headed up an alley, running, and now he knew that he had really made a mistake but he couldn't stop. How could he stop?

The cop was yelling, "Stop! Get back here!" and though it flashed through Jules's mind that he was in danger, he still could not stop. He dashed around a pile of junk and fled across the barren back yard of some high building, turning his ankle, not even crying out, and behind him the cop was muttering something loudly. Jules thought that he had to hide, but shrewd and fast as such thoughts came, his body kept on running in panic and would not be brought to earth. *Jesus Christ help me!* Jules thought, reaching out for a building's rough brick wall and trying to flatten himself against it. *He's going to kill me.* He knew enough not to cross back to the street again, where the other cop would be cruising with the car, but fled along a side street he had never seen before, past small, darkened one-story homes. Behind him the policeman fired his first shot. Jules had no idea how close the bullet came. He lunged for someone's porch, thinking maybe he could crawl under it, but, panicked, he had no time to stop and kept on running into the back yard of the house. There was an old doghouse there but luckily no dog, and just as the cop shouted, "Stop!" and fired another shot, Jules dived through a broken fence. He got to his knees and then to his feet and found himself running alongside another small house out toward another street. He was sobbing. He had no idea what was happening. On the street a car's headlights flashed, and he thought madly the squad car had doubled back and was about to run him over, so he turned to the side and smashed through someone's bushes, getting scratched on the face. He ran panting across a row of front yards. His heart was pounding violently. He felt pain in his side, in his chest, but more than anything his brain seemed to be throbbing with surprise and anger, asking, *How did this happen? How did you let it happen?*

"I got you!" cried the cop, and Jules felt sure the bullet would get him in the back, but he felt it whiz by him. Nothing to do but run. Keep going. If he could get over to his own neighborhood where he knew places to hide . . . basements, warehouses, sheds, garages, his own house . . . but the cop would not let him run in that direction, he seemed to be steering Jules, herding him off into the dark. Though it was dark Jules was becoming visible: he could feel himself becoming visible. Two or three shots rang out. Jules burst his way into someone's shanty and there, panting, weeping like a child, he fell to his knees and embraced his own body, which was shuddering. He was safe. He would not be found here. Then suddenly he heard the cop's footsteps again; he could hear the man muttering right up to the shanty itself. The footsteps thudded against the ground. The door was kicked open. "Don't shoot me!" Jules cried. He was bent over, kneeling, with his shoulders hunched as if he were trying to bend himself in two. "I didn't do anything!" Jules said, sobbing. He shut his eyes and leaned toward the ground, his hands hard on the back of his neck, gripping his neck.

"Hey, you little bastard, little motherfucker, trying to run away on me!" the cop cried. He put the barrel of his pistol against Jules's head. "You know what I'm going to do? Going to blow out all your brains, kid, you smart-ass kid, running me all over the goddam neighborhood!" And he pulled the trigger, but it clicked upon an empty chamber. In disgust he raised the gun and brought it down on Jules's head.

Jules fell. He felt himself being kicked, being turned over onto his back; he felt his pockets being turned inside out and something taken, and he began to weep with his eyes closed, too terrified to play dead.

When the cop left, Jules did not move. It was strange that so much noise hadn't brought people out back, or maybe it would not bring them out of their houses but make them hide under their bedclothes. Nothing happened. He heard boat whistles from the river. He lay still. Time passed. He shivered convulsively; his head felt soft and wet where the gun had struck him. He had better get home. But for a while he could not move, as if he were paralyzed—his legs too weak or too cunning to move. Finally he got onto his stomach, then onto his hands and knees. He was breathing very hard. He found his empty wallet lying a few inches away and put it back in his pocket. He got shakily to his feet. His head pounded violently, but it was something he could stand. Punishment for his mistake. Being stupid was a mistake. One false move, a guilty step, running when he should not have run, should have met that cop face to face. He wept silently, in pain, ashamed, and made his way back out to the street.

It was after three when he finally got home. He washed his face in the bathroom, wincing with pain. Maureen came to see what was going on. He said, "Go back to bed, mind your own goddam business." He pushed the door shut so that she couldn't see him, but when he came out she was still standing there.

"What happened?" she said. "Did somebody beat you up?"

"No. Nothing."

Maureen stared at him. "They didn't take your money, did they?"

He tried to get by her.

"Jules, did they get your money?"

"Yes." He pushed past her on his way to bed.

She said, "That's going to drive Ma wild."

He fell onto his unmade bed and slept. The next sound he heard was an alarm clock going off in his parents' room. He got out of bed. He hadn't undressed so he didn't bother to change. He looked all right. There was some dried blood on his head, a bruise. His head pounded. But that was all right, he could stand it. What sickened him was his stupidity. He tasted vomit, thinking of how stupid he was.

After his father left for work he went out into the kitchen and had some coffee, standing. Loretta was sitting at the table. She stared dully at him. "What time did you get in last night?" she said.

"The usual time," he said.

There was a pause as she waited, dense with politeness, for him to say something more—didn't he have a few dollars to give her?

But he said nothing.

She watched him, sleepily and a little sullen. "When are you coming home tonight, if I may ask?" she said.

"The usual time," said Jules. He escaped from her and got outside, though he had two hours before school started. He walked around. He ran and reran in his imagination that chase behind buildings and through alleys, wondering how it would look in the daylight. The cop had yelled at him, warned him. *I'm going to get you!* Jules had been too stupid to get away and too stupid to turn around and face the cop. That pistol had slammed down on his head, hard. Jules had bowed his head and down onto his head had come the pistol, very hard, meaning to crack his skull. That was almost that. Almost the end of Jules.

The high school was fenced off from one of the city's busier streets. Against the fence, blown up to its full height, were scraps of newspapers and bags. Jules leaned against the fence and smoked a cigarette. He tried to get himself calm. At a quarter to nine he made his way inside with a crowd of other kids. He inched by instinct toward his friends, who were already idling in the corridors by their lockers, hating school but somehow drawn by its walls and noise and its scent of prison, an instinct with them too. They were joking about something. They banged their lockers shut. Jules's head ached, and he turned away from them and went to his homeroom just as the final bell was ringing, not a second before. He did this every morning. It was all right; he hadn't died.

Three seats over to his right was the girl he was in love with, a blond, small-nosed girl who wore pleated skirts and white wool socks and sneakers and who rarely looked at him, being for some reason nervous of him and his side-burns and smirky stylized grin. He allowed himself to fill with an eerie, mystical desire for her, dazzling himself with desire, while his homeroom teacher—a woman in her fifties, frail and spidery—talked to them about filling out health-card forms. *When was your most recent dental examination?* Jules looked over at the girl. She was no better off than he was, her parents were just as low, but she carried herself carefully, with an eye for what was neat and proper and clean; her friends were good girls, like herself, though more given to horseplay than she; her name was Edith. Jules loved her. He dreamed about her . . .

When the bell rang, he made his painful way to the front

of the room to say to his teacher, "My ma forgot to write my excuse for yesterday," and the woman dismissed him, a little nervous of him and his friends and put off perhaps by his glazed eyes. His breath too—it tasted stale. Everything about him was stale—but at least he was alive. He walked slowly and carefully to his first class, English.

At first he could not remember where his assigned seat was, and a daring girl giggled at him, Jules so clumsy this morning, but finally he located the seat and fell into it. English class. He opened his notebook. He had forgotten, or lost, his English textbook. He groped around in the desk and came across someone's book, not exactly the English text but near enough in color to it. Jules stared toward the front of the room. The teacher was already talking. The blackboard was watery. Something was being written on the blackboard—handwriting large enough but strangely jumbled. Jules squinted; he brought his fingers to his eyes and pressed them, trying to see. What was all that? *Coming around the corner the firehouse . . .* Jules leaned forward and let his elbows grope against the desk top, seeking support. He felt his mind go blank, then come back to life. He was slipping off. With his fingers spread around his eyes he tried to hang onto consciousness, desperate and ashamed, but still he was slipping off. The teacher turned his head, then turned it another way, a bald head, talking, and Jules felt himself falling. Something scuffed against his thigh, maybe a rat, and with dreamy loathing he recalled a rat jumping up against him when he'd been about seven or eight, fooling around somewhere, and a rat had leaped toward him and ricocheted from him in a panic, pushing off violently from his thigh. He remembered it now, vividly, and felt the rat leaping crazily against his thigh and pushing itself off in terror, and in a numb terror of his own Jules began to lean forward, his head slowly dropping, his forehead slowly moving to the top of the desk.

10

When Maureen was thirteen they moved from the house on Twentieth Street to another like it on a street named Labrosse, still in the same neighborhood but closer now to Tiger Stadium and not far from the New York Central railroad terminal, a great gothic building with hundreds of windows. She was getting too old to explore buildings and vacated houses, too conscious of herself as a girl to run yelling through warehouses with a bunch of other kids. She held herself back, she carried herself cautiously, afraid but not knowing exactly why she was afraid. Moving from one house to another disturbed her. She couldn't sleep for many nights in the new house. All those boxes, the trouble, her mother sweating and angry and her father grunting with the effort of carrying things, everything in a turmoil, up-rooted—she was frightened.

Even Jules lost patience with her. "Oh, come off it," he said, poking her to get her going, growing up himself now and always in a hurry. Even sitting down he had a distracted look, as if he were making plans for what he would do when he got up. She admired him, she resented him. She went through the pockets of his trousers when he hung them up in his room, looking for evidence of his larger, mysteri-ous life, a life lived away from her.

The house they lived in now was like a barn, a square box of a house set close to the sidewalk. There were only a few feet of yard, without grass; a few broken bricks, some rocks, unidentifiable junk, ruts and footprints hardened in the earth. The house had once been painted gray. When you ran up the front steps the third step sagged. There was a closed-in, sly feeling to the whole neighborhood, that put off strangers —policemen or plainclothesmen on the prowl, water-meter men, gas-meter men, welfare snoops, social workers—the welfare bumps, as Loretta called them. The women would yell from one back yard to another, "The Investigator is coming!" when just about anyone showed up who didn't belong in the neighborhood. Sometimes Jehovah's Witnesses came through and argued with the Catholics.

Her mother sank into the neighborhood and made friends at once. On any morning women just like her, older or younger, pregnant or not pregnant, were to be seen hurrying out in their cotton dresses, their hair wound up on plastic rollers, anxious to talk—what happened last night next door, what was all that noise? what happened with that nigger in a car down the street, did he run into someone? "Oh, them niggers," Loretta would complain pleasantly to her neighbors, being understood at once. "Them niggers have a birth rate twice as much as white people, or ten times, I forget which, and they're all on ADC and play poker with the checks. I know all about it." She complained about the new house, about her mother-in-law, about her kids. She complained about her husband. Everything she said was understood at once; she sank into the neighborhood and might have been living there all her life.

They had had to leave their old house because part of a block was to be torn down—for a reason, they weren't sure why. Someone said a park was going to be built there. But years were to pass and no park appeared, only a half-block of demolished houses and pipes and miscellaneous rubble, open basements, jagged jails. . . . Maybe a park hadn't been planned, or maybe it had been forgotten. Anyway, the Wendalls had had to move. Not that Loretta really regretted the move, once she made friends. It was just that she hated to be kicked around. She told Maureen and Betty every morning at breakfast, "Look, don't you let anybody kick you around today. Jules I don't need to tell, he knows what's what in this world. But you two, you're dumb enough to get pushed around, and just don't stand for it—tell them you don't take no mess. Don't ever let anybody push you around."

"Oh, Ma," Maureen would say in embarrassment, "pushed around how? Who's going to push us around?"

"Not the nuns and not any other kids. Remember that," Loretta said.

"Nobody's going to mess with me," Betty said.

Maureen emerged from the house onto the sagging veranda with a cautious, befuddled sense of alarm—who was going to kick her around today? It *was* true that somebody always kicked her around—an older girl or an older boy, a nun patroling the corridor, or Betty—Betty might push her around, having the strength of greater simplicity and tighter, tougher muscles. Maureen thought it was all crazy, this worry about being kicked around, when all you had to do was recoil with the blow and start to cry as soon as possible—not like Jules, who had refused to cry for years now, no matter what happened; not like Betty, who always seemed to be asking for more. Maureen walked out onto the veranda each morning, clutching her books and her lunchbag, and let her eyes wander out onto the street to see if there was any danger.

The veranda was so long that all the kids who lived in the house and kids from next door could play on it, making forts of crates and arranging them into two camps. On one side of the veranda was the Wendalls' door and on the other side the Stanleys' door. When it rained the kids slammed in and out of those doors and hung around the porch, the little kids busy with their noisy games and the older kids like Maureen and Betty and Faith, from next door, reading comic books. After the Wendalls had lived there a month the Stanleys moved and another family, with six children and a deep drawling accent, moved in. They said they were from Kentucky. All their things were in a truck, loaded up and covered with sheets, and Jules and Maureen and Betty helped them unpack, excited with their new neighbors. Six children! On moving day Maureen felt giddy and out of control, so much was happening, so much was always happening, so much noise! So many faces! So many footsteps, so many mothers and fathers and children to keep straight! Loretta brought out some beer in cans. Maureen and the kids ran through the rooms of the other part of the house, overturning boxes and shrieking with laughter. Then, suddenly, Maureen wished that no one had moved in. She wished they might live alone in a house for once. So with a nail she made jagged little marks in the wallpaper of what had been Faith's parents' bedroom.

After a while everyone forgot about the Stanleys, who had moved to Grand Rapids. The new people were named Stonewall. Mrs. Stonewall came over to talk with Maureen's mother all the time, and they sat on the veranda and sipped beer or coffee and smoked, the two of them exactly the same age, wearing slacks that were a little too tight across the back or skirts that were a little too long for this year, while behind them small children played and the radio squawked with no one to listen to it. On Saturdays, Maureen had to get out of the house because of all the noise; she walked two miles or so to the library, where it was quiet. The library was like a home should be, quiet. As she walked she muttered to herself about what she would do if she was old enough to be a mother: how she would take care of all those kids, punish them when they needed it, give them a good slap and a good spanking and even, for the worst of the kids like her sister Betty, find some dark wet place— the "dungeon" under the veranda—and nail her up in it until she was good.

She wondered what was wrong with being quiet—people were always saying she was too quiet. Loretta was always after her for having "secrets," which meant that she was quiet, and Grandma Wendall talked about her "long face."

"She has a long face and she eats with long teeth," the old woman said sourly. Maureen was puzzled at her grandmother's dislike: hadn't the old woman liked her at one time? Hadn't she liked Jules at one time? Now she sat around, sick and sour, leaning on a cane even while she sat, as if to emphasize her swollen legs and feet, her evil condition, brought so low in a household of enemies. Maureen thought her face was no longer than anyone else's, and it was not a bad-looking face. She tried to be quiet and composed and orderly, and this perhaps irritated people. "Oh, what a fuss you make!" her mother sometimes screamed when Maureen insisted upon counting every stamp in the stamp-redemption book, or inspected dishes to see if they were really clean, or asked if she could wash her hair more than once a week. But her mother screamed at everyone, her own kids and the Stonewall kids and the kids across the way—it meant nothing. Mrs. Stonewall screamed too. It meant nothing. In the next instant they flopped down and lit cigarettes and forgot about being angry. Maureen's heart would still be pounding but already her mother had forgotten, would forget anything, and that was why she trudged up the street alone, muttering to herself, and why she daydreamed at school, thinking of punishments that would keep everyone good and quiet so that her mother would never scream again. Those little brats! At school the Mother Superior, a nun with a man's wise, gnarled face, called Maureen into her office one day and said, "Maureen, it's up to you to watch your sister at recess. You're the oldest."

"Yes, Sister," Maureen said.

"Your sister is quarrelsome and impudent. She's like your brother. It's up to you, your mother said, to watch her during recess."

So she hated Betty and hated them all and wished they would die. She would like to shovel all their bodies under the veranda, in that dark, musty, leaf-strewn dungeon where spiders and other nasty things lived. Or maybe she would crawl under there herself and hide, let her mind go quiet and blank, give herself a good rest so that she could get her life straightened out.

In the public library the ceilings were so high she was always glancing up nervously. It seemed to her that the ceiling sometimes floated away. The floors were old but well polished. They were a little uneven. Maureen could not quite believe in the silence—it was like a beautiful glass vase that might be shattered at any moment. She took her books far into the reading-room, where she could sit at a table by the "Great Books of the Western World" and by a hot radiator, and read for hours. The silence in the library really was not broken often, though she expected it to be. People even walked quietly here. There were few children. She read through the Young People's Shelf, book by book. She did not allow herself to pick books at random, because that way she might miss something important. And each week she made herself go back to the beginning to check whether any new books had been put on the shelf, books returned that week or brand-new books with blank cards in the pockets at the back. Discovering these books, she smiled with a kind of cautious surprise.

The librarian reminded her of the principal of her school, so Maureen knew that it was best to be shy in front of her. Because she controlled the library she had a terrible authority over Maureen's life. One day, at the desk, she leafed idly through a book Maureen was returning and discovered a large tear down one page. "How did this happen?" she said.

"It was there when I took the book out," Maureen whispered.

"It was not there. All our books are checked."

As if to prove this, she turned a few more pages and came across a mended tear. It had been mended with transparent tape that had turned yellow. "See? Like this. It would have been mended," the woman said.

"I don't know how it happened," Maureen said. "I didn't do it!" She saw the woman's eyes move coldly over her, Maureen in a sweater of loose knobby wool, worn at the elbows and uneven in back; Maureen looking guilty, with her legs absurdly thin and exposed.

"I'm afraid this book was in good condition before you took it out," the woman said.

Maureen began to nod, frightened. She must be guilty. Someone must have done it at home, by accident, but it was her fault. Her fault. She should not have brought a library book into such a house.

"You'll have to pay a fine, I'm afraid," the librarian said. "Twenty-five cents."

"I'll bring it tomorrow," Maureen said.

"All right. But you can't take any books out today."

"I'll bring it tomorrow," Maureen said. In her relief at

being released so easily, she forgot her disappointment at not being able to take out any books. For a moment she felt the desperate gloating of a criminal. She was allowed to walk out of the library and walk home and nothing had happened to her.

At home she did not bother to ask Loretta for the money but waited until Jules came in. She hung around the bathroom while he washed his face. He took off his shirt and leaned over the sink. She saw that the hairs on his arms were thick and dark and that his chest was hairy. He looked very tired.

She said shyly, "I got in some trouble today and need some money for a fine."

"How much?" said Jules.

"A quarter," said Maureen.

"Okay, here," he said, giving her a quarter, and she felt a little sickened to think that she was deceiving her brother. She really had a few cents saved, out in a tin can in the garage, but it was money for something special and she had made a vow to the Virgin not to use it for a year. Saving money was a secret no one else was to know about and a secret that made her different from all of them.

She wondered if Jules too was saving money: he was like her, secretive beneath the prominent open bones of his face.

There were so many crowded in their half of the house— besides Grandma Wendall, from time to time there was Aunt Connie, who was sick off and on but who worked in a laundry when she was well. Aunt Connie had had a *bad life*, Grandma Wendall said in a whisper. (Her insides operated on? Her husband killed in a car accident or run off to California? Which was it?) Aunt Connie was heavy and seemed very old, older than Loretta, and sometimes her very sluggishness brought her so low that Loretta wanted to help her up again, and therefore liked her, but at other times her sluggishness got on Loretta's nerves so that she ran next door to Flora Stonewall and cried, "That bitch! That fat-ass bitch! Either she goes or I go, tonight I'm telling him for sure!" And of course Betty, who shared a room with her, and Jules was in and out of his room, not making much noise but still a presence, a human being, crowding upon her. Their father had a job that paid well, he said, but where did the money go? Where did it go? He was a stout man who carried a lunch pail and wore the same pair of grimy dark trousers all the time, on workdays or days off.

His shirts were blue. He seemed often to be contemplating his own big hands, lying on the kitchen table or on his lap. He seemed to approach everything with a sideways look: food, ale, people, the television set. He was cautious, suspicious, closed. Then, as minutes passed, he opened himself up to supper or television, moving in, beginning to sweat— he liked to eat and drink, he ate and drank passionately, and he liked all television shows. He was suspicious at first and then he opened himself up. Maureen had learned this. His favorite place was a tavern a few blocks away, the Holiday Grill, which had two large dusty plants in its windows, plants with spearlike leaves—seeing plants like that always made Maureen think of her father, even years after he was dead and no longer any threat. Leaves like spears. There was something dense about her father and, beneath the density, a sharpness that was frightening.

One night he'd moved sideways into supper, eating and sweating, and only when supper was almost over did he look at Jules. Then he said, "What's this about Malone?"

Maureen had noticed her brother's alarm, which was a giveaway. He tried to cover it up by saying smoothly, "I don't know, what about him?"

"He got himself roughed up, heh?"

"I don't know."

"What do you mean, you don't know?"

"Duane Tracey was saying something—"

"You little shit, don't you lie to me! You know all about it!"

"I don't know all about it!" Jules said.

"What the hell happened to him?" said Loretta.

"He got beat up. He got his goddam smart-aleck face kicked in for him," Maureen's father said angrily. It was hard to tell why he was angry: was he happy that Ramie had been hurt, or sorry?

"Yeah, what happened?" Loretta said.

"That punk thought he'd pull something smart—I heard it down at the corner—he stopped a nigger kid over on Hastings who was carrying a bag with some cash in it, and the stupid goddam bastard never thought he'd get caught! Them niggers caught up with him in an hour!" Maureen's father said. His face was shining and vicious; again he was not looking at Jules. Jules was not looking at him either. "What kind of a stupid son-of-a-bitch of a punk would hustle a runner for the numbers, eh? What kind of a punk?

A nigger kid twelve years old that's running with four thousand dollars in a bag ain't no kid on his own, you stupid bastard! You think a kid with four thousand dollars in a paper bag is out on his own *going shopping?* You think he's maybe buying his mama a present?"

"Don't call me names, I wasn't mixed up in it," Jules said.

"You'd better as hell not be. But if you were, they'd of got you by now. Kicked your teeth in for you, how'd you like that?"

"I didn't have anything to do with it."

"No, you're too smart! Jesus Christ, that's one good thing," Maureen's father said, but without relief, still with a kind of perplexed anger. "They kicked the kid's teeth out. Half of them out. They banged up his eye for him. They broke four of his ribs for him. What they did to the rest of him I don't know, but they didn't hold back, I bet, and even if they are niggers I got to admit he got what's coming to him—that smart-aleck little bastard always roaming around on the street!"

"Look, I didn't have anything to do with it," Jules said.

"But you know all about it, don't you?"

"No."

"You sit there and lie to me, eh?"

They were not looking at each other, and Maureen could feel the tension building up between them. She wanted to put her hand on Jules's arm and whisper, "Give in," but Jules, his pale face strained, showed all his hatred in the very set of his mouth.

Loretta steered them out of it by saying, "Hey, I made some pudding tonight. You all want pudding?"

Later on that night Maureen's father said with a sullen sigh, "Them niggers will get control of this city yet. They'll put a padlock on it and put up roadblocks and, brother, that will be the end!"

Loretta sat watching television with him, in her spangled straw bedroom slippers. She said, "The police should get them for beating Ramie Malone up. I don't care what you say, they didn't need to kick his teeth out. He was sort of a nice-looking kid."

"I wouldn't be surprised they cut him up fine. They like to cut people up," Maureen's father said slowly. "Down at the plant, if you fool around in the parking lot after the other guys have gone, you're taking a chance. They don't just take your money, they cut you up. They like to do that. It's what they do for fun."

On other nights Maureen heard him talk about the Po-lacks, who stank, and the greasy spics, who were moving into one end of Bagley Street itself, all of them jabbering away like crazy, carrying knives, drinking and fighting each other right out on the sidewalk . . .

Jules, making fun of his father to Maureen, said, "Them niggers, them Polacks, them spics! Jesus Christ, how I'm sick of having to hate them all! What a pain in the ass it gives me!" When he imitated their father he made his face turn gross and his jaw droop, so that his eyes took on a moronic expression. Maureen had to laugh, but then she felt a warning, which had to do with their grandmother's constant remark: "Make a face and your face will freeze." *Make a face and your face will freeze.*

She saw them all with their frozen faces, her mother and father, her sister, her brother, her grandmother, her aunt, the faces of the nuns at school, the faces of the priests, the faces of the kids in the neighborhood, the faces of all the world—frozen hard into expressions of cunning and anger, while she, Maureen, having no hardness to her, crept in silence among them and waited for the day when everything would be orderly and neat, when she could arrange her life the way she arranged the kitchen after supper, and she too might then be frozen hard, fixed, permanent, beyond their ability to hurt.

Her mother concentrated attention on faces, as if she'd learned this style from Grandma Wendall while, having no knowledge of its origin, she adopted a singsong joviality when she and Maureen went out shopping, indicating people by saying, "Look at the horseface!" "Look at the sow's-face!" "Look behind you and see the monkey!"—getting Maureen to look over her shoulder and into a mirror. Loretta's face was sometimes flabby and ugly, sometimes rather pretty, sometimes the pores of her nose loomed large and black, sometimes not, it was up and down, ugly and pretty, messy and neat, and who could tell which Loretta would step out of her cluttered bedroom? All this made Maureen concentrate upon herself. Her mother directed attention that way anyhow; she often said, squinting at Maureen, "Is your face breaking out? You're about at that age now for lots of pimples."

Around the five rooms that made up their half of the duplex everything was in Loretta's domain. She presided over them all. As soon as their father returned in the early evening his bulk fitted into the overheated rooms; he made his way around the piles of clothes that needed to be washed or ironed or were just lying around, and Betty's junk underfoot, and Maureen hunched over the kitchen table trying to do her homework. He ate the food Loretta made for him. Even when Maureen actually prepared it, it was still Loretta's food, and the house smelled of her—her "bath salts," her perfume, her cigarette smoke. Even when he ran out of silence finally and slapped her, shouting something into her face, she was still at the very center of the house, passive and indolent and vicious.

Through all this, Maureen worked at her homework and tried not to be distracted. She was fairly good in school. Betty was no good at anything except showing off. Jules hadn't even brought a report card home in months. His eyes looked dark and hollow and he lived a life of secrets: a girl at school told Maureen that Jules went out drinking with other boys, that he went out with a girl named Rose Ann, that he was a friend of Ramie Malone and you know what happened to Ramie. Maureen looked through his pockets and found odd things—a broken black plastic comb, filthy, a matchbook with "Manhattan Lounge" on the cover, Kleenex crumpled and smeared with lipstick, a broken key chain, loose coins, slugs, peanuts, various junk. She knew he was flunking out of school but did not dare ask him about it. And Betty, Betty was a little brat—she was so loud and dopey that Maureen would rather take the long way home from school so she wouldn't have to walk with Betty, though that meant she would miss the store windows and the Rialto Theater, whose posters changed once a week and were of great interest. Monday was her mother's day for having her hair washed and set by her friend Ethel, and plucking her eyebrows and doing her nails. On Monday her lips and her fingernails would be the same shade of dark grape. So Maureen understood that her mother was a woman like the women on those movie posters; they wanted certain things and were willing to take risks to get them. Maureen's mother took her shopping in a supermarket and they brought back food in paper bags with red and black squares, and yellow stamps for the book; that was her mother's way of getting things.

On those Saturdays when it was too cold to go to the

library Maureen had to stay home. She hated home. She sat for hours looking out the window. There was nothing to see. Just the partly crumbling concrete base of the house next door, a house as old and ugly as theirs. Not that this house was *theirs;* every month Maureen's father grumbled about paying the rent. What he paid was a secret. Adults had many secrets, mostly dealing with money. It could be shouted out that Loretta was a bitch or Howard was a lazy bastard, anything might be shouted out that had to do with people, but nothing about money—the facts of money— could be mentioned out loud. It was a secret to all children. It was a secret how much her father made every week, and how much he gave her mother; it was even a secret how much some things cost. Aunt Connie complained about making only fifty dollars a week when she worked, but that was just like her—she was always whining, always coughing up things you didn't want to hear. When she came in the kitchen to complain about her life to Loretta, Maureen sighed and moved closer to the window of her room, wanting to get out, to go deaf, wondering why the winter glare that made everything so hard and colorless was somehow better than the close, stale odor of their house. After all, she did love her mother and father. She loved Jules. She even loved Betty, if only Betty would wise up, and so why did she want to see them all dead and buried under the front porch? Even Jules, dead and buried and put to rest.

Most of the time Maureen daydreamed. In her mind she shouted commands, like a soldier; all the kids obeyed her and lined up. There were no adults anywhere to punish or even to praise. It was peaceful and good without them now that she was taking their place and doing what they should have done. Or she closed her eyes and played school. She was the teacher, a nun, and all the kids on the block were sitting in rows; she made them read their lessons one by one, going up and down the aisle. She made them go to the blackboard and add up long columns of figures. If they made mistakes they were scolded in front of everyone and not allowed to make excuses—if they were allowed to make excuses they would only say, "I couldn't do my homework last night, there was some trouble at my house," or "I had to go out last night and I couldn't get any sleep." No, this was like no other school. "Here you've got to work. To work," Maureen would tell them. Her heart would begin to pound, thinking of the captive children and herself watching over them, guarding and bullying them, a different Maureen from the girl everyone knew. Why couldn't people be perfect? Why did they make such mistakes? Doing her homework, Maureen checked and rechecked everything, fearful of making mistakes. Even when she played, even in her imagination she was somehow afraid of making a mistake.

A year ago she'd still played horses, but now she was getting too old. She had played the leader of a herd of horses, a great black stallion. She had dug her heels into the earth and kicked into the air, playing alone, concentrating painfully on being a horse—she had played in secret, shaking her long hair like a mane. Around the house or in the presence of other children she never let herself go like that. She didn't "play." She was not large for her age but she seemed somehow older, and that was why, when something went wrong in the kitchen, she never tried to escape but said calmly that she'd fix it—spilled food, a broken plate, something Betty might have done. She never made excuses. One time when her mother and Flora Stonewall had spent the whole day drinking beer and telling stories about their childhoods, and her mother had done nothing about starting supper, Maureen had taken over in the kitchen and both women had teased her. "Look at Maureen, she's going to make somebody a good wife," Flora said. She was a handsome, lazy woman with long red hair, sometimes tied back from her face. Her arms were big, big-boned, and her legs were rather thick. Her voice was musical in a slightly accusing, singsong way: she seemed to like Maureen. Scraping garbage into the smelly pail under the sink, doing the dishes until her face was flushed from the heat, Maureen forced her mind to concentrate upon the schoolroom she presided over or upon the ravine in which the wild horses lived or upon the library with its waxed, smooth floors and the occasional clicking of the librarian's typewriter. When she was by herself her thoughts wandered to these things. She sometimes woke to find herself standing in a doorway, absent-mindedly caressing her own arm, while Loretta sailed past and said, "Wake up, kid, the house is on fire."

She woke to see her family at supper, shapes inside clothes, weighed down in their chairs. It made her dizzy to think of them this way. Her father was a dense object, his shirt partly unbuttoned; her mother was a fluttery, insubstantial object; her grandmother was thick, heavy, brooding, dressed in black. One time, downtown, she had seen her own sister with a wild bunch of girls, fooling around by a bus stop. The girls were all dressed in blue jeans and sweatshirts. They surged around a corner and signaled a bus, and when the bus pulled over to stop and the door opened they ran away. Betty was shrieking with laughter, a hard, wiry little object, like a puppet or even like a top, spinning out of control, turning round and round on the sidewalk until she bumped against a passerby and her friends all laughed at her. Maureen had shrunk back, not wanting to be seen. Was that her sister, that awful girl with the dark blond hair cut short as a boy's, shorter than Jules's hair, that girl with her hard, muscular legs and her hoarse voice? And she often watched Jules when he walked through the house, always tired, narrowing her eyes until her brother became a shadowy object passing her, bringing out no response in her, no love or kinship. He was growing up and had to do the things grownups did. He had to entwine himself around some girl, he had to do certain things with her and with the crowd he ran with, he had to work, he had to make money, he had to shave, to fuss with his hair, to run his hands wearily across his eyes, to answer in a sharp, ugly voice if someone bothered him—"Go to hell, Maureen," he would say, or to Betty, "I don't have time for screwing around, get away." He was always pushing himself off from them, always escaping.

One day in spring, on her way home from the library, Maureen scared up a toad near a house on her block. She chased it under a nearby porch. She found a stick and tried to poke it into jumping, but the stick wasn't quite long enough—there the toad sat, its body puffed and gulping, terrified but not moving, in a pile of leaves. She felt mean. She thought, *If I crawled under the porch I could get that toad,* and there was something in the very kinship between them, their similar breathlessness, their terror, that made her want to crawl under. She poked around with the stick, leaning forward on her hands and knees, but the toad did not move; they eyed each other in silence.

When she got home Flora Stonewall was sitting on the front steps. She said casually, "Oh, Maureen, where you been? I'm spost to tell you something."

"What?"

"Your ma and grandma have gone somewhere. They didn't know where you were. Jules drove them. They told me I was spost to wait for you—"

"What's wrong?"

"I guess your pa had some trouble."

Maureen stared at her. "What kind of trouble? With the police?"

"Honey, no, don't talk like that," Flora said, pained, drawing her lips and eyebrows up in the same instant. "Your pa had some trouble at work. An accident. He got hurt at work."

"Hurt? How?"

"I don't know, honey. Why don't you go inside or something? You want a Royal Crown? I got some in my refrigerator. You want one?"

"No."

"Loretta told me to wait for you. I'm real sorry to tell you bad news, it just makes me feel awful, honey. You sure you don't want no Royal Crown? Why don't you come in my place and relax?"

"No, I'm all right," Maureen said.

She went past Flora, dignified and cold with fear, and the very silence of their house told her: the end. The end of something. The front room looked like hell, the sofa's slipcover was loose on one end and the lamp shade was crooked, sunlight from the side window fell upon a worn brown rug; it was all familiar, the very staleness of the house was familiar and should have been a relief, but suddenly Maureen realized how temporary it was—even if it was ugly it was still temporary and it could still be lost. She went to lie on her bed, which was unmade. She looked up at the ceiling. She waited.

After a while the back door opened and someone ran in. "Hey, Maureen," Jules called.

She did not answer.

He came to the door of her room and looked in. "Did *she* tell you, next door? Tell you what happened?"

"Is Pa dead?"

"He's in the hospital."

Maureen stared at him. It was a surprise to see how tall Jules was now. He didn't wear the tight-pegged pants of a year before, his hair was brushed back impatiently from his face, he looked shaken and sick. He said, "He's going to die maybe. Another man did die who was with him. A ton of some stuff fell on them, two tons—"

"Fell on them?"

"Something happened and it let loose. It fell on them."

They stared at each other. Finally Maureen said, wondering what to say, "He's in the hospital?"

"They took him to the emergency ward at Ford's."

She saw the hospital suddenly, a heavy building. "In the hospital?" she said vaguely.

"We're going to go over. First I'll take you out for a hamburg or something."

Maureen covered her face with her hands.

"Hey, kid," Jules said quickly, "hey, don't cry! You don't have to have a hamburg. It was Ma's idea. I'm supposed to take you and Betty out for some supper and then over to the hospital. Don't cry—you want me to start bawling myself?"

Maureen took her hands slowly away from her face and Jules was still there. His face was pinched and white. "You wouldn't ever cry for anybody," she said.

"That's a hell of a thing to say!"

Betty was nowhere around so they drove out to a Biff's restaurant on Woodward. Maureen felt liberated, daring, in the car—it was as if a holiday had come unexpectedly.

"Did it really happen?" Maureen kept asking.

Jules glanced over at her. "Yes, sure. You think I'd kid about something like that?"

"But, I mean . . . did it really happen like you said? A ton of stuff fell on him?" she asked.

"Two tons, it was," said Jules.

If Jules could only keep driving forever! Up north along the avenue, turning north continually, following any roads, getting them out of this city and away from the hospital where their father lay and had nothing to do with them, already changed, distant . . . Maureen kept gripping her face with her hands, feeling it, uncertain of her own face and skull, wondering at it. This skull could be crushed too. Jules glanced at her but said nothing about her odd behavior. Instead he said, as if knowing her thoughts, "It would be damn nice to keep on driving, huh? Up to northern Michigan where there's lots of lakes and woods, past the tree line, someplace where nobody has been yet but that's cleared off and ready for us to move in. I can imagine the sky there, and a lake. I can imagine a moose drinking from the lake. Or maybe it was in a picture I saw, in a magazine or on a calendar . . ."

It frightened her, the way his voice ran down suddenly. It seemed to lose energy.

"What's a moose exactly?" she said.

They went into the restaurant. Maureen had no appetite but, sitting next to Jules at the counter, reading through the menu again and again, she thought that she had better eat; it was a privilege, being in a restaurant. They had hamburgers and French fries. Maureen ate everything, even the last burnt, wrinkled French fries. She rubbed her finger on the plate and licked salt from it.

Jules said, muttering so no one else could hear, "Maybe he's dead already. I hope so. Then we can get over waiting. We might come in the door and they'll say he's already dead! And Ma will be bawling, and Grandma Wendall mad. We'll just park the car and walk in and they'll say, *Your father is dead*."

Maureen was ashamed now of having eaten so much. She had forgotten, in a way, why they were at Biff's and not at home.

"You never liked Pa, did you?" she said softly.

"It's a rotten mess. Those women bawling . . . The hospital stinks, I can't stand that smell. No, I didn't like him, Reeny, but shut up about it. Don't you ever say that again. If I kidded around it was just for the hell of it—I mean, about wanting him to drop dead—for the hell of it and because . . . because I couldn't stand it, him being so quiet! I had enough of his quiet." Jules wiped his hand under his nose suddenly. "It got next to me and almost drove me crazy sometimes. Jesus Christ, he taught me all I need to know about quiet!"

11

After his father's funeral Jules went for a walk downtown. He looked in store windows like everyone else and allowed himself to be brushed by people passing him in a hurry, feeling himself invisible, floating. He was almost sixteen years old. He could not understand what that meant: sixteen years of age. His father's death had sloughed off onto him the heaviness of his father's spirit, and his heaviness, like a gas, was filling up inside him. He had heard that the dead collect gas, internally. Yet he was strangely lightheaded, though his feet ached. His head felt as if it might float away. The dirty sidewalks around him and the hurrying feet of other people were going one way; and his brain seemed to be straining another way. There was something he had to get straight, come to peace with, but here he was, cold and disordered, lightheaded, crossing over to the Grand Circus Park, alive and dressed unnaturally in a good dark suit, while his father was dead and set in the ground.

Who had his father been exactly?

I can't remember his face or anything he said, Jules thought in a panic. It was his father he had to come to grips with. It was not right that a man should live and die and come to nothing, be forgotten, with his own son unable to really remember him—it did not seem right. As Jules passed a park bench an old man watched him closely, as if about to recognize him. Jules looked away. He did not want to be recognized. His mother's sloppy, whining grief and his sisters' fear chilled him; he did not want to be a part of it. He had to get away from everyone. So his father had been killed, so it had happened and was now quite naturally being passed by, and maybe his father had never really recognized him either, what difference did it make? He tried to absorb it all. His mother could absorb nothing, everything spilled out of her like those hot painful tears and so he, Jules, would accept everything and make it normal. He lingered by the movie houses, looking at posters—the handsome, made-up faces did not seem to mean anything to him. They could absorb grief, pain, joy, without strain—no lines appeared on their faces, nothing. Jules wondered if these faces would someday betray him. Inside the big old movie houses everything went on as usual, thin crowds came and went, there was the usual odor of soiled carpeting and stale popcorn and that musty darkness of old, large, downtown buildings, inexplicable. Jules stared at the posters, waiting to become interested. He stared at a photograph of Marlon Brando. Much of his life had come from movies, much of his language and his good spirits. From the movies he had sensed that life is backed by music, but now, out on the sidewalk, he felt depressed and lifeless, and there was no music anywhere around him or the promise of music.

His father had been—how old? What pain had he felt? And the body that had felt pain—had it really been his father's, the man who had sat for so long at a certain place at the table, the man who had eaten supper in a certain way every night, anxious to get it over? The man Jules had always hated?

He walked slowly home. It was a long walk. The weather

was cool, and he could not think of which season it was—spring or fall. The river looked steamy, but that was probably from factories on the west side. Smoke billowed up from a number of points. It rose and flowed gently across the Ambassador Bridge, passing through the bridge, making it look unreal; cars and trucks drove through the smoke. Jules could not remember why he'd come so far for a walk, what he was looking for, what he had hoped to figure out, when he had many things to do at home—his mother needed him—and he was uncomfortable in this suit. His mother needed him at home and would need him permanently.

He began to sweat. Out in the river there were maybe bodies beneath the surface of the water, or at least there were stories kids told about seeing bodies bob to the surface and then disappear again . . . The dead, the drowned, so silent and patient. . . . Jules felt that these dark mysterious people moved about in ordinary air, corpses that looked alive. You might stumble into one of them, fall into an embrace, feel that cold heavy breath upon you and that ratty, stringy cold hair. . . .

Just what had his father been like, anyway? Jules remembered suddenly his father trying to fix the toilet, trying to stop a leak. The bathroom door was warped. The linoleum was of various levels, bloated and worn smooth, so that when he sat in the bathroom Jules stared down at this landscape and had the vague idea that it was a relief map of something, a secret land. His father had tried to fix the toilet many times, the faucets many times. No luck. The heavy breathing, the muttering, the minutes and minutes of silent struggle, and then, "Goddam it!" and the noise of something being thrown down, a wrench or a pliers, whatever. The silence, the breathing and then the noise. That was his father. Never any luck fixing things. Roaches came out of the secret edges of the bathroom at night and sometimes they were still out in the morning, lazy things, and often they were in the kitchen cupboards and under the sink, very often—they made his father swear. The floor must have been a real landscape to the roaches. Jules narrowed his eyes and tried to think about his father. What had his father to do with roaches? Why was it easier to think of them than of his father? His father and money: that was important. That was maybe the secret. He had complained about money. He hadn't complained about much, but when he did it was usually about money. Where did that money go, a paycheck's worth? Where did that twenty dollars go? And on and on, the misery over money, the worry over money, not having enough, too many people to feed, a sick mother in the house, and every year the kids got flu and the anti-biotics were very expensive. Pills were expensive. Loretta had had some trouble with her kidneys and had to take pills every six hours, and those pills were expensive, like every-thing else in the United States, very expensive, so that Jules's father would say viciously, "One of these days I'm taking off! You can all go to hell!" Or he would say, looking up from the newspaper where he'd read something, "All the niggers are on welfare, why not me? Us? Everybody can go to hell!"

Jules had thought of his father's anger during the Mass said for him. No special Mass, a funeral Mass. A dreary church. Jules had sat beside his mother, immensely weary of her sorrow, which was as confused and lightheaded and un-controlled as her anger usually was. If only he could depend upon her. . . . Jules hadn't paid much attention to the fu-neral Mass. He no longer went to church. He felt the churches of the city drag at him as he passed, a melancholy lure. They were like vast legendary caverns in the sea, luring swimmers down, breathing them in with mysterious currents —promises of secrets, rewards, a special knowledge that no longer mattered. He did not care. His father had not cared. There hadn't been any anger in it, there had been only nothing. His father's face smooth and blank as a skull with white skin stretched over it—that was his father. Jules could almost remember him. The Mass had obscured him, the dead man, but now he was returning to Jules, painfully. Anger was at the core of him. That was his secret—anger.

But Jules hadn't killed him.

Yes, anger was at the core of him; his soul was anger, made up of anger. Anger for what? For nothing, for him-self, for life, for the assembly line, for the cockroaches and the dripping toilet. One thing was as good as another. Anger. No money. Where had the money gone? Where would the money come from? Anger, money. His father.

Jules felt a flash of satisfaction, almost of joy. No, he hadn't killed his father. His own anger had been kept back for years, kept successfully back; he hadn't hurt anyone. Money was an adventure. It was open to him. Anything could happen. He felt that his father's essence, that mut-

tering dark anger, had surrounded him and almost penetrated him, but had not quite penetrated him; he was free.

A few days later, on his way to school, he was thinking
about this—his father, his father's fury, his father's money,
his father's death—when he saw something that jolted him.
Then, a moment later, he realized that it was Edith. She
was with two other girls. For an instant he could hardly
move, staring at her, feeling the same sense of despair and
wonder he'd felt at his father's death rising in him now at
the sight of this girl. She was going up the concrete steps
to a viaduct overpass with her girl friends.

Jules ran to catch up with them. "Hey," he said, "where
are you going so fast?"

They looked around in surprise. One of the girls, the
boldest one, grinned at him. She was the prettiest, but Jules
was faithful to Edith; he lurched over to her side of the
walk. In their presence he had become slightly swaggering.
"You always walk this way?" he said.

Edith shrugged her shoulders lightly.

She had pulled her hair back into a ponytail. She had
blond eyebrows and blond eyelashes, a chaste cold girl with
no smile for him. Jules walked with his weight on his heels,
his hands stuffed in his pockets, conferring his presence upon
them as if it were an important gift; he felt a slight tugging
between him and the girls, a nervous exhilaration. He
glanced at Edith sideways. She looked very nervous. The
other girls began to talk to him, teasing flatly, gaining courage, and Jules answered them in the same style: *Yeah, is
that so, you wouldn't kid me?*

"Where is your girl friend, Jules?" they asked him. They
stretched their mouths in a sweet accusatory way, and Jules
made a face to show that he had no interest in this question.
He did have a girl friend, his own girl, and so really had no
need of Edith. His girl, Rose Ann, was no friend of girls
like these; her friends were knowing and sly and very sure of
themselves. They wore stockings to school. Their ears were
pierced, and their secrets were razzing and exciting and
sleazy, while these girls, anxious to imitate their sophistica-
tion but afraid of it, tried to talk in the same singsong, flat,
melodic patter. Jules had a slightly contemptuous smile for
all of them.

They were halfway across the viaduct. The wind was
quite strong. Edith's frail bangs whipped about her forehead

and she had to narrow her eyes against the flying dirt; Jules saw tiny lines appear at the corners of her eyes. She had pale blue eyes and very pale skin. She wore no lipstick. Her coat was a yellow-and-white-check and already a little soiled from Detroit's air and buses; she carried a purse with a long strap that went over her shoulder. Jules thought she looked delightful. He did not know her at all. He took hold of the strap of her purse suddenly, thinking of the strap of her slip, and tugged at it. She pulled away from him, frightened. He could see the muscles move in her throat. He wanted to tell her not to be afraid of him, but instead he said, teasing, "What's in here, ammunition? This is pretty heavy."

"Oh, it's just . . . my purse . . ."

The three girls seemed to be dancing about him in the wind, though their feet in standard brown loafers were really not very graceful; Jules smiled at all of them, at their shrill expectant faces. He did not let go of Edith's purse. He said, "Hey, you got some pictures of yourself?"

"What do you care?"

"Do you have some? Can I see?"

"Why? What do you care?" Edith said.

She turned to face him. Her hair fluttered in the wind. "Give me a picture of yourself, huh? Will you?"

It was the fashion that spring for high-school girls to have "portraits" taken of themselves, $3.99 for a number of prints, the portraits in brown tone with fake velvet props and single strands of pearls and heavy makeup. They all went to an Italian photographer near school. Jules ached suddenly to get a photograph of Edith. He tugged at her purse.

"Oh, all right," she said nervously. "I don't know why you want one, probably just to be . . ." Either she ran out of courage or could not think of anything more to say. She took a blue plastic billfold out of her purse, and out of this, as Jules watched lovingly, she extracted a photograph and handed it to him. He was suddenly very excited. He wanted to take her hand, he wanted to kiss her, but she was already sidestepping as if she knew what was in his mind, and the other girls closed in upon her, as if protecting her.

One of them said spitefully, "Don't ask me for a picture because I wouldn't give you one!"

Jules paid no attention. He was staring at the photograph.

It was brown-toned, and Edith sat rigid against a background of what looked like a starry night. Around her thin shoulders was a dark velvet cloth, a V in front, moderately daring. It was supposed to look like an evening gown. She wore a single strand of pearls and her lips had been outlined too heavily; her eyes looked pale, faded, overpowered by the heavy lines of her mouth. Jules thought that he could not help loving this girl, though he had no idea who she was.

She was moving away, embarrassed and hurried. The other two girls looked back at him.

"Thanks a lot! I mean it, thanks!" he called after them.

Jules lagged behind. He stared at the photograph. *Edith. Edith Kamensky.* Having the photograph, he felt that he could afford to let the girl get away; what could he say to her anyhow? She had cool, cold, uncertain eyes. The lashes were scanty. There was a mole near the left side of her mouth. Wisps of hair lay about her temples, passing down high on her forehead. Jules wondered if she ever laughed. What was she like when she laughed? He felt lust rise in him, a desire to get her alone, to get her to himself, though he really did not want to approach her again in the next few days. He could not imagine approaching her again at all.

He stopped to put the picture in his pocket, but somehow it got loose. The wind snatched it away. Jules lunged for it but it was blown over the railing. "Jesus. Shit," he said in surprise. He watched it being blown rather languidly down and across the street, above the tops of trucks and cars. He ran to the stairs and slid down the embankment to the street and right down through the mud, and only a few feet away a police car sped past him. It passed him at maybe eighty miles an hour. Good luck. They must be after someone. Jules looked around for the picture—it was just coming to rest. There was an opening in the traffic; he calculated and began edging out. Someone honked angrily at him. He jumped back onto the curb, which was not exactly a curb but only a raised narrow ledge. No one was supposed to be down here on foot; it was against the law. Jules waited. The wind made his eyes burn. His face too was burning, with shame and exasperation, but still he would not give up, he'd set his vision now upon a small white piece of paper that was fluttering on the other side of the street, lifting and falling violently as cars passed. He edged over again, waited until a car sped by, then ran blindly across the street. Someone put on his brakes and a terrible honking began. Jules waved them away and jumped to the other curb. He snatched up the piece of paper but it was not the photograph. "What?" he said aloud. He threw it back over his shoulder in disgust. Then he saw another piece of paper. This had landed in the near lane a few yards away and was already crumpled. He ran over and picked it up.

Edith Kamensky with her pale, pale lashes . . .

For a while he stood there on the curb, at the foot of the muddy embankment, staring at the photograph. It was dirty, it had been bent in two. Weariness rose in him, a sense of wonder. There was always something about life he could not figure out.

Now that he had retrieved it, he thought, he had to be faithful to it.

12

She was fourteen. She sat in the kitchen at the table while her mother's friend Ethel combed out her wet hair and rubbed hair-set lotion on it. The lotion was green and had a peppermint smell; Maureen liked that smell.

Loretta sat across from them, her chair turned outward, her legs crossed. The two women were smoking. Loretta said, "The boss isn't so bad. I like that car of hers—that red car, you seen it?"

Ethel was putting one strand of Maureen's hair onto a big pink plastic roller. She said with a preoccupied air, "She took me for a ride in it one day. No, she ain't so bad, but she gets every penny out of the place. I'd rather have a man boss. And Dora May, that little suck, she runs and tells her if anyone leaves early. The other day I got finished with my customer at four-thirty, so why the hell not leave? So I left, and the next morning . . ."

It was summer now and Maureen's father had been dead for months. She did not miss her father. Sometimes she began to cry when she was alone, crying for no reason; but she did not think this had anything to do with her father. It had to do with Ford Hospital and all the corridors and all the people, every one of them helpless as her father. It had to do with the cemetery. It had to do with her brother, who stayed away from home most of the time now. All these changes, this geography of change, she could not keep up with. So she sometimes cried when she was alone. In front of other people she was learning not to cry.

"Mrs. Foster is a nice lady," Loretta said. "She came back specially to me to give me a quarter. Wasn't that nice of her?"

"Yeah, she's nice. And Mrs. Abrahams is nice. But that Mrs. Freer or whatever her name is, she's a bitch—she thinks she's so glamorous but I got a surprise for her, if she ever asks my opinion."

Ethel was a lanky, energetic woman in her forties. She had taken a course at a local beauty school and worked at the La Marvel Beauty Salon on Vernor. Loretta, who had no training, worked there also but could only wash hair and help clean up the place. She had worked there since the beginning of June. Suddenly her looks had changed; she came home with her hair tinted a light airy blond, puffed out about her face, her eyebrows were arched in a new and important way, her nails were expertly done, without the half-moons showing; she had a new working-woman's way of smoking, with the cigarette held urgently between the thumb and forefinger, poised, always ready to be brought to her mouth. Maureen noticed that Ethel smoked the same way. Ethel had hair that was tinted red, set into heavy waves about her face, and she always wore certain colors that she thought went with red—brown, green, dark blue. She and Loretta leafed through magazines when they sat in the kitchen having coffee—*Hair Design, Vogue, Salon & Boutique*. They brought these magazines home from the La Marvel Beauty Salon and forgot to return them. Maureen had gone down to the salon one day just to see what it was like and had been a little depressed at the unclean front windows, but it was a job, it was something. Her mother seemed to like it.

"I wish I could get myself to go take some course, some lessons," Loretta said. She was watching the way Ethel did Maureen's hair. "I'd like to cut hair and all that. I think I could do it real well, don't you? I wouldn't have any trouble setting it, it's just cutting it that would scare me."

"Nothing to it," Ethel said.

"Next month I'm going to get myself downtown to that place, what's-the-name, and see how fast I can get through."

Maureen touched her head. There were four large rollers set across the very top of her head, pulling her hair tight, but she did not want to complain. Ethel was working on the sides now. This had been Loretta's idea: she'd said, looking critically at Maureen a few days before, "You'd better let Ethel fix you up. Them bangs don't do much for you, kid. It looks like you bought them from the Fuller Brush man."

And now, on newspaper laid on the floor around her chair, lay snippings of her dark brown hair. The damp clipping scissors, brought home from the La Marvel, lay on the table with clots of hair stuck to it. The setting lotion and the hair spray and the rollers themselves had been smuggled home from the La Marvel.

"How's your mother-in-law?" Ethel said.

"You saw her. I don't ask."

Grandma Wendall, though no better, had taken over the living-room. Maureen did not know how this had come about. Gradually the old lady had taken over the sofa, half lying there with a quilt over her knees, watching television. She woke up every morning at six. They heard her in the kitchen, making herself breakfast, and when they got up, her breakfast dishes were all in the sink, soaking, and Grandma Wendall herself was in the living-room with the television set turned on rather loudly, watching the "Today" show. The blinds were drawn down so that there was no glare on the screen. When she wanted to go to the bathroom she called Loretta, if Loretta was home, or Maureen, if Maureen was home, or Betty, and, leaning heavily upon their shoulders, walked to the back of the house. She seemed heavier than before, though she was not well. She ate a lot of ice cream. Her hair was frizzled and white, very thin, and her face was a mass of wrinkles. Still, there was a certain youthful antagonism about her. Right now, at nine-thirty in the evening, she was on the sofa with the room darkened, watching a television program; Maureen could hear the artificial applause and laughter roaring out of the darkened front room. In the kitchen the two women were strangely silent.

"Well," Ethel said slowly, "it was like that with my ma too—I mean she had her mother-in-law with her. For thirty years. How'd you like that, kid?"

"Jesus Christ," Loretta said.

"That old lady was batty all her life. I swear, her brains were scrambled or something. She come over from Czechoslovakia when she was seventeen years old and never bothered to learn English. Said it was too much trouble, it was too late for her. She lived to be eighty and never knew anything, I mean not one thing; she never knew about the Second World War or Hitler or anything, it was just crazy. She wasn't a bad old dame, but how'd you like that, Loretta?"

"Jesus Christ, no."

"We lived over on Lycaste then."

Maureen sat obediently, bending her head. Ethel finished another row of rollers. She fixed them with steel clips. Then she lifted the can of hair spray and sprayed Maureen's head all around for quite a while.

"God, that stuff stinks," Loretta said.

"This stuff is nothing. At work we got a real strong mixture, not like this," Ethel said. "It comes out of a gun like, you seen it? God, is that strong! I got a coating of it in my lungs, I bet. It makes me want to puke. For four years I been using it, and what you want to bet my lungs are coated with it, huh?"

"Oh, I bet they aren't."

Now Ethel combed Maureen's bangs down flat on her forehead and fixed them there with a strip of Scotch tape.

"Bring the hair drier in and get that hair all dry. You don't go to bed with wet hair," Loretta said.

They hooked the hair drier up, and Maureen sat holding it in her hand; it was a hand model, bought for under ten dollars. She liked the warm air blowing against her head. The kind of tears it brought to her eyes were innocent tears, without pain. It was like when she yawned. It was not like the bitter tears that surprised her, coming upon her with such power; sometimes in the library, back in the stacks of books, she found herself beginning to cry in a passion of shame, not understanding. Her mother rarely cried now and her sister never cried. And Jules, who had cried only a few times in her memory, was never around now and so she knew nothing about him.

He had flunked his sophomore year of high school and had said he wasn't going back.

The two women drank coffee and talked now, evasively and quietly, of someone Maureen didn't know. She gathered that she was not supposed to listen. A woman who'd gotten in trouble and her husband kicked her out, and . . . Maureen thought about Jules. She felt safe between these two women, her mother and her mother's friend, oddly safe in their intimate, gossipy warmth; let them talk about anything,

anything! At such times she could think about her father or about Jules or about nightmare things that would ordinarily frighten her—for instance, a girl dragged into a car not two blocks away and raped and pushed out the door, ending up half dead, and the girl was someone Maureen knew. Jules had started to stay out overnight back in April. He told Loretta he was staying at a friend's house, spending the night. He gave them a name. Loretta had wept but hadn't looked up the name or made a telephone call, and gradually Jules began staying away two or three nights a week. Maureen heard from other kids that he was cutting school. But what he did during the day, whether he had another job or spent his time roaming around, whether he was getting in trouble, no one knew. He told Maureen, "Those kids at school get next to me, they're so goddam dumb. They're little people. I can't stand them." The boys he had hung around with for years were dumb now and he avoided them. If he had new friends, Maureen did not know who they were.

One night when Maureen asked him what was wrong, didn't he like her and Ma and Betty any more, he had said impatiently, "It's this house I can't stand. I can't stand this dump. I come in the front door and keep thinking I'm going to see *him* there. . . . Instead it's always the old lady. I keep thinking I'm going to hear him drive into the driveway. Or hear him get up in the middle of the night and go to the bathroom. There's too much left over of him here, I can't stand it."

"She had it done three times, I bet you. There was three separate times," Ethel said.

"Wouldn't you think she'd learn? Jesus!" Loretta laughed.

"How's that what's-her-name, Connie? She still come around here?"

"She's got a place in Highland Park. She got a job doing something, don't ask me what, you'd think it was some big secret or something the way she talks. Actually, Maureen and I think she's a waitress. What else could that cow do? Yeah, she comes around sometimes. Her and the old lady sit in the front room and if you walk in they give you the fish eye, like it was their goddam house. Connie must weigh two hundred pounds—what a cow! She comes over here from Mass and has the goddammest lace thing, black lace, draped over her head like some Spanish bull or cow or something. The two of them keep whispering in the living-room, gabbing their heads off. I know they're talking about me but I don't give a goddam. Let them. If I didn't have a job I'd go crazy with that old bag's stink and her crap and that television set on all the time, but look, I figure it this way: when the television breaks down next time I'm not going to bother fixing it, but until then she might as well watch it. Why not? She wouldn't be a bad person if she'd just let up once in a while. I mean, I can remember when we were all out on that god-awful farm, in the country, and she was a lot younger and did all kinds of things—oh, she made bread and noodles and did a lot of canning, she worked like hell, she was real nice to Jules and just was a different person. Now her face is always set the same way. Like a bomb. She looks like a bomb. But I don't like to speak bad of her because . . ."

Because she's going to die soon, Maureen thought.

"Because she was Howard's mother, you know," Loretta said lamely.

"Yeah, I know. Like I told you, my own ma had the same problem. For thirty years."

"Your mother must have been a saint."

"Yeah, she was sort of a saint, now I think about it. All us kids think she was real good. I wish I hadn't given her so much trouble—"

"Trouble! Jesus Christ, there's nobody that doesn't have trouble."

Loretta fixed her eyes on Maureen. She was beginning to look at Maureen in a certain way now, seriously and thoughtfully. This had begun a few months back, when Maureen had turned fourteen. "Fourteen years old! My God!" Loretta had said, and Maureen had been uneasy at her words.

"Yeah, that's a fact. That's a sure thing," Ethel said.

"In the front room I got trouble, when Howard was alive I had trouble, back living with my father I had trouble—one thing after another, all my life. But I don't let it get me down."

"You sure don't. You look real good, Loretta."

"Oh, the hell with that," Loretta said, pleased, brushing this compliment away with a wave of her hand. "I'm just not going to let them get me down. The guy came about the water meter and said somebody broke it, some kids. I said, well that ain't my fault. He said it hadn't better be broke again. I said, go next door, it's their water meter too, ain't it? I tell you, Ethel, every half-assed bastard comes down the street winds up here trying to give me a hard time. He said, are you Mrs. Howard Wendall and ain't this Labrosse Street? I told him have a look at the street sign if he could read. I told him none of my kids broke that meter and he could go to hell if he thought I'd pay for it."

"Yeah, they always try to push you around. They got a badge or something and come in a truck, think they can push you around."

"I'm telling *you* nobody is going to push me around. Just because I'm a widow. Now, this one cop, this Italian what's-his-name, he gives Jules a hard time and for no reason whatsoever. What's his name, Reeny?"

"Joe Mattuizzo."

"Yeah, him. His kid brother used to be a friend of Jules. He picked Jules up in the squad car last week, or two weeks ago, and Jules was doing nothing, not one thing. Him and the other cop searched him. They said they were cleaning up the street and looking for kids with knives or dope. Jules don't have even a knife, what the hell would he want a knife for? Anyway they had to let him go. When I saw that bastard the next day, hanging around by Vernor, I told him, go feel up some nigger and leave my kid alone! He tried to act real polite but I told him he'd be sorry if he bothered my kids, to remember that."

"He wasn't the one, about Betty?"

"No, that was some old cop, that wasn't a bad old guy," Loretta said. Her face took on a slightly irritated look, and Maureen knew that Ethel had done wrong to bring up this subject. "No, he was nice. He understood. He just brought her home and talked to me. I gave him some coffee. He was a real gentleman and not like that bastard Mattuizzo or whatever the hell his name is."

Betty had been brought home by the police one day, caught with a gang of kids who were breaking into cars parked near Tiger Stadium. It had been the afternoon of a baseball game and all the parking lots and even the front and side yards of private homes had been filled with cars. No charges had been made against her. Loretta had wept about it for an evening and had finally slapped Betty around, and that was the end of it. It hadn't been mentioned again.

"But I'm telling you they ain't going to get me down," Loretta said angrily. "There's not enough bastards in this city to get me down for long."

The one job Maureen's grandmother was supposed to do was the ironing; that had been her own idea. While Loretta was gone during the day she was supposed to iron, sitting out in the kitchen with the ironing board stretched between two chairs so that she could reach it. On the kitchen counter was a radio that played continuously, little fifteen-minute stories. But she usually felt sick, and so Maureen did it for her, giving in, feeling the surface of her skin rise in tiny prickles at being so weak. When Loretta came home from work she would say, "Oh, I see you got the ironing done, Ma, *thank you*," but her grandmother never spoke up to say that Maureen had done the work.

"I hate her! I wish she'd go away," Maureen whispered to Betty.

"They should come and take her away and throw away the key," Betty said.

Part of Loretta's new life was a certain fast rollicking blindness; she did not seem to see what was going on. She was in a hurry. She came in the house and changed her clothes, she went down to the drugstore, she went shopping just before the grocery store closed, she went out to the movies with Ethel or other "girls" who worked at the beauty parlor, she went bowling with them, she was always in a hurry and seemed to have a big-sister's mocking strength. Toward Grandma Wendall she was ludicrously formal. She said, "Reeny is going to do the kitchen and the bathroom this morning, Ma, and we would both appreciate it *very much* if you didn't walk on the floor. So if you want to go to the bathroom maybe you could go now. I'll help you in."

She appeared in the kitchen in her slip, the odor of sweat and perfume about her, the straps of her slip fixed with safety pins and its skirt tight about her thighs so that you could see where her stockings were fastened. She often hummed to herself. When she complained about her low pay at the La Marvel it was not real serious complaining but a kind of song, another kind of humming. When Maureen tried to explain things to her, why she needed a new skirt or fifteen cents for the Red Cross Drive at school, Loretta often didn't hear her. Or she said, "Blah-blah-blah." She developed a habit of standing with her hands at her hips, her mouth fixed in a patient, disbelieving smile. Perhaps she listened to the wild stories of the other beauty-parlor operators with that same smile. Perhaps she listened to the wild stories of her customers with that smile. Sometimes when she came home late, having been out at a movie or bowling or maybe at a bar, she'd wake Maureen and Betty and give them a bag of pretzels! Other times she woke them up to complain about something. Why was the house so dirty? Why couldn't that big dope Maureen keep things cleaner? She was going to turn Betty over to the reformatory, the girls' jail, yes, she was—and Betty, with her wise, crinkled eyes and her tough skin, would watch her mother with that exact disbelieving smile, her mother's smile. Sometimes Loretta sailed into the house with her hair newly done and her face all fixed up, an almost-pretty woman with a slightly sullen, perplexed forehead, and announced that she was *going out for dinner* and would Maureen please take over and try not to leave the place a mess.

The more Loretta was away, the more powerful Grandma Wendall became. Maureen had to run down to the drugstore for her. She had to telephone the clinic to report her grandmother's new symptoms. She had to go next door to tell Flora Stonewall that her grandmother would like to borrow some cocoa to make hot chocolate. If she went outside to get away, just hanging around the front veranda with a girl friend, her grandmother lay in the living-room and called, "Maureen! Maureen!" in a voice of pain. In the summer she played parcheesi with a girl in the neighborhood and the games were always interrupted. Under her breath she murmured, "Oh, hell," as she ran back into the house, thinking, *What next? What's she want now?* And it was always something surprising, something she would not have imagined.

One morning after Loretta left for work Grandma Wendall began talking about her. "You know she's running around with every man she can get," the old woman said. Betty snickered and shoved her chair back from the table. "Oh, yes she is! You think your grandmother is lying? Making things up? I sit in this house and I don't go out but I know everything that's going on. I know everything. I can look right out the window, through the side of the window, through the side of the shade, and nobody knows I can see what's going on but I can. I know all about that little girl friend of yours, Maureen—that girl with the bad skin and the oily hair, her. I know all about her. And I can hear you talking. I can hear everything you say."

Maureen looked away.

"She's just making it up," Betty said.

"I can hear everything. I can see everything. And when your ma comes home it ain't alone. I see them out front on the street, in the car—I know, I'm watching. She thinks I fall asleep in here with the television on but I'm not asleep. I know just when she comes in and I know everything about her. She doesn't fool me—"

"You're crazy," Betty said.

"Don't you talk like that to me, you little jailbird!"

"I'm not no jailbird," Betty said in a whine. "I never got arrested once! Don't you call me that!"

"I can hear everything they say. Oh, your ma says all kinds of things, she's got no shame. She tells them men anything they want to hear. I wouldn't tell you girls what it is. She talks about meeting them the next night, she makes promises—them men are probably married and just running around with her for the hell of it, to see what they can get out of her, and she's so dumb she thinks they'd marry her. Well, nobody's going to marry *her*, with her hair all bleached like a bone. She looks just like one of them roosters with the blond feathers on top."

"I think Ma looks nice," Maureen said.

"I do too," said Betty.

Their grandmother pushed herself up from the table. She was stooped over but still fairly tall; what had been muscles hung in folds from her arms, visible through the overlarge armholes of her cotton dress. There was an odor of unwashed flesh about her. Really, she was a very dirty woman; she did not like to wash. She was so hawkish with her sharp eyes and mouth that Loretta did not dare to mention it.

"You just like to talk back, you two. One with a long face and the other a jailbird—"

"Betty was never in jail," Maureen said.

"I never even got arrested," Betty said again.

"You will," the old woman said.

"I don't care if I do! I can take care of myself. I ain't no crazy old bag," Betty said. She wore blue jeans and a boy's shirt and she was barefoot. She and her grandmother stared at each other, nearly the same height. Betty snickered like a boy.

"One of you two help me now—I got to go in the bathroom."

Maureen went obediently to her grandmother and helped her walk. The old lady leaned upon her. She said, "You wouldn't stand around telling your grandmother to go to hell if your father was still alive. You'd see what was what then. Or if your mother didn't run around with every man she could find, anything in pants—"

"Shut up," Betty said.

"—if she didn't stay out all hours of the night running around in cars and getting drunk!"

Maureen went to open the bathroom door, but Betty got there before her. She slammed the door to and held onto the knob. "Don't let the old bag in! You're always letting her boss you around!"

"Betty!"

"Let her go in her pants! She's all dirty anyway, the old bag, the old bitch! Or let her go out in the yard like the dogs, shove her out here, here!" Betty opened the back door wide. She was shouting. "Come on! Shove her out the back door! She ain't no better than a dog! Come on, Maureen! Let go of her!"

"Betty, are you crazy?"

"I had enough, I ain't taking any more! She ain't going to push me around, let me tell you! This door is standing wide open and she can climb right down the steps here and do her business in the back yard, she thinks she's so smart. Come on! Come on!"

While their grandmother cried out, Maureen and Betty struggled over her. Betty seized the old woman's wrist and began yanking her toward the door. Maureen pulled her back. She was amazed and yet there was something funny about it, Betty's anger and her white-rimmed eyes and her grandmother's sudden weakness. The old woman was really weak. She had no strength. Betty yanked her forward and Maureen had to let go. "Now go outside! Go on! You do what I tell you 'cause I am now your boss!" Betty screamed. When the old lady grabbed hold of the door frame, Betty raised her foot and brought her knee back, like a man, and gave her a hard solid kick right in the small of the back.

The old woman fell forward onto the top of the back steps, then over the steps and down a few yards to the ground.

They looked down at her. She lay writhing in silence.

"Come on, get up! You ain't hurt!" Betty screamed.

The old woman's silence terrified them. Maureen could not move.

"She's just pretending, she fell on purpose! You saw her fall on purpose!" Betty said. "I ain't taking nothing more from her or from nobody! Nobody is going to push me around! Let her lay there and die! Let her! You saw yourself she fell on purpose to get me put in jail! You saw it!"

13

That September, Maureen was elected secretary for her homeroom. During homeroom meetings she had to sit at the table at the front of the big room, beside the president. She had to take careful notes. In her slanted tiny handwriting she took everything down, anxious not to miss anything; she sat hunched over, writing, while the boy who was president, in a frightened, faltering voice, tried to conduct meetings, and Sister Mary Paul, their homeroom teacher, looked sternly around the room to see that nothing was going on.

Sometimes things did go on, not during meetings but outside or in the corridors—Maureen tried not to know about them. In the yard at noon hour boys said certain things to girls—it was better not to hear.

After school, on the long walk home, she and another girl, Carol—a kind of friend—were careful which way they walked. Passing by an old warehouse one afternoon Maureen had seen an old man waving to her, and she'd known enough to stay away, to hurry away. Some of the girls told wild stories. Carol's mother told wild stories. Maureen tried not to listen, her face burning, everything in her confused.

Carol's mother trapped her and Carol sometimes and made them listen. Everything about her was strange: greasy, mussed hair, already gray, a slovenly, smelly body, a very shiny, hard-looking face. She told Maureen and Carol about *certain things,* talking rapidly and angrily, without looking at them; Carol would stand in an agony of embarrassment, a heavy-set, worried, plain girl in a soiled school uniform of blue jumper and white blouse; Maureen, a little more polite, would nod *yes, yes,* to Carol's mother's warnings about how girls should never go into cellars or dark places, never sit on toilet seats in public places, or look at men on the street, or hang around anywhere, or wash their hair during that time of the month—or else they would get very sick and everyone would know why—and did they know how easy it was to get pregnant and have a baby?

Maureen was afraid of Carol's mother, yet she did not

try to back away; she remained polite and listening while Carol shifted her weight from foot to foot, ready to cry. Around school they said that Carol's mother was crazy. Carol herself never talked about it. Maureen felt a dizzy, dangerous sensation, unable to move away as the woman came closer to her, always talking, muttering warnings, warnings; it was clear that this woman knew everything about life that was ugly and this knowledge obsessed her. It weighed her down. It seemed to be bulging out of her, making her talk so fast. Knowing such things had made her sick. Once she put her hand on the back of Maureen's neck and said angrily, "That brother of yours, that smart-aleck kid? Where'd he get that car? How old is he? He thinks he's pretty good, eh? I saw him with a woman the other day right out on Michigan, walking along. A woman. Who is that woman? Does your mother know what's going on? Or can't she handle him?"

Maureen stammered, "I don't know . . . anything about it."

Every Friday, Sister Mary Paul's homeroom had a "meeting." At this time Maureen became the "secretary," and rose shyly from her desk to come to the front of the room. She was very proud of her job. The rest of the week was confusing, and on her way home anything might happen and at home anything might happen, but being a secretary, having a special job, was safe. And she had the idea that this would give her experience so that she could become a secretary after high school. Her mother had liked that idea. She would get a job and make money and live by herself.

At the start of the meeting the president would ask her to read the minutes of the previous meeting. She would read them slowly and carefully. The secretary's official notebook was a plain one with a blue cover and lined pages with wide margins. On the front was a sticker that said *Room 202*. SECRETARY'S MINUTES. Sister Mary Paul, a massive woman in her fifties, taught Maureen exactly how to take down the notes. It was an important responsibility, being homeroom secretary. Sister, sitting at her desk with her eyes closed, told Maureen what to do, very serious, nodding as she spoke. First of all, no ballpoint pen. A fountain pen only. Dark-blue ink only, not light blue ink or black ink. That was important. Every line had to be blotted carefully. The blotter should be clean. The minutes had to be written out on an ordinary piece of paper, handed in on Monday morning to Sister Mary Paul for checking, then copied with great care into the blue book. Each word had to be written slowly and carefully. No word could be crossed out: if a mistake was made it would have to be erased. And it was difficult to erase dark-blue ink.

Maureen was terrified each time she had to copy the minutes into the blue book. What if she dropped a big blot of ink . . . ?

She had so much to do that her mind was a little confused. The secretary's job was the most important thing in her life, but there were many other things she had to do. She had to get up early, while her mother slept, and get breakfast and start the coffee. Loretta was often out late because she had quit her job at the La Marvel Beauty Salon and now worked at the Checker Grill, which was on Michigan Avenue a couple of miles away. The pay was better and the tips were better. People were lively there, Loretta said. But the work tired her out and she had to sleep late, so Maureen had to take over in the mornings. She had to get Betty up, and sometimes Betty was mean in the mornings. She had to rinse the breakfast dishes; if she let cereal dry on a dish it was hard to get off and her mother would give her hell. She had to sweep the house when she came home from school and on certain days clean the floors, especially the kitchen floor, which got sticky, and she had to start supper because Loretta was always out at that time of day. On Saturdays she did the laundry and the rest of the week she did the ironing, depending on how fast things were needed. Sometimes Loretta hugged her and said, "That's my good girl, you're a great kid!" And sometimes she was in a hurry, stomping around in her high heels and looking for a blouse or something, and she might say, irritated, "You mean that blouse is still in the basket? On Wednesday, still in the *basket?*"

She wrote out the secretary's minutes at school, staying late, because at home the book might get soiled or rumpled.

One day her mother paused and came over to sit by her. It was a Saturday. She put her hand fondly on Maureen's shoulder. Maureen wondered what was wrong. Was Loretta drunk at this time of day? Her hair was done up in pink plastic curlers. She smelled of bath powder. "Well, you're getting grown up, huh?" Loretta said, confidential. "You and I have got to have a talk one of these days. Jesus, the years go fast! And that brat Betty, she's getting big for her age—

where is she always running off to? Who does she hang around with?"

"Oh, a few kids. I don't know."

But Loretta forgot about Betty. Betty with her muscular legs was in and out of the house, bumping into things, and it was always better when she was gone, so why should Loretta nag her into staying home? Loretta stared at Maureen in a tender, critical, curious way. Maureen drew back slightly. There was silence for a few seconds, then Loretta said, reddening, "You . . . you better watch out for them boys, huh? Boys ever fool around with you?"

"Ma, *no*."

"You tell the truth now."

"I said no," Maureen said miserably. She stared down at her feet.

Loretta tried to laugh. The moment grew unbearably warm. Finally she said with a pleasant harshness, "Kids your age never tell the truth. I don't believe one word you say, kid!"

Maureen could not think of anything to say. She was very ashamed.

"You want to ask me anything? I mean, about anything— you know," Loretta said.

"No."

"Well . . ."

They sat for a while in silence. Loretta was picking the polish off one of her nails. She made a tsk-ing sound, as if the fingernail polish had disappointed her.

"You get bad cramps or anything?"

"No."

"Well, you always did keep to yourself. You got a lot of secrets for a kid your age," Loretta said with a laugh, relieved, dismissing her.

But half an hour later she came out of the back bedroom and handed Maureen a sweater, one of her own. "Here. This is too small for me—how about you? You want it? Go ahead, take it. Try it on."

"Can I have it?" Maureen said, surprised.

"I said take it. Try it on." She sat in her silky green kimono, her arms folded, watching Maureen.

Maureen put the sweater on.

Loretta said, "If you'd stand up straight you'd be all right. You'll have a nice shape, but I might have to put a harness on you—you know what that is?"

Maureen stared at her.

"A harness to make you stand straight," Loretta said.

"What . . . what is it?"

"Oh, Christ, I'm just kidding! Can't you take a joke? Always a long face! Christ! Aren't you going to thank me?"

"Thank you, Ma."

"Your face isn't bad for a kid your age."

Maureen turned away.

"You tell me if any boys bother you or anything. Around school or anything. Okay?"

Maureen nodded.

"If Jules wasn't always bumming around . . ."

Jules had quit school. He worked for a trucking outfit and had his own car, a 1950 Ford, and he came home to sleep only once or twice a week. Where he ate, who his friends were, where he stayed on the nights he didn't come home, Loretta didn't know. When she asked him he would say, "I get along all right, don't worry," and the conversation would drift off idly to something else. Loretta did not think that anything was going wrong because, after all, Jules gave her twenty dollars a week, every week. He was a good kid. The only bad thing that had happened was back in August, when he'd been picked up with some other boys and booked for something or other—burglary, trespassing, "suspicious behavior"—but he was let out in three days and nothing had come of it. Maybe they had lost the records. He'd been in Children's Shelter off and on, and once he had been kept there for a day and a night before Loretta had even known about it; Jules had told them he was from Toledo, a runaway. "Christ, what a crazy kid! What an imagination!" Loretta had cried. But those charges had been dropped and so Loretta forgot about them. There was so much for her to think about.

For one thing, they had to move again.

Now that Grandma Wendall was in a nursing home and gotten rid of, Loretta was able to do what she had always wanted: move into an apartment. She was fed up, she said, with running a house. It took too much of her time. The bathroom plumbing was always backing up, the furnace was always stinking up the rooms, everything was getting dirtier and dirtier and falling apart, and it was dangerous to live here now without a man. If only Jules didn't bum around so much, but you can't do anything with a kid that age . . . She found a corner apartment over a drugstore not far from the Cadillac plant. It was a better neighborhood, Loretta said. She liked it. She liked living in an apartment. It turned out that there were more cockroaches there than in the house, but Maureen kept saying that it was nice because Loretta seemed anxious to hear that it was nice—she wanted nice things—nice things!—after all the crap she'd been through! She deserved them. What she deserved was a vacation, or a fur coat, or a bigger television set, or some wonderful surprise—she didn't know what. Then, one day, she mentioned "Pat" for the first time.

She kept mentioning "Pat"—Maureen thought in the beginning "Pat" was a woman, then realized it was a man. "Pat knows the inside story on that, the Mayor's kid," she would say. Or, "Pat said that fire was really caused on purpose, the owner is a Jew, he collected a million in insurance."

Maureen and Betty exchanged looks but Loretta never explained. It was part of her new fluttery style to talk fast, excitedly.

At school Maureen thought with dread, "Who is *Pat?*"

She ran into her brother one afternoon on the street. He was wearing a dark trench coat; he looked handsome. Broken away from home, he must have been, at last, free at last, to look so handsome on the street! She tugged at his arm, overjoyed at seeing him.

"Honey, I'm in a hurry, I'm going in here to get some cigarettes," he said. He sounded a little guilty.

Maureen looked around in disappointment. She saw a car at the curb, not Jules's old car, and in the car was a woman with very short blond hair, cut straight across her forehead and across her ears. She had a boyish, cold look. She looked at Maureen but her face showed nothing.

"Jules, there's some guy Ma is going with—his name is Pat. You know anything about it?"

"I'm in a hurry—"

"When are you coming home? What's wrong? You ever heard of this guy Pat?"

"It's just some guy. He's all right."

"You know him?"

"He's all right." He pulled away from her gently and went into the drugstore.

Maureen followed him. "Don't you like us at home any more?" she said. "Do you have your own place now?"

"I'm doing all right."

"Don't you like us any more?"

"Sure I like you."

"You're never going back to school?"

"I'm through with that crap."

"Aren't you going to visit us, Jules? Why not? I don't like the place we live in now. I can't sleep. I keep thinking we're somewhere else—I get mixed up. I keep thinking I hear Pa walking around, you know, like when he would get up to go to the bathroom at night. Why did Ma want to move?"

"You're better off where you are."

"Don't you like me any more, Jules?"

"Hey, do you need any money?"

"I don't want money!" Maureen cried.

Jules turned from her, annoyed. She was talking too loudly. He went to the counter and bought some cigarettes. Maureen stared at his back, something was happening, something terrible—she was losing Jules or had already lost him . . . was losing something or had already lost it.

When he came back she said politely, "Yes, I could use some money. Can I borrow a dollar?"

"Sure, sweetheart." Jules smiled, relieved, and took out his wallet. Maureen noted that it looked new. "Here," he said, giving her three dollars, "go see a movie or something. Buy a dress. Be good."

"A dress for three dollars?" Maureen laughed.

He gave her another bill—a five-dollar bill.

"Oh, Jules, thanks! Thank you!"

They stared at each other, suddenly embarrassed. Jules put his wallet away. Maureen put the money in her army-surplus purse, a small boxlike purse of the kind all the girls had; it had been used to store bullets, so they said.

They left the drugstore. Maureen did not dare ask about the woman in the car.

"Hey, how's Ma these days?" Jules asked, backing off.

"Real good."

"And Betty?"

"I don't know, the same."

"Grandma?"

"I guess the same."

"Take care of yourself, kid!"

Maureen did not look toward the woman in the car. She felt as if she were in some peculiar danger, yet not knowing what the danger was. In Jules's nervous, cheerful manner there was something that frightened her.

It was on her way home that afternoon that she realized she had lost the secretary's notebook. It was gone. And why was she bringing it home, what had she been thinking of? The notebook with the blue cover, the official notebook. . . . Minutes had gone back to 1953 in that book, recorded by other secretaries; Maureen had lost it. She had been carrying several books and the notebook, but now the notebook was gone. She kept looking through the books again and again. She found nothing.

In a panic she ran back to the drugstore. She looked inside. She looked out on the sidewalk. The strange thing was: why had she been bringing the notebook home? She could not think. She hurried back toward school, her heart thudding. The blue notebook was so real to her that she kept thinking she saw it, in a doorway, in an alley, in the gutter . . . she was going crazy, seeing it when it wasn't there, her eyes beginning to water. . . . But how could she have lost it? She must have left it in school.

She set her books down on the curb. She looked through them again. Her fingers were trembling. *It's got to be here,* she thought. A few people passed her. They glanced down at the girl in the nuns' school outfit, her coat undone, her hair thick and blown about her face in the air of that wide, windy, evil Michigan Avenue; a girl going through the worst experience of her life. They glanced at her and glanced away. It seemed to Maureen that her life was coming undone. The world was opening up to trap her, she was losing her mind, she was coming undone, unfastened. It was like that time her period had begun in school, a hot flow of blood, a terrible sickening surprise yet not really a surprise, and she'd gone in the girls' room and, trembling, nearly in a convulsion, she had tried to fix herself up but hadn't been able to think of what to do, only that blood was coming out of her and would not stop, and she felt in the presence of Carol's mother . . . the heavy winking ugly wisdom of the insane, knowing everything, prepared for everything, no surprise so sickening it can't be mastered with a lopsided grin. . . . It would be the end if she started to cry. So she picked up her books and ran back toward school. She crossed a vacant lot she had crossed earlier. Papers and junk everywhere but no blue notebook. She looked along the path, kicking things aside: nothing. She looked in an alley. She turned in a strange suspended terror and looked around at the buildings all around her, used-up, without features, the empty buildings of grownups that told her nothing: *Michael-son Brothers Towel Service, Lenox Photographs, Detroit Furniture and Refrigerator Resale.* The wind blew tiny bits of dirt against her. Her eyes watered. She thought again of Jules, who had driven away, and of Carol's mother, and of Room 202 and Sister Mary Paul. Sister's face knew everything. Maureen's life was in her keeping. Maureen was guilty and never, never would she be forgiven, there was no way out, no escape, no help—oh, she would give up everything, give up her mother, her brother, her own life just to be innocent again, to have things back the way they were at two-thirty that afternoon!

Out of breath, crying, she reached the school. Sister Mary Paul was still in her room. She was disgusted. "Go look for it," she told Maureen. Maureen ran out to look for it. She hurried around the concrete yard, though she knew the note-book could not be there; but perhaps Sister was watching from a window. She looked around by the fence, all along the fence: nothing. She looked in a pile of trash. The yard was empty. The walls were dirty with scrawled words, half mysterious and forbidden. Maureen usually did not look at those words but today she stood staring at them dully. No one else was in the yard. Everything was over, finished—the future was finished. The wind, high above the old church steeple, was making a curious hollow noise. Maureen could not think what to do. She hardly knew what to think, what to occupy her mind with.

Finally she retraced her steps to the corner where she'd met Jules. Maybe he had seen it? Maybe he had it? She looked everywhere, everywhere. She walked back and forth on the sidewalk. Could the notebook already be at home? Somehow at home? Or had someone at school stolen it? Could she buy a notebook like the one that was lost? But she couldn't make up the old minutes, the many pages of minutes from other years—it was hopeless, a trap—discussions about paper cups, about who had taken someone's mittens, all those minutes of old talk conducted in Room 202, all of it lost, all of it her fault.

She felt that her mind was coming undone. She ran back to school.

Sister Mary Paul was at Mass, they said. It was already four-thirty. Maureen waited for her. "I couldn't find it!" she said, beginning to cry again.

"Keep looking for it," the nun said coldly.

Maureen tried to seize the woman's hands. "Please forgive me! Forgive me! I didn't mean to lose it—"

"Go look for it. Keep looking."

She kept looking around on the street until it was dark. At home she wept. The next morning she got up at six to go out and look again—a blue notebook, lost, a blue notebook, she had to find it. She thought of nothing else. Every morning of that week she had to report to Sister Mary Paul that she was still looking. Still looking. Sister Mary Paul said, "Keep looking. Those are important records." The week passed slowly, in a dream. Maureen's head ached constantly, she could not sleep; she lay on her bed and wept, until Betty told her to shut up.

One day another nun stopped her in the corridor and said, "Sister Mary Paul would never say anything herself, Maureen, but she's very pleased with the way you're looking for the book. Keep looking."

Maureen could have wept with gratitude. She wanted to kiss this nun's hands. She kept looking, but she never found the notebook.

14

Maureen was brushing her hair. She leaned toward the mirror with a critical look that was something like her mother's. She had been ready for school for some time and had nothing else to do: she had eaten breakfast an hour before and now the rest of them were eating, making noises at the table. She tried not to listen to them but their noises could not be shut out. At night she had to listen to them, she had to listen to *his* snoring. Once she had had to listen to her father's snoring. She'd had to listen to her grandmother's snoring—raspy, choking, vicious gasps for air, hardly human. At night she slept and woke, slept and woke, dreaming while she slept that she was awake and terrified of never being able to sleep, hearing the noises of her family eternally, never being free. There were dark shadows under her eyes, reproachful marks. She contemplated herself in the mirror critically, hearing through her tentative reflection *his* voice rising out in the kitchen.

"Guess I'll go down to the garage today," he was saying. "See what's up. There's . . ."

Maureen did not call him "Furlong," which was his last

name, and she did not call him "Pat." There was nothing at all to call him. Loretta said she should call him "Dad" but Maureen had said nothing, having nothing to say.

Betty called him *that guy* behind his back.

When Maureen went out he was still sitting at the kitchen table, which was pushed into a corner. His shirt was off. His chest, broad and yet a little sunken, covered with thick curly gray hair, rose and fell as he breathed; he was drinking coffee noisily. He held the cup in both hands. Loretta stood behind him idly massaging his back.

"Don't you go lifting anything, somebody wants a hand," Loretta said. "You got to get over this trouble. A slipped disk would be terrible."

"A what?" said Furlong.

"A slipped disk, something in the spine. Men get it from lifting heavy things." She glanced at Maureen. Her face was pursed into a pretty, worried look.

"Yeah, well, the goddam cold weather don't do it any good," Furlong said.

His back was "acting up." When it had been better—a few months before, Maureen gathered—he had driven a truck. He belonged to the Teamsters Union. But now he just messed around at a garage where some friends of his worked, though that kind of work wasn't good enough for him. He had a lot of time on his hands. He seemed to examine his hands often, seeing them empty, puzzled and a little angry, a big man getting fat. As soon as his back got well, he was always saying, he'd be on the road again and making good money.

Betty, who said she hated him, was crowding around him this morning. She was asking him about trucks. About fights. What did he think of Rocky Marciano? (Rocky Marciano was one of Betty's heroes; she had a picture of him taped up in her room.) Did he ever fight himself? Did he ever handle a gun? Weren't there shootings sometimes? Wasn't a truck driver killed just the other day? He knew all about it, didn't he, the inside story? A truck driver who hadn't belonged to a union had been killed driving to East Lansing; a large piece of scrap metal had been knocked off an overpass and through his windshield. The *News* had a big picture story about it. Didn't Furlong know all about it, know who had done the job?

He rubbed his hand hard over Betty's head, as if she were a boy, a kid who bothered him and yet pleased him.

Betty tried not to wince with pain. "Sorry, kid," Furlong said, "that's secret stuff."

He turned to Maureen, smiling. "Well," he said awkwardly and yet with the same bossy smile he used on Betty, "well, where are you going? Out to Hollywood to get in the movies?"

"This is what we wear at school, this thing," Maureen said. She tried not to look at him; his foolish teasing made her miserable.

"That old jumper's been around for years. Reeny's worn it to school for years," Loretta said, her voice high-pitched and surprised. She let her arms slide across Furlong's chest and she looked at Maureen over his head with a certain tenderness. "The nuns make them wear it. You know."

"I wasn't kidding or anything, I think it looks nice. You had breakfast yet, Maureen?"

He was trying to be friends.

"Yes. I'm going."

He had a thick, muscular body, and because he was so often without his shirt—either in his undershirt or with his chest bare—Maureen mixed up the graying, matted hair on his chest with his face. She had a confused idea of him as hairy, with curly hair like shavings, very stiff, gray, unreal. But his face was always shaven. It was clean and frank. His head, like his body, looked hard and muscular; his curly hair was clipped short up the back of his head, very neat; his nose was small but clearly defined, because the nostrils were so large and dark. Tiny hairs emerged from them, just visible. Maureen supposed he was a man women would call handsome. But when she had to pass near him she could smell the smell that was always with him—not just dirt and grime and grease but the personal, private smell of his body. She did not remember her father smelling like that—he had had an odor of tobacco mostly. She did not think this man was handsome. She hated him. In her daydreams she imagined him dying as her father had died, crushed by metal. Hot metal. Deaths of men had to be brutal, the death of tons of metal cracking through ribs, through skulls, because the men themselves were so brutal. Even their breathing was brutal. Their snoring was brutal. Hard, rhythmic, deliberate, their breathing at night or during the day, their eating and their talking, the way they sat at the table, were brutal. Furlong was always teasing her, half teasing her. Trying to be friends, with those blunt thick fingers and those

dirty nails. Sometimes, at Mass, Maureen found herself thinking about him. She thought of a flashing movement she could
not quite explain to herself, the falling of metal, something sharp. An artery severed. One arm crushed and mangled. An accident, an accident—once happened it can never
be undone! And with his chest bare, this man could with-
stand nothing, he was open, vulnerable, waiting—he would
cry out in pain, calling for help, but no one could help
him. A man on his way to death cannot be helped.

And she would come to herself, shaken and ashamed,
and remember that she was in church and that she was
happy for her mother: why shouldn't Loretta get married
again and be happy?

"Hey, Reeny," Loretta said as Maureen went to the door,
"be sure you come right home today."

"I will."

"Don't you go fooling around or anything, I need you
back home."

"Betty's the one that fools around," Maureen said with
dignity.

"Go to hell," said Betty.

"Just you come right home, Maureen," said Loretta.
"There's all that ironing laying in the basket—"

"I said I'd come right home."

Maureen wanted to get out, but Loretta seemed to be
hanging onto her. Loretta said in a high-pitched, critical,
and yet not unpleasant voice, "There's a lot going on, so I
hear. I hear lots of things. I don't want you hanging around
the five-and-ten or with that Carol what's-her-name, her
mother is absolutely nuts. They found her in her slip running around outside in a storm, what d'ya think of that?
She said somebody was in the house, somebody was trying
to get her. I don't want you walking home the long way
either, there's too many smart-alecks on the lookout for
kids like you."

Her name was now Mrs. Furlong. She was no longer Mrs.
Wendall. Maureen and Betty and Jules, though, were still
Wendalls; Maureen was glad of that. She thought it over
and over, the meaning of her name. She thought about her
mother's new name, Mrs. Furlong, and she kept waiting for
things to change, to straighten out and get quieter, but
nothing happened. Nothing changed. Mrs. Furlong stayed
with her job at the Checker Grill and Furlong went out most
of the day, hanging around somewhere, making connections,

catching up on news, telephoning people, doing who knows what, keeping himself busy, secretive. Then he came back home.

"Carol's mother isn't so bad," Maureen said sullenly. "It's somebody to live with."

"Yes, well, I didn't mean anything bad," Loretta said, fluttery and feminine. "In fact the nut-house would only make her worse. But you better stay away from them or people will think you're nuts too."

"People think she's nuts now," Betty said loudly.

"They do not," said Loretta.

"They think she's stuck-up, she's always got her nose in the air. She's a real big deal." Betty, trying to get Furlong to look at her, spoke brazenly. To show that she knew something none of them knew she ducked her head as if the impact of her knowledge was too much for her, a joke that was also terrible.

"You, what do you know," Maureen said contemptuously. She opened the door.

Loretta said, "Remember what I said about coming home early, kid? Okay?"

"Yes, Ma. Yes."

"I don't like to see girls hanging around places like the five-and-ten," Loretta said seriously, more to Furlong than to Maureen. "They're just in there to pick up stuff and it shows all over. They can't hide it. If I ever caught Maureen stealing junk, like that . . ."

Maureen sighed in exasperation. Maureen, always Maureen! Why didn't her mother let her go?

"But she probably meets boys instead," Loretta said.

She was maybe trying to tease, affectionately; maybe not. There was something bright and nervous about her this morning. The mention of Carol's mother had done it, Maureen guessed. She knew that Loretta's father had died in the state hospital, that he'd been crazy at the end, very bad, and that Loretta kept bringing it up somehow—when Maureen's father had been alive he was sure to bring it up himself. "They're all nuts in your family," he had said.

"I don't meet boys," Maureen said.

She left. She didn't know whether to be hurt or angry or to forget about it. Her mother was always picking on her, and yet it wasn't in the way she picked at Betty, it was something different. It made her nervous, not exactly resentful. She couldn't understand it. These days Loretta was not herself. She and Furlong had been married on the first of October and had gone away for four days, to Chicago they said, and now it was October 25 and there was still a dizzying excitement to the air, something strange. What did marriage mean? What was going on? Was the marriage legal and permanent, or was he going to walk out one of these days?

Everything was busy, noisy. Maureen thought that life should be quiet and sensible, but there was always too much happening at their place. The apartment was too small. Wash and ironing and dishes lay about until Maureen put them away. Clothes lay about. Towels, sheets, boxes of cereal carelessly closed, knives with food stuck to them, Furlong's shoes, Betty's junk—everything lay around, waiting to be taken care of by Maureen. Sometimes Furlong had friends of his over, men who played cards and drank in the kitchen until early in the morning. Betty stayed out until late. Jules was always gone, never came to visit. Maureen would sit in her room, trying to do schoolwork. She shut her ears against the noise from the kitchen or from the television set or from Loretta and Furlong arguing or fooling around or laughing together, two big kids, two fools. It was harder and harder for her to do her homework. Since moving to this apartment she hadn't been able to sleep right—she slept part of the night, but not well. She kept waking. Her heart seemed to flutter, as if it had heard something she hadn't. It took her an hour to do a page of math homework, sometimes more than an hour, sitting with her hands pressed over her ears, staring at the book, trying to make sense of what she was reading.

She was in the ninth grade now. Assignments seemed harder to her. Her mind seemed to work backward, strain backward, resisting what it should do. A crease or speck of dirt on the page distracted her, caught her eye again and again until in exasperation she would have to cover it up with her hand. She wanted to please her teacher—there seemed nothing more important to her now. But her mind seemed to resist. It wanted to break loose. Furlong's friends stayed for hours, and at about two in the morning, when Loretta came home from work, no one bothered even to go and unlock the door for her, she had to unlock it herself. Maureen, lying sleepless and exhausted in her room, could hear all this but could not figure out exactly what it meant. Why was there always so much going on?

Maureen hurried outside. It was always good to leave the apartment. She walked to school alone now, walking fast. She could not think whether to be hurt or angry over Loretta's teasing. "I suppose you got a secret boy friend," Loretta was always saying. Loretta had grown slightly thinner since her marriage. You could see the outline of her shoulder-blades when she leaned forward in her green kimono. Her face had a pale, bluish look when there was no makeup on it, and sometimes she dropped things. The evening before she had dropped the scissors and Maureen had had to pick them up for her. "It makes me dizzy, bending over," she had said.

Maureen felt a peculiar tenderness toward her, partly resentful, partly protective. But she was measuring everything against the time when she would leave home, like Jules.

She drifted down to the library whenever she was free. Growing up and moving away from home was somehow linked in her mind with the library—the library at night, its silence and openness. Anything might happen. Nothing happened but anything might. She sat at the long, shiny, empty tables, reading, leafing nervously through books, glancing up when someone came into the big reading-room, waiting. She liked to go to the library in the evenings, when her mother was out working. Furlong didn't care where she went. If Loretta were home she'd never let Maureen out, so Maureen began to think that it was good her mother worked, it was good to be left alone.

She leafed through magazines, curious and alert for what the rest of the world was doing. In a glossy magazine she came upon an advertisement for a paperweight, a small cat made of glass; it sold for $500 and was "to hold down your important papers." She sat staring at this advertisement for some time. She looked at what women were wearing, long-legged and sullen, their faces more beautiful than hers and remote, as if they were women from another planet, speaking another language. She stared at these pictures, aware of having failed though she was still young; her failure was tied up somehow with her being unable to sleep. She would not grow up into a normal woman: something would catch her and hold her back, some snag, some failure to have dreamed her way out of childhood.

Most of all she liked novels. She liked novels set in England. As soon as she read the first page of a novel by Jane

Austen she was pleased, startled, excited to know that this was real: the world of this novel was real. Her own life, up over Elson's Drugs or back on Labrosse, could not be real. The birdlike chatter of her mother, Betty's grunts and bad temper, the glimpse Maureen had to content herself with of Jules out on the street were not so real as novels, not so convincing. There was nothing permanent about them, as there was about people in novels. And when her mother made those ugly accusations about Maureen meeting boys when she should be in school, how could that be real? How could such words be real?

The rest of the day, the following night, were hardly enough for her thoughts. She was bewildered amidst the confusion of all that had rushed on her within the last few hours. Every moment had brought a fresh surprise; and every surprise must be a matter of humiliation to her. How to understand it all! How to understand the deceptions she had been thus practising on herself, and living under!

These words were real, and very real the person behind them. Maureen, dreaming over them, could feel herself begin to dissolve into nothing, nobody, an eye in a head, a blankness. The suffering of such a character in such a novel was much greater than her own. How could she or her people be raised to this level of suffering? Grandma Wendall's grunts and groans made her hated. Nobody felt sorry for her, not really. Nobody would ever cry over her as they would over the unhappiness of a woman in a novel.

On Sundays, when they went to visit Grandma Wendall, Maureen took a book along for something to do. Often Aunt Connie came with them. Furlong drove them and let them off at the nursing home, then went down the street to have a few beers while they climbed the steps and ascended through layer after layer of stale, disinfectant-stinking air, peering without curiosity through opened doors that showed bed after bed, aged woman after woman, all of them sisters in their soiled white nightgowns of flannel and their anxious, jealous eyes. Sometimes an old woman would creep out into the corridor to stare after them, fascinated by Loretta's patent-leather high heels and Maureen's long shining hair, or angry about some fantastic wrong. "Come here and look, it's filthy! Not fit for people! They come and do their business in the corner of my room, look at the roaches, little girl, come look!" Maureen always kept going.

"Them poor old things," Loretta said, shaking her head. "It's really awful when you get old."

It was a world of women: sick trays, skeletal hands, wet paper napkins. Maureen stared at the smooth, innocent curve of a skull beneath thin white hair. She felt very young, remote. But she also felt threatened. The crucifixes on the walls were the same as the one her mother had on the living-room wall at home. Everything was the same in this world outside of novels.

Connie, in her broad-shouldered cloth coat and her Sunday hat, was always calm. Or perhaps she saw nothing. She led the way up to the fifth floor and to the old woman's room, no nonsense about her, no lingering over elderly women in the corridors who wanted to register a complaint with the bishop. Maureen was both nervous and bored by these visits. She felt very young, even threatened. She hated to be stared at. In the room they always sat in the same place— Connie and Loretta on either side of the bed, Maureen on the window sill, half sitting and half standing. She was glad to be out of the way. Grandma Wendall looked very old. She did not look like the same woman. Her body, big beneath the bedclothes, had a stationary, welded look, as if nothing could move it. Maureen tried to feel sorry for her but could not locate any sorrow. The odor of flesh and spilled food was too much; it ruled out sorrow.

"They told you, eh, about my stroke? Whole right side paralyzed, *paralyzed?*" the old woman said to Maureen.

She was alert and spiteful, not wanting Maureen to open that book and escape.

"How is Jules? Jules is my favorite!" the old woman said.

Connie and Loretta, who now saw each other only during these visits, faced the old woman with a certain strange enthusiasm. Climbing up the steps made them breathless, and this breathlessness turned into a kind of anticipation. They began to talk. They talked to Grandma Wendall and to each other with ironic, womanly smiles, moving gradually into the areas of their real interests, gaining enthusiasm, momentum, as the minutes passed. They talked about work. Loretta was still a waitress and Connie worked in a laundry. They talked about religion, about the priests at their churches. They talked about the price of food, about the baby Loretta was going to have (yes, a new baby—due in four months!), Loretta's apartment and Connie's apartment, the troubles on the street, the troubles in the city, Betty and her gang, Maureen herself ("She's got secrets of her own, like a sneaky cat," Loretta said in Maureen's hearing), and finally, as if this were the target they'd been circling, men. Furlong and his job. Furlong and his back. Furlong. Men. Connie's boy friend Stan. His job. His ex-wife. His crazy ex-wife.

Off to themselves, safe and lively, women always talked about men: their eyes and their voices seized hungrily upon men.

After about an hour and a half of this, either Loretta or Connie would get to her feet and clap her hands lightly together in a confused gesture of satisfaction at having seen Grandma Wendall and having found her "better." But it was time to go! Time to go, sorry. They had jobs the next day . . .

"I woke up and my whole right side was paralyzed. Like stone," Grandma Wendall said bitterly. "How would you like that for yourself, you two? Always strutting around!"

"Ma, what do you mean by that?" Loretta cried, hurt.

"You say hello to Jules for me. Don't forget. Jules is my only favorite."

"Jules says he'll be over to see you real soon, maybe next Sunday."

"Doesn't matter if he comes or not. I know him. He's my only favorite."

Though they were anxious now to leave they always hung back. Loretta might think of something more to say. Connie might think of something. Only Maureen, carefully marking her place in her book, would be ready to go, frightened and bitter at the old woman's power even now. Some people, even in their dying, had power; others never had power.

"You say hello to Jules and to Betty and to what's-his-name—"

"Ma, you know his name is Pat! Patrick Furlong!"

"And to him too, what's-his-name . . ."

They found Furlong down the street in a bar. He had gotten to know the bartender there. The three of them sat with him in a booth. After a few minutes Loretta and Connie would be weeping lightly, and Maureen would sit in idle misery, wishing it was light enough for her to read. Loretta would say, drowsily affectionate, her hand on Furlong's arm, "Boy, she used to be something, that old gal! Wasn't she? A real tough old gal! Wasn't she something, Connie?"

"Yeah, she was pretty tough."

"It's hell to get old . . ."

After they dropped Connie off at her place Loretta would always say, shaking her head, "That poor dope! It'd make me sick, washing the crap out of other people's clothes. She can have it."

"Wasn't she ever married?" Furlong asked.

"Yeah, but he run off. Left her."

"Why'd he leave her?" Maureen asked.

Loretta said nothing for a while. Then she said, her face pinched, "What do you care? It's none of your business, you're too young!"

"I feel sorry for Aunt Connie."

"Oh, hell, you don't feel sorry for anybody!"

Maureen stared at her, hurt. She could not understand. She wondered if maybe her mother was talking to the real Maureen, a girl who was hypocritical and selfish and sly. Was that the real Maureen? Sometimes when she was alone, walking along the street, she was taken by surprise seeing her reflection in a store window, a remote, ghostly reflection she never quite expected or recognized; it did not really seem herself.

Later on Loretta teased her about cutting school, and Maureen said with a tired laugh, "Go ask the nuns, then, if you're so sure!" And Loretta teased her about using some of her new lipstick, and Maureen said vehemently, "Ma, I assure you I did not! I'd never touch that stupid grape lipstick of yours!" She felt set upon by her mother and unable to locate any center to her mother's assaults, any reference point. Furlong often looked on with a faint smile, making no sense of it either—not knowing that Loretta was wrong or knowing it and taking no part?

But one day Loretta tossed a small gold tube onto Maureen's bed. She said, "Here. Here's your own, no need to sneak mine."

It was a tube of lipstick.

"Oh, Ma!" Maureen said. She picked it up cautiously. She opened it: pink.

"Go take it, try it on," Loretta said. Puffed and slowed down, wearing a maternity blouse, she stood in the doorway with her arms crossed, tapping her fingers impatiently on one arm.

Maureen went to the mirror. She dabbed on some lipstick, still cautious, and in the mirror she caught sight of her mother watching her. Her mother's face was thoughtful behind the usual razzing smile, a kind of good-natured, lopsided smile she had picked up while being a waitress.

"Okay. That looks nice," Loretta said.

"I look funny," Maureen said.

"No. You look nice."

"But I can't wear it to school. They don't allow——"

"Aren't you going to say anything?"

"Thank you."

"Now you can leave my stuff alone, eh?"

"Oh, Ma!"

She turned to catch her mother's eye. Her mother was staring toward her, not exactly at her; the thoughtful, unsmiling look on her face seemed not like her and alarmed Maureen.

Maybe it was because Furlong had begun to stay at the garage later, sometimes missing supper. Loretta no longer worked and she hadn't much to do except sit around. It was winter now. She would sit silently at the table, staring at the oilcloth covering. Maureen would come home from school and find her there. The television set would not be on. Maureen would turn it on for her mother. Then she would begin to make supper, fooling around in the kitchen, taking her time. She liked to make supper. It was easy to please people, to please men, just by giving them food. In the old days she had made her father's supper too. It was the same supper. The same food. She would chat with her mother, opening and closing cupboard doors, looking in the refrigerator. She would always ask her mother how she felt. Loretta would always say, "I'm all right." Then, sourly, she might add, "I'm too old to go through this again." But Maureen pretended not to understand. There were secrets of female life open to her, ready for her to learn, but she rejected them. She did not even look at her mother's stomach if she could help it; magically, her eyes glanced away.

After supper she cleared the kitchen and did the dishes by herself, since Betty was never around to help and wouldn't help if she were around. Then she worked on her homework until Furlong came home. He came home later and later as the winter went on. No one said anything. From the kitchen Maureen could see her mother padding around the other room going to change the television channel, or going into the bedroom, opening a drawer, closing a drawer, making at times a sound that could have been sobbing. The two of them, alone so much, drifted to opposite ends of the little apartment. Maureen thought of them as two women with nothing to say. She herself was a woman, but in disguise as a child; if they saw that she had grown up, they might want to talk to her. Maureen pretended to hear nothing, not even her mother's sobbing. Was that sobbing? Loretta was too strong to cry, no man could make her cry. It was unthinkable. But still Maureen pretended to hear nothing, pressing her hands over her ears, trying to make sense of her schoolwork. Why should her mother cry? Did the baby hurt inside of her? What would it feel like to have a baby? Maureen daydreamed about being pregnant herself. She would have a baby someday. She would get married and have a baby, dress herself in the puffy big blouses her mother wore, the same kind, a woman like her mother; she could not escape. She did not want to get married but there was no other way. She did not want to live with a man, sleep with a man. It made her angry to think of a future in which she waited in an apartment for a man to come back from whatever it was men did, all those hours spent with other men somewhere, talking about something, swearing and laughing angrily, letting their half-closed fists fall onto table tops, peeling the labels off bottles of beer, looking at clocks, shifting their shoulders restlessly inside their clothes. When they were together, men talked of things that could not be told to women.

One night Furlong didn't come home until late. Maureen waited around—it was eleven o'clock, twelve o'clock. She had to sit up and wait for him, to get him supper. Her head ached. She sat in the kitchen with a book in front of her, waiting. Loretta and Betty had both gone to bed. Maureen made marks on the oilcloth with her fingernail, writing out her name and trying to erase it. She thought of Loretta lying in bed, waiting. The clock said twelve-thirty, then one o'clock, and still he wasn't home and still she waited. She had to get up for school the next day. "That dirty bastard," she said to herself, writing "Furlong" in the oilcloth cover.

One night Furlong didn't come home until after two. He was drunk. He stumbled against a chair, sending it clattering, waking Maureen from her fitful sleep. She could hear him in the kitchen—he was moving something around. She called Loretta and woke her. "He's home," she said. "I'm going to bed."

"What time is it?" Loretta called.

"I'm going to bed."

She went into her room in a hurry. She lay down on her bed, wanting to sleep at once, feeling how urgent it was that she sleep. She had to wake up the next day at seven-thirty . . . but her mind was racing in a panic.

She thought of Furlong hitting her mother: she thought of that startled furious cry, her mother's cry.

She thought of Jules in jail again. What if he got arrested again?

She thought of her father. He was mixed up with her father, the two of them mixed together, stumbling home late at night. It was no surprise. Two tons of steel had fallen down on him, her father. And if Furlong died? Any money? What about the baby Loretta was going to have? Aid to Dependent Children? A check a month? Welfare? What then? Jules had quit school and worked. He brought Loretta twenty dollars a week, a secret from Furlong. Twenty dollars! Maureen should work and then she could make money; she needed to *get out*.

In the other room they were arguing.

She needed to get out, the way Jules had . . . she needed money . . . she had to get out . . . She was mopping the kitchen floor. She had to make sure she didn't step in the wet, because that made the linoleum dirty again. Black and white squares. The mop splashed soap onto the floor. She had to move the table and chairs out of the way, then mop the floor . . .

"Maureen! Maureen!"

It was confused with mopping the floor: she felt the handle of the mop strong in her hands. She ached to clean the floor. She liked the smell of soap, she liked cleanliness that was harsh and bright . . .

"Maureen," Loretta said angrily, "come out here! You're only pretending to be asleep!"

She rolled over. In the other bed, about a foot from her own, Betty lay asleep. She heard nothing. Maureen heard everything and had to get up. She saw that her mother was very angry, very upset.

"I know you're pretending, you're fooling around!" Loretta said. She was about to cry. "Come out here! He's in the kitchen sick and I'm not doing one more thing for him, the hell with him! I'm fed up!"

Maureen stumbled into the living-room. She rubbed her eyes.

She must have fallen back to sleep. "What do you want? You want to sleep in my bed?"

"Sleep out here on the couch. Come on."

"What?"

"Stop pretending or I'll slap your mouth!"

"What's wrong?"

"He's out there puking and the hell with him. I've had enough," Loretta said. Her eyes were streaked with tiny red veins. "I'm going to sleep. I'm sick."

"What's going on? You been crying?"

"Shut up."

"I got school tomorrow—"

"Oh, you and your school, you and your library! Go tell *him* your troubles, you and him have all the troubles in the house, to hear you talk! Go make him some coffee."

"What?"

"Make him some coffee."

"You woke me up to make coffee?"

"I said make the bastard coffee."

She slammed the door behind her. Maureen looked through to the kitchen. The clock said two-thirty. She could see Furlong's legs. He must have been sitting at the table, listening.

In the dim light the room looked clean and unfamiliar, like the surface of another planet, or the cold, smooth surface of the moon. The soiled walls did not look soiled. The oilcloth gleamed white. On the stove the coffee pot looked as if it might be made of silver.

She went to the stove.

Furlong said, "What happened to your mother? What was all that?"

"She went to bed."

"Where?"

"In my bed."

"Why'd she do that?"

Maureen did not look at him. She got a jar of coffee down off a shelf.

"She says you're sick."

"Why'd she wake you up? Are you making coffee?"

"She told me to make it."

"Is that why she woke you up?"

"She wanted to sleep in my bed."

She saw him out of the corner of her eye, sitting heavily, too tired to move. Like a dog, he shook himself unconsciously and without meaning. He said, "You mean she kicked you out of your room? Good Christ!" But he remained sitting at the table, waiting for his coffee like a man sitting at a diner counter. Maureen got a cup for him. It was easy to please men, to stay out of their way. He was a little drunk, but there was always a slightly drunken, clumsy, agreeable quality about him. It was hard to understand that he was dangerous: he could knock things around, break things.

Maureen served him coffee.

After a while he said, "Your mother says you been running with some bad kids. That true?"

"You mean Betty."

"No. You."

"Not me."

"Some store manager caught you shoplifting?"

"*No.*" She turned to look at him, fully. He had fine lines on his forehead and at the corners of his eyes from laughing too much. There was silence in him, but it was not like the silence her father had had; it came in chunks, thoughtfully.

"Your ma didn't make all that up," he said coaxingly.

"I don't know what she did."

"I just want to know if it's true or not."

"I told you it wasn't!"

"Look, I'm your stepfather now—"

"You are not."

"What?"

Maureen stared at the floor.

"You calling your own mother a liar?"

"I'm not calling anybody anything."

"What about me, you calling me a liar?"

Maureen poured the rest of the coffee into the sink.

"What are you doing?"

"Cleaning up."

"I wasn't finished with that."

"You didn't want any more."

"Yes, I did. I did want more. You did that on purpose."

"I did not."

"You did too."

They were silent. Maureen stood with her back to him, at the sink. She waited. Her face was very hot. Then, abruptly, he leaned forward and knocked the coffee pot out of her hand. It clattered on the floor. Maureen shrieked.

"You poured that out on purpose!" Furlong said.

She picked up the coffee pot, not looking at him.

He said, "She told me she'd make some coffee and there better be some or I'll smash the place up—you won't recognize this dump when I'm through! Put that back on the stove!"

Maureen put it back on the stove.

"Put some water in it!"

Maureen was afraid of him, but she was more afraid of her mother: her mother's silence. Loretta was listening to all this, listening in silence, and would not get up to help her.

"I said put some water in it. What are you standing there like that for—are you crazy?"

"You're the one," Maureen muttered.

"What? What did you say?"

Maureen did not answer.

"Do you want your teeth knocked out?" Furlong said.

"Nobody's going to knock my teeth out."

"Just now your mother said, five minutes ago she said I'd better teach you something before it's too late—I don't want the police sticking their noses in around here."

"What about the police?"

"Don't play dumb!"

"I'm not in any trouble."

"Look—"

"I'm not! I'm not in any trouble!"

"Well, you better not," Furlong said. He was breathing hard. "Like that goddam smart-aleck brother of yours, you can get out and on the street. I won't stand for it. I don't want my name smeared up in anything. I'm not getting mixed up or taken down to no police station, believe me."

"I'm not in any trouble," Maureen said feverishly.

"Stealing lipstick from a five-and-ten?"

"I didn't steal any lipstick!"

"You calling your mother a liar?"

"Ma is maybe sick . . ." She was silent. She could hear Loretta listening to them. She could picture her mother's face there in the darkness, in Maureen's own bed, listening to all this.

"Did Ma really tell you that—you should teach me a lesson? Before the police come around?"

"Yes."

He was drinking his coffee. He was still a little drunk

and his shoulders were hunched toward the table. "Your mother tells me lots of things about you."

"Why?"

"I don't know why."

"But why does she hate me? I don't hate her—why does she hate me? I can't stand it! I don't know what to do. She always liked Jules better than me. It didn't matter how good I was. Then Jules left and she still likes him better, everybody does. Now she acts so strange but I didn't do anything, it's Betty who hangs around places and steals things. Ask Betty yourself. Look in her side of the room, look under her bed! She takes all kinds of junk—she steals stuff she doesn't even want; she says it sticks to her fingers—just for fun. I don't hate Ma—why does she hate me? Why does she say things about me, make up things?"

"Go to bed. Forget about it."

He pushed his chair away from the table, but not to face her. He was facing the wall instead, looking at the wall, his neck and shoulders tense.

"I'm going to run away if she doesn't quit. If she hates me I'm going to run away. I'll live somewhere else like Jules—"

"You're not going anywhere, so shut up."

"I'll get a job and run away."

"You're not leaving this place! You're not getting into trouble! Shut up and forget about it!" Furlong said loudly.

"Then ask her why she hates me—"

He turned suddenly, with an effort, and slapped her. He hit her on the side of the face, a surprise to them both. What she felt about his hand was its sudden cracking pressure; the blow had not hurt.

"Now shut up!" he shouted, furious. "Get out of here and go to bed!"

"You dirty bastard," Maureen said.

He jumped to his feet and slapped her again. The chair was knocked aside. Maureen started for the door but he jerked her back. He shook her so that her head bobbed and she thought her neck would snap. "Get us in trouble and see what I'll do to you—see what happens!" he yelled, then let her go.

Maureen ran into the living-room, too surprised to cry. She could hear her mother listening, she could see those pinpoints of eyes there in the dark. Why didn't Loretta get up? Why didn't she come out here? Why that silence from that room? Maureen opened the door to the stair-

way and stepped outside. Now that she was safe she began
to cry. She sat down with her back to the door. She pressed
her fists against her eyes and drew her knees up to her
chest, feeling herself safe on the drafty stairway, alone.

After a while she stopped crying. Hours passed. She made
her way back into the apartment. The kitchen light was still
on. She lay down on the sofa and fell asleep. When she
woke up she had a headache. Her mother was leaning over
her. She said, "I told you lots of times he's got a bad temper.
I told you not to provoke him."

Maureen lay exhausted on the sofa. She stared blankly at
her mother.

"You better get up," Loretta said.

"What?"

"It's morning. Time to get up."

"Morning?"

"Stop looking so stupid. You asked for trouble, don't drag
me into it."

"I didn't ask for any trouble—"

"Reeny, you have that snippy-snotty look—you should see
yourself in a mirror! When you look like that there's always
somebody going to slap you."

"I didn't provoke him. I didn't say anything."

"Well, he'll be sorry tonight. He'll apologize when he comes
in."

"I don't give a damn about him."

"You'd better give a damn." Loretta looked at her critically, yet with a kind of affection. It was a wavering, hesitant look that made Maureen shiver; she could not understand it. "Maureen, you should even out those bangs of
yours. They're too heavy on one side. You look like a goddam dope that way."

"What?" Maureen said, surprised.

"Your hair. Go get me the scissors and I'll do it myself."

"What's wrong with my hair?"

"It needs straightening out."

"I'll do it after school," Maureen said. She was very confused.

"Get me the scissors. Come on." She went out into the
kitchen and Maureen followed, in a daze. Loretta reached out
and made snapping motions with her fingers. Maureen got
her the scissors from a drawer. She sat. Loretta leaned over
her, leaning against her with her swelling stomach, and began to cut her hair. Maureen sat in a daze, obedient.

"I'm sorry about last night," Loretta said, "but you know what he's like. Men are like that. They don't put up with crap. Now, keep these bangs trimmed, don't let them get too heavy. Too much hair up here gives you pimples. It's from the oil in the hair. You should know that at your age." Loretta leaned around to look at Maureen's face. "There are some blackheads on your nose, kid. Take care of yourself. You got a nice face so take care of it, right?"

Maureen wanted to hide her face in her mother's dirty old kimono and ask *Why? Why?* Why was everything so loud and confused? Why was everything ready to fly into pieces?

She knew she would have to leave home.

Late that afternoon, when she got home from school, Loretta was wearing a dress and her face was fixed up. The intense red of her lips was matched by two oval spots of rouge on her cheeks. Furlong was home. Loretta said to her, "Reeny, your stepfather has something to say to you."

Reluctantly Maureen went into the kitchen.

Furlong was sitting with an untidy pile of newspapers around him; every day he bought two newspapers. When she approached he glanced up as if he hadn't known she had come home until now. He said, embarrassed, "Guess I had too much to drink last night."

Maureen stared boldly at him.

"There's too much going on all over," he said, gesturing toward the papers with their headlines and photographs. The face of Eisenhower looked up at Maureen. "Well, I'm sorry," Furlong said.

Maureen said nothing.

Loretta came into the kitchen and clapped her hands together lightly. "All friends again?" she said.

"Sure," said Furlong.

"What about you, stuck-up?" Loretta slid her arm around Maureen's shoulders. "You're not mad any more, huh? It's all over?"

"Sure, Ma," Maureen said.

"Sure," said Furlong.

He and Maureen glanced at each other by accident and looked away at once. The shame between them was strong and sharp as the bath powder Loretta always dabbed on herself.

15

It came to her at night, when she thought she was sleeping: she had to get out. She had to get money. In her dreams she caught up with Jules on the street and asked him, *How do you get money?*

She dreamed about her father. Her dead father was sitting at a kitchen table in a room without walls, reading a newspaper. His eyes were vacant and alarmed at the headlines. Maureen came over to see what he was reading, but there was nothing there—they didn't know the secret, she and her father, to what was in the newspaper. But money was behind it all, surely. Money was the secret.

Now that she and Furlong were "friends," it was Maureen who had to get him when he stayed too late at the garage. In the past he had drifted home by way of several bars, taking his time, but now Maureen went to get him to see that he got home. His back was not good. It wasn't getting well the way it was supposed to. So Loretta sent Maureen out, never Betty. "Look, you're the favorite," she would explain. "You're his favorite. Get him to come home and eat." Maureen hated going the three blocks down to the garage, hated the risk of going out on Michigan Avenue at twilight, hated approaching the cluster of men inside the gas station, whether Furlong was there or not. Sometimes he wasn't there. Standing in the cold halo of light from the garage doorway, she watched the men before they noticed her, wondering what men did talk about when they were alone—what secrets they had. She hated their looks of surprise and then their smiles, their knowing smiles. She was Pat Furlong's stepdaughter. She was Maureen Wendall, standing out in the cold and waiting, come to take her stepfather home. Furlong, reluctant and swaggering, always took time to say goodnight to his friends, ignoring her.

Sometimes she waited out by the gas pumps for ten, fifteen minutes, while snowflakes fell slowly about her and traffic out on the wide street dwindled, the car headlights misty and expanded in the moist air. She wondered where those cars were heading. Would one of them stop to give her a ride? She caressed her arm through the thickness of her coat sleeve, puzzled, unable to figure out why she was puzzled, as if the feeble pattern of traffic before her held some knowledge she should have possessed. In the deepest part of her was a question: *Why was she herself and not someone else?* But then, as if to muffle this question, she would think, *I might as well be here as anywhere else.*

When Furlong finally came out she often glanced up in surprise, not exactly remembering that she had been waiting for him. "Okay, come on," he would say, already in a hurry. She had to walk fast to keep up with him. He took impatient, yard-long strides, as if trying to escape her.

One evening she said to him, "Why won't Ma let me get a job?"

He glanced over his shoulder at her. "Won't she? I don't know."

"Will you ask her if I can get one?"

"Sure."

"Please, will you ask her? She says she doesn't want me to work. She doesn't want me out of the house. But I need a job, please, please ask her." She was conscious of her voice annoying him. It was a mistake to talk too much to men, to this kind of man. They didn't want to hear the voices of women pleading with them. "Now that she has the baby she says I should stay home to help her, but I could help her at home and have a job too. I could do it all, I could do everything. Will you ask her?"

She was pleading with his back. He wore a short jacket, zipped up to his throat. Maureen leaned forward as she walked, and Furlong, though in a hurry, seemed to be about to turn back to her.

"Okay, I'll ask her."

"If she says no, ask her again. Keep asking her. I need to make money."

But Loretta was against it. Maureen was needed at home. "Anyway, I don't like her hanging around places. I don't like her running around any more than she does, like going to the library like she says." The words *like she says* were ironic; Maureen caught that but did not understand. What was wrong with the library?

She woke up at night thinking about a job. She thought about it constantly, a job, having no job in mind but only the idea of it, only the word itself. Loretta stood in her way, stubbornly. She needed a job, needed money. But Loretta would only say, her face closed, "I need you around here, I said! You'll get in trouble soon enough."

"Ma, I don't get into trouble!"

"Don't you talk back to me, Reeny. I told you my opinion."

"But you never believe me. You make up things. I go to the library, that's the only place I go—not even to the movies —here, look at the books in my room! Aren't those library books?"

"Now, don't start bawling. You always did have a long face, like Grandma Wendall said. You always take things too serious."

Maureen wandered away, clutching at her head. She thought something was going to snap. She needed to be free, out in her father's car with Jules driving it, the two of them liberated, in the open, on their way out of the city and up north. "Why can't I get a job?" she shouted back at Loretta. "A part-time job? After school? Why not? Why do I have to be home all the time? Why me, why not Betty? What's there to do with the baby you can't do? How come Betty can run wild all she wants but I have to stay home? Why is it? Why is it all so crazy?"

"Don't you yell at me! I told you my opinion and that's that."

The baby's crying began to get on Furlong's nerves, or so he said. He wouldn't come home when Maureen went to get him. "The hell with supper," he would say. So she stopped going to get him and instead waited up for him. Everything had to do with *him,* with that man, and nothing had to do with Maureen herself. She had to stay up late to warm up his supper and make his coffee. He couldn't do it himself and Loretta was too tired; she was always in bed. Sometimes he stayed out overnight, and around two o'clock Maureen would go to bed herself, giving up on him. But then she would have to stay home the next day, cutting school, because Loretta would feel sick and wouldn't want to face Furlong alone. So Maureen had to stay home from school and wait out the morning until he came back. She hated him. Her hatred for him was so violent that it was always with her, in the foreground or the background of her mind, everywhere with her. She felt that he was turning into her real father, being always with her in her imagination.

On these quiet, dopey mornings she read through books she had already finished, her mind desperate, her body sluggish and sullen. Loretta moved the television set into the bedroom, and since Maureen did not want to be in the same room with her she couldn't even watch those stupid daytime shows—there was just nothing to do, no escape.

The old daydreams were all finished. She could not summon up out of her imagination the classroom scenes she had once gloried in, with herself as a teacher. She would never be a teacher. She could not make herself imagine Furlong dying in an accident—the vision faded, she forgot to keep it going. There was nothing in her but a hatred for him so diffuse that it was like her own blood, coursing mechanically through her. She ransacked her mind but there was nothing in it. Everything was emptied out, exhausted. She might have been inhabiting her mother's body. The only richness was in books, but the books lay on the sofa, read and reread, emptied. They could no longer stir her.

Sometimes she thought idly about earthquakes, fires, buildings cracking in two. She thought about accidents in which automobiles piled on top of each other, one after another.

She thought about money. At first she thought about the idea of money, as she had thought about the idea of a job. But then she began to think about the feel of money; she took a dollar bill out of her room, out of a hiding place, and stared at it. In this way she could pass an hour or more. She remembered how easily Jules had given her eight dollars; it had happened so quickly, like magic! Furlong carried his wallet in his back pocket. It was tight in that pocket, wrinkled and worn out. In it he had lots of bills. She wondered how much money he had. He got a check twice a month and Loretta got a check once a month. How much money did they have?

She imagined a hiding place for money: the veranda of the old house on Labrosse. She could crawl under the veranda, into that dirty secret place, and hide everything there. No one would find it. She could stay there herself, hiding, and no one would find her.

Her schoolwork began to come back to her with grades of D. Even in English, her best subject, she got D's. She sat stunned and ashamed, sliding her test papers into her desk, hiding them quickly. Everything was so precarious. She had always gotten A's and B's, but now she had slid down to D and could honestly not understand why. It just happened, by itself. She should have asked her teacher about it but instead she remained in her seat or hurried quickly out of the room when the bell rang, anxious to get away. She walked home daydreaming. She sat in school daydreaming. She was getting slow, silent. There was a slight insolent edge to her stare when she was scolded. What the hell did it matter? Homework, schoolwork, oral questions, all that junk . . .

She imagined finding an old paper bag on the sidewalk—with money inside! No one would bother to pick it up except her. She imagined finding an old paper bag next to her on a bus, in a movie house, in a corner of a restroom—filled with bills, all kinds of bills!—money that was all hers and that no one else knew about.

There was something aching behind her eyes that told her she had to get this money, had to get out, never mind where, had to escape—as if, while she tried to read her homework or a novel from the library, a certain passage struggled to make itself clear to her. It was magic that did not quite work. She might open a book anywhere and let her eye fall upon a paragraph and *that* would be the paragraph that could tell her what she needed to know—but when she read it, she could not understand. Sometimes she could not even understand the words. What was this code? Did it make sense to other people?

She said to her friend Carol, "Do you ever think about running away?"

"Not any more," Carol said slowly.

"Doesn't it bother you—I mean, at home?"

Carol shrugged her shoulders.

"But you don't want to run away?"

"They just bring you back again. To the same place," Carol said.

Maureen talked to another girl, an older girl, who had run away and was caught in Buffalo. "Where did you get the money for the bus?" Maureen said.

"Stole it," said the girl.

"Why did you run away?"

"I wanted to. You know."

"Are you going to run away again?"

The girl was slightly embarrassed at Maureen's attention. "Naw, it was too much trouble. They just think you're going to have a baby and they take a test of you. They got minds that low," she said with a laugh, measuring a foot or so off the floor.

She tried to hunt Jules on the street. He was seventeen now and should know everything. Sometimes she believed she saw him ahead of her, but it never turned out to be him. She found the brother of a friend of his, a kid with greasy hair and tight pants, and asked him about Jules; he looked evasive. "Tell him I want to see him. I want to talk to him," she pleaded.

And then, after time passed, something happened to her. A change came over her one morning as she sat staring out the window of the apartment at nothing. The baby was crying, Loretta was bathing him. Maureen felt a certain hardness come over her, as if something invisible were blessing her, as if a shell were shaping itself out of her skin. She drew back from the window, thinking it was a draft of cold air. She shivered. Her muscles cringed and then relaxed in acceptance. She felt herself change.

The next day she left school early, soon after lunch. She told Sister Mary Paul that she had a bad headache, which was true. Her head always ached. But on the way home she dawdled—it was a clear sunny day—and as cars passed she glanced up at them, mildly surprised, as if she had no idea where she was going or what she could expect. Her expression was pleasant, wondering. When she had walked about a mile, aiming toward downtown Detroit, she saw a car slow in front of her and pull over toward the curb. She walked along the sidewalk without hurrying and without fear. When she was passing the car the driver leaned out and said, "Would you like a ride?"

She thought for a terrifying moment that he was Furlong, in a different car. But then she saw that he was a stranger and that he looked nothing like Furlong. She took in his face at once; it was all right. It did not matter who he was. "I could use a ride maybe," she called out. She got in.

The man said quickly, "Do you live around here?"

"Oh, I live back there. I was just going for a walk."

"School's out now?"

"Yes."

"Are you in high school?"

"I'm a senior."

"What's your name?"

"Maureen."

He smiled nervously, not hearing any of this, and she too smiled—but not nervously. She let her long chestnut-colored hair fall forward. Under her coat she wore her navy-blue jumper, a little short for her now, and loafers like all the girls wore; she carried her books cradled childishly in her arms.

Once in the car she felt relieved, as if she had safely crossed a boundary line. She let her books fall onto the seat between them. She said softly, "On a nice day like this I like to go for a ride, but we don't have a car. My parents don't have a car; I don't know anyone who has one."

"Nobody at all?"

"Oh, maybe somebody."

"No boy friends?"

"I'm not interested in boys," Maureen said.

"You're in—high school? What year are you?"

"My last year," she said, lying with a dazzling smile, letting herself relax. The sunlight was like honey. Somewhere she could smell cologne—she imagined it. Notes of music drifted into them from passing cars. She felt as if she were in a boat, being borne gently along a stream, without effort.

He drove toward the river. Maureen thought it was strange, how familiar everything looked. She stared at everything; she was blank and smiling. The very odor of the air was familiar. They passed warehouses, vacant lots. On the river there were boats—great barges, lake barges that moved slowly, without sound. She was free. No one could even see her. Freedom came to her like air from the river, not exactly fresh, but chilly and strong; she was free and she had escaped.

The man was maybe thirty-five. She couldn't tell. He was silent, and in his silence there was pleading. Shrewdly she recognized it but gave no sign—like a man, she was contemptuous of pleading. He stopped the car somewhere. He took out his wallet and took snapshots out of it, showing Maureen pictures of his family. She stared past the pictures to the wallet itself, which was cracked and worn, like Furlong's. One of the snapshots showed a man in a soldier's uniform—the man himself! Maureen smiled at the pictures. She thought, *I'm not afraid at all. I don't feel anything.*

After a while, nervously, clumsily, the man kissed her. Though she could feel his mouth against her own, she did not really feel anything. She felt the pressure of his mouth. She kept thinking clearly, *I don't feel anything at all . . .* Past his head was the sky. It was normal. The man leaned over her, breathing sharply, and in a strange eager haste embraced her and kissed her again. There was pleading in him, in every part of him. She put her hands up against his shoulders, not to push him away but just to complete the embrace as she supposed she should. Still she felt nothing. She was untouched. In another minute he was kissing her throat; he clutched at her and pressed his mouth against her, and Maureen felt a little uneasy for the first time—but only for an instant. They were out in the open. The blue sky faced them above the Detroit River.

After a while he moved away. He was very nervous. He said, "I better drive you home."

"All right," said Maureen.

"Do you get a ride home from school most days? A boy friend?"

"I don't have a boy friend," Maureen said.

"Why not?"

"I don't have time for boys."

"Will you be out there tomorrow? I mean, where you were? Tomorrow around this time?"

"All right," said Maureen.

There was silence between them. She did not look at him. Finally he said, "If I came by tomorrow again, maybe we could go for a ride. Would that be all right?"

"All right."

"We don't have to go far."

"All right."

She met him on the street the next afternoon. She was not wearing her school outfit since she had cut school; instead she wore a skirt and sweater. Her hair was loose in the wind.

The man stared at her when she got in the car; it was a hard, helpless stare. She did not look at him. She smiled toward him. They drove out along West Jefferson; the day was slightly overcast and seemed to press them together, to urge them together.

"Sit closer," the man said.

Maureen moved over closer to him. "Can't you sit any closer than that?" he said.

Maureen gathered her skirt up about her knees and moved over again. The man took both her hands in one of his, at once. She felt again a slight uneasiness, almost a memory of fear, but it passed. At the very center of him was the money he had that he would give to her—she thought about that.

They drove along. They passed trucks, cars, buses. Maureen looked around as if she'd never seen all this before, and the man kept glancing from the street to her, to the side of her face. He was jumpy and his driving was a little clumsy. Maureen wondered what would happen if he had an accident. A police cruiser passed them, in no hurry. Maureen glanced over into the car. Three policemen, smoking cigarettes. They wore sunglasses in spite of the dull air.

He took her to an old hotel on West Jefferson. Maureen did not bother looking around. She climbed the stairs ahead of him, feeling him behind her with that eager intense stare. Still she felt nothing. It was not personal. If her heart was beating fast, it was in imitation of what she ought to be feeling but did not quite feel, as if her body were at a safe distance from herself. She believed that her teachers, the nuns who had cautioned the girls about certain things, would have felt nothing more than she was feeling—it was not possible to feel much. Even fear was too much.

They were entering a room. The man closed the door behind them and fastened a chain. Maureen looked around and saw a bed, a chair, a bureau, then she gave up looking.

"I wish you'd take this off," he said, meaning her coat.

He was as tall as Furlong, a tall man, but he was very nervous. What she could see of his face was all right. He had fair, ordinary skin. So long as the fear was on his side Maureen did not have to be afraid at all. He helped her off with her coat politely and hung it up. Then he came to her and embraced her. She cried out a little in surprise. Her hands rose to his shoulders, as if to push him away, but she stood facing him and did not push him away. There was no fear in her. She did not feel anything really; she was at a distance from this. She closed her eyes. He pressed himself against her, all the length of him, an adult man pressing himself against her. As if they were familiar to each other, she began to move her hands behind him, up to the back of his neck. He was kissing her mouth. She felt the short sharp hairs at the back of his neck. So close together, they could not see each other now; he would never be able to remember her face.

In five minutes it was over, and she lay beside the man, not even looking around the room. She had not felt much pain really. She had imagined that she would feel great pain but it was mild, she could not quite concentrate on it. Everything in the man had been concentrated, vivid and quick; in Maureen everything was vague. There was so much feeling on his side that she had not needed to feel anything.

After another hour they prepared to leave. He tried to smooth out her clothes, which were wrinkled. He was like a father. "Oh, it doesn't matter," Maureen said, surprised that he should care—what did her clothes matter? His concern touched her. She began to cry, surprising herself and him.

She covered her face, crying; but it was not serious. She was able to make herself stop. She forced herself to stop. She didn't know why this had happened—she had felt no pain and no fear. It was over. Nothing had really happened.

He pulled her onto his knees tenderly. He seemed like someone's father.

"I need money," Maureen said. "I need to buy things of my own, clothes and things."

He hugged her. He told her to stop crying. He wiped a teardrop from her cheek with his finger and brought the finger to his mouth.

"I need money, money," she said. She understood that he would give her money. He was anxious to give her money. But it would take a certain passage of time, a few minutes, several minutes . . . but he would give her money. That fact kept her from breaking into pieces.

16

"She had a baby . . . the bottom part of the spine wasn't right, what-ya-call-it . . . it kept dripping out, some water . . . . the baby only lived a few weeks . . ."

"That's really lousy . . ."

Maureen sat on the edge of her bed, leafing through a book. From time to time she glanced up at the door to her room, which could not be shut tightly enough to keep out the voices from the kitchen. Loretta had a visitor, a woman named Rita. Maureen hated to hear their voices, hated to hear the things they said, yet at the same time she yearned to be out there with them, understanding everything. They talked in bright patches of sound, rhythmic, robust, in total sympathy, very much together: Maureen did not know if she hated them or envied them. All her life she had heard women talking, together, almost out of earshot but never out of earshot. But the talk did not make sense: she sat on the edge of her bed, alone, leafing nervously through a library book, understanding nothing.

This woman Rita had bounced up the stairs that morning out of nowhere, "just back from Florida and for good," wearing a black sweater with spangles on it and black slacks. Her hair was too black to be real. Her ears were pierced and she wore gold knobs in them. Loretta, opening the door to her, had cried out in surprise and delight, and the two of them had embraced, very excited, affectionate. Maureen had ducked back to her room to get out of the heady air of their excitement and affection. She did not like excitement and she did not understand affection.

The book on her lap was *Poets of the New World*, just the right size and with the right title to keep out snooping people. On page 200 were a number of bills. One of them was a fifty-dollar bill. On page 300 there were more bills. Maureen sat leafing dreamily through the book, not watching the page numbers to see if she was coming to her hidden money but letting herself come upon it by surprise. She felt a mild shock every time she came upon it. That was the strange thing about money; it was always a surprise.

She sat for a while in her room, waiting. Betty's side of the room was a mess; they had divided the room in two, and Betty's junk lay right against the boundary line, where Maureen had pushed it back with her foot. Betty's clothes lay everywhere in a jumble, clean and dirty clothes, and the junk she collected—comic books, even small traffic signs—lay in uneven piles. Betty's husky, hurried presence was almost audible in the room, while Maureen's was not; this neatness on Maureen's side of the room, the made-up bed and the small row of books along the floor, suggested that no one lived here permanently. And this was almost true: on nights when Loretta fought with her husband she kicked Maureen out of bed and Maureen had to sleep on the sofa. This bed had become Loretta's bed as much as it was Maureen's. Maureen did not really own it. Like everything else of hers, it was precarious, and anyway it seemed to her right that she should now be sleeping or lying awake on top of so many strange beds since she had never really had one of her own.

At exactly five o'clock she put *Poets of the New World* back in its place on the floor and picked up three other books. In the kitchen her mother and her mother's loud friend were still talking. They were drinking beer. "This is my Reeny, my Maureen, you remember her?" Loretta said, reaching out for Maureen's hand. "Isn't she grown up real pretty?"

"Sure I remember her. She's real cute. She was real cute then, a little kid." Rita smiled with affection at Maureen. "How old are you, honey?"

"Sixteen."

"Sixteen, Christ!" The woman screwed up her mouth in a pleasant, bewildered look. "You know, your ma and I were real good friends when you weren't even born yet. In fact your mother was about your age. What do you think about that?"

"Isn't that something?" Loretta said enthusiastically.

Maureen looked toward the floor. Her mother was still holding her hand, expecting something from her. She was trapped by their clumsy good will. What was it about affection she now hated? Was it having to get close to someone, having to look clearly in someone's face? She did not want to look into anyone's face.

"That's real nice," she said.

"Yeah, your mother was only your age. Believe it or not."

"I had long hair then, real long. Down my back," Loretta said.

Maureen smiled and eased away from her. She waited for Loretta's permission for her to escape; she was obedient and polite in her school jumper and her clean white blouse. She seemed not to want to look up at her mother and this friend. She did not want to imagine, either, her mother at sixteen years of age, with long blond hair.

"Well, kid, where are you off to now? I suppose you're going to the *library* again?"

Maureen wondered at her mother's meaning.

"Yes, Ma, I have three books to return."

"Oh, you—you and that library!"

"She's a real pretty girl," Rita said warmly. "I like the way kids these days wear their hair. Only what's that outfit?"

"The nuns' school."

"No kidding, Loretta? You're sending your kids to a nuns' school after what we went through? Those stupid bitches—?"

"Oh, it's good for the kids, it does them good."

Maureen said good-by and got out.

It was spring now and she wore no coat. She walked over to the library, almost happy to be out of one place and not yet in another, suspended and free for a few minutes. When she entered the library she felt a shiver of anticipation pass over her. She went to the librarian's counter to return the books. Then she went into the reading-room where a few people sat at tables, reading, daydreaming. Someone caught her eye. He held up a copy of *Newsweek* before him and on the cover of the magazine was a woman's face—Maureen did not recognize the face but it was a beautiful one. She returned his look and turned again and left the library.

Outside, on the sidewalk, she waited until he caught up with her.

"Did your mother give you any trouble?" he said.

"No. About the same."

She walked alongside him, swinging her purse gently, smiling, and he crowded a little against her. She had met him about three weeks before, seeking him out because he had a certain safe, restless look. She could draw near to a man and through half-closed eyes assess him, never really looking at him; it was a feeling in her blood. She lowered her head in a certain way, she let one foot slide out so that the ankle touched the floor, she pretended to be thinking seriously about something in her own life, and in this way she felt his attention move upon her like a strong light, bathing her in it and marking her.

"It's a nice day today. It's a good day." He leaned against her slightly as they walked, touching her arm. She felt his body leaning toward her. He was not a shy man or a very gentle man but he understood her; he gave her money. She was greedy for the money he would give her today, stuck away now in his wallet. It was supposed to be out of sight and out of her concern for the moment. But she thought keenly about it, its passing from his hands into hers, its becoming her money. The bills would not change in any way and yet they would become hers. Its power would become hers. The man's giving her his money was not a simple act but a transformation of the money itself, so that it became another kind of money, it became hers, it was magical in her hands and secret from all the world, and yet it was unchanged.

He was saying, nudging her, "What are you thinking about? You look so strange. What are you always thinking about?"

"Nothing."

"Nothing? Not about me?"

"No."

"Sure, you're thinking about me!"

He was joking, and she glanced up at him, smiling. She did not quite see him. She had seen enough of him that first day to know that he had a rather hard, demanding face, that his hair was trimmed short, that his fingernails didn't seem dirty, that the clothes he wore were fairly good—at least she thought they were fairly good. She had known that when they were alone he would grab her, and that when they tried to talk to each other their words would come

out nervous and warm, like slaps. It was like talking to Loretta sometimes: not really talking. About his private life
she never thought and had no curiosity. She did not wonder
if he was married or not or if he had a good job or not.
He might have had no job at all. She really did not think
of him except as a man she met a few times a week who
gave her money and who was carrying now the money he
would give her later that afternoon—that was the secret and
central part of his being, which would be opened up and
given to her.

"You want to go somewhere?" he said.

"Anywhere," Maureen said.

"My car's parked here. You want to go for a ride, kid?"

"All right."

He rubbed his hand across the back of her neck, now
that they were in the parking lot and off the street. He
opened the car door for her. She got in, passing near him,
and he bent down to kiss her. At this point it began: a
kind of beginning. He changed, she could feel him changing.
He said against her mouth, "I've been thinking of you all
this time . . ." And it was not any particular truth he was
saying—in fact she supposed he was lying—but it was the
truth of his needing to say it that made her know that everything was all right.

He embraced her. Everything was all right with him. Sitting in the car, she let the strength flow out of her body,
as if it were Maureen herself flowing out, escaping, disappearing into the air, and clumsily the man leaned over her,
trying to define some need of his with his own body, his
hands. There was something gay and extravagant in his passion—sparks that seemed to flirt with her, leaping about her,
sparks of excitement she could not quite grasp and had a
little curiosity about sometimes but could not get hold of
herself.

Shaken, he drove out Woodward Avenue, driving fast as
if to exhibit his power. She let her eyes trail along the string
of familiar buildings. On the radio a popular song was playing. The air was good, as this man had said, touched with
spring. Maureen wondered why it didn't mean more to her.
She couldn't quite remember the spring before, the year before. She thought she'd always liked spring, relieved at having lived through another winter, but now this feeling belonged to her friend, who was steering the car with one
hand and squeezing her hand with the other. He had taken

up all the strength of spring and was giddy with it, while Maureen sat calmly and looked out at the stores and the people, all those people with money in their pockets going in stores to buy things, to lay out money on counters, to give money to other people, a cycle that never stopped.

He was talking to her and she had to listen. "Are you still a homeroom secretary?" he said. "Tell me about that."

"There's nothing to tell."

"I remember being in school—my homeroom—we had a president and a secretary too. Tell me about it."

"Really, there's nothing to tell."

After a while he said, "Tell me more about your mother. Do the two of you fight all the time? She doesn't really believe it, does she?—that you're running around. What about your father, what does he think?"

"I don't know. I don't know anything about them."

"Did somebody try to pick you up once and she found out? Tell me about it."

He drove out past Palmer Park, where small crowds of people drifted in the spring sunshine, looking dazzled by it. An unruly mob of ducks and geese were scrambling for food around the pond, fighting with one another. Out in the water benches had been thrown, one of them on end, and a pigeon was perched on it, watching the spectacle. The sunlight glinted beautifully on everything. There should have been music. People were on the tennis courts, playing tennis or hanging around. Maureen put her hand over the man's hand and stroked his fingers. This might keep him silent. She wondered what it was like to be a tennis player; not to play tennis, she had no interest in that, but to be a tennis player, one of those girls in a white outfit with a sweater slung over her back and its sleeves tied in front of her . . .

He drove past the State Fair Ground. Negroes were waiting for buses in a large shelter; a few of them, women, stood out in the sunlight.

The man took her to a motel outside Detroit, a place painted white, with pink neon lights. There were several cars in the parking lot with out-of-state license plates. Maureen got out of the car and waited for him to come back from registering, then went with him to the room. The Venetian blinds were already drawn.

The man helped her take off her jumper and, with a gentle, kindly pretense of authority, drew the skin taut at the tips of her eyes. "You should get more sleep. Is your family still so crazy?" he said.

Maureen said nothing. Standing in her white slip, she drew the covers back from the pillows, thinking that this scene, the pillows and the sallow light, were so familiar that she no longer had to place herself among them. She was here and yet not here. But an accident disturbed her—she happened to catch sight of the man's face in the mirror. She hadn't meant to see it. He was unbuttoning his shirt, looking down, and she noticed that he wore a platinum stretch-band watch and that there were tiny buttons on the points of his collar, holding them down neatly; his face looked a little coarse with hurrying.

He came to her and they passed into another part of the cycle, now that they had stopped talking, and Maureen felt the flesh of his back dutifully as if only now was she beginning to recognize him. But this too was familiar. She had memorized all the parts of the cycle, the route the machinery took to its inevitable end; she wanted to hurry it along. His skin was a man's skin, a little rough. It felt almost sandy beneath her fingers. He himself was a little rough, and so she seemed to be guiding him with her hands on his back and her mouth near his. A man was like a machine: one of those machines at the laundromat where she dragged the laundry. There were certain cycles to go through. The cycle had begun when he had opened the door of his car for her, and in a minute or two it would end with his sudden paralyzed tension, his broken breath against her face, the familiar urgent signs of a man's love. For he spoke of love, groaning against her, "Jesus Christ, but I love you . . . I'm crazy about you . . ."

Afterward they lay together under the cheap cotton cover and he talked in another voice. He was cheerful and energetic, a little loud. "Your mother doesn't really believe it, the crap she says, does she? Why would she let you go out then?" He was setting a certain argument before her, certain blocks of logic. It did not matter what they meant.

"I don't know," Maureen said.

"You should get more sleep. Get to bed early."

"All right."

"Do you need much money?"

"Yes."

"Why, to buy things?"

"Maybe."

"What kind of things? Skirts and dresses?"

"I don't know."

"You want to buy pretty things for yourself, huh?"

Maureen closed her eyes.

"I could buy them for you. Let me buy you something."

"No," she said simply, "I would rather have the money."

"But I could buy you something nice myself. You could pick it out."

"I would rather have the money."

"If I didn't give you money, you wouldn't come with me?"

Maureen didn't answer. She felt too weary to answer.

"Then you don't like me, huh?"

"I like you."

He laughed. He was in a very good mood. "Do you love me?" he said.

"Yes, I love you." She spoke in a dull, vacuous manner, perfectly obedient.

She could hear traffic getting louder outside on Woodward; it was getting late. People were heading out of the city, heading north. She felt a shiver pass over her, thinking of men in cars heading out of the city, north to the suburbs where they lived, a steady, noisy stream of cars. So many people, so much urgency. It was strange that she had to lie still on this strange bed, in a room this man had rented, while everyone else was escaping, driving away from the city. She eased away from him a little. Her heart had begun to beat quickly.

When she got home, around seven, she went right to the bathroom and got her mother's jar of cold cream out of the medicine cabinet. Loretta followed Maureen into the bathroom. "Help yourself, don't bother asking. Feel free," she said. Rita was gone now but her chattiness was in the air and had infected Loretta.

"Well, can I have it?" Maureen said patiently.

"Why not? We got to live together."

She slid past her mother and went to her room, where she sat on the edge of her bed. Loretta followed. Maureen could see *Poets of the New World* from where she sat. She had more money to be put in the book—that night she could count it all up. She could lock herself in the bathroom and count it.

She put cold cream on her face while her mother slouched in the doorway, smoking. Maureen did not listen to her mother's chatter but thought about her own face. Maybe it was getting older, changed, by the friction of those rough faces against hers. Something would change in her face. She wondered if all women who gave themselves to men felt the imprint of faces on theirs—how did you get them rubbed off? They were like shells enclosing her face, hard and ugly. Her own skin would get rough.

Loretta was saying a little drunkenly, "That Rita is a real sweet kid, she's my heart, that one. Two times she helped me out, *two times,* when I was in bad trouble . . ."

Maureen wiped the cold cream off her face with a tissue. On the tissue there were no particular signs—just cold cream, a little dirt. Specks of dirt. No sign. She did not dare to be relieved, however. It was bad luck to be relieved when danger was past; danger was never really past. What about the money in her purse? What if Loretta snatched up her purse, in fun, and looked inside? She was nosy enough to do this. A shudder began low in Maureen's spine. She wiped her face and crumpled up the tissue, wondering if her mother could guess. Yes, her mother would guess if she opened the purse. No, she wouldn't guess anything. Did she know already? Or was it all a joke? Maureen's spine felt cold and brittle as if it were turning to ice. It felt as if it might break suddenly. And then all the spinal fluid would gush out. She thought of that man hanging over her, his weight on her, all that love pushed into her and released as if it had been just too much for him and he had to get rid of it, the sooner the better. She thought of her mother and Furlong. She thought of her mother and her father, her dead father. Very slowly she wiped cold cream off her throat, thinking of these things. It was good to feel clean, yet there was a greasy, clammy feel to her skin from the cream. It was not really clean. Her back was very cold, brittle. If a man fell upon her now he would break her in two, her spine would snap. She could not understand these things. She could not understand the weight, the force that drew men and women together, of their own free will. What she could understand was the money in her purse, and the money in that book. It was something that could be counted again and again; it was as real as a novel by Jane Austen.

Loretta, lounging in the doorway, chatting, smoking, gave no sign of going away. "So how was the library, kid? Learn a lot?"

"Ma, you should turn off that stupid television and read something yourself. There're all kinds of books in the library," Maureen said suddenly. "You'd learn something."

"Oh, the hell I would! What?"

"There're books on all kinds of things."

"Like what?"

"I took out a book of poems, it's right there on the floor. Poems."

Loretta looked down at the row of books.

"Poems, hell. Shit," she said, and left the doorway.

Is she real? Maureen wondered suddenly. *Is any of this real?* She remembered hearing her mother talk once about being a mother, about having children. Loretta had said that it was strange to be a mother because if the kids weren't in the room with you—were they really around? Did you really have them? And maybe the main kid you were supposed to have, the important one, was someone you never got around to having—what then? Loretta had spoken slowly and seriously. She'd been talking to Connie, across Grandma Wendall's body. And Maureen, half listening, had been struck by something pathetic and frightening in her mother's voice. *If the kids weren't in the room with you, did you really have them?* And she herself, Loretta's daughter, could not have said what the answer was.

Maybe the book with her money in it, and the money so greedily saved, and the idea of the money, maybe these things weren't real either. What would happen if everything broke into pieces? It was queer how you felt, instinctively, that a certain space of time was real and not a dream, and you gave your life to it, all your energy and faith, believing it to be real. But how could you tell what would last and what wouldn't? How could you get hold of something that wouldn't end? Marriages ended. Love ended. Money could be stolen, found out and taken, Furlong himself might find it, or it might disappear by itself, like that secretary's notebook. Such things happened. Objects disappeared, slipped through cracks, devoured, kicked aside, knocked under the bed or into the trash, lost. Nothing lasted for long. Maureen thought of earthquakes opening the earth in violent rifts, swallowing city blocks, churches, railroad tracks. She thought of fires, of bulldozers leveling trees and buildings. Why not? While she had lain with that man, only a short time before, it had come to her helplessly that she was there, not out on the avenue, she was in bed with a man and not in a car traveling somewhere. It was her fate to be Maureen; that was that. But the Maureen she was in the presence of that man she'd been with—he said he was crazy about her and he needed her violently—did not last. It came to an end. As eagerly as he switched himself onto the cycle of loving her, still he was sober and eager to switch himself off and drive her home and get rid of her. That was a fact. He was very real to her for about five minutes, that was all. Her clearest memory of the men she'd been with was their moving away from her. They were all body then, completed.

That night Furlong came home early, around ten. Maureen heard him. Then she heard Loretta calling her—"Hey, kid, come out here. Got a job for you." Maureen got up at once and went out, not even making a face to herself. She was in her bathrobe. Furlong was standing by the kitchen table with one hand on the small of his back—a gesture of defeat that looked strangely tender. Maureen had never thought much about men feeling pain but she could see that this man felt pain.

"Honey, can you rub his back for him?" Loretta said. "It's acting up again and I'm real tired myself. I been feeling dizzy all day."

Maureen looked levelly at her mother and nodded.

"I'll get the stuff for you," Loretta said. "It's a real nice favor, Reeny. He won't be able to sleep otherwise."

Furlong sat. Maureen waited. The two of them did not speak or look at each other. Loretta came back from the bathroom with the rubbing alcohol and unbuttoned Furlong's shirt for him, breezy and bullying. "Reeny might as well make herself useful," she said. "The baby was sick twice today, the poor kid. It's about all I can take. Now, Reeny, come here. Here's how you do it. Watch me."

Her mother showed Maureen how to massage Furlong's back. "Use your fingers hard, you have to do it hard. Around in a circle," she said. She gave off an odor of something cheap and powdery and pleasant. Furlong smelled different. Just as his body was solid and heavy and fixed, so the odor of his being, the mysterious odor of his soul, was heavy, dark, opaque. There was nothing light about it, nothing powdery.

Maureen felt a little dizzy, as if her mother's dizziness had become her own. It was strange: she did not mind her mother's hands over hers, guiding her own narrow hands on Furlong's back, the fingertips moving slowly and with a kind of wonder over those strange little bones that make up the spine. Though she was very tired she did not mind any of this, not even her mother's leaning against her.

"Like this, like this," Loretta said, pleased. To Furlong she said, "How does it feel?"

He nodded gratefully. His face was sweaty with pain. Maureen stared at his thick, smooth flesh beneath her fingers and understood why he was silent. Her father too had been silent. There was too much flesh to men, too much weight to force words through.

"Okay, Reeny, you know how to do it? I'm going to bed," Loretta said and left.

Maureen heard her in the bedroom, talking to the baby. The baby whimpered. These sounds, coming from another room, were like a wall: Loretta was on the other side of it. Maureen watched the back of Furlong's head. She stared down at his neck, which was very still, and his solid back, the pale flesh marred with tiny blemishes and moles that were like secrets of his weakness, something you would never know unless you stood this close. She felt an overwhelming, sharp sense of dizziness.

Massaging him became hypnotic. Yet her weariness slowed her hands; the muscles high on her forearms ached. She paused. She leaned down toward him, as if to whisper in his ear, but instead she laid her cheek against the warmth of his back, near his shoulder. She remained that way for a moment.

Then she said, backing off, "Good night, I'm going to bed."

17

The next week, at about five o'clock one afternoon, Maureen happened to glance out of her friend's car window as they waited for a light to change on Livernois. On the sidewalk, standing with a group of men who looked as if they'd been standing there all day, was her mother's husband, and he was staring at her. Maureen shielded her face with her hand and turned away.

"What's wrong?" said the man.

"Nothing. Never mind."

He drove on. He was in a different mood today, quieter. She did not bother with his moods and kept herself still, waiting for everything to be got over with, for the routine to run itself through, exhaust itself. But suddenly she was very afraid. She began to tremble. That curious sensation in her spine began again, as if it were the start of paralysis; the coldness spread through her body. She wondered what was going to happen. He had seen her, yes. She had shielded her face with her hand. It had happened in an instant and was over with and yet none of it was over with. She gripped her head with her hands, feeling the actual skull, wondering if she was going to faint in this stranger's car.

He was talking about something. She sat very still and stared out at the running landscape of sidewalks and stores. Everything was too bright. Her eyes hurt. She did not think about the man beside her, or about Furlong, or about what would happen when she got home. Instead she fixed her mind upon that book, and the money in it, saved up week after week. It couldn't be taken from her, not so easily. It was not possible that she might lose it. She began to breathe quickly, thinking of her money. It was *her* money. A stream of air from the car window stirred her hair and made her eyes ache. Why was it so cold? She could not quite remember where they were going. Had they already gone to bed together this afternoon or were they on their way? She'd been with this man two days before, or three days. She could not remember. Cautiously she shifted her body and tried to think, testing herself—was she sore from him or hadn't anything happened yet? One way or another, she really did not care. Everything was so empty in her that she felt nothing; her body forgot faster than she herself did.

His car smelled of leather and metal. It smelled of some cologne she'd dabbed on herself, her mother's stuff in a pale blue bottle. Her hands lay limp on her knees, a schoolgirl's hands with long fingers and knobby knuckles and a few ink stains. Her hands were very cold. She tested her feet and discovered that they too were very cold. But it was not winter any longer—no lopsided dirty mounds of snow remained—it was well into spring, people walked out on the street in their shirt sleeves, without coats, and yet it seemed to her very cold. She stared out. She could not think which street this was. Gates were lifting slowly in front of them— they had been waiting for a train to pass. Maureen stared at the lifting gates and felt terror.

"Hey, what's wrong? You sick or something?"

"No."

He took hold of her hand, concerned. He switched off

the car radio, which Maureen hadn't heard until he switched it off. She began shaking her head, *no*, it was always no regardless of what he asked her, she lied automatically and without spirit. Then, reversing herself and lying again, she said, "I have a little headache. It's nothing." He squeezed her hand. He pressed it against her thigh. She looked down at his big hand, at the hairs on it, and wondered why women gave themselves to men when it only came to this: a hand or another part of the body.

At her high school girls ran around with boys their own age, wild kids. They did anything and they got no money in return. She could not understand them; their excited talk in the washroom was as incomprehensible to her as another language. The girls were always saying, "Oh, I love him so, I'm crazy about him"—and Maureen, curious, vaguely repulsed, could hear through their words a ragged tenderness that was mysterious. They were like creatures of another element, these girls, wild and pretty, with their hair teased high on their heads and their lips bright red, their stockings, their shoes, their clothes bought tight to show the trim bulk of their bodies. They wore identification bracelets that left dull green marks on their wrists. They wore boys' rings on chains around their necks, chains that left faint green marks. Sisterly in their passion, their need to fall into the maniacal grasp of some boy and give up everything to him, they gathered in nervous, delighted groups and talked. Sometimes they talked in whispers, as if in church. The regulation jumpers of the school could not contain their excited breathing. Their hands flurried in identical gestures, showing helplessness, a stricken delight, a crazy, extravagant falling. It was incomprehensible.

Maureen stared at this man's hand, his fingers entwined with hers. She did not understand why human beings willingly entwined their bodies together, what need had to be so greedily and violently satisfied, why there was such a rush at the last moment to come together, to get it done . . . His skin was coarse. Yet there was something tender and vulnerable about it. Beneath the surface of the skin were three large blue veins, looking swollen, and four bones that led out from his knuckles, raising the surface of his skin. Maureen stared down at his hand. She felt that she was going insane. . . .

He was a man, a stranger, looking up at her over a copy of a magazine. His eyes continued on her the way they had run along the line of print, pointing her out, assessing her.

She was walking home from school and a car passed her. The car slowed. She did not slow her walk or quicken it but continued along the sidewalk. A prickly feeling began on the side of her face. What danger?

Her mother and another woman chattering: about the Negro man who sold Bibles and got into women's homes and slashed at their breasts with a knife. He wore a trench coat and dark glasses and was well groomed. He attacked both white and Negro women. He himself had light skin. He was attractive. He wore a trench coat. He was on foot. He could turn up at anyone's door, selling Bibles. Behind his dark glasses there were probably ordinary eyes, though no one had seen them. He carried a paring knife.

They were driving near the expressway construction. The expressway was cutting its way north through the city. Everywhere there were mud and giant orange girders. Some were erected over the expressway, some lay in the mud. Men worked in the mud. There were several steam shovels and trucks and many men. Maureen saw a man who looked like Furlong, standing by the side of the street, staring out, smoking.

She was scrubbing at the kitchen floor, the linoleum. You could never get those black and white squares clean. The soap had a harsh, pleasant smell. The floor dried unevenly; some parts shone, others dried and looked dirty right away. The white blocks of linoleum were yellowish.

A friend of Loretta's, talking in the kitchen with her: "His father is dying of cancer, so I said we'd like the car when he dies, and the old bitch got mad. Who else deserves the car more than us, with Bob working all the way out to Ford's?"

Some hillbillies were standing on the sidewalk waiting to cross the street. Maureen could tell them by their pale, strained, sleepy, suspicious faces; they were lean and yet clumsy. A man of about thirty stared toward her. His face was pale, as if finely powdered, a soft, rodent-like face. She wondered if he was someone's brother. . . .

The motel was made of concrete blocks painted beige. A neon sign with large looping letters stuck out toward the street. Because of an overpass nearby the motel looked sunken, and a large puddle had formed in front of its driveway. Two cars were parked at one end of the court, license plates from New York and Ontario, Canada. There were beige drapes of a synthetic material, fireproof, in the room. Maureen drew them. The bedspread was tan with strips of red and black. It looked familiar. The man was unbuttoning his shirt, looking down. Maureen shook her head to get her vision clear: she was thinking about the girls at school, huddled in the restroom, smoking forbidden cigarettes and talking with joy of forbidden things . . . she was thinking about the Negro Bible salesman who carried a paring knife.

The man came to her and embraced her. She put her arms around him. She was deathly afraid but could not remember why.

They were driving back home, along the expressway. Overpasses were half constructed; the expressway itself ended, suddenly. Great chunks of the city had been taken out, houses and earth. Trees lay toppled over where they had fallen, still. Their roots were a cluster of thin threads and clods of mud. Maureen realized slowly where she had gotten the idea of an earthquake from. Beyond the houses that still remained standing, beyond the trees that had not yet been plowed over, the sky had turned a late afternoon pink, stained by smoke from downriver. Maureen's eyes took this all in and tried to appreciate it; it was precarious enough, any kind of beauty.

The man said, "I wish they'd get this damn expressway finished!"

"Sometimes we could keep on going maybe," Maureen said. Her voice was weak and shrill. "For a ride, a long ride."

He glanced at her. "Sure. A good idea."

"I'd like to go for a long ride sometime, maybe over to the bridge and into Canada, and along in there—I've never been to Canada."

"Sure, we'll do that sometime."

He let her out a block from home and she hurried home. She was carrying her schoolbooks. Her body had become numb. Halfway there she saw a girl in jeans jump out of a doorway; it was her sister.

"Hey, Reeny," Betty said, "what the hell gives? The old guy is mad as hell. He's waiting for you up there. You'd better not go up."

Maureen stared at her. She hugged her schoolbooks against her chest.

"What's it all about?" Betty asked, frank and curious.

"Ma says to tell you to come where she is, at Ginny's. I'm going to spend the night there too. You better not go home first, he's mad as hell. He's drunk."

Maureen went on by.

"Reeny, why is he mad at you? Is he just drunk? He was knocking some stuff around in our room, the bastard, and he found some money in a book of yours. Where'd you get all that money, Reeny?"

"Never mind."

Maureen was hurrying toward the corner where they lived. She wondered if Furlong was looking out the window, waiting for her.

"Did you steal it, Reeny? Where'd you get it all from? Them big bills?"

"Never mind. Shut up."

Maureen got away from her and went up the stairs to the apartment. She walked slowly. She heard nothing.

Betty shouted up at her, "You're crazy! Come back down! He's madder than hell—you want your teeth kicked out? Says he's gonna turn you over to the cops, on account of that money . . ."

As Maureen pushed the door to the apartment it swung open.

He was coming toward her. She could see a mess behind him—the sofa wrenched sideways away from the wall, a cushion on the floor, the coffee table knocked over. He was wearing the same jacket he'd worn a few hours before, out on the street. It was still zipped up tight. He came toward her and seized her by the neck and dragged her into the room. He was shouting something she couldn't catch. She heard the words but they were so close to her, battering her, that she could not make them out. With his free hand he began striking her. He held her up so that she couldn't fall and struck her, again and again, while she tried to get away, to fall backwards, away from his hand. She screamed. He began to strike her body. He let go of her and she fell. She put her arms up over her head and screamed against the floor, the linoleum floor, while he bent over to pound her flat on the back with his fists.

2

To Whose Country
Have I Come?

The air thickens suddenly. She shuts her eyes. A haze sweeps upon her, a horn sounds close by. MAUREEN, WHAT THE HELL ARE YOU DOING! *Someone takes her arm. Good. To be held safe, good. Her arm is held tight, impatiently, and she feels her body emptying out, her head emptying out . . . her body turns into a delicate, fleshly shell and is very thin. A man's voice is saying something near her ear. The tinkle of coins. Traffic, horns. The smell of exhaust smoke. She is already on the bus, with her mother still gripping her, when she turns and sees her self step out of her body, with a sudden convulsive movement, freeing itself, escaping. This self is her. It steps down to the sidewalk again, pushing past other people who want to get on the bus. It glances back up at her. Everything rushes out of Maureen now and joins that other body, that free body, running away . . . it is like the terrible pressure of water wanting to burst free. How she yearns to join that body, get loose, scream with the pain and terror of getting loose . . .*

SIT HERE, SIT STILL. FOR CHRIST'S SAKE, *says her mother.*

She sits. She turns wildly to look through the window, to where her other self stands on the sidewalk. Crowds pass. People, strangers, seem to break around her, not touching her. They pass around her. They become invisible while she herself, that other self, becomes vivid and dazzling, standing on the sidewalk with her head turned back at a painful angle, looking at Maureen on the bus, her face guilty and wild.

1

Jules was sitting in the kitchen of the small cluttered apartment, staring into his coffee cup. On the table beside him was a potted plant with large dyed pink flowers.

"Don't worry, she's going to be all right," Loretta was saying. "She's getting a lot of rest, she's feeling low and broken-down, but who the hell doesn't? A woman grows up to take all the shit she can from men, then she breaks down, that's the way it is but kid *I* am not going to break down. He can rot in jail."

"Four months isn't any rotting in jail."

"Four months! Four lousy shitty months!"

Jules acknowledged this with a twist of his mouth. He was eighteen now and carried himself up into this apartment like a man carrying something breakable, with a look of regret and apprehension. He loved his mother. He loved his sister. He hated fearing them and their contamination, thinking it showed up a weakness in himself, and so he sat stiff at the kitchen table, aware of his mother's angry, heavy breathing and the ticking of the eternal clock on the refrigerator. He longed to jump up and break into a routine of horseplay. Most of the time he was kidding around. Why not imitate Furlong's apish smile, that forlorn try of his at being a *good man?* Why not dance around the table the way he did with other people, showing off, a bright young kid who never took himself seriously? People said to him, "Jules, you're crazy!" as they rocked with laughter, or they said, "Jules, you ought to be on television!" But now he could not imagine why anyone thought him amusing. He sat in his mother's latest little apartment, on edge with the prospect of seeing what was in the next room, clothed in being a son, a brother, someone dragged to the bottom of the river by chains of blood and love. . . .

"You think it isn't too bad then?" Jules said, stirring. "I was talking to Betty the other day—"

"The hell with her. What she knows goes on the head of

207

a pin. I'm about ready to wash my hands of that little brat, let me tell you."

"Ma, you feel all right yourself, don't you?"

"Why do you ask?"

Since Maureen's beating back in April, and Furlong's arrest, and the various stages of the divorce, Loretta had changed: she had a haggard look all the time. Sometimes, Jules thought, she looked almost intelligent, as if this suffering had taught her something. He leaned forward against the table and rested his chin in his hands. Energetic elsewhere, almost feverish with energy, he felt tired and old in his mother's presence. He felt that he was gradually aging while she remained the same age; he wanted this to come about, simply so that he could guide her life. They'd been together so long, Jules and his mother, he'd known her consciously before she had even noticed him, he was shrewder than she, he could see around corners and Loretta of course could barely see in front of her. This morning her face had a subdued, cautious look to it, and her thin eyebrows, above her sharp eyes, gave her a delicate look. Jules could see a ghostly image of Maureen's face in her. Maureen was going to grow up into this face.

"Well, can I talk to her?"

"She's probably asleep."

"Last time I came she was asleep. Does she sleep all the time?"

"No, not all the time," Loretta said impatiently. She picked her baby up from a kind of crib in which it had been lying. Its face and arms were reddened, as if with a rash. Jules looked at his half-brother without much interest, wondering why he had no interest. "She watches television. I talk to her, we get along, it's just when that brat Betty makes trouble that things get bad. Look, Jules, I had a talk about Reeny with a doctor down at the clinic, and he says she'll snap out of it."

"When was that?"

"The end of April."

"Well, it's June now—is she any better?"

"She's lots better."

"Why won't she come out of that room?"

"She's resting. She's getting back her strength. She eats everything I make for her, so she's all right. She's got a real good appetite, Jules, and a nurse told me that was a good sign."

"Which nurse where?" Jules said impatiently.

"Oh, a real nice woman I met on the bus, a registered nurse. We got to talking, and I told her a little about Maureen—"

"Jesus, a nurse on the bus!"

"What's wrong with a nurse on the bus? What do you want? You want me to get your sister dumped in some nuthouse somewhere, you want me to forget her? What the hell do you know about it? My father wasn't crazy until they got hold of him, then after that he went to pieces, he was always sitting around in dirty underwear and he stank and they were all like that, up there. Besides, do you know that women get pregnant in those places—yes, they do— there are only a few nurses and what-d'ya-call-it, attendants, and a couple of doctors, and at night all kinds of crazy things happen. It's a dump, that place, all those places!" Loretta said, drawing anger out of herself as if to justify everything to Jules. "All kinds of things go on! Dirty things! Things you wouldn't believe! All he did was beat her up, kid, but in that dump she'd get a lot worse and she'd never get back to normal again. I know. The things a woman has to take from men can drive her crazy, and Maureen needs to stay away from them until she can figure them out."

"But Betty told me—"

"The hell with her! She's like you, running around! She spends half her time with so-called *friends* and one of them is a nigger girl seventeen years old!"

"Ma, don't interrupt me, please," Jules said. He tried to smile. There was always some weakness in his mother for a smile, for a touch of courtesy. "What Betty said was that there was a lot of money in her room, Maureen's money. That's what she said, she told me."

"That wasn't Maureen's money, it was *his* money."

"Betty said it was Maureen's. She kept it in a book."

"No, it was *his* money he was hiding from me. He hid it, the bastard, and got drunk and tried to say that Maureen had stole it from somewhere—he said that both of them, Maureen and Betty, had stole it—that's exactly what he said—"

"Betty's story is different."

"She's lying! She's a goddam brat on her way to jail, and when they come around with her I'm going to tell them to lock her up and throw away the key! Her and her goddam nigger friend and her ugly face! No, he tried to say it was

Maureen's money that she stole, but it was his own money that he got from some place and was hiding from me."

"Then it isn't true what Betty says that . . . that Maureen was out on the street?"

"Jesus! Of course that isn't true," Loretta said.

Jules looked over toward the closed door that led to Maureen's room. He could hear his mother breathing quickly. He said after a moment, "Well, I didn't believe it exactly but . . ."

"But what?"

"But Betty said, and also another kid. . . ."

"They're crazy! And anyway Betty has always been jealous of Maureen, you know that."

"If she had money, why would she hide it? Why hide it all?"

"Sure, why hide it?" Loretta said quickly. "Kids don't hide money. It isn't natural. I know Betty is getting money from somewhere but she won't let on. I'm through with her. She spends it right away on clothes and junk. In fact, her and that nigger bitch are going to buy a motor scooter—how the hell do you like that? It's going to look nice, my daughter riding around with a nigger on a scooter! But kids all spend money right away, Reeny wouldn't be any different. No, it was *his* money all along and he got drunk and tried to blame it on Maureen because they never did get along. He was jealous of her and you too, because of me . . . he knew I loved my kids more than I did him and that used to drive him wild. No, she wasn't doing that. Christ, if I thought—"

"Okay, Ma."

"A prostitute—"

"Okay."

"Don't listen to what they say back in the old neighborhood. They shoot their mouths off all the time. I'll be glad when it's all torn down, then those fat bitches won't be able to stand around gabbing about people's troubles . . . I'll be glad when they dig out for the expressway right through it, those goddam drunk Irish anyway! Half of them are nuts. The niggers are moving in from down town and the Mexicans from the other side, so it's going to be a hot time one of these days. Who do you hang around with from back there? That Ramie Malone?"

"I don't hang around with him or anybody."

"Who are your friends now, Jules?"

"I didn't come over to talk about them."

"Jules—"

"Can I talk to Maureen?"

Loretta looked sadly at him. After a while she said, "Sure. But watch this kid, will you? I mean, if he rolls over or anything." She put the baby back in the crib; it was neither awake nor asleep. It had a plump, dopey face, with surprised tufts of hair on its head. Jules thought her request was strange, that he should watch over the baby though she was only going to look in Maureen's room—was everything so precarious to her now? She had seemed so reasonable all this time.

She got up and went into the other room. Jules, uncomfortable, looked into the baby's face. Furlong's baby. Left behind for Loretta to raise. It slept and took in nourishment and even had a name—Randolph—and was much heavier than it had been the last time he'd seen it; so many babies being born! On his way to this dump of a building he had seen a Negro girl of about fifteen chatting with two Negro boys, toeing the sidewalk, passing the time of day, the boys with big knowing eyes and wild hair and the girl with a dark merry face, about seven months pregnant, just passing the time of day out on the street. His mother's remark about women getting pregnant at the state hospital had startled him. He had never heard that. He'd heard plenty of other things about that place and about the various jails, but he had never heard that. One time, put in Children's Shelter overnight, he had gone through something terrible and he did not often let himself think about it, and he was a boy, a boy. What might happen to a girl he did not want to think about either. Enough had happened to Maureen already.

Loretta leaned around the door. "Okay," she said. "Come on in. She wants to see you."

The room was a shock to him: peeling wallpaper, plaster fallen out in queer patches, a light bulb fixed in a socket overhead. He felt suddenly very warm. Maureen, sitting up in bed, staring toward him, was also a shock.

"Hi, Maureen," Jules said. He held out the pot of flowers to her. When she gave no sign of noticing them he set them on the window sill. "How are you?"

She stared at him. She was sitting up, propped against a pillow. The covers were drawn up around her though the room was warm. Her hair had grown long and straggly, worse then the hair he saw on broken-down women in the city, and her face had a puffed, plump, shiny look to it. It had been about a month since he'd seen her last and in that short time she had put on a lot of weight.

"She feels fine," Loretta said.

Loretta hovered behind him, moving the flowerpot on the sill. She went to the foot of the bed and tugged at the covers, trying to make them even. "Sit down, Jules, take a load off your feet," she said, giving him a poke.

Jules sat on the window sill. He looked toward his sister and tried to smile. Maureen was fumbling with something—not fumbling but just working her fingers on the edge of the blanket. Her fingers moved nervously but she herself was not nervous. She stared at him in a sleepy, steady way, unsurprised but rather cautious. He might have recognized her had he seen her out on the street, but maybe not.

"It's a real nice day today, you should come outside," Jules said. "I'm going to buy a car with a top that comes down—"

"A convertible!" Loretta said, poking him again—he shouldn't *talk down* to Maureen. "Isn't that nice, Reeny? You always liked to go for rides. When it gets warmer he can take you out, huh?"

Maureen's eyelashes seemed to flutter, yet she was not responding to her mother or to Jules. They waited, but nothing happened. She looked down at her fingers. Her face, once very pretty, was now gross and blemished; blotches had come out on her forehead and cheeks. On her left cheek was a rash of pimples that was nearly solid. Jules stared at her and could not look away.

"Say something, talk, tell her about yourself," Loretta said. "Tell her about driving down to St. Louis."

"Yes, I'm driving somebody down to St. Louis. It's a job. I'm driving a man who's in business down there," Jules said hollowly. "I mean, he's in business up here and needs to meet with someone down there . . . he's paying me a lot . . . he won't ride on planes or trains . . . and . . . and he's paying me a lot." He stared at Maureen, and she looked toward him, but their eyes did not meet. He felt as if he were on the brink of a terrible revelation. Suddenly trembling, he felt for his wallet. It was there. He was relieved that he hadn't lost it, that somebody hadn't picked it out of his pocket.

"I don't want to forget to give you something," he said awkwardly. He looked through the wallet. "You could probably use a little money. . . . Do you like this new place? The apartment?"

"It's okay," Loretta said.

"Why'd you move here, this particular place?"

"To be nearer downtown, nearer the welfare place. You got to go down there and argue with them, you know. . . ."

"It isn't dangerous around here?"

Loretta made a snorting, contemptuous noise. "You know what Detroit is," she said, laughing.

Jules tried to smile. He thought instead of this dump being broken open and the furniture in it—moved over the years from place to place, faithfully—stolen by niggers and hillbillies, and Loretta would do nothing about it, wouldn't even notice.

"How do they treat you at welfare?" Jules said.

"It depends if you get a bitch or not. Some of the guys are okay. I can handle them. You just get there early and wait in line. But this one fat guy, he wears sunglasses out on the job and is real sharp—*he* can trip you up on the price of shampoo and what's on sale at Kroger's this week. He asked me why *I* needed razor blades, who's in the family to use them, he said. Is there a man in the family not reported? The smart-ass bastard, I don't know if he was kidding or not. You got to be careful with them, joking with them. The joke always stops sometime."

Jules was nervously taking bills out of his wallet.

"I could maybe use a little something. Till next week," Loretta whispered.

She was shy: it was against welfare regulations for her to accept any money unless she reported it.

"You got enough for food? What's the rent here?"

"I could use a little," Loretta said, urgent and embarrassed.

He took a handful of bills out. He would have liked to shake them under Maureen's nose, to wake her up. *Didn't you do it for money? Didn't you? And now you're turning backwards into a saint, a pig of a saint . . .* But Maureen noticed nothing. Her eyes were large and drugged. He could not believe, glancing at this heavy, ugly girl, that she was the same girl who had been his sister. "Here, Ma," Jules said, handing her the money.

She took it from him and put it in her dress pocket, quickly. The transaction left them both breathless and a little ashamed.

"I got to answer all kinds of questions about you down there," Loretta said. "He wants to know how much you make. I told him you didn't come around, you left home and never bothered with us. Everybody says that, you know—I mean, all the mothers with kids bringing in money, as long as they don't live at home. They know you got a police record so they believe it. Well, kid, thanks a lot. I really mean it."

Maureen sat without moving. Only her fingers moved on the edge of the blanket. She might have been waiting for them both to go away.

"You want some coffee cake and some more coffee, Jules?" Loretta said. "Reeny and I usually have something to eat around now, doughnuts or something."

"I better be going."

"So soon?"

"I got to meet someone at noon."

"Let me get you something, it won't take a minute."

She went out, and he was left alone. He felt alone in the room, unwatched. Maureen did not see him and he could not bring himself to look at her any longer. His body felt unclean. His clothes were damp from perspiration. He thought of Maureen bloody and unconscious, and he thought about himself that night in Children's Shelter, where he'd been fooling around to show that he wasn't afraid, and all that punkish joyful violence had turned around on him . . . three kids had cornered him in a lavatory, drawn by his showing off . . . and so . . . they had slashed his arm with some glass, but that wasn't the part that sickened him . . . anyway it was over. He thought of Maureen in the hospital, with her blackened eyes and a large yellow swelling on her forehead, a rotten yellow. He thought of her teeth edged with blood. Furlong had really beaten her up and must have been trying to kill her. Now he was in jail for four months. Jules felt a terrible anger rise in him, a sense of madness—in four months that man would be out! He pressed his hands against his eyes, kneading them. He thought of Furlong and he thought of his own father, mixing the two together. He thought of the Children's Shelter, all those whining, whimpering, snot-nosed kids; he thought of himself prancing among them and showing off and of what they had done to him . . .

He jerked around, repulsed by the memory. But Maureen gave no sign of noticing him.

Loretta came back with a cheerful smile and offered him

some coffee cake. He shook his head no, feeling weak, and this weakness increased when he saw how greedily Maureen reached out for some coffee cake and how quickly she ate it. No, he wasn't going to sit here and watch her eat, not like that. He couldn't take it. Blundering backward, fixing his face in a bright awful smile, he said good-by to them and he'd be back soon and bring them a little money.

Loretta followed him out. She said anxiously in a low voice, "You take care of yourself, Jules. Don't worry about her. She has such a good appetite, that's a good sign. Some of them, when they get like this, you know, they have to be fed by tubes and things, by needles, and they get all skin and bones and weak and that's very bad, but Reeny eats everything I give her—"

"That's good," Jules said.

He escaped.

2

The car wasn't his but belonged to a man named Bernard, whom he had met through Faye.

Sitting up in his mother's smelly flat had made him feel rocky, and now he drove aimlessly around, staring at the unfamiliar buildings and houses. Gangs of kids were playing out on the street. White and Negro, mixed. More Negro. Jules could remember having been a kid who played in the street but the memory was from the outside, as if he'd seen himself playing and the memory had stuck to him, photographed.

So she had a good appetite, which was a good sign . . .

The weather should have been mild, but its mildness was oppressive; bits of soot fell against the windshield of the car. Jules had had the car washed just recently. He felt as if he himself were being soiled. Faye was a fastidious woman, fastidious about her body. He could remember Maureen making supper, working with food, rinsing food off dishes after supper, cleaning up, wiping up, her face slightly flushed and content.

He needed to buoy himself up. He needed to get high on driving this excellent car, and the jumble of Detroit and the anticipation of the drive he'd be setting out on that evening should have done it but somehow failed, something in him was sinking lower, lower . . . He could smell Detroit about him, a kind of stretched-out hole, a hole with a horizon. Had he ever lived out of this place? Or was that memory of the country a fraud?

He thought of the money he'd given his mother, the rumpled, soft, filthy feel of bills; that at least had happened.

He telephoned Faye but no one answered. He thought about going back to see his mother again, to ask more questions about Maureen. Better not. He hadn't enough time. He put the dime back in and dialed Faye's number again. No one answered. He had met Faye downtown, not long ago. He had stepped off a curb and almost been hit by a car, and a woman behind him had cried out. She yanked at his arm, pulling him back. The car sped on by, turning the corner, and Jules was left trembling on the street.

"That was pretty close," the woman had said.

She looked shaken and yet amused. Jules, who hadn't eaten for some time, felt dizzier when he turned and saw what she looked like. He turned blindly away, upset by her face. He had seen a vague, beautiful face, he hadn't been able to believe it. As he stumbled toward a drugstore entrance someone came out and bumped into him.

"Watch out!" the man shouted.

The woman stood watching him from the curb. Finally she said, "Are you all right?"

She had blond hair that was nearly silver, a metallic color he thought could not have been natural; she was about twenty-six and stood watching him. So they had met. She had children somewhere, put away somewhere; she had taken him up into her life out of a languid, cynical indifference, seeing something in his face, feeling sorry for him, though she was attached permanently to another man, who lived in the suburb of Bloomfield Hills and who was permanently married. It was Faye who decided that she and Jules would meet. He had stood trying to collect his wits, and she had stood eying him, still amused, wondering. He was a little frightened by her. His face burned from his having made such a fool of himself, two times in her presence, two times in one minute. He believed that he had never seen a woman with such sharp, attractive features, a woman almost manly in the level flat look of her eyes. She wore a dark fur coat and nothing on her head, and her blond hair was cut very severely to frame her face, coming down in small delicate points before her ears, exposing the ears, giving her an ascetic, impatient look. He was intimidated by her face and her coat.

She came up to him. "Let me get a cab," she said.

He was unable to speak. He could not have turned away if he'd wanted to. He stood shy and alarmed, waiting for her, until she got hold of a cab and the two of them climbed in, suddenly together. She sat in the back seat of the cab, beside him, entirely used to such services and not very daring; there was a terrible impersonal dignity about her. She told the driver a number on East Jefferson. Jules felt a stab of pleasure, for his body was shrewder than his imagination —it recognized the worth of East Jefferson, the worth of this woman's manner and the rings on her fingers.

They got out at her apartment building. Across the river was Belle Isle, very still. The woman paid the cab driver. Jules began to breathe quickly and shallowly, wondering if the world had suddenly become perfect or whether he was reading everything wrong. She turned back to him. Her face showed a sisterly amusement, yet a kind of superior affection.

"Do you want to come up?" she said.

Jules narrowed his eyes at this. It must be a trick. Half of him lunged for surprises, the most unlikely of treats—he was still waiting for his rich Uncle Samson to give him a job— and the other half drew back sour and knowing. "Up there? Up to your place?" he said. "Isn't there somebody at the door—somebody watching?"

She laughed. "Well, come up or not. You look pretty bad," she said.

Her voice was level and really not adventuresome. So that first day she brought him home with her, and he gave in, shaken and elated, looking hard at the gleam of good dark wood—he supposed it was good, at least it looked old and expensive—trying to fit himself in with this adventure, to adjust himself. New places made him nervous, put him off. He had to adjust his breathing. Glancing sideways at her in the elevator, he caught her eye and, quick to exaggerate any mood of his, he brought his fingers to his forehead in a gesture of helplessness, expelling his breath—and it was a successful thing to do, it worked, she broke into a smile and liked him. He could feel her liking him. He needed that. "My God," he said, pretending to be overwhelmed at the same time that he was truly overwhelmed, not able to figure her out. Once in her apartment she began to talk, chatting, but still he could not figure her out.

"Yes, I should get a job. I've worked since I was fifteen

and always liked it. Jobs are healthy. They're releases for aggression." She opened the drapes to her windows and the sky above Belle Isle hurt Jules's eyes, too brilliant. "My name is Faye," she said, suddenly coming to him. She shook his hand.

"My name is Jules."

He was really very weak.

"The apartment is a mess because I sleep late. Then I go for a walk," she said. She walked around, fixing things, arranging cushions. He could not see that she was straightening out anything. "I don't eat until around four. I hate food. It's disgusting, when you consider it. And the need for food, having bodies and being reduced to *eating food*—did you ever think about that?"

"Yes. No," said Jules.

They sat in two chairs, facing each other. He was alert and very nervous; she was becoming calmer all the while. She looked almost bored. Under her coat she wore a yellow wool dress; the yellow blurred in Jules's vision and confused him. She had let the coat fall onto a sofa and it was sliding slowly to the floor. He sat on edge, wondering what would happen. Why did she talk about food?

"Sometimes I send out for Chinese food. A restaurant down the street, very nice," she said. "If you stay a while we can send out for food from that place . . . I don't want to bother going out for a long time."

Jules got up and lunged for her coat, which was sliding down. "Your coat—" he said.

"Oh, let it fall. Why are you so jumpy?"

She herself sat calmly eying him, unsurprised. Now that she sat with the coat off, her legs crossed, at home, she had a kind of sloppy, brittle quality about her; she was almost boyish. She stared at him.

She reached out to straighten a pile of magazines. "I do a lot of reading, there's all this here—you can look through them if you want. Actually I've got nothing planned until Sunday afternoon. What about you? I do a lot of reading. I'm alone a lot. But no, I guess I don't really read. I look through the magazines and lose interest. I can't seem to make myself get interested in anything all the way to the end."

Jules shifted his position in the chair, trying to calm the beating of his heart. He asked himself, *Is this really going to happen?* He searched her face for some clue of a joke, some ironic smirk. Nothing. She was very serious and at the same time very casual.

"Why are you staring at me like that?" she said.

"I'm sorry—"

"What are you thinking about?"

"Nothing."

"Tell me."

"I'm thinking, is this a trick or not? A trick—"

"What's a trick?"

He got unsteadily to his feet. Then, after a long and very awkward pause, he knelt before her. He began to kiss her hands, trembling.

She touched him on the back of the neck. "No, it isn't a trick," she said, not gently, but just explaining.

Later that night she told him about her family. She talked quickly and with an air of detachment, as if Jules were not particularly close to her, as if his infatuation for her meant little. She had come from a small town in Ohio and had been married there for five years, to a man she couldn't remember very well now. "I don't remember his face exactly," she told Jules. "Do you think that's strange? The face of my grade-school teacher is much clearer in my mind."

Jules was already in love and eager to agree that it was strange, everything was strange, what she said and what she didn't say. He was in a daze. He had forgotten his hunger. While she talked to him he embraced her and lay with her, in her thoughtful arms, and wept with the sweetness of her body and its remoteness. He felt as if the very bottom of his soul had been stirred. There could be no threat to him because the woman was so detached herself, wanting nothing from him. She did not want to know *him*. The sensations he felt made his own body seem unreal to him. *Did this really happen? How did this happen?* She talked casually about her family, and he felt with jealousy how this family tugged at her, though she could not really remember them. Two daughters. A husband. Parents. The burdensome center of her life was back in Ohio, not here with Jules, and she had to talk about it in her cool, wistful, indifferent way, getting nowhere. Jules thought, dazzled, *Is everyone like this, trying to get free? To work themselves out of other people?*

He had thought that first night that he would fall deeper and deeper in love with her, and the thought frightened him, but it turned out that he felt nothing more than what he had felt at first. Nothing stronger followed.

They became friends. He drove her around. He had coffee with her at odd times of the day. They drifted together, so that Faye could talk about herself; they were drawn together for no reason that Jules could figure out, except this. When she had nothing else to do in the evening, he came out to visit like a cousin or a brother. He was dark, slender, abashed. She was fair and cold, as impersonal as the hostess of a cocktail lounge. At this time Jules was living in a single room in a boardinghouse, a few miles from his mother's place, though he had not told Loretta his address. His freedom was important. He was free. Every thought dragged him back to that mess of a family but technically he was free. "I think that if I could get enough money to fix them all up," he told Faye, "to get some good doctor for my sister, then . . . I guess I'd take off for California and see what's out there."

"There's nothing out there," Faye said, yawning.

"Nothing?" cried Jules.

She drank liquor and he drank soda pop. He hated the taste of liquor and beer, remembering how Loretta had given him beer to shut him up years ago; it was associated with his mother. He hated any kind of alcohol. It was important for him to be alert always. Being in love deadened his alertness and at the same time made his skin tender, as if the very outer layer of skin had been peeled off to leave his flesh exposed. But he was not really in love. He kept slipping in and out of love with this woman, who showed only affection for him, and that strangely genial affection; he carried her presence with him everywhere, dreaming of their evenings together and trying to imagine what she felt. He no longer saw any girls his own age. He had forgotten them. In love with Faye, he would wake suddenly in the morning to think that it was impossible—he had to extricate himself, with a laugh. He couldn't love a woman older than himself, he couldn't love a woman who was the mistress of a married man . . . it was impossible . . .

"How can you stand it? Your arrangement with him?" Jules asked.

"I don't know what you mean."

"I couldn't stand anything like that myself."

"You don't have to stand it."

"But even if you liked him, if you wanted to marry him, seriously—after a beginning like this it would be all rotten, wouldn't it?"

"You don't know what you're talking about."

"But don't you ever get low? Want to kill yourself?"

"I wanted to kill myself off and on when I was married, but not now. Now I never think about it," she said. "I had all that straight life back home. I went through all the stages. I had two little girls, you know, they're in good hands. I just fell out of it, I lost interest. You have to believe in all that to keep it up. My ex-husband married again, I heard, and I wish him well."

"You never think of him any more, of loving him? All that is gone?"

"Of course."

"But isn't that strange?"

"Why is it strange?" She laughed.

There was something steely in her that alarmed Jules, because she was a girl from the country and he, he liked to think, was a tough boy from the city, very knowing. But he hadn't her hardness. "So you don't worry about your kids? And this guy you see now, you never worry about him—going back to his wife, changing his mind?"

"He can't go back to his wife because he hasn't left her. She doesn't know anything. They get along very well. I know all about her, everything. This is something in the air here," she said with a small smirk, "they're all crazy with it, in this town. They live out in Grosse Pointe or in Bloomfield and they want to keep something hidden somewhere else—they're willing to pay a lot for it. My God! I could tell you about a woman I know, like me she came up here by herself, and she's rich now and would never have to fool around or worry about anything, and the crazy thing is that there was something wrong with her all along, inside—she'd had an operation and her womb is partly supported by metal or plastic or something, and if any of those men knew it they'd be sick. But how could a man know it? They don't know anything. She gets along very well." All the scandals of automotive Detroit, the anguish of millionaires and half-millionaires, living in homes far from the city's fumes and danger but terribly restless in those homes—Faye had no particular interest in this anguish but knew enough to recognize its value.

It was through Faye that Jules met Bernard Geffen.

Jules was with her one evening when the telephone rang. She answered it and said, "Sure, come on up. No, he isn't." Jules was very hurt. In a few minutes a shaggy, nervous man in a raincoat appeared in her doorway, wet from the rain. Faye embraced him languidly, in a gesture so ritualized as to strike Jules as lovely. The man brushed her cheek with his lips. He was already smiling over his shoulder at Jules.

"This is my good friend Jules Wendall," she said. "This is my good friend Bernard Geffen."

"Wendall, is it? Wendall? I'm very pleased to meet you!" the man said, shaking Jules's hand. Jules sensed something odd, unbalanced; this man was over fifty and looked prosperous, but he was shaking Jules's hand as if Jules were an important person. "Are you the one Faye has told me about? You keep her company, go to movies and all that? You're very young. It's very nice, I'm sure—I mean—"

"Take off your coat," Faye said coldly.

They spent an awkward hour or more, Bernard still in his coat, Jules wondering why he didn't leave, Faye leafing through a fashion magazine and trying to keep up a mysterious conversation with Bernard. Jules could not make out what the conversation was about. A trip to Florida? South America? Someone's yacht?

"I'll put it to you, son," Bernard said, turning his watery gray eyes on Jules, "do you think I should make the investment? Another boat? It's a fifty-thousand-dollar investment, but, more than that, you have to consider that I would get no interest on it, which of course I'd be getting even if it was just in a bank."

Jules stared.

"There are various kinds of investments. Some depreciate, some grow. Look here," Bernard said, taking Faye's hand to show Jules her ring, "this diamond is worth—let me guess —nine thousand, ten thousand? Or don't you know, my dear? Whatever it's worth, it will be worth more in a few years, obviously, and in the meantime it can be worn, it's very beautiful, and does justice to your beautiful hand."

"Is this worth ten thousand dollars?" Faye laughed.

"Certainly. But it isn't yours, you simply wear it, you exhibit it. You have no problems, you pay no insurance, you couldn't even sell it if you wanted to. That's one kind of investment. A boat, on the other hand," he said, sighing like an old mariner, "a boat—did I show you this snapshot, Faye?" He took out his wallet and extricated a picture. Faye looked at it and passed it to Jules without comment. It was a color picture of a woman standing on the deck of a large pleasure craft, dressed in white, a rather dumpy though pretty woman no longer young. "That's my wife there. Ex-wife," Bernard said. "She died of cancer last year."

"I'm sorry to hear that," Jules said politely. The woman in white struck him as doomed, even then.

"We were together for a long time, off and on," Bernard said. "Her trouble was that she didn't understand me and therefore didn't trust me. Everyone in her family had money but they also worked. They held down jobs. She didn't understand my family, my father. I felt trapped inside her head." He looked up at Jules, smiling. "My boy, would you be interested in working for me this summer? On my new boat? Maybe on my new boat?"

Jules handed him back the snapshot. A certain movement of the man's fingertips made him suspicious.

"Doing what?"

"Helping out. A cabin-boy."

"I drive a truck."

"I could pay you much more."

"But I have a job. I enjoy driving." Jules felt his mouth growing tighter, and he was puzzled at this caution. So he said with forced enthusiasm, "But it might be a good idea, being on the water. It would be healthy."

"We could go down to the Caribbean!" Bernard said. "Your dear friend Faye could make me very happy if only she wanted to—maybe you could convince her? If the trip interested you, perhaps it would interest her? If I put you on my payroll now, months ahead of time?"

"Bernard, are you crazy? I thought you didn't have any money," Faye said.

"I have money as of last Saturday," he said. He was very nervous.

Jules, anxious to escape, looked with concern at Bernard's warm, damp, rather broad forehead; there was something childlike and yet weary about this man, whoever he was, as if the peculiar energy that inspired him to talk for minutes on end might shake his feet into dancing and drive him to a frenzy, only to let him fall limp again. Rivulets of sweat ran down his forehead.

"A certain loan came through. I admit that I have no fixed income like your friend, and I have no desire for it," he said to Faye. "I like adventure. I don't dare prophesy where my liking for adventure will lead. I think you know, but still it mustn't ever be spoken between us, for your own sake and for the sake of your young friend here."

"What do you mean?" Jules asked in alarm.

"Both of you, good night. I'm going to bed," said Faye.

She got them to the door. There Bernard slipped his arm around Jules's shoulders and said, "She's like a northern princess. A fairy-tale princess, very cold, enchanting. Jules, my boy, let me put you on my payroll right now. I feel shaky tonight and I'd like you to drive me home. What do you think about that, Faye, is it all right?"

"Of course. Good night," said Faye.

They were standing together in the corridor. Jules looked back at the door, puzzled. He did not know whether to be angry or not, whether his honor demanded that he pound on the door or push Bernard away from him.

Bernard was saying, "But you do have a driver's license?"

"Yes."

"You'll drive me home then?"

"Where do you live?"

"Not far. Hardly a mile."

He was shorter than Jules, an agitated, busy man. He needed to move his hands in order to speak. The expensive trench coat was rumpled and stained; his trouser cuffs were spotted with mud; his shoes needed polishing. Going down in the elevator, he talked into Jules's ear confidentially and rapidly, as if talking into a telephone receiver. Jules wondered if he was crazy.

"I like to have people on my payroll whom I can trust. Friends of friends. Faye was mistaken about my not having money—women don't understand these things. They only understand money when they can see it. They're very crude essentially. They don't understand where money comes from or what it means or how a man can be worth money though he hasn't any at the moment. But a man understands such things."

"I suppose so," said Jules.

"What kind of people are your family?"

"My uncle is Samson Wendall, maybe you've heard of him?"

"Isn't he in . . . in trucking?"

"Tool and die."

"Tool and die, yes. Wendall. The name is familiar, a nice name," Bernard said. "And your name is Julian? Jules! Yes, good, Jules, my problem is that I take things much too seriously, I get very excited, a kind of faintness rises in me— it might be high blood pressure. But I conceive of life as drama, I conceive of history as a tragedy unfolding, and . . . and I need someone to drive my car for me, I have difficulties just in getting around, the most mundane things. I had a driver, a Negro, but he was always having accidents. I had to let him go. He set fire to the back seat of the car. I still haven't gotten around to fixing it. What would you say to one hundred dollars a week?"

"One hundred?"

"Two hundred, should we say two hundred dollars a week?"

"Do I just drive a car? Just around the city?"

"I will want to go to Toronto, St. Louis, and Buffalo sometime soon, depending upon how business works out," Bernard said quickly, as if he didn't want Jules to check any of this, "but in general it would only be around Detroit. I need someone who can keep secrets. I need someone who's intelligent, like you—it's obvious from your face that you're intelligent. Let me take you somewhere and get your hair cut."

"My hair cut?" Jules said.

"It's too long. You need a new suit. You need a coat. It doesn't matter how I look, I'm beyond all that, but you should look right. Drive me home and keep the car overnight and come back in the morning with your hair cut. All right?"

"Keep the car?"

"Yes. Overnight," said Bernard. They were out on the street. He was both enthusiastic and worried. He kept glancing around over his shoulder, as if he expected someone to run up behind him and put an end to this folly. "Here's my car," he said as they approached a Lincoln parked at the curb, ticketed, "and here are my keys."

Jules saw that he tore up the ticket, very agitated, but probably without knowing what he was doing.

"I live at a hotel downtown. It's very convenient to Faye's place but, you know, she rarely lets me see her. Her life is terribly simple and yet terribly complicated. You must tell me about her sometime, your subjects of conversation with her."

Jules drove to the hotel, and before Bernard got out he leaned forward against the seat and handed Jules something. "Here's a check. Cash it in the morning and take care of yourself and come back to get me. We'll take Faye out to lunch if she's up. Get your hair cut. Get a new suit."

Jules looked at the check: it was made out to Jules Wendall for one hundred dollars.

At ten the next morning Jules went to the National Bank of Detroit, and there he sweated out a teller's suspicions for some fifteen minutes, though he had a driver's license to show who he was. "Just a moment," the girl said. Jules, so close to one hundred dollars that his stomach had begun to ache, lost himself in staring at the frizzy hair of a Negro teller at the next window, counting out bills. Endless bills. One hundred dollars was coming to him . . . a gift . . . an enchantment. His teller was making a telephone call. Jules tried not to hear what she said, for what if she were saying, *Oh, the account has been closed? Oh?* Jules thought of the one hundred dollars, which he needed. Bernard would be like a father to him. Already he had recognized Jules's intelligence and was willing to invest in him and put him on his payroll. . . . His teller was saying, "Thank you," brightly, and, as if nothing had happened, as if she'd never been suspicious, she went to a money drawer and began taking out bills. Jules watched. She took out four bills, then two bills. She came to Jules and counted them onto the marble-topped counter, near Jules's itchy hand.

". . . one hundred dollars!" she said.

"Thank you," said Jules hoarsely.

He went out into the overcast Detroit morning. The hundred dollars was safe in his wallet. His wallet was safe in his back pocket, pressed against his body by the pressure of his tight trousers. He braced the wind across the way to the Sheraton-Cadillac, where he had his hair cut. It was important to him that he have it cut here, though it was an ordeal to sit in that perfumy, silent barbershop—too aware of himself, Jules Wendall getting his hair cut and worrying about how much to tip the barber—and, a while later, it was an ordeal to get himself out of his tight trousers in a fitting room, trying on new clothes. He needed a new suit. "This is exactly you, this is exactly right," the salesman said solemnly.

Jules believed anything. He was still in a daze, in love with Faye and with the promise of a new, chaotic, open future. "It's obvious from your face that you're intelligent," Bernard had said. Jules wanted to be loved and prized for that, above all—his intelligence.

He was very disappointed when the salesman said the suit would have to be altered; he couldn't wear it out of the store! It wouldn't be ready until Friday! So, clumsy and chagrined, he got back into his cheap trousers and coat, the back of his neck reddening.

He went down to pick up Bernard. The ache that had begun in the bank had spread through his whole body; it wasn't himself, Jules, who had quit one job for another, crazy job, an outlandish job, who was going to pick up someone named Bernard whom he wasn't sure he would recognize. Luckily Bernard was out on the sidewalk waiting for him. Jules managed to get the car to the curb without running it up on the sidewalk, and his shakiness didn't show when he leaned over to unlock the door to the back.

The Negro doorman opened it with a flourish, and Bernard swung in, sighing. "Oh, this morning air! This smog!" he said. He tipped the doorman—Jules couldn't see how much—and settled back onto the burned seat. "Drive straight ahead. I want to think. I have got to plan the rest of my life this morning," Bernard said.

A nerve in Jules was touched by that remark: planning the rest of his life that morning! He was sorry he had doubted Bernard. And why couldn't Jules plan the rest of his life too that very morning? Wasn't he free to make nearly anything happen?

3

When they called for Faye she wasn't in, or wouldn't answer her door. Bernard said sadly, "I don't know how I met that woman or what she means to me." He had a dramatic flair that would have been embarrassing in anyone else; but, sucking on his fingers in his nervousness, tugging at his collar, Bernard looked like a man involved in an invisible drama, helpless in his fate. They went back to the street. Bernard led the way, talking about the morning's stock-market report, and about the weather predictions, and the stuffing that was stuck to the back of his coat, from the car.

Jules felt a rush of affection for him, he was so unlike the men Jules knew.

"Yes, I must plan everything. I must get everything straight," Bernard said. "The trip to Toronto is off but the trip to St. Louis is more urgent than I'd thought. I have to make a connection there. And you, Jules, can you be ready to drive me in a few hours' notice? Do you have any family, anyone to take care of? How much money do you need?"

He got into the back seat. Jules, settling down behind the wheel, happened to glance into the rear-view mirror and saw the man's gray, serious face. Bernard's watery eyes were moving restlessly over the back of Jules's head.

"Money—do you need any? How much?"

"I guess I don't need any right now," Jules said, embarrassed.

"I'll give you something for your mother. For groceries." He made out a check, balancing the checkbook on his knee, and passed it up to Jules.

It was for two hundred dollars. Jules, surprised, took it from him and stared at it. "But, for groceries . . . ?"

"And now we must get started. I have a busy schedule this morning."

Jules started the car off with an energetic jerk. But almost at once Bernard said, snapping his fingers, "Wait! I want to run in here for a minute." He got out in front of a drugstore and motioned for Jules to drive around the block.

Jules drove off. He felt giddy from the surprise of this second check. It lay beside him on the seat, and he glanced down at it to make sure it was real. He thought he saw a mistake—the "hundred" was spelled wrong, spelled "hunred"? And would a teller accept that mistake or would the check be worthless?

He snatched up the check. No, "hundred" was spelled right. Someone honked at him angrily, a cab driver. Jules wrenched his car over to the right just in time. Yes, "hundred" was spelled right.

The third time he circled the block Bernard came out of the store on the run, his jowls shaking. "Quick, get in the left-turn lane. We've got business to do!" he said.

Jules had the idea that his driving was clumsy. He could not seem to calm himself. Out here in morning traffic and in an expensive car he hardly deserved, he was taking great risks—he might end up being worked over by some policemen, a punishment for his daring. But he guessed Bernard would notice nothing, not even a minor accident; and a minor accident wouldn't matter much. Bernard was in a hurry, sitting in the back seat. He seemed to be straining forward. There was a damp, sad, doggish smell about him. "Jules," he said dramatically, "something is going to happen within the next few hours that may change both our lives."

"What is it?"

"I can't tell you but it has to do with currency. With the gold market. Now do you understand?"

"I . . . I guess not."

"What day is it today, Jules?"

"June 18, 1956."

"Now do you know?"

"Know what?"

"Don't you read the papers?"

"I don't understand."

"Turn right here. No, watch out for the bus—yes, go ahead—get in the right lane."

Jules found himself swerving onto East Jefferson again.

Bernard said petulantly, "This afternoon we're getting a new car. I'm sick of this one! Look at this stuffing, it's all over my coat and in my nose—I have asthma—waiting for the insurance will take years, I'd just as soon take a tax loss. We'll get a new car this afternoon. A new Lincoln."

While Bernard talked Jules felt his heart swell with the idea of . . . something intangible and lovely . . . not just connected with money, but perfumed with the gray-green metallic odor of money, its power, and, more than that, its mysterious essence.

"Turn in here and get gas, we need gas!" Bernard cried.

The tank was nearly empty, and when it was filled Bernard cried, "How much is it? Who do I make the check out to?"

"I don't know if we take checks," the attendant said sullenly.

"Of course you take checks, nobody carries money today," Bernard said. "Who do I make it out to?"

"We just take cash."

"Jules, give him the money then. Hurry."

Jules paid for the gas, handing the boy a twenty-dollar bill. "That's fine, keep the change," Bernard said. "Let's get going!"

They drove out Lakeshore Drive and into the city of Grosse Pointe. Houses fell back from the street at once, brick homes uneasy in the gray light, their lawns blemished by scraps of newspapers blown over from Detroit. Everywhere scraps and strips and whole pages of newspapers blew. Dots of white danced in the eye. Bernard told him where to turn, and where to turn again, and Jules found himself moving slowly in a world of foliage and dark red brick; he had forgotten to eat that morning and such sights went to his head. Such lovely homes! Quiet, clean sidewalks and streets, with no one on them—that was always the surprising thing, this emptiness—as far as he could see no one was walking, no one existed!

"Drive in here," Bernard instructed, and Jules turned into a circular drive that led to a large, pale brick home, of an elegant style, with columns, far too big for an ordinary family. Jules would have thought it a funeral home or a fancy restaurant. His body began to tingle in the presence of such a sight. Bernard jumped out of the car as if he lived here. He bounded up to the door and rang the bell. Jules pretended not to be watching closely.

Another car turned into the driveway behind Jules, a blue station wagon. It stopped to let a girl out, then the driver continued on past Jules and out to the street again. Jules admired all this movement. The girl who had gotten out of the car was about sixteen or seventeen, dressed in plaid Bermuda shorts, with long black hair that swung past her shoulders; she was carrying a straw purse. In no hurry, she strolled past Jules in the black Lincoln and gave not the slightest glance at the car, only at Jules, moving her dark, serious, critical eyes over him. He stared back at her. He felt that look of hers shoot to the very back of his head. Out of the corners of his eyes he saw her stroll on past and approach Bernard. The two of them began to talk. The girl lifted her hands in a gesture of helplessness. Bernard was insisting upon something—he made short, chopping motions, arguing. The door was opened by a Negro maid. Bernard moved to go inside, still arguing, and the maid hesitated, then let him in. The girl followed. She had not even glanced back at Jules.

The house was closed behind them. It rose up pale and overwhelming, a small mountain of brick that set Jules's teeth on edge with wonder. Who could bear to live in something so big? Wouldn't the space make echoes? Wouldn't the pressure be too much on one's brain? And who had the money to build such a home? Agitated, a little resentful, he looked about and saw the precise look of a lawn no one ever bothered to walk across, hedges, small ornamental trees, flowers—everything was hazy as if under enchantment.

Anyway he had another check. He picked it up. *Two hundred dollars . . .*

Loretta had given him a few things for birthdays and Christmas, never much. Maureen had given him a few little things. But never had he really been given a *gift,* a surprising gift of the kind that stuns the heart, that lets you know why people keep on living—why else, except in anticipation of such gifts, such undeserved surprises?

The girl who had gone into the house was like that too, a surprise. Jules could not stop thinking of her. Yet he could not quite remember her face. He remembered something curious and penetrating about her look, an idle scrupulosity, and a turning inward of the foot—she'd been wearing sneakers—and her slender pale-pink knees. She went with the house. It was no surprise that she lived there. She was someone's daughter, unassailable.

Jules stared at the big front door and waited. After fifteen minutes Bernard appeared again, alone, in a hurry. His coat was unbuttoned and flopped about him. Jules leaned around to get the back door open, responding as mechanically as if he'd been bred out of centuries of subordinate flesh, and he had time to take in his employer's face: was that man crazy or not? "Those people! Those parasites, themselves, *they* are parasites, without imagination, people like that!" Bernard muttered. "As if I didn't know they were home—*she* was home at least, my dear sister, hiding, so I wash my hands of them forever!"

"Where do you want to go now?" Jules said humbly.

"Drive on! Get out of here!"

Bernard had an intelligent look but there was something jagged and glazed to it. His eyes wandered everywhere. His forehead, broad and sloping, seemed of paler skin than the rest of his face, skin not just lighter but somehow stretched thinner, of a different texture. It might have been that the upper part of his skull was swelling slowly out of shape. His jowls and jaw were flabby and on his cheeks tiny veins had worked their way to the surface, giving him the flushed surprised look of the many bums and rummies Jules saw every day of his life downtown.

"Move!" Bernard said loudly.

Where the night before he had been brotherly with Jules and almost intimate, in Faye's apartment, now that they were alone he tended not to look at Jules and to draw himself back into a dignified and slightly absurd preoccupation with the buttons on his coat, or his long, unkempt fingernails, or the bits of singed white fluff that were coming out of the back seat's holes. His voice, shaking and commanding, sounded to Jules like the voice of an actor, tuned up a little too high for personal contact.

"They always took my wife's part," Bernard said. "No trust. I showed them the bills and the receipts from her doctors—twelve doctors, believe it or not, my boy!—and waved them in their faces. They imagine themselves American aristocrats because they *work,* but I, I deem myself of no class whatsoever . . ."

Jules listened eagerly to all this, hoping for facts. He wanted to find out more about the girl. Finally, after about five minutes of it, Jules lost patience and said, "Who was that girl?"

"What girl?"

"The girl who went in the house with you."

"Oh, that was my niece Nadine. She must be ten or twelve by now, no, she must be older than that—time goes by so quickly—I'd say she was fourteen, maybe fifteen."

"She's older than that."

"Is she? I don't know, I hadn't noticed. A nice little girl, when you consider her parents—a successful but unhappy marriage, a very common kind of marriage . . . the girl nearly drowned in the club pool, I remember that as if it were yesterday, though she must have been about two or three. I really haven't noticed her much since then. I was the one who rescued her."

"Did you rescue her? From drowning?"

"Yes. It was the Yacht Club pool."

Jules was absurdly envious.

"Now, Jules, let me tell you one thing I'd like you to remember all your life: never trust anyone. Will you remember that?"

"Sure."

"You're too young to realize how life is. At my age you'll know."

"I know all about life," Jules said cheerfully.

"I have to make several telephone calls, I'd almost forgotten. I have to contact people who are difficult to contact, who are always on the move, like myself. Drive me back to the hotel now and you can go out by yourself and get a new car."

"Did you say . . . a new car?"

"Yes, but not a Lincoln after all. I want a Cadillac."

"You want me to buy a new car?"

"Leave them this one. They'll give you a little money on this."

"But I don't know how to buy a car, a car like that," Jules said.

"Then you'll learn."

"They might not let me in."

"I like you, Jules, I like your face and your intelligence and a certain grace about you," Bernard said. "To be frank, I wish I'd had a son like you. Men need sons, it has to do with genes, with the passing on of dreams. It isn't just that you've been Faye's lover, which is a miracle, but that I like you for your own sake—if I'd seen you out on the street I would have trusted you immediately, there's something sympathetic about you, you have an intelligent victim's face. When we're finished with this project I'm working on, when all this pressure is off, I'll finance your college career."

"College career?"

"Yes, certainly. You can major in . . . in philosophy, or art, or anything you like."

"But I flunked out of high school."

"You really can't get much out of life directly. That's one of life's ironies," Bernard said quickly. "You have to learn about life out of books. I'll send you to the East. You can compress centuries of wisdom in a few books. Turn left here. Watch out for that truck!"

So this is the way life happens: a sudden ballooning upward. Jules swerved around the laundry truck in a dream, not even seeing the other driver's sour face. He was on his way up and nothing could stop him. The fluttery sensation in his chest was his heart expanding, or maybe his lungs giddy with too much oxygen. Jules in college! "I'd like to go to college, sir, yes, I'd like that, I'd do anything for that," he said excitedly.

"Turn left again. No, right. You can make the light if you hurry . . ."

Downtown Bernard handed him another check, torn hastily out of his checkbook and ripped unevenly along the perforated edge. "Here. Get a handsome car. Meet me back here at three," he said. He slammed the car door and bounded away. Jules lifted the check to his eyes. Ten thousand dollars? He had to squint to keep the figures on the check from swimming away. A check made out to Jules Wendall for *ten thousand dollars?*

For a while he could not move. Then, not knowing what

he was doing, he started the car clumsily and blundered around a corner and onto a one-way street. He was going the wrong way. A yellow taxicab nearly ran into him, its horn blaring. Not chagrined but only giddy, his head smooth and bouncing as crockery, he began to back up. The cab driver was honking his horn. Jules thought the sound was like music. He got his long car back around the corner, backwards, then started off again. Halfway down the block he nearly collided with a city bus, pulling away from the curb. Gracefully, magically, he swung out around the bus and did not hit anyone approaching in the left lane, which opened up for him strangely and let him through, and so he drove around for perhaps ten or twenty minutes, unsure of the time, not even thinking thoughts cast in the form of words but only basking in the music of that check on the seat beside him, made out to Jules Wendall for ten thousand dollars.

He would cash the check and take off. For California.

It was a temptation but he couldn't do it. Never. He liked Bernard and could not steal from him. Also, it would be sinful to bring this adventure to an end so abruptly. His fate might be in riding out the adventure. And there was the girl, Bernard's niece, whose face in his memory was so tantalizingly unclear. He kept seeing her move across his vision, around the front of the car, out there beyond the shining black expanse of the hood. He tried to see her face but could not quite remember it—only the level, serious, impertinent stare, and his ears rang alarmingly. Was she thinking of him? Speaking of him? It was not enough to get such wonders thrown at him, Jules thought sternly, he had to be equal to them. What a disaster, what a shame for all of his life, if he turned out unequal to what happened to him!

He drove around a while longer, in a daze, wondering if he might stop at his mother's place to show her the check— but that was a crazy idea. He wanted to stop people on the street and show it to them. Better to think about the more serious side of his new life: finishing high school. It would be difficult to finish with so much money being thrown at him. He'd have to resist distractions, resist even the excitement of Bernard's niece, whom he might someday see again . . . he would have to finish high school at night . . . he could finish quickly, and then . . . and then he would go *East* to school, somewhere in the *East* to college, though his mind buckled at the thought and the ringing in his ears grew shriller. All he knew of college was Wayne State University, a bunch of modern glass-and-aluminum buildings in the middle of the rubble of Detroit, and all he knew of the East was the gentle swooping line it made on a map, worn out by the Atlantic Ocean. Still, it was a turning point in his life, he knew, the very beginning of his life. He would have to be equal to it.

"This looks like Chapter One," he said.

He managed to park the car—in his zeal getting the right back tire up on the curb and then bouncing violently down again, going through his pockets twice before he could find the right change for the meter, and he was off down the street to the National Bank of Detroit, hoping for the same teller. When he entered the bank its high ceiling assured him: they'd have enough money for him here. But what if someone ran up to him and asked, "How did you get a check like that, Jules? We know *you*, Jules, of all people *you!*" What if the policeman in the corner began strolling toward him, casually unsnapping his holster and taking out his gun?

He waited in line. The line at the next window was moving faster but he did not cross over to it, being very good, very virtuous. He was a good citizen; with his new trim haircut, he was on his way! He waited.

He wasn't going to get the same teller he had gotten before. This one was a middle-aged man, a suspicious man. When Jules's turn came the teller looked right into his face. He stared at the check, looked back at Jules, and said, "Are you Jules Wendall?" Jules smiled to show that this question gave him no discomfort. He took out his wallet and slid out his driver's license, leaving the wallet on the counter so that the man might see, if he chose, more money inside, folded up, bunched up. Then Jules remembered the other check, the check for two hundred dollars. He searched his pockets for it. He laid it on the marble counter, smoothing it out, wondering if it was worth cashing—two hundred dollars, after all, was not much. The teller picked up this new check. His mouth was thin and sour. "You haven't endorsed this," he said.

Jules signed his name with a bank pen and was surprised to see that his handwriting differed from check to check. He had even begun putting a second "n" in his last name but realized what he was doing just in time. On the ten-thousand-dollar check "Jules" looked buoyant and youthful; on the second check, signed under the teller's gaze, "Jules" looked humble and middle-aged. The teller stared at the two signatures. He looked at Jules's driver's license.

"This driver's license has expired," he said.

"What?"

"It's expired. On your birthday, in April."

"But . . . but I didn't know, I forgot . . . I mean . . ." He managed to get hold of himself. He said, "Thank you for reminding me. I'll go to the police station right away."

The teller turned away, taking both checks. Jules watched him while pretending not to watch. What if the money was not available? What if none of this was real? He was only eighteen years old, and it was not enough for these surprises to fall into his lap, he had to be equal to them. He had to be equal to Bernard's expectations. Finish high school. Go to college. Major in philosophy. He had to be equal to a supreme Jules, a dictator who expected even more than Bernard did. He had to be equal to Bernard's niece, who at her age already knew more than he could learn, probably, just by living in a house like that.

Now the teller was conferring with another man. The two of them stood back near a big vault door, which was closed. Over their heads Jules saw a camera. Was his picture being taken? What if there was a robbery in this bank in the next few minutes and Jules's picture somehow got taken in the midst of it? It might be that Bernard himself was a criminal, a forger. The two of them might be arrested. And it would be assumed that Jules had been his accomplice for years of crime, his bodyguard, his chauffeur, his son . . . But the teller might give him the ten thousand dollars after all. And a crowd of people would gather around him in silence, watching as the money was counted out into his quaking hands.

Then it occurred to Jules that no sane person asked for ten thousand dollars. He should have opened a checking account in his own name. How did you open a checking account?

Too late. The teller was on a telephone, the other man was sending a cautious look Jules's way, and the line at the windows on either side of him moved along, people were served, money and papers were given out or handed in, people turned and got out of the bank and disappeared, the gears were in motion and he, Jules, was caught up helplessly in them. The man was still on the telephone. He looked over toward Jules. A babble of voices rose suddenly in the bank, coming clear to Jules. Everyone was talking at once. The bank's high ceiling sent back echoes to him, making his pulse race.

The teller returned with the other man and a portly, severe-looking woman. The three of them looked at Jules. The teller smoothed the two checks down on the counter and said, "There is some question at the other end about a check made on this account two days ago, Mr. Bernard Geffen at the Bank of the Commonwealth, a check that was certified by Mr. Geffen for twelve thousand dollars. We'll be getting a call on that in a minute or two. Would you mind waiting?"

"Did you want this in cash? In various denominations, in cash?" the woman asked.

"I guess so," said Jules.

Behind him, in line, people shifted from foot to foot, murmuring, impatient with the back of his head and his tight-fitting clothes, not liking the dull shine to the back of his coat and thinking little of his scuffed shoes. Shoes! He needed to buy shoes! His mind reeled with all that he needed to buy and to do. He would have to drop over at the high school and see about night courses, sign up, rush into all those old courses he'd given so little thought to before, all the courses he'd flunked, with a punk's smirk. Jules Wendall, a punk.

He waited. Finally a buzzer sounded. The teller picked up a telephone receiver and listened. Jules tried not to listen. The woman moved away, adjusting her glasses. The teller nodded briskly. He put down the receiver. "Did you want this in various denominations or mainly in large bills?"

"Yes. I mean, yes, in large bills. There won't be enough room . . ."

The teller opened a money drawer. He began counting out money, now and then putting his fingers to a large red sponge set in a glass dish. Jules saw this and felt suddenly very dizzy, as if he were going to faint. Then the money was coming to him? Ten thousand dollars on its way?

He stumbled backward slightly and bumped into a woman with a shopping bag. "Excuse me, please," he said. The woman muttered something. Jules pressed his cold hand against his forehead, steadying himself. The teller was counting money. The other man folded his arms and smiled at Jules. Voices rose everywhere in the bank. Jules looked over at the camera, thinking that maybe they would take a picture of him as he accepted the money from the teller, maybe that was necessary for legal evidence. He cast his eyes upward to the golden ceiling of the bank, for a moment confusing it with church, thinking he was somehow in church. It was not too late to get out of this. The magic moment had not yet come about. As soon as he touched the bills he would be contaminated, flashbulbs might go off, everyone in the bank might duck to the floor so that only he, Jules, would be left standing for the police to shoot.

It was too late to get out. He had kept everyone waiting in line. He stood, sweating, while the teller counted out some fifteen or twenty bills onto the counter, then scooped them up and counted them up again. It was obvious that Jules had to take them.

Ten thousand two hundred dollars . . .

He mumbled thanks and turned blindly to leave.

When he got back to Bernard's car—he had not quite remembered where he'd parked it—he saw that someone had bumped its left rear fender, nothing much, but the paint was scraped off and the metal dented slightly. He tried to straighten it out with his hands. No use. Maybe Bernard wouldn't notice. Anyway he had to trade in the car, what did it matter? Jules drove away. He was still a little blind. His eyesight was besieged by particles of light and dust, so that he had to keep blinking to get rid of them. He drove in downtown traffic, soundlessly. Now for an automobile showroom, a Cadillac dealer. He couldn't find one for some time. He drove around for miles. He wondered if he might be going blind.

He located a Cadillac showroom and went in. In his wallet, in his back pocket, he had over ten thousand dollars; he had become immortal. "I'd like to buy a new car," he said politely. "I'd like to trade in my old car." It occured to him that he would have gotten a better trade-in at a Ford dealer's, but that was not his fault, that was Bernard's fault. The salesman was talking to him. While he explained certain things—his sentences were faultless—he kept eying Jules with a certain curiosity. Jules noticed this but did not let on. He was being told about a car that was in front of him. The car itself escaped his fullest attention. It was too big, resting heavily upon its white-walled tires in the center of the gleaming floor, very still, gleaming itself and overlarge, so that Jules was tempted to close his eyes. He had become an ant, a flea, crawling on the surface of an enormous piece of curving metal.

The salesman opened one of the doors ceremoniously. Jules was instructed to look inside at something. He did close his eyes for a moment. He was thinking of the nights in the country, himself as a child, when his mother had fed him beer to get him a little drunk and ready for sleep; he felt almost that way now. He hadn't slept much the night before. He thought he might never sleep again really.

The salesman was very articulate and handsome, but Jules had the strange idea that the man was about to grab him and do something to him—stuff his mouth with the brochure he held in his hand maybe, and drag him inside the Cadillac. He'd been dragged somewhere in the past. Three boys had dragged him . . . but it was wrong to think of the Cadillac salesman in connection with that—Jules knew he had to wake up. The problem was that the salesman was not as real as the car or any easier to look at. Jules was hungry for something to look at clearly, without flinching. How had he gotten this job? Jules would have liked to ask if there were any other jobs open, for a kid like himself. It might be better to hide here, to stay clear of the life fate seemed to have arranged for him. Was there rapid advancement here?

He found himself sitting in a small office while the salesman went somewhere on silent feet, silent as white-walled tires. Jules was smiling fixedly. Maybe they were getting the car ready for him? Maybe he would be expected to drive it away while they watched? The salesman returned with another man, a wise, gentle, gray-haired man who looked sympathetic. He began asking Jules questions.

"I work for a trucking firm," Jules said, "that is, I did, but I've just quit. Now I work for a private person. He instructed me to buy this car."

They asked him for identification papers. Jules took out his wallet and was startled at how heavy it was. He showed them his wrinkled driver's license.

"This expired last month," said the older man.

"But isn't it still good? I'm still the same person," Jules said, nearly jumping from his chair.

"Of course, don't be alarmed."

They smiled at him and at each other. They asked him about his employer: what address?

"I don't know exactly," Jules said.

What about the automobile registration for the other car?

"It might be in the glove compartment, I don't know. And

I should tell you, I guess, there was a fire in that car, a small fire—it did a little damage to the back seat but nothing bad," he said.

They looked at his fixed smile. What was his address?

"It's just a room. I plan on moving. I think it's on Bagley but I don't know the number—I mean, it isn't important, I can find it myself without any trouble. I know the neighborhood," he said.

There was silence. He eyed the door to the office and wondered if he shouldn't make a run for it. He had not stolen the ten thousand dollars but still there might have been a robbery earlier that day of ten thousand dollars, so they might arrest him for it. They had to get someone . . .

"On second thought," Jules said, "I better get the car later." He stood. He went to the door of the office. The middle-aged man took three fast steps toward him, alarmed, and Jules automatically raised his elbow to protect himself. "I'll come back later!" he said shrilly.

"But your license, and your wallet, here on the desk—"

"Oh, yes." Jules went back to get them. He had some difficulty in stuffing the wallet in his back pocket.

"You . . . you said you might be back later? Later today?" said one of the men.

"Later today, yes," Jules said wildly. "It's time I got somewhere. I have to see someone. The lighting in here, the fluorescent lighting, makes my eyes ache."

He got out. He managed not to bump into the cars on display. Above the two men who stood watching him was the imperial crest of the Cadillac, a coat of arms fastened high on the wall. Jules made his way to the front door, walking carefully. He walked carefully out to the sidewalk. When he looked back he saw the two men watching him from the show window.

Bernard was wearing the same raincoat when Jules picked him up. He was in the same hurry. He swung into the car and gave Jules an address, already talking about something urgent, something about precious minerals in the Congo. Jules could hear only every third or fourth word. He was driving with his eyes nearly closed, very exhausted. Bernard seemed to have forgotten about the car and the ten thousand dollars. He was agitated and bullying, thumping the back of Jules's seat to make his points. "They are not going to crowd me out before I've begun. I'm fifty-five years old, and if I don't begin now, when, when will I begin?"

"I don't know," Jules said.

He was thinking of Faye, of loving Faye. Out of her mysterious cool body all this had come. A car, a man, a wallet bulging with bills. She herself was untouched by all of this, and uninterested. He thought of the hours he had spent lying in her arms, of her long slender legs touching the length of his legs, and he wanted to weep bitterly for everything that was being lost to him in this nightmare of a city. Faye had said to him, one night when he was clowning around, "You're always showing off and joking, but you're always serious." He had been struck by that. It was true. Now he wanted to turn to Bernard and say, "You're always serious but it's a joke, a joke! You're always joking!"

If he wanted to spend that ten thousand dollars he would have to spend it five dollars at a time, passing five-dollar bills. Otherwise he'd be caught.

Bernard was talking angrily about the pollen count.

Jules took him to what looked like a private club and Bernard got out. A Negro with a desiccated face hurried to help him, obviously recognizing him. So Bernard did exist.

Jules waited. It was a clear June day, and high in the sky an airplane was doing mysterious maneuvers. Long fuzzy streams of white trailed out behind it. Jules wondered what it would be like to be up there, free and floating, sailing above the earth, making marks in the sky.

Bernard came hurrying back, carrying a package. His face was mottled with red, flushed. He said, "Drive over to the east side again. Hurry."

At the next stop Jules had to wait quite a while. He was parked near a well-known restaurant, and it interested him, in a way, to watch people coming out from their drawn-out lunches, people with nothing to do on this mild June day except drink and eat and talk. What did people talk about? Surely they didn't talk about money during all those hours?

All that day, driving Bernard around, Jules wanted to explain his failure to get a car but he hadn't the nerve. Anyway Bernard seemed to have forgotten about it. He was talking more and more about St. Louis now; they'd be driving down there the next day.

"Is there anyone—your parents maybe—anyone you should say good-by to? Nearest of kin?" Bernard asked.

"My mother," Jules said slowly, struck by something odd in this question but too tired to figure it out. "I'd better see her."

"Oh, your mother! You have a mother? She's dependent on you?"

"I give her a little money, but mostly she's on welfare."

"Does she have money for groceries?" Bernard asked, concerned.

"Yes, I think so."

"But she's on welfare?"

"Since April."

"I don't approve of welfare, frankly," Bernard said. "Doesn't welfare encourage her to be idle?"

"It might."

"But do you need any money for her? Let me make you out a check, my boy."

"No, really. I don't need it."

"Nonsense! I'll make you out a check and you can run over with it, of course, but you should tell her to get off welfare if she can. You can bring her to live with you and I'll support you both, gladly."

"I could maybe go to college here, at Wayne State, instead of in the East," Jules said.

Bernard ripped the check out and passed it up to Jules. It was made out to *John Wendall* for *twenty-five dollars*.

"I really don't need this," Jules said uneasily.

"Nonsense, take it. I don't mind. I'm glad to give it to you."

They had dinner around five o'clock in a Howard Johnson's. Bernard brought the package in with him. Jules ordered the same dinner Bernard ordered: hamburger plate with French fries. Bernard was moody. He ate with his shoulders slumping forward, disappointing Jules; he ate like a truck driver sitting at a counter. Jules thought of the adventure before him as he chewed his hamburger. He tried to re-experience that ballooning sensation in his chest; how had that felt? Across the way he could see a waitress mopping up something that had been knocked onto the floor. It seemed to him that this scene might drag him down forever if he wasn't careful, if he didn't look aside. . . .

"I forgot! This is for you!" Bernard said, snapping his fingers. He brought the package up on the table. "It's a very necessary part of our equipment—I hope you won't be alarmed."

Jules watched as he unwrapped it. It was a gun. Jules, in a panic, reached out and drew the wrapping paper back up over it. "My God! Jesus!" he whispered.

"Of course I shouldn't open it in here, of course," Bernard said wisely. "I'll give it to you outside."

"No, not to me, no thanks," Jules said. "I'm not carrying a gun!"

"But why not?"

"I don't want to get put in jail, I don't want to get my teeth kicked out for possession!"

"We'll put it in the glove compartment then."

"But that's the same thing!"

"We won't talk about it any more at the present."

"But . . ."

The next morning he went to see his mother. She gave him coffee and they chatted. It was the usual conversation: chatting about Maureen's appetite. *She eats everything I make for her, so she's all right* . . . And then he had to go in to see Maureen herself, lying in bed, forever lying in bed and stuffing her face with coffee cake and cookies and whatever sweet crap Loretta gave her, so that her face had broken out, her body grown disgusting. Maureen was going to drive him crazy too unless he put distance between them. St. Louis wasn't far enough.

He went to pick up Bernard at noon. Bernard did exist; he appeared in a small crowd, materializing out of it. He wore the same coat. Jules leaned back to open the door for him and had the idea that the two of them had been together for a lifetime already and might be sentenced together for another lifetime, an eternal lifetime, like conspirators who wind up together in hell, a sad joke their being together for eternity . . .

Bernard said, "To the airport!"

"Which one?"

"Metropolitan. Hurry."

It was a long drive. Jules nearly fell asleep. To keep himself awake he tried to explain about the Cadillac, but Bernard was reading a newspaper and did not seem to hear. Out at the airport Bernard had Jules drive around while he went into one of the terminals to check something. Jules wondered why he hadn't simply made a telephone call.

Bernard came back on the run. He sighed cheerfully. "It's all on! Our plans for St. Louis!" He struck the back of the seat with one flat-handed blow, as if to make a point he didn't really believe in.

Jules drove back to Detroit.

And then . . .

Though he was to have plenty of time to think it over, the event that followed never really became believable to him. Lying in a hospital bed some years later, having nothing to do except regain his strength, he was able to think and re-think that afternoon but he was never able really to believe in it. Bernard instructed him to go to a certain address on Livernois, which turned out to be a sleazy-looking muffler shop. Then on to another address near Grand Boulevard. Jules was able to park on the street in front of the house, since this was a residential neighborhood. "I have to finalize something here," Bernard said. Jules reached over and got the newspaper out of the back seat and read it, beginning with the comic page.

Time passed.

After a while he looked up uneasily. The street was fairly crowded. People were strolling around. No Bernard. The house he'd gone into was made of brick, old and decrepit. An awning on the front porch was rotted. Jules let time pass, maybe an hour, before he prodded himself into getting out of the car. He stared at the house and a terrible feeling came over him: is this as far as he would go?

He rang the doorbell several times. No answer. He tried the door and it was open. A hallway, a stairway. Plaster-board showed. A few coat hangers were lying on the floor. The house was empty, yet cluttered with boxes and old clothing and junk, the remains of a family. It smelled. Jules poked around downstairs though he felt instinctively that what he was looking for was not downstairs.

He went upstairs. "Mr. Geffen?" he said. At the top of the stairs lay a dead rat, very stiff. Its tail was long and rubbery but still. He stepped over the rat and looked into the first room, where a card table had been set up. Two chairs were drawn to it, close together. A ruffled pink curtain lay on the floor. A *Captain Marvel* comic book lay near one of the chairs. Jules could smell a terrible cold smell, inside him, that had nothing to do with this dump of a house or with the dead rat out on the landing.

He went to the next room, leaned in through the door-way, and there he saw Bernard. Bernard was lying on his back near an opened closet door. His throat had been cut. Jules leaned farther into the room as if someone had given him a shove, but he did not move his feet. Bernard, a gray-ing man in his fifties, lay on his back on the bare floor with his throat freshly slit and the butcher knife placed in his hand, the fingers loose about it. "My God!" Jules said aloud.

Now he was beginning to wake up, though slowly enough, and his eyes danced around the spectacle of that bright blood, streaking the floor and staining Bernard's raincoat, the red so bright that it gave Bernard a look of youth and energy. Blood was everywhere, smeared up onto his cheeks, even onto his forehead. His eyes were open and blood was even smeared across one of his eyes and clotted in the eyelashes.

"Mr. Geffen?" Jules said feebly.

He tiptoed over to the dead man. Yes, the butcher knife had been put in his hand and had fallen out again slightly. Bernard seemed to have no interest in the knife. He had a surprised, though dignified look, even with all that blood. Jules stared into his face and saw that the blood was smeared onto the eyeball of one eye, the left eye. That was strange. Jules shut his own eyes, feeling pain in them. When he opened them after a moment nothing had changed.

He took out his wallet and in a slow, cold panic took all the money out of it, a thick handful of bills. Distastefully but with dignity, he bent over and put all the money into Bernard's inside coat pocket, stuffing it in. He remembered the car keys; he put them in the pocket too. The odor of terror was rising sharply about him. He straightened. He got out of the room. Out on the street he bypassed the Lincoln, which had attracted a small crowd of Negro kids, and headed off on foot for his room many miles away, leaving behind his fingerprints and any evidence of himself that existed for fate to handle.

He did not pick up the suit on Friday.

4

September 1956. Jules was driving a truck filled with flowers around the unflowery streets of Detroit. He had become so accustomed to driving that the motor's drone was confused with his thinking, his energy. In a sweet flowery daze he thought about Bernard's niece, though he had nothing to think about her, no reference point.

When he had the opportunity to drive out to Grosse Pointe he cruised near her house, unafraid of being seen, feeling himself invisible. His hair was combed down flat beneath his delivery boy's hat. Of Bernard he did not often think because the sight of that man had a little unnerved him. So much blood, and blood smeared on an eyeball . . . But of Bernard's niece he thought constantly. She was the opposite of the sight of that dead man, she had somehow to do with the fragrant burden of flowers he hauled about the streets, their stems and leaves and heads nodding in rhythm to the demands he made on his truck, in a constant hurry but without any destination. He had no clear reference point. He thought about the girl and mixed her up with the cool, disdainful lovely distance of Faye's body—Faye had now disappeared—and the futility of Bernard's quest, a mystery to Jules.

He tried to avoid close thoughts about anything. Better to stick to himself, to keep driving. He liked to be tired at night so he could sleep without any thoughts, except thoughts of Bernard's niece; but these were not really thoughts. Still, it had puzzled him that Bernard had died so quickly and so permanently. One minute he had been bounding up to the car, the next lying flat on his back, and that was the end. It was no surprise to Jules that the police never picked him up, since he knew how they smudged fingerprints and lost evidence, working in a hurry, but he was surprised that he never found out what had happened—he'd searched through the newspapers for weeks, looking for notice of Bernard's death, but found no mention of it. So a man could die and disappear? It was like the rifle shot that had been fired through the window of a friend of Loretta's, in August. A shot had rung out, a bullet had crashed through the window and gone into a wall, and nothing else—some screaming, some alarm, but nothing else. A rifle is fired, but most of the time a rifle is not fired. Nothing follows.

He was drawn to Grosse Pointe though it was out of his way; he made up for lost time by driving fast along ordinary streets. Grosse Pointe was for him a paradise of evergreens and brick. There no one fired through windows; doors were left unlocked; the officials of the Detroit Mafia, seeking genteel lives, bought mansions and hired nursemaids for their curly-haired children; everyone settled down, settled in, breathed deeply the air that blew from the lake. Jules wished his employer did more business in the Pointes. Jules liked nothing more than delivering flowers to a home in Grosse Pointe, carrying out a gilt-wrapped heavy bucket of mums, the flowers light and their containers heavy, expensive, ringing a golden doorbell, hearing golden chimes deep inside. He had dreams in which Faye's body was confused with the bulk of a house, one of those beautiful ornate houses, and this in turn was confused with the body, the being, of Bernard's niece, who, innocent as Faye was not, had the right to live in such a home. Faye would never live in such a home. And he dreamed, sleeping lightly, of the mysterious golden interior of one of these homes, its rooms and corridors and its softness, like the fragrant softness of a woman's secret body, a mystery to him. He was still eighteen.

This job was a lousy one, he knew that. Yet he was reluctant to quit and find another. He was locked in a cheerful inertia, in love as if hypnotized by long distance; he imagined his routes around the city and into Grosse Pointe as an ingenious cobweb of crossings and crisscrossings, leading him inexorably to that girl. She would not have known him. She could not have remembered him. But he sat in his driver's seat preparing for her, his face made gentle with plans of love, his eyes working intelligently under the asinine green cap he had to wear, or wore out of indifference.

"I don't like you in that uniform. I don't like uniforms," Loretta would say, drunk, maybe put in mind of a cop's uniform. "At least take off that goddam cap!"

"I don't put on airs. I'm happy driving a flower truck," Jules said with exaggerated politeness.

"Take off that goddam cap in the house!"

So Jules would bow and snatch off the cap with a cavalier-like gesture, irritating his mother even more. "You're crazy!" she would say.

Autumn was lovely in Grosse Pointe though it made no mark on Detroit. Jules noted the leaves about to change, he noted the autumn flowers arranged in symmetrical patterns around driveways, he noted the teen-aged girls, newly returned to school, in plaid skirts or Bermuda shorts of dark material, sometimes wearing knee socks on their slender strong legs. His lust for one girl flowered generously over them all; if he had fallen in love with Bernard's niece, he had fallen in love with all the nieces and daughters of the Pointes, those fair-skinned, thoughtful girls with their shining clean hair.

At fourteen he had been older than he was at eighteen. At eighteen, in love, vulnerable, he had to prod himself to think about a new job, about money, about his sister. Bernard's niece freed him from thoughts of money because no amount of money could ever get her. It was hopeless. One hundred dollars might have bought Faye a while ago, but even Faye's price was higher now, and in any case Faye had disappeared—and why did he need a new job, didn't he live in the present? What else mattered? And, living in the present, how could he bear to make himself think about Maureen?

He brought her odds and ends of flowers, but she lay around the house in a soiled nightgown, unseeing. He avoided the apartment to avoid her and Loretta and the squawling of that brat, Furlong's kid. If he could get over this girl and become the old Jules again, cagey and on the lookout for advantages, he'd get hold of some money and take Maureen to a real doctor and be free of them all. But he was afraid of stealing and getting caught, especially now. Anything might happen now; he couldn't afford to take chances with his freedom. He stopped thinking about Maureen and began to think about Bernard's niece. She was with him constantly. He wondered if he was losing his mind, giving himself up to the memory of a girl he had seen for half a minute, when there were other girls who came with the enthusiasm of popular love songs into his arms, at home there, and he had the idea that never, never would that other girl be at home in his arms.

But he prepared himself for her with other girls: he was rehearsing Jules Wendall, her lover. He watched himself critically. He admired himself. Wasn't he Jules Wendall, knocked down and kicked around but not counted out? Hadn't he escaped from danger all his life? Hadn't his luck always bounced him back up to the top, as if he were a rubber ball, all one texture, one foamy, happy, invulnerable, rubbery texture that nothing could kill?

No, of Maureen he would not think, his other, darker self, his sister, lying around in silence, unwashed, drab and coarse—he could not let himself think of her because he was eighteen and in love and he knew better than to think. He reeled with the drowsiness of imagined love, his mind fixed upon a girl with long black hair and a straight, inquisitive look, bound to him by the violence of her uncle's death but totally unknown to him, and innocent of everything, innocent of the other women in his life, whose arms always threatened to pull him down. But he was still free. Everything lay before him. But sometimes, beneath the frothy odor of the flowers in his truck, he caught a whiff of something harder, more permanent, the stench of failure that was blown back into his face from the exhaust of a city bus or a big auto carrier, the sour, foul stench of failure, of the foul, dark joke of a world in which he had lived all his life and might never escape.

One evening, broke, he stopped off at Loretta's to see what was up, and there in the kitchen a man was sitting.

Jesus, another baby on the way, Jules thought.

Loretta jumped to her feet. "Jules, guess who! Guess who's here!"

The man, shaven so recently that a few clots of blood were still fresh on his chin, got to his feet to shake Jules's hand.

Loretta cried, "Jules, this is your Uncle Brock! Your uncle! My brother! And, Brock, this is my son Jules, my big son. What do you think of him? Isn't he handsome?"

They shook hands energetically.

"It's nice . . . nice to see you," Jules stammered.

"It's nice to see you. What's that uniform?" Brock asked.

"Jules delivers flowers. In a truck."

"That's nice."

"It's a very steady job. Jules works hard."

Brock smiled and could think of nothing to say. He was very uneasy.

Jules felt shrunken by Brock's height and the bulk of his shoulders; he could not decide what to think—what did this guy want, what was up? Or was this a good thing, Loretta's brother showing up?

"It's the craziest thing, how Brock found us! My God!" Loretta cried.

Jules flinched at her excitement, which was a little liquory, and tried to figure out what was behind it—was she serious or putting on a show? It looked as if she was serious. She was so fluttery and pleased, and anyway, Jules thought, he should be grateful that this wasn't another Furlong come along to move in with her and impregnate her with another little bastard. At this moment the kid was fooling around by the table, about to knock over a can of beer. Jules watched impassively.

"Sit down, both of you! Jules, have some beer. My God, what a surprise! Brock knocked on the door an hour ago, he just walked up the stairs like nothing! I knew him right off even though we didn't see each other for—what was it? —nineteen years. Jesus Christ, nineteen years! Isn't it the goddammest thing, how life goes?" Loretta laughed. She pulled at Jules and got him to sit down. Brock sat down awkwardly.

Jules watched him with a cautious smile; he did not trust him. This brother was a mystery. Loretta had hinted from time to time that she had a brother who had done something and had to run out of town, whatever town that had been, and she'd never laid eyes on him since, telling all this with a bright, malicious excitement. Brock must have killed someone. He looked like a man who might kill, who might hitch up his trousers and raise a rifle and shoot through someone's window, an incidental window, and then go strolling down an alley. Brock wasn't stupid-looking but rather dense-looking, with a hard, sour, grainy face, and eyes that Jules realized were very much like his own eyes. He found that he was looking into his own eyes, in this big, lardy man's face. He grinned foolishly.

Furlong's kid, Randolph, knocked over the beer can and beer splashed onto the front of his shirt.

"Damn it, look out! He's always pulling something over, always making a mess!" Loretta cried. She grabbed Randolph and slapped him.

Brock paid no attention to this. His big arms rested on the table and he tried to smile at Jules, as if guessing that Jules's opinion was important. Jules, agitated by the noise with Randolph and this unexpected uncle, stared blankly and wondered what he should do. He forced himself to think of Bernard's niece—she was a kind of oasis of thought. He would think about her. What was there about girls, about women, that one could fall into thoughts of them the way one fell into their arms, surrendering everything, suffocating, plunging to a warm, feathery death? He imagined himself a soldier in some land remote as the moon, Korea maybe, returning from the dirt of a man's war and falling into the arms of a woman, stroking her hair and her long smooth back with the fingers that had worked so hard at killing and which were as well suited for this, killing or stroking . . . His fingers rapped nervously on the table. He had another night to get through, and maybe the next day he would encounter Bernard's niece. He took nights one at a time.

". . . so Pa died in there? That's too bad. When did it happen?" Brock was saying.

"A long time ago, he never knew nothing—he didn't recognize me when I went up."

"And Howard Wendall? You married him, huh? The one that was a cop?"

"Yes, Howard Wendall," Loretta said.

Jules watched her, fascinated. She pronounced the name carefully, as if fearful of getting it wrong, frowning, fastidious in her pink dress, locating her husband and the father of three of her children as if picking someone coolly out of a police lineup. "Howard Wendall. You know, he was a cop for a while."

"So he got killed, huh?"

"Got killed at work," Loretta said slowly.

"Not shot down?"

"He had another job then. A factory."

Jules listened. He was miserable and yet fascinated by this pair, a brother and sister tied together by obscure memories, bumping heads over them, sitting like ordinary people at an ordinary kitchen table. Well, life was mysterious. Jules wondered why the mystery was cast in the forms of such diminished people.

"I better be going," he said.

"Aw, Jules, stick around. Don't you want supper tonight? I'm going to make us all a nice supper."

"No, thanks."

"Don't you want to talk to your own uncle? You just came up and now you're running off again. What goes? What's so important?"

"Nothing."

"You're not in any trouble these days, are you?"

"Hell, no."

"You ever run into Betty?"

"No."

Betty stayed out most of the time now. They heard things about her, exaggerated things, maybe, but they rarely saw her; she was staying with friends in a building on Second Avenue, below Wayne State University.

"Well," said Jules, "how is Maureen? Should I say hello?"

"She's asleep but you can stick your head in. Go on."

He stuck his head in her room but it was dark. Anyway, he said hello to her or to the darkness and got out.

The next day, turning off Kercheval in Grosse Pointe's shopping area, Jules saw the girl on the sidewalk. He knew it was Bernard's niece at once. She was alone; she wore white slacks and a pink sweater. He cruised alongside her without much alarm, staring out at her, making sure she was really the right girl. She glanced over at him, just once. He himself wore sunglasses and, he remembered, that green cap. He snatched the cap off and tossed it behind him . . . and passed at once into a blizzard of excitement. There are times when the air breaks into dazzling particles, blinding and lovely, and when one's lungs ache with the sudden steely coldness of the air; so it happened with Jules. It was the same blizzard that swept across the highest part of the globe, killing everything, and in Jules's vision everything was killed except this girl. Her hair swung without effort beside her face.

Jules, trembling, braked his truck to a stop and jumped out. "Nadine," he said, "I have something for you, some flowers . . ."

She stared at him. Still, she approached him, with a kind of hesitating confidence, the confidence of Grosse Pointe and its clean sidewalks, approaching this trembling boy from the city whose face was beaded with sweat and whose anxious fingers were obviously ready for her. "I have some flowers for you. A surprise for you," Jules said.

"How do you know my name?"

"Isn't it Nadine?"

"Nadine, yes, but how do you know me?"

Jules raised his shoulders cheerfully and helplessly. "Your uncle. I was an associate of his."

"My uncle Bernard? You were what?"

"I drove his car for him."

She stared at him. She was quite safe on the sidewalk, in the open.

Jules said, smiling, "*I* didn't kill him."

"Did somebody kill him?"

"Don't you know that he's dead?"

"They said he died of a heart attack—isn't that right? What happened?"

They stared at each other. The girl, put off by Jules's smile, had begun to look apprehensive; he could see her lips slowly parting. In his vision she was nearly blotted out by that blizzard of lust that came at him now from all sides, pressing him toward her. What they were talking about made no sense, it was nothing. He hardly knew what he was saying. He would have liked to grab her in a glassy-eyed embrace; she might not resist. But he said instead, smiling idiotically, "Lots of people die and in strange ways, in Detroit—it's especially true there. I didn't kill him and don't know who did. I would rather he hadn't been killed, though."

"He wasn't very nice. He went away when my aunt was dying of cancer."

The girl laughed nervously, not paying attention to her own words. Jules smiled. How he loved her! He moved toward her in the splotched sunlight and said, as if reciting the words to a catchy tune, anything to hold her interest, "The last time I saw your uncle he was lying on his back in a pool of blood . . . his own blood . . . he had a big butcher knife in his hand . . . *I* didn't put it there, honey, and I was very sorry to see it. He told me you were his favorite niece."

"His favorite! I'm his only niece," she said, lowering her eyes.

"Anyway he liked you very much, he told me your name was Nadine, and we've seen each other before, Nadine, though you don't remember. One day I drove him to your house—do you remember?"

"No."

"I drove his car and you were wearing shorts and carrying a purse and you looked right at me, as if you were putting a sign on me, a mark. And the next day your uncle died. I was very sorry."

She shook her head, as if lightly confused. She could not erase a trancelike little smile from her face. "Oh, him, he was so strange. I'm not surprised. He was always asking my father for money. He wanted to be a criminal, a gangster —all his life he wanted that but he didn't know how. He had a lot of books on criminals, he admired Willie Sutton." She laughed. There was something abstract and giddy about her, as if Jules's presence were a threat she couldn't really understand but could sense. "So he died like that? That's such a strange way to die, it isn't like dying in a hospital where they wait on you."

"Well, I didn't slit his throat for him, or anybody's, I promise you that."

"I didn't say you did." She spoke with the faintest hint of coquetry, an almost mechanical intonation.

Jules was rocky now with excitement and wondered how

he could get this girl to some safe secret place . . . the back of the truck? He felt that if he pawed her and rubbed his face against hers long enough she'd give up everything to him, seeing how gentle he was and how deserving of love, he would need no knife to convince her of anything. . . . But he controlled himself. He put his weight back full on his heels. He said, "I want to see you sometime. What about now? Could you come with me right now?"

"You mean, to a movie or something?"

"Yes, a movie."

She began to smile. Then she frowned. After a moment's hesitation she said cautiously, "No, not now."

"Why not? Down to the lake, I'll drive us to the lake. Why not?"

"I don't think so."

"Five minutes?"

"I have to go home," she said.

She was suddenly nervous. She sidestepped him in a slow but patterned maneuver; he could measure with his eyes just where it would take her, how many feet from him. Too far.

"I have to go home," she said.

"I won't hurt you," he said, lifting his hands for her to see how empty they were, how clean, and even as an after-thought opening the jacket he wore to show that nothing was stuffed inside his belt. She laughed at this. "I could drive you home. After all, I know where you live. I won't hurt you, I would never hurt you." This was true. A blast of music seemed to back up his words, washing crazily at his head. He felt faint. Did he hear music? He shook his head to get it clear again and said to the girl, who was staring at him now with a fixed, frigid, desperate stare, the look of a girl about to scream, "On second thought maybe you better go home."

She maneuvered around him. Behind her, out of a fuzzy technicolored background, a woman appeared in a beige suit, with strong hiking legs. Jules backed toward his truck. He didn't want anyone screaming or calling for the police. None of that. He backed away, his lip caught in his teeth, forcing a kind of grin, which the girl involuntarily matched, her own small white teeth showing in a fast shy smile. *Jesus, that girl is going to bite my heart in two,* Jules thought musically, one foot groping backward for the safety of his truck, and he seemed to see quite clearly before him a stretch of terrible bone-dry hours he would have to live through before he saw this girl again and got her alone in some secret corner of Grosse Pointe.

The woman walked on past. Very suspicious. Jules said softly, "I'll see you again tomorrow—right here? About this time?" She gave no indication of hearing. "Remember, I won't hurt you. Don't stay away or I'll have to come and get you. I don't want to get in trouble. I don't want to get shot. Does your father have a gun? I love you, I'll see you tomorrow. Remember I didn't kill your uncle or anyone, and I had only the best thoughts of him."

The truck he drove off was heavy as a giant iron-cast truck, a monster like Detroit's giant iron stove, that freakish landmark, cast out of prodigious insanity and forever after a drag upon the very earth . . . but he drove the truck steadily with a consciousness of being watched; his foot turned iron, his forehead ran with sweat, a cold erotic storm of particles all around him. It panicked him to think of having to live until the next day.

5

Like all lives, Jules's was long and richly tedious, vexed with prodigious details of physical existence he would have been ashamed to record, were he writing his own story; his story would deal with the spirit exclusively. He thought of himself as pure spirit struggling to break free of the morass of the flesh. He thought of himself as spirit struggling with the fleshly earth; the very force of gravity, death. All his life he thought of himself in this way, and only during certain bleak unbelievable periods—hustling around the Southwest, for example, or lying in a hospital bed trying to come back to life—would he have sighed to himself, *My life is a story imagined by a madman!*

Of the effort the spirit makes, this is the subject of Jules's story; of its effort to achieve freedom, its breaking out into beauty, in patches perhaps but beauty anyway, and of Jules as an American youth—these are some of the struggles he would have thought worth recording. All of Detroit is melodrama, and most lives in Detroit fated to be melodramatic, but Jules's fate was to fall again and again into astonishing shrill spaces of craziness, all of it overdone physically and aborted spiritually, but somehow logical. Of his experiences as a boy there hasn't been much time to speak, and anyway we have enough of these memories in other books. Of the many thousands of hours spent around kitchen tables—those eternal kitchen tables of the poor!—there is not much to say, and of the glancing knowledge he had of hoodlums and sub-crooks, petty thieves, con-men, pimps, men with no incomes and no jobs and no futures but with money, there is nothing much to say; Jules didn't really know them that well. Of his hours spent in bed dreaming, his hours at work, the way in which he put on his shoes—no one cares—though these things are closer to the heart of the real Jules than his delirium of love. For love, being a delirium and a pathological condition, makes of the lover a crazed man; his blood leaps with bacteria that shoot the temperature up toward death. The real Jules, a cunning boy with a sweet look about him, was drenched and overcome by the sweat of the crazed Jules, a Jules in love.

He drove back the next day, ready to pick up his girl, but she wasn't there. He waited. Then, not surprised and not disappointed, he continued down the street, his eyes grabbing at each girl he saw, waiting to see her. He did not have his delivery boy's uniform on. He wore a white shirt; a necktie was stuck in his pocket just in case. He had shaved carefully. His long hair had been combed neatly back. As if on a merry-go-round, and in no hurry, he drove around the block several times looking for her.

When he did not see her, in that press of after-school girls and boys and the hard-walking figures of Grosse Pointe matrons, he wound his way back toward her house, traveling by instinct. There was a sweet lassitude in his driving to her house, as if he were coming home. Block after block of elegant brick homes seemed to hypnotize him; yes, he was coming home. Let the girl barricade herself behind a locked door fronted with an iron grating; let her run up the staircase and hide behind another door, and then another; let her run to the attic to escape her fate—still, he would break everything down and find her and with his hands and body and voice convince her that all was well, she couldn't escape. He had taken on some of Bernard's relentless optimism, a little glassy-eyed, unswerving, perhaps doomed but enthusiastic to the end. *The worst that can happen is death,* Jules thought.

A police cruiser marked "Grosse Pointe Police" rounded a corner and, seeing the delivery truck, believed that all was well: a truck filled with flowers, an anonymous driver inside. Jules overtook a mashed squirrel in the street. He turned his wheels in order to avoid the animal. He did not want to contaminate himself, coming to Nadine. Yet his face was fixed in a kind of smile even for that dead animal, accepting it, linking it up with his inevitable path to Nadine's home—just one more thing he would have to see and pass by before he came to her. He wondered if he might be shot down. Did people shoot other people in Grosse Pointe? How did people die here—in hospitals, waited upon? He had read that there had been no serious crimes here in a whole twelve-month period, which seemed to him whimsical, maybe a mistake on the newspaper's part. And yet, what a lovely world for Nadine to live in!

Her house was approaching. Dreamlike, it seemed to be gliding toward him, without sound. His eyes fixed themselves upon that miraculous front door, not only fronted with an iron grating but covered chastely with a pane of glass, and behind all this a medieval-looking wooden door, meant to keep out all strangers. He parked the truck in the circular driveway. Alert enough to carry out a heavy potted plant—it was wrapped in red crinkly paper and a white bow, hospital-bound—he jumped out and saw out of the corner of his eye the police cruiser gliding past, out for a ride no doubt and enjoying life. No trouble!

Jules rang the doorbell. He remembered Bernard, fated to die, ringing this same doorbell. A Negro maid answered. "I have a delivery here for Miss Nadine . . . Nadine . . . I can't read the last name," Jules said, looking at the card.

"Greene?"

"Yes, Greene. Nadine Greene. Is the lady home?"

"I'll take it to her," the maid said sullenly.

"But it's a special delivery, she has to sign for it in person," Jules said.

He was breathing hard. The maid looked at him frankly and saw the hungry look of a city boy, undisguised by the flowers he held; she hesitated so he could see it.

Finally she said, "I'll see if she's home. Just a minute."

Jules edged into a small foyer, between the front door

and an inner door, not so heavy. Another foyer awaited him. He stepped through the second doorway, and the maid, glancing back at him, said, "You spost to bring that around to the back door, don't you know?" She looked at him with indifferent contempt, as if she saw through his plot and found it shabby. Jules would have struck his forehead if he had thought it might be convincing; deliveries were always made to the rear, he knew that, he'd known that for all of his servile life! Yet, come for Nadine, dressed in his civilian's clothing, he had forgotten and come directly to the front door like a suitor.

"I'm sorry, I'm new on the job."

The woman disappeared. He stared after her, down a corridor. The floor was highly waxed. A chandelier hung down from another story, a thousand tear-shaped bits of glass. He looked nervously up at it. He half expected the wind to jostle it and call attention to himself, Jules, an intruder. He expected a door to fly open somewhere and a man to rush out at him with a gun.

Still, getting this far inside the house was an accomplishment, already farther than he had seriously dared to hope, and he had only to remain there, committed and smiling, for the adventure to open before him. Bold and calculating, Jules believed at the same time in passivity; he thought of events opening before him, crashing about him, sweeping him up, as the act of love itself swept him along and made of him a Jules he would never have imagined himself.

The girl's voice came from somewhere. A sound of music ... tinkling glass?

"Downstairs. Front door," the maid said in her urban drawl.

Jules felt footsteps though he did not hear them. He saw a girl's figure appear at the top of the stairs. The stairway was covered in thick beige carpeting, every step and under the step, elegant, fastidious, rich, and he longed to be the carpet beneath her feet, feeling that delicate pressure. She came down only a few steps. She hesitated. "What is it?" she said.

"A special delivery."

"From who?"

"The card says, 'From your aunt,'" Jules said, looking at the card. It said, 'To Tanya, with love, Bessie.'

He held out the plant. He had no idea what it was—sickly white flowers nodding above dark, waxy green leaves, looking unreal. A plant for the dead. Nadine stared across the expanse of floor, disbelieving. Jules had not yet seen her clearly, being nervous himself, but over the tight bunched flowers he dared a look.

She had a pale, fated face.

"My aunt is dead," she said.

"From another aunt. From someone else's aunt," Jules said at once.

She remained on the stairs, still. Her fear inspired him. With so much fear in her why should he feel anything?

"I know who you are. I remember you," she said.

Jules said generously, "I'll put the plant down here on the floor. You can get it when I leave."

"I thought I had to sign a card."

"You can mail it in."

"You're crazy!"

She wore white. The dress was of coarse cotton, sporty-looking, very sweet. Jules loved her. He put the plant down on the floor and pushed it a few inches toward her with his foot. "See? There's no danger."

"Is that plant real?"

"Is your father home?"

"No."

"Your mother?"

"No."

"Where are they?"

"My father is in Chicago and my mother is out for the afternoon," she said, staring at the plant.

"Is there a room we could talk in?"

"A room?"

"Can we talk in your room?"

"No."

"Why not? Would you rather go out to a movie? A ride in my truck or a ride in a balloon or—"

"No!"

"Are you busy? What are you doing? What were you doing just now when I rang the bell?"

"Looking through my homework, figuring out my clothes—"

"Figuring out your clothes! But what is there to figure out with clothes?"

He took a step forward, charmed. She retreated a step upward on the stairs. Jules wondered where the maid was.

Behind him, the delivery truck was a weight dragging him down; it had been a mistake to leave it there. So he said, retreating. "Well, I'll leave this here and say good-by. I have five hours' work ahead of me."

She stared at him, surprised.

"Just fill out the card and mail it in," Jules said.

He drove the truck around the block and parked it on a side street and walked quickly back. In the newspaper article about Grosse Pointe in which he'd learned about their low crime rate, he had read also that few people bothered to lock their doors, even at night, and so it was a natural thing for him to stroll right up to the front door and open it. Nadine was now bent over the potted plant. He saw her through the inner door. Her head was bowed, her hair was very black around her face, her face was serious, pale, doubting, but still not quite real to him. He hoped his face wouldn't make hers raw. He tapped on the glass of the inner door and opened it slowly.

She jerked around.

"Can we talk in your room?" Jules whispered.

"What do you want?"

She seemed frightened, yet a faint smile drew her lips apart.

"A few minutes."

"You can be arrested for this," she said.

"Why should I be arrested? I love you—what is my crime?" Jules said.

"Then you're crazy, you can be put away!"

"Is your room upstairs?"

"What do you want with me? What are you doing?" she said.

"I'm just doing what I have to do," Jules said.

With one hand she seemed to be warding him off, as if warding off the blow of an ax. The other hand was motionless, helpless. Jules wanted to seize both hands and kiss them hungrily. He sighed. "If nobody is home, why can't we talk? Talk upstairs? I can help you figure out your clothes."

"Are you going to rob the house?"

"Rob the house! Why?"

"Is somebody else with you outside?"

"Why would I bring somebody else along?"

She laughed. Her laughter was abrupt and high-pitched; it stopped suddenly. She said, "You came here on a bet.

They're outside watching. Take me outside and introduce me to them."

"Nobody's outside."

"Yes, yes, there's somebody outside! From school, from somewhere! It's a joke—let me in on it. I want to know what the joke is, I don't want people to laugh at me."

"It's no joke. We're all alone."

"We're not alone!"

"We're all alone right here, talking."

She shook her head. "No, it isn't funny. You shouldn't play tricks on me. Sometimes I lie in bed all night crying— it's bad enough to cry over nothing, but now, now I'll cry about this, you playing a joke on me!"

"What is the joke? That I love you?"

"You don't love me!"

"Why is that a joke?"

"You don't love me, you're just laughing at me. How can you love me?" she said angrily. He saw how very white the whites of her eyes were, making the iris darker; she had an unnatural stare. Her face might harden into beauty in her late twenties, perhaps. There was a slightly unfocused, uncoordinated look to her; she was edgy and near hysteria.

"Why do you cry all night in bed?" Jules asked gently.

"I don't know—don't people cry in bed? Why do you want to play a trick on me?"

"It's no trick. I won't hurt you."

"About my uncle—you said—?"

"I don't know anything about him."

"You said you saw him dead! His throat cut!"

"Somebody else's uncle."

"No, you said so. You were the one. You saw him lying dead."

"Did you tell your father about it?"

"He hasn't been home. Why would I tell him anything?"

"Your mother?"

"No, of course not!"

"Can we go upstairs?"

She stared at him with a peculiar half-smile, a drugged smile.

"Is anyone home beside you and the maid?"

"Nobody."

"I won't hurt you," Jules said softly.

"Anything could happen to me and I wouldn't know it,"

she said. Jules took her hand. She looked at his hand, holding hers. "I feel so far from everything. It could happen to me, pass over me, doors opening and things like that— slime getting on me—and I wouldn't even notice at the time. Then afterward I would remember and start to scream. I thought all night about you, what you said yesterday. At the time I didn't think about it at all. I hardly noticed you. Then, as soon as you drove away, I began to think about you and what you said, my uncle and all that, and you were coming back today—"

"You didn't call the police?" He caressed her hand, which was quite cold. "Five minutes upstairs? In secret. I want to introduce myself to you."

Like Jules, she seemed to be in a kind of trance. But he could not count on it lasting. He kissed her hand. The action was deliberate, stilted, very tender, so that Nadine's head moved forward slightly, mechanically, as if preparing to submit itself to the heavy edge of an ax.

"I don't know you," she whispered.

"In five minutes you'll know everything. I'll turn myself inside out for you."

He scooped up the plant and walked with Nadine, his arm around her shoulders. Pieces of furniture seemed to move backward from them, against walls, giving them room. Such furniture, Jules supposed, had no function except to take up space—there was a lot of space in this house, and no one around. Everything was silent, in awe of his daring. Would it be a lovely life, lived out in a museum of a house? He would make money after all. Why not money? A million dollars? He had no direction in which to go except up . . . everything was above him, all of America . . . and on his way why not try for it all? He would make a million dollars before the age of thirty and marry this girl, Nadine Greene.

"I love you," he whispered. "I've been in love with you since that day I brought your uncle here. You walked around the front of the car and I fell in love with you. I can't explain . . ."

She leaned toward him, listening. She was very tense. He could see her pale forehead beneath a childish, feathery bunch of bangs, hair he wanted to brush impatiently aside, wanting to get a full look at her face. He was afraid of her innocence. Maybe it was evil for him to draw her into his love, out of this gleaming house, these rich pieces of silent, empty furniture. "I won't hurt you. Never," he said, and at the same time he was thinking, involuntarily, of a closet back in his childhood where he'd fooled around with some girl for several hours, just a little girl and himself a little boy, not yet innocent. He thought of Nadine locked in a closet and him locked in with her, for eight hours.

Jules drew a line with his fingertips from her ear to the tip of her chin. "When will your mother be home?"

"I don't know."

She led him upstairs and into her room. He saw now that this was the first room he had ever been in, the first room anyone had seriously lived in. His sisters' rooms had not been real rooms. This one was decorated in white and yellow. His heart thudded suddenly, seeing it, understanding that it belonged to Nadine and had been built around her, built for her and her alone. Her price was beyond estimation. He put the pot of flowers down on her bureau, glad that they were white and pure, an offering worthy of her. He was silent.

She put her hands up to her face. Jules's senses seemed to move together in a sudden urgency, an explosive urgency; he went to embrace her. She was stiff in his arms but did not resist. He kissed her lightly, wanting to put her to sleep with kisses, comfort her, his mouth light against hers like the petals of roses or the fluttering wings of moths, nothing substantial. It was all so airy, even this embrace. He kissed her eyes, her hair, her throat, her mouth, breathing softly through his mouth and through hers, desirous of her sweet breath, prepared to become intoxicated by it. How he wanted that intoxication! But at the height of his tenderness he felt that he was losing his mind and that this could not last. He stumbled with her backwards to the bed. He pushed her down on the bright yellow bedspread and lay on top of her, suddenly anxious, surprised at how real she was, not squirming or fighting but just a small density of flesh, very warm. Her eyes were closed. He felt her terror. In silence she moved her head from side to side, not avoiding his lips but not quite ready for them. He felt as if he were on the brink of madness or of some terrible act the other Jules would perform and then withdraw, leaving him behind. He seemed to black out and then return to consciousness, in the same instant. Consciousness was delicate. He framed her face with his hands and stared down at her. His heart was pounding, urging him on, that thief's heart of his, but her stillness urged him to go slowly, to love her. If he did not cherish her he would never forgive himself.

"Are you all right? Am I hurting you?" he said.

She did not answer. She seemed nearly unconscious.

For some time he remained that way, pure and in awe of her face, though the violence was building up in him and his hands moved from her face to her throat, groping, caressing, wondering . . . to her small breasts, which seemed to him terribly unprotected, right against him and close to his own heaving heart, and with his thighs he held her tight . . . could feel the slight cleft of her loins, the lean muscle. With his legs he held her legs tight together, protecting her from him, but a sudden frenzy drove him to fall heavily upon her, his teeth seeking flesh, anything to rub helplessly against, and his face in a grimace that wasn't anything of the real Jules. And all of his senses finally rushed together, out of control, so that he moaned and had to grind himself against her rigid body in order to bear it. And so that was over.

He lay beside her, waking. He hadn't been asleep, but still he seemed to be waking, coming back to life. His breath was jagged. Nadine, lying stiff, with one arm flung back across her forehead, did not look at him. Now he could look around. He saw that he was in a girl's room, a lovely white and yellow room, a picturebook room. On the bureau were some things—among them white flowers. The rug was fluffy and yellow, meant for bare feet. Yet, being in this room, lying on the bed, he had a peculiar sense of not truly being in it but only looking at it.

She did not move her arm. "Nobody ever did this to me before," she said.

"Honey, I'm sorry."

"I never even thought of it. Some things I don't think about. Then if they happen I don't know what they are, I have to let time go by so that I can figure them out . . ."

He was anxious that she keep on talking, because she seemed to find talking so difficult, almost painful. He could see her mind casting about for a thought, for words, anything. But he could not help her.

"People don't touch me," she said. "I don't let them near

me. I don't want to get them mixed up with myself, everybody so close ..."

"I hope I didn't hurt you," Jules said, feeling sluggish and sweaty, all body.

"I ran away two times. The policewoman, a nice woman, asked me both times if I had been with a man. They think you won't run anywhere, won't bother walking out the front door, unless it has something to do with a man. She never needed to ask me anything more because she could tell by looking at me. Nobody ever got this close to me before."

"I didn't hurt you?"

"I don't remember what happened. It's mixed up with my uncle."

"Forget about him."

"I can feel myself lying on my back somewhere, like this, in some strange room in Detroit, with my throat cut and the blood down under my back, getting me wet. I can almost see it. And you're squatting over me, looking at me."

"But why?" Jules asked, shocked.

She lowered her arm and opened her eyes experimentally. She looked at him. Her stare was frank and inquisitive and a little flirtatious, though Jules thought he might be mistaken. Maybe she was getting ready to scream instead, and would he have the good sense to put his hand over her mouth?

"So you ran away from home?" he asked quickly. "Where did you go?"

"Downtown."

"Why downtown?"

"It's far enough, it's like any other city. Why should I go all the way out to Los Angeles? Detroit is big enough."

"I live downtown."

"Alone?"

"Yes, alone."

She tried to smile at him. Warmed, reassured, Jules leaned over her again and caressed her face and shoulders. At once she closed her eyes. She seemed to be getting rid of herself, abandoning herself to him. A pinprick in his brain began swelling suddenly, and he moaned and moved upon her again, one arm around her head very gently, kissing her. He had no idea where he was. He forgot everything— bed, bedroom, house, street, police cruiser—he could not remember, and beyond her soft, pale skin he could believe in nothing. He took her arm and kissed it. He raised it to his lips, running his tongue along it, in love with her delicate flesh; he tried to put her arm around his neck, in an embrace, but she was limp. Her neck arched, her head yearned backward. He shut his eyes and pressed himself against her, feeling all the clarity of a second before—they had had a conversation!—whirl out of him and leave him no wiser. *Ah, Jules,* he thought, able to remember his own name, *this is worth dying for!*

He believed he would truly be her lover in a few minutes and that their lives would be forever entwined, irrevocably, and so he began to explain himself. His voice was feeble and rushed.

"I know that only good can come of this. Only good. You were right to let me touch you and not anyone else . . . It's because you know who I am, you feel it. I will set myself a few years to make enough money, I won't fail. We'll be close together all of our lives and nothing can undo it . . ."

The girl did not open her eyes. She was listening tensely, silently.

"All my life I've trusted to certain signs, hunches," he said. "For instance, I happen to be walking along and something comes to me, like a dream, an idea comes to me, and I feel a terrible need to make it come true right away. My heart starts pounding like hell. Once when I almost lost a picture of a girl I had this feeling. I had to get the picture back, it was a sign of something, I don't know what, and anyway I forgot about the girl afterward, for some reason, but I had to get the picture and I got it. It would have been the end for me if I hadn't. I don't know how I know this."

The telephone rang beside her bed.

Jules, terrified, nearly jumped up to escape. The ringing got in the way of his thoughts: he could not think. Nadine, sleepily, reached out for the phone. It was yellow. He watched her groping for it, wanting to guide her hand. She pulled the receiver off and let it fall onto the bed. A tiny voice questioned them. "Pick it up! Say hello," Jules said, alarmed. The receiver began to slide down, about to fall on the floor. Jules picked it up himself. "Who this? Who on the other end?" he said in a vicious Negro accent, then slammed the receiver down.

Nadine laughed.

"Who was that? A friend of yours? Your mother?"

"I don't know. Why would it be my mother?"

The telephone rang again. This time Nadine sat up and answered it; she surprised Jules with her sudden coolness. "Hello, Brenda," she said, her eyes already veiled from him at the sound of that small, strange voice that meant something to her and nothing at all to him. "No, I can't. Something came up. Call Sue. What? Why not? I don't know. Mother doesn't want me to. I guess not. No."

Jules wanted to snatch the phone out of her hand and slam it down. It seemed to him offensive that she should talk so casually with a friend of hers, bruised and stained as she was from Jules's passion.

"Hang up!" Jules said.

She said good-by abruptly and hung up.

"What is your name?" she asked Jules.

"Jules."

"I like that name. That's a beautiful name for a man. But you can't push me around like that. You can't tell me what to do."

He did not hear most of what she said, trying to ease himself gently upon her, feeling himself heavy and awkward. He did not want to surprise her with his body. She was so naïvely opaque, so passive and unwondering, that he supposed she hadn't much idea of what was going to happen to her—the skirt of her white dress had been pulled up onto her thighs and Jules had a longing to pull it back down again, to protect her.

"I'll never tell you what to do, never again," Jules said.

They lay with their faces pressed together. Jules was drenched with sweat. Nadine's forehead was wet, with her own sweat or his, he couldn't tell. He felt as if the boundaries of their bodies were melting with the heat of his love. It was a phenomenon that happened apart from him, from them, a natural fact. He had never been so close to anyone before—as if he were lying with someone he had made up, a girl he'd dreamed into being.

She seized his wrist and stopped his hand. "Don't," she said.

They were both trembling.

After a moment, unmoving, she said, "Could you take me somewhere?"

"What? Where?"

"Could we go away somewhere? You and me?"

"You mean run away?"

"Yes, run away. Could we? Could you take me? Could we go to Mexico?"

Jules thought for a moment. "All right."

"Could we leave today?"

"Today?"

"Could we pretend we were married?"

"Do you want to get married?"

She said seriously, feverishly, "We can pretend. We could tell anyone who asked . . ."

He touched her legs, and she brought her knees hard together, in panic. "No, don't, " she said.

She lay sweating in his arms. He had never seen anyone so agitated—it crossed his mind to be afraid of her. Tears made Jules's eyes ache—for her, for the misery he was enduring, which was part pity, part delirium. He rubbed his face against hers. His own lips were a little sore and his body ached now with a passion that had turned skeptical. They seemed to be together on a boat, a small raft, which was being carried along swiftly, out of Jules's control; he could not even see where it was headed. The girl murmured, "Jules, Jules," as if she were somehow making him up, giving him a shape out of her own imagination. There was something halting and experimental about her, but he tried not to think about it. He did not want to be frightened of her. At the height of his joy in this was a strange premonition of madness, his own madness or hers—the fear of madness, Maureen's blank stare, which might turn out to be his inheritance as well. Their bodies, so sore from the clothes they wore, and so damp, seemed to be drifting somewhere with the pull of a river's gravity, dragging them miserably downstream, to a climate of black intense heat.

"Let me come to you," Jules said.

She moved from him in terror. He seemed to lose consciousness again, borne rapidly downward and clutching her, feeling the texture of her cotton dress against his straining fingers, forgetting her. It was as if, in a movie, on camera, the tension had grown so strong as to become unendurable: hence a blackout, the end. Jules heard himself groaning as if in pain, surprised at the pain.

After a while she began to sob against his face, "You'll

take me away from here. I'll get in your car and close the door. They won't be able to follow me. There's no mark, nothing left behind . . . just highways. I'll kill myself if I can't get out of this place."

Jules could not make sense of her words. He pressed his face against her, not hearing.

"It doesn't matter if we get married or not, I don't care. I want to keep driving and get out of this country and into Mexico—I've seen pictures of Mexico. I want to live where people speak another language, so that they can't talk to me and I can't talk to them."

She seemed not to have understood what had happened to Jules or what was happening yet. Her own excitement was almost violent, but it was in her head and nowhere else—Jules could very nearly feel it, a pressure more painful than the one he had endured.

"In school I try to make myself sleep. I sit at my desk but I shut my mind off, blotting out part of the room. It's like a picture puzzle, with parts. I blot out one piece, then another, then another. I can sit there without sleeping and yet my mind is asleep, it's neutral and not even upset. The girl who called me on the telephone—I don't have any connection with her, not really, or with anyone. I don't know why. And now you came along—I don't even know how you got here. You're in my room and I can't remember. People should come along like this, by accident. Nobody else in my life is an accident," she said and Jules saw himself being marked up as if with a dab of red paint, marked off, a kind of freak. "I'm going to be seventeen but I'm really older than my mother. I don't want to be like this but I can't help it. Jules, are you listening to me, do you believe me?"

"Yes."

"Why do I want to sleep all the time? Why am I too old for everything? When my mother gets excited about something, it embarrasses me to see how childish she is. You won't meet my mother. But she's happy and I'm not. You won't meet my father either. They're good people, I like them, but when you're with them you lose interest in being good. You think, well, if they're good people I might as well do something else. It makes your head ache. It's all played out. My father is always in a hurry but he has time to plan things. He sits planning things, drinking milk late at night . . . he makes plans for five, ten, fifteen years that way, in his business. He's a vice-president in charge of public relations. You probably don't even know what that is. He travels all over. I used to love him but now I think I love you. I can hardly remember him when you hold me. I think I'll forget them all with you. If we could just get out of here and drive somewhere, fast, down to Mexico or Texas."

Jules wiped the sweat out of his eyes. "Honey, why Mexico or Texas?"

"Just an idea I have."

"You're not making this all up?"

"No."

He caressed her vainly, feeling the numbness in her pass over into himself. He understood why ordinary men—gas-station attendants, taxi drivers—killed women, feeling the numbness in them flow violently into themselves, bringing it all to an end.

Nadine brought herself sharply up on one elbow. By the tension of her body Jules knew she was hearing something he couldn't hear. "My mother is home," she said.

He heard a rumbling noise, then a dull thud.

"She's coming out of the garage . . . she's in the kitchen . . ."

Jules heard nothing.

Nadine got up slowly. She disengaged herself from him politely, as if not wanting to hurt his feelings. He saw with surprise that she looked sick—her face rubbed sore, her hair damp and mussed, her dress wrinkled and smudged. *Am I in love? Is this love?* Jules asked himself. He was intoxicated with lust but a little soured over it too.

Nadine brushed her hair angrily back from her face with her hands. "I have to go out or she'll come in and talk. You can wait for me."

If he had wanted to escape, Jules thought, he was too exhausted; his will was flattened out.

He waited for her. Half an hour passed, an hour. He was not at all afraid. His body was the body of a drowned man, motionless. The worst that might happen would be death, a second death . . .

After a while Nadine came back. She approached the bed. "Some people are coming in now for cocktails. I have to talk to them for a while. I didn't do anything wrong. I didn't cry or start to scream. It's because I can't believe what's happened, I can't make sense of it yet." She smiled at him. "So you're safe. Will you wait for me?"

Jules lifted his arms to her. She bent over him and they kissed.

"Or maybe I'll call the police, I don't know," she said as she left.

Jules must have slept; when he came to it was nearly dark outside. He sprang to his feet, testing himself. He was still himself. His face was sore, his body ached, when he stretched his mouth his lips cracked in several places, yet it was all recognizable. He felt cheerful. His fate was obviously prepared for him and could not be averted now. He looked through her bureau drawers to get to know her—pajamas, sweaters, slips, underwear—a real girl after all, an ordinary girl. He opened the door to her closet. A light came on automatically. He looked through her dresses, handling them gently, pleased with their bright colors. He touched her shoes with the tip of his own shoe, pleased. He supposed he did love her. She was accessible in these objects, clothing and shoes, in spite of her high price. Perhaps he could fill up the vacuum in her with something of his own. Why not run away with her? It was time for him to run away again, permanently, to Mexico or Texas. Fate had arranged it. He gnawed at the flowers he'd brought her, in idleness, joking to himself, and then spat them out on the carpet.

She returned. She came to him silently, and they embraced. Old friends. Old lovers. She said in a bright, tense whisper, "You're very handsome. Are you going to take me away?"

"Sure."

"Do you have any money?"

"Don't you?"

"Just in the bank, but the bank is closed. Don't you have any?"

"A little."

"We don't need much, do we?"

They lay down again, gently. Jules kissed her and at the back of her mind saw something that frightened him, but he lost sight of it. She stroked his hair. She stroked the back of his neck. They smiled at each other as if just meeting, just catching sight of each other. The house was dangerous,

Jules knew, but he was wooed by inertia; he did not care to move. The thought of Mexico seemed improbable.

"I could stay here. I could live here, in your room, for the rest of my life," he said.

Nadine left him reluctantly. She went to the mirror and looked at herself. "No wonder they stared at me. Mother asked me if I'd had anything to eat today. Well, I won't have to look at myself again, not here," she said with satisfaction. There was something hard and intelligent about her after all, Jules thought. She began to heap pieces of clothing together, swiftly and impatiently, as if alone.

Jules lay on the bed and watched her. "You're not really serious about this?" he said.

"I'm always serious."

He liked that answer. "Good," he said. "And you have your mind set for Mexico?"

"I would rather leave with you than go by myself," she said. "I had it in my mind to leave anyway. I kept thinking of leaving, going away. I don't know why. I don't want to bum around exactly. I don't want to see other kids—all that crap. I want to get out somewhere empty, where they speak another language. I'll try it. And I didn't choose you, you came along. It isn't my fault. It must mean something, it must be a sign. I couldn't stop you from coming up here and I love your name and your face. I don't love anyone else, I'm dead to them, asleep to them. I didn't make this happen though. You did. You came in the front door. It isn't my fault."

"Not my fault either," Jules said cheerfully.

They waited a few more hours. They sat side by side on her bed, Jules smoking a cigarette and Nadine waving the smoke away, as if setting up a pattern for the next forty years. She talked. From time to time he saw her face contract into a mask of tiny, impatient wrinkles, irritated by something. Jules leaned over to kiss her shoulder. She caressed his face lightly, tenderly, with a kind of surprise at herself for being so tender. Around one o'clock they prepared to leave. Jules felt that he was leaving a room in which he had spent a good part of his life.

"Are you nervous?" he said.

"Yes. Are you?"

"I'm ready."

They went downstairs. A single light was burning in the foyer. Jules respected the house, felt humble inside it, and yet impersonal; it was quite right that he should be stealing this girl from it. Nadine took his hand and led him up to the front door. "And now—now what are we going to do?" she said.

"Steal a car, honey."

"Steal a car? Where?"

"I only need it to get back to Detroit to pick up my own car. I have a car. Are there friends of yours, neighbors?"

"Right next door. I don't know their name. But how can you steal a car?"

"Just go in and steal it if the key's in the ignition."

"It will be in the wife's car, in that ignition," Nadine said. She carried her clothing stuffed in a paper bag, not very large. It was the lightsome burden of their new life.

Without fear, trusting to fate, Jules went around the back of an immense home to its garage. The door was open. There were three cars and in one of them the keys were stuck, waiting.

Everything was under an enchantment.

Minutes later, free and rushing down Lakeshore Drive, Jules reached over to take hold of her hand. He kissed it, like a new husband. She had begun to cry. "Nothing can stop us," Jules declared.

6

His breath was drawn from him in slow, languorous, painful sighs. He could not get the object of his yearning into focus. Sleeping, he tried to shake his way free of sleep, wanting to get this clear—what was so painful, what penetrated him so bitterly? He wanted nothing more than to understand. Pictures of undreamed dreams flashed to him, like cards. He remembered first grade, cards with words and numbers on them. He remembered Sister Mary Jerome. Her pale, vivid face flashed into his mind and was then lost. He thought of his mother, unpacking groceries from a bag. He thought of Maureen. He woke.

It was very early, too early to wake. From the window a steamy bright light outlined the shade; in several cracks light was outlined. It looked as if they had been made with a magic pencil. Jules closed his eyes quickly, hoping to sleep longer. The days of driving, of being on the run, were too much for him, and he would feel, half an hour after getting up, as if he hadn't gone to bed at all. But outside on the highway traffic was noisy, awake hours ahead of him. He had felt the vibrations of big trucks passing all night long. And, very late, there had been shouts out there—kids, probably drunk, hitchhiking or on their way out to farm homes, exactly Jules's age but no kin to him. The highway was a big black line on the map he and Nadine studied, but he could not remember its name or number. Were they already in Arkansas, or had they passed through Arkansas? Were they in Texas? Jules opened his eyes suddenly, afraid that the maps lied. Once you were running you might never make any progress, and one landscape might blend into another. Michigan, Illinois, Arkansas, Texas—there were no signs in the earth to show where one left off and another began.

Beside him Nadine lay with her back to him. Her tangled, shining hair was mixed up with the pain of his sleep. He would have liked to move against her, sliding his arms around her, burying his face in her, and sleep again, but he couldn't do this. He could not disturb her. For some reason he was reminded of a child he had come across in Detroit once, lost, at night. It wasn't that strange to see kids wandering around and most of the time they knew where they were going or where they belonged and they'd go back home, after a while, but this kid had touched Jules's heart because he was really lost and his terror had set him apart from everything around him. He had been about six years old, a white boy. His hair had been long and matted with days of neglect, his clothes filthy, but when Jules had asked him, "You lost, kid?" he had been afraid to answer. The boy's eyes had been liquidy with a spread, exhaustive terror, and he had seemed not to hear or see Jules though aware of Jules's presence. It had been about three in the morning, the street fairly busy with stragglers, and there the boy had stood by the doorway of a darkened liquor store, in front of the grating, just standing. He had stood a few feet away from Jules but in a terrible vacuum, in a dream Jules did not dare to enter. He had the idea that if he were to touch the boy the boy would sink his teeth into his hand, like an animal.

Nadine was like that, he thought. Her prettiness was distance in itself. If he were to bury himself in her, finally, throwing his body on hers in a last demand for mercy, she would wake from her lethargic sweetness and change at once into an animal, ready to struggle to the death.

"No, don't touch me. I can't. I'm afraid," she was always saying.

He touched her hair with his fingertips. She slept. Every night she fell off to sleep like a drugged child, leaving him awake; out on the highway trucks roared past and made the cabin or room they had rented for the night shudder. Jules certainly could not sleep, awake with his thoughts and with all this noise. He was growing keener, more intelligent, as his flesh was wearing away from him—he had lost weight, but there seemed to him a kind of spiritual leanness also, an intensity. What did he want except this girl? But his brain could do nothing with her, could not reason with her or dismiss her. He could not reason with himself. She was eerily sweet, lying in his arms, fully dressed though her clothes were always rumpled and pulled awry and Jules's own clothes wet with the anguish of his body, but still she kept pure her own image of herself, *if he loved her he would not hurt her*—making plans for them that dissolved every evening when Jules made her understand they could not drive any farther that day, he was finished. Her sad, evil vision of purity kept him pure. He could not contaminate her with his lust; she seemed to feel nothing.

"What time is it?" Nadine said, waking.

Jules pressed his face against her back. They had not undressed the night before, sleeping without covers in this southern autumnal heat, and so there was never any real sleep for them, Jules thought, always this uneasy, temporary resting, as if they were both prepared to jump up and run out of the cabin at a moment's notice.

"It's early," said Jules.

"Shouldn't we get started?"

"In a while."

She twisted to look at him. Her face was puffy with sleep. How she trusted him, her lover Jules! It was a sign that never in her life had anyone offended her, manhandled her, betrayed her, and that her body had passed through seventeen years of life in America without having been insulted. He loved this about her, her stupid purity. He loved her trusting him as she did. What was entrusted to his hands, so completely, was a gift of his own opinion of himself—a good person after all, not vicious, able to fall farther in love than he had ever imagined.

She slid her arms around his neck. They kissed. Jules, his pain newly awakened and eager, looked at her misty, half-closed eyes and wondered if he would get out of this alive.

"Today let me drive. Please," she said.

"You don't have a license. What about the police?"

"Why should they stop us?"

Jules, driving a not-very-new Ford that looked exactly as if it might belong to a kid who looked like him, still felt danger everywhere. He was astonished at how many police he saw. Whenever they passed through small towns he was sure to slow down, for there the police were, two or three idle, uniformed men in a squad car, behind a billboard and doing nothing except staring out at traffic and quick to note out-of-state license plates; on the deserted highways Jules sped along at the best speed his car could make, around sixty-five, and there the state troopers were—lean, anonymous men wearing sunglasses, patrolling endlessly, making illegal U-turns to speed back after some lawbreaker or imagined lawbreaker, having nothing to do with their days but cruise up and down the highways, enjoying life, given over entirely to cruising, assessing, clocking. He feared their pulling up alongside him and shouting, "Get over to the side!" And there, at the side of the road, they would lean into his window and shout, "Where did you get that girl from?"

He imagined Nadine crying, "He made me come with him, he kidnaped me from Detroit!"

She sat up. "Before we start out we should buy some food. And some shampoo. I want to wash my hair."

"Does it need washing so soon?"

"I want to be clean. Could you get those things?"

Wearily he tested his legs; they moved. "I wish you loved me," he said sadly.

"I do love you. What do you mean?"

He swung around to get up. Everything changed and yet each morning was the same: he had faith in the future and believed that eventually they would come to an ideal landscape, something to please Nadine, but it was not here. Arkansas, or Texas, whichever state . . . a condition of the sky and earth that was somehow not right . . . it didn't test right to Jules. His instincts told him he had to keep running; he was irritated to recall a dream he'd once had, of a wilderness and a clearing like an island in it—for how could there be a clearing in a wilderness without someone's labor? Without someone being betrayed?

"Where am I going to get money from, my love?" Jules said. "I'm down to two dollars."

She said nothing.

"All right, I'll be back in half an hour," Jules said.

He dabbed water onto his face in the smelly little lavatory with its damp, dripping shower stall. Everywhere there were the remains of bugs, and a few bugs that moved sluggishly. When he went out Nadine was lazily drawing her hair back from her face, smiling at him.

To have her with him, traveling with him as if she belonged to him—what triumph!

He never got out of the reach of his love for her. It followed him around, it was breathed in and out by his aching lungs, it gave to the hollowed cheeks of old women on the streets an enchanted look. On this morning, a warm September morning, everything looked mistily enchanting, cast into an off-golden hue, both threatening and promising. Really, Jules thought, walking fast along the highway toward a small town nearby, really he was an enchanted person. Nadine would someday wake up to his love for her; he had faith in her intelligence. It seemed to him that she was truly extraordinary, that the very intensity of her strangeness corresponded to something in him, a wildness he had never exactly acknowledged. Surely the two of them were marked for a special fate.

Special fates were of two kinds, both miraculous, but one leading to wealth and power and prominence, the other leading to sudden death, a throat slit by a stranger's knife or a hard, resistant skull sheared off half an inch at the top. You had to pay a kind of price for your fate. Jules thought amiably, *Jules Wendall is my fate*, knowing it was not Nadine who shaped him but himself—for another man wouldn't have fallen in love with her . . . only Jules could have loved her so violently.

Nadine fed his idle dreams of becoming rich as if he were giving her the words himself. He would become rich, she felt sure, how could he fail? "Because there are so many stupid people I know who are rich," she told him. And Jules, who had brains and good luck, could not fail. Jules secretly agreed with her. He had faith in an automatic upward swing, once he got really on the bottom; clearly, there was no future not open to him. Why not? He would locate himself in the Southwest and begin in a growing area . . . a salesman, for insurance? real estate? oil? With his looks and his brains, he thought, why couldn't he make as much money as his Uncle

Samson had made? That is, on his way to becoming a millionaire?

The tourist court they were staying in looked shabby in the daylight, and along the highway, off the raw, red, eroding shoulder of the road, various buildings shared that look. Jules scanned the flat horizon and could locate nothing anywhere of promise. Where was the beauty he had waited for? There were scatterings of pine trees but they looked anemic and second-rate. The blighted elms of Detroit were not less beautiful. He passed a bowling alley that looked closed. On its gravel driveway boys were playing, riding bicycles. Their shouts excited Jules. Hadn't he also been a child, in the country? But this was not the country. It was not the city either. Raw, gaping hunks had been cut out of the earth—in preparation for a shopping plaza maybe—and trees were overturned, dried out. Vacant fields. A tavern painted pink. The neon lights, turned off, looked chipped in the daylight. As he stared at the tavern the sun came out, or burned through the mist, and a sudden blow of heat struck him. He was truly in a foreign country. He was a stranger; it wasn't necessary not to understand the language.

Though he took care to wash himself every night, anxious not to disgust Nadine, still the southern sun made his pores ache with sweat. He felt filthy almost right away: there was nothing he could do to stay clean. Nadine was fastidious about herself, as careful to keep her hair and face and body clean as she was to keep herself, *Nadine,* clean of the pollution of love. She washed her hair every other day, that head of long thick black hair he loved, and let it dry, and brushed it out, thoughtfully, frowning, like a child to whom the troubles of the world are scaled down to snarls in a brush; something to be worked over and solved. He loved her so much!

Loving her, alone in this strange country, he walked in a warm humid daze. The sun caressed his back the way Nadine naïvely caressed him. He was certain that she did love him, but she was afraid of him. Certainly she should be afraid: there was too much in him waiting for her, too much violence. But he wanted to give her the pleasure that was stored up in him, for her alone, to wrap her in his arms and deliver her over to an abandonment of love, losing her in love. His own desire for her, which was slowly driving him crazy, was partly a desire to please her and make her a slightly different person, a young woman in love. Still, she said self-pityingly, "You want to hurt me," and he tried to explain to her that he would never hurt her—except, of course, he would have to hurt her a little. "But why do you only think of *that?*" she said uneasily. "Isn't it enough for us to be friends? Close friends? Don't you love me enough this way?"

As he walked, trucks and cars threw bits of dust onto him. The dust stuck. His shirt was wet already and he was just entering the town. He found himself staring at a farm girl in a truck, in the passenger's seat, looking out at him. She waved. The truck roared past. Jules felt a pang of excitement, wondering if she thought she knew him or whether it was just a friendly sign, a sign of his being handsome, likable. The affection of other people was like a fishhook in Jules. He could be drawn up eagerly by any kind word. And might it happen that Nadine, carried farther and farther south, would turn affectionate and buttery to his touch as the memory of Detroit faded? In Texas, in a small town, she would become his bride the way the fourteen- and fifteen-year-old girls of the South became brides, without much fuss.

He walked by a laundromat. A whiff of air from inside nearly suffocated him—what heat! A few housewives, girlish and chattering, stood around inside, stuffing laundry into holes, dragging laundry out. A little girl squatting in the doorway smiled at Jules: a good sign. Now he passed a Piggly-Wiggly store. Shopping carts were bunched up outside, against the building. A few were scattered around the lot. As soon as he got money he would buy some food in this store, right here. It looked safe.

He walked on, trying for the shade when he could get it, passing parked cars and strolling shoppers and kids, passing a drugstore, crossing a street, his eye attracted by a woman in slacks and a yellow blouse who was talking to a cop. Jules couldn't look away from her, he had to turn his head, passing her, though he thought this might be dangerous—after all, the man was a cop. He had a head of brown-blond hair, very curly. He was chewing gum. He did not notice Jules.

Excitement had entered Jules in a rush. Jumpy, his vision jumpy, he hesitated in front of a sporting-goods store and pretended to be interested in camping outfits. Fishing rods of glass and metal . . . high boots . . . mosquito netting . . . It seemed to him prodigious, all these things, unthinkable; their maleness pleased him. In the store window he could see, reflected clearly, the shapes of girls passing behind him. His blood surged with ambition for the future—he would sell oil wells, he'd be an architect and build buildings, spectacular skyscrapers, he'd be a politician, a governor, a senator, he'd speak on television and nothing would be beyond his grasp . . .

He came to a cigar store. It reminded him of Detroit and so he went in, liking the masculine odor of tobacco and newsprint. A rack of magazines caught his eye. He pretended to be seriously interested, frowning. He should be on his way but still he lingered. The covers of paperback books attracted him. *Lust and Love* was the title of one book; Jules thumbed through it, hoping for some advice, some consolation. Another cover showed a girl with wild red hair stepping on a man who lay in chains, a man with a face something like Jules's. What a fate! Jules moved on reluctantly. Magazines on display, a hundred covers. *Detective Annals*—on its cover a girl in a tight red skirt being dragged into a taxicab. "The Lust-Mad Cabbie of Memphis" was a headline. Jules picked up the magazine and leafed through it nervously. The pulp pages did not move with grace. He came upon another story: "Jail-Bait Slashed, Raped, and Slain in Boise." The story was illustrated with several photographs of a fourteen-year-old girl with a snippy face, long blond hair, a strange, demonic pleasure evident in her mouth, her parted lips. *Her mother went into hysterics when police. . . . Neither parent knew of her secret life. . . . Hitchhiking up and down the highway for fun. . . .* Jules scanned the story, looking for a crucial paragraph, but he had no luck, and when he tried to turn the page he turned too many pages. The girl was lost to him. He came upon another story, trembling: "My Baby's Father Was Killed in My Arms!" A photograph of a muddy trailer, a woman in slacks, her face undistinguished, men in the background who looked like state troopers. *One minute after my baby was conceived his father was shot to death in my arms—my ex-husband broke in and killed him, pumping five bullets into him!* Jules scanned this story, feeling both excitement and disgust. He scanned the paragraphs that led to the couple's meeting, their wandering back to the trailer court, their love-making, and, finally, the blast of bullets, the end. Then, in disgust, he put the magazine back. He felt dizzy. All around him were photographs of girls, on magazine covers, on book covers, on cards propped up for display, girls without clothes and unprotected even against Jules's anguish. He stared at them, sweating.

The proprietor of the store edged toward him. Jules left.

Oppressive air on the street. The sun had disappeared. The air hung heavily about him as if crowded with the exhaled breaths of too many girls, too many men. A girl of about twenty, passing him, glanced with a country girl's open friendly interest at his face, and he felt weak immediately, as if struck. He thought of her thighs in her tight skirt, her mouth opened for a scream, photographed. He went on, a little blind. He loved Nadine so much . . . In front of a Greyhound bus station a woman brushed against him, scolding her kid, and he felt the danger of women like a terrible blow and drew back from her. It was a kind of poison, accidental contact.

He wandered into the bus station. Walls painted thinly white. A candy machine. A popcorn machine. He pretended interest in them, cagily. He looked around the room. Babies were fretting. An old man leaned over to spit with care on the floor. Jules did not dare to look at any women but confined himself to the faces of the men, which seemed to him gross. Yet his temperature was soaring. Small clots in the blood, like spores from feverish spring plants, dandelions maybe, floating and suffocating in his blood. If only he didn't love that girl so strongly! He saw a man in a cheap gray suit cross over to the men's lavatory.

He went over and entered the lavatory himself. The man was standing by one of the sinks, staring at himself sadly in the mirror—he was an old-looking young man with parchment-like skin. Jules saw his eyes flick onto Jules's face in the mirror just before Jules moved—Jules grabbed him by his rather long hair and jerked him backward, one hand going over his mouth, and tried to knock his head against the tile wall. He missed. He grabbed the man by the throat and this time did succeed in knocking him back against the wall. The man fell heavily. Jules reached inside his coat to get his wallet, thinking just at this moment that there wasn't much point in stealing from someone who looked like that; but too late! In a few seconds he was back out in the waiting-room again, on his way out.

His sweat had turned to a film of frost on his body.

In the Piggly-Wiggly, like a young husband, he bought a bag of potato chips and some cheese and white bread and a few other items, including shampoo for his young bride, making his way patiently behind lady shoppers. Where else would he be as safe as in the Piggly-Wiggly store? He was dizzied by the bare legs of young wives who dawdled with their shopping carts . . . but he was faithful to his love, to Nadine, who kept herself faultless and put her childish hands on the back of his neck and talked to him, whispered to him late at night. "Now I never stay awake and cry at night," she had told him, surprised. She slept while Jules stayed awake, not exactly crying, dry-eyed but very thoughtful. He toyed with the idea of throwing himself upon her and finishing it all, kicking her out, slashing his own wrists—but she was all he had, after all, with her selfishness and her purity. He couldn't hurt her.

At the check-out counter he looked through his new wallet, a stranger's wallet. It was a sign of his confusion that he hadn't bothered until now to see how much money he had. But a pleasant surprise: two twenty-dollar bills, someone's, enough money for a while. He was safe. He took out a twenty-dollar bill to pay for his purchases and felt rather proud of himself.

"Here, your stamps," said the cashier, handing him some saving stamps; and Jules gallantly turned to the lady waiting in line behind him and offered them to her. She smiled in surprise, thanking him.

When he returned to the cabin Nadine had the door open and was waiting for him. "I was worried about you," she said. "Did you get some shampoo?"

"All kinds of things." His smile ached but he did not flinch from her embrace. On the way back he'd thrown away the wallet, but certainly he was in danger. "Maybe we could get out of here?" he said.

"As soon as I wash my hair."

"It would be a good idea if we left now."

"Jules, please . . ."

In the lavatory she bent over the sink with a towel around her shoulders, and Jules himself washed her hair. She had lovely thick hair and he loved even the strands that came loose, wrapping themselves around his soapy fingers.

They drove into Beaumont, Texas, buoyed along by waves of heat on the highway. Jules's eyes had a permanent parched feel to them—so much land, so much sunlight, all of it mixed up with the swaying of his own brain. These several days with Nadine had resulted in his beginning to talk like her, shaping his mouth like hers. Perhaps the faint delirium he felt was a girl's hysteria, unavoidable. How could he stop from changing himself into her?

She snuggled against him in spite of the heat, needing affection, attention. She said petulantly, "Something always seems to be pulling at me, tearing at me. I don't know what I want."

It was an invitation for him to answer her, and he answered in spite of a sense of wild hopelessness, the futility of talking to her at all. "Maybe you want love?"

And she said, "But then what? What comes after that? Doesn't anything come next?"

They had been driving for hours. Swinging down to the Gulf of Mexico, Nadine's whim, they were a little baffled by the flat, dismal land and the long stretches of oil fields—oil derricks in fenced-off rectangles of dry land, with stray cows grazing nearby—and the surprise of a great thicket of trees. Beaumont was on the Neches River, a river that did not impress Jules. He had never heard of it before. To the east were the Sabine River and Louisiana; he felt a tug at his imagination, a yearning to see the towns behind such names as Sulphur and Creole. But the map had disappointed him enough; the tearing folds in it were like the disintegrating seams of his own mind.

"If you don't want love, why did you come all this way with me?" he said.

She kept up a curious childlike expectancy, while Jules labored just to stay awake; she was always ready for a surprise in the town just ahead, on the alert for historical markers and homes that looked historical. Yet they never bothered to get out of the car. Cruising by, they stared at what presented itself to them and were always vaguely disappointed; Nadine found most things disappointing. Jules was glad they hadn't been caught yet by the police.

"What you should do, honey," he kept suggesting, "is telephone your parents and tell them you're in California. You're healthy and well and happy and in California."

"I can't talk to them any more."

"Sure you can. For my sake."

"I can't even think about them."

It startled him to see with what frigid casualness she dismissed them all—really, she never thought about her family except as subjects in the long monologue of her life. Was it possible to forget people that easily, Jules wondered, or were the effects taking a while to get to her? It chilled him to think that this young girl, the daughter of wealthy parents, sweet and delicate and well mannered, could be so shallow. The farther he ran from his own miserable family, the more immediate they appeared to him. Even on the road as he was, nobody's obvious son or brother, he felt weighed down by their troubles. He was still responsible for them.

"But if you loved me," Jules said wearily, in the car or in a diner or in bed, and Nadine sometimes answered wearily, "But I do love you. What do you mean? Why do you keep saying that?" She really could not understand. Sometimes she said in exasperation, as if trying to make herself understood by someone who spoke a foreign language, "You talk about love so much! I don't know what you mean—why do you keep at me with it? Why is it always love, love, love? I never heard of anyone who talked about love so much, outside of books."

Beaumont, Texas. No mountains, no beauty. Jules was sick of Texas. The city was larger than he had desired and already crowded on its peripheries by shopping plazas and outdoor theaters. The spread of land from Detroit to Beaumont was similar in the cities and in the country—in the country drainage ditches and dirt that ran from brown in the North to a fairly rusty red here in the South; in the cities miniature golf courses and rows of cheap new homes, American colonials, all of them colonials, colonials with aluminum siding, acres and hillsides of colonials, the distance filled with bright new colonial homes. Out of all this traveling Jules wanted at least to put together some kind of personality for himself, the personality of a young man in love or a born criminal or a millionaire on the first stretch of his "career"; all this land had to add up to something!

When they hit Beaumont, Jules said, "This is the end for today."

"Can't we keep going to the Gulf?"

"There's nothing there, on the Gulf. Nothing to see. Look at the map and see what's there. I can't drive any more today."

The air in Beaumont stank. It must have been gas from refineries; there was a faintly sickish taste borne on one wind and a faintly acrid taste borne on another. Nadine sniffed in her innocence and kept glancing around, puzzled.

Jules, who had lived long in Detroit, knew that there would be nothing to see.

The gas gauge showed nothing left. But they hadn't run out of gas yet. What made Jules worry was the fact that he was like the gas in the car's tank. He, himself, was the gas. He had to keep them going; he was running down; he had to be juiced up. What was happening to him? He laughed and kissed Nadine's ear. "Find us a place, honey, so we can get some sleep. I really am finished."

They were passing giant palm trees. Rose bushes were still in bloom. A heavy, cobweb-like dampness hung over everything. The palm trees were too thick, too large. Something about their blunt squat thickness made Jules's eyes pinch. Also, the look of white frame houses and rainwashed shanties, side by side, jostled him and made him wonder how real all this was. Texas? Were they really in Texas? He got stuck behind a grimy bus, a city bus. The road had potholes in it—first the bus lurched, then Jules lurched. Nadine looked around in amazement. "Is this Texas?" she said. The road turned suddenly to dirt. It branched, and one branch led to what must have been the city dump. Jules followed the bus on the other branch. The smell of gas grew stronger. A gang of Negro children darted across the street in front of the car. Wood and tar-paper shanties appeared beside the road, chickens pecked in the dirt, a skeletal dog stared out mournfully at Jules with Jules's own eyes.

"Now it's starting to drizzle," Nadine said. "This is a place to die in."

She picked out a motel when they found the highway again—the same motel they had been seeing all along, made of concrete painted pink, with neon lighting and a few lawn chairs scattered out front. Jules was quick to note, with his parched eye and parched brain, that it was near a residential area of ordinary homes and a few stores.

He checked them in, not hesitating to sign his name in the register, happy to write down the number of his license plates. He was no criminal, not really. He had nothing to hide. Yet, signing his name, he was overcome by an immense weariness, and when he went back to Nadine the earth felt precarious beneath his feet.

She was still in the car. "It looks like the place we were in last night," she said.

"That's all right. We both need rest."

"I don't want rest."

"What do you want?"

"I don't know. Why is it so early? It's only five-thirty and you want to stop for the night. I don't understand."

He opened the car door and she got out slowly. They embraced. Though it was bright daylight and traffic moved on the highway not far away she did not resist; she was inert and abstracted. "You seem so tired," she said. "You know, I do really love you. I love you for bringing me all this way."

He unlocked the door to the room. The room was dark, damp. It smelled strongly of insecticide. Jules switched on the light and a swift movement in one corner caught his attention—a cockroach—but fortunately Nadine hadn't seen it.

She tested the bed with one knee. "Why is it so damp in here? It smells so damp."

"It's not bad."

He sat down shakily on the edge of the bed. He tried to smile at her. He had been waiting for her to break down but she had never wavered, had shown nothing—what a triumph of nerve! Now he, Jules, seemed to be breaking down. He felt something move painfully in his bowels. Even his lust, on this hot drizzling afternoon, had grown feeble.

She knelt beside him and put her arms around him. She liked to kiss his eyes. She liked to be kissed by him—she brought to it the same vague, pleased expectation she showed in the car, awaiting a new landscape. It was a way of moving successfully through time. Seeing her young face and her dreamy eyes, Jules thought of *Detective Annals* and wondered if there was someone to whom Nadine would be no more than a flash of arms and legs, a stifled cry, a frantic insignificant body. She was talking happily to him about something. Her words washed against him but made no sense. Jules was conscious of his body perspiring, his clothes rotting on his filthy body.

"Do we have money for something to eat?" Nadine said.

The thought of food made Jules nauseated, but he gave no sign. He washed up in the little lavatory and went out again, out to the road. *This is Jules in Texas,* he thought. No, they hadn't money but that was no problem of Nadine's; it was his problem. Like a dog, he was drawn to alleys and corners. His bowels felt sick but he acted out of habit. Mechanical movements seemed to Jules magical and therefore blessed, almost invisible—you couldn't get caught doing something for the tenth time—surely he would never get caught. He smiled, thinking of Jules the born criminal, an invisible young man, never caught. *Police swore the robberies had been committed by a large gang* . . . He was in a white neighborhood but it looked poor; nothing worth hauling away. So he wandered on and crossed a series of railroad tracks and found himself in a better neighborhood, a subdivision erected upon spongy, swampy land, made up of brick ranch homes with high, narrow, horizontal windows. A housewife in a green shift walked barefoot across her lawn to pick up a folded newspaper. This sight pleased Jules —it was so ordinary and reasonable. Walking alone here, even in his sweaty clothes, he was close to the secret workings of things, the way people lived when they were not being observed. In himself there were no secret workings: he had no ordinary, reasonable life.

He passed a home with shades drawn and front porch littered with papers—a temptation—but next door a dog was barking. Jules hurried on, thinking of Nadine, her arms, her lovely face, the slightly damp look of her eyelids, wondering how it had happened that he was in love and brought so low by love, when nothing connected him to Nadine or to anyone else. He had only to keep walking to be free . . . Another housewife, thick-waisted but sprightly, hurried across another lawn to rap at the door of the next house; she called a name, someone opened the door, she went inside. This looked right: the hairs on the back of Jules's neck stirred. Instinct drew him to her house. His legs moved him up the walk without hesitation. No mistake here. He was safe. He went right to the front door and pretended to ring the bell and, after a moment, for the benefit of anyone who might be watching him, he pretended to be greeting someone as he pushed the door open.

Once inside he had no time to waste: right to the kitchen. The house was cool, air-conditioned, and smelled of insecticide. He walked quickly through a living-room, through a dining-room, into the kitchen. In a nearby room a television set was on. Children were probably watching it. But he had no fear of them, and in the first second of entering the kitchen his eyes located what he wanted—a woman's purse. He went to open it, moving silently, without fear. He took the billfold out and slipped it into his pocket. An open door drew him: a bedroom, the bed carelessly made, his own reflection looming guiltily in a bureau mirror. On an impulse he lay down on the bed, his feet side by side. He smiled. So this was what it was like.

After he'd left the house, a few minutes afterward, he broke out into a sickening sweat. He counted the money in the billfold—over fifty dollars. But the money did not make him feel better. He was still sweating. He headed back toward the motel, retracing his steps. He had a certain moronic instinct about directions, never making a mistake. Back past the railroad tracks, down into the shabbier neighborhood, on his way, nervous but unhurried, a kid who might belong around here. A local kid. Doomed by Texas heat. His hair had grown long again and gave him a countrified, sleepy look. He appeared harmless.

He entered a small grocery store. Already, he knew Nadine's likes; he wanted only to please her. But near the counter stood two policemen, white, and a colored man, chatting in an explosion of drawls and surprised exclamations. One of the cops bent over nearly double, laughing. It was worrisome to Jules to see a cop laugh, as it had bothered him in the old days to see a priest laugh very hard. Jules picked out some milk, some cheese, bread, a box of chocolate cookies for Nadine. Still the cops hadn't left, and he wandered around at the back of the store, feeling his bowels begin to writhe with pain, waiting for them to leave. The pain was not more than he could bear. He tried not to let his face show what he felt. A white woman in slacks glanced back at him from the cash register, watchful of her customer at the same time that she was delighted with the cops and the Negro, their hilarious conversation, and Jules felt that he must go to her and pay for the food and escape. He had to walk up there, right by the cops. The pain in his stomach turned sharp and hot.

"Here," one of the cops said, reaching out for Jules, "you wouldn't never believe what this boy is tellin' us!" Jules did not flinch. The cop looked no more than his own age; he was shaking his head helplessly. Both cops were grinning. The Negro, who might have been in his forties, or his sixties, shook his head in bewilderment, trying for a comic effect, protesting in a high, raspy voice of the kind Jules had often heard on the Detroit streets, "I ain't never told any lies! What you think! Ain't goin' to start that kinda thing now!" It made no sense to Jules, it was like music he hadn't heard the beginning of and had no interest in; he smiled at them blankly and put his things down on the counter. The woman giggled and looked past Jules, waiting for more.

"This boy is a real bugger," the cop said to Jules, tapping his arm, "he ain't goin' to last out the year!" There was a gracious, jovial brotherhood here, the cops and the Negro and Jules, a kind of dance, but Jules couldn't dance; his body ached so that he was afraid he might keel over into the cop's arms. "Lookit what his wife done to him! You ever goin' to let your wife treat you that way?" the cop said to Jules, raising his eyebrows dramatically.

Jules looked politely at the Negro. He saw that his face was scarred—strangely scarred, in long, thick patches, like dribbles. The skin of part of his face was thickened like an alligator's skin. Jules stared. He saw nothing funny. The Negro held in his laughter for a moment, then surrendered in a surprised, soprano giggle, as if it were too much for him, himself and these two cops who were making so much of his face, and even Jules, a newcomer who obviously wanted to hear everything.

"What happened to his face?" Jules said.

"His wife got sick of him runnin' around," the cop explained, still clutching Jules as if to help Jules restrain his own laughter, "and she got a nice big pot on the stove boiling and she put some sugar in it—you know, some sugar—and when he come home she didn't waste no time sayin' where-you-been or nothin'—nosir, she just dumped that water right on top of him—ain't that the craziest thing you ever heard?"

"Why did she do that?" Jules said, trying to grin, "I mean, why the sugar?"

"Let him tell it," said the other cop, and they all looked at the Negro.

He shook his head wonderingly. "She put sugar in it 'cause that sticks to you, boy, that's what makes it stick—water don't stick, it run right off. Sugar *stick*, boy, you better remember!"

The cops broke into hoarse laughter, and Jules managed a wheezing laugh, to show that he was one of them. He took advantage of their good will to push his items toward the cashier. Jesus, would he ever get out of this dump!

"Sugar *stick!*" one of the cops cried, overcome with laughter.

Their laughter followed him out to the street. He had to go to the bathroom violently now, and that was enough to

capture his imagination. He forgot the cops. Their laughter
thinned out, then thickened again—so much to laugh at in
this world! He could not remember having laughed honestly;
stuck in a body like this, a body burning with pain, how is
laughter possible?

He got back to the motel room and put the things on the
bed and went immediately to the bathroom. The door did
not quite shut, not firmly. In desperation he yanked it but
still it did not lock. He carried the image of Nadine with him,
Nadine out in the other room—surprised when he'd passed
her by and said, "I've got to go in here," alarmed at the
look on his face, not thinking he was handsome now. In
this miserable little room he groaned with pain and tried to
rid himself of the foulness that had formed in him, but he
could do nothing—nothing happened. He pressed his forehead against the warped wood of the bathroom door and
began to weep.

After a while he came out shaking. "I guess I got the flu,"
he said.

"Are you sick?"

"The flu."

She looked away from him. The loaf of bread was opened,
on the night table. "That smells of insect spray, that bread.
I can't eat it."

"I'm sorry." Jules was too weak to talk. He lay down on
the bed.

Nadine said, a sense of sympathy stirring in her, "I can
prop these pillows up for you."

"I won't be sick long."

"Should I do anything for you?"

"Maybe you could get me some . . . some aspirin at the
drugstore."

"Where is the drugstore?"

He had begun to tremble violently. He crawled under the
covers, his eyes shut. It was all he could do to keep from
groaning aloud.

"Should I get a doctor?" Nadine said, frightened.

"It's just the flu."

"You look so sick."

The pain was so sharp that he opened his eyes, startled.
Then, throwing the bedclothes off, he stumbled back to the
bathroom. The diarrhea seemed to scald him. Shaking, overcome by the stench of his own bowels, he rocked back and
forth on the toilet seat and pressed his palms against his

ears. What had he wanted from that girl in the other room? What did human beings try to get from each other? He could think of nothing but his foulness.

When he came back to bed Nadine was standing in the doorway of the motel room, as if ready to leave. "Jules, please let me get a doctor. Please."

He lay down, feeling very weak. He did not quite hear her.

"How did it happen?" she said. "Is it caused by germs or something? Is it in the air?"

He made no sense of her words but was grateful for them; they filled up the space between himself and Nadine. Time passed. He wanted to sleep.

Nadine sat on the edge of the bed, holding his hands, kneading his hands. She worked the fingers, staring sadly into his face. "Oh, I love you, Jules, please get better. I'm afraid. I can't stand it with you sick."

"I'll be better tomorrow."

But the night was miserable. He kept lurching up to go to the bathroom, amazed and terrified at the way his body had gone out of control, doubled over with pain, shuddering. He had never been so cold. "But it isn't cold, it's hot in here. It's terribly hot," Nadine said, but still he was cold, trembling with cold. He wondered if he might die. That was an imaginable ending. Toward morning Nadine fell asleep in the chair beside the bed. Jules was grateful for this—he wanted to be alone with his misery. He was ashamed of it.

In the morning she went out to get some things for him. Now he peeled off his filthy clothes and let them fall on the floor. He lay in bed in his underwear. This too was shameful, and he felt a wild irrational fear of Nadine hating him, hating his body. He drew the bedcovers up around his face. He hated himself. *Jules dying.* His obsession with Nadine he recalled vaguely, in patches, but he could not recall what love itself was. His body shuddered repeatedly. The revulsion of his body for itself paralyzed his spine.

Nadine returned. She gave him pills to take, she chatted with him. He began to shiver again, his teeth chattered. Nadine cried out in desperation, "What's happening to you! What's wrong!" She pressed her face against the top of his head. "Don't die, don't leave me!" she said.

"I won't die." Jules tried to laugh. Then something happened . . . he must have become delirious. He was very hot, then his teeth were chattering again.

Nadine, approaching him out of a mist, bent over him and stared. "Jules, your teeth are bleeding. Your gums. Why is there blood around your gums?"

He wondered if these words were real or part of a dream. He wiped his gums and, yes, there was blood on his hand, but his hand too seemed unreal. In his veins tiny bits of grit were expanding. His heat rose. Never had his lust for Nadine fired his blood the way the flu fired it, stoking it higher, higher, until his brain seemed to float weightlessly loose of his foul body, aching to be free of his body, which had become a pit . . . a pit in a dungeon, corrupt with evil smells, slime . . . a sudden hot flow about his thighs was like a miracle, an outlet of pain. The foulness of his body was now outside him, a miracle. He lay in this stench and wondered if that was a sign of hope.

He lost consciousness, he dreamed. His dreams were disturbed by light. He woke and found the bed wet, excrement in the bed, and in terror he tried to get up. He was too weak. His body was weak but still not emptied out. A new storm of pain was working itself up in him. He groaned aloud, paralyzed by a coil of hot pain, and he thought of that Negro man with a pan of boiling water dumped over his head, with sugar to make it stick and burn. How much pain could a man feel before he stopped being a man?

When he came to himself, at some unknown hour, his mind clear of fever and his body strangely weak, he was alone. He felt this, then he saw it. No Nadine. He called her; no answer. After a while he dragged himself from his filthy bed and looked out the door. No Nadine. No car. She had left him in southeastern Texas and that seemed to him the end of the story of Jules and Nadine.

7

A person, a girl, imagines the mirror will show no reflection to her. So she does not dare look. Her body has the hopeless feeling of having become weight, a bulk; it has been loved too much, used and used up. It is weak from months of sleep. It has no reflection, no face. A headless body.

The ceiling is arranged in a certain way. It does not move up or down. Wallpaper pasted over wallpaper, thickness upon thickness. Curls form. Patches are about to fall. If the girl allows herself to think about the wallpaper she will get sick. It is enough to be a heavy weight, sweating in bed.

Someone sits and talks to her: her mother. Chatter, chatter . . . all the words are shrieks . . . like little vicious birds. Birds sometimes chatter outside the window but they are invisible. She can't turn her head that far. She doesn't trust windows—looking through the glass frightens her. Someone else sits and talks. A man. He reads newspapers. The rustle of newspapers, their particular smell, the fluttering, panicky sense of things happening outside the room. Better not to listen. She does not listen.

The television set is on in the other room. Muffled sounds, swellings of laughter. Laughter?

Her mother is unfolding an orange piece of paper. "I can't figure out this goddam eggbeater," she says.

Her mouth waters. She is hungry, hungry. A terrible hunger rises in her. Food is something to fill up her entire body and keep it heavy and peaceful. Sleep follows. The television set recedes. The baby's crying recedes. Her uncle, Brock, sitting in the easy chair, reads the comics out loud and his voice recedes.

A cookie, a gingersnap, out of the box. It falls onto the floor. She waits, thinking of it on the floor, out of sight. Her mouth waters. Finally she leans over, grunting, to pick it up. She picks it up. She eats it quickly. The flat, bland taste of stale gingersnap awakens her. Her mouth waters for more.

She does not think but occasionally words form in her, against her will. *What is the other Maureen doing now?*

Drawing her hair up in thick, snakish strands above her head, eyes closed, fingers very graceful . . .

Oh you little bitch . . . you running around with that nigger is all I need . . . get out of here . . . I'll call the police to kick your ass . . . this ain't no nigger whorehouse for you to hide out . . . get back on the street . . . go to hell . . . dirty little jail-bird, you horse-face!

Loretta is screaming. Betty runs past her and into Maureen's room, in blue jeans. *Hey, Reeny! Get this old bitch off my back! Snap out of it! There's nothing wrong with you and you know it!*

Loretta tries to pull Betty away. *She's sick—*

Well you made her sick then with your crap!

Loretta slaps Betty. Betty brings her arm around and knocks Loretta backward. Loretta screams. Betty shouts something and runs out of the room. More screaming. Loretta leaves. Loretta is shouting *Running with a nigger . . . I don't care if it's male or female . . . you can go straight to hell!*

Brock reads the comic strips: Rex Morgan, Gasoline Alley, Brenda Starr. He shows the comic page to Maureen but she does not look at it. She does not look away.

Brock says, "Your mother went to the A & P. There's a surprise in the mail. You want to hear it?"

Maureen is silent, lying cold and heavy beneath the covers, not waiting. Sometimes she looks at Brock, sometimes not. This is her uncle. She is not certain what an uncle is. His face, his groping voice, the frequent jiggling of the bed as he passes by remind her of something, someone. She does not pursue the memory. Stubborn, heavy with sleep, she lies disguised in a body not her own and waits without waiting for anything.

Brock opens a letter:

Dec. 14, 1956

Dear Ma and Maureen,

Well look, here I am in Houston, Texas! I will write more when I have time. Don't worry about me because I am doing OK. The second day looking for a job I got a job with a co. that does business in real estate on the Gulf. Enclosed a brochure explaining their work, pictures, etc. I will be a salesman going out to visit clients as soon as I finish my training. I got to buy a suit. How is everyone? I hope well. I think of you all often. I am pretty well now that the winter is beginning. The heat kept me low. It really got next to me. In Texas the winter doesn't begin until Dec., I mean where I am in Texas. The state is very big. You should see it on a map sometimes. The bugs are just about gone now, dead or hiding. I go out without a coat even though its Dec. but I can take it, unlike the hot weather. All is well with me. I think of you. Take Maureen to a good doctor, take care of her. I will send money when I can. Im sorry not to write for so long.

Love,
Jules

Her mother is taking the letter from Brock, very surprised. *What, from Jules! A letter from Jules!* she cries.

She unfolds a booklet. *Hey, this looks like something,* she says in awe. Brock, with his hairy face and his slightly apologetic, clumsy body, looks at it with her. *Golden Triangle Retirement Paradise. Acres Still Available on the Gulf.* Loretta reads the booklet to Maureen, who lies without looking at her, without listening. Still, she hears some of it. She blocks off her mind from what is behind the words: Gulf of Mexico? Texas? Her brother Jules? She does not want to think about these things. She does not want to be hurt.

Now she is being urged up, out of bed. "Now come on, honey, that's right," says her mother. She has forgotten how to put her arms through sleeves. They have to show her how—her mother and another woman. A woman with short dyed red hair, a friend. She and Loretta are the same height. "Honey," says Loretta, "you're doing just fine. Isn't she doing fine? Don't be afraid. Watch out for my African violets there . . ."

Brock is sitting in the kitchen. He smiles and the smile turns into Furlong's smile. Maureen draws back.

"What's wrong?" cries Loretta.

Maureen pulls back from them, desperate to get back to her room, to bed. She must get back to bed. The red-headed woman lets go of her, Loretta hangs on for another second, tugging, and then lets go in exasperation. "Oh, hell! Shit!" she cries. "I'm fed up with this life and this kind of never-ending crap. I don't care if she is sick or not, what about me? What about my life?"

Maureen can hear her, from bed, her mother weeping out in the other room.

"What about my life?" Loretta says. "When is it going to begin?"

Brock reads another letter:

Feb. 1, 1957

Dear Ma and Maureen,

As you can see from the postmark I am no longer in Houston but am now in Dallas. The real estate business did not agree with me! I did not get put in jail or anything, not even overnight, so dont worry about me. Anyway I take care of myself. These crazy people! Enclosed is twenty dollars. Take Maureen to some good doctor not just the clinic. I hope she is better. Write me at General Delivery, Dallas, Texas. I think of you all and miss you, I love you all. I have come to the conclusion that people are all lonely, each one of us, now being alone doesnt bother me so much. I can take it being alone better when I think things out. Right now I am working substitute for a guy who is sick, its building work on a house and good work as long as it doesnt rain. The rain can get pretty cold. There are two guys I am kind of friends with here, my age. I dont hang around with them much though. Everybody is pretty friendly but I dont get too close. The Golden Triangle Retirement thing went under. I dont know where the president took off to. I went to meet some client, a old guy all crippled up, with a real mean face, and it looked fishy around the house and I saw some cops down the street so I took off. I got to Dallas by hitch-hiking. My health is much better now. I feel good most days. Dont worry about me and take care of yourselves. I think of you often which people do when they are away and by themselves.

> *Love,*
> *Jules*

A memory: driving along the expressway. Great gouges out of the earth, mud, lines of cars, orange signs saying "DETOUR." She is sitting in a car beside a man, not her father, not Furlong, not Brock. He is a stranger. He is saying, *Well Tuesday's out . . . what about Wednesday?* His hand covers her hand. His hand moves onto her thigh. Her flesh moves toward him, like grains of sand easing downward, without haste. It gravitates that way. Now they are somewhere else, a darkened room. He is above her. With his legs he spreads her legs . . . anything can happen, any sharp swift surprise . . . she feels the muscles of her face freeze with waiting . . . he enters her and everything in her body freezes, fixed by him, by what he is doing, all the quivering cells of her body are urged to that frozen center, to him, helpless.

In the other room the television set is on. She lies alone, not sleeping and not awake. In her memory is the constant smell of semen and the feel of it, easing out of her body . . . warm from her body. There is so much of it, a flow like the flow of blood, endless. She is paralyzed by it. She imagines it now, between her thighs. The ceiling is threatening . . . but if clumps of wallpaper fall off and onto her face she will not be able to move or scream. She closes her eyes.

The other Maureen is out on the street, swinging her purse. Slits for eyes, a pretty mouth, everything soft. As if in a dance she pauses to fix the white scarf about her head, and a man, passing by, a stranger, pauses to help her fix it: he knots the ends beneath her chin. She lowers her eyes. With his hands he grips her face, her throat. He stares into her face. He leans down to kiss her. He kisses her mouth and his hands grip her shoulders, fixing her. He kisses her mouth slowly out of shape.

Betty, in the doorway, fresh from the cold air outside, her short shapeless hair damp, says, loud and laughing, *There's nothing wrong with you and you know it! You ain't the first one in the world some bastard beat up!*

And Loretta screams at her, *Get out! Get out!*

Betty shouts, *No son-of-a-bitch's ever gonna beat up on me, let me tell you. I ain't putting up either with all that fuckin' like you or Reeny and you can go to hell, Ma, you think you're so goddam smart!*

They are talking of Betty, and Maureen finds herself listening. Loretta says to the red-headed woman, "She's just wild, nobody can keep her down. She's got a hard heart. It ain't my fault where she ends up, what did I do wrong?" Her friend says, "Honey, you didn't do one thing wrong. If they're going to go bad they'll go bad. You know that. Look at Jules, ain't he done good for a boy his age? Went off on his own to see the country and got a job and sends money home." Loretta says forlornly, "I used to talk to Betty, I really did. Used to tell her to wise up. But she always talked back and kept running around with a real bitch of a crowd, mixed black and white and you know how I feel about that. I might turn her in one of these days myself."

Maureen closes her eyes and sees Betty, a kid of eleven again, fooling around downtown with a bunch of girls all dressed in old blue jeans, laughing and shrieking. A private language. She, Maureen, cringes behind some people, not wanting to be seen.

The air thickens suddenly. She shuts her eyes. A haze sweeps upon her, a horn sounds close by. *Maureen, what the hell are you doing!* Someone takes her arm. Good. To be held safe, good. Her arm is held tight, impatiently, and she feels her body emptying out, her head emptying out . . . A man's voice is saying something near her ear . . . the tinkle of coins . . . traffic, horns . . . the smell of exhaust smoke.

She is already on the bus, with her mother still gripping her, when she turns and sees her self step out of her body with a sudden convulsive movement, freeing itself, escaping

. . . This self is her. It steps down to the sidewalk again, pushing past other people who want to get on the bus. It glances back up at her. Everything rushes out of Maureen now and joins that other body, that free body, running away . . . It is like the terrible pressure of water wanting to burst free . . . how she yearns to join that body, get loose, scream with the pain and terror of getting loose . . .

Sit here, sit still. For Christ's sake, says her mother.

She sits. She turns wildly to look through the window, to where her other self stands on the sidewalk. Crowds pass. People, strangers, seem to break around her, not touching her. They pass around her. They become invisible while she herself, that other self, becomes vivid and dazzling, standing on the sidewalk with her head turned back at a painful angle, looking at Maureen on the bus, her face guilty and wild.

Now watch your step!

Stepping heavily down, in a dream. The bus is stopped. Why doesn't the sidewalk rush up on all sides and crush her? She is so heavy and so dead, this Maureen! Disguised as Maureen! No man would come up to her and play with the ends of her scarf. No man could penetrate this flesh. She weaves on the sidewalk, dizzy from the air and the wind.

Maureen, come on! We're already late on account of you!

A building, concrete. A certain acrid odor . . . medicine? She sits. Chairs like kitchen chairs with aluminum tubing and cracked plastic covers for the seats. Across the way a fat child, white bulbous face, very fat. Eyes slightly bulging. Fixed on Maureen. A fat snowsuit, red, soiled, limp, bulging eyes and a bulging mouth, drooling. Maureen sits sleeping in her body, knowing that she is safe. Her mother, beside her, leans over now and then to whisper the way mothers do to daughters. *That's a cute purse, see it? You have to go to the bathroom or anything? Don't get anybody mad by looking at them too long.*

The fat girl hangs onto her mother's chair, one of the legs. She falls. Whimpering viciously, she falls and will not get up. The chair is jerked out of its place. The child kicks, blubbering, drooling . . .

Isn't that a shame, Loretta whispers to Maureen.

A pane of glass at the receptionist's counter, to protect her. The nurse is looking through some papers. *Wendall? Are you sure you've been here before?* She is very young but her face is already lined from looking through too many papers.

Dr. Morris will see you now.

Who? Where's Dr. Stein?

He's no longer in Detroit.

But I was supposed to see him again. Every time we came in I was supposed to ask for him—

Dr. Morris will see you now.

Oh shit!

Brock is reading them both a letter:

March 8, 1957

Dear Ma and Maureen,

Thank you Ma for your letter but you didn't say much. How is Maureen doing? Better I hope. Enclosed is five dollars. How are the checks coming along? I hope OK. Dont let them push you around at welfare. You got the same rights as anybody else. Is your brother still in Detroit? How are you all? The weather is getting nice here. I been doing odd jobs. When I get back to Detroit I am going to finish high school. You cant do anything without finishing high school and going to college. I think Ill take a business course. My health is very good. Im not mixed up with anybody here. I keep by myself. I dont talk so much like I did when I was a kid, fooling around. I wised up. Does your brother have a job? Im looking for a regular job but its hell making telephone calls, all those dimes. I follow the want ads. Everything is well here. Soon as I get things lined up Ill write again. Dont worry. I love you.

Love,
Jules

"He's a funny kid," Brock says.

"Yeah, he was always kind of funny. But smart," says Loretta.

"He sounds real smart and it seems like he loves you, he keeps sending money. He's a real strange kid," Brock says, embarrassed. "I mean, how he keeps saying that he loves you."

"He always loved me, it wasn't like with other kids running off and telling their mothers to go to hell," Loretta said. "I treated him good."

"It's nice the way he keeps in touch too."

"Yeah, I treated him right, I always gave him lots of love and paid attention to him, not like *our mother*—she didn't know the first thing about having kids. Now I look back on it, it's a wonder I was able to have kids myself!"

Maureen thinks of Jules, but, thinking of him, she is suddenly weak. She wants to cry out, *Jules, Jules . . .*

No no no no . . .

Not Jules but a man bends over her, someone else. Before he can strike her she falls asleep. She is no longer lying on the floor but in bed. She sleeps.

"Hey, can I take a bath here? It's all shot to hell at my place, the water don't work." Voices in the other room, a friend of Loretta's. Women, women. Friends. They are always talking, chattering. Talking about men and sick stomachs and lettuce that turned rotten as soon as it was brought home, talking about buying a burial plot . . . "my crazy father-in-law finally died, he went out to the track just the night before and won the daily double. . . . the old bastard always had the luck! . . . and then the next day at noon he dropped over! . . . he always had bad luck too, coming right after good luck. That was his way . . ."

Sometimes they are in the room with Maureen, smoking and chatting. Maureen sleeps. They are "keeping her company." Loretta says, excited, "If that son-of-a-bitch thinks he's getting anything out of me he's crazy. I been through it all too many times." Her friend says, "Oh, he ain't such a bad guy. His kid, that ten-year-old, got picked up for 'stubborn child' and he feels real bad about it. He's just been drinking too much. He thinks the world of you, Loretta, he told me so himself." Loretta says, in her husky voice, "Shit!"

Midge has her short red hair up in pink rollers; her face looks puckered, pulled up. Tobacco and perfume. Maureen, asleep in her body, not watchful, uncautious, lets her eyes move slowly over this woman, without interest. What does it mean to be a woman? How do these people endure it, how do they keep going?—dragging about in the envelope of their bodies, their skin puffy over their bones, living. They keep on. Sleeping. Maureen herself is sleeping. A bulk at rest. In her body nothing moves, in her brain nothing moves, everything is bloated, gluttonous, at rest sleeping.

"Everybody says the niggers plan trouble," Midge says. "New Year's Eve I was worried like hell. What if they set fire to all these dumps?"

"Jesus, it was funny back in—what was it—1945?" Loretta laughs. "We all been hearing about the trouble and I went to see it, took one of the kids that could hardly walk—that was Betty. And the cops stopped me by Hudson's and told me to go back. They yelled at me. Jesus, I could of been killed! I didn't think it was nothing like it turned out."

"That was really something."

"Wasn't I a dope, going out with a kid? My God, I do the dumbest things!"

"I remember that, that was really something."

"Everybody went wild. It was crazy."

"I'm afraid of these places catching fire."

"Somebody told us, a friend of Howard's, how there was real blood in the hospital, running on the floor. You believe that? Blood running down the hall, what do you think of that?" Loretta says earnestly.

Dr. Morris will see you now.

We want some blood for a Wasserman.

How long has she been like this?

There is no file on you . . . Miss Greacon from Wayne State . . . social work . . . social worker. She opens a purse, opens a file. She wears stockings . . . a coat not taken off. She says to Loretta, *How long has she been like this, Mrs. Wendall?*

Brock opens the window.

"How about some fresh air?" he says.

Loretta slams the door behind her. "That dirty bastard, that fucker, if he thinks he's gonna push me around! I told him I needed emergency money, that ass-hole, and he makes me wait four hours on the floor—Jesus Christ I could strangle somebody! And a fat nigger woman right next to me slobbering about something, with her kids hanging around and they got that *rule* about not bringing kids! And he makes me wait—he made me sit there and wait for four hours, and nobody else could help me. They said, 'Who's your case worker? You got to wait!' I'm going back there and set fire to the whole shitty place!"

"You better calm down."

"Don't you tell me to calm down!" Loretta screams. "I'm the one that goes out, not you! It's my money not yours! What the hell do you mean, telling me what to do?"

"You just better—"

"I better do nothing! *Better* you keep your opinions to yourself, you bastard! All this is your fault so you keep your opinions to yourself!"

"How is it my fault?" Brock says.

"Your fault! Your goddam fault, *you!* Why the hell did you have to kill him that night? You smart-ass bastard, showing off! Showing off with that goddam gun of yours!"

"Loretta—"

"You caused it! Shut your fat mouth! He was just a kid and you, you had to show off with that gun, you didn't give a damn who you shot, so you shot *him*—you killed *him*—now look at me, look at my life, you caused all this and you show up here for supper, a big goddam joke! I should kick you out on your ass! My life is a joke and I can't even get a laugh out of it!"

Something falls, a plate. Brock says in a whine, "You got food on my shirt."

"I'll put food on your shirt, you bastard! I'll stuff your ass with it!"

After supper the television set is turned on. Brought into Maureen's room. Loretta goes out and Brock watches television and talks to Maureen. He says, "Don't mind your mother when she gets too excited. She has a hard life. She worries about you, honey, that's why you got to get well. On May first you try to get out of bed, okay?"

He is reading a story to her about dogs. Performing dogs. She does not listen, and she does not turn her mind off. She lies still.

He is reading the newspaper to her.

He is opening a letter, he reads it to her:

April 24, 1957

Dear Ma and Maureen,

In Tulsa where I am I have a job for six weeks, with some other guys. Ill write more when I have time. Here is twenty dollars. The job is very interesting but I dont know what it is exactly, I stay in a dormitory with some other guys and every morning at six we go to a place, like an office, and wait until someone lets us in the next room. A doctor is inside. He checks us, tongue and heart etc. What I have done to me is, he puts some drops in my eyes. It only stings a little. I have to keep out of the sun then come back the next day and he checks me again. I got plenty of time for stuff like reading in a library here and listening to some records they got. You should get some records and a record player for Maureen. Music is nice when you are alone. One of the guys is a lot worse off than me, they give it to him in a needle. His arm is all sore and broke out.

Love,
Jules

PS. I think this is connected with the government or the army or something like that. Real crazy people!

Brock is brushing Maureen's hair. He is serious, a serious-faced man. Maureen holds herself stiff. He says, "I know you can hear me and I don't mind no games you play. Your ma explained to me what was going on and how he beat you up, and it ain't none of my business, it all happened before I came. But I want you to know that when I get a job we'll start sending you to a real doctor. You got to pay for good doctors. *He* should have to pay for it but he's took off, they can't find him at Friend of the Court or nothing, but what the hell. You made a promise—May first you're gonna get up, okay?"

He is saying, sitting in the easy chair dragged into Maureen's room, "Life is just the craziest thing! I spent a year down in Indiana, in jail, but don't tell nobody. I didn't want to upset your mother. How it happened was this: I felt so low inside I wanted to die. I couldn't shake myself out of it, couldn't change. So I thought to myself I will get shot down by the police because by myself I would make a mess of it. I went right in some restaurant and held them up and didn't have no gun either. Well, the girl gave me all the money. She was just a kid. Then when I got the money in hand I had to leave, there wasn't anything else to do. So that kept me going for about three days; I had a lot to drink, kept me feeling pretty good. Then it wore off and I got bad again and was determined to get finished off. So I went right downtown in some flea-bag town, forget which one, and walked into a drugstore. I made out I was going to buy some whisky, got myself a few bottles, then told the old guy running the place that it was a stick-up, he should give me all his money. A woman in there with a kid started screaming. I told her shut up. So she shut up. The old geezer emptied the cash register and give it all to me, so what was I to do? I sort of waited around, walking slow to the front door, but no cops came, and so I got away. I made a hundred dollars, about, from that drugstore and never once planned on it. So that kept me going good for a week. Near the end somebody rolled me. I woke up real sick and my face beaten up and this time I made up my mind to get killed. I was fed up with life. I was fed up with my face—I always hated it anyway. So I went in a bank and waited in line and got up to the window and said it was a stick-up, and the girl there, she just about fainted and had to hang onto the marble thing, the counter, but she didn't faint and kept kind of looking at me like she was going to scream, but she didn't scream either, and finally she gave me some money in envelopes. I cleared six hundred. The alarm bell didn't work, I read in the paper next morning—she was pushing it with her foot but it didn't work, the wiring was bad. I had half a mind to go back and scare the hell out of her—here I felt sorry for her, being so scared, and she was pressing that goddam thing with her foot!

"But I left town and stayed feeling pretty good for a few weeks, and then I come crashing down again. I was going to hitchhike somewhere by a lake I heard about, where there was a lot of good times in the summer. I was going to get good and drunk once and for all and drown myself. I felt real optimistic about this. But on the way out a guy stopped to pick me up in his car, I was hitchhiking, and he was real nice to me, offered me cigarettes and something to drink he had on the seat with him, and I drank it, and then he started acting sort of funny and was patting my hand, so I said, 'You better let me out, mister!' and he says, 'You're not getting out of this car yet!' and started laughing like he was crazy. Oh, my God, was I scared! I was only twenty-five or so and just a kid, not like now, I like to wet in my pants I was so scared, and this guy kept on driving with one hand and with the other hand was feeling around me, and I was pressed against the door and wondering if I should open it and jump out, right on the highway, with him going about seventy, and he started to sort of twist my skin on my neck, and it hurt like hell, and I pushed him away and he pushed me back, breathing real hard, and I give it to him on the side of the head and the car just about crashed, but he was a fighter, that guy, and he got the car going straight again and slammed me one back on the side of the head and I saw stars, and I went for his neck to strangle him, I was so scared, this crazy goddam bastard wanting to kill me, when I never done anything to him, and just then some police car comes over the hill and we like to run headfirst into them. We ended up in a field upside down and the cop car was in a ditch on its side and they come running over to us yelling, and the guy goes crazy and tells them how he picked me up hitchhiking and then I tried to rob him and was trying to get the car away from him, we were fighting right when the cops arrived, so they took a look at his car, which was pretty good, and his clothes, and he was wearing glasses too so that he looked like a teacher or something, and they looked at me, a bum, and naturally they knew who to believe—and that's how I ended up in jail. One whole year of my life—and when I came out I forgot about killing myself, it was too much trouble."

He reads a letter:

May 16, 1957

Dear Ma and Maureen,
 Dont be scared, I am all right. I had to be put in this hospital where I am writing from because something was hurting my head. The experiment program is all over. I got paid. But now I need to pay the hospital so I have nothing to send you after all, in fact I owe them fifty dollars already, and in here on Monday night I got an infection and Tuesday morning was very sick. Its a hospital infection, the nurse said, lots of people were getting it. It goes around the hospital. I was real sick and had to be fed in my veins, through the blood, this had nothing to do with my first trouble which got cleared up, I guess. My eyes are better now. Im not supposed to go out in the bright sun for a few months. My head doesnt ache too much now. How are you all? I am anxious to get back up to Detroit as soon as things get settled here. Or maybe I should stay down here a while, I heard of a new job just before I got sick. Is the weather nice up there? In the bed on one side of me is a man with bleeding ulcers, his wife says very sick, and on the other side a man died just the other day. Now there is an old man there tied down. I dont know what his trouble is. He cant even use the bedpan. Hes pretty old. The only trouble is he asked me to help him sit up the first night, after the lights were out, and I tried to get him up then discovered they had him strapped down or something. That scared me. So I told him I better go back to bed. But I am not discouraged by any of this, in fact when my headache is gone for good and my eyes are better I will be better than new, all checked out by a hospital and all. Anything can

happen once I get out. I have lots of hope. In here I been reading some books they pass around and looking through the Bible which as you know I never bothered with much, and dont care much about now, but there are some interesting things in them. My main discovery is that people have always been the same, lonely and worried and hoping for things, and that they have written their thoughts down and when we read them we are the same age as they are, its like time hasnt really gone by. Do you still go to church, if so pray for me, I like to think of you doing that. I dont pray to God but only pray to myself, I mean I think the words to myself, or sometimes I pray to different people I have known—it sounds crazy I guess. I like to think thoughts out clearly. What they mean in the books by the Spirit of the Lord is something I like to think about. I know I have this in me. Being in pain and hurt pretty bad I had a lot of time to think it through and I am certain that there is a Spirit of the Lord in us all, it makes us able to talk to one another and love one another. I trust my luck. I know that things are going to turn out well. There are lots of jobs here and everything in the U.S. is going up. As soon as I get checked out of the hospital I will write you again, dont worry, I love you,

Jules

"I don't know what to make of him," Loretta says, excited and proud. "You ever heard anybody talk like that? When he was a kid it looked like he would end up in jail like the rest of them brats, but now look—"

"You should be proud of him, honey," Midge says.

Maureen dreams, a little restless with spring. The open window shows sky to her. Her slightly bluish arms lie without movement on the covers of her bed. A foul-smelling bed. A winter of a bed. The stupor about her is thick with pellets, air thickened to grit, raining upon her. She yawns, she sleeps. A door opens in her brain. She says to herself questioningly, *Where is Maureen now?* But looking out through the door she can't see anyone. No Maureen. She thinks, *Then what about Jules?* A sensation of fear opens in her, for Jules. Why isn't Jules here? Jules with tubes taped to his arms, being fed blood, Jules all the way across the country, down in Texas and Oklahoma . . . She sleeps and tries to get away from these thoughts. But she finds herself mouthing words to a man on a street corner. She has lost the secretary's notebook for her homeroom and Sister Mary Paul is angry, she tells him. The man slaps her face to bruise it. Or is it Sister Mary Paul slapping her? If her face is bruised she will never make any money. If her body is kicked and bruised, no money, no money. Grown sluggish and stinking and fat, no money. She says to a stranger on a street corner, it looks like Michigan Avenue, she says in a whining child's voice, *Did you see my notebook?* The man is well dressed, good, he must have money, he bends down to her and embraces her so that she can feel the whole length of his body. *My notebook,* she says, looking over his shoulder and into the sky, *did you see it?*

She remembers a day on Belle Isle, driving aimlessly around the park with a man, in a man's car. He is talking, talking. He is very sad. "I've known the woman who is my wife for twenty-five years . . . twenty-five years . . . a quarter of a century we've known each other . . . we've been married almost that long . . . we have four very wonderful children and . . . and I love them all . . . my heart breaks when I think about them . . . I feel as if I'm being torn into pieces . . . I love you and think about you all the time . . . I feel as if I'm being torn into pieces with it . . ."

The pieces of Maureen's body, damp and warm, are fitted together into the bulk of her body, a disguise. She sleeps uneasily. She is alert for sounds she doesn't want to hear. Beyond the television's droning she hears new sounds, outer sounds, people talking on the stairs, people outside . . . so many people . . . windows are open with warm weather, letting people out. Against her will she listens. Curious and shy and a little angry, afraid, she listens. Brock reads to her from the newspaper. Rex Morgan. Gasoline Alley. Brenda Starr. His favorites. Loretta goes out and Brock stays home to watch Maureen. He keeps her company. He talks for hours. He talks about Indiana, about getting rides on trains, about working on farms, about being in jail . . . he talks for hours, hours. Maureen falls asleep and wakes up to his talking. His bulk is like hers, safe. She begins to trust him. Her eyes focus upon him. He reads her letters from Jules, over and over. "I'll read the one about the bus ride he took, that's a nice letter," Brock says. He takes the letters out of a cigar box and looks through them. He shows her the comics. He puts the television set by the end of her bed, on a card table. He tries to play cards with her but she won't play. She lies stubborn and cold beneath the covers, awake but not willing to play cards, hiding. Brock plays solitaire. Loretta comes home, her high heels noisy in the kitchen. She opens the refrigerator door to see what's what, on her way to Maureen's room, and Maureen hears everything she says.

"Guess who I ran into downtown," Loretta says.

My God, Maureen thinks, *am I waking up?*

She is afraid. She feels open, as if her legs have been yanked apart, anything can happen. She shuts her eyes, wanting to sink back, but it doesn't work, and she lies instead with her heart pounding dizzily, unable to sleep, awake. She is awake.

One day she is impatient with her mother and Brock. They are out in the kitchen having coffee. Maureen sits up and listens; she can hear that the mail has come. She hears the mailman downstairs. Sweating, in a panic, she twists beneath the covers and mouths silent words. *Why don't you hear him downstairs? Is there a letter from Jules?*

The silent words are painful. She feels them large in her throat, distending her mouth. Exasperated, exhausted, she tries to keep them back and to lie dead on the pillow, heavy and cold. Then suddenly she finds herself sitting up and calling out, "Is the mail here? Is there a letter from Jules?"

Loretta and Brock come to the doorway at once, staring in at her.

Out loud again she says, childishly and impatiently, ready to cry, "Please look downstairs. Don't you hear the mailman has come? Maybe there's a letter from Jules."

She has awakened for good.

8

February 11, 1966

Dear Miss Oates,

Years ago I was a student of yours, you don't remember me. I am writing this letter knowing you won't remember me.

Why do I want to talk to you? You are in a hurry in your life and won't listen to me. When I was your student I did poorly, why should you remember me? I was not fat then but changed back to what I had been. I had been fat before. Never mind. I want to send you a message but I don't know what the message is.

I take hold of my skull and try to remember my life, how

it happened, the order things happened in. But everything is a jumble. So I went to the library the other day and got out the newspapers for the time between April 1956 and May 1957 and read through them.

While I was asleep everything had kept on!—no end to it, a jumble of people and things—photographs of tanks and soldiers, people lying in the street, I don't even know what people they were, lying dead in the street—everything keeps going, keeps going. The books you taught us didn't explain this. The jumble was hidden somehow. The books you taught us are mainly lies I can tell you. But I am not criticizing you.

I think I am writing to you because I could see, past your talking and your control and the way you took notes carefully in your books while you taught, writing down your own words as you said them, something that is like myself. My name is Maureen Wendall. I hope you remember me but why should you remember me? I did not do well in your course and dropped out of school and should be ashamed of myself for writing to you like this. Please don't think bad of me. Is it an insult to say that I am writing to you because there is something like me, in you?

Sincerely yours,
Maureen Wendall

9

March 11, 1966

Dear Miss Oates,

Thank you for answering my letter. I was sorry I had written it and wished I could take it back, but now I'm glad, it's just as well. I wish I could write down my thoughts not in a mess like most of my life but in some order—I want to explain something, I want to get it clear. Yes, it was in 1964 that I took your course at the University of Detroit. Did you remember that or did you look my name up in a class book? It would mean so much to me to think that you remembered me, but I don't expect that, why should you remember me when I can almost not remember myself? I went to the library last Thursday after work and looked through newspapers again. You can't see what has happened day by day, reading the newspapers, you must look at them for a whole year. Then everything comes rushing at you.

You see how the year was a waste. Faster and faster the headlines come, one day has nothing to do with the next, suddenly someone has been killed or a nation is on the front page, the photographs change of people lying in the streets, the names change, everything goes up and down jiggling the eye. In the library I started sweating, so afraid. How can I live my life if the world is like this? The world can't be lived, no one can live it right. It is out of control, crazy. I felt this right in the library though everyone was sitting quiet at tables. I looked around. Those people would like to throw the books out the windows, break the lamps and chairs, hit one another over the head with anything they could grab. But they are quiet, sitting and reading. I don't want to sound crazy to you. I am only saying what I believe. The library is very clean and modern, I love that kind of place, there is nothing behind it or not much—not much history. I love people walking quietly and very polite. At my house nobody was quiet or polite.

I want to tell you about my family, how we lived. I want to tell you about myself. Now it is March 1966 and I can't believe that date. It is like living in the future—not real. It is so many years later, after what happened to me, but I am still alive, and I am about to begin a new life, start over again with a new life. My heart is frozen so afraid at the thought of going out to begin again, I want to talk to someone. I want to send you a message.

What will happen after today? I am sitting here in my room in Detroit, writing this down for you to read. It is ten at night. I am alone, I live alone. My life is quiet. When I was your student in that night class I had a day job as a secretary, full time, now I have a better job and I am taking a course at Highland Park Junior College two evenings a week. It is supposed to be a much easier school than the University of Detroit. But I want to continue my college career. I want to learn whatever I can, maybe it will help me not to be afraid. Asleep or awake I am afraid, and how can you live that way, always afraid? I am afraid of men out on the street if I see them or don't see them, I am afraid of cars hitting me, of people laughing at me, I am afraid of losing my purse, of throwing up in a store, of screaming out loud in the library and being kicked out and never allowed back. I keep sitting here thinking of the time. Fifteen minutes after ten on March 11, 1966, and I know that should be a sacred time because it will never come again, but I don't feel anything for it, I am numb. What will happen in the future? I am afraid. I am afraid not just of my own future but of all the world. When I read the newspapers I feel that I am losing myself, my own self Maureen Wendall, and becoming like the world itself, not knowing what will happen the next day and never ready for it. Maybe I am writing to you not because you are like me—I sound a little crazy!— but because you are the exact opposite, you are never surprised, you foretell everything, and inside all the mess of the newspapers you live your own life in peace, prepared.

The students in our class, some of them, thought you were a little strange. They think most professors are strange. That was in 1964, January and February, the second semester. They thought you were very intelligent but cold. You were happy about the books we read, you were happy reading passages out loud to us, we could tell that the happiness in the room for you was in the book and not in us. I don't know if I even liked you at first. Sometimes I like women a lot and other times I hate them. You were not much older than me so maybe I was jealous. I always wanted my teachers to be older than me, in fact I would like everybody to be older than me so that I can follow their example. Now I am getting old myself, I am twenty-six years old!— which seems a terrible age to be alone, not to have a career, not to be like everyone else with a definite life. But I have gone through so much that instead of being twenty-six I should really be forty or fifty. Inside my body and face I am an old woman, not even a woman or a man but just an old person; maybe I am writing to you to get rid of all this to make myself young again, to feel the way I should feel at the age of twenty-six about to fall in love.

There is a man I want to marry—I want to fall in love.

We were curious about you, your marriage. You were so calm and intelligent and your sense of humor kept us afraid. How could you be in love and married? That's what I wondered. You reminded me something of my brother Jules. Jules could have been intelligent like you—I mean, he could have been educated except for the way things turned out. I have told Jules about you. My brother Jules is the most important person in my life but what can you do with people who mean a lot to you? Love them? How do you love them, exactly what does that mean? Is it sitting and thinking about them, wanting to protect them? In that case to keep Jules safe he would have to be dead and buried. I want to marry a man and fall in love and be protected by him. I am ready to fall in love. But my heart is hard and my body hard, frozen.

Probably you don't remember me. The course I took with you was "Introduction to Literature." I always loved reading books but in that classroom, in the Commerce and Finance Building, everything seemed cold and strange, a threat. The other students were a threat. It was a night class, that made it worse. At night everything is exaggerated. We could tell you resented teaching a night class. I sat in the third row and I had long hair then, long dark hair, but now I have short hair and I noticed from a photograph of you in the paper that you also have short hair now, short dark hair. That was all three years ago. Did you ever look at me and think about me? Did you think *That girl is something like me?*

One night you read something from *Madame Bovary*, which was our assignment, about the woman going for a walk in a field with her dog. You seemed to think that was important. Out in the field she looks around, she sees—I don't know what. I don't remember. Then she feels a cold wind starting to blow, and she goes back home. You read that passage to us and pointed out something about it, and I could tell you were thinking *That woman is something like me,* like you yourself, a stranger to us, and I sat there hearing myself think, *This is not important, none of this is real.* I felt weak and dizzy, thinking of it. Those days I liked to fast, to make up for the days I ate so much, so I got dizzy sometimes at night. I ate crackers in the morning and some bread after work and a banana or orange or something, that was all. I liked to feel my stomach ache with hunger, knowing that I was hungry and not filled up, not fat any more. I used to get dizzy in your class a lot. Why did you think that book about Madame Bovary was so important? All those books? Why did you tell us they were more important than life? They are not more important than my life.

I loved books when I was a different person, before I went crazy. I was crazy for thirteen months. Nobody put me away, they let me stay at home. I lay in bed crazy. I could hear things but I wasn't listening. I was not Maureen Wendall but a certain mass of flesh, lying on a bed. All of my life I could have lain there, but I came back, I woke up. I don't know why I woke up. It happened.

Now I am writing this in a library, not my room. It is

dark out. Tomorrow night I will see the man I plan to marry, the man I want, but tonight I am a young woman in a library in Detroit, a small library, alone, sitting alone at a table, writing a letter to a woman named Joyce Carol Oates, a former teacher of mine. There are only three other people here tonight because it is snowing hard out. Almost a blizzard. There is a woman with an overcoat on, still buttoned, with a fake-fur collar that is matted and ugly, a coat that looks like a man's coat; and a man who is maybe seventy, bent over the *Detroit News,* with a very empty face, reading the paper very slowly; and another man, around fifty, I don't want to look at him much because his nose is running and he doesn't have a handkerchief, he wipes it on his fingers. Then there is the librarian, with her white-rimmed glasses. I come in here all the time but she pretends not to know me. She works at her desk. We are all in here and outside it is snowing hard and we should feel close together but we don't. We don't talk or look at each other.

This letter is a crazy idea but I don't care. I don't care what you think. Maybe you get lots of crazy letters. I have given up on what people think, I can't change them. All around me there are shelves with books on them and none of those books are worth anything, I know that now, not the books by Jane Austen I used to love or the book about Madame Bovary you liked so much. Those things didn't happen and won't happen. None of them ever happened. In my life something happened and I have to keep thinking about it, over and over. For a while I was very sick. It was my mind that was sick, it gave up, it got cloudy and slow, it drew back from people talking. You always talked too fast in class, that was a bad thing about you. We would sit trying to make sense of it, your words, and faster and faster you would talk, getting away from us. Did you hate us, that you talked so fast? You left us behind. I wanted to come up to you after class and ask, "Why do you want to leave us behind?" but I had no nerve for that.

When I got well my uncle took me out for walks. He brought me back from where I was, crazy. He woke me up, my uncle. I haven't seen him for years now but never mind, it is Uncle Brock of 1957 I remember, and my mother of 1957 I remember, otherwise everything will be a jumble. My face was a mess. He brought me back by talking to me. He had a sad, serious face, a mess himself, a failure of a man, with no nerve. Ma made hints that he had done something once, something bad, and had to leave town. I don't know. But he brought me back from where I was. I love him no matter what a wreck he is in his own life or no matter that he doesn't even have a life himself.

Why do I keep remembering a lady walking in a field in France, somewhere in the country, walking a dog and shivering in the wind? I don't want to remember that when I've forgotten so much else. You read it to us, you read it with a certain serious look and serious sound to your voice that almost made me shiver, it meant so much to you, and you never talked like that to us; that was because you believed the book was more important than your students were. Isn't that true? You hung onto your books and we students came and went, night students and day students, in and out, and you quit that school and went somewhere else, but you took your books along with you and they all had your name written in them, I bet, and they were more important to you than any of us. That's all right. I didn't know the other students, I didn't have time for them. My life was a flurry. I wanted to succeed in school and find a place, make my way along, get married, but my life was a flurry and I was too nervous to do well. One year I was crazy in bed and a few years later I was in college, in your class, sitting there in the third row staring at you, afraid of you and of school. One year I lay in bed in silence and a few years later I was writing papers for you, trying to write. You failed me. You flunked me out of school.

I don't blame anybody. I never blame anybody. I am like a piece of wood being carried along in the water, drifting along, meeting things and passing by, not judging, not calling anybody names. The man across at the next table sniffs that loud fast sniff that certain men do, in public places, so that you want to scream at them, *Get a handkerchief, you filthy pig!* but I think, *No, he's just a man, don't pay any attention.* My father was like that. Clearing his sinuses in the morning, in the bathroom next to the room Betty and I shared. Let them. They do such things, they do other things with you, hurt you, breathe their private breaths into your face, and then they die, it's all right. I don't blame them. I don't blame you.

My other English teacher at that school, Mr. Kovack, was very hard when he corrected my papers and I thought he had to be pretending, making things hard when nobody gave a damn, when outside on Livernois brakes were always squealing and the air stank and the Negroes were standing out on the street corners all day long, thinking what to do, making plans. Fires and shootings. Burn Detroit down. But he handed my papers back marked D and F, and in red ink he explained all my mistakes. You gave me F, for the only paper I handed in, but you didn't bother explaining what was wrong. *Lack of coherence and development,* you wrote at the bottom of the paper. You wrote in blue ink, Mr. Kovack in red. Your handwriting was, it still is probably, large and dreamy with circular letters and long crossed t's slanting straight up and down and very clear, but what did you say? I couldn't understand your meaning. You knew what you meant but I didn't. You are not a woman who would lie paralyzed for thirteen months because a man tried to kill you, you are not a woman who would give herself to men for money or for anything, not even love, you don't spend your nights like this in a library writing a letter to a stranger.

I don't ask to turn into you but to see myself like this: living in a house out of the city, a ranch house or a colonial house, with a fence around the back, a woman working in the kitchen, wearing slacks maybe, a baby in his crib in the baby's room, thin white gauzy curtains, a bedroom for my husband and me, a window in the living-room looking out onto the lawn and the street and the house across the street. Every cell in my body aches for this! My eyes ache for it, the balls of my eyes in their sockets, hungry and aching for this, my God how I want that house and that man, whoever he is.

I am thinking of the months I went back to high school, to night school, making up for what I had missed. It was then I began to dream about my future. I went through school, I made up for the months I was crazy. I did it. But how do you fall in love? I heard Ma say to a friend of hers that there was nothing in life but men, nothing but love. "Jesus, when you come right down to it, what else is there?" she said in her flat, amused voice, as if she'd gone through everything and had to admit this truth. But how do you fall in love? I am thinking of Ma throwing things around the kitchen, drunk, crying, her face twisted ugly and the words ugly coming out of her mouth, when some man let her down—they were always letting her down, poor Ma, and she was kind of a pretty woman. Why did she open herself up to that pain? Again and again she opened herself up.

I am going to fall in love. Tomorrow night I'll see the

man I have picked out to love. He is already married; he has three children. I want him. I want him to marry me. I am going to make this happen and begin my life. We will have a bedroom together, we will have children, he will leave his own children behind. I am telling you these things even though you are a married woman and would not want any other woman to take your husband from you. But you are a married woman, I think, who would not mind taking someone else's husband, so long as it happened well enough, beautifully enough like a story. Once in a while, though, I don't believe my life will change. I don't believe he will marry me or even think of me. I don't believe something so strange could happen. And I fall into a sad state and can't get out of it. I lean forward and my head droops between my shoulders, my bones seem to turn helpless, I think *Why didn't I die? Why didn't he kill me?* For thirteen months I was an animal. Ma uses other words, she says I was "going through a phase," but I remember it all, I know. Never did I think anything in those months, but pictures floated through my mind, like a nightmare. Even when I was awake I was asleep. Even now, sitting in this library with time ahead of me, so much dangerous time, I feel in my arms and legs a strange soft sensation which is like a memory itself. I can't get such memories out of my body. I felt no love for those men but I put my arms around them. They entered my body in its most secret place, those strangers, and the space between us was only a slick surface of skin and sweat. Is it different with love? What is it like to give yourself with love? Or do you lie there and feel terror to know that, love or not, a husband or a stranger, it is all the same and no words can change it? I was never in love. They did not love me. They embraced me again and again; in my mind I will always see a man embracing a girl who is me. I can see a man's hands upon her body but the bodies are strangers. I can't get rid of this memory. My body is like the body of an animal, or one of those things that are just one cell, very tiny, that keep everything in them of all their history and are always the same age, I mean in any century, at the time when Christ was alive or right now those things are always the same things, the memory is hard in them and it has nothing to do with their brains. I remember. I will live very long and remember.

So I came back. I woke up. I finished high school, I moved out of my mother's place, I worked as a typist and got a room near a bus stop, I enrolled at the University of Detroit for one course in Fall, 1963, Composition, Mr. Kovack gave me a D. I enrolled for another course, yours. I came to class, I listened to you, I lay awake nights thinking of how I must not fail, how I must get a C in this course, how I must take hold of myself become like other people. But I did fail anyway, you failed me. You gave me an F.

You failed me.

That year at the University of Detroit was strange for me. During the day I worked. Three other typists, myself, a secretary. Downtown. I took the bus both ways. I hated it. I sat by myself. I was afraid but I kept on. I didn't look for another job. I didn't go anywhere except to work and to school. I didn't dare go to the movies. I was afraid of those first few minutes when you can't see well in a theater. At night, from seven until eight-thirty, two nights a week, I took a course at college. I tried to look like other girls. By then I had lost weight, my face had cleared up. I washed my face twice a day, I put cold cream on it, I did everything to it, and the face you saw, if you bothered to see it, was a nice face again. I bought shoes and clothes like the other girls. I put my hair up in rollers, I washed it all the time. I was a pretty girl. Now, at twenty-six, I think I am prettier. I deserve to fall in love and be married. In those days I didn't dare to think about anything so distant, it was enough just to get through a day without breaking down. I never thought of marriage. I was afraid of men. What I envied in you was your easy way with men, the way you talked to them, like friends, other teachers I saw you with in the hall, friends with men? I didn't think that a woman could be friends with any man. One day before class I saw you walking to the building with a man, a professor like yourself, a tall handsome man with gray hair, very well dressed, the two of you talking, smiling, like it was no accomplishment, and the two of you not seeing me, and another time I saw you, in a black Volkswagen, your husband driving you to school, coming up the driveway, your husband.

Everything in me aches for a husband. A house.

I carried this ache in me all my life, not knowing what it was. Everybody is flawed with it, a crack running through them. In you it is filled in for a while. You feel no pain. I know you feel no pain right now. I don't envy you or want to be like you, I only want to escape the doom of being *Maureen Wendall* all of my life. I dream of a world where you can go in and out of bodies, changing your soul, everything changing and not fixed forever, becoming men and women, daughters, children again, even old people, feeling how it is to be them and then not hating them, out on the street. I don't want to hate. There are too many strangers. I am writing this to a stranger, writing in a library about to close. You, the stranger, my ex-teacher who failed me, are reading this as fast as you can, you're impatient with it. You don't want people to make claims on you. I know. I don't blame you or judge anybody. You said, "Literature gives form to life," I remember you saying that very clearly. What is form? Why is it better than the way life happens, by itself? I hate all that, all those lies, so many words in all those books. What I like to read in this library is newspapers. I want to know. The old man is reading a newspaper, so is the man with the runny nose. Like me they want to find out what's going on, what is real. They don't have time in their lives for made-up things. But I remember you saying that about form. *Form.* I don't know what that word means. Maybe my brother Jules would know. I don't know. I myself am a certain form, a shape, sitting here with my head emptied out and afraid, that is all.

In the hospital, after her husband beat me up, a doctor was trying to take blood out of me. I was conscious. He had a big needle and was poking in my arm for a vein. He couldn't find it. He took the needle out and put it in again, poking for a vein, and he squeezed my wrist to make the vein swell so he could get inside it, but still that didn't work, so he tried my other arm, holding my arm out now because I was crying. I keep thinking of that, the needle going in and trying to find my vein, the doctor, a man, poking in my arm for a vein and not finding it. I would have made the vein big and soft for him if I could, but how can you do that? Finally he got the blood. He said, "She's got to have a Wasserman," to someone, not talking to me. I would make myself open and ready for love but how can you do that, how can you change yourself?

It is almost closing time in the library.

There is no end to this.

What form is there to the way things happen? I wanted to run up to you after class and ask that question, cry it out at you. Your words were wrong! You were wrong! One day the secretary at work ran in our office. She said to us, "My God, the President was shot! the President was shot!" Mandy, the girl next to me, jumped up and knocked some papers off her desk. They all began asking questions. The radio was on in the next room. Our boss came in, he was very upset. I straightened up the papers and while I was bent over my mind ran along as fast as a train, thinking, *There is something happening here I should understand.* In the restroom Mandy was crying and I didn't want to look at her, those tears, her shoulders that were shaking. I said to her, "But people die every day. Right here in Detroit they get shot like that." Some terrible invisible thing was passing close by me. What was it? Why couldn't I understand? Out on the street people were strange, all upset. I wanted to run up to them, grab their arms, I wanted to shout, "But why? Why? Why is everything stopped? Why now? What has happened? What is it?"

When I got to school that night everybody was talking about it. Some girls were crying. A boy made a joke about Mrs. Kennedy's pink wool suit, something about strawberry jam. The girls drew back from him, making faces. I sat alone by myself, alone, silent. But people die every day, I thought. Who was John Kennedy that he couldn't die? A bullet entered his skull in a certain way and what was inside that skull was ruined. It will happen to us someday. It has already happened to some of us, and it is happening right now in Detroit. A girl said, very excited, "Did you hear about some professor in Finance? I think it was Finance. He came into class and said, 'Thank God somebody had the guts to do it!' That's what he said, right to the class." The girls exclaimed over this, shaking their heads. One of the boys laughed. I touched my face to see how my skin felt, hoping no one would look at me, hoping they wouldn't find out my secret.

A few minutes to nine. The librarian switches the lights off and on, to warn us. Time to get up, get going. Put on your overshoes. It will be very cold outside. The man with the runny nose looks up, surprised. Is he afraid? Nowhere to go? He has a pale, pouchy, freckled face and a rumpled shirt. Better not look at him. The clock hand jumps another minute, the old man folds up his newspaper with care, returns it to the shelf. So much for that day. His hands are fastidious. He lingers there, arranging other newspapers into piles. By the radiator the woman sighs a sigh I can hear across the room, pushes a magazine away from her as if pushing a plate away, stares at the table top. And I, I am sitting with my heart beating steady and slow, writing all this down out of hate, because it seems to me now that it's you I hate, my ex-teacher, a woman, but that's crazy because I didn't know you and I didn't do any work for you, maybe I could have passed the course and maybe not, how was it your fault?

But yes. I hate you and no one else, not even those men, not even Furlong. I hate you and that is the only certain thing in me. Not love for the man I want to marry but hate for you. Hate for you, with your books and words and your knowing so much that never happened, in a perfect form, you being driven to school by your husband, and now there are even photographs of you in the paper sometimes, you with your knowledge while I've lived a lifetime already and turned myself inside out and got nothing out of it, not a thing. I don't know anything now, anything more than I knew before. Those men taught me nothing. I don't even hate them. I lived my life but there is no form to it. No shape. All the people who lie alone at night squirm with hatred they can't get straight, into a shape, all the women who give themselves to men without knowing who those men are, all of us walk fast with hate like pain in our bowels, terrified, and what do you know about it? You write books. What do you know?

The woman by the radiator gets to her feet. She is heavy, she seems pained when she stands: thick cream-colored fat-marbled old legs, poor legs, veins cracking and rising to the surface, a woman of middle-age. Oh, we women know things you don't know, you teachers, you readers and writers of books, we are the ones who wait around libraries when it's time to leave, or sit drinking coffee alone in the kitchen; we make crazy plans for marriage but have no man, we dream of stealing men, we are the ones who look slowly around when we get off a bus and can't even find what we are looking for, can't quite remember how we got there, we are always wondering what will come next, what terrible thing will come next. We are the ones who leaf through magazines with colored pictures and spend long heavy hours sunk in our bodies, thinking, remembering, dreaming, waiting for something to come to us and give a shape to so much pain.

10

July 1966. Jules was still so glad to be back north that he didn't mind driving his mother every week to the hospital where his uncle was—had been for some months—sick with a mysterious sickness and not getting any better. He told himself that part of life was driving people back and forth to hospitals, visiting hospitals, occasionally getting stuck in one yourself. While in the Southwest he had been in hospitals three times for various troubles. The climate had weakened him, made him prone to headaches, eyeaches, dizzy spells, and once he'd been hit hard with a tire iron, his knee nearly smashed, and while in the hospital he had tried to clear an island of quiet around him so that he could think, plan his life. But the hospitals were all so noisy—night and day were mixed up, sleepless nights and sleepless days, too much eating, too much exposure to other people—he came to the conclusion that it might be better to have no brains at all, to lie there and wait.

Now that his mother was going out with a new man, things were looking up—still, things should look grim for a hospital visit, so she looked sad. Jules could read her mind. He was fond of her, loving her for all the things that had exasperated him when he had been younger. He liked his mother's bouncy step, going up the stairs to the hospital. It was something he could count on.

"You'd think I'd be fed up with this city by now," Loretta said, "but on a day like this it's hard, the day is so goddam nice. If Brock would just get back on his feet again—"

"He'll be all right."

"Now they say liver trouble. Liver, kidneys, what is it? He reminds me of our father, your grandfather. There are men like that all over the world, they just can't get back on their feet, they can't get going, they stumble and fall and if you're a woman you got to try to raise them again. But you can't. A woman spends most of her life on her hands and knees scrubbing up after them and washing their dirty clothes and shaking mud out of their shoes and cooking up big dump-piles of food for them—they eat like pigs and they drink like pigs, they drink like fish. They'll talk your head off with what they're going to do when they get well but in the end you're the one who gets the job, you yourself, and that's the only way you know where the money comes from and if there's going to be any. That's the only way. With them it's all talk and puking in the sink from them drinking too much, and their breath stinking from their rotten yellow teeth, and any whore that walks by in the street can get them to follow her, while somebody else stays home cooking and cleaning up all their filthy mess. Now this one is down sick. What the hell is wrong with him?"

Her anger had accelerated steadily. Now she turned to face Jules.

"I don't know. They'll fix him up, don't worry," Jules said with a cheerfulness that went no further than his smile.

They passed the reception desk in the foyer, walking on old tile that was not very clean, headed down a corridor cluttered with carts of linen, carts with dirty dishes stacked on them, carts with soiled bedding, making their way quickly along past the X-ray room, past the vending-machine room, to a dark corridor in which an elevator was just discharging some nurses. Jules stuck his hand into the elevator to keep the door from closing and he and Loretta stepped inside, familiar with the greenish light of the small car and its mellow hum.

"I hate hospitals, they give me the creeps," Loretta said.

"Be glad for hospitals," Jules said.

His life now was not unpleasant. He had a job with his uncle, his father's brother, Samson Wendall, a man of caution and flabbiness and bad temper, the kind of man Jules imagined he could handle. A job with Samson Wendall! No matter if the job wasn't much, didn't pay well—Jules believed in the future. The old man had come around one day, nosing around for Jules; his own son had gone from one college to another and was now hitchhiking through Europe, lost somewhere in Europe, baffling and angering the old man, and so he had turned up looking for his nephew, of whom he had heard extraordinary things in the old days of Mama Wendall, who carried tales from household to household. At that time all the prophecies of Jules's superiority had gone unremarked or had been greeted with scorn, but now, mysteriously, some flower had bloomed in Samson's head and Jules had a job at his plant in Wyandotte. He was growing up at last. He was twenty-seven years old.

This part of the hospital was for welfare cases mainly, and therefore many Negroes were about in various stages of undress, sitting up, reclining painfully, lying motionless beneath stark white sheets, bed after bed of sick, harmless people. Jules steered his mother along. He dreaded her whispering to him, "Aren't you glad you're not a nigger, at least?" which she had said to him in the past. They passed open wards, a long line of beds. Loretta looked around pityingly. She was so conscious of being white! And finally she did turn to Jules and say in a low voice, not quite a whisper, "Jesus, how'd you like to be a nigger and sick on top of it? I did that much for you at least, kid." Jules expelled his breath to show sympathy, humor. Actually he was immensely grateful for being white. In Detroit being white struck him as a special gift, a blessing—how easy not to be white! Only in a nightmare might he bring his hands up to his face and see *colored* skin, *Negro* skin, a hopeless brown nothing could get off, not even a razor.

Brock's bed was between two unhappy beds, the occupants dying slowly and without beauty or mystery; in one, an aged Negro man who had had several heart attacks, a fat man become skinny; and in the other, a middle-aged white man, Greek or Italian, who lay in a stony silence and stared up at the ceiling, emitting a strange odor, almost the odor of the grave. When someone came to visit him they were silent, everyone was silent.

Well, here we are! Loretta's face took on her hospital-visit look, a broad, false smile, and Jules stood attentively behind her, feeling himself ten years old.

"Well, Brock, hiya! You think we weren't coming?" Loretta said, almost shouting with good will.

"Hi. Hello. Good to see you," Brock said, trying to smile.

So the visit began. There had been eight, ten visits so far. Brock was not an old man; nevertheless his body was old, the doctor said; his heart was the heart of an old man, his kidneys and liver worn out, his stomach weak, all from drinking, drinking, or running around, or just living—the doctor had said this, or someone who had appeared to be a doctor but was maybe just a student; it was hard to tell. They were giving him tests. The tests alone had aged him, Jules saw. He had a worn, perspiring face, his hair sparse and receding from his faintly astonished, sullen face, his mouth slack, his cheek slack, the very look in his eyes slack and unfocused except when someone in white drew near—then he took on an uncanny look, almost a demonic look, as if he were prepared to fight. He'd told them a little about the tests but in the main had been secretive about them. Better not to know, Jules thought wisely. Better not to think about what was done in hospitals.

Jules felt a tragic bridge between himself and his uncle, a bridge of kinship and despair. But he, Jules, was only twenty-seven years old and on the verge of a new life, feeling himself immortal, with a decent job for the first time in his career, wearing decent clothes, having put behind him the red dirt of the South and the Southwest, reborn in the North—for a month he'd been so down on his luck, so miserable, he had hired himself out in Texas as a dog- and cat-napper, catching stray pets at the edges of suburban lawns or in alleys and bringing them to a veterinarian who, in turn, sold them to an experimental medical laboratory at a profit Jules never quite found out, though he had tried, wanting to go in business for himself; he'd sunk that low; and, for a while, on his way back up, he'd hired himself out in St. Louis to a combination used-car sales company and finance-loan company, his job being to steal back the cars of debtors behind on their payments, a most adventuresome and thankless job, though needing brains and skill—he'd done all these crazy things, but now, after his twenty-seventh birthday, it looked as if he was going to turn out well after all.

Activity down at the other end of the corridor—some nurses, an attendant. A patient seemed to be throwing up . . . or hemorrhaging. Jules kept his eyes upon his uncle, forcing Loretta to stay facing him also, wanting no fuss. The visits were bad enough, awkward enough—let them get no worse by bringing in the miseries of others. He dreaded Loretta's exclamations, *Oh, is that blood, look!* or *Where is that man's leg?* He judged her as not quite that stupid but playing a woman's trick, unconsciously playing at ignorance and surprise in order to suggest the great distance between such horror and herself—she was a flowsy blond woman, good-humored, that was all, not marked for horror. Horror surprised her. But she had sense enough not to exclaim over Brock's appearance. She was quiet about that. Something was going on in Brock's face—his upper lip seemed to be eroding away, dissolving slowly. Week after week. The lower lip was normal but the upper lip tapered off on the left, sandy and grainy, very dry. Jules remembered having seen this before on other visits, noting it and not quite noting it, feeling that it was none of his business and why hadn't the doctor mentioned it? Of course they hadn't seen the doctor for three weeks. Maybe his uncle had leprosy. All the talk was of heart and kidneys and liver, mysterious internal devices. He tried not to notice his uncle's lip.

"And Maureen is fine, Brock, just fine, doing so well with her job, and she's still going to school," Loretta said. Actually Maureen had flunked out of the University of Detroit and she had a lousy job as a typist, but Maureen out catching city buses was a miracle after Maureen lying in bed for a year, and everyone knew it. "And she's real pretty now, bought herself a spring coat, she's never looked prettier. Or more healthy."

"Is she happy?" said Brock.

"Oh, real happy! Sure she's happy!" Loretta cried. "She would of come today except she had to go somewhere. It's just wonderful how Maureen is back to herself again and ... and all because of you."

Brock took this gravely. He believed it. Breathing raspily, lying in silence, he seemed to be contemplating the slender, mysterious Maureen. It was strange that she never came to visit him. They made excuses for her. But Maureen, frightened and abrupt, would never come to the hospital. "I want to see him but I can't, I can't! Let me alone!" she would cry angrily, anxious to get away, off on her own lonely life.

Brock lay in silence for some minutes, thinking of her. "Well, I'm glad she's got a job and all that," he said finally.

Now Loretta began to chatter again, about tenants in their building, kids with head-lice, bastards of kids who would steal you blind if you didn't let them know who was boss, trash living upstairs and trash living downstairs, a window in the bathroom broken all winter and never fixed, water pipes leaking, a step in the stairway broken out, ADC mothers with bellies like watermelons and if you didn't give way to them on the sidewalk they'd bounce right into you with those bellies—all of them nigger whores, of course —and she, Loretta, trying to get off the rolls if it killed her, and if it killed her trying to get Betty back home again, trying to get the family back together again, and she, Loretta, was scared to death just driving down here, for what if Jules ran into a nigger kid in the street? They swarmed all over the streets, everywhere. What if he ran into a kid and everyone piled out of the houses onto him and tore him apart? And what would they do to her?

"Ma, not so loud," Jules said.

His attention was taken up by a nurse who made her way through the ward. She was younger than he but confident in her walk, silent in her white rubber-soled shoes, a honey-faced girl he would have loved to embrace, surprising her. He smiled at her; she glanced at him and lowered her eyes. He remembered having seen her before. His heart gave a pointless little leap. He had never gotten over his love for Nadine, though his misery should have ended that, and now all his relationships with women, whether public like this or private and physical, were darkened by the memory of Nadine, loosing in his veins a stupid melancholy. How he'd loved that girl! Hating her had only been a form of his love, hopeless as that love, and his obsession had fed upon itself for many months, for years, until the idea of Nadine was fixed and permanent in his head, so rigid that he could be unfaithful to her with any number of women and she, Nadine, remained not betrayed but somehow honored. He did not know whether to hate this weakness in him, this love, or to be grateful for it.

While his mother went on to chatter bitterly about some one upstairs Jules excused himself and followed the nurse out of the ward. He walked fast, conscious of looking good, a pleasant young man, with a slight limp yet from a terrible blow he'd taken on the knee a while ago (in a fight with a man whose car Jules was reappropriating for the finance company, a Negro who had tried to smash his kneecap with a tire iron), and in the corridor outside he caught up with her. He approved of her clean white uniform and her shining hair.

"Is there a coffee shop around here?" Jules asked.

She stared at him, flustered. Jules was disappointed in the first instant by something unimaginative in her look, but he went on, walking with her slowly, heading her down the hall. "Every week we come to visit my uncle, but my uncle doesn't seem to be getting better."

"Yes, I remember seeing you."

"My uncle isn't getting any better. I wonder if he's dying. Do you have the inside story?" Jules asked with a smile.

She glanced from side to side. Her forehead was furrowed. "What do you mean, the inside story?"

"Can you have coffee with me somewhere?"

"No."

"Why not?"

"I'm on duty, I have to work."

"When do you go off duty?"

"Six."

"Let me come back and pick you up, then you can tell me the inside story," Jules said, touching her elbow lightly. "Isn't there always an inside story? About the doctors and the nurses? What goes on in surgery?"

She reddened, not looking at him. "You're not serious," she said. "You're making fun of me."

"I'm very serious. I'm not critical, I just want to know. Everyone wants to know about hospitals. People on the outside have great faith in hospitals and doctors but still we wonder. I spent a few weeks in a hospital in the South and found cockroach legs in my soup—the whole cockroach would have been one thing, I could just have flicked it out onto the floor and gotten rid of it, but pieces of a cockroach mean something more serious—you can't hope to get to the bottom of it. What do you think?"

"I've never seen a cockroach in anybody's soup," the girl said.

"My uncle's lip is eroding away. Nobody mentions it. I noticed on his arm a lot of red dots, needle dots. Are you people injecting cancer into him?"

The girl stared straight ahead. "I'm not injecting nothing into nobody, except under orders," she said.

"Oh, not you, I don't mean you, and if you were doing it it wouldn't be on purpose," Jules said cheerfully. "I mean some of the interns, the night shift maybe, aren't they all experimenting? All those niggers in there, why not? A few cancer cells here, a new cancer drug here, one bed and then another—why not? The welfare people are anxious to cooperate."

"I don't know what you're talking about," the girl said.

"I'm just talking to pass the time of day because I like you," Jules said, his good mood wearing out slowly. "It's nobody's business what the doctors do to them, niggers or white. Why not experiment? I don't judge anybody. If I were a doctor I might do the same thing myself. I'd always be trying out something new, and on the night shift nobody could stop me from transplanting toes and fingers, ears onto stomachs, for a laugh, sponges left inside wombs, a stainless steel fork poking out of a guy's eye, in the interests of medical science. I'd discover new diseases and their cures all in the same night. I'd have a hell of a good time. I'll meet you out in back at six then."

"I don't know."

"Yes, six. I'll be there. My car is white."

"I don't think so. I don't know."

"Six o'clock," said Jules.

He left her and turned back to his uncle's ward, a little depressed. The perfume of the hospital was not Jules's perfume; mixed with the light smell of a woman, it grew perverse and heavy. It blotted out the woman's smell. He

walked back slowly, his hands in his pockets, hearing a typewriter clicking somewhere and hearing beyond it a low dull
mumble as of mumbling in a cave, mumbling in hell. *We've
been here for years! Waiting for you for years!* a chorus of
the dying might cry out as he entered the ward, eager for his
youth.

His youth . . .

The night before, lying in the arms of a woman who was
married to an acquaintance of his, he had had a terrible
thought: the entrance to these women was all the same,
every one of them the same, and yet he had never really
entered, was always rejected. He was left outside, dismissed.
He had never completed anything.

A man in a bed near Brock's sat up with a black rosary
dangling between his fingers, gazing at Jules as if about to
say, *Yes, we men are always rejected.* Jules looked away. It
could not be possible that he, Jules, was growing up into a
man like every other man—that there was no special skill in
him, no grace or delicacy, no destiny in proportion to his
desire. He wanted so much! Now, heading for his dying
uncle's bed, his mother's bobbing, gossipy body, he felt that
he wasn't in a hospital so much as in a prison, loosed for the
grounds, handed a minimal freedom. He would have liked to
light a cigarette. Fear began in him, nothing serious, but
when he returned to Brock and gazed upon that wreck,
seeing accidentally again the red spots on his uncle's arms, it
seemed to him probable that the doctors were really experimenting with cancer cells—it wasn't a joke but serious—
injections followed by the growths of cultures, stained cells
beneath microscopes, a sequence of antibiotics, anti-viruses,
anti-germs, secret potions brewed in the night by the bright-
est intern on the staff, destined for fame. Anything was
possible.

How triumphant to be a doctor!

11

Jules drove his uncle to the London Chop House for
lunch and surrendered the car to the Negro parking attendant, himself above being a parking attendant and a little
above being a chauffeur, but carrying some of their amiable
servility about his shoulders—it was a way of getting along.
He was dressed well, in a light summer suit that had cost

over one hundred dollars, with a tie of steely light gray, his shoes polished, his hair neatly trimmed, his eye on his uncle's belligerent, unsteady walk. Uncle Samson was not really Howard Wendall's brother—it seemed hardly possible Only the drinking linked them.

Samson Wendall had his own tool-and-die plant in Wyandotte, Michigan, and he was on the market, money poured into him; he lived now in an immense Tudor mansion in Grosse Pointe itself with his fat wife and daughters, who must have spent most of their time gazing out the baroque windows onto the long, dipping, showcase lawn, waiting for Grosse Pointe ladies to call. None called. The Grosse Pointe Yacht Club did not beckon, neither did the Detroit Athletic Club, though Samson sneered viciously enough at that great building as Jules drove by it. "Look at that, take a look! One block behind them there's nigger whores out on the sidewalk, hair bleached to hell, and there's the DAC itself—how d'ya do?" Jules smiled and drove on. It was his duty with Samson not to be smart or inquisitive but only to be a son, a replacement for his wild lost cousin: he had popped up as his cousin, a boy named Joseph, had disappeared. To hell with Joseph, Joseph in Europe. Jules was in Detroit, driving Uncle Samson around adroitly. All he had to do, Samson said again and again, was to keep his mouth shut and his eyes and ears open. He was to work with the plant manager. He was to hang around Samson himself, learning things.

"Hey, did you know I fly by jet now? Jet airliner?"

"That's wonderful," said Jules.

"Times sure have changed from the old days. God, they sure have," Samson said with a sour smile.

Of Jules's father they never spoke.

Of Jules's mother Samson said, "Hear your ma has a little boy. Well, that'll keep her young—women like to fuss around a little kid, eh?"

Only of Jules himself did he speak, with the enthusiastic rush of words that Jules sensed might mean nothing, as they had meant nothing with Bernard Geffen. "First thing, we put you through college, take the right courses, get that out of the way. Cram it into your head, boy, and the rest you learn straight from me. I need someone I can trust. I like your face."

"Thank you," said Jules.

"Don't thank me! I said I like your face. I trust you."

They entered the Chop House, descending into the expensive dark, and Jules bent politely to the hostess's ear to ask for their table. Yes, he must have had a good face, everyone responded well to it. But was it the same face he himself saw? At the table with its red-and-white-checkered tablecloth, back in a corner, lost in the rich winecellar dimness of the place, sat someone named Yates, waiting for them. Samson was forty minutes late, having coughed up something in the bathroom off his office, while Jules, numb with a certain professional numbness he was cultivating, stared out the window at the suety air of Wyandotte, Michigan. Now Samson grunted hello to the man, shook hands, introduced Jules, sat down heavily, with that look of irritated expectation that belongs to portly, up-from-riches businessmen in Detroit, lunching at the London Chop House.

"What a dark hole! They hiding something here?" Samson muttered.

The other man responded at once with an appreciative bark, and Jules unfolded a napkin with a smile meant to be Joseph Wendall's smile. He felt responsible for this uncle; though Samson was a hundred pounds heavier than he and decibels louder even in his breathing, an enormous-chested man with gray hair, undistinguished except for his arrogance, carrying Howard Wendall's assembly-line gut around with him above a straining, expensive belt. Jules hoped he would not drop dead before Jules's job was more secure. Jules's blood circulated freely in this uncle's presence only when he, Jules, nodded *yes* to everything, however fanciful. The leading joke this noon was about Lady Bird Johnson. "It seems that Lyndon Baines was stepping out of his bathtub one morning, when who did he see . . ." Jules smiled ahead of time, taking the opportunity to look around the crowded restaurant, wondering if his face was growing thin with all the smiling he had to do. He did admire his uncle. He had always admired him for his money, spurred on by Grandma Wendall's admiration and jealousy and his own mother's hatred, knowing that success, for a man, must stir jealousy and hatred in the unsuccessful. He had gone to lunch with his uncle many times like this. At expensive restaurants downtown, at restaurants near the Fisher Center, in Dearborn, out Woodward, out at the airport, all of them business lunches at which he, Jules, was to sit and listen, a son, dutiful and quiet, with an intelligent, reliable look, having one drink and then allowing his elders to pass on to second and third and fourth drinks, as they always did.

"This place sure is dark! If I knock something over there'll be hell to pay for somebody," Samson said. Like a character in a comic strip, he latched onto a certain observation and kept tossing it up with a petulant grin, as if everyone else were being gifted marvelously with it, a lifesaver to keep them afloat in the dangerous waters of conversation. "In these dark places they add up the bill and throw in the day of the month," he said.

The other man made an abrupt, hacking sound meant to be a laugh.

Samson had begun as an unskilled worker at Ford's decades ago; he had gone into tool-and-die work; he had left to begin his own business, a supplier to larger businesses. He had made his way without blundering, without stupidity, rising, drawing in investors, until now he could boast of having made six other men besides himself millionaires. Jules was sitting beside a millionaire. Yet it did not seem convincing: Jules might have been sitting at a lunch counter beside a stranger.

"The hell of it is, it's six hundred thousand dollars' worth," Samson was saying to Yates, flicking his thumb angrily, "so what do we do? The bastard says some entertaining. I said to him, 'What entertaining?' But you get nothing out of them —they got their own kind of language up in New England! So I called Mike and told him and he says, well, there's this guy at Metro Airport, you contact him, and what he does is arrange for some girls that are at the University of Michigan—"

"At the what?" said Yates.

"The University of Michigan. Girls. Students. It's thirty dollars a night, but I said to Mike, are we expected to pay for it?—because six hundred thousand is six hundred thousand but I never got in this kind of business before, and maybe it's too late to start. So he says let's keep still about it and see who wants to pay the thirty bucks, *that* will decide it. Not a question of thirty goddam bucks for how many— how many is it? four or five guys?—but Jesus Christ nobody's going to push *me* around."

"Where'd you hear the University of Michigan? Are you kidding?"

"I don't have time to kid," Samson said angrily.

Their drinks arrived. The restaurant seemed lighter. Sam-

son leaned forward against the table to talk into the face of
Mr. Yates, a man something like himself, and now he began
to talk about his boat. Jules was always hearing about this
boat. It was fifty feet long and had cost many thousands of
dollars but did not always work; the motor did not always
start. Samson kept inviting Jules out on the boat but never
got around to giving him any specific time.

Samson said to Yates, "I was on the phone five times this
morning with my lawyers, and the hell, do you think they
can straighten a simple goddam thing like that? Jesus! What
she did was a damn fool thing, tossing a big watermelon
overboard—it was spoiled and rotten, the goddam thing—
and there were these kids water skiing, so wouldn't you
know it, but all hell broke loose, and my wife, she keeps
wanting to call them up, the parents, and cry over the
phone or something. I told her that's exactly what they
wanted . . ."

Jules's gaze drifted wearily to one side, and there he saw
Nadine herself. She was sitting with two other women, looking at him. His heart jumped in his chest. He looked away at
once.

His uncle was talking about the boat and the lawsuit. One
lawsuit followed another. A new lawsuit on Monday. Law-
suits. Lawyers. Judges. Court. "Life didn't used to be so
mixed up," Samson said, screwing his face around so that it
looked almost like the face of Jules's father, brought back
horribly from the grave, a sour, perplexed, suspicious look.
It seemed that he had hired a bright young man from a
certain company—this outrage blended in with the yachting
accident—and this young man had turned out to be a thief,
a common thief, "a son-of-a-bitching bastard of a thief, the
little cocksucker!" Samson said loudly. A new lawsuit. A
company in New Jersey was suing him, Samson Wendall, for
hiring that man, and already the man had quit and was
working for another company out in California, the bastard,
and was this what life was coming to?

Mr. Yates ate celery noisily and sipped at his drink and
said, "I heard of the exact same thing happened to Indiana
Floeman. The exact same thing."

"How'd they make out?"

"Went bankrupt."

"I didn't know he was stealing plans from them. I didn't
know anything."

"Can you prove it?"

More drinks arrived. Jules, very nervous, looked back toward the woman he believed to be Nadine but could not decide: his vision was too jumpy. He felt as if he were suffocating. His uncle's cigar smoke maddened him. Then she glanced over at him again and their eyes met and he knew that she was Nadine, Nadine herself. He let his gaze fall from her heavily, as if struck by a blow.

Now Samson was saying something about George Romney —was he a crook or a saint? Yates joined in loudly. One of them hated Romney and the other admired him. Jules could not make out which man had which opinion, perhaps they traded opinions or confused them, but still the discussion rushed on in an amiable, loud manner, while Jules sat transfixed.

He looked back at Nadine.

She was sitting with two other women, older than she. She was no longer looking at him. Half turned from him, inclining her head to someone's words, she was very still, her arms and throat were bare; she wore black, with her black hair drawn up onto her head and wound about in an elaborate manner. Jules felt his heart sink to see it, it seemed to him so beautiful. He wanted to press his mouth against the thick, shining coils of hair. He wanted to come up behind her and embrace her, for, after all, hadn't she lain in his embrace years ago? hadn't she accepted his kisses, his caresses, his passion?

"You, boy, what're you staring at?"

Jules looked back at his uncle.

"Kid, you look like somebody sat you in the electric chair."

"I'm all right," Jules said coldly.

The air of the restaurant surged and ebbed. Jules could feel it pulsating. He tried to eat and watched the men at his table eating, ready to imitate them. A strange deeper darkness rose out of the restaurant's pretentious subdued light, a sense in Jules of evening, of nullity. It frightened him because he could not understand it. It was as if a door were being opened deep inside him but it was not a true opening, not a true beginning, an opening instead onto nothing.

But a steady excitement began to rise in him, coating him with sweat. *She won't leave without talking to me,* he thought. He was aware of Nadine at that table, eating lunch with two women, strangers, leaning forward toward them, smiling, talking, a deathly woman standing at the very brink of Jules's life, prodding him with the toe of her expensive shoe. His head was heavy and dazzling. He realized that he still loved her and that his desire for her was stronger than it had been. She herself had changed, she was older, more elegant, with a peculiar translucent, uncanny beauty, as if she had now imagined herself a different woman, exactly the woman to win Jules. In spite of the attentive pose of her spine there was something trancelike about her, as if she were listening to her friends' words too closely. Like Jules, she was always pretending—he felt that truth about her. She was eager, the back of her neck bent to hear, and Jules felt himself slowly disintegrating.

When he answered his uncle's questions his voice sounded slow and heavy. He could hear it from a distance. Fortunately his uncle and Yates had had enough to drink and were themselves in a kind of buffoonlike trance, stamping and pawing, lurching forward to concern over the slow car sales, lurching backward to a muttered remark about someone's yacht, someone's watermelon. Jules could make no sense of it. He saw Nadine get to her feet. He wanted to call out to her but did no more than watch helplessly as she reached for her purse, exactly as the other women did. Then she turned, slender and arrowlike, as if surveying the room from a vantage point that was invisible and invulnerable, undisturbed by the various eyes that moved upon her. He saw her approach him. She wore fashionable shoes, in the extreme style of the day, open heels with thin straps, small knobby heels, a tortoise-shell decoration on the front. He let his eyes move slowly up to her face, as if reluctant really to see her, and his uncle and Yates gaped at this strange woman who came up to Jules and handed him a piece of paper. He took it at once from her fingers and put it in his pocket, not surprised. She walked away.

"Jesus Christ, what was that?" Uncle Samson cried.

"We went to high school together," said Jules.

"High school!" Samson cried. "Jesus, some of them look like boys, flat in the chest—my Gawd, that won't do—you went to high school together?"

"High school together," Jules repeated.

"Jesus, they look like boys, I don't approve of it. What was her face like? Everything is changing . . ." Samson's eyes went slowly out of focus. Jules wondered if his uncle would fall asleep at the table, as he had at the last luncheon, snoring softly as the busboy wiped crumbs silently away, careful not to disturb him.

"Order us all a little brandy, son," he told Jules.

Her last name was no longer Greene. She no longer lived in Grosse Pointe; she lived in Bloomfield Hills. It was a long drive out Woodward Avenue. The drive began for Jules in a frenzy of excitement and nervousness but changed gradually to a strange serenity, a sense of floating, as if he were driving a car whose mechanism was set for a certain fate and would not fail to get him there. At first the traffic alarmed him but at about Six Mile Road the buildings fell back and the ragged green of Palmer Park began, followed by the city golf course and a series of cemeteries. Seeing cemeteries did not bother Jules; he thought them the most beautiful of the sights in Detroit. Woodward Avenue was divided by a strip of green, littered with junk but still green, a delight to the eye. As he drove along his despair lifted. So long as he owned his own car he could always be in control of his fate —he was fated to nothing. He was a true American. His car was like a shell he could maneuver around, at impressive speeds; he was second generation to no one. He was his own ancestors.

Nadine drew him with a strength he could not resist. A foolish sap was flowing sweetly in his veins. What could he care about his dying Uncle Brock, a body in a welfare-ward bed, his lip eroding away and his eyes bright with disaster and hope? What could he care about his sister Betty, who'd been picked up on an L & L charge—lewd and lascivious behavior, which could mean anything at all; he had an idea dope was involved, but what could he care about her when everything in him rushed toward Nadine, a stranger? Of his mother, his sister Maureen, his half-brother, it was impossible to think seriously. He thought only of Nadine.

The drive was long and the day warm. He tried not to speed. Past the suburbs north of the city, along the long, long avenue, through Birmingham, into the city of Bloomfield Hills—which was no city at all, which had no business section and seemed to have no homes, all of them set far back in the countryside on quiet lanes—he steered his way with a sense of jaunty doom. She had handed him a piece of paper with her name written on it, with an address. She had suggested no date. He had waited one day, two days, and on the third day had risen shakily with the conviction that he would tell his Uncle Samson he had to see a doctor that afternoon, and so escape the old man's authority, his promise, his cold sane eye . . .

Along the edge of the highway, past the neatly mowed wild grass, were wild weeds past their prime. What sent him rushing out to Nadine was a terrible desire to sink himself in her, to fulfill himself in her, to get to some avenue straight and clean as Woodward but more permanent, an avenue of clarity in his mind: what was the truth about himself? What was the meaning of his life? He felt that his life's meaning was irrevocably linked with that woman.

It was a conviction he'd come to on one of those Sunday visits to his uncle. Maureen had come along reluctantly. Loretta was level from a week of no spectacular defeats, her mouth pursed for sympathy. Jules had felt it, their sympathy—women at their best, their most healthy, giving sympathy to a man, their eyes growing moist with love for the death of a man. He felt that, he understood. This sympathy women drew up from the deepest, most private part of their beings, from a frightening sense of doom, of mortality, and now it was being directed toward his uncle—a man without worth, a failure!—and someday it would turn onto Jules himself, searching him out like a beacon, precise and knowing and forgiving but not personal. It was this impersonal, blind compassion, almost a yearning for physical union, that he felt in Nadine though she hadn't the body of a mother or a sister but the body of a stranger.

He found her house. It startled him to see how much it resembled the other house built by her father. Set back on a larger lawn—land being more plentiful here than in Grosse Pointe—it had a raw, expensive look, a look of newness totally impersonal. Jules drove up the oval driveway and parked in front of the door, dizzy with a sudden sense of *déjà vu*. He saw himself sharply from a distance, a character in a photograph or in a film. An X hovered over him, near him, pointing him out. He was aware of a lawn mower somewhere, a sharp, persistent droning. As he took the keys out of the car's ignition he felt a strange sickness rise in him, the dread of the foreigner in a neatly cultivated land. He had come too quickly to the fulfillment of his desire.

The sound of the lawn mower grew louder, but he could not see where it was coming from.

Nadine herself opened the door. She reached out to take his

hand, but some hesitation in him made the gesture into a handshake. "Hello," she said.

Jules nodded. She was breathy, strange, in a dress of some aqua silkish material, showing the soft flesh of her upper arms. To offset his nervousness he said, smiling, "This all seems familiar to me."

With a swing of his eyes he indicated the hallway, the white table with its bowed legs, the scarlet-cushioned chairs, the heavy mirror near the stairway. In that mirror he and Nadine were reflected unnaturally, their faces expanded by the curve of the glass.

"I've lived here for three years," Nadine said, anxious to please him but not knowing what he meant. "It isn't familiar to me yet."

The handshake ended. She drew away slightly, embarrassed. He closed the door behind him and they embraced, though formally. She stepped aside with an apologetic laugh. She bumped against the white table—it looked like an antique, off-white, brushed with gold.

Jules said, "Did you hurt yourself?"

She laughed again, shaking her head. How could she hurt herself in this house?

"This is a beautiful place," Jules said. "It's just like you. Everything in here is like you, exactly." He half wanted her to deny this, but she did not understand; he could sense how his words, his presence, cowed her.

"I don't know about that. I don't understand," she said.

She led him somewhere. Jules, stunned by her face and her body, allowed himself to go slack as soon as she turned; though he was only a few feet from her now he felt full of dread. Had he this essential dread of other people, was that his secret? He wanted Nadine and yet dreaded her? She turned. She sat down on a small sofa. Jules sat beside her. A cloud of abstraction came over him—one of the most peculiar, freakish experiences of his life—a few frigid seconds of dissolution, of immobility. He might have been led through an open door into a temple and there confronted with a faceless and soulless being, or he might have woken as if he were himself on the raw, blank, lighted side of the moon, everything smooth and unreal, where his own soul would be lost, flowing out of his terror and into nothing. She seemed to him nothing—he could not recall her. He felt chilled, faint, as if he were undergoing a physical transformation she could not help seeing.

Her face was fuller than he remembered. Her skin was lightly flushed now, rosy and excited, particularly along the ridge of her cheekbones. Jules could not move. He began to imagine, reluctantly, the beating of her heart and the pulsing of her rich blood. He stared at the woman as if he himself were not really here, not beside her, but as if he were peering at her through a telescope. She had the tense look of a woman aware she is being spied upon. She seemed terrified but not of anything she could see.

"You don't seem real to me," she said. She reached out and touched him.

The moment passed for Jules. He began to breathe again. Nadine, catching his mood, took hold of his arm childishly and tried to smile at him. She seemed to be staring out a window, hopefully. "You're not going to ruin my life?" she said.

"Never."

"Why didn't you come earlier?"

"When, today?"

"No," she said impatiently, "earlier—the other day, the day I saw you. I went home and waited for you. I waited for you all day."

"You mean Monday? You waited for me on Monday?"

"Yes, of course. What did you think? I couldn't think of anything else. I went home, I got rid of those women, I waited for you."

"I didn't think you would want me so soon."

"Yes, I wanted you."

"But now it isn't too late?"

"You're so strange. You make me afraid of you."

"I'm afraid of you," said Jules.

He brought her hand up to his lips. He kissed it, closing his eyes. He was really afraid of her, afraid of burying himself in her body and breaking her bones, killing her. She seemed so ready to be killed. Her body had a precarious look to it, as if it were always on the verge of physical hysteria—a man had only to touch such a body to destroy it. He said, "Nadine, look. Tell me what you want. Tell me what your life is now. Keep talking to me and explain everything, will you?"

"There's nothing to tell."

"Who did you marry, what are you doing, do you have any children?"

"No."

"When did you get married?"

"I went to college off and on, then dropped out to get married."

"Who is it?"

"That isn't important."

"It certainly is important!"

"A man, a nice man, a corporation lawyer—"

"What kind?"

"Corporation law, tax law," Nadine said. "Everything is taxes and how to get out of them." She was staring at Jules's hands, which held hers, and it seemed for a moment that she knew far less than he about herself. He would have to lead the way. "He's gone now. He left on Monday for New York. He'll be back tomorrow."

"Tomorrow is so soon," Jules said, disappointed.

"No, he's always gone. He flies to New York all the time."

"What is he like?"

She brought his hand up to her face. She pressed her cheek against it. Jules wanted to laugh hysterically—a broad grin actually broke across his face but shattered into something else. He had a sudden vision of himself strangling this woman. He put his hands around her throat, and the two of them sat very still, looking down, breathing swiftly. She seemed to acquiesce, allowing him to lead the way. But he only said, "You're very beautiful. It's much more than before, much different. I don't think I can stand it."

"Would you marry me then?" Nadine said.

"Yes."

"If you ruined my life, I mean my life here," she said, confused, looking around the room, "would you give me another life? You'd marry me?"

"I'll marry you right now."

"You won't abandon me?"

"How could I abandon you?"

"But I abandoned you, I left you."

Jules waved this aside.

"I left you in that room. You were sick—"

"I shouldn't have gotten sick," Jules said with a laugh.

"I loved you. I don't know why I ran away."

"Forget about it."

"I loved you. I did love you. I was sick with love for you and I tried to get over it, but I never did."

Jules, in the presence of a woman, felt a certain dizziness, a golden glow that seemed to emanate from her, a warmth that was unconscious and comforting; it was a little dangerous because it was unconscious. He was drawn to women as if toward something warm, drawn out of the cold, gravitating forward and eager to lose himself in such warmth. With Nadine the instinct was richer and blinder. He felt the danger more sharply, as if, through half-closed eyes, he were really making out the shapes of rocks underfoot while pretending to see nothing. He was deaf with the expectation of joy. Sounds came to him as if through rocking waves of water, his own blood muffled and inarticulate. He did not want to see or to hear. He wanted to be violated in a strange, light, painless way, violated without his understanding.

He said in confusion, "Well, I loved you too, of course. I still love you. It isn't any choice of mine. What can I do about loving you?" His agitation took him back to those sweaty hours in motel rooms, lying on top of sleazy bedcovers. With his fingers he caressed her throat. He thought to himself, *Now this woman wants me,* and the knowledge calmed him. He could sense her paralysis. He could imagine her waiting for him for several days, a woman waiting for a man, sitting and standing and walking about in a lovely house, her face just so, made up to be fragrant and lovely and yet alone, waiting, incomplete; a woman's mind might crack under that. He felt her blindness too, her strange deafness. A sudden vision came to him of the two of them afloat on a river—sitting on this sofa of green velvet—rocking gently, floating downstream, hearing and seeing nothing on shore. He could not recall the years when he hadn't seen her and in a way he could not recall that younger, less important Nadine.

"I won't ruin your life,", he said. "Everything will be the way you want it. Just tell me what you want."

She seemed to be sensing his words, caressing them. He felt the two of them drifting relentlessly downstream. . . . He said, "But you do love me?"

"I've never forgotten you, or anything. I love you."

"I'm a different person now. I don't run around stealing cars and things, knocking people on the head. It all seems fanciful, all that, but I know I did it. I'm older. I never thought I would live to be thirty," Jules said. He was uneasy; his words did not really convey his feelings.

"I wanted to see you again," Nadine said. "I tried to write to you but I didn't know where to write. I looked up some names in the telephone book—it was very confusing. When I got back to Detroit I was sick myself. They took care of me at home for a while and then put me in a hospital."

"How were you sick?"

"I couldn't sleep or eat. I kept crying all the time," she said impatiently. "All I could think about was you. I tried to starve myself. I felt sorry for myself and I wanted to punish my parents. I kept thinking about you, only you. Jules, I had to leave you, I had to get out of that place. I remember the way I was. You were so sick, it wasn't even you, it seemed to be a stranger. And I kept thinking about you sick, a stranger, so that I wouldn't have to love you, but I could never really believe in it. I wasn't free. I had to leave, but when I left I never got over it. I took your car a few hundred miles, then it broke down. I called home. They both flew down to get me."

He wanted to tell her, *Forget about the car,* then he realized that she had forgotten about it; she had never thought about it.

"I had to get out and leave you. I had to escape. I'm sorry."

"I understand."

"I wrote long letters for you, crazy things. They put me in a kind of hospital, a very nice place. I didn't ever go back to school in any ordinary way but took courses by myself. Well, it wasn't very nice, I don't know why I said that, it was a place for people sick in the head. We all carried ourselves like glass, we were very breakable. My father got me tutors from the University of Michigan. It wasn't far from there. I kept looking at these men and listening to them, but I didn't see them or hear them, I kept waiting for them to change into you. I couldn't think of a man who wasn't you, they all seemed to be you."

Jules stared at her.

"It was very strange to me how a man, a young man, could have a face of his own that wasn't yours," Nadine said dreamily. "I would look at the parts of his face, his eyes, his mouth, and figure out how they could be yours, belong to you. I don't know what makes faces different. The eyes might be the same except for color. Mouths look alike. I don't know—how people are different people, how they keep separate. But none of those men was ever you."

Jules felt a sensation of danger. He said, "Is there anyone else in this house?"

"Not today."

He felt as if he were going to explode and the violence would kill Nadine. She was motionless and dreamlike, leaning against him, her arms around his neck. Their embrace was formal. If he were losing his mind it was an accident of her presence, her voice, the green sofa, the persistent waves that bore them along. But what if this woman were not Nadine, what if some other woman had put her arms around his neck and was hypnotizing him? What if in another moment the spell broke and she reached around under one of the sofa's cushions and drew out a gun?

"I'll come to you somewhere else," Nadine said. "Downtown. Somewhere else, not here."

"A hotel? When?"

"Tomorrow morning."

"When does your husband get home?"

"Around three, but he won't call, the car is at the airport—"

"Which airport?"

"Metro."

"He won't expect you to be home?"

"I will be home when he gets home. I'll be back by three-thirty."

"Will you come downtown then? The Sheraton-Cadillac?"

"Yes."

"You really will do this?"

"Yes, yes."

"Should I get a room, should I wait for you? How early can you come?"

"Eleven."

"But don't do this if you . . . if you're going to be upset."

"I won't be upset."

"I think you will."

"No, I have to do this. I need you," Nadine said.

He felt a helpless, painful sympathy for her. But could he believe in her? Her limpness, her sense of doom, her frightened breathing, seemed to him unnatural, an exaggeration of his own fear. The trembling he felt in her body was exactly like the trembling he held back in his, as if the two of them were fated for some final convulsion, locked in each other's arms, their mouths fastened greedily together in a pose neither had really chosen—like gargoyles hacked together out of rock, freaks of mossy rock. Jules said quickly, "We don't have to do anything right away. We could see each other a few times—"

"No, I'll come down tomorrow."

"We can talk—"

"There's nothing to talk about."

"I think there is. Do you really want to marry me?"

She pressed her forehead against his shoulder. She thought.

"You want to get a divorce and marry me? Jules Wendall?"

"Yes. I think so."

"Anything you want then."

"I want you. I can't stop thinking about you."

"What about your marriage?"

"It's a good marriage, he's a good man, but . . . but he isn't you. I married him a few years ago when it was time for me to get married. He was like those students from Michigan, those graduate students; he never turned into you. There's nothing for me to say about him. As soon as I saw you in that restaurant I began to lose connection with other people, even with what I was saying. Everything is jerky but dreamlike, not connected. I sound crazy. It isn't really like me to be this way, I'm much older and different from the way I was when you knew me. I had to go through some bad months to get over that. But I got over it. But now . . . With you, Jules, I can't think of my life or remember what it is. I can't remember myself. It's as if I were walking somewhere and music began to play very loud, making me deaf, and someone took my hand to lead me away—why not? How can I remember who I am, what does it matter? I've been waiting for you for three days. Every hour or so it would become clear to me that I should get out, go to my mother's or just get out, go somewhere. I shouldn't have to go through all this again, with you. But I couldn't leave. Then I thought you weren't coming or were going to insult me by coming a few days late, which you did, but still I kept waiting. Everything in my life seemed to lean toward you—it was like something falling slowly over. I realized that I didn't care about anything else, though I wanted to care. But I didn't."

They were silent. Jules said finally, "Well, I've thought of you. In those years."

"You did?"

"I didn't exactly love you, it was something deeper. I

wanted to get hold of you again, like this. No, not like this. Not like we are now. I wanted to get hold of you . . ." He could not explain.

She said, "I understand."

"Have you been lonely?"

"Yes."

"Even with your husband?"

"Yes, very lonely. With him and with everyone."

"Is it hard for you, for a woman, to be lonely?"

"I've survived. What about you?"

"I've survived."

They smiled at each other. Jules felt the possibility of their becoming friends!

"What did you do after I left you?" she said.

"I got well after a few days. Got some jobs, bummed my way around, got back on my feet. I had to make money to eat. I kept going. Finally I got back up to Detroit, when I was ready for Detroit again. I tried not to think of you but you were always there, in the back of my mind."

"Thank you," she said.

She began to kiss him. Jules embraced her eagerly. They seemed to fall stony-eyed into this embrace, breathing with relief and pain. As soon as he kissed her he wanted to speak: he wanted to explain to her how unfulfilled his life was. Blinded by her, he felt a sudden clarity about his love for her—it was not really his own, nothing he could control, but a torrent of emotion he had somehow been trapped in, an old-fashioned fate. A lovely golden light seemed to blind him; he moved his hands desperately upon her body. The light was a radiance that came partly from her face and partly from the furniture of this gleaming room. He said, very excited, "People are always falling in love with me, or they want something from me I can't give. I have to pick them off me. I have to get rid of them. None of them are ever you," and his voice cracked with this truth.

"You're very good. You're not selfish like me."

"Couldn't we go upstairs here? Right now?"

"No."

"Nadine?"

"No," she said miserably, "not here. I can't. I'm married to him, I—"

"All right."

"Jules, please—"

"I understand, all right. Should I leave now?"

"In a minute."

He laughed. He framed her face with his hands and laughed. "You're so beautiful, this can't be happening. What is the good of it after all? Is there any way to use it? What good will it do for us to be in love again? What can we do with love?"

"Don't talk like that."

"I'm face to face with your female ego—your soul—what can I ever possibly do with it?"

"Don't make jokes. I never cared for your jokes."

"Jokes are the sign of a desperate man," Jules said. He stood up and smoothed down his hair, straightened his clothes. He was a desperate man. "Just tell me what you want, Nadine, and I'll give it to you. Make up your mind."

She looked up at him. The skirt of her dress had been pulled up to her thighs. He saw her skin, smooth under the material of her stockings, this private Nadine that was in his possession—like a rag doll she seemed, in his possession, reckless of herself. Yet he did not really own her and had no idea what she was thinking.

"Tell me what you're thinking," he said.

"I'm thinking this," she said wearily. "A woman is like a dream. Her life is a dream of waiting. I mean, she lives in a dream, waiting for a man. There's no way out of this, insulting as it is, no woman can escape it. Her life is waiting for a man. That's all. There is a certain door in this dream, and she has to walk through it. She has no choice. Sooner or later she has to open that door and walk through it and come to a certain man, one certain man. She has no choice about it. She can marry anyone but she has no choice about this. That's what I'm thinking."

"You mean that?"

"Yes."

"It isn't exaggerated?"

"That man isn't you, exactly. It's what I need to do with you, in order to keep alive. I need you for myself, for my life. I need to love you."

"You won't run away afterward and leave me?"

"I'm older now. I'm a married woman."

"But I won't share you with another man."

"All right."

She followed him out to the door. They were both shaky, yet their movements were light and airy. Jules felt intoxicated. He took her hand and covered it with kisses, delighted at the freedom he had with her, this limp, warm hand, a part of the body that was going to belong to him, and even the big diamond on her finger was going to belong to him.

"Tomorrow morning then. And you're not going to be upset?"

"No."

"All right. I love you. We'll see what happens."

"I love you, Jules."

Driving back home, he saw everything clearly: billboards, restaurants, gas stations, other cars. He saw everything and left no imprint of himself upon them, so free had he become and so strong. It was only at about ten o'clock that night, alone in his room, that he realized what was going to happen, what had already happened. He was overcome by a sense of depression.

Would he get out of this alive? Would anything remain in the world to astonish him?

12

He checked into the hotel at nine the next morning. His room, at sixteen dollars a day, was a disappointment; the window looked out upon a nearby wall. It surprised him to find himself in so ordinary a room, nothing magical about it. A steady sound of running water came from the bathroom and he couldn't see what was wrong, or if anything was wrong. He walked back and forth from the window to the bed, trying to calm himself.

Last night his mother had given him a pathologist's report about his uncle. He had read it swiftly, and certain key words had stuck in his mind—*cytology, Leukeran, blood count, remission possibility*—and amazed him, for now it seemed that his uncle was dying of a kind of cancer. Was that possible? To enter the hospital for one reason, to die for another? He had felt a kinship with his uncle, their being inescapably married to one fate—what did it matter how they got there? Jules lay on his bed as if awaiting his own fate, waiting for it to flow into him and drown him. He stared at the ceiling. So his uncle was dying. One less. His father was already dead and forgotten. His other uncle, his healthy uncle, Samson Wendall, was dragging himself forward every morning—he left Grosse Pointe every morning at six-thirty, anxious to begin the day, impatient with sleep and with the very conditions of sleep, the bed he owned, the bedroom in which he and his wife slept, and maybe his wife as well—with his hacking cough and his bleary, suspicious eyes, this uncle was not yet dying and had he a choice in the matter he would never die. Jules understood that: he wished never to die, himself.

He lay very still. Though he had not slept most of the night before he was not ready to sleep now. His mind raced. He had the idea she would not come, and it would have greatly relieved him to know this; but she herself was so uncertain that perhaps she would show up, after all. He tried not to think of her, but still her face formed and re-formed itself in his mind. Her beauty was a reward for him, for him alone. He had been faithful to her and now he was to be rewarded.

Out in the corridor there was arguing, a man and a woman. Jules imagined them married, middle-aged. Their argument was not exciting, did not excite them truly. He tried to listen to their words but could make out nothing.

He felt lines forming in his face. Concentration. He was ready for a sudden release of energy, a flowing into him, a softness. A process would fulfill itself through him, through his body. He felt as if he were floating in a strange darkness, in silence; the people in the corridor had gone; down on Washington Boulevard traffic was remote and tedious, unimagined. He pressed his hands against his eyes and wanted to cry out that he was lost . . . was this the way you died, giving everything up, shamed out of living? He felt his will draining out of him. It was draining away like the leak in the bathroom, an error too trivial to correct, the sign of sleazy merchandise. *Time is passing,* he thought. He, did not move.

By eleven he had resigned himself. She would come or she would not come; the choice was not his. Perhaps her husband would come instead. He was too lethargic to be concerned. A cold flame ran over his body, and he tried to concentrate upon conversations out in the hall . . . the sound of a toilet flushing nearby . . . traffic down on the boulevard . . . something to fix him to himself, to draw him out of being only a body waiting to fall in agony upon another body. It was shameful to be Jules and to be such a creature. It was a betrayal of the true Jules.

The telephone rang. It was twenty after eleven. It rang

one short ring, and Jules picked it up at once. "Hello?" he said shakily.

"Hello," said Nadine.

"Well, where are you?" he said.

She said, "I'm still at home—"

"At home? Why at home?" he said. His exasperation gave him something to get hold of—he felt that he hated her.

"Do you still want me to come down?" she said.

Jules said nothing.

"I haven't slept all night. I don't feel well. I . . . Jules? Are you there?"

"Sure."

"Do you still want me to come down?"

"It's up to you."

"Yes, I'll come down."

He hung up. His anger aroused him. He paced back and forth from the bathroom to the window to the bed, rubbing his cold hands. He had been in a state of near shock, his body hadn't been his own, and this flood of anger was like hot liquid streaming through him. Yet his hands were cold, his feet were cold. He looked at his watch and calculated it would take her at least half an hour to get down, probably an hour.

He went downstairs and had a glass of beer. He came back upstairs, thinking she might have arrived while he was gone. He opened the door of his room: an empty room. He lay on his bed again. He waited.

Someone knocked at the door.

He jumped up to let her in. Now everything was simple, hurried. They embraced, they exclaimed greetings.

"You really came, you're really here," he said.

Nadine laughed. "Didn't you believe me?"

"But you're trembling. Sit down. Sit over here."

Graciously he led her to the only chair in the room. He knelt beside her. He kissed her knees. Nadine put her hand on the back of his head, leaning over him. He could feel her fear and his own exaltation, teasing each other.

"I wasn't going to come, that's why I called you," she said quickly, "because I don't feel well this morning. I'm sort of sick—"

"What's wrong?"

"I couldn't sleep all night. I was awake all night."

"I was awake too."

"Now I'm sort of sick. I mean . . . I'm not well."

"Honey, sit still. Don't be so nervous. We can talk to each other, we have years of talking ahead. What do you want me to do for you? Room service? Do you want lunch, champagne? Is it time for lunch? I can have them send up some out-of-town newspapers. I can stand on my head for you, sweetheart, only don't look so miserable."

"But I'm not well. It started last night."

"What?"

"Cramps. It started last night."

Jules caressed her long silky legs in silence. He stared at them, then at the carpet. It was a dull colorless gold, not very clean. He stared at the individual bits of yarn, pressed down by Nadine's white shoes and his own knees.

"I shouldn't have come down here then. Probably . . ."

"It's all right."

"Jules, I love you so, I'm sorry."

"Do you want an aspirin or something? Something to drink?"

"No."

"How bad is it?"

"I feel a little faint, I . . ."

Jules remained kneeling. He pressed his face against her knees in submission and felt a terror at his own helplessness. Even the pain in her loins was something he had no control over, something he could not stop. Everything was private. Nadine caressed the back of his neck eagerly. "I couldn't seem to get hold of myself last night. I was very upset—it was like a nightmare. I kept walking around the house, wondering how people get through the night, particularly women. You know, Jules, a man's love creates a woman's love. You've made me the way I am. I'm certain of that. There are men who are permanent in a woman's life, everything in them is permanent, and terrible, nobody thinks about them *That's something I set out to do;* there's no choice about it. You love me and I love you, I don't have any choice about it."

Jules made an exasperated sound, a kind of laugh. "I suppose that makes sense," he said.

"But don't you want me to talk to you?" she said. "Are you angry?"

He got up. "Of course I'm not angry."

"It's so strange for me to be here, to be saying these things to you. You're one of the people who couldn't visit me if I was sick, or come to my funeral."

"Why not?"

"You wouldn't come. Probably you wouldn't know about it."

"Probably not. Nobody would tell me. Are you thinking of dying?"

Nadine laughed nervously. "My husband has a gun—"

"Where?"

"At home, a gun. I took it out last night. I looked at it and thought that it was a mysterious thing, a gun. I went to the mirror and put the gun up to my head and stood looking at myself for a while."

"Why the hell did you do that?"

"Don't be angry, there wasn't any danger. But it was very interesting, seeing myself like that."

"What's wrong with you?"

"I'm just afraid."

"But it's just me, Jules. I'm only a man. I'm a wreck. Why should you be afraid of me?" He sat on the edge of the bed and faced her. He felt a moron's good will showing on his face.

"I do love you," Nadine said softly.

"So much that you want to shoot yourself?"

"I don't want to shoot myself."

"Who do you want to shoot then?"

"Nobody. I don't want to do anything. I want to live a good, simple life. I want to put my faith in things that are simple and clear. That's all a woman asks. I want to put my life in order."

"That isn't easy to do," Jules said.

"Can I ask you something?"

"Sure."

"About your past?"

"I don't have any past, sweetheart."

"Don't make jokes."

"That wasn't a joke."

"Your past—what you did last week, last year. I want to know about your life."

"In terms of what?"

"You never got married?"

"No."

"Were you close to getting married?"

"Never."

"What do you think about . . . about getting married?"

"To you? I want to marry you."

She smiled shyly. "But I really don't have much money, not really, maybe you'd be sorry. I'd be off on my own, divorced. Would you want me then?"

"Of course I would."

"But . . . have you ever been in love? With anyone else?"

"No."

"Are you serious?"

"I haven't been in love, no. Except with you. This is it, the end. I don't want to be in love or even think about it any more, except with you. This is the end of it."

She leaned toward him and pressed her lips against his cheek. He could not make sense of Nadine or of himself. If nature was driving him toward her, forcing him to an act of love with this particular woman, the excess of feeling he had to endure was overwhelming as lava: suffocating and preposterous, a kind of joke. Surely all this was not going to end in the conception of a child? Detroit was packed with children.

"Have you made love to many women?"

"No."

"Haven't you?"

"I can't remember. I've forgotten."

"Why don't you tell me the truth?"

"All you want to hear is dirt, so why should I tell you about it? Your idea of the past is dirt," Jules said. "Forget everything that's over with. It doesn't belong to us."

"But I want to know everything about you."

"Well, you're not going to. It's over."

"Don't you want to know about me?"

"As conversation, yes. For the next thirty years. But it isn't essential. I can't concentrate on it. I can't even ask you whether you've had any lovers since your marriage, or before, because that isn't any of my business."

"Of course I haven't."

"All right. Good."

She was silent. She drew back from him. "Well," she said. "I think I should leave now."

"Leave?"

"Someone downstairs recognized me, I'm sure of it. She looked at me in a certain way."

"So what?"

"I . . . I think I should go back home."

Jules made a sad, sucking noise with his mouth.

"Jules, listen," she said quickly. "Don't hate me. But I've always thought, I've always been afraid, that you might have some kind of disease. You know."

Jules felt as if something cold had been dumped over him. He stared at her. Then, turning it into a joke, he tried to smile. "No, sweetheart. I'm all right."

"I was always terrified of that."

"I don't have syphilis."

"I was thinking of where you lived, the way things are in the city, and Negro women, girls—"

"No."

"Have you ever . . . with Negro women?"

Jules rubbed his eyes. Since the experimental program he'd hired himself out for years ago, his eyes often ached, particularly when he was troubled. They began to water. "Why is everything in your mind dirt, your imagination all dirt?" he asked in anguish.

"Don't say that!"

"Oh, Jesus!"

They were silent for a while, not looking at each other. After a while Jules said, "You can leave if you want to."

"I'll call you in a few days."

"You'll never call."

"Yes, I will."

She lay back in the chair, one hand across her stomach. "I will call you, Jules. It's just that I'm sick. I took some pills to keep the pain down but they didn't work. I should be in bed. I shouldn't have come down here to bother you. How can I help it that this happened to me?"

"Did you expect it?"

"Not until next week."

"Well, obviously you made it happen," Jules said with an effort toward tenderness. "Not that I blame you or have any special opinion. I'm sorry you're in pain."

"I parked my car just across the street."

"Did you? Let's see the stub."

"Why do you want to see it? Don't you believe me?"

"Let's see."

She showed him the little cardboard stub.

"Yes, the same place. I used to work there," Jules said.

"In that parking lot?"

"Parking cars, yes. When I was a kid."

Nadine looked through her purse. "I don't think I have

enough money to pay for this. I didn't bring any money along at all."

"I'll pay for it," said Jules.

"But . . . why didn't I bring any money? I went out without any money." She looked through her purse, exasperated. She seemed quite helpless.

"I'll be glad to pay for it."

He saw a single tear fall from her cheek and into the purse, and was touched by the sight. He did love her after all.

"I don't know what's wrong with me," Nadine said.

He gave her a ten-dollar bill.

She thanked him and put it carefully in her purse. She took the stub back from Jules.

These gestures signaled to him the end of their meeting. He felt depressed at once. "You're really going to call me?" he said.

"Yes."

They stood. Jules's sadness flowed into her, and she stepped into his embrace, weeping. They held each other. Jules felt her warm, slightly damp, intense body beneath his hands and wondered if, inside her, still, was that deliberate perverse purity, that obscene purity, she had prized years ago. Did she go about the objects of her life thinking, *Nadine Greene is walking here undefiled, to the left of this, to the right of that, precise and virginal?* He understood that his rival was not her husband, who was a kind of ally, being a man, but this woman's image of herself as a woman, her melancholy frigidity.

"You don't want to love me maybe," he said softly, accusingly.

"That isn't true."

"You want to make a pattern of us. Like moving children's blocks around on the floor."

"I don't understand that."

"You don't want to give yourself to me."

"I love you, I think of you constantly, I'm sick with love for you—what more can you want? I'm trapped by my love for you."

"That doesn't sound good."

"I feel that I could go crazy with it, Jules, it's nothing I had any choice in and I resent it."

She stood weeping in his arms; they had nothing more to say. Jules looked around for their image in the bureau mirror as if to prove to himself that they were standing here, just so, this woman in his arms, the two of them rigid and baffled.

After she left he checked out of the hotel at once and went to a bar, where he had several drinks. A dark depression was upon him. He hadn't the energy to drive out to his uncle's plant, as he had promised the old man; instead he telephoned. He said, "I have to go out to the hospital again today. Drive my mother out. Yes. No, not yet. Pretty sick. Yes. Cancer." A respectful pause. Uncle Samson respected cancer and money. "Yes, thank you. I'm sorry about today. I don't particularly like what I have to do. Thank you. Yes. Good-by. Yes. Cancer of the lymph nodes or something, some kind of cancer. No, not from smoking. No."

13

Two weeks passed. Jules waited.

When she finally called he had grown skeptical, and her voice sounded improbable: a chance connection. She seemed to be reading off to him a certain address, a certain time. Writing this information down, he leaned forward to press his forehead against the wall. In his entire body there was nothing firm, nothing to stop him from falling except that wall.

He left early so that he would not have to drive fast. His mind, filled with inconsequential news of his uncle's office and public life, kept back the excitement that threatened to overtake him. Driving, he seemed to pass into a kind of trance, keeping the vocabulary of his ordinary life but absolved of its meanings. No matter what he did, Jules felt, he could not be blamed, he could not bear the consequences of real life; he was not a character in "real life." He put on the twelve o'clock news in order to check up on the real world, which seemed much the same. So he could think with relief, *I've been through this before.*

His life for the past two weeks had not been properly lived. He had struggled with Nadine as with a drowning woman, imagining her constantly. The battle was silent and secret and had no true adversary, because Nadine had dropped out of sight—he had tried to call her but she hadn't answered. He had hung up, relieved. But her presence was all about him, the way the scent of her had been on him, a light, airy touch of doom. He argued with himself. He spoke of himself in the third person; he addressed himself desperately, saying, "Jules, you've got to get out of this!" But the essential Jules, the deeper, wiser, Jules, did no more than say constantly, *How could you live with yourself if you weren't equal to this?—To this emotion?*

The apartment she had rented was on the fifth floor of an old apartment building near Palmer Park. It was made of dark red brick, heavy and pompous, with small useless balconies of wrought iron. The balconies were only symbolic, ceremonial. At the four corners of the building were grimy turrets, inexplicable. To Jules they had a military look, but he knew nothing about architecture and could not have said what they were or what they had once been, in another century. They made him apprehensive. Only pigeons fluttered heavily about them, but he expected to see the nervous movement of weapons. His chest flinched at the thought of such a death. Did he want to die shot down, or did he want to die in a hospital bed like his uncle? His imagination had been heated by the memory of movies, stark black-and-white deaths of men shot down, always shot down; it was the price that had to be paid for being important. Jules was too important to himself, too much alone. As a child he had sensed that in the movies a sudden noisy death would take place whenever a man was alone for two or three minutes; he unwisely left his companions, he whistled to himself as he opened a safe or changed his shirt, alone, and in a minute the camera would shift slyly to show a gun barrel . . .

This building impressed him. In the air, as if stirred by his presence, there was a sudden odor of dust; it was an odor he thought strange and elegant. He had smelled dirt often enough but never this kind of clean, acrid, clear, invisible dust. The elevator was antiquated. It moved reluctantly. He was accustomed to fast-moving, silent elevators, he was accustomed to escalators, to the functioning of efficient machines. The very slowness of this elevator charmed him.

When he got out on the fifth floor he suddenly lost his nerve. It was in a dream he moved toward her door . . . he saw the door open. The crack widened, teasingly. He stared at it as if staring at a movie screen. The symmetry of the door was being destroyed; it was a door of dark wood and it looked expensive to him. Everything looked expensive to him here. He reached out to touch the door, and Nadine took his hand. He came to her, wordless, and buried his face against the hollow of her shoulder and throat.

He felt formless in this embrace, unable to recall himself. Nadine, in his arms, seemed to him formless and very warm, yearning toward him. He could not have said her name. He seemed to be watching himself, Jules, grow smaller and smaller like a dying light, extinguished in the confusion of her body. Everything else passed out of his range. He had no vocabulary. Nadine's face and body and the anguished movement of her hands against his back were like words shouting at him. She was saying something, she said "Jules," —and he hadn't the strength to answer her. She drew him somewhere. He felt the blindness in her body, her stumbling against something, and his own legs were numb and blind. She sat down on the edge of a bed. Jules knelt before her and embraced her. He pressed his face against her. He felt her fingers in his damp hair and imagined her staring down at him, as if not comprehending his passion but giving herself up to it, recognizing its power. She drew him up. It was with an impersonal, abstract strength that he rose to her.

Jules made love to her, still without words and without any memory of his having done this before with other women; his body led him forward while his brain, in a swoon, cast about for some hold, some fixed point, so that he would be able to come back to himself. He needed a style; he was terrified to lose hold of himself. But everything gave way in him. He felt as if he were in a wave of violence that bore him along, Jules Wendall, a kind of victim, burying himself in Nadine with groans of surprised love, while Nadine submitted to him, embracing him, her softness delivered over to his impersonal strength. Yet he felt a horror at not knowing what he did. He would not remember it.

"Jules, I love you," Nadine said.

He opened his eyes. They looked at each other.

"Jules, do you love me?"

"I love you."

He was trembling, covered with sweat. He felt beatific with it, absolved of the heaviness he'd been carrying around for weeks. Now that density, that impurity, was gone; he felt that he had shed everything in Nadine's arms. They lay together in silence and looked at each other, Jules pretending sleepiness out of a kind of courtesy. Nadine smiled. She had a sudden, surprising smile; she seemed happy. This dazzled Jules. He stared at her mouth, shaped into that gift of a smile. He could not believe in her beauty. She brought her arms around his neck and touched his mouth with her own, shyly. In a kind of terror Jules gathered her tight into his arms again, wanting to bury himself in her. They clung together tightly.

Jules lay on his back and looked around. A ceiling, a room. He had never seen this room before and now it opened itself to him in a swift series of patches of light—white ceiling, white walls, a window with filmy white curtains. Everything was bare. There was a sense of an echo here, an indefinite emptiness. Jules wiped the sweat out of his eyes like a swimmer wiping away drops of water, desperate to see, afraid of the element he was in. He felt as if he had surfaced from a great, dangerous depth.

"I didn't think this would ever happen. Like this," he said.

"You do love me?"

He did not want to drown in her closeness—her closeness was uncanny. Everything in him might have resisted but he had no hold on himself, no clear memory of himself. So he had made love to this woman? She was his mistress?

"How did this happen?" Jules said.

"Oh, don't make jokes!"

"But it's a wonderful joke. It's wonderful. I'm going to die with it." He felt the room's sunshine penetrate the deepest part of his brain, dazzling him. Light flooded everything. "Where are we, honey? Did you rent this?"

"Yes, for a month."

"You rented it for us?"·

"Yes."

"But I didn't hear from you for so long, I thought it was finished. I thought you'd given up."

"I didn't."

"Why didn't you call, Nadine?"

"I thought of you all the time. I couldn't think of anything else," she said.

Now that they were lovers even the barrier of her cool, rapid, nervous speech was gone; she spoke softly. The gentle hot stroke of her breath was a marvelous intimacy to him. Jules was amazed at her sweetness. He kissed her body, he caressed her, he marveled at her smooth skin. His own hand made him ashamed, his hands, his body; he felt shame at touching her.

But Nadine drew him to her, saying, "I love you. I love you," like a woman in a trance. "I didn't want to see you again but I couldn't go through with it. You could have called me. I kept waiting—"

"You weren't waiting—I did try to call you."

"You did? But I . . . I didn't hear from you either, and I was afraid to call you . . . I wanted to die, it was so miserable. I thought about you constantly."

"I thought about you constantly," Jules said happily, remembering the misery of those weeks as if another man had suffered it, someone ludicrous. He rose and came to her again, and Nadine, gracious and startled, pressed her open mouth against his and waited. He entered her as easily as if all those years of distance and deprivation had not existed. He did not think of this woman as someone else's wife and therefore practised in love, but as the deepest, essential Nadine, always prepared for him and only him, Jules, the only man her body would really accept. In his passion he saw her blurred pale face, too close to be seen; they clung together, very warm; the boundaries of their bodies were uncertain. Jules pressed himself down again and again on her soft cries, comforting her. He felt as if his head had become hollow and her moans were echoing inside it. A great joy began in him; he wanted to gather her violently into his arms and penetrate her to the very kernel of her being, to her deepest silence, bringing her to a release of this joy. But she seemed to slip from him, too weak or too stunned, and he felt his love emptied violently into her again while she held him, her hands tight against his back, tight as if with alarm, her own body grown rigid at this crisis.

"Nadine?"

She drew the back of her hand across her forehead.

"Are you all right?"

"Yes. Wonderful."

Jules saw the pillows for the first time: white with dark green stitching on the edges. Everything was strange. He felt the slim curve of her body with his hands, fascinated with her skin. He could not remember any other woman, was not certain that he had ever done this before. Everything was washed out of his mind; there was nothing authentic in his experience; what was his personal history might have been stolen from movies and books, the imaginations of other people.

The room had one large window facing the park. The window had been redone and was newer than the rest of the room, which was old-fashioned. Up at the ceiling the molding looked ancient, like mummified cake; it was a shock to see a black telephone on the floor, very modern, stark and purposeful.

"Why do you have a telephone?" Jules asked.

"It isn't connected."

"It came with the apartment?"

"Yes."

This pleased him immensely. He was light-headed. His legs seemed very strong suddenly, urgently strong. "Then no one will call us. The phone will never ring," he said.

"Never."

They lay for a while watching each other, smiling. Jules felt the strength flowing back into his body. It was a curious sensation. Nadine stroked him, and the skin beneath her fingers lifted itself in tiny bumps.

"Where is your husband?"

"Don't worry about him."

"Is he gone away again?"

"Yes."

"But when is he coming back?"

"Don't ask."

They lay pressed together. Jules, in love, contemplated her body with some fear—he could not quite believe in all this beauty, this gift of beauty, this perfection. He was afraid that he had won her through some mistake, a misunderstanding. Covertly he stared down the length of her body to her bare feet. His throat constricted with emotion: he had never been so moved. He said with a desperate lightness, "Can we both live here? In this apartment?"

"Yes," said Nadine.

Late in the afternoon they rose shakily. Jules stared at the bare floor, a shining waxed floor. He saw everywhere around him the result of labor not his own, a kind of magic. Nadine herself was magical. He felt embarrassed, getting out of bed in so ordinary a way, crossing to the bathroom, while Nadine sat up, her elegant white backbone slightly bowed. She did not look at him. Naked, Jules wanted to hide himself from her, from her incidental glance. But she did not look around. Her hair had come down in dark shining tangles

onto her shoulders. She looked as if she had just risen from
the sea, deranged from hours of breathlessness.

The bathroom was radiant with light—white curtains,
white tile, a white shower curtain. This room had been redone also, remodeled. Jules staggered to the sink and stared
at himself. He looked wild. Nadine's lipstick was smeared
faintly across his face but still he recognized himself. Jules in
love, sick with love. . . . He'd seen that face before, a hint
of it, but had never felt its desperation so strong in his
bones.

When he came back out she was putting on a yellow
robe. Her movements were slow, lethargic, trancelike. She
seemed really to have emerged from another element, an
airless element or a world in which air was thick and creamy.
Her skin looked creamy. It looked as if there was a gentle
coating to it, something languorous, soft. She went to the
closet where, inside, lay an open suitcase filled with clothing.
On the closet's several hooks were other pieces of clothing.
Jules swallowed drily, seeing her clothes hanging there. They
looked so intimate. For the first time he considered her belonging to him, the two of them belonging to each other,
living out their lives together. The thought rocked in his
veins.

"Nadine?"

He felt such a sharp love for her that his body seemed
to turn into a crystal of love, a work of art, his bones
stunned and hard. Nadine, turning shyly to him, not looking
at his body, seemed to him also a work of art—fragile
in her silk robe, with her sky rosy, startled, shy. He felt
panic in his need to possess her. He himself was possessed
by her, by his love; it was a frantic burden, a pressure
like electricity, needing release. Jules could not think at all.
He embraced her as she stood by the closet door, hesitating
between him and the closet, about to break out into some
casual, embarrassed remark of everyday life. He took her
in his arms and felt how he was translated beyond himself,
transfigured. He drew her back to the bed, feeling how
his own wildness enticed her, silencing her. She put her arms
around him and gave herself up to him.

When Jules woke he saw that Nadine was gone. She came
to the doorway at once, as if sensing this, a shadow of
yellow moving into his vision.

"Are you awake, Jules? Come out here," she said.

He got up. He got into his trousers, dreamily, and came to her.

"Look at the sun setting. Look at the park," she said. She leaned heavily against him. They were in a long, broad room, evidently a living-room. There were only two chairs —one an old-fashioned chair with a green silk seat, perhaps an antique or a reproduction, the other an ordinary straight-backed chair. On the floor were some magazines, a newspaper. The sun shone through the leaves outside the window and blossomed into a thousand glimmering dots.

"We're in a painting. People in a painting," Jules said hungrily, thinking of a nameless painting he'd seen once in the art museum, years ago, on one of his wandering, curious days around that part of the city. It had seemed, then, to hold a secret for him—the way out of Detroit. Now, standing with Nadine in this empty apartment, he found himself back in those days. He felt that his life now surpassed anything he could have imagined, even with his energy. He had gone beyond himself. He was being in a painting, embracing a woman in a painting. Their love, so sweaty and violent at its height, had exploded into a thousand clean glimmering dots and golden leaves.

"I feel that I'm possessed by something. By you," he said.

"Are you joking again?"

"I never joke."

"Yes, you always joke and you're always serious. Both at once. I remember that. But I was too young to really love you then. I had to grow up."

"I loved you then."

"I know. That's what I remembered about you. There was never a day in all those years that I didn't think of you."

"Will you always think of me?"

"All my life. I know I will, no matter what happens to us."

"What's going to happen to us?"

She laughed and pressed her face against his. She was cool now, gracious. She had combed her hair and put on lipstick, fixing herself up for him. The gentleness of this woman, unexpected, seemed to Jules to dislocate him from the world he'd known, throwing him into some queer dimension in which his style of living, his words, his very self had no power.

"Come out in the kitchen. I'll make you something to eat," she said.

The kitchen was small and old-fashioned; its sink was a little tarnished. At the heart of a building, in its plumbing, certain secrets crop out—this sink's faucet had a slow silent drip. Jules brought the two chairs in, and Nadine sat on the elegant one, he on the ordinary one, prim as a guest. She sliced cheese for them with a dime-store paring knife. Jules's hunger was overwhelming. He had never felt so healthy. "I have rye bread too," Nadine said happily. She was rosy with joy, childlike, almost giddy. She watched him eat, covertly, and he felt embarrassment—everything was so heightened, to the point nearly of being painful. He laughed. He sat a few feet from this woman, in a daze of love, very hungry, eating cheese.

From the living-room came splotches of golden light, touching one side of Nadine's face. She looked young, her skin slightly raw. He had worn it raw with his own skin. Around her lips, worked into her soft skin, was a pink hue—her lipstick. Jules ate the pieces of cheese and bread she handed him, staring at her. It was a miracle, this transformation. He stared at her face, a woman's private face, in its way impersonal and lovely as any work of art, absolved of personal anguish. A finely wrought face, and yet not heavy with intelligence—reflecting light, sunshine from the window or the light of Jules's fierce attention. He looked at the opening in her gown. He could not see the top of her breasts but he understood that she was naked beneath the gown, an intimacy that stunned him, so strange and undeserved a gift.

"Will you love me? Will you let me love you?" he asked suddenly.

"I have no choice about it," she said.

Her skin was translucent, a victim's skin. But she smiled. Her teeth were even, white, ordinary. Her smile slowly revealed these teeth. Jules's own teeth were not so white and not so good-looking, but at least none of them had been knocked out. He smiled slowly at her, taking her hand. There was something brittle and jewel-like, pearl-like, in her impersonal perfection. What he had done to her, all that lust, lay quiet inside her and gleamed through her pores, waiting.

"This doesn't seem real," she said finally.

"Not to me either."

"You've made me so happy, Jules."

"Yes."

She brought his hand to her face and pressed it against her cheek. He saw the pale blue veins on the back of her hand. "I can feel what you've left in me, inside me," she said dreamily. There was something lethargic, almost labored in her voice; she sounded drugged. Jules was a little startled by her words and then charmed, then excited. He wondered if, like himself, she felt annihilated by the sudden expansion of love—too much suffocating light, too much violence. He took hold of her by the shoulders and kissed the opening of her gown.

"You won't leave me, Jules?"

"Where could I go?"

She was slow and hypnotic, like a child fascinated by something unexplained. Her hair was loose about her face. Jules felt a desperate lust for her but was ashamed of it. Her body, so obedient to his own, seemed to him too fragile a vessel for his desire; he didn't want to destroy her. He kissed her mouth, her face. He felt as if he were kissing bruised skin. She closed her eyes and brought her hands up to the back of his head, caressing him. Her touch drove him wild. He remembered her touching him like that while he had made love to her, so gentle a touch urging him on, inviting him.

"Could we . . . ? How do you feel?" he said hoarsely.

She stood. He embraced her eagerly. "I want to make you happy. I don't want to hurt you," he said.

Walking with her into the other room, he had a kind of hallucination—a flash of a blown-up photograph of himself. He sometimes thought ironically of himself as being photographed, in the act of running, in a foolish situation, grinning idiotically, eating. Now the flash came to him, came and went. He did not really see it; he imagined it. He imagined himself leading this beautiful woman to a bed, his arm around her in an intimate, husbandly way, his face fixed in an expression of confidence and tenderness. He had become a husband. But the Jules of this photograph had been imagined in other roles, other positions less flattering. Endlessly Jules had pursued Jules, in endless stories and dreams: now he had come to this polished, waxed kingdom, and the immediacy of Nadine's body was so miraculous that he wondered at his own daring. He opened her robe. He bent to kiss her body. She stepped back from him as if startled, but not really startled; he followed her, he let the robe fall to the floor. The closet door was partly open. He pushed it shut. He had always been afraid, as a child, of an opened door inviting trouble.

Jules knelt above her and came to her gently. She arched her back. He gathered her in his arms and clung to her, as if fearful of someone tearing him away. The white walls of the room seemed to draw back from them. Had there been a mirror somewhere near it would have shown Jules's straining form in a mist of white, straining to achieve some permanence. He knelt as if he were falling endlessly, and only her body kept him from plunging down. *A photograph of Jules falling.* The darkness of her body, its warm secrecy, but also the cool external whiteness of her body, its clean, washed skin—this astonished him. He was being urged out of himself. Fearful of ending too soon and leaving her, he drew his head back wildly, very young. Nadine's hands, on his back, were the hands of certain possession, urging him ahead. He said, "My darling . . ." and hoped that his words would put him at some distance. There was a terrible pressure in him that he feared, being unable to control it with her. He was not a machine but an urgent mass of flesh, shameful in a way, an unnamed mass of hunger.

Nadine embraced him. She moved her mouth against his as if she were talking to him, desperately; she had no words. Lost inside his love for her, helpless beneath his body, she lay straining for the pleasure that he had won so easily. She began to breathe in sharp, ragged breaths. Jules's face was contorted. If only now, only now . . . if she would only be drawn up with him, like this, like him, and like him released from this struggle. But he could feel her rising and failing. He could feel the tension in her rising to hysteria, then falling, as if her body had not the strength to sustain it. In a kind of delirium Jules made love to her for many minutes, desperate in his desire to help her, but suddenly the desperation faded, he could not remember or could not care, and everything in him was driven in a rush toward emptying itself into her. His nerves were caressed to a pitch of madness. The core of his being, the *Jules* of his body, was frantic to be released and could not be held back, though Nadine writhed in his arms and said, "Don't leave me, please, Jules," and clung to him with her feverish hands, gripping his back, his thighs, his shoulders. Jules slipped from her. He felt as if he were falling through her, evading her. Their skulls, through their flushed skin, rubbed hard and mute together.

She began to sob. She was feverish in his arms, close to hysteria. Jules said, "I'm sorry." He kissed her forehead and brushed her hair back from her face. His failure was queer, set so vividly beside the airiness of his body. He knew that he had failed her, but his own body, pressed against hers, felt only victory; this lingering, ebbing passion, the acute memory of passion, did not allow him to believe that he had really failed her. Yet she wept. He hunched himself over her and moved his mouth against her body. She was wet, silky. She shivered beneath him, and he could feel her rejecting him before she gripped his hair and said sharply, "Don't."

Jules stopped. He pressed his face against her stomach. "Let me. Let me kiss you," he said. But she began to sob in long, shuddering gasps. "Don't, please," she said. He was afraid of disgusting her—he was afraid of her, her passion, he could not understand. They clung together blindly. Jules caressed her thighs and opened his mouth against her flesh, but again she drew away, she rejected him. "It's inside me, it's deep inside me, where I need you," she said faintly. She urged him away. He lay carefully beside her, strange and uncanny, still airy, weightless, dazzled. Fear touched him, that he had failed this woman so utterly, and yet she lay perfectly docile in his arms, light-boned, delicate, a part of his own body. She would not look at him. "I'm sorry," Jules said, covering her hand with his, "I love you so much."

"I love you," Nadine said.

They were silent. This intimacy was magical to Jules—he could not believe there was such distance between himself and Nadine as her misery indicated. He felt that she had become part of him. The memory of her body, the experience of her body, was silky to him, mysterious, warm. There were no complications. Yet there were complications he could not understand. The very urgency and power of what he had felt frightened him, for coming to her, loving her, did not satisfy him but stirred him to wanting her again, locking her to him in his imagination. . . . The way out of such tension was release from it, but the violence of this release was intoxicating. He could not shake his mind loose of it. It was as if his brain were infected with the fever that had seared his body, to purify his body.

She was exhausted. He felt a heavy silence between them and was relieved when she fell asleep, her head on his shoulder. She slept uneasily. But it was a relief to be free of her consciousness. Jules looked around the room, holding her. Because it was so bare the room held no threat. It was a room that had no past and belonged only to the future; it would be fulfilled in the future. Now, in the present, it was blank and unreal. Anything might happen in it. The weight of Nadine's feverish body against his seemed unreal. He kept seeing her at a distance, his vision swooping up to take in her face, her eyes, the delicate line of her body—this body, so close to his, was a puzzle to him. Everything was locked inside it. He had not the words to release her, to wake her from this uneasy sleep. Her breath was labored. He was keenly aware of the subtlety of her bones beneath her wet skin, the slimness of her neck, even the fine lines of her face. But her hair was wild. Even in her exhaustion and sweat she seemed to him elegant, a mystery. Her long, smooth body was a challenge. He felt himself turning slowly blind, drawn inward by the hot silky challenge of Nadine's body.

He lay half asleep. It was night. Nadine's arm was flung back on her other side, in a child's gesture of abandonment. Her breathing was now quiet. Jules tried to get his thoughts clear. Everything was damp. The sheets were twisted. He could not think, lying here. A strange fear came to him: might he be forever bound to this woman, the two of them locked together in passion that could come to no end? Had he the strength to perform a miracle after all? Sodden, satiated with the miracles of his own body, he felt lacerated with having lived through so much. His eyes burned with the experience of miracles like the eyes of a Biblical prophet, a bearded, wild-eyed prophet of some nameless desert, wandering through a hot eternity of deserts, flaming bushes, apocalyptic cracking skies, rearing white waters, the purposeful flights of imaginary fabulous birds . . . He was slowly losing his strength, his soul.

He woke to her touch.

"Jules?" she said. "Are you dreaming?"

"I don't know . . ."

He opened his eyes, confused. She leaned over him. The air of their bed was stale and sweet. He felt her hair on his chest, her presence above him milky and sweet. In a rush all his love for her returned; he felt almost faint. "I love you so much," Nadine said, but her words were girlish and unthreatening; when she kissed him it was without anguish. Jules put his arms around her head, pressing her face against him. It was curious and exciting to him, his bare forearm against the back of her head, bunching her hair up against her neck.

"Talk to me and tell me about yourself," she said.

"There's nothing."

"Jules . . ."

"No," he said shakily, "nothing, I don't remember my life. How long are you going to be able to stay with me like this?"

She hesitated. "Why can't I stay forever?"

"Do you mean that?"

"Yes, I mean that. Forever. I'll stay forever." She pressed the length of her body against his. Settled, warm, she lay as if thinking over her own words, precisely. "I've always been lost inside the love people had for me. My husband— I would say his name, a particular name, and I thought I loved him. I told him that. But I was just saying the name of that, the name *love*. I was saying it against everything in the world that wasn't him, that didn't know me, where nobody would give a damn what I was or how much I suffered, trying to love somebody. I was setting his name against that. I've always been terrified of that."

"Of what?"

"Of everything, of going over the edge."

"Nadine, you? Do you really mean that?"

"You have to take me seriously, Jules."

"I want to take you seriously but I can't believe it. What has ever happened in your life to frighten you?"

She was silent.

"I mean it," Jules said gently. "Tell me."

Her silence was hostile. He caressed her face, as if trying to read her expression.

"What's wrong?" said Jules.

"You seem so distant to me."

"That isn't true. What do you mean?"

"You love me but you don't listen to me. You draw back from me. All your life you'll take refuge in having been poor, having been kicked around, to make you superior to people like me. You don't want to think that we're real."

"That isn't true!"

"I remember being alone with my father, on a train. He

started vomiting. He vomited blood and there were things in the blood—bits of flesh. I remember that—"

"My God, I'm sorry. Don't think about it."

"I want to think about it. I know what the edge is, just as you do. I might know it better. But you don't believe in me, you don't believe that I'm real. I'm something you made up, even my body is something you made up."

Her very voice excited him. There was truth in what she said—he had made her up, imagined her. But she was also real. "Don't talk like that," he said.

"Because it sounds as if I'm crazy? But that's the edge I mean most of all, going over the edge . . ."

He heard their voices and their words but his brain did not quite take them in. He wanted only to embrace her but he feared her drawing back. Slowly, gently, he ran his hands over her body as they talked, as if these caresses were not important, were only a part of their conversation. She was saying, "I imagine you out on the street, walking somewhere. Hitchhiking. These men walk along the edge of the road, sometimes walking backward, watching for cars. They seem very wise, very nasty. They put their thumbs out and wave for a ride, watching everything, mocking. They're very dangerous, I think. Or maybe they aren't dangerous, maybe they're tender, how do I know? I don't pick up hitchhikers. But you came right into my father's house. I couldn't say no. For years since then I've had the nightmare of you breaking into my house again, climbing into my window . . ."

Jules was so nervous he could do nothing but laugh.

"But why are you laughing? It terrified me."

"There's no reason to be afraid. Don't talk like that."

"I love you, I want you so badly, so bitterly, I don't think I can stand it," Nadine said suddenly. "If we were on a boat I would break it in two, I'd sink it under us. We'd drown. I can't control my feelings for you and so we would drown. If we were in a car, driving fast, I'd take the wheel away from you and make us crash."

"Why are you saying those things?"

"I don't know."

She was breathing quickly. Jules ran his hands along her shoulders and back, frightened of her, unable to stop. He could not understand her. The slightest wedge between them opened at once to a great gusty distance, and he had the idea that, at a distance, she hated him. Because he did not believe in her? in her terror? Because, like his sister Maureen, she was a woman who had to lie down to terror, submit to it, not having enough strength to escape?

She said, "Once a dog went after me, a German Shepherd. It went crazy, biting me, on the ankles, the legs, on my arms. It went crazy, and I screamed and screamed, trying to get away, but the dog kept lunging at me and knocking me down. It was in a fury. It was like something whirling out of control, flying at me. I didn't think I was going to die, I didn't have time to think of that. I was too terrified. The dog just kept throwing itself at me and saliva flew all over, from its ugly mouth. I can still see that mouth—the black lips, the tongue, the teeth—it was in such a crazy rage over nothing, wanting to tear me to pieces. For months after that I wasn't able to sleep without dreaming about that dog. Sometimes, even when I was awake, I could feel it taking shape in the air beside me—a dog getting solid out of the air, a very tense, heavy, awful shape in the air. My arms and legs were all bloody. I still have some scars. But it wasn't the biting that frightened me afterward. It was all that power. It was power getting shaped out of the air right beside me, a terrible danger. I thought it might pass over into me and I might do something awful, I'd kill somebody or myself . . ."

Jules held her. "Jesus, that must have been awful," he said.

"The shape of the dog was awful. I thought I would go crazy."

"I wish you wouldn't think about it now."

"I don't know why I even mentioned it. To impress you with the danger I've lived through? But you yourself are my worst danger—what can I do about loving you?"

"What can we do?"

"Other people have loved me and I knew what that was, exactly. But you love me like somebody calling out my name in a crowd—knowing me, coming right up to me. I can't escape. I want only to lie in your arms like this, I want you to make love to me, I'm driven out of my mind with wanting you." She spoke quickly, with a faint, desperate urgency. She might have been confessing something too ugly to be spoken aloud.

He felt her calling up the excitement in him, her nervous, warm body moving against his, as if challenging him. He ran his hands hard down the length of her body, as if assessing her, fixing her. He felt himself taking shape be-side her, the power of his lust giving shape to his entire body, outlining him in the dark. There was a strange clarity to his sensations. His mind flashed to him an image of him-self and Nadine, entwined together, a woman's long, pale arms lashed about his body, and Jules's strong back arched over her, in a grip of death. Hadn't he always put his faith in such bizarre images? Jules risking this, Jules leaping to that, Jules plunging in? He was the hero of countless stories. The conclusion of one story faded into the beginning of an-other, all of it imagined. That had been his life. But through these endless chapters he had been pursuing a woman who turned out to be this woman, a woman under an enchant-ment like his own, fated to wrap herself about him and give everything up to him.

When the poor get rich, Jules thought, they fall into a stupor of luxury and their eyes are filmed over with miracles —so Jules, impoverished for life but now sodden with the luxury of love, could not quite shake himself free of a sense of unreality. The clarity of his lust pinpointed all that was unreal. Nadine, his beloved, his mistress, a woman who had somehow married another man, drew him to her and put an end to all his questions, but not to the wonder behind them. "I love you, I'm crazy about you," he said in anguish, entering her, losing the shape of his words. He was afraid of what he felt, inside her. He felt as if his soul might be lost, drawn out by her love, her hunger. *I can't stop it, I can't control it,* he thought.

She strained against him. It was a terrible tension, the tension of her legs and arms. A power like the power of lightning rested in her graceful bones and was drawing them to the breaking point, but still they would not break, nothing broke, nothing released her. Jules kissed her. They struggled together, grappled together. In her desperation she began to claw at his back. The divinity in him, so vio-lently aroused, was distant to her, and she could do nothing but claw at him, wanting it, in a hellish agony. "I love you, I love you," she moaned, but her body seemed to fight him and held no love for him, only a kind of baffled dread. Jules stayed with her, holding her. The moment was so strange that he was able to draw back from it, on the brink of climax and yet guiding this woman, able to direct them both in spite of the heavy, quick pulsation of his lust, which she now sensed and wanted. She seemed to sense in him a rich, violent power that should have been hers, since it came from her body, but somehow was not hers—it was denied her, mysteriously. She drew her teeth hard against the side of his face.

"Jules, don't leave me!"

"It's all right."

Her cries were high, terrified, like the cries of ocean birds. He felt her turning into a wild, cruel bird. He felt her sinking and rising and sinking again in the frenzy of her own mind, unable to draw herself up, weighed down to insensibility. He wanted to turn his face away from her. But he kissed her instead, hungrily and wildly himself, in imitation of her passion and out of courtesy, to hide it from them both. If she were able to smile, Jules thought, a thin, sinister smile would illuminate her face—how she wanted him, how she needed every part of his body! What he had thought elegant in her was only her distance from him, a female distance. Really they were trapped together, struggling together. They were enemies. He imagined her body lacerated with deep red gashes, the frantic maniacal slashes of a dog, and the idea of her blood, the sight of her blood, excited him. He knew he was hurting her, though she could not feel any pain. He knew that her face and body were already rubbed raw by him, but he hadn't the strength for this, for this cruelty. He was sorry for her. He did not really want to hurt her, though she wanted him to hurt her, she wanted her blood spilled by him, but Jules could not keep it up, he did not want to be shaped out of the air by her violent imagination. She said, pleading, "Jules . . ." and it was already too late, he buried himself in her with a cry of pleasure and defeat.

"Oh, don't leave me! How can you leave me?" She wept.

He felt as if she had struck him with these words. He had failed her again. Exhausted, almost insensible himself, he could say nothing, he could not think at all. His body was fading from him. He could not imagine himself or Nadine. Her frustration, the desire she felt for him, was now beyond his imagination. He felt that he was near to dying while Nadine, miserable with life, still clung to him and pressed her damp, contorted face against his, accusing him.

"You don't love me, you don't care about me!"

She grew quiet. Jules did not speak. As consciousness came back to him he realized the depth of his failure, he felt ashamed, he really could not understand it. He was ashamed and baffled. He would have liked to say, "Of course I love you. What does this prove? So what? We'll have twenty or thirty years together, give me time to love you." But he said nothing. The idea of twenty or thirty years, the marriage of Jules and Nadine, struck him now as unlikely. He was afraid he had misunderstood her. And now, thinking him distant from her, unloving, she was prepared to reject him. He could not understand how he had failed her. Her own body had failed her, but her body was in his keeping, in his trust. He was her lover and yet could not make love to her, not truly, for everything was secret in her, tense and hidden. He could not understand. Every part of her, every cell of her brain, was infatuated with him and had given itself up to him; he could have sucked the very essence of her sweet blood, everything had been so open to him, and yet there was failure between them. Her body took on a kind of sinister radiance to him. It opened and closed upon him, driving him to an excess of lust, almost of madness, but still he had failed. It numbed him. He was exhausted, heavy. Even the faint light from the street hurt his skin.

He wanted to kiss her, between her thighs, but she drew away. She seemed to feel his pain; she had grown abstracted; he opened his eyes upon the pale street light that covered her body and thought for a strange moment that he did not even know this woman.

After a while she sat up. She said, "I don't feel well. I'd better take a bath or something."

Jules sat up and stroked the back of her neck. He could only say, "I'm sorry . . ."

She let her head rest briefly on his shoulder, then turned away. When she got up Jules felt for the first time a sharp stinging on his back, from her nails.

He followed her into the bathroom. She turned on the faucets to fill the tub with hot water, steaming the air. There was a murky, satisfying violence in the sound of this rushing water. Jules stroked her slight, slender body, and she stood without responding, staring at the water. He knelt to inspect a yellowish bruise on her thigh. "Did I do that? I'm sorry," he said. He was genuinely sorry. She turned vaguely to him as if his words were hardly audible to her. Jules felt his heart sink but he said cheerfully, putting his arms around her, "I'm sorry. I'll never do it again."

She said nothing. A nerve twitched in Jules's eye. He was in love and he knew that Nadine loved him. But, standing here, a little blinded by the steamy air, he felt distance opening between them and could do nothing about it. She leaned over the bathtub, away from him. He put his hands around her waist. Obviously her body belonged to him; she had given herself up to him, and yet it did not make much difference. He could not guess what she was thinking about. Love, this gravitation toward unity, this terrible fusion —why did it mean so much?

He was baffled and frightened, thinking of it. Why did it mean so much?

Nadine stepped into the tub, holding onto his arm. She sat awkwardly, as if afraid of falling. Jules looked down at her as if looking at a child, one of his sisters as a child again. "You'll feel better now. I must have made your skin pretty raw."

She leaned back. Her body was white beneath the water. Jules was reminded suddenly of a statue of the Virgin Mary he had stared at as a child, imagining he had seen it move. He had wanted so badly to see it move—he had needed a sign of friendship, of recognition. Now he knelt by the side of the tub and pressed his forehead against the rim. He said nothing. Nadine said nothing. They remained like this for some time. He could not think why his feelings for this woman were so violent. Why did he want nothing else except to love her, again and again, when she herself had drawn back from him, accusing him of failure? He did not truly believe in failure, any kind of failure. And so this did not make sense. How could he have failed her when she was himself, the two of them were one, in love? But her body did ache from him. Her skin was sore. His back ached from her raking fingernails. He could feel in her a rising tension, not the tension of love, turning her away from him although she was not looking away.

He looked up at her. She lay perfectly still in the water, her body growing pink from it. Jules tested the water with his finger and said, "Jesus, that's hot." She did not look at him. She seemed drugged, in a trance. He believed that she felt what he felt—locked in a desire for fusion, unity, but turned back rudely, baffled. He had not quite been able to believe in her terror but he was prepared to believe in it now. There was a terror in this white bathroom, the gleaming porcelain sink and tub seen at four in the morning, by artificial light. One's veins might be opened here, drained away by dawn. Should he kill Nadine and then himself, to fix their love properly? But he could not kill her without hurting her; he did not want to hurt her.

"You don't believe that I love you?" he said.

There was a tyranny in the tension she held between them, making them both victims. They were not free. Nadine lay like a victim in the hot bathwater, a woman in her middle twenties, slender, intense, baffled. Her hair was wild. Tendrils hung down onto her forehead and cheeks. Her eyes were livid, also a little wild, but with a dilated, drugged, stormy look. A rash had broken out along her chin, reddening as if the warm air were shaping it. Jules could imagine the rashes on her delicate skin that his hands had made. Exhausted himself, he felt her exhaustion. The damp air clouded his mind. He could not make out what she wanted or what he himself wanted.

She drew her hands up before her, covering her breasts. She looked down at herself slowly. "You're thinking of me—that I'm a pig, aren't you?"

"Nadine, what?"

"You're thinking that I'm a pig? For all of this? A pig, a slut?"

"Don't talk like that. You know better."

She was silent. He wanted to lean over suddenly to kiss her, but there was something still and deathly about her. She had control of the tension between them; it lay in her body. Jules's head ached with the enchantment he had labored under for so many years, and he saw helplessly that, for Nadine, it had moved on, it could not be reclaimed. The metamorphosis continued. Her face, which had seemed luminous to him the other week, at her home, was now very still, turned inward. She seemed absorbed by wonder.

"What's happening?" said Jules. "I love you. I don't want anything to change."

"You're thinking of how I am, how disgusting I am," she said slowly. "Like some little slut of yours. Some Negro woman. You've seen what I'm like and now you'll never forget it."

"I don't know what you mean."

"I always wanted you," she said in a slow, emphatic voice, as if confessing. "I couldn't think of anything else. I wanted you, only you. I wanted you to make love to me but not for it to end. I was in misery, wanting you. I walked around the house out there and was in misery while everything was so beautiful, all the things I owned and couldn't use. There was nothing I could do about loving you, nothing. My body ached. Everything in me ached. I wanted to die, I was sick with it. Did you think women could feel this way? It was heavy, dragging me down. I couldn't think of anything else. I couldn't sleep. Everything weighed me down, my body, the air pressing on my body, everything. I thought only of what it would be like when you entered my body, and time stopped for me, my heart stopped, just thinking of it. So now you know what I'm like."

She was to him a small, solid object, a statue made of some white substance, drawn in upon itself furiously and selfishly, complete. Her words were completions of something, a kind of ending. Jules said, desperately, "But so what? What the hell? What does that mean?"

"I'm a pig," she said slowly.

"Jesus Christ, what does that mean? A pig! I've never met a pig, never; that expression means nothing to me. In all my life I've never met a pig in human form, let alone you, never!"

She seemed almost to be listening. But she did not look up.

"You're exhausted, you don't know what you're saying," Jules said shakily. "I've upset you by coming here and staying so long."

"Yes, I'm upset."

"It's natural for you to feel like this. I stayed with you too long, I should have been gentler with you."

"Yes."

"And your husband, you're probably thinking about him. Do you want me to leave for a while, a few hours? Then I'll come back again and we can talk this all over."

"You want to leave me?" she said. For the first time in several minutes she turned to look at him. Her eyes were opaque, baffled. He felt a sickness in his body, seeing her so strange. She said, "Do I disgust you, Jules? What are you thinking? Are you comparing me with other women?"

"Of course not."

"Do you think, *I made her commit adultery?*—do you think that?"

He pressed his forehead against the rim of the tub again; he began tapping his head against it as if he wanted to smash his skull.

As it was above, so it went below—Jules thought giddily of his jokes and his flightiness, floating upward to an innocent sky, and of his passion and heavy, black, feverish blood, dragging him down. He was a criminal. His secret was that he was a born criminal. Her body was someone else's property he had ransacked, but he could not carry it off; he had the power to ruin it but could not escape with it. He had made of Nadine a soiled conspirator in his lust. He knelt on the bathroom tile, trying to think, tapping his head against the porcelain rim. Finally he said in exasperation, "So you've committed adultery! So what!"

"I don't want to think about it."

"Don't think about it then."

"I can't stand to be awake."

"You only want to make yourself sick. You're driving yourself to a breakdown. Why are you doing this?"

They had been together too long. Their intimacy had lasted too long. Nadine lay very still but there was no relaxation in her, no peace. He could feel her tension. It was like madness, gone beyond words or explanations. He had set it into being but could not touch it now, could not change it, as if he were no longer the man she had once desired.

"I committed adultery. I went to bed with you. I called you here, to come here, and all along I knew exactly what would happen," she said slowly. "I didn't think of anyone except you. I'm not thinking of my husband. What is there about you, why are you so strange? You might be married, I don't know. You might have some kind of disease after all. I don't even care about it. I don't care where you live or where you work. I don't give a damn about you but only going to bed with you. Now you see what I'm like. I should die."

He felt sickened, hearing this. He said nothing.

"You've degraded me but I wanted it to happen. Everything is dirty in me, inside me. My mind is filthy. I should die, I shouldn't live . . ."

Sickened, Jules got up and left. In the other room he stood perplexed and stunned, not remembering—not remembering where he was, what had happened. He looked out the window. There was always a promise in windows, the possibility of surprise. It was dawn, very early. A few cars had been parked on the street overnight, at the corner his own car was still parked. Escape. As long as he had his own car he was an American and could not die. But the room tugged at him—he had to turn to it, acknowledge it.

The sheets on their bed were a mess of wrinkles, stained from his semen, terrible to look at. He felt stunned, hypnotized, by the sight of that bed. What had happened between them could not be undone, and yet she was trying to reject him, trying to end it. How could her body reject him after so much love? He felt the heavy, trancelike lethargy of her body, its lust powerful beyond anything he could feel, a lust beyond his own. He was weak, stunned, by this failure.

He stumbled around looking for his clothes. He was a little blind, his eyes were filling with tears. He had the sudden fear that she would kill herself.

He knocked on the bathroom door. "Nadine? Are you all right?"

"Yes."

"Why don't you come out now?"

"I will."

He got dressed. He brought her bathrobe to the door, he opened the door shyly and leaned in. "Here," he said, handing it to her, but somehow it fell on the floor. She thanked him. He withdrew.

Waiting for her to come out, he paced the room and out into the larger room, depressed by all this emptiness. His brain could not manage in such dim empty rooms. Even the shining floor depressed him. He was too much alone without Nadine. He thought of loving her, he thought of her anguished, dilated eyes, he thought of her saying, *Now you see what I'm like.* But he did not see, he did not understand. What was she like? What had he seen? He could recall nothing except his own love, his burying of himself deep in her body and his need to stay there, dying in that mindless, suspenseful wonder . . . but, thinking of her, he began to want her again and the desire was a harmful one.

He heard her in the bedroom but did not go in. He was afraid of offending her, disturbing her privacy. After a few minutes she appeared behind him, dressed.

"Jules?"

"Yes?"

"Are you leaving now?"

"Wouldn't that be the best thing for me to do? I'll come back later, when you feel better. After you sleep. Or don't you want me to leave?"

"Yes, I think you should leave."

She smiled at him, a meaningless smile.

"Can I see you later today then? This afternoon?"

"I don't know."

She came to him and touched his arm gently. Surprised, pleased, Jules leaned to kiss her. His body yearned for her but he did not dare to touch her; he felt that this would destroy her. She kissed him in return, touching his lips cool-ly with hers. He felt his soul going blind at her touch.

"Nadine, I love you so much. I love you," he said.

"I love you, Jules," she said slowly.

But it was as if she had spoken against her will. They stood for a moment staring at each other. Then she said suddenly, "I'll walk you down to your car. I haven't been out of this apartment for . . . for over a day."

"All right. Good."

"I'd like to walk out in public with you, on the sidewalk. I think I'd like that," she said.

He felt that she was hurrying him out of the apartment now, guiding him along. But when he took hold of her shoulders to kiss her she turned her face up to his at once, without resistance. He kissed her for some time, gently. He felt how blind his kisses made her and yet how little effect they had upon her stubborn, hypnotized soul. He kissed her eyelids, to close them. He did not want to hurt her. The sullen morbidity of her words had passed from him, he did not choose to remember them, he put his faith in the magic of love to carry them on—why not, if she stood so obedi-ently to be kissed, allowing him to kiss her eyelids, kiss her blind? Why not? His kisses must have felt to her like gentle moths, butterflies . . . If this metamorphosis had come upon them, binding them together in love, why not another? Why must there be any end to change? She had loved him vio-lently once and he had the conviction that she would love him again, that her love would be stronger than her re-vulsion.

"Please remember that I love you. That I think of you constantly," he said.

"Yes."

"And I want to marry you. I have to marry you."

"I want to marry you, yes," she said.

He drew back from her, uncertain. She tried to smile. Then they went to the door together, Jules with his arm around her shoulders, trying for a certain jaunty intimacy, a casualness. They were lovers. She walked alongside him, pressing easily against him, in a dress of some dark, coarse material, a stylish dress with a sailor collar. Her legs were bare. On her feet were black shoes with knobby heels. He smelled soap, he smelled dampness in her hair. A sense of love rose in him, sickening him with its urgency. At the door he let her pass before him, weakened, feeling absurd.

"I'll come back this afternoon then," he said quickly. "Should I call you first?"

"I don't have a telephone."

"Yes, that's right, I forgot. You don't have a telephone here."

They went to the elevator. Jules pressed the button; it glowed red. Down. A down button, to take them down to the street. It would be delightful to walk with this beautiful woman on the sidewalk, in public, right out on the sidewalk. Why did that seem so dangerous? He kissed her neck. He kissed her hair. Why was he leaving her exactly? He could not quite remember. They decided something in their words. He had said something, she had replied. If he had not said those particular words, she would not have replied as she had, determining their fate. But he was less apprehensive of her now. He moved his face gently against hers, weakened, loving. He did love her.

Out on the street he saw that the city was waking up. A gentleman in a handsome suit crossed the sidewalk before them, on his way to a car. On another street a car pulled away from a curb. The early morning air was cool, invigorating. Jules glanced sideways at Nadine and saw that she was staring at him. She was shivering; she walked with her arms held rigidly against her body. "You should have a coat on or a sweater," Jules said. "What's wrong?" She was staring at him so oddly. He leaned toward her to take her arm but she drew away, still staring at him.

"Nadine, what the hell? Why are you acting like this?"

They were walking slowly past apartment buildings, one after another. Spaces of green lawn, expensive shrubs, wrought-iron fences. A man and a woman, dressed for traveling, the man carrying a suitcase, the two of them crossing the street to a large black car. Good. Their intimacy looked good. Everywhere there were expensive cars, which must have meant something, something good, peaceful. But still Nadine stared at him without recognition.

"Nadine?"

She continued walking alongside him, but on the far side of the sidewalk. Then, out of her pocket, she took an object —Jules looked and saw at first a small black purse. Then he looked and saw a gun. She held this out toward him as if waving him away.

"What are you doing? My God!" Jules said, more in alarm for her than for himself, fearful of her being seen. "What are you doing? Nadine? Put that back, hide it!"

She walked alongside him as if forcing him along. With the gun she kept him at a distance, assessing him. But there was no recognition in her face. Her beauty had gone all into hardness, in vacuity.

"Nadine, you're not going to shoot me, not me," Jules said, astonished. "You love me, I love you—don't you love me?"

She pulled the trigger. The bullet struck him somewhere in the chest, a terrible blow. Jules reeled, seeing the sunshine shattered in the windshields of an acre of large, gleaming, expensive cars.

The spirit of the Lord departed from Jules.

3

Come, My Soul,
That Hath Long
Languished . . .

1

April 1966. A girl in love is standing before a mirror, very still. Her gaze is fixed upon herself. The name *Maureen Wendall* is attached to this reflection, a clouded reflection in a cheap bureau mirror, and she stares at this reflection because it is all she has. Love, she is in love, sunk in love . . .

Outside a group of boys are playing baseball in the street. This is a street in Highland Park, which is in Detroit, a section surrounded by Detroit and shot through by Woodward Avenue, Second Avenue, Third Avenue. She lives in a large brick building on Third Avenue, in a single room. A single girl in a single room. Her face is heart-shaped and very pure, knowing nothing. A cautious face. It is pale as if with dust, with cheap powder, even the flesh beneath the eyes curiously pale as if she has seen nothing, nothing. Nothing has happened to her.

She presses her flat stomach against the edge of the bureau; she brings her face up close to the mirror. Doomed to be Maureen all her life? It seems to her a mystery that she should always be herself, this particular person; there is no way out. But she will escape into love, sink into love, fall backward into an abyss of love that will obliterate most of what was Maureen.

In the hospital, after Furlong had beaten her, she had worn a narrow plastic bracelet with her name on it: MAUREEN WENDALL. It is not possible to escape your name.

She is wearing a white slip. Her hair is cut short about her face, curly hair, giving her a girlish look. In her mid-twenties, now, she looks much younger. She watches herself closely, cautiously. Outside the sky has turned from blue to gray, a midwestern sky, changeable but monotonous. Maureen has spent too many years beneath that sky. She flinches from it, is nervous of windows, has thought much too often at work, *What if I fall out that window?* (She works on the seventh floor of an office building downtown.) Something draws her to the window and then teases her, *What if you fall out this window?*

The man's name is Jim. The name is too short. It does not seem to her enough to catch hold of, to keep her from toppling out an open window. His name is Jim Randolph. Randolph is also her half-brother's name; he is a brat of twelve; she tries not to think of him, her mind is closed against him and his dirty mouth. She thinks of him only when Loretta brings up the subject, complaining. When Maureen goes to visit her mother, Randolph is usually gone, running around somewhere. Too many kids on the streets. At twelve years of age they are grown up except for the terrible energy in their legs. Maureen has only to glance at Randolph (the kids call him Ran) to know that this loose-limbed smart-aleck kid knows everything, everything. Loretta complains, "He's just like Betty was, I can't do a thing with him or talk to him, but he's worse than Betty—he's got more energy." Loretta, now forty-six, must spend hours dreaming of a life without children dragging her down. Maureen's sickness was bad enough, thirteen months of it, but Randolph in perfect health is worse; he is making her a wreck, she complains, pouting, very serious with her pouting. What the hell has all this been for, all these kids? And Betty is always in trouble. And Jules, look what happened to Jules . . .

Jules almost died. But he did not die. A woman tried to kill him, firing two shots into his chest and then turning the gun on herself, but failing to kill herself also—the important thing should have been that Jules hadn't died, but somehow he did not seem to have survived. He does not seem to be alive; he has disappeared somewhere into Detroit. They hear about him, but rarely. Why did a woman try to kill him? Why would anyone want to kill Jules? Maureen remembers him as gentle, too gentle. She loves him but does not want to see him. She is afraid of what she might see—Jules changed, Jules worn out. He is almost thirty. A lifetime of being a kid and now—almost thirty! So Maureen tries not to think of him but thinks instead of the man she hopes to marry.

She looks at herself in the mirror, seeing herself as he must see her. She loves him. Her life is set for him, for loving him. She supposes that her body is set for loving him. She feels herself to be a cheap plaster figure set out on a lawn, the Virgin Mary or a deer, something that looks strong but is really brittle and can be broken easily. Out the window she can see children playing. They slam the ball at one another, they never seem able to catch the ball—it flies out of their hands, stinging them, and crashes against someone's front porch . . . so many thumps, so many jarring noises, vibrations . . . it is mixed up with her dreams about Jim, this sense of permanent alarm, caution. How is she going to give herself to him? How is she going to embrace him when that time comes? She closes her eyes and imagines. But her body tenses with fear, with panic.

Maybe she has chosen a married man because there is the hope she will fail?

He is her teacher in a night-school class at Highland Park Junior College. This college is in the same building as a high school. Maureen takes the Third Avenue bus and her route is simple enough; there are plenty of street lights and plenty of people getting on and off buses; plenty of traffic. But one day she saw a crowd of Negro kids, circling two boys who were fighting. Everyone shrieked and clapped hands. *Come on! Come on!* The kids who were fighting circled each other with a terrible adult caution. One had a knife and the other had his jacket, to slap into his opponent's face. A knife! A green canvas jacket! Maureen stared out at them, and that day she did not get off the bus, she was paralyzed and could not get off . . . her hatred for Negroes paralyzed her. She hates them violently, obsessively. She hates the teen-aged boys, those loud-mouthed hoodlums, she hates the teen-aged girls, the smaller children with their running and shrieking, the men, the women, all of them. But the next day she forced herself to go back. She went back. Nothing was going to stop her from getting to that classroom, not the men cruising the neighborhood in low-slung flashy cars, white or Negro men leaning out car windows to ask her if she'd like a ride, not the policemen in squad cars eying her, not the dirty drab old men riding the city buses perpetually, staring at her, vaguely staring at her, not all the newspapers blown in a mild whirlwind into her face, not the heavy air, the changing sky, the melancholy exhaustion of the other students in her class —nothing was going to stop her.

She is dressing now for class. Preparing for it excites her. Her mind is obsessed now with the thought of attracting this man, pleasing his eye, drawing him to her. She, Maureen, is a window that will draw him to it, stupefy him. He will fall in love with her and leave his present life. He will leave his family. She wants him so badly that the man himself fades from her mind and she can only think of wanting him, wanting *it*, marriage. She wants to love him, with her heart and with her body, but there is no time for love to rise in her; she does not know how to work it up, cultivate it, she's heard too much about it from her mother and other girls and from the movies, and it has been breathed into her ears too often, from men who did not love her but supposed they did. So Maureen supposes she will love this man, once they are married. She stares longingly into the mirror, as if staring into the future. Her face is the way into the future. Nothing can bring her into life, into the world, except that face.

Jules in the hospital, his face pale and thin, his eyes dark and melancholy in their sockets. What is a face, some bone and skin and gristle? What is the mysterious substance of the eye, what magic comes out of it? Maureen does not understand. This magic is a terrible cruelty, because it wears out. In America it wears out quickly. She feels a sense of alarm, of panic, staring at her face and knowing that it will not last, and that the loss of that face is more terrible than the loss of flesh and bone, rotted into the earth.

A guarded, cautious game with this man. He is her teacher and must keep himself at a distance. She is ready to love him and perhaps he understands? He shuffles papers, he is nervous, he is kindly and gentle; she understands again and again that he is a man to marry, a perfect husband. She wants to marry him and take him from his wife and three children —*his wife and three children* are a sign that attracted Maureen at once, for he is settled down, a good man, he has prepared his future and seems content with it, he is a perfect husband. If he leaves his family for her he will have proved his love, making this change, and never, never would he dare to make another change. He is thirty-four years old and she is twenty-six. Good. The difference is just enough, and the family he must leave for her is just enough—proof of what she can do, of her power, proof of his love if he comes to love her, a way of closing him off from the past and insuring the future.

She grows nervous and greedy, thinking of this.

Last fall she went for a walk up around Gesu Church, which is a block above Six Mile Road, a block from the University of Detroit, in a neighborhood of large brick homes. These large homes! these lawns! And in each house people lived, families lived, mothers and fathers and children, going about their lives as if such living, in such homes, were nothing extraordinary. It astonished Maureen to realize that these people did not comprehend their own lives. They did not comprehend the distance between themselves and Maureen, who was walking through their neighborhood, pretending to have a destination. She was eager to see people, to hear them. Occasionally a woman was working outside on her lawn, occasionally children were playing on the sidewalks, and Maureen's heart leapt up eagerly to see what these people were like. She wanted to go up to them and say hello. Two women, young mothers, were talking excitedly about something, and Maureen wanted to be a third young woman, talking with them, a young mother talking out on the sidewalk casually, aware of nothing extraordinary in her behavior. She stared at the women. Her envy was not hatred but something like love: she loved them. This was as close to love as she could come.

Toward men she could really feel no love, not really. She would have a baby with her husband, to make up for the absence of love, to locate love, to fix herself in a certain place, but she would not really love him. And yet there was the possibility that, once he was her husband, she would learn how to love him.

She couldn't be like her mother, always ready for the next day, always curious, cheerful, even in her complaints anxious to see what was going to happen next—she couldn't be like Loretta, ready to begin all over again. Loretta was always ready to begin all over again. She was not her mother's daughter. She felt an almost physical revulsion for that kind of woman, Loretta's kind, their hair in curlers and their monkeyish faces set for a good laugh.

I will fall in love, Maureen thinks, *I will make him love me.*

2

That morning something disturbed him, before he woke, not quite a thought but the apprehension of a thought, the fading conclusion of a dream. Asleep, most himself, he was alarmed at the great range of his desires, and waking was always a relief to him. Waking, he understood who he was and what he was. He moved to embrace the woman sleeping beside him, his wife, taking comfort in her warmth.

At this time they had been married for nine years.

The depth of her sleep seemed to him a great trust, a treasure. She slept silently, in his arms. It stunned him to think that for nine years they had slept together, himself and this woman, that their lives had become inextricably bound, that he could not clearly remember a time when he had not known her. That time belonged to another, younger, more helpless self. He got no pleasure from thinking of it.

She was thirty-two. She had had three children, and the children slept along the corridor of this small apartment, two in one room, peaceful and miraculous to him in their sleep, a perpetual surprise, because he could recall a time in his life when they hadn't existed, when he himself had been no more than a child and unnaturally wary of the traps of permanence adults accepted so quietly. He had always been a wary person, beneath his kindliness and his gentle, patient smile. Before waking, drifting in a gray tangle of sleep that was like the tangle of a woman's hair, he felt his wariness rise in him to become a kind of evil. What is he waiting for? What is going to happen? Is he going to do something to his life, something irreparable?

He found himself waking again, out of a muddle of a dream, something about a train crossing an icy continent. It was time to get up. The day stretched before him suddenly like a continent, full of dangers and petty jokes and humiliations, something to be crossed. His wife was awake. She pressed her face against his wordlessly. He thought of the rickety train setting out across a wasteland of ice and a sensation of fear rose unaccountably in him; he began to sweat. "I don't want to be late," he said, drawing away from her. He got up. She got up from her side of the bed. The shades in the small room were drawn but he could tell that the day was going to be another overcast day, a monotonous day. He was thirty-four years old and the sky of Detroit had burned its way into his brain, searing it with gloom and grit and something relentless, monotonous, and powerful.

His wife was talking to him. She had a solid, muscular stance, buttoning her bathrobe. There was something efficient about all her movements, even her gestures; she knew how to get through the day. They had been married for nine years. He tried to listen to her but something failed and his face took over, smiling an early morning smile, showing strain, affection. She was talking about going shopping that afternoon. About money. Frowning, apologetic, she spoke to him about money.

Out in the kitchen he sat with his head in his hands, at the table, until his wife whispered, "What's wrong? Do you have a headache?" He told her no, nothing was wrong. While she made breakfast—he would take only coffee—he sat thinking guiltily of that dream of his, himself wary and shrewd, in a gray wild tangle of sleep. That was not his true self, yet he preferred it to himself. The self he lived in was familiar and familiarly treated, by his wife and his children and his friends and the people who were his superiors and by the entire world, seeing in him a kindly man with lines in his face caused by kindliness.

His wife said, whispering, not wanting to wake the children yet, "I can get Brenda to come down and sit for me. When will you be home tonight?"

"I thought I'd go right from school out to the college and skip dinner."

"Do you think you should skip dinner?"

"I never feel much like eating before that class."

"But don't you want to come home first?"

"It would be easier the other way. The long drive . . ."

He was in love with this woman, set in the condition of love, entwined in the history they had lived through together, and responsible for it; he could see himself from a short distance, perhaps through the window of this cramped kitchen, a man sitting at an ordinary breakfast table, watching his wife closely. Of such a man what can be said? He would squint desperately at himself, hoping for some recognition, some certainty. So he was Jim Randolph. He had an older brother, Tony, of whom he'd been jealous all his life. His mother had several sisters and they all had families and so he had many cousins, some of whom he'd liked and some he'd hated, and two of his grandparents were still living, all people to testify to his identity, should any question arise. And of course his mother and father. They all knew him.

He pressed his hands against his eyes, wondering.

A woman's magazine lay on the kitchen counter. On its cover was a bright color photograph of a cake, a birthday cake. What colors, what breadth, what a peculiar, squat, outrageous authority in that cake! Headlines: *Spring Comes to Your Home, A Shower for Someone Close, A Doctor Looks at Intimate Problems of Marriage*. His wife bought these magazines occasionally, and it had been years since she'd stopped apologizing for them. He was curious about the magazine and wondered what it could possibly have to say about the problems of marriage, but he would never bother to open it—he was too intelligent and fixed, too scornful of such things. His wife was whispering again, about clothes for Terry. Terry was the five-year-old, a girl. He smiled at his wife and agreed with her. Sometimes his amiability was like a hand thrust into her face and she grew silent, offended, and he was forced to ask her what was wrong, why was she angry? And she would say coldly, *"Because you don't really listen to me!"* The bond of their love was a puzzle to him, a sweet puzzle. It decided his life; he was fixed within it. He was not the kind of Catholic who believed that divorce was impossible, and he was not the kind of Catholic who took religion very seriously, but he felt the bond between himself and his wife was irreparable, a permanent condition, as permanent as his own name. But something had happened once that had alarmed him. He had been on his way home, when they had lived in married students' housing at another university, years ago, and he had noticed several young wives talking out near the mailboxes by a muddy road. His imagination had touched upon them lightly enough, wanting to admire them, noting their slim legs and their nervous laughter, that trilling catch in their voices that showed how close to the surface of their young bodies hysteria lay. Some distance from them, he thought them desirable enough, but as he approached and one of them made a tired, cynical gesture, a pushing of the air outward with her hand, he had thought suddenly that it was all a loss, a mistake, this combining of lives and bodies, this wretched joking camaraderie of being poor and being in perpetual uncertainty; people were better off apart. Then the woman turned and it was his wife herself, catching sight of him. It was a commonplace happening and yet it alarmed him, being so commonplace, so ordinary.

He had married to settle himself into a certain life, to place himself in a certain relationship to his own family and to her family, whom he liked well enough. He liked everyone well enough. He had wanted to come to the end of uncertainty. He had wanted an end to the confusion of emotions that had made his adolescence miserable, and it frightened him to think that, at thirty-four, he had really settled nothing. He could not control his emotions. They broke and flooded about him, teasingly.

Still, nothing would happen.

His wife went to take care of the baby and he picked up her magazine. He leafed through it hurriedly. *Have a Gala Birthday Party for Your Child!* He passed this by. *How to Create Happiness.* Drinking his coffee, he skimmed through an article, *The Five Basic Don'ts:* "Don't worry needlessly. Don't expect too much, particularly from your husband. Don't compare yourself to your friends. Don't take anything for granted. Don't daydream." He was irritated by this: why not daydream? He turned the page and came upon another article, no, a short story about a wedding . . . a soft, somber drawing of a big-eyed girl in a wedding dress . . . the first paragraph went, "Elinor was certain that the telephone had rung, but now she heard nothing. Bitter tears filled her eyes . . ." Over the page, an article by a doctor, *Intimate Problems of Marriage.* "The most destructive problem in a marriage is lack of communication, particularly concerning love, sex, and money . . ." And pages of hairdos for spring, girls with glossy healthy hair smiling out at him, girlish girls, no threat, with ribbons, with tiny buds in their hair, with gleaming white sanitary smiles, not threatening him or any other man, about to break into a chant: *Love us, only love us!*

Behind everything lay love, a hunger and a mystery. He was in love himself, he loved his family, and he loved himself, in a sense, as a man in this family; he loved that role. Of himself apart from that role he did not think since that self did not exist, nor was there the possibility of its coming into existence. A sudden thought: why not move out of Detroit? He wanted to see another landscape. To Europe? A trip to Europe? He wanted to see his family by a foreign river, by an ocean, he wanted them joyful with freedom and the knowledge of their being totally, permanently loved. He wanted to escape Detroit with them.

And now, would his car start? He went out to see. It was always a surprise, and he felt both an exasperating helplessness and a kind of detached, amused contempt, wondering if it would start. His fate lay out of his hands. That morning they would investigate the complex causes of European decay in the eighteenth century. Decay always had complex causes whereas health was simple: was there a riddle in that, or was it a lie? His friend Max had left one of his books on the floor in front, a paperback copy of *King Lear.* Max was working for a Ph.D. in English and was harassed, lonely, inarticulate . . . always losing things. It was good to have such a friend, to invite him to dinner, to talk out his problems with

him. All this was familiar, familiar. Out of habit, he leafed
through the book. Books attracted him. There were many
footnotes, many marginal notes in blue ink. He felt a vague
apprehension, glancing at the lines of poetry. He did not trust
Shakespeare. Tragedy had always terrified him with its blunt,
raw stops and starts, its elegant language and bloody endings
and calm revivals. A sense of apocalypse followed by an ordinary morning. Horatio and Fortinbras playing chess in a
drafty, velvet-hung room, yawning and patient, good men left
over to fight a good fight, ignorant enough to survive. And
there was always a Cassio left over, bruised but energetic,
and Kent dazed with the past but optimistic enough to take
on the future, the long rise of history. He leafed through
the book, not letting his eyes linger too long on anything:
"But yet thou art my flesh, my blood, my daughter;/ Or
rather a disease that's in my flesh . . ." "Hang him instantly.
Pluck out his eyes . . ." "My sickness grows upon me . . ."

Making so much out of death! So much out of life! He
felt a little sick himself, closing the book. No, it did no good.
It was pointless to think about death, about life. Getting
through the day . . . The day was a part of the enormous,
indecipherable granite block of his life, which he had to chip
at, chew at, tease and plead with, having no instruments sharp
or powerful enough to do what another man might do with
one blow; *love, sex, money* . . . The dream of Europe had
become slightly stale. He and his wife had talked it over too
many times, had played out their mutual roles with too much
enthusiasm; that was that. The future. But at least his car
worked, it started at least—wasn't that a good omen? A chip
the size of a splinter off that great granite block, a tombstone
of a block with his name on it: the car starting this morning.
If he was late for this class again and the students trooped
out to complain, then what, what might happen next semester? He owed money, he had three children.

He tossed the copy of *King Lear* into the back seat. Bad
to glance at such things so early in the morning. He was
too sensitive. Weak. What did he have to give to anyone,
even his wife? He was closer to his wife than to anyone in
the world, yet what did he have to give her that was uniquely
his own? His permanent love, his intelligent, serious, permanent love?

The day passed. Evening came. At the school in Highland
Park, before class, the girl was waiting to see him. He had
asked her to come down early. He was nervous, approaching

her, anxious to see whether she would be there at all and then mildly gratified that she was—standing in the dim corridor, very much alone, waiting for him. He wanted to draw his hands roughly across his eyes but he kept his face serious, smiling a serious smile.

They said hello. She was quiet, shadowy. He sat at his allotted desk (shared with a daytime instructor, whom he never saw) and the girl sat across from him. Gentle, very quiet. He grew cheerful and boisterous, imitating an uncle of his. What weather! What air! He had to say a few things, a few foolish things. Then he took her compositions out of his briefcase and glanced through them, though he was perfectly familiar with them. The girl sat watching him. After a few minutes he said, smiling to comfort himself and her, "I'm afraid you have a problem with writing, Miss Wendall."

"I'm sorry."

"No, don't be sorry, that's why you're a student." A friendly smile, a poster smile. Put her at ease; she is a student. "That's why you're taking the course, but I can anticipate some difficulty in your handling the next assignment. You seem to have a definite problem with writing, with . . . expressing yourself in words, on paper."

He smiled, feeling his eyes crinkle, feeling the lines deepen in his face. Both jaunty and old tonight, jaunty in the girl's presence but old from a long day of work, rushing around, a little put off by the girl's youth. She did not look much more than twenty. He was excited by this and resentful, both. His head began to ache. He said, "I wish I could see some improvement from paper to paper, but you seem to be making the same mistakes. They're not mistakes exactly—"

"I suppose it's the way I think," she said.

"It might be that, I don't know. No, I don't want to say that," he said quickly, alarmed. He avoided her still, sad look and shuffled through the papers again. He was too clumsy a man to handle this. He looked through the papers helplessly.

There was silence. The girl did not move, very obedient, respectful. As he looked through her papers, staring at the handwriting that now made no sense to him, saying nothing, he had a sudden sense of her restraining an impulse to reach out to him, to call out to him. But no. Nothing. He looked up and all was ordinary.

He cleared his throat. "Do you understand my comments

on your papers? Do you feel they're fair? What do you think of my criticism?"

It was a ruse of his, a familiar plea: pretending to be at the mercy of a student. But really he was in control. The girl did not go along with him. She looked confused.

She said, "But I don't know enough to think anything."

He laughed. "Miss Wendall, that isn't true. Not at all. For instance, do you understand what I mean by . . . lack of coherence?"

And then, as if giving up suddenly, he saw that she was a beautiful girl, sitting across a battered desk from him, helpless. But her beauty had nothing to do with hair, skin, eyes—it seemed deeper, a kind of wound, a bewilderment. He could not make sense of it—he felt only helpless before it, himself. No one would ever take a picture of her for a magazine; she wasn't clear, she couldn't come into focus, she was a threat. Her look was uncanny. In class, while he droned on for an hour and a half, sneaking looks at his watch, the class of students listened quietly to him and among them the girl listened, watching him, seeming to open herself to him continually, apart from the others. But was it true that she was unlike the others? Wasn't there something sleazy and unsubstantial about her, something that might rub off under the thumb?

Her silence made him nervous.

"Well, forget about that. Tell me something about yourself," he said.

She stirred, coming obediently to life. She almost smiled. "There isn't much to tell."

"Nothing in your background to explain this? I mean, this problem, the way your sentences don't make sense—don't follow one another logically, I mean," he said, embarrassed, afraid of seeming crude. "I mean, is there anything in your past to account for your being confused maybe? Uncertain about anything?"

"I don't know."

"Has anyone ever discouraged you from expressing your own ideas? I mean, a teacher or someone in your family? Argued with you? Rejected your ideas?"

"I don't think so."

"You seem so hesitant."

"I'm sorry."

"No, don't be sorry," he said, laughing a little noisily. "My God! I only wonder what's holding you down. Obviously you have something to say. You're intelligent. But this—this"—he tapped her papers in a hearty gesture—"this doesn't show it."

"I'm sorry," said the girl.

"I wish I could help you more. I wish I could do something."

"I never had trouble . . ."

"Go on, don't stop. You never had trouble?"

"I never had trouble except after my father left."

"Your father left?"

"He left my mother."

She spoke shyly, yet there seemed to be a strange pleasure in her confession. It was the first intimate fact about her he had learned and it gave him pleasure too. Her coat was still buttoned, a cheap yellow coat that looked lemon-colored in this light.

He leaned forward gently. "So your father left your family?"

"Yes. I was fifteen then."

And how old are you now? he wanted to ask. Her youthfulness irritated him. But he said, "I'm sorry to hear that." It showed in his voice, that he was sorry. She glanced at him in surprise. The moment weighed strangely upon them, and he felt that this face might break into a stupid grin. "But you . . . you're all right now? Do you live at home?"

"Not now. I moved out."

"Do you live alone?"

A strange question. Shouldn't have asked . . . Into the kind, patient, generous range of his life many people had come, students and friends, and he had always opened himself to them all: he was a good man. He looked like a good man. His father, who had run a dry-cleaning store, had been a good man also for fifty or sixty years, and it was in the genes, fated. The careless and the lonely were drawn to his shabby, pleasant looks, assured by his uncut hair, his squinting, his groping after words, his soft uncertain voice, even the frequent trembling of his fingers early in the morning. His eyes were blue, a little prominent, and he felt them get bloodshot as his long, exhausting day wore on, tiny threads of blood cracking to the yellowish surface of the eyeball. The backs of his large, square fingers, which sometimes trembled, were covered with fine golden-brown hairs. It seemed to him suddenly that his wife was with him in this office. She was leaning forward to peer into his face, watching and judging.

"Did you say you lived alone?"

"Yes. Alone."

She had the appearance of a certain kind of student—night classes, courses stretched out over a number of years, hopeless. Lost and thoughtful. Her eyes were clear, surprising, self-conscious. What to do? For some seconds they had been looking at each other. Between them, on the nicked surface of the desk, lay her latest paper with red marks on it. He was alarmed to see how cruel they looked, his marks—red, angry exclamations shouting out against the small, regular, mediocre lines of her handwriting.

"Is my writing hopeless?" she said.

"I wouldn't say that, no. No, of course not."

"Is it . . . is it the writing of an insane person?"

"Of course not!" he said, shocked.

He fell silent, wondering at her perception. The writing of an insane person? Yes, that was true, true enough. And yet she was not insane. He was certain of that. He avoided her troubled look as he avoided her gaze in class—it opened too much to him, it disturbed him. Shy and naïve but strangely knowing, a puzzle. What did she think of him? Intelligence. Tenderness. His wife might glance over at him and see everything there was to see, having heard years ago everything there was to hear, helpless herself to change this fact, a fact of history. She saw through him—why not? She had constructed him, partly. She had helped imagine him for himself. She could not help seeing through his try at calm, elegant language (in imitation of a favorite professor) to his panic, his exhaustion, to the shabbiness of the tweed jacket he wore, the feeble exoticism of his necktie of red and green scimitars, or parrots' beaks, this crazy necktie he had had for too many years. Did his students notice his shabby clothes, or him? He taught English composition here two evenings a week, from eight to nine-thirty, and the fifteen adults enrolled in his class watched him on those long evenings as if he were a figure in their restless dreams, incomprehensible in his smiling irony and verbiage and perhaps worth listening to, of value, if only they could keep awake. On those nights the air was heavy with fatigue and futility. They all liked him very much, he knew that. It was part of their fatigue and futility. Several housewives, a sour-faced taxi driver, a milk-delivery man, three men who worked at Ford's on the day-shift, all of them worn to the bone by other lives, other identities, so that their shoulders were permanently rounded. He would have liked to toss his book aside and say the hell with it and caress their aching shoulders, pass a cool hand over their sad aching eyes. To save them! To change their lives!

"Is there any hope for me?" the girl said suddenly.

He awakened. For a moment he thought she was asking about her life, any hope for her life? But they were talking about her *writing*. She was his *student*. Nervously he said, "Of course there's hope. Of course, you have to keep reading and writing, practice writing. I'll give you some books you might like to read. You'll improve, please don't worry."

He caught in this girl's alert, dreamy look a peculiar kind of intelligence—not much surprised her. A sudden pang of desire for her ran through him. He leaned forward and brought his arms down on the desk, in front of him.

"Why . . . what made you say that, about your writing? Like an insane person's writing? Why did you say that particular thing?"

"I just thought of it."

"Are you troubled about something?"

"The usual things."

"What?"

"How to live, what to do, how to get through certain days," she said. She smiled slowly.

"Do you get a ride home after class, or take the bus?"

"I take the bus."

"It isn't dangerous?"

"Nothing has happened to me yet."

"But it might be dangerous, a girl like you—"

"I can't help that."

"No, I suppose you can't help that," he said slowly .

He knew he ought to dismiss her. Time to stop this. Out in the corridor someone was waiting, another student. He glanced through her papers again, frowning, though he was tired of this pretense and tired, really, of this girl, whom he had been thinking about for too long. It was absurd, his thinking about her. He did not need her in his life. He did not even have time for her. And, being himself, he had no idea of how to approach her had he wanted anything from her—he had been married too long.

"Someone is waiting to see you, I think Mrs. Thibodeau," she said.

"All right."

She left. He had got through it: he hadn't offered her a ride home. A little relieved, he prepared himself for Mrs. Thibodeau, one of the class talkers, nervous and defensive.

She came to him with a hefty, imposing need, sliding onto the chair Maureen had vacated.

He said very genially, "How are you, Mrs. Thibodeau?"

Only a few minutes before class.

That night, after class, he stood around talking with a few students and did not watch the girl leave. Walking to his car, he did not glance over at the small crowd of people waiting for a bus. She was protected by that crowd. She could take care of herself. He drove home and felt his attraction for her lessen, stretched out thin. He was a husband, a father of three small children, a man with a certain identity. This identity drew him home. He knew where to go. It was the girl's voice that struck him most, perhaps, a slightly drawling, dreamy voice with a certain authority and expectation. Did it remind him of something? What did it remind him of? When he read her assignments he could almost hear her speaking in that small thoughtful voice: *It is the elaboration of justice out of man's control, it is in the hands of God.* That was the way she wrote. Where did she get such words from, such nonsense? It was insane and yet he understood it. And it was touching, he thought, that she believed in God.

Very dark out now, a long drive. Shopping carts from a supermarket out on the street. Dangerous. A few Negro boys were fooling around on a corner. Their hair grew bushy and wild, as if their heads had been forced out of shape by some exotic ritual, giving them secret powers. Tumbled vacant lots . . . a mattress lying near the sidewalk . . . a look of blowy, blowsy disorder . . . a block of apartment buildings. Did Maureen Wendall live in one of these ugly buildings? How to attach the ugliness of her life to her, to drag her down with it? He wondered if she saw these same sights, one after another, as she rode the bus back and forth in that pack of tired, helpless people.

He had come by accident into the lives of such people, his students. He was studying at Wayne State University for an advanced degree in sociology, having switched out of history because he had grown despairing and impatient with the dead, eager for contact with life, with the living. He had married fairly young, he had three small children, which amazed him, and because of this—the children—he had hired himself out for part-time work through the university's English office, dignified and desperate in his old tweed jacket and his trimmed, neat brown beard, a gentlemanly young man, a gracious victim. He impressed his superiors as a victim who was not self-pitying but gracious: in short, the kind of man they wanted. So he had hung around the English office asking for work, any kind of work. He was qualified to teach at any dismal extension center or community college or junior college because, six years before, he had earned a Master's Degree in English, when he'd had other plans for his life—of all these "other plans" he tried not to think. His years in English studies were his blue period, best forgotten.

He was taking three courses at the university this semester: a graduate course in social-psychological aspects of organizational theory, a seminar in human ecology, and another seminar in sociological methodology. He was a research assistant for one of his professors, a stern, busy man, and he spent many hours of his valuable day in the library, charting statistics. He ate his lunch in the library stacks. In the afternoon he ran across campus to teach an Adult Education course called "Introduction to Sociology," which met three times a week from four-thirty until five-twenty, in a decrepit university building marked for destruction, overlooking the Lodge Expressway. Then he ran back to the library and to his carrel and took notes on his own reading, scribbling on note-cards in different colors of ink—red, blue, green—writing very fast. Each color indicated a different kind of information. His dinner was what remained of his lunch, maybe an apple. He had no time to be hungry. Sometime between five-thirty and seven he spent a dime calling his wife, who got lonely at the apartment. They talked fast, exchanging news. One of the children had a cold. A letter from her mother had come and she was afraid to open it. How did *he* feel? Was his throat still sore? He couldn't afford to get sick again. When was he coming home tonight? Often close to tears, bored and exhausted herself, his wife pleaded with him in her sensible voice: why was he always running around? why were they so poor? and please, please, he mustn't borrow money from Fred again, that was shameful, she wouldn't stand for it . . . Why was life such a mess? Under stress her voice took on a stubborn, melodious sound; he could imagine her skin growing flushed.

He loved life, he loved living. But certainly it was a mess. It was jammed up, bottled up, impossible. On Tuesdays and Thursdays he had to drive up to that junior college, located in a high school, through a cluttered waste of sad-eyed buildings; when his car broke down, as it frequently did, he

had to catch a bus himself. At least he could prepare his
lesson on the bus and always put it off until then, when he
could run through it feverishly. He was paid $250 a semester
for this course. "What is wrong with this sentence? Can anyone explain what is wrong with this sentence?" he would
ask his sunken-eyed housewives and truck drivers, gazing
out into their furrowed, honest faces as they struggled over
a mimeographed exercise he had borrowed from someone
in the English Department at the last minute. His students
hung onto the mimeographed sheets as if these papers might
explain everything that was wrong, as if they were keys to
the enormous ultimate mistake of the universe. Maureen
Wendall was among them, waiting. Was everything about to
be explained to her? Was a revelation near?

He thought it touching, her belief in God. He was a
Christian himself though he didn't want to push it too far;
he never pushed any of his beliefs too far.

When he finally got home that night he went into the bedroom at once and lay down. He seemed to have collapsed.
His wife leaned over him, frightened. He heard himself mut-
ter, on the verge of crying, "I can't do it. I can't keep up
this goddam schedule, this life is killing me. I can't keep it
up any longer . . ."

Crazily he thought his wife might change everything by
telling him he could stop. They could all go away somewhere, escape around the world! Why not? But she said instead, not so confident now, suddenly frightened of him and
his weakness, "What can you do? What else?"

So in the morning he was ready to go again. He was a
man of thirty-four who looked years younger, perhaps because he had no choice. He was in perpetual motion.

3

He was perpetually waiting for something to happen—
anxious that it might happen and that it might not happen.
He had no idea what it could be. He had begun waiting for
it early in life. For a while it had had to do with the priest-
hood, then it had had to do with marriage, now it was connected vaguely with the mystery of dreams, those disturbing
dreams that seemed to belong to another man but had to be
his own. During the day, awake, he had no time to dream.
He rushed about from one enormous glass-and-concrete

building to another, cutting across university lawns, past the white concrete walks and spaces and benches, having no time to see anything, crossing streets against traffic, caught out in the November rain without an umbrella and comically, horribly alone among the thousands of hurrying students—a man who was waiting for something to happen, in spite of his hurry. At the back of his mind was a premonition of blankness, an ultimate disappointment—that he was no more than the ordinary man he had always tried to be, and that his fate was to be ordinary.

His car was working. Tuesday evening again, another Tuesday evening. He drove out to Highland Park and felt the tension rising in him—not concern for the weary class but concern over the girl, whose face he had been trying desperately to recall all weekend. If she did not show up . . . ? On the several evenings when she had been absent he'd felt an unnatural irritation—a gnawing ache, an embarrassment. Too sensitive. His wife sometimes complained that he was weak, that his being nice was only a phase of his being weak, and he understood that this was true. Everything was true. But he resented the fact that this girl, helpless as she was, had a life of her own and had no real need of him. She was beyond his influence. His feelings were somehow in her control, but she herself was beyond him. And he felt not just this unreasonable apprehension about the girl but a sense of disorder, of danger, that had something to do with the space through which he had to drive—up along Third Avenue past the Fisher Center and Ford Hospital and into the ominous congestion of Detroit's residential streets. Too many shapes in the corners of his eyes . . . too many buildings, gas stations, kids on bicycles. There was the pressure of too many people. Pressure. A pressure on the eyes and on the brain. Where, in this dangerous landscape, could he be going? It did not seem right that he, the son of his father, should have been born for any destination of this type. He said to himself, *I want . . . I want to . . .* but he could not think of concluding words, he could not complete his thought. He was too exhausted, he could not think clearly. His life was a joke. The variety of shapes and colors along this street was a joke. Illusions danced before his eyes like the relentless strips of paper pennants decorating gas stations. He was driving from one woman, his wife, to another woman, whom he didn't know. Yet his heart pounded with the need to get to her.

Always, he had been a man drawn to adventure—to the longing for it. His mind was filled with movies and books. He loved the commonest of things, movies on television, movies at third-run neighborhood theaters, not just because his life as a student was taken up so savagely with the uncommon, the intellectual, but because his body felt a natural gravitation toward the excitement of the banal. He was an intelligent man, yet he was perfectly ordinary and anxious to remain ordinary. He was ordinarily good-looking. He felt at times gaunt with normality, happy with it and yet distressed, wanting to call out to people on the street, "Yes, this is me but not really *me*. Look again, look closely!"

And if the girl didn't come that evening?

When he hurried into the classroom, already five minutes late, she was not there. Not coming. He picked up a gnawed pencil left behind on the desk, examined it with an unusual concern, and put it down again. Time to begin. Everyone else was in the room, waiting. No, not everyone else—Hendrix the cab driver was absent. He cleared his throat. Then the girl entered the room and everything was all right: everything became perfect.

He talked. Maureen sat with her coat unbuttoned, looking tired; he tried not to glance at her. Overhead the cheap fluorescent lighting flickered. Bad for the eyes and bad for the brain. Objects lost their correct outlines and substance its dimensions in such light. He felt a foreign disquieting strength in himself, an almost giddy sense of power. Mechanical talk, a familiar lesson—he knew this all so well, had known it for years; he was in control and talking to them, talking, exerting power over these strangers. And yet alert, expectant. He liked teaching. He loved teaching. He loved the pull of their eyes upon him, the pull of his voice upon them. He seemed to be transformed into their idea of him, losing his own familiar shabby outline in the light from the fluorescent tubes.

When the long session came to an end he felt a sense of excitement but also of loss. He was baffled at this, his excessive weariness. He gave so much to his students, even the most helpless of his students, and in turn they gave him nothing. Not really. His life was rushing by, days were being snatched from him in handfuls, he was nearly thirty-five years old . . . Maureen stood and began to button her coat. Each movement of her fingers was a secret movement, with meaning: he believed desperately in signs and symbols. For weeks, hadn't this girl been trying to communicate with him? Had he misunderstood? Had he imagined everything?

He had to get to her before she escaped. He said, "Let me drive you home tonight."

She looked only mildly surprised. Very pleased. She smiled and said, "Thank you."

And so that had happened. He gathered up his books and papers and dropped them in his briefcase. He had no idea what he was doing. Most of these things were props—he didn't need them, he felt that students expected books and papers on a teacher's desk, it looked better. Under the girl's scrutiny he glanced down at himself and saw, or half saw, that he was dressed no better than any of his students. The same green and red necktie he'd worn the other day, a shirt of narrow blue stripes, a jacket of dull plaid, trousers of dark gray, and his shoes were brown, a scuffed suede. But there was comfort in being so mismatched. There was a kind of innocence to it.

He took her to a restaurant for coffee. He asked her if she wanted anything else and she said no, nothing else. He himself had a piece of pie; he was suddenly hungry, violently hungry. The girl watched him eat. She was very slender, thin. Why did she live alone? Did she really live alone? He tried to keep the excitement in him under control. Here they were. Maureen with a peculiar birdlike poise, waiting. Her face slender, slightly angular, her skin translucent.

"Tell me more about yourself," he said. "Where do you work?"

"Nowhere special."

"Last week you were saying, about your father . . ."

"That was just to explain why I'm so stupid."

"But you're not stupid."

"I'm slow. I have trouble."

"You said that your father left home?"

Her face colored slightly. "Yes, he left us."

"Why?"

"To get married again."

"Did he just . . . leave?"

"He walked out. He got fed up and walked out—it happens all the time."

"And what about your family?"

"Oh, we got along. Ma never had any trouble getting along if she had to."

"Did you ever see your father again?"

"Oh, sure. He got married. I see them sometimes."

"You don't mind seeing them after what he did?"

"I don't hate him or anything, why should I mind seeing him?"

"You don't hate him?"

"No," Maureen said. She smiled slightly. "He fell in love with a woman and left my mother—he said he couldn't help it. He tried to explain it to my brother and me, how he'd fallen in love, but we already knew. We knew."

"You and your brother—you didn't hate him?"

"Why should we hate him?"

She crossed her arms shyly. The sleeves of her yellow sweater were pushed up and strained, the cheap wool pulled tight. It crossed his mind that a girl like this, with the same bright pink lipstick and the same sweater, was the kind of girl often found dead in some remote lonely place—there was something permanently doomed about the heart-shaped locket she wore on a thin chain around her neck. It had perhaps belonged to many girls and had been passed down to this one. He could imagine headlines on an inside page in the newspaper and he could imagine lurid pulp-photographs in a detective magazine: here is the shed in which the body was found, here are the "articles of clothing" found two hundred yards away . . .

Maureen was saying, "I love my father in spite of all that. He's all right. It was over between them, my father and my mother, and he was still young, and he just fell in love with someone else. I can see that. So I moved out on my own and started school. I had a hard time making myself go through with it. More than anything else I want to get through college and get a good job, you know, not like typing all my life, I want to make something of myself. I had to force myself to come into class that first night, but I did it. That was your class. It was very important in my life, it changed my life."

He was unable to follow all this but he heard the last part. "How did it change your life?"

"You. The way you teach."

"I . . . I'm glad to hear that. But you're not afraid any longer, are you?"

She made a fluttery gesture with her fingers, to show disgust. "Oh sure. I can't help it. I start thinking about how I'm going to fail, how everyone else knows more than I do, or I think about someone following me home. I live alone and I get afraid."

"I'm sorry to hear that."

"It's nothing I can help. I don't know how."

"Couldn't you live with someone? Another girl?"

"I don't know anyone that well."

She lowered her eyes as if she were conscious of his fascination. Was it that obvious?

She said, "I shouldn't tell you this because you might think I'm crazy. But sometimes I feel . . . I feel as if I could die, everything is so lonely. But I don't want anyone near me. I think that nothing will ever change, that my life will go on like this forever. I think that someone might be waiting in the hall for me, when I come home. It's crazy. I know better. But it seems to me that I can't keep going, unless there is the promise of something better, a new life. There has got to be more for me than this, but I've got to do it myself. I have got to make it happen myself."

He stared at her. "Many people feel that way."

"You don't feel that way, do you?" she said shyly.

"Sometimes."

"But aren't you married, don't you have a family?"

"That doesn't make any difference."

"It doesn't?"

"I don't know any answers."

"I'm sure you do."

"No. Not me. No answers," he said with a smile.

He drove her home. The girl said nervously, not sitting back against the seat, "You don't think it's wrong, driving me home like this?"

"Wrong, why?"

"If the other students found out?"

"They're not going to find out."

She looked over at him. He made his mouth stretch into a kindly, reassuring smile, but he was very agitated.

They parked in front of her apartment building. It was hardly more than a large house. Unpromising, a little shabby. What he had imagined for her. "Would you like me to see you upstairs?" he said. He was afraid she would open the door suddenly and leave.

"You don't have to."

"I want to."

"I'll be safe enough."

"Do you go out with anyone in particular? Any man?"

"No."

"Why not?"

"There's no one I like. No one I know."

"No one?"

"I haven't gone out with anyone, like that, since I was sixteen years old. Do you believe me?"

She looked at him sideways; it might have been that she had revealed something bizarre. He did not understand. "I . . . I believe you. But why not?"

"I'm afraid."

"Of what?"

"Of men."

He felt oddly touched by this. He could not quite understand. "But don't you want to get married?"

"No."

"Why not?"

"I just don't."

"But is something . . . wrong? What's wrong?"

"Sometimes I think I would like to be like other people; I would like to see men sometimes, go out places, whatever people do, but then I can't go through with it. I'm afraid of being too close to people, I don't want to get hurt."

"Why would anyone want to hurt you?"

"But people hurt you. It happens. It happens," she said, glancing at him.

"It's so strange of you to be afraid. Don't be afraid!" He spoke nervously and jestingly, as if teasing her. She stared at him in silence. He leaned over and rubbed her cold hands. The action took no preparation, no special nerve. Between the two of them there arose a sudden agitation, a breathlessness that was almost painful. He remembered first touching his wife, he remembered their wedding night, the birth of their first child: agitation, this kind of agitation. "Let me come upstairs," he said, begging, "I want to see where you live. I won't stay long."

"I—"

"Please? I won't hurt you."

She seemed very confused. He reached past her and opened the door. "All right?" he said.

"But it's—"

"All right. Just for a few minutes."

In the dingy foyer of the house there were two brief rows of mailboxes, exactly the same kind as in his apartment building. This pleased him. Cheap fake-brass mailboxes. They were nicked and dull, with openings in sunburst patterns to show if there was any mail inside. His eye jumped to *Wendall* and he saw that it was empty. Nothing.

Upstairs she fumbled for her key as if in a dream and he stood beside her, his brain in a commotion, thinking, *What is going to happen now?* It was funny and not funny. He might have smiled, but he did not smile—to be on your own like this, always on your own! A strain on the heart! The girl's shyness and the jumpy aggression of his own body led him on; he felt that he no longer had to think, to plan, everything was decided. The girl opened the door and led him inside. She switched on a light and glanced back at him anxiously, to see whether he thought this room was ugly. . .

"So this is where you live," he said.

He had meant his tone to be hearty but it sounded faint, tense. He sat down. The small room unfolded itself to him in blotches—a brown sofa, a chair, a cheap, shiny-topped table with a few plates and cups on it. She hadn't expected visitors. A breakfast table? Was this room a kitchen too? Yes, he saw a small refrigerator in a corner, and a sink . . . and this sofa obviously turned itself into a bed by strenuous magic . . . the room's walls shuddered and lost their shape before his eyes. He smelled perfume or food. He said again, numbly, "So this is where you live."

"Yes. I spend my nights here."

"And on the weekends?"

"I spend my weekends here."

"I can't believe that."

"Why can't you believe it?"

And now it seemed to him that a new man was coming to take his place, taking over. This might have been a scene out of a magazine story or a movie. A movie, yes. He was a detective searching for someone, and she was the girl who somehow stood between him and his goal, possessing crucial information, this frightened, lovely girl in a lemon-colored coat and pink lipstick. Or he was an ordinary man out to revenge himself upon someone, a murderer, and the girl was the murderer's girl, or perhaps his sister; that sounded better. She was chaste and frightened and could belong to no one. Or perhaps he was only pursuing the girl, himself, on his own, having trailed her remorselessly to this city, checking hotels, apartment buildings, bus stations, working a private fantastic logic, foreseeing everything. He had followed her to this particular house, which was nowhere. Metaphorically it stood for nowhere. Its essence was nowhere, nothing. It had no being. They were meeting now upon an X which was located at no particular spot in the universe, and they seemed in terror to be recognizing each other . . .

He reached clumsily for her hands and upset a coffee cup on the table.

"No, please, don't get up," she said quickly.

He sat back, alarmed.

In her coat, buttoned up in her coat, she sat down and stared at him. He forced himself to lean back against the sofa, to relax. He tried to make his face relax. But he felt the skin of his face prickling, gathering itself up into tiny terrifying dots. The girl's eyes on his face did this. His head and body felt very heavy and yet his mind raced along feverishly. He understood he was committing adultery and that he was daring everything, risking everything his life had accumulated. He was risking himself. He was moving toward an ultimate act, like murder, which could never be negated. It was an act to be done without any particular reference to his wife, whom he couldn't quite remember. It was an act to be done in this girl's arms, a stranger's arms, and if he did not stop he would be inextricably bound up with her, his life with hers, a stranger's life. His mouth had gone dry. He stared at the girl's pale face and down the length of her coat to her slim legs—stockings made her legs shine slightly, appealingly—and to her narrow black shoes. He saw a faint waterline on those shoes. He was moved by this, by her silence and her sorrow and her beauty, which was turned toward him and yet turned away from him, open and shy at the same time, wondering as he was wondering, baffled. She had fixed her stare upon him as if she had hypnotized herself with fear.

After some minutes he said hoarsely, "Tell me about yourself. Please."

She said nothing.

"You don't like men?"

"I . . . I can't talk about it, I don't know how to talk about it."

"Please tell me. Talk to me."

"I'm afraid."

"Of what?"

"What can I say? I'm not intelligent, I can't explain myself like you and the people you know. I'm afraid of life, of how confused it is, I'm afraid . . . of Detroit but also of leaving

Detroit because I don't know anything else. My Uncle Brock
was dying in the hospital, we all thought. He looked bad.
He lost fifty pounds maybe, and looked very bad, and we
thought he was dying, but something happened and he walked
out—one day he got out of bed and got some clothes and
left the hospital, by himself; he walked out . . . and . . .
and nobody knows where he went, he just walked out. The
nurses and the doctor and everybody were surprised, he just
. . . just walked out when he should have been dying. I guess
he got fed up with the hospital. But I can't do that. I don't
know how. How could I leave Detroit? My Uncle Brock was
dying but he changed his mind and walked out of the hospital, just walked out! How did he do that? I want to know
how he did that, how it happened that he woke up and said
to himself that he would leave, that he'd get his clothes and
walk down to the elevator and escape, just like that, and not
even tell anyone where he was going. Even my mother, he
didn't tell her, he didn't tell anybody. He's gone. But how
can you do that? What I wanted all my life was to be one
person, a success of a person, something firm and fixed,"
Maureen said slowly. "Not mixed up with dreams. Not just
junk. My mother is like that—she seems wide awake, she's
always going somewhere and she's always ready for a laugh,
but really her life is all asleep. My Aunt Connie's life too.
All their friends, men and women both, they're all asleep but
I can't explain it. My father and my stepfather too, all asleep,
men who are asleep. I want to be Maureen Wendall but I
want it to mean something. I want to be awake. But at the
worst times I know that what seems to me to be myself, a
certain person, isn't any person at all but a confusion of
things . . . what I can remember, what I'm seeing, what I'm
thinking. I can't control it. Everything is seething and boiling
and I'm afraid of it."

He stared at her, amazed as if physically struck. She spoke
slowly and yet her eyes were heavy with an almost sepulchral
passion, a drugged, occult look. He had never heard anyone
speak like this in his life. He wanted to reject her words,
reject that heavy, drowning, intense look, but he only stared
at her, unable to speak. This was the insanity he had feared
in her but also the insanity he had been drawn to; and yet
it was not insanity, not really. He understood her words as
they passed through him, easily.

"I don't want you to think that I'm crazy but I can't help
it," she said calmly, watching him. "I want to tell you. Some-

times I sit by that window there and look at the sun. I watch it go down. It seems to take a long time but every day it happens, it gets over and done with, that's that. It can't come back again. I have a lot of time to watch the sun go down. I have time to read and I keep reading, books from the library, things you mention in class. I'm looking for something in them so I keep reading. A person who lives alone has a lot of time. It has to be filled. So I look out the window. I keep waiting to see something there, in the way the light changes, I want to see some . . . some law."

"What?"

"A law. Something that will come back again and again, that I can understand."

He nodded quickly, helplessly.

"Now maybe you should leave," she said. She passed her hand before her face, as if his stare alarmed her.

"Leave? Should I? Should I go home now?" he said.

"Shouldn't you go home?"

He got to his feet. It seemed to him that he was passing by a scene of terrible mystery without quite seeing the mystery, without being able to touch it.

He came to her and embraced her. Breathing heavily, helplessly, he gripped her shoulders and bent over her. She seemed so small to him, a child. Excited, agitated, he pulled her to her feet.

"No, please don't . . . no," she cried.

"Don't make me leave," he said.

"Unless you love me, don't . . . I can't stand it . . ."

He let go of her.

"You should leave," she said. "Please. Unless you love me, you should go home. Please don't hurt me."

"I'm sorry," he said. He stumbled backward, reaching for the knob of the door. Where was the door? His senses rushed backward and forward, trying to direct him. He could not remember how this had happened, where he was, how he had come to feel so violently propelled toward this girl. The sensation in him was turbulent and heavy at once, dragging him toward her. He did not move. "Should I really leave? Do you want me to leave?"

She put her hands to her face.

"I don't want to leave you here alone," he said.

She said nothing.

"Why should I leave you?" he said wildly. "Don't make me leave!"

Maureen turned from him. He could see that she was frightened, exactly like a girl in a detective story, like a girl in the most common of dreams. But she said shrilly, "You're going to hurt me! If you don't love me you'll hurt me! How can I stand it? I've been alone too much! I've been afraid too much, and now you, you make me afraid, you're like the rest of them, how can I trust you, what if you hurt me, what if I can't make myself get up to work in the morning because I feel so broken down, a wreck, what if you do that to me—what then? What will I have left? I haven't been near a man for ten years! That's ten years! It all happened in another life, I can't even remember! If you come near me you'll begin it all again and I—I'm not strong enough, I can't take it. When you suffer the way I did you don't learn anything from it, it doesn't teach you anything or make you a better person, it just breaks you down—why do you want to hurt me?"

"I don't want to hurt you," he said.

"You want to hurt me!"

"I want to love you . . ."

She did not turn to him. He came to her in silence; he put his arms around her and clutched at her. *So now what is going to happen?* he thought. He was terribly afraid. But he could not stop, and the girl did not stop him, and his fear did no good, the high ringing beat of her heart did no good, warning him off, drawing him to her.

4

In late May, Maureen went to see her mother. Loretta was sitting with a friend; the television set was on. The friend, Bridget, had a bright, curious smile for Maureen.

"Well, if it isn't the stranger," Loretta said. "What are you doing? What's new?"

Maureen sat on the edge of her mother's chair and looked mechanically at the television screen. "A few things," she said.

"You're looking good, Maureen," said Bridget.

"Thank you."

On the television screen was a jumpy picture of a crowd of people blocked off occasionally by a line of police. The police were holding the people back.

"What's that?" Maureen said.

"Oh, some sons-of-bitches making trouble," said Loretta, "picketing against the war."

"Twenty years ago they'd all been put in jail," said Bridget.

"They'd of been *hung*," said Loretta angrily.

"Is that what it is?" Maureen said, looking at the screen. "I thought I saw a priest there."

"Honey, what's wrong with you? You walk in here and sit down and don't explain nothing—it's been how many weeks since I saw you, three or four? You're looking very nice. Is everything okay with you? How's your job?"

"Okay."

"What's your opinion on the war, Reeny?" Bridget said.

"People like this shouldn't make trouble. Marching around like that, it makes things confused," Maureen said slowly.

"That's exactly right, they shouldn't make trouble. We got enough trouble," Bridget said.

"I don't like to see things confused," Maureen said. She felt sluggish, yet a grave certitude gave her energy; she knew that she was right.

"Look at that kid," Loretta said, laughing. "Is that a boy? With all that hair? If that was my kid I'd sit him down and get the scissors after him. Jesus!"

"They certainly are funny-looking," Bridget said.

The news switched to a man sitting at a desk.

"Oh, the hell with that, turn it off. I saw this all before at noon," Loretta said.

Maureen leaned over and turned off the set.

"So what is your own personal news, kid? You're not in trouble?"

"No," Maureen said, making a face.

"Then what?"

"Maybe I just came over for a talk," she said. "Why not? You don't need to look at me so strange."

"Sure, talk to me. Say something."

"How's Randolph?"

"Sprained his ankle."

"When was this?"

"Couple of weeks ago. Goddam thing won't heal. He keeps running around on it. And Bridget here, she got a real bad deal, her husband's back out and hanging around the neighborhood."

"Oh," Maureen said. She looked politely at her mother's

friend, a woman of about fifty, heavy-set and pleasant. "How did that turn out?"

"Lousy. They put him on some special program, Jesus Christ," Bridget said, rolling her eyes, "acting like he's fixed up fine and not nuts. They said he could come back on probation or something, whatever they call it, and I told off the supervisor and said that he was crazy and couldn't be trusted and if he started drinking there'd be hell to pay. I told her, 'Am I supposed to hide out from him the rest of my life?' She said they found a job for him. So he's out, hanging around. I can't figure when he works or if he got fired already or quit. He told somebody he was going to cut my throat. That's how it is at my house. And my mother-in-law, she's been over too. Must be eighty years old and sharp as hell. You got to put your purse in a safe place when *she* drops in."

"No kidding, is she still coming around? How is she?" Loretta said.

"I guess okay. She keeps going."

"Howard's mother, she was a great old girl. Wasn't she, Reeny? Big and strong and really knew her mind. She wouldn't take no backtalk from anybody."

"Yeah, but this one don't talk, herself. She just sort of sits there and looks at you. So that's how it is at my place, Reeny. What about you, how's your job?"

"I'm quitting."

"Why?"

"I'm going to get married."

Everyone was silent. Then Loretta shrieked, "What! My God, Reeny! Married! Are you kidding?"

"No."

"But who is it?"

"The man who teaches me at night school."

"Jesus, a college teacher? Are you kidding?"

Maureen tore her eyes away from the blank television screen. She looked down at her mother's grimy bare feet and Bridget's large, comfortable feet in Indian moccasins. "Why do you keep saying that? Is it such a surprise that anyone would want to marry me?"

"You're really getting married?"

"Yes."

"Honey, you're a beautiful girl, it's no surprise. But I . . . I thought you didn't hang around with anybody. You never told me one word!"

"This is the first one, the first man."

"What is he like?"

"He's very nice, he's intelligent, he loves me very much and wants to marry me."

"Is he Catholic?"

"Yes, Catholic."

Loretta laughed with surprise. She threw her arms around Maureen. "God, I never expected this! Jesus! Never told me one word and here you are going out with a teacher, a college teacher! I always sort of thought you didn't want to get married, you had your own reasons or something—"

"I thought so too," said Bridget happily.

"But I'm real happy, it's real good news, only why such a secret? Why didn't you bring him around here or something?"

"I don't know."

"Bring him over for supper on Sunday then! Okay?"

"I don't know."

"On Sunday I'll fix up something real nice, you bring him over. Just the three of us. We can get acquainted. My God, what a surprise!"

"What nationality is he?" said Bridget.

"Nothing. American."

"Sure he ain't a Polack?" Loretta said, nudging Maureen.

"Yes."

"So what's wrong with him then?" Loretta said. "What's the matter?"

"He's married."

Loretta got to her feet. Still smiling, still surprised, she stared down at Maureen and could not seem to understand. "Married?"

Maureen nodded.

Loretta stared. Then suddenly she slapped Maureen's face.

"Ma!" cried Maureen.

"A married man—you and a married man!"

"Honey, let her alone," said Bridget, jumping up. "Why do you want to make trouble? Let her alone—"

"She's a whore! A little whore!"

"You shouldn't say that, how do you know what's what?"

"Are you a whore or not, Reeny?" Loretta said. Maureen sat with her hand to her cheek, trying not to cry. Loretta spoke with a curious irony, heavy and sour and yet a little affectionate.

"Are you a whore or not?" said Loretta.

"I talked with his wife the other day. She came over."
Maureen began to cry, soundlessly. Her expression was composed, as if she were still in the presence of that woman.
She kept darting little glances up at her mother as she spoke.
"She told me to leave him alone, that he couldn't get a divorce
and marry me and so I should leave him alone, and she
started crying and saying things to me about the children,
and I could see . . . I could see that he did maybe love her
at one time but now he loved me more, he couldn't help
it and I couldn't. So she started screaming at me, a nice
woman like that, ready to call me names she'd been thinking
up all along. So I explained to her that I was going to marry
him and that she could go to hell, what if she is educated
or not, what if she has three kids that are his and had two
miscarriages, I'd have kids for him too and I wasn't going
to be talked out of it! I heard myself saying all these things,
and I was surprised, but it was all true—she said things to
me that must have been a surprise to her—and it ended with
me saying that I would never give him up, never, that I loved
him and that was that, I was in love with him, I was going
to marry him, and she could do anything she wanted but
she couldn't change that."

Loretta stared. "Jesus, you said all that? You? To his
wife?"

"Right to her face."

"My sweet little Maureen?" Loretta said, ironic and surprised.

"I found the words for it. They came from somewhere."

They paused.

Loretta sat down again, slowly. She expelled her breath
and sat at attention, her gaze bright and ironic on Maureen.

"Well, it sounds like you did what you had to do, honey,"
Bridget said.

"So . . . you're getting married to another woman's husband?"

"Yes."

"And you knew he was married all along? Did you?"

"Yes."

"Right from the beginning?"

"Yes."

"But you didn't let it stop you, huh?"

"No."

"When's the wedding?"

"When the divorce is final."

"How do you like that," Loretta said waggishly to Bridget, *"when the divorce is final!* Talking like that, eh? I should drag you down to see Father Burney, see what his opinion is. *When the divorce is final!"*

"These modern things are very complicated," said Bridget.

"No, she's a whore, it's nothing modern but she's just a whore. She set out to be one and she succeeded," Loretta said. She clapped her hands and then rubbed them energetically. "So. So you're all set. *When the divorce is final . . .* and how many kids do they have, did you say three?"

"Yes, three."

"What about them?"

"How do I know what about them?"

"They stay with the mother, eh? He pays child support?"

"Yes."

"Aren't you going to mind that? Child support and alimony?"

"No."

"So you got it all sewed up. How'd you do it?"

Maureen wiped her tears away. She said, "There's nothing more for us to talk about tonight. I just wanted to tell you this."

"But you don't think you're a whore?"

"Not now."

"What's that supposed to mean, not now? You a smart-aleck too?"

Maureen looked shyly at her mother. She was a little afraid of what she might see, but Loretta's face was ruddy, indignant, and at the same time reassuring—there was a bond between them, after all. Maureen stood. "Well, thank you," she said.

"Thank you for what? You being a smart-aleck again?"

"I never was a smart-aleck. That was someone else, Betty or Jules," Maureen said.

"Jesus, don't mention *them!"*

"But it was never me. Not me, not Maureen. I was someone different."

Loretta made a snorting noise. Bridget, embarrassed, walked with Maureen to the stairs. "You're a real nice girl, real pretty," she said, not understanding Loretta's anger and embarrassed by it. "Don't you worry about your mother. She'll come around. You sort of surprised her, that's all. She don't want you to make any mistakes, like she did herself.

You understand? But she loves you a lot, you understand? Right?"

"I know it," said Maureen. "I love her too."

5

One afternoon in June of 1967 a young man caught sight of himself in the window of an empty store—he thought for a moment that he was seeing a stranger, possibly an enemy, then he recognized himself. He passed on slowly. He always walked slowly. Where he had come from was a room in a brick building a block away, but the room and the building had passed out of his mind already; where he was heading was a movie house out on Woodward, which changed its bill every Wednesday, yet the movie house had not yet entered his mind. Everything was in a pleasant, fluid suspension. On the corner was a Revco Discount Drugstore, a small dark grocery store . . . some Negro kids crossed the street in front of him, in a noisy flock . . . two white girls with long hair sidled toward him . . . they wore slacks. He let his vision go vague and the girls slipped out of focus as if teasing him, their long hair bright in the sunshine and their hands, gesturing, precise in some melodious language, about to tell him some secret, meant to attract him. But he could not bring them back into focus. He passed by them, indifferent. At the very moment at which his eyes should have moved up onto their faces, taking them up and considering them, showing some agile knowledge, he had forgotten them and passed on.

The pavement was hot. Only mid-June and already the air had a used-up, flat taste to it. So he had survived for another summer, he would live through another summer! Last fall he had nearly died, carted into a hospital's emergency ward, blood leaking out of him, but he hadn't died, he had survived for another summer. He thought of the summer as interminable, though it had only begun. Had it only begun? He could not truly remember any other summer and yet this one seemed endless. The energy of a boy on a motorcycle, speeding past, made Jules flinch—noise, energy, the flash of light on chrome! He had never been that young.

For many months he had inhabited a body . . . sewed up, plugged up, maybe stuffed with bloody cotton pads. They had gotten him ready for use again. But gratitude? Did he have to feel gratitude? His mind went dim. He'd outlived himself, in a body. He had become a weight, Jules, an object, throwing a shadow uncertainly before itself but taking up no room . . . not much room, anyway. Before him was an old man or maybe an old woman . . . trousers, gray-haired, shaggy, shabby, sleepwalking and throwing a shadow onto the pavement. He fixed his gaze upon this shape. Its legs moved as if fifty or sixty years of practice had made it all easy, a shape with a certain weight and a certain displacement of water, should it ever tumble into water. Walking was a habit . . . . living a habit, mechanical. Shapes, weights! Jules felt them in the very balls of his eyes, irritants. A pressure upon the eyes like the pressure of that big cold machine, wheeled right up to the eyes to take a reading.

What had those doctors read, looking into Jules's brain through his bloody eyes?

Every day he passed the Discount Drugstore. He remembered that now. The store had a fake bright front, very clean and shiny. Inside was a small crowd, Negroes and whites. And every day he headed either to the left, which took him by the smelly Greek grocery store and the three stores in a burned-out block, one of them evidently a laundry, what had been a laundry; or he strolled over toward the right, which took him past big apartment buildings where students from Wayne State University lived, crowded and noisy, in the midst of a clutter of garbage cans and cardboard boxes that the city workers didn't bother to collect. And he passed Crater's Pub, where students hung out, on the fringes of student life and nearly in his own kind of life, nearly on the fringe of living itself. A few other burned-out buildings, mysteries. Posters: VOTE FOR . . . VOTE FOR . . . VOTE . . . *Vote and change your life,* Jules thought. One of the men running for office had been defaced, unfaced. His eyes inked out. Teeth inked out. The sky would look to him as if he were staring out through a piece of rotten fruit. Some Negro boys were fooling around . . . lime and grape colors . . . one of them was shuffling, snapping his fingers, singing in a breathy, anxious voice . . .

> "Tell me where you're going
> Ain't I got a right to know . . ."

A mild thought for Jules: nobody asked where he was going, nobody had a right to know or any interest.

He himself was a man inside a piece of rotten fruit—it

kept getting in his mouth. The sky had a melony, overdone, orange-brown cast, a rotten cast to it, unmistakably. The Negro boy's voice sounded soft, rotten, peeling, decaying, breathy and effeminate. Better not to listen. Jules walked along. He was like the invisible child he had tried to imagine himself years ago. But now he had become truly invisible. In his slightly soiled, worn clothes he had nothing for anyone to envy; his unhurried but unlazy walk, with a slight drag to the heel, spoke of a certain distraction; maybe he was on drugs and might be dangerous—that kept people away, drew only the eyes of reckless girls to him. His face was neither moronic nor shrewd, holding nothing, promising nothing, his eyes fixed and dark and without light. Impressions flowed through him. Nothing caught hold. He was safe from his own past, kicked free of his own past like his uncle walking out of the hospital, disappearing. Jules had disappeared too.

To have an emptiness in the midst of this city—to keep it to himself, but without selfishness—that had become Jules's desire. It would be nice to walk out like this every day for the rest of his life, unhurried but not truly lazy, with a certain destination. His feet were drawn along. Promise of some dark movie house and a few hours of movies. Buying food afterward at the Food Fair, or not buying food. Eating or not eating. If he went into the store he would stroll along as if passing through a park, slowly along the aisles, seeing neat wrapped packages of food and mountains of cans, cans in their colorful jackets: it pleased him to know that he wanted nothing. At the front of the store, lounging against the gritty counter, there'd be a Negro policeman, sharing with Jules a certain mordant, agreeable calm. The policeman's pistol would be holstered and the holster snapped shut. The policeman, a young man with a moustache, would glance at Jules as he glanced at all men who wander about alone, but some confidence in Jules's step would reassure him. Down here white men were more suspect than Negroes. What were they doing down here? Down here? Had they chosen to live *down here?*

Jules crossed the street. A broken-down building, housing the Students' Revolt Against the War in Vietnam. Angry white lettering. Out front, a few kids loitering. Were they part of the Students' Revolt or just hanging around? Their eyes were glassy and curious, moving hard onto Jules as if onto a mystery, then dismissing him. In their front room a few days ago one of their people had been killed, an organizer shot to death. An angry cab driver had run in and shot him in the chest. Dead. The cab driver told newspaper reporters that he had a son in Vietnam and was proud.

One of the girls called out something, maybe to Jules. Part of a song. These girls were always singing, drawling musically. Jules did not look around. Yes, he did look around. The girl was barefoot and he looked only at her foot—a red plastic ring on her little toe. She said something but he did not respond. He did not really hear her. Her voice floated musically upon the air but without weight; it did not seem to be a human voice. Only sound.

A sign nailed overhead: *Hey Friend Now Smile Upon Your Brother Let Me See You Love One Another Right Now!*

Police in a squad car nearby. Waiting. Jules tried not to look at them. He felt a certain pressure on his eyes from them, from their shapes . . . their weights. The letters in *Police* danced whitely in his eyes. Someone was looking at him. Jules could not resist; he turned and looked back—a bland cold look exchanged with a policeman, a wondering look. There was something massive and ponderous about the man's face, a thoughtfulness that made Jules uneasy. Balding, large. Or, rather, in the place where Jules might once have been uneasy, a dull bewilderment stirred; it was not quite an emotion. He smiled. The policeman did not respond. Another policeman, as if sensing danger, turned to watch Jules walk by. His back to them, he felt more vulnerable.

Halfway across the street he felt someone grip his arm. Not one of the policemen, though, someone else. A young man. "Hey, Jules, I thought that was you! Didn't you hear me calling you?" This face was grinning and excited. Too hearty. Jules was reluctant to stop but couldn't pull away. He said something. The two of them crossed the street together. The young man talked. Jules felt a dull anxiety. He didn't want people to call out *Jules!* Had he given out his name so freely? He felt a weight beside him, the weight of this young man whose name was Mort. Busy and charming, Mort, his hands zigzagging with talk.

"You walk in a daze or something, but you're not high!" He seized Jules playfully by the back of the neck. "You just don't answer to your name!"

Jules pushed him away. "I'm in a hurry."

"But . . . but I want to talk to you," Mort said, hurt. "We want to talk to you, some friends of mine, friends of Marcia's. I saw you on the street yesterday, heading up Cass, but then you disappeared. Did you go into a store or something?"

"I don't remember."

"Where are you in a hurry to?"

Jules said nothing.

"My friend," Mort said, leaning toward him frankly, "the fact is that you have nowhere to go, like me, and that's exactly what we all want to change—our not having anywhere to go. Oh, I don't mean love or anything because we're all in love, more or less. I think even you have a woman and are 'in love.' I mean instead something more permanent, something transcendent—"

"Don't touch me," said Jules.

"I'm sorry. I got carried away," Mort said. He was olive-skinned and sickly beneath his energy; he tried to smile at Jules. As they walked his swinging arm came close to Jule's arm. An itching. An irritant. The touch of other people, the sudden glimpse of teeth in smiles, slightly decaying, rotten . . .

Mort talked. He talked about the black population. The Afro Commune. Heckling, walking out of a rally on campus by the Students for Peace. The UUAP. What was the UUAP? Mort said, his voice level and serious, "It's almost sure to be this weekend. I heard it from Coleman himself, he's the president of the, you know, the UUAP, and when it comes we've got things ready, we've got certain plans, only I'm terrified things will get out of control and he doesn't seem to realize the extent of the . . . the possible damage. We can't seem to get organized. People come and go. After all, how much practice have any of us had? It scares them. What do we know about fighting in the streets?"

Jules looked at him.

"What's wrong?"

"What do you mean, fighting in the streets?"

"When the riot comes we're going to stop the city. But I worry all the time. I can't sleep at night—I take sleeping pills and they have no effect at all—I keep thinking, what if this gets out of our hands?"

"What riot?" said Jules.

"The riot is set for this weekend, we're almost certain. Saturday night. Unless it rains or something."

"A riot?"

"A riot—you know."

Jules laughed. "There isn't going to be any riot," he said. They were standing in front of an antique store, a junk store, and the quiet dusty furniture behind the dusty window showed how correct his words were. How could anything happen on this earth? How could anything begin to move? Everything was stationary, weighed down. Mort was an object of a certain weight. It had a face—yes, a face—of ordinary proportions, dull olivish skin, dissatisfied and excited, with a short-trimmed black beard that gave it an outline, a fixity. The street seemed to Jules very flat and open and yet nothing could move upon it without great effort.

"Jules, come with me and we can talk! I want so much to talk to you—and some friends of mine want to talk to you—where do you keep yourself? Marcia says you come around but she never knows when to expect you. Is she at work now?"

"Yes, at work."

"She's a wonderful woman! You're very lucky, but . . . I don't want to offend you—I'm always offending people with my big mouth. Come with me, Jules?"

Jules hesitated. Then he said, "Could I borrow twenty dollars?"

"Twenty? Why do you need so much?"

"Twenty dollars."

"But didn't I lend you fifty dollars the other week? Was that you or was that someone else?" He looked genuinely baffled, as if he could not remember.

"I don't remember," Jules said.

"Well, if you really need it. I cashed my check this morning, so I suppose . . ." Embarrassed, he took out his billfold and counted out twenty dollars for Jules.

Jules took it and wadded it and put it in his pocket. His own billfold had been missing for some time, probably stolen.

They walked along, Mort leading the way. "I admire you and I admire Marcia—not that I know either of you, certainly I don't know you—but I want us to come together, to have a dialogue, to help each other. All of us would like to help you. And I feel you would like to help us, that you know things we need to know. We've got to talk! Organize! Time is running out for the city, and if we don't take control other people will. The Afros are splintering off—they won't communicate except for their president, who's a very intelligent young man but emotional, and the rest of them are emotional also—we've got to get things settled, organized, assigned . . ."

Jules thought of Marcia. He visited her occasionally; it surprised him to hear their names mentioned together. Why had Mort mentioned their names together? Thinking of Marcia, he began to think of Faye . . . cold and silvery, a blond whose face he had seen back in April on the society page of the newspaper . . . Faye metamorphosed into someone's wife, of Bloomfield Hills . . . arriving at Meadowbrook Theater with her husband and another couple . . . she had ended up a face in a newspaper yet no less real than Marcia. There was something of Faye in Marcia, whom he wouldn't have time to know, some waspish, self-effacing, self-confident blondness, inexplicable.

Mort was speaking excitedly, his elbow bumping Jules's arm. "All hell is going to break loose!" he cried.

Heaviness. What could break loose out of this heaviness? The temperature was rising to ninety-five. Humidity high, dense. Such heaviness, such flat, baking, oppressive heaviness, as if the soul of the street itself were melting to vapor, losing all strength, disappearing. What was there to distinguish black from white in such a mist?

"Everything will crack, crack open! It needs to be cracked open and pitted—the pit spat out! Why should everything stay fixed? We're on a roller coaster and the car is rocking. A little wind is all we need. Jules—what's your last name incidentally? Did you ever mention it?"

"No."

"Jules, I want to get to know you, don't put me off. Look, I know I talk too much and I'm just an amateur, I'm a guy who hasn't been around, a lazy bastard, but I have hopes, I have dreams—for all of us, blacks and whites, the kids in Vietnam, the Vietnamese—I have these dreams, I can't sleep at night for thinking of what could happen if only we made it happen! I don't want to spend my whole life getting by. Money from a university, money from the government —getting by, getting along; I mean, I don't want to *think* about myself while everything around me is rotting, going to hell. I want to get rid of it all, like a snakeskin sloughed off. I really want to see this city burned down and built up again. Jesus, I can hardly wait!" He paused, breathing rapidly. "Jules, you never get high? You said before you never got high, eh?"

"Never."

"That's your trouble maybe. You never get free of yourself. Never take a flight, get a new view—the scenery changes as fast as you can snap your fingers! How can you live without getting free of yourself once in a while?"

"I'm always free," Jules said. His voice sounded hollow, echoing in something hollow. He had the idea again of inhabiting a giant, rotting fruit—breathing in the rot, his skin soft with it . . . a hollowness inside the decay, scooped out and brown.

While Mort talked the police cruiser passed but Mort did not notice. They entered a bar on Canfield. The smell of rot was closer, darker. Mort introduced Jules to several people, three men and a young woman. The woman slid over in the booth to make room for Jules. "What will you have, Jules? Beer? Have something, please, drink with us," Mort begged.

Jules shook his head. No. Nothing. Drinking upset him. Any loss of control, even an instant's loss of balance, upset him. It made him recall the sound of gunfire close to his head . . . an echo in his head. It made him recall falling to the ground. He said no, Mort sat down clumsily, abruptly. "You don't trust us! You won't drink with us because you don't trust us! Jules, I know we seem very different from you but we are all brothers of yours—"

Jules waved his hand at Mort, to silence him.

Mort laughed. "Well," he said to his friends, "he has a certain oppressed look. I don't mean beaten down or unhealthy or ugly or anything like that—in fact, I would say he is a handsome man as far as that goes—it isn't anything that simple, but he has the look of being permanently out of the sunlight, a depression baby—"

"Jesus, he isn't that old!" the woman said contemptuously. She wore slacks and a mannish shirt, round-shouldered yet not unattractive. Jules remembered that she was a teacher at Wayne. He had met her at someone's apartment. "I would say he isn't thirty-five yet. Are you thirty-five, Jules?"

"No, not yet."

"Then you aren't a depression baby."

"Not necessarily the *historical* depression," Mort said. "I mean another kind of depression. A permanent depression of the spirit."

The woman snorted. Jules lit a cigarette and began to concentrate on the taste of smoke inside him. Did it really go into his lungs, outlining his fleshy, bloody, weak lungs? The parts of his body could be outlined . . . X-rayed . . . photographed . . . ill-smelling. He could not be bothered connecting the parts together; let them breathe in unison, let them pulsate. Occasionally his body gave him pleasure, but the moment of pleasure did not last and its memory was mysterious. What was the pleasure of the body except a mystery? It could not even be photographed the way his heaving heart might be photographed. Once he had been a fountain, a glowing fountain, and sunshine had broken beautifully upon a polished floor . . . but now even the memory of that pleasure was a puzzle.

"This society obviously gave you a raw deal—we won't go into any details," Mort was saying brusquely, a little fearful of Jules's look, "but the rest of us . . . the rest of us have been, frankly, blessèd children of sunlight—"

"What bullshit! Speak for yourself!" someone said.

The memory of pleasure did no good. Memories of the body did no good, not being housed anywhere, not even in the flesh. The photographs of the parts of Jules's body, put together, would add up to a body but not to Jules. Better to sit in a dim, smelly bar, to pretend to listen to these people. Untidy, earnest people. Words animated them. Flesh strained away from their Adam's apples, these urgent men. Words seemed to be teasing them up from their seats, preparing them for battle.

"I'm serious about this! I am serious!" Mort exclaimed, his beard very black against his pale face, "I'm fed up with being stabbed in the back and I'm serious, may God strike me dead otherwise!"

"Shit, you just like to talk, all of you like to talk," a man said. Jules had met him before—he was a professor of something, maybe English. Dark and Jewish and irritable, dressed like a child in a soiled turtleneck shirt and blue jeans, he had a prematurely aged, lined, bitter face; his eyes were rabbity. "You sold yourself, Mort, so you try to disguise it with words! Talk, talk, talk! It's all shit!"

"Mort isn't to blame for you being fired," the woman said.

"Nobody is to blame for me being fired, I am a free agent and I choose to remain free of anyone's influence, thank you, but it may well be another person's fault that he is *not fired*, that he prepared his actions so carefully that no photographs even exist of him in the University's files—what about free will in that direction, what about that?"

"—and I don't approve," the woman went on, solidly, "of you giving all students in your courses A's—it might very well have been an act of principle, to destroy the grading system—"

"Of course!"

"But it might also have been for more personal reasons."

"Such as what?"

"Such as your attachment to . . . well. . . ."

"Your attachment to your boys!" Mort said. "All those boys you entertain in your apartment!"

A dark glow of a grin appeared on the man's face, and then disappeared.

"You're talking shit," he said coldly.

"We won't go into your motives. The hell with private life," Mort said. "And so please don't go shooting your mouth off about me, the rest of us, tenure or not—I haven't been given a contract yet and I could lose everything, as you know very well. What if they kick me out too? You know what a setback that would be. We've got to stay in here, stay in the place of power, not give up. Don't hang me up with your middle-class notion of honor, please; my friend, we can't afford honor. Yes, I'm sorry you were fired and we all did what we could, but they had you and they had you good, it couldn't be broken. Honor is too abstract! The hell with all honor, with talk—I'm as fed up with talk as you are. What we've got to do is get into this community, I mean really into it. We've got to get where people are living, where they're trying to live, in all this shit! We have got to learn how to hate, to *hate* with energy, and not how to talk, to prepare for the revolution in our guts, not in our heads—"

"By taking money from the government through the UAAP," one of the other men said, snickering.

"Could you get the job, you yourself?" Mort cried. "Could you get cleared for it?"

"Are you proud of getting cleared by the CIA?"

"Yes, I am proud, I am proud of getting cleared by the CIA because it means that *I* have not abandoned myself to impulse, to emotion, because *I* will remain in the seat of power where I can be something while *you* will be on the outside whining and complaining—"

"Please stop this. Please," said the woman, clutching her head.

"Where would the community be without that money? Where?" Mort cried. He pounded the table. "Money is money! A loyalty oath is the way to money, to ammunition and guns and leaflets—don't look at me with your wounded middle-class eyes, your Boy Scout's sense of honor betrayed, because I didn't allow myself to get broken the way you did—"

"Really, I mean it. Please stop," said the woman angrily.

"A lot of us took jobs with the poverty program—why not? I have a Ph.D. in sociology. I am eminently qualified to sell my brains, goddam it, and figure out a way to burn it all down—how much money do you think we're promised? Huh? I've been giving the money I got freely enough, you should know that—just stop picking on me!"

They were silent for a while. Then someone said, "Why is everything so slow?"

"Well, the black population has waited over a hundred years, patiently, like good people—or is it three hundred years?"

"We're all good at waiting. Too good."

"I keep seeing a figure in a story, I think it's a story of Poe's—a man goes through something terrible, some grotesque experience, I think he falls into a whirlpool or something, and out of the center of the whirlpool he sees a great white figure, a giant, all white—"

"So what?"

"That's how we must look to the blacks, like that. All mist."

"But that's mysticism, the blacks don't want to fall into *that;* what we call white is just the ego, the selfish, puking ego, and we've got to get rid of that—white and black people both. Black Power is just more power, we don't want power, we're fed up with people and power, power and people, as if the human soul couldn't operate without it—"

"The soul can maybe, but the body can't!"

"Mort, the trouble with you is that you *do not* listen! You have no sense of innuendo, of nuance. That degree in sociology cost you your soul—"

"The hell! The hell with mist and heaven and all of us lying down together, the hell with it!" Mort cried. "When the cops run for you, tell it to them, not to me! I don't want mist and I don't want crap about honor! I want action, I want money and guns, I want an organization where people show up *on time* and have a sense of responsibility and are not forever thinking about their goddam twerpy egos, their *egos,* their *egos!*"

Jules noticed a girl approaching them. In the first instant of seeing her something in him seemed to move, rising almost to a moan, but then he saw that she was no one, no one he knew—a girl of about twenty, dressed in the familiar slovenly style of the neighborhood, a shapeless dress and bare legs and sandals. But, like the rest of the students who played at being poor, she had good teeth; being poor stopped at teeth.

Mort got to his feet. "Vera, right here! My dove!" He seized her hand and clumsily introduced her to everyone. "Vera is my best student, my most promising student—sweetheart, sit down . . . sweetheart, let me buy you something! Did you move down here now? Where are you staying?"

"No, I'm still living at home."

"Where is that?"

"Out on the West Side, way out on Six Mile. I'm staying with someone down here for the weekend, a girl friend."

"You know the riot is scheduled for this weekend?"

"I *heard* that! I was so excited I came right out to look for you!"

She sat pertly across from Jules. Her face was pretty, moist-looking, rather childish and daring. Her hair swung about her face. She smiled a wide smile around at everyone, feeling both welcome and unwelcome, pleased with herself. "So what are you going to do? What are your plans?" she said.

"We haven't organized our plans yet," said Mort.

"Is it going to be secret?"

"Honey, not from you—you're one of us."

Mort rubbed his hands together in excitement. He was shorter than Jules, with a solid, round face, busy lips, an air of robust nervousness that was endearing. Jules closed his eyes slightly and Mort became a blur, talking into the air. Beside him the girl with the long swinging hair became a blur, listening. Jules tried to concentrate upon her. Through the voices clammering around him he could occasionally hear her voice, a throaty, self-conscious voice . . . she sounded like someone at a costume party, in disguise, embarrassed and pleased with her disguise . . . what did he care? While something inside him was running down he sat leaning slightly forward in his chair, trying to interest himself in her. Lust was delicate in him, delicate as the wings of butterflies. It needed air, sunlight, a gracious wind; it could not rise through the crust of ordinary air.

He sensed her as an object. Slight, soft. A delicate object with a delicate weight. Its voice was low. Its skin was moist.

Jules's hair had grown long and thick, and he could imagine the fingers of that childish hand stroking his hair, the way other fingers had stroked his hair, sometimes idly and sometimes in passion . . . Someone handed her a glass of beer; the fingers closed around it. Jules opened his eyes and looked at them.

"Yes, I believe it will draw him here. I believe he will make a special trip, heavily guarded, by special airplane, yes, I believe that, I have definite reasons for believing that!" Mort said, breathing heavily. "The President himself, that filthy motherfucking son-of-a-bitch, that fascist bastard, and I would be willing—I mean this—I would be willing to trade my life for his, as simple as that, if it wouldn't just be a waste, if I could stand not to see how history turns out—"

"A bullet. One bullet," someone said faintly.

"One goddam bullet!"

"They can't guard them that heavily. Not all the time. But what if he doesn't come?"

"I don't think that bastard would come."

"Johnson? He won't come! Not for any riot, not even for a war!"

"I have reason to believe he will come—for votes! Politics! To make the Governor look like an ass!"

"How could he make Romney look worse?"

"Just who's going to shoot him?"

"You think you're a good shot, like Oswald? You think you could pull it off, a direct hit, and not get caught?"

"Maybe not me, maybe not me," Mort said in a furious, low voice, "but it could be that I have some young friends who could."

"And sacrifice themselves?"

"Why not?"

"Look, we could have alternate plans, five or six plans. We could have a lot of buildings ready, people on the roofs, on the top floors, all ready with guns. Listen, I can get hold of rifles at any time," the other man said, warming. "I'm not kidding, I've got contacts that make yours look like shit—which is not to say that I could handle a rifle myself but I could learn, and some of them have night scopes on them, a telescopic sight that can see in the dark."

"Jesus, do they have things like that? Is that possible?"

"I think it's possible."

"No, really, is it possible?"

"Isn't it—?"

"I could handle a rifle myself! I want to do it!" the girl cried. In her excitement she almost upset her glass of beer. Jules caught it. "I don't mind what happens to me—I'm fed up at home! Listen, I'd be willing to burn myself up in front of that bastard, like a Vietnamese nun, or I'd be willing to dose him with gasoline myself and light him—it would be on television and in all the papers!"

"But if we kill him—assuming that can be done—if we kill him," the other woman said sourly, "how can we focus our meaning? Look at Oswald—that was really nothing! He had nothing to say! Shot down Kennedy—and by the way Kennedy deserved to be shot, but much earlier—shot him down and had nothing but a vacuum surrounding that act, one of the most heroic acts of the twentieth century, but nothing to say! A waste! Nothing to say!"

"Would it be for Vietnam or for the black revolution?"

"Vietnam is more important."

"How could we let him know why he was dying? Wouldn't it be better to let him know, to explain?"

"We could write a letter to . . . to the newspaper afterward," Mort said. "We could mail the letter before the assassination, so everyone would know it was legitimate, a legitimate letter . . . and . . . and state that it was a formal protest against the Vietnam situation."

"The hell with Vietnam, what about right here? I mean Detroit! Right here, Detroit, this crap-pile, it stinks to the sky, what about blowing up Detroit? You think killing one son-of-a-bitch is equal to burning down a great city? Humphrey would just take office—look at him! that jerk! Then you'd have to kill him, and who's left? Jesus, I don't even know—Everett Dirksen? Then what?"

"I don't think it's necessarily Everett Dirksen—"

"I'd like to kill *him*."

"I'd like to kill any of them! It would be so easy, once it was set up. I wonder why more people don't try it! Did you know that assassination as a political method was revered in the Middle East, in Biblical times? Sure! A ruler ruled for life and the only way to get rid of him was to kill him. So they were all killed off."

"Then who took over?"

"Someone else."

"But we don't want to kill too many people," Mort said, sweating, but very pleased. "Look, you don't want this to get banal! I have a terrific fear of banality—it's my melodramatic temperament—we must keep death sacred, very terrible! Then if Johnson is killed it will mean something!"

"How can death be sacred? Talk about being middle class!" the woman said angrily. "Haven't you been reading the papers? Thousands of people are dying over there, thousands of *people!* Bombs, napalm, burning gasoline—flaming gasoline, it runs along in a stream, and if peasants are hiding in a ditch it runs into the ditch like water, flaming water, and burns them up alive! How can you say death is sacred? The death of a bastard like Johnson *sacred?* He should be put through a meat-grinder and fed to hogs! He should be plowed under and used for fertilizer!"

"Don't talk so loud, please—"

"I don't give a damn who hears me!"

"But if someone is listening—"

"Who's listening, there's just us in here!"

"Let's return to the initial problem. Let's not get excited. The problem is assassination—a political method that is respectable or not? Is it?"

"Yes."

"Yes, along with burning everything down."

"I don't want my books burned down!"

"I don't mind my books being burned! I'll give them up!"

"But if Johnson doesn't come, what then?"

"Then Romney. Kill the Governor of the state."

"Won't that make him a martyr?"

"So what?"

"What would he be a martyr for?"

"I don't think that Romney is significant enough to kill. Listen. Well, yes, he is worth killing, speaking in general political terms . . . as a way of breaking down the existing structure . . . and though I dislike him I think—"

"I'd rather kill Cavanaugh actually."

"Why?"

"Because he's more immediate, he's the Mayor."

"But you're working for him!"

"I'm taking his money. Actually I despise him. He has some good ideas but he doesn't move fast enough. None of them moves fast enough to keep up with history—"

"He's gotten too fat. It's a bad image."

"Well, we can always kill *him*. He'll be in the city for a while."

"But if Johnson doesn't come—and I doubt that that bastard is stupid enough to come here, after a riot, even for votes—I don't think we should bother with Romney, that's just flattering the Republicans. I think we should kill someone significant like Keast—"

Everyone laughed.

"Keast! Kill Keast! Why, nobody's ever heard of him! Who gives a damn about the president of Wayne State? My God!"

"He has more significance than people know—he's a symbol. And the black revolution and the youth revolution should converge on the university, should get together on the campus. The campus will be the battlefield, not the slums—"

"You think a university is that significant? A university president in comparison with a senator?"

"Which senator?"

"After the riot they'll both come, everyone will get into the act, certainly Hart will show up—"

"He's a good man."

"Shit! There are no good men in government. It all has to be destroyed!"

"But do you think Hart is important enough nationally?"

"Who's heard of him outside Michigan?"

"What about a Negro leader, what about King?"

"Yes, he might show up if the riot is bad."

"If King was shot—"

"King is a half-assed bastard, he's betrayed every Negro in the country, he deserves to be shot," Mort said angrily. "Actually, the kids in the community—the Canfield Babes we were working with, that gang—they'd all love to be in on shooting King. They don't give a damn about Johnson or even know who he is—"

"But what has that got to do with Vietnam? King is against Vietnam."

"We could change the message from Vietnam to just the race issue, or to doing away with existing leaders—"

"Why Martin Luther King?"

"What have you got against him? Isn't he as important as Johnson? Just because he's a black, isn't he important? It would be very dramatic, killing him, and it would be blamed on the right wing."

"Then we don't control the assassination! We don't give it its meaning!"

"Yes, we control it, but very cleverly."

"The message will be lost!"

"It will not be lost! We'll control it, we'll write a letter!"

"Blaming it on the right wing? On the National Rifle Association?"

"But it would be more logical to kill Stokely Carmichael if you wanted to blame it on the other side," someone said impatiently. "Jesus, you don't know what you're talking about! Everyone knows that King is working for the right wing, why the hell would *they* shoot him? Talk, talk, talk! Carmichael is the man—he's a saint—he won't be afraid to show up here, and his death would be worth something!"

"But, excuse me, to go from Johnson to Carmichael—I mean, haven't we sort of gone down? I mean, not morally, but in terms of publicity? Frankly, nobody will give a damn about Carmichael except the people who are already prepared to burn this country down."

"What's wrong with that?"

"The headlines will look wrong, won't they? Or will it be better? It would show the other nations how racist America is, like when the CIA killed Malcolm X."

"The other nations know all that and don't give a damn! Why should they? They're being paid off!"

"I have an idea. We could kill them all, everyone we mentioned! We could kill all the bastards who come to Detroit to make speeches! Why not? It would teach them to respect a riot, to stay the hell out of a riot area—"

"For a dramatic effect—"

"No, it would not be for a dramatic effect, it would have the opposite effect! You don't have any sense of balance! Let's say that Robert Kennedy shows up here and we shoot him, and also the others—who do you think would get the headlines? Him and Johnson! The others would only go on the inside pages. It would just be a waste! You're talking bullshit! I wish you people had a slight sense of theater, of history!"

"This is giving me a headache," Mort said. "The way you throw things around! I supply the money, I've got the know-how, I've got the kids anxious to pull some triggers, but you won't let me organize it! You fight me, you're always picking on me!"

"Nobody is picking on you, Mort," the woman said.

"Jesus, this depresses me. Sometimes I'm up, now I'm down; now I soar, now I'm plunging; poor Mort is plunged to the very bottom of the sea. I'm lost in some miserable icy channel up by the North Pole, the stars are very small.

How can I find my way back to earth? Jules, have you been listening to all this crap?"

Jules had just noticed the *Bhagavad Gita*, in paperback, under someone's restless elbow.

"What is your opinion, Jules?"

"I don't have any."

"Who should we kill, Jules? If you had your finger on the trigger, who would you kill?"

"Nobody."

"Why not?"

"Why? Why kill anybody? People die anyway, sooner or later," Jules said. He looked at the colorful cover of that book, remembering something urgent about it . . . he must have wanted to read it at one time. "It wouldn't change anything."

"Wouldn't change anything! What? Everything can change!" Mort said. "Everything can be changed with the right people in charge! You should meet the kids in this gang of mine—we're trying to find jobs for them supposedly—kids who've been working all their lives running numbers and pimping, pimping at the age of ten, handling dope—trying to find jobs for *them!* This one kid, his life has been so lousy, somebody in his family fed him ground glass when he was four years old, and he grew up to be thirteen and a first-class little pimp—he just bought his mother a fur coat. You think their lives shouldn't be changed? You think everything should continue the way it has been for centuries?"

"He sounds like a goddam Catholic or something, this Jules of yours," said the woman, shaking her head at Mort. "The futility of history—what crap! The gears of history must be oiled with blood or nothing will move. History isn't a natural sequence, it's made by man. We create it. Man does and undoes everything. I could change a small part of human history by just tossing a bomb into someone's window, believe me. According to Fanon—"

The girl across the table from Jules giggled suddenly, covering her face.

"What are you laughing at?" said the woman. "What's so funny?"

She peeked out through her fingers. "I'm afraid."

"Oh, Christ!"

Everyone began talking at once. Mort pounded the table. His forehead was greasy with sweat, so was his nose, his lips worked busily and hungrily . . . the woman next to Jules

smelled strongly of perspiration, in her excitement very female, husky and female . . . the other men pulled at their
chins, their lips, their noses, as if hating their faces, nervous
and irritated and impatient, bewildered, while Jules caught
the girl's eye and saw that she was a pretty girl and that
there was no future to her face, nothing. She was like the
hot, humid summer itself, which had hardly begun—it was
only mid-June—but which seemed to have lasted months already and had blotted out all memory of cooler weather. The
floor was very flat, like the sidewalk and the street. The summer seemed to Jules flat, its horizon flat. He reached out slowly and put his hand over hers.

Her eyes jumped to his face.

"Don't be afraid, why are you afraid?" he said softly.

She pulled her hand away. Mort, watching them edgily,
pretended to see nothing and interrupted someone's argument
with an explosive laugh, almost a hiccup. "Burn everything
down! I offer my books into the bargain—a couple of thousand dollars' worth of books! My parents' house in Grosse
Pointe! Fine, fine! Everything for the fire! Burn it all down
and at the very bottom, fine white bone dust at the very bottom, let it not be Johnson or Romney or any of those bastards
but a very ordinary person, a black kid, a victim and martyr
to the whole establishment we call civilization—isn't that the
way it is? Symbolically and literally? The whole establishment
resting on the pulverized bones of a kid?"

"You stole all that from Thomas Mann! From *The Magic
Mountain!*"

"I've never read Thomas Mann," Mort said, offended.
"Where are you going?" he said as the girl rose.

She was on her way out. "Good-by," she said.

"Where are you going?"

She waved him away. Jules got up to follow her. Mort,
deflated, sat and stared after them while his lips worked silently.

"Hey, friend," Jules said in a singsong voice, hurrying after
the girl, "why don't you smile upon your brother? Hey, wait."

She did not look back.

"Where are you going in such a hurry, honey?"

On the sidewalk, in the sunlight, she stopped to look at
him. "I felt afraid in there, all of a sudden. I don't know
why."

"Nothing to be afraid of."

"The things they were talking about—I just started trembling."

"Where are you trembling? Your knees?"

"Yes, my knees. I'm only eighteen. He was my teacher in Intro to Soc, you know, Mr. Piercy—I mean Mort. I sort of fell in love with him last semester but now I don't know, I don't know what to think. He made us read *The Wretched of the Earth* and it changed my life."

"Are you still trembling?" said Jules.

"A little."

"Why don't you walk this way, along here," said Jules. His voice was not hollow now but kind; it sounded kind. "Walk along here," he said, pressing with his knuckles the firm column of her backbone, urging her along. Vacated stores, old election posters, his everyday walk. He was walking it backwards now. "Tell me about yourself, honey. Talk to me."

"I don't know what to think. I came down here with a suitcase and some things, a few dollars. I had a bad fight at home. I'm fed up with them, they're hopeless, and I was thinking maybe I would . . . well, I would live down here permanently. But I don't have any money. Your name is Jules? I know you, I've met you before. You go around with a woman named Marcia? She's got a little kid? Why can't I stop trembling, I feel so strange."

"You'll feel better in a few minutes. The sun will warm you up."

She shivered. Her teeth were chattering.

"Honey, why are you so afraid? You're not afraid of me, are you?"

"You . . . I was watching you all the time, in there. I could hear them talking, but you were looking at me. But where is that woman? She's a nice-looking woman, your girl friend, do you live with her? Her and the kid? Do you all live together?"

"Off and on," said Jules. "But tell me about yourself."

They were walking slowly in the sunlight. Jules watched their shadows. The girl's legs made long, filmy shadows, very graceful shadows.

"I don't know what to say. Jules, I met you before. I don't know why I'm walking this way, I should be going the other way. Maybe I should get the bus up to Six Mile, or telephone my father. I had to drop out of school because I got so mixed up—I failed English composition, I couldn't organize my thoughts. What a hell of a break it must be, to be born with brains, like Mort and that what's-her-name and the rest of them. I admire all of them, and you too. You never get afraid."

"That's true. I never get afraid." He touched her backbone again, more gently. He stared at her back and ran his fingers down it.

"What are you doing?" she said, drawing away. "You're so strange, acting like this. I don't know what to think. I met you one other time but you didn't remember me—"

"I'm thinking about you now. I can't think about anything else."

"But you shouldn't touch me like that! What are you doing?" she said weakly, moving away. Jules's hand fell free. "What can I say about myself? Are you listening? I want to come alive and be a real person, I want to love—I want to love in a strong, permanent way, I want to give myself up entirely to it, but it has to be worthy of me and I'm afraid, I'm afraid I won't be able to tell, I won't know how to recognize it—I could be locked in a coffin and never get out. I don't know the right words. I know that I'm pretty but people like Mort don't give a damn about that, they want the right words and I don't have them. I feel all locked up in a coffin."

"This way. Turn this way," Jules said as they reached a corner.

"But I don't want to go this way."

"Yes, this way," he said, taking her arm.

She walked with him up the street, stumbling a little. "I haven't eaten since last night. Supper last night. I ran out this morning without eating. I feel so faint . . ."

Some Negro boys ran past them, shrieking. The girl bumped into Jules, in a panic. He touched the back of her neck and caressed her, beneath her hot, heavy hair.

"I know how Mort feels," she said, shaking her head to be free of Jules's hand, "I know what he means about burning everything down. There can't be any other way. A big bulldozer to even everything, to level it all down, people and trees and houses, and what's left after the fire, piles of rubble, white and black both. Sometimes I sit up, wide awake, and have a dream when I'm high, of a building on fire falling to pieces, every brick falling away from the rest and falling by itself down into the street, far below, tilting over and then collapsing . . . all so beautiful . . . and the firemen, crushed beneath the fire . . . and in every room people waking up, trying to run on stairways that burst into flame beneath their feet and collapse, and everything would keel over, burning, the people themselves burning . . ."

Jules caressed her back, leading her along.

"But do I want to be one of those people? I don't know what I want, I can't think straight, I don't think I'm well. My mind is all mixed up. I have dreams about blood and the insides of people coming out, from my high-school biology class, where we had to dissect a frog and I hated it, hated it—my God, Jules, please don't do that!"

He stepped around to her other side, shifting his hand. "Let me protect you from the street, honey. Too many people."

"I can hear cars but I can't see them. I can smell them."

"There are too many cars on the street."

"I don't want to go home."

"Tell me about yourself, anything," said Jules. Inside him, far inside him, something was dissolving and falling. But he did not let it fall. He said, "Do you like to sleep? Do you dream at night? What do you dream about?"

"I used to like to sleep but now I'm afraid of it. I could dream anything, I'm free to dream anything . . ."

"Don't you want to be free?"

"Yes, I want to be free, there's nothing I want more, but . . . I'm afraid of the kind of dreams I have, I can't control them. I have one dream where I'm armed with a belt, carrying a belt! Why am I carrying a belt? Why is everything so crazy!"

Her teeth chattered. She gave Jules a frightened sideways look, strangely coquettish.

"Cross the street here. Wait for this car," Jules said. He put his arm around her shoulders to guide her. She stared up at him and then broke off her gaze with an effort, looking around. She stumbled at the curb. Confused, neutral, she stood on the sidewalk looking around.

"Where is this? Detroit? Is this still Detroit?"

"Yes, honey. Always Detroit."

"Are you on that program with them—what's it called—action against poverty? United Action Against Poverty? Do you work with them on that, getting money and faking reports, buying guns? Or are you one of the poor people?"

"I'm one of the poor people."

"But you're not black. Are you very poor?"

"You can't get much poorer."

"Then how do you live?"

"I get along."

"But, for a poor person, you talk as if . . . as if it didn't matter. I thought poor people were different, I thought they were mainly black . . ."

He took her hand as if charmed by this and tried to raise it to his mouth, but she drew away. Then, confused and embarrassed, she reached out to him and allowed him to take the hand. Jules gnawed gently at the knuckles. The girl laughed. "Stop that. Go away," she said.

"But I live here. I can't go away."

"Here? You live here? Do people live here?"

She looked around, staring. "I'm sorry," she said, "I don't know what I'm saying. It just looks as if they're tearing things down here. Buildings. But some buildings are still standing, people can still live in them. I've been feeling strange since Saturday night, I haven't been able to eat much . . ."

For a moment she stood motionless. Then, suddenly, she pushed past Jules and ran back across the street, in the direction they had come from. A Negro driving a junk truck shouted at her.

"Hey," Jules cried, "where are you going?"

He ran after her and headed her off, driving her toward a doorway. She ran with her hands pressed up against her face. "You don't want the police to pick you up, honey. You've got to be careful," Jules said. He knew he had to talk to her, to say a certain amount of words. A familiar wheel was moving, a wheel of physical logic, and he felt himself carried along with it. The girl huddled in the doorway, hiding her face. Jules took hold of her shoulders from behind.

"You'd better let me go," she said. "I want to call my father."

"I'll find you a telephone then."

She turned. She tried to get past Jules, but he blocked her. "That's the wrong direction," he said. "No telephone there."

She tried to get away but he took hold of her hair, gripped a handful of it and wound it around his fist. The girl stood motionless. She closed her eyes, her face screwed up into a look of pain and concentration. She took hold of his fist and tried to open it. She pried frantically at the fingers. "I'll call the police," she said.

"Honey, the police will do worse than this. They'll get you in the precinct garage and when they're through nobody will give a damn about you, not even your father."

"That's not true!"

"It's all true, everything I say is true."

She looked at him. Laughter rose in her, she couldn't help it. Jules smiled. He felt his smile like a strip of magnesium across his face.

"Where is there a telephone? Is there a store near here, or something with a telephone?"

"I'll find one for you."

"You won't find it! You won't help me!" She managed to loosen his fingers and pushed his hand away. "I think I've been down here, lost, for a long time. I have this feeling that I've been down here, with you or someone like you, and with *them*." She looked sideways, hatefully, at people in the street, Negroes mainly, who were passing her and Jules without paying much attention to them. "I can't remember my own telephone number at home. All sorts of numbers deliberately fly into my head to confuse me."

"If your father's name is in the telephone book you could look it up," Jules said.

"I don't have a dime."

Suddenly weary, with that peculiar drawn smile, she stepped backward into the doorway. A slanted shadow fell across her body. Jules followed her. He crooked his arm around her neck and kissed her. He pressed himself up against her, sensing his agitation as if from a distance, vague and dull in spite of the girl's frightened warm breath and her warm mouth. He kissed her eyelids. He caressed the back of her neck, under her hair, and twisted the top button of her dress; it came off at once and fell away. Both he and the girl straightened jerkily, as if someone had shouted at them. Jules stepped back to let her go.

"I can find a telephone by myself," she said.

She started off again, but he took hold of her arm to turn her in the other direction.

She gave in. She hurried that way, and Jules stooped to pick up the cheap button that had fallen from her dress. He followed her, wondering at the hysterical energy of her legs and thighs. Her hair blew in the wind. He could imagine her shrewd terrified eyes, her still face. At the next corner she waited, looking from side to side. She looked like a frightened horse, covertly frightened. The neighborhood was partly burned-out, partly demolished. Jules came up behind her and stroked her head, as if she were a frightened horse. "I have something for you," he said. He tried to force the button through her buttonhole. She pushed him away, laughing. The button went through the hole and fell out again and rolled on the sidewalk.

"I can't stand this," the girl said. She looked as if she were about to run blindly out into the street, into traffic. Jules put his arms around her. She did not move. Over her head the sunlight looked filmy, as if photographed. In one direction the avenue was closed off by black and yellow blockades. Pavement was torn up. Great barrels of refuse lay tipped over; children were playing in it. A long-haired boy on a motorcycle slipped past the barriers, bouncing on the rutted ground, heading away. Jules embraced the girl from behind, feeling her heart beat and wondering why it did not mean more to him. Her heart was beating. She was alive.

"If you come this way I can find you a telephone, anything you want," he said. He led her down the street to the building he lived in. An old man, a white man, was sitting on the bottom step but did not bother to glance up. Jules and the girl stepped politely around him. He led her up to the first landing, where she stopped. She stumbled as if faint. Jules stroked her head and shoulders, frowning down at her; he was waiting for something to begin in him. In another second it would begin. The vision of that broken-up street came to his mind, filmy with sunlight, crossbars and blockades of yellow and black stripes, and a big diamond-shaped shield that said DEAD END. He took hold of the girl's ear with his teeth. He ran his tongue around the whorls of that ear, wondering if it seemed a familiar shape and a familiar taste.

"I can't stand it, please . . ." the girl whispered. She was leaning back against the railing and she turned clumsily to him.

Jules embraced her lightly. They smiled at each other. "Which way were you going, here? When I met you?" said Jules. "Were you heading upstairs or downstairs?" He helped her up onto the next step. With his hand at her elbow he walked with her to the third floor, then steered her gently to the right.

"What is this place? Where am I?" the girl said.

She flicked the ends of her hair out, in the same gesture flicking out the tips of her fingers. He saw that she was not carrying a purse. Her dress was badly wrinkled in back. The muscles of her legs showed white and dangerous, and at the backs of her knees tiny blue veins grew sharper, then indistinct, as she walked. He wanted to bend down to kiss the backs of her knees.

"I could leave now," she said. "I could be back home in time for dinner."

Jules pushed open the door to his room. It was unlocked. The room had only one window, without a curtain. Jules's eyes were drawn to a dark shape on the edge of his unmade bed—maybe a cockroach?—and his instinct made him turn the girl around so that she wouldn't see, and, stooping over quickly, as if in a mock bow, he knocked it to the floor. A dead cockroach.

The girl closed her eyes. Jules took hold of her. He knelt down before her and rubbed his face against her. Gradually he was overcome by senseless dreamy violence that had become his best instinct, his emergency instinct. A vision of that excavation site flashed to his brain again and again. He could very nearly see the motorcyclist bouncing up onto the broken concrete, readjusting his grip on the steering wheel, heading off to ride along the edge of the expressway; he was sorry he hadn't looked more closely at the cyclist . . . The girl began to push at him, but not hard, her fingers uncoordinated and wild as Jules's rising passion. She was saying something, telling him something important. A warning! He had to stop! But Jules knew he did not have to stop. He did not have to do anything. He pulled her down onto the bed and lay with his palm hard against the base of her skull, holding her sweating and hypnotized, and he felt himself an impersonal force holding her by the back of the neck, not especially Jules and not anyone else, hardly even a man, but in the shape of a man.

He thought of Mort, Mort saying, *Now I soar, now I'm plunging . . .* , and the urgent fancy of those words matched his passion, which surprised him with its violence, and an instant after it was over he removed himself from the girl and lay beside her. A coating of sweat had formed on his body, like a miracle.

The girl was whimpering. "I didn't want to come here . . . I don't know what place this is . . . I don't know who you are . . . I don't love you . . . I can't even think who you are . . ." She began to cry.

Jules's eyes ached. He lay still and waited for his heart to slow.

The girl said, "If I could love you it would be different . . ."

"It's all right."

"But I don't even know where this place is . . ."

After a while he got up to look for his cigarettes. They

had fallen out of his pocket and were on the floor, tangled in a bed sheet. He said, "Once I thought it wouldn't be possible to live without love, but it is possible, you keep on living. You always keep on living."

"You what? . . . What?"

"You always keep on living."

6

"So you copped that mousy little girl? Where are you hiding her?"

"I'm not hiding anyone."

"She's white, at least? At least she's white?"

"I wouldn't touch a Negro," said Jules.

"You bastard, I know you wouldn't. I know it."

Jules looked out the window. A car was passing idly in the street: he fixed his attention on it. Who was in the car, where were they going? Was it a worthy destination? When the car passed out of sight, Jules's attention was fixed upon a neutral, empty space, harmless.

"What did you do today, Jules? All afternoon?"

Jules was fascinated by that empty space.

"Go to another movie or what? Jules?"

"Went to a movie."

"Which one? Where?"

He shrugged his shoulders.

"Is something wrong, Jules?"

He said nothing. Silence began to fill up inside him.

He turned from the window. The heat in this apartment was oppressive; outside it was steamy, in the 90's. June was past and now they were in July of an interminable summer. Jules kept wiping his face but there was no use, a new film of perspiration appeared; his eyes stung. He sat down on the edge of Marcia's bed. In the bathroom Tommy, her four-year-old, was leaning over the bathtub, playing. Jules was helpless before a vision of that child falling and cracking his head in the tub. He could see the blood. His vision backed to the vision of a woman settling herself in a shining white tub, into very hot water. The water shimmered about her body. Her body was pale and beginning to flush from the heat of the water . . . Jules felt sick and his imagination buckled.

Marcia was stroking his hair. "Would you like something to eat?"

"Not particularly."

"I'm going to make Tommy and myself some sandwiches, just sandwiches. Do you want one?"

"No."

"Some potato chips?"

"No."

Marcia was silent for a while. Her silence was not quiet; he could feel her nervousness. Then she said angrily, "What do you do all day? I don't believe you're exhausting yourself with that little bitch—she's all doped up, everybody says. Where are you hiding her? Did you make a deal with the police? Not that I give a damn, but I have to face people. Mort is always latching onto me and asking where you are."

Jules closed his eyes. He felt her stroking his head but there was no pleasure in it; she continued angrily, as if afraid to stop. He was running down, running out. The very air was distorted. Objects might melt in it. His body might turn to fat, melting, while the pinpoint of energy at its very center— Jules Wendall—became hard and bitter and useless, like a grain of sand or grit.

"We've known each other for five months," Marcia said. "Do you realize it's the middle of July? Already? Doesn't it mean anything to you—this, me?"

Jules tried to piece together her words.

"Doesn't it?" she said.

"Yes."

"And Tommy, do you love him too?"

"Yes."

She stood for a moment, leaning over him. He heard her sigh. She said, "Well, I've got to make something for us to eat. Come out in the kitchen, talk to me."

Jules did not follow her. He remained sitting on the edge of the bed. On the window sill was a small plant in a bright brown ceramic pot; its leaves were a little limp. The earth in the pot, dried, had shaped itself into tiny, vivid, hard-looking balls. Like pebbles. Jules went into the bathroom and took Marcia's plastic cup and filled it halfway with water, then returned to water the plant.

Marcia leaned around the corner from the kitchen, peering in at him. "Oh, thanks for doing that, I keep forgetting," she said. Jules left the cup on the window sill and sat down again on the bed. "Jules, are you all right? Are you taking something? Please tell me."

He said nothing.

"Are you taking something?"

"No."

"I'd be afraid for Tommy if you were. Please tell me—"

"No."

"But what is this about a girl? Is there a girl? Her name is Vera?"

"There might be."

"And what about her?"

"Nothing."

"Do you love her?"

Jules had an unclear, sudden hallucination of beasts—transparent beasts in the space between himself and the kitchen doorway.

"But what does it mean to you?" Marcia said.

"What does what mean?"

"Anything."

"I don't know."

The animals in their transparent shapes melted back into the damp air. Jules felt slightly relieved.

"I'm sure they're going on strike," Marcia said, "those goddam Teamsters, going on strike again, and if they do he'll lay me off, I know it. I'll be the first to go. Out looking for a job in the middle of the summer, Jesus Christ! I wish I could get out of here."

Jules said nothing.

"Anywhere would be better than this, anything. I don't know how the hell I ended up in this filthy city . . ."

Tommy slipped on the wet floor but did not crack his skull. He picked himself up. Jules saw that he was in pain and he felt the impulse to go to him, but he did not move. The boy began to cry.

"Oh, God!" cried Marcia. "What did he do now?"

She ran to him and bent down, to hug him. Now Jules looked at her. She was a strong-boned woman in her late twenties, with blond hair so light as to look unreal; it was cut short to show the bottoms of her ears. On the street, walking, she had a swinging, open, healthy look; inside she had a slightly harassed, impatient, look. She hugged Tommy and made a face at Jules over the boy's shoulder.

"Oh, you're always falling down! You dope! Aren't you a dope? Well, you're all right now, you didn't get hurt at all. No cut, no scratch, nothing! All right?"

She stood. Tommy went back to his play.

"Why is he always so hot? He must have a fever. I don't

know what the hell she feeds them at that place. I should take him out of there, but if I get laid off I won't need her. I can lie around here and do my nails. I can go to the movies with you."

Jules noted how strong the bones of her face were, even in this warm air. He himself felt no strength. He felt as if all his strength had drained out of him, dissipated into the air of this room and of other rooms, adding up to his past. Marcia, more desperate than he and more cunning, had lost none of her strength though her husband had left her two years before, walking out, saying he was headed for Canada. This struck Jules as somehow familiar but he could not say why. Had Furlong mentioned Canada? It was strange to Jules how familiar everything seemed, as if like the walk to and from his room, the entire world added up to a few sights and sounds that had to be used over and over again. With Marcia, lying in bed with her, he could feel his soul browsing idly amid the tumbled sheets and pillows, gone blind, even his fingers blind to the body of this woman, who could have been any woman. His own desire for her was a desire for any woman. He was lost in it, but not seriously lost. He could return. He recalled playing a game with some kids many years ago, himself a kid, leading them with wooden swords through a warehouse basement, and at that time the Jules in himself, the essential Jules, had been strenuous and impatient, already formed. Now, thirty years old, this Jules lay asleep or dying, drained of himself. He could sit forever on the edge of this bed, which belonged to Marcia. She was talking to him now. She came home after working all day, typing out order forms for a trucking concern, typing all day long, taking the bus back and forth, and now she was home with her son and her lover, who was Jules, her face slightly flushed with . . . with what? . . . concern for her son's mishap, or love and anxiety for Jules, for her "family"?

"Well, maybe it will turn out for the best if those bastards do strike. Maybe we could get out of here," she said.

Jules did not answer. He did not look at her.

"We could go to another city, maybe. Jules? My God, what kind of a person are you—I mean, what kind of a state are you in? It's hopeless, with you—you just sit there. I must be crazy trying to get something out of you, anything." She drew both hands up against her forehead in an impatient, masculine gesture, rubbing her temples with the palms of her hands. Jules thought of how impossible it was to love her, to love any woman who rubbed her forehead that way, rubbing perspiration off it. "What are you thinking about, Jules? Why don't you look at me?"

"I have to go out in a few minutes."

She was stricken.

He looked away.

"Go out where?"

"To see someone."

"Someone, who? Who is it?"

"I'll be right back."

"But who are you seeing? Should I go along with you?"

"No, I'll be right back."

But he felt no energy to get up and go downstairs and face the street again. The air between himself and the door was opaque and dangerous, as if crowded with invisible shapes.

"I don't know why I'm always at you," Marcia said, "I love you. I don't mean to keep at you . . ." He was hearing now her flat wistful voice, the second and less attractive of her voices.

"That's all right," Jules said.

"I just keep thinking if you got a job somewhere else, I could get one too, and we could maybe get out of here. I keep hearing there's going to be trouble, every weekend there's going to be trouble. Mort and those stupid friends of his, those big-mouthed bastards, they think it's going to be a carnival. I ran into him on the way home and could hardly get away. I think he's going crazy with all this. He and those jerks are going to be like generals, guiding everything—fires and bombings—they plan on blowing up the bridge and the tunnel and the expressway intersection, and he said something about the water supply. Jesus, he looks bad too. He must be about ready to crack."

Jules nodded.

"He says you're working for him. Is that right? That community project thing? What are you doing for it?"

"Nothing."

"What are you supposed to do?"

"I don't know. Nothing."

"But you're on the payroll? For how much?"

"Not much. I haven't been paid yet."

"But how much, approximately? A few hundred a month?"

"I don't remember."

Marcia laughed. "One hundred a month? Fifty? It isn't

going to last long, him and his money. Or else one of his
contacts is going to kill him. Don't they know the niggers
don't give a damn about them? They don't trust them and
can't understand their big words. A nigger is a nigger. I
don't mind a nigger, but it isn't the same as a white man,
and they don't *want* to be the same as a white man. Mort is
always so nervous, giggling. He wasn't always that bad."

Jules got up. "I'll be back in a few minutes."

Tommy ran out of the bathroom. "I'm coming too," he
said.

"No, honey, he's just going out for a few minutes. Be
still. I'm going to make supper."

"I don't want supper."

Tommy had fair, curly hair; his eyes were blue. From so
many hours at one nursery or another he had developed a
crouch, as if expecting to be hit or shouted at. Jules could
never think of anything to say to him, though he liked the
boy. But perhaps he did not know how to like children at
all—his imagination blanked out on them.

Marcia followed him out into the hallway. "So you're
angry with me?"

"No."

"You don't want anything to eat?"

"No."

"Why can't you look at me? Why can't we talk? I don't
want anything much from you. I'd like to talk with you now
and then, that's all. All I want is someone to talk to, someone
intelligent and not . . . not crazy, you know. Jules, why
isn't it working out?"

"It's working out fine."

"You don't think about next year?"

"What about next year?"

"I mean the future. I mean leaving here, getting jobs
somewhere else, getting married?"

"No, I don't think about it."

On his way down the block he ran into a small group of
Negroes on the sidewalk. Several of the men wore handker-
chiefs around their heads. A Negro in workclothes, very
drunk, was being arrested by a Negro policeman. There was
an air of festivity, of murmuring, hilarious silence. The
drunken Negro was swaying from side to side, and the policeman was trying to straighten him up.

Suddenly there was yelling, whining, the scuff of feet. Jules
made his way around them politely. The drunken Negro was

trying to fight the policeman, who looked like him—it was surprising how they looked alike, both in their thirties, with very black faces and vicious eyes. The policeman knocked his man back against a building and the man's head bobbed foolishly. He took out his club and began striking him. One blow, another blow! Jules kept going. He wanted distance between himself and them.

There had been a fight downstairs in his building a while ago, and out of curiosity Jules had gone down to look when everything was quiet. A few bloodstains on the floor. Someone told him that the landlord had beaten up someone with a baseball bat. The landlord was not really a landlord but a caretaker, a husky, light-skinned Negro who always wore a hat; the landlord was said to be another Negro, who lived up in Palmer Woods in a mansion. There were many tales. Behind one Negro there was another, more successful, and behind him another even more successful: everyone was proud of him. Jules did not believe these tales or disbelieve them. His own thefts were so small, so unimaginative, that he had no envy or interest or ability to rejoice when he was told about the exploits of fabulous thieves. Everyone was struggling, climbing up, but Jules was sitting off to one side in a daze, happy, unhappy, not waiting. In retirement. He had seen Faye's photograph in a newspaper, after so many years, and it had not disturbed him. He had been her lover for a short while. What did that mean, to be a woman's lover? What difference did it make? She was now someone's wife and surely she never thought of Jules, could not remember him. He had seen, once, his own sister Betty on the street, in the company of other tough strangers, Betty dressed in very tight, chic, suede clothes, trousers and jacket and a silk scarf, looking both conservative and bizarre, her homely face done up to a look of raw contemptuous confidence—that cruel mouth was her best feature. And Jules, suddenly fearful of her, had turned away. So much for his childhood.

Of his sister Maureen he no longer thought. Someone's wife at last: she was saved. Nor did he think about Loretta, except when some dumpy loud woman on the street reminded him of her—and there was no mystery to his forgetfulness, nothing. He was like the weeds that grew to a height of three or four feet right through the sidewalk's cracks, struggling upward but without cruelty or design, mindless and content. Or those weeds in vacant lots, growing up amid the rubble, squeezing around the rubble. They were permanent though they had no consciousness. Everywhere around them were things or parts of things that had been man-made at one time, and still bore the signs of someone's consciousness, but the weeds were more permanent, being without design.

Jules looked through a few bars. In the Lucky Horseshoe he had good luck; Vera hurried to him. She said, "I've been waiting here for you. Is there any trouble?"

"No, is there trouble with you?"

"Well, maybe. I don't know, I can't figure it out."

"Come on."

She was so wheedling and pathetic, with her long hair that bored him and her sooty over-large eyes, that face that was hopelessly young, that he could do no more than slip his arm around her shoulders.

She leaned against him gratefully. "It's just hell . . ."

Jules said nothing. He walked her back to his room. She was unsteady on her feet or pretending to be, leaning against him.

"I feel so beaten down," she said, "so low. I've been waiting for you for hours and that place is filthy. I don't feel well."

"Where?"

"In the head, in the neck."

"How did you do?"

"You won't be mad?"

"No, honey, how did you do?"

"I got a little, but I didn't feel well, so I went to Sheila's place where some kids were. I don't know what the hell they were talking about, it was all fanciful and wild, you know. That bunch is really crazy."

Jules made a sound to show that he was listening.

"There's this Benny, he's really crazy! He went over to Wayne today and walked around the professors' offices and stole an electric typewriter, a big heavy one, and walked right out with it. He took the staff elevator down! And he sold it, he got fifty dollars. He's always doped up, you can't even talk to him. He looks like hell. I'd rather die than look like that, honey. I don't look bad yet, do I? Do I look nice?"

"Yes."

"You won't be mad at me then? Because I really didn't feel well and Sheila had some stuff to eat there, I thought I might as well eat there."

Up in Jules's room she lay on the bed and covered her face with her arms. "My head hurts. The back of my neck is stiff. Do you think I might be getting polio?" she said.

"Where's the money?" said Jules.

"In here," she said. She sat up. She took a change purse out of her dress pocket and handed it to him. "I guess there's forty or fifty dollars in there. Please don't be mad at me . . ."

Jules counted out sixty-five dollars, sixty-six dollars. He took fifty dollars for himself and handed her back the purse.

"Honey, you're not mad?" she said.

"No, I'm not mad."

"You told me to get one hundred . . ." She looked at him with her wistful black-rimmed eyes.

Jules sat on the edge of the window sill and tried to smile at her.

"So you're not mad after all."

"No, never."

He had an imprecise memory of beating this girl with a twisted coat hanger. He had been careful to beat only her back. This had happened a few weeks ago. Her back had bled slightly and had become bruised. But he had not been angry with her. It was for another reason, to make her understand something; but had that really been Jules beating this girl?

"Can I tell you some things? You want to hear?" she said.

"No, not particularly."

"Something real crazy. This one guy wanted—"

"No."

She smiled in bewilderment at him. He saw how young she was and this did not move him, but settled him back farther, settled him down. His body weighed four hundred pounds, a thousand pounds. He could never move it. The girl's delicate body, grown thinner since June, weighed maybe ninety-five pounds and was so flimsy that he could not quite believe in it. Could she feel pain? Feel anything?

She said, "Are you staying here tonight?"

"I don't know."

"Are you still seeing *her?*"

He could not quite make sense of her question, though the words were clear enough. He felt himself growing very heavy, very hot. The girl's mouth smiled, her eyes pleaded something complex and troublesome. *If you get hysterical again,* Jules thought, *I'll have to push you out the window.*

But even here his imagination had done no work; a week ago on this block a Negro prostitute had been pushed out a window by her pimp, and Jules had gotten the idea from that. He felt very weary.

"Jules, come here? Come over here?"

He lay down beside her but could not close his eyes. She began kissing him. She began to cry. "Jules, I love you," someone was saying. "Jules, I love you!"

Love, there was so much love! He felt her arms around him, he felt his own arms sliding around her. Flimsy ribs. Her beating heart. She was demented with too much love, too much hysteria. And if Marcia lost her job, what then? Then they had no money, nothing; then they could all live on Vera, or on Marcia herself, why not? He thought of Tommy cringing in play, alone. Tommy squinted perpetually as if sizing up threats. Invisible adults must hound him at all times. Wise and agile for his age, with airy blond hair and a patient look, the child of a man who'd taken off, a lost child . . . Jules could not help him and so he stopped thinking about him.

He tried to concentrate on Vera. In her thin wheedling tone of love she spoke to him, calling him by an irrevocable name, calling him Jules—why hadn't he thought to change his name when he got out of the hospital?—and moaning, "Jules, I'm in pain, for you, I love you and I need you inside me. Jules, only you, please, Jules . . ."

After a few minutes Jules said, "Sorry, I can't."

His veins burned with desire but he did not know what this desire was for. A woman? He was not sure, not any longer. Vera sobbed in his arms. Her knees were drawn up as if to protect herself, being wounded. Jules's blood pounded, wanting some knowledge, some intensification of itself. The other night a woman had given him a shot of something, bent over him lovingly and with sly, cruel love sinking a needle into the vein that ran down the center of his arm, and Jules had come near to loving her for the pleasure that shot had given him, striking him high in the backbone and radiating outward, overwhelming him. So that was it—that was how it felt! But the memory of that shot left him adrift from himself, curiously light, uncommitted.

Vera wept. She was one of his transparent beasts, helpless. Very warm. Slick with sweat, below the waist a helpless beast; he felt sorry for her. And Marcia had also wept in his arms. He had emptied his body in their bodies and the very violence of his love had shaken him free from them. The needle had sunk in and jolted him out of himself but that was not it, not what he wanted. He wanted only himself, nothing false. He did not understand what he wanted. He clung to Vera, forgetting her, and in her misery she seemed to be forgetting him, sinking into herself. Why couldn't he think yet of that other woman whom he had loved for so long? He did not think about her. Around her being there was a deadly fog, a mist he did not dare to penetrate. Pleasure has no memory but love seemed to him all memory, a fatality of the mind, worse now than when he had lain with that woman in his arms . . . and now he was lying with another woman, the two of them sweating and miserable. He felt suddenly very sleepy. Vera's sobs were muffled, she was falling asleep. He loved her at once for this, for falling asleep and leaving him. *So you copped that mousy little girl?* Marcia had asked, wisely and with irony, knowing everything. Well, he had her. He slept.

7

Jules, having lost count of nights and days, woke suddenly with his heart pounding. "Who's there?" he cried. For a moment he could not remember where he was, what time it was, whether he was eighteen years old or thirty.

There was something empty inside him and outside him . . . a slow motion. He lay very still, testing himself. He could see objects in the room, though dimly, so he was not blind. He could see. His lungs did not ache very much. It was his skin that ached, as if he had been burned. He scratched himself and flecks of skin came off under his fingernails. He peered down at himself: he was sunburned in patches. How had that happened?

Drowsily he recalled a park, a field of mowed weeds with their brown stubble fragrant, and himself wandering through it. Slow motion . . . moving. He must have fallen asleep in the field—a city park—and got burned by the sun. Or had that happened years ago? He rubbed at the sore patches on his skin and tried to figure out what they were, then forgot them.

It was important for him to remember what had happened yesterday. He had left Marcia, but that might have been several days ago; it did not help him to remember that now. Her angry, tear-stained face, her reddened eyes . . . a muscular neck, that girl. A good woman. Too good for him, he had to admit it and make her admit it, he'd woken up long enough to get that said. *I'm not the one! Not me!* he had cried. A barrage of pop bottles . . . slowly, as if dreaming, he remembered a barrage of pop bottles. Had he wandered into a fight between some kids? Or had Marcia thrown something at him? The end of the world would come in slow motion, drifting over the horizon like a sail. He felt peaceful in this knowledge. Even the ache in his body was peaceful.

The sailing pop bottles had come from the park: some kids fighting one another. Then, for some reason, they had all turned on Jules. He hadn't the energy to run away. He'd lain down in the stubble. They had screamed at one another and not at him, throwing bottles, sticks, rocks, all of them Negro kids and not very big, stamping around in an enchanted violence. One pop bottle, only one, had struck Jules on the side of the head. A Coke bottle, returnable. The blow had made him fall into the stubble, into the heat. "Now you killed him!" someone yelled. Jules in mowed grass, fragrant and wild, lying in the sunlight with no one to see him . . . Yes, that had happened a few days ago.

He got out of bed. Rising, moving his back. His backbone was stiff. The window shade was tangled at the top of the window, as if it had snapped up viciously by itself. Was it twilight or dawn? He went to the window and looked out. Only then did he hear what had wakened him . . . a siren. The siren seemed to curl through the air, a red curl, a metallic red curl, striking him. He put his hands to his ears. "Jesus Christ!" He thought for some reason of his boyhood. He had heard too many sirens.

Down on the street a Tactical Mobile Unit car raced by. Heavy with cops. Jules leaned out the window, dizzy, empty, waiting to be filled with news. But he had no faith in news. It must have been the other night, only Friday night, that he had been sitting on a door stoop somewhere and a man had sauntered up to him and said, "Your little girl's been busted. You interested in getting her out?" Jules had not seen Vera for two days. He thought she must have gone home. But really he had not thought of her at all. In his wallet was five dollars, five dollars remaining . . . from something . . . a handout from Mort or money from Vera or Marcia, he could not recall. So he had not thought of

Vera. "I said, your little girl's been picked up, kid," said this jaunty Negro, putting himself out to be Jules's friend. "Don't nobody keep you informed? How you operate, kid? A & S they got her for, just ask me. I know everybody up and down the street."

Jules had gotten to his feet and staggered away, confused. He felt sorry for Vera, in jail, but since she had already been in jail for two days it was really too late to think about her. The Negro caught up with him. His voice was a little impatient. "I said, kid, look here—you gonna do the thing for her? You tell me, huh? How much money you got?"

"Five dollars."

"Five dollars? Shit. You got five dollars, that's all?"

"Five dollars."

"How you gonna do the thing for her with five dollars? Damn shithead!"

Jules gestured for him to go away. The very thought of Vera wearied him. He imagined her posed before a window, wavering, faltering, falling out . . . better to die, to get it over with. Her dreams had been too violent. Somewhere a window awaited him. Or a gun. But he would have to borrow someone's gun. Vera in jail, leaning her head against a damp wall, waiting . . .

"She's cleaned up by now, you wondering," the Negro said irritably. "Was she on a bad habit, son? You want her cleaned up all the way, is that it?"

"I don't have any money."

"Jesus, if you got one hundred to begin with, and the rest on installments—"

"No. Nothing. Leave me alone."

And now he remembered the slowness of his walking away. Hard to walk away from a black man who is staring contemptuously at you. He walked away.

His neck hurt, the skin of his neck. Sunburn. There was no mirror in this room. He rubbed his neck. It was strange that he could still feel pain, so far on the surface of his being, when deeper inside him there was nothing. Another police car sped by. Jules waiting, pale and unshaven, dressed like a bum . . . waiting at the window.

Outside, on the street, he decided it was almost dawn. The air had an odd taste to it. He smelled smoke. People were gathering at the corner, their shirts unbuttoned. A strange smell to the air. Jules, very weak, puzzled, walking along at dawn. A few young Negroes were arguing over a car. One of them shrieked. One of them brought his fist down hard on the windshield . . . a flying spurt of blood. He walked past and felt again that strange sinister slowness, slow motion. No one saw him.

Then, turning the corner, he saw that the street was milling with people. Why these people, why awake so early? Wasn't it before dawn? There were Negro men and women and a few white men. They milled back and forth and around, talking excitedly. They were gathering out in the center of the street. Someone climbed up on the hood of a car, to yell at them. Jules could not make out his words. Above, far above, the sky was getting ready for another hot, misty day; Jules could tell. He wondered if he could be wrong and it was really twilight. Sunset. His brain whirled. Someone took him by the arm and cried into his face, then drew back with a shocked politeness, saying, "You ain't him!" Jules shook his head, no, he wasn't.

He moved down the street. The street itself was moving. Heads bobbing. One block down there were trees arching over the street. No shade here. Someone knocked over a trash can, and it rolled angrily past Jules. He stepped out of the way. His agility was a surprise.

The papers inside the trash can burst into flame. A miracle. Something shattered, Jules didn't know where. He rubbed his forehead. Why was he so slow? He would have liked to run up to a store window to get a look at himself, at his reflection, but the crowds had become too dense. Maybe there was a parade beginning somewhere and they were lining the streets. A siren wailed nearby. The crowd began to surge away from it. Jules saw himself stumbling into the burning trash can, though it was obvious he would be burned. He cried out in pain. His pants leg was smoldering.

A squad car appeared at the intersection ahead but did not advance. Its red light was whirling. Then, slowly, as slowly as Jules himself, the car drove off and out of sight.

The crowd gave a happy yell!

In one surge it carried him up to the sidewalk, and there he saw a window smashed. DR. PALMER RALSTON, OPTOMETRIST had owned that window. The slabs of glass fell slowly. A Negro boy ducked out of the way. The glass hit the sidewalk and shattered, someone screamed, a trash can was thrown into the showcase, knocking plastic-rimmed sunglasses in all directions. It was an explosion of glasses.

Husky, energetic men in sports shirts galloped up to a liquor-store window and took hold of the iron grating, heaving themselves upon it, yanking at it, twisting it. Someone was cheering in rhythm. *Come on! Come on!* Glass broke behind the grating. The men got the grating loose at one end and twisted it down, their muscles bulging. Then, bending it down, they placed it neatly over the broken glass and everyone scrambled inside. *Come on, come on! They afraid!*

Jules held onto a lamp post. He could not remember where his room was. Better for him to crawl back there, get sick there or die, where at least he wouldn't wander so slowly about, in a daze. Already men were emerging from the broken window with bottles of liquor! Already! In the time it took Jules just to figure out what was happening, everything had happened, completed itself, and had rushed right on by. A child of about ten scrambled through a maze of broken glass, clutching a bottle. Jules caught him as he slid. The child righted himself and ran away.

He was standing near a sign that said KEEP CROSS STREET CLEAR. It was a fixed point. From there he could see in three directions, though not well. More people were milling out onto the street. Some stood in the center, watching. Others were struggling on the sidewalk. Another trash can rolled out into the street, on fire. Someone shouted. Jules hung onto the post. CANCELLATION SHOES had been broken into. Shoes flew jubilantly. A small Negro boy ducked under a fat woman's arm, carrying a bunch of shoes. "You gonna wear all them, boy?" someone yelled in delight. Jules wandered around the corner. More mobs attacking stores, making the street vibrate. A holiday. The very pavement shook with the energy of their enchantment—such people! Jules picked up a stray shoe and threw it into a broken store-window . . . a drugstore. Kids were scrambling inside, knocking over the faded cardboard advertisements of shampoo and toothpaste. The air was heady with cries, like music. It vibrated with their music. Jules caught sight of another white man, about his own age, and tried to keep within a few yards of him. The white man was screaming, his shirt was open, his chest bleeding as if from an enraged lady's fingernails . . . he had a bottle of whisky. Jules felt the slowness of his own being in the midst of all this urgency, Jules himself inching along, a white man, half-asleep. Sleeping. He could not really believe in it. He was probably asleep, dreaming. Everything vibrated. Was this real? More sirens, a smell of bitter, thick smoke, the rollicking cries of looters . . .

Down a cross street flowed a great mob, and in front of it something was flying . . . many things . . . rocks, bottles? At the other end of the street, its target, was a police car parked sideways, as if it had skidded into this position. Its siren blared helplessly. The barrage of rocks and bottles rained upon it, the car backed up onto the sidewalk with the spryness of a toy, someone fired a shot, the car rushed away . . . a flood of bottles and rocks followed it. Everyone was rushing to two positions: stooping to pick something up, wrenching an arm around to throw it. Stooping . . . throwing . . . The street was breaking up into pieces.

Jules found himself being carried in one direction. The neighborhood around him looked familiar, but with the familiarity of a snapshot—he did not quite seem to be in it, walking in it. Faces on all sides of him shared this sensation. Behind the faces was disbelief, but on the surface of the faces was an immense excitement. *Get this one! Right here!* came the repeated cry, and the muscular outer rim of the crowd ran forward, sweat-glistening boys and men with flapping shirts, in a hurry to throw something through something else. Jules thought of fireworks. He thought of a telephone ringing, a continual nervous jangling. Calls were coming through for everyone. It was everyone's birthday. The sky was lit at the near horizon, a few blocks away. Jules was being pushed from one side to the other, sometimes grasped and released, and he felt in these hurried fingers an alarm that was turning out to be his own.

Through the smashed window of a grocery store women were stepping carefully, their arms already filled. Someone dropped a cantaloupe and it smashed onto the sidewalk. A boy with too many jars and boxes dropped everything on the curb and cried out in disappointment. A woman carrying an infant stepped gracefully inside the store, looking around. Her hair was fixed in buoyant red curls. She had a querulous, dissatisfied look, a regular shopper. Jules waited until the front door was broken so that he could enter in this way, properly.

"You the manager or something?" a woman said, laughing at him.

He went to get a carton of cigarettes and stuffed packs in his pockets. He felt no hurry, though everyone else was hurrying. The sirens were all around them. Red lights flashed on the inside of the store, a few people ducked, nothing happened. "They afraid! Look at that, they afraid!" a man yelled. Jules took a jar of peanuts and tried to open it, but the lid was too tight. He knocked it against a counter, smashing it, then selected a few peanuts from the broken glass, picking them out carefully. He must not have eaten for some time; he was weak with hunger. A white woman, her nightgown showing sloppily beneath her raincoat, pushed past Jules to get hold of some cans . . . shrimp. The woman reminded him of his mother, though she was rather ugly, maybe crazy. She stood flat-footed, snatching cans of shrimp off the shelf and stuffing them into a shopping bag. Not even the rowdy little Negro boys could push her aside; she knocked them back with a blind sweep of her arm.

In a sparkling dream—sparks were flying now everywhere—Jules made his way back out to the street. The crowd had thinned out here. People were standing on rooftops, at windows, watching. Some Negro women were crying into their hands. Thick curls of smoke rose from the back of the street, back somewhere, and Jules heard more sirens. A milk bottle flew past him and smashed on the sidewalk but he thought it nothing personal, nothing. He was a white man but the kind of white man who didn't count. "You got a camera?" someone cried. Jules lifted his hands to show that he had nothing. *"He* ain't no cop!" someone cried. Jules sat down on a porch step, having a step all to himself, and watched. A few fires burning down the block. Some distance away a firetruck had stopped and firemen, white men, were milling around. A knot of Negroes watched them. The very air, lovely with sparks, was melodious and bright; Jules could hardly accustom himself to such festivity. So this was really happening? The end on its way? It was like flaming gasoline poured out onto a flat surface, free to run in any direction, in all directions, urgent and beyond help. Jules smoked cigarettes and watched.

The fires were spreading. People were running up the street, their arms filled with clothes and bedding and kids. A couple, arms entwined, ran by. Running, running! At the other end more fires waited. Some kids turned over a car and set it on fire. They wore their hair long and kinky, their shoulders were muscular beneath their dirty shirts, and their shoes had cruel pointed toes. They cried out to one another in a language of shrieks, like large, dangerous birds. The couple paused to watch them, arms around each other. Jules could see their joy. He felt touched by it, drawn to it.

Let everything burn! Why not? The city was coming to life in fire, and he, Jules, was sitting in it, warming to it, the flames dancing along his arteries and behind his seared eyes.

Hadn't he understood all along that this would happen?

A few blocks over toward Woodward police had already come into the area, stationed in front of stores. But the stores were being bombarded anyway. A young cop, his arms folded and his hand nowhere near his gun, leered at Jules as he approached. Around the cop, behind him, kids of six and seven were smashing a dime-store window. "What're you waiting for, you?" the cop cried to Jules. "Come and get it or it ain't gonna last!"

"Why should I?" said Jules.

"It's all for free! C'mon! It ain't gonna last, none of it, you ain't gonna get another chance!"

"I don't need anything."

"The Mayor says give it away! Christmas presents, Christmas time! He thinks he's Santa Claus! Everything's for free!"

A spray of glass hit the cop and Jules. For an instant Jules thought a piece had gone into his eye, but he was all right. Someone screamed. It was a little boy, bleeding from the face. He staggered on the sidewalk, his eyes shut, streaming blood. He bumped into the cop's legs and the cop gave him a shove.

The next cop, a burly man, stood with his arms crossed and legs apart, guarding a store that had just been set on fire. His hair was wild. He was middle-aged, with a high, heavy stomach. He fixed his eyes upon Jules and said something, moving his lips. Jules cupped his hand to his ear politely. "Go help yourself, you nigger!" the cop said, staring at Jules. "Soon as we get the word everyone is going to get mowed down, so help yourself now, get it while the getting's good!" His manner was husky and secretive and furious at once, oddly confidential. Jules thanked him but did not linger.

For some hours he wandered the streets, smoking cigarettes, smelling smoke. Everyone's lungs would be coated with soot, he thought. It was now a solid hot morning, Sunday morning. He felt the need for sleep back of his eyes, but his body could not have slept. It vibrated, feeling the street shaking. His knees and fingers tingled. On certain streets nothing was happening. People waited, with baby buggies and umbrellas. On other streets fires were blazing noisily. Firetrucks were at work. The firemen seemed sluggish, burdened by their outfits and their white skin. Even the water from their hoses, rising mightily in the air, could do little against four stories of flames. Jules felt something rush past his foot and saw a rat. It sped by him. On another street, in the rubble of a grocery store, several large rats were feasting in spite of the smoldering junk and all the commotion around them. Rats! People! Sirens! Gunfire! Jules felt suddenly intoxicated. Someone touched him and the intoxication was complete: he understood that the old Jules had not truly died but had only been slumbering, in an enchanted sleep; the spirit of the Lord had not truly departed from him.

A girl was tugging at him. He recognized her. "This way! Come on!" she cried. She wore cut-off jeans and a man's shirt. Her hair was fixed in pigtails. They ran through the street, ducking through smoke, careful to go around patches of glass. Everything had been cleared out here and now the buildings were on fire. Jules held the girl's hand and caressed her fingers. She led him upstairs, in a building not yet on fire.

"Jules, where've you been? Looting? Wasting time looting?" someone cried. It was a friend of Mort's whose name Jules could not remember.

On the rooftop of the building a group of white people were standing around, drinking beer. One boy was very drunk. Just as Jules came up the stairs he dropped a heavy pair of binoculars over the edge of the building.

"When is this one going? You sure this one isn't marked?" someone cried. It was a small red-headed man in a shirt and tie, pulling at someone's arm. His face was distorted, droplets of sweat ran down his cheeks.

A transistor radio was giving out news.

"Is there a place for me to sleep? I want to sleep," Jules said.

"Sleep, are you crazy? This is a revolution!"

He caught up with the girl who had led him here. She was yelling at a boy with a blemished face who had started to cry. Jules pulled her around to face him. "Take me downstairs. Show me the way," he said. The shirt she wore was too big for her, the collar far too big. Jules reached inside and touched her collarbone, which was prominent and nervous. What an articulate girl! A lovely girl!

She pushed him away without interest, screaming at her boy friend. "Oh, Jesus Christ! You make me sick!" she cried.

It was a playground. The sky was orange, burning, vile and sweet at once. Someone ran up the stairs, shouting. Someone surged against him. He tried to go downstairs, wanting to get back to the ground, but the stairway was too crowded. A man whose name Jules remembered was Fritz clawed at him, pushing by. "They're coming! They're here!" he yelled. Jules stepped aside. The roof shook with the pounding of feet. Police followed Fritz up onto the roof, clubbing at him.

Screams. Rushes. The girl with the pigtails began to scream at a young policeman and he clubbed her in the face. She fell forward, still screaming. Blood poured out of her nose. The policeman stood with his legs apart, clubbing her. Two policemen got Fritz against the edge of the building and worked him over, clubbing him. Jules saw the man's blood fly up in a fine spray, like a fountain. When he fell they propped him up again and clubbed him again, the face, the cheeks, the nose, the head, the back of the head, and someone tried to stop them and they turned impersonally and clubbed at him—Jules saw the man's nose broken. A spray of blood, a drooling of blood . . . Another policeman rushed up to the roof, knocking people aside, in a frenzy. The boy with the blemished face ran at him. He paid no attention, pushing the boy aside, yelling. The other policemen heard him and stopped. They backed away. They ran down the stairs.

Jules, thinking they might clear the way, ran after them. They paid no attention to him.

He ran all the way down into the basement. His heart was thudding. He had been very frightened. A box fell over. The air was stinging down here. Sparks and pieces of blackened paper floated everywhere. Jules liked the taste of ash and could not remember a time when he hadn't tasted it, floating everywhere in the air. He walked into a nail that grazed his thigh.

After a while he climbed out of the basement. A solid mass of flame across the street . . . firemen slipping in the wet streets. Someone shot up into the sky. There were other shots. A rat ran past him, in a hurry and knowing where it wanted to go. Rats. He did not mind the rats, they did not mind him; rats in a hurry were never any bother. The sparks in the air must have dazzled them as they dazzled Jules. The very movement of the air, the shivering patches of heat from the sun, told him that all was well.

He would not die.

In a burnt-out block he got some food, left behind on smashed shelves. He had to dash in and snatch the food out, away from the rats. They were everywhere now. A helicopter passed overhead, at some distance. Jules squinted at it. He wished he were in that helicopter, moving so proudly and easily over the fires, lifting itself up into the sky. The sun was almost down. Jules could not remember if he had spent a day on the street or if he had only now awakened, having lived through hours of flamboyant dreams. He crossed to an alley . . . very much alone, in all this noise . . . Jules always alone. A police cruiser spotted him but did not pause. He was drifting with freedom, intoxicated with freedom. That was what he had tasted in the air . . . freedom. The roofless buildings, already burnt-out, looked up into the sky in a brazen, hopeless paroxysm of freedom.

Not far from home he passed a Packer Food Store, still being looted. Women were using shopping carts and taking their time. It was still Sunday. Sunday night. And tomorrow, would a long work week begin in Detroit? Jules paused to watch the ladies shopping, stomping back and forth through the big broken windows. One boy was carrying a gum-ball machine under his arm. The metal base kept bumping into people, who reached around to give the boy a shove.

Jules was standing there when a boy came running at him. He had a peculiar lurching, hopping run; he held a rifle in his arms.

The air jangled with cries and laughter. Sirens in the distance, distant. The horizon was livid with light. Electricity popped. A car lay overturned, burning in the street; the smell of burning rubber was suffocating. Too close. The boy with the gun was approaching him, lurching. Was Jules going to be shot? He had felt the unbelievable impact of bullets and he had known that sickened, immediate denial: *This didn't happen!* So he watched the boy with respect. The boy's face was no longer the face of a boy. His hair had been shaved from his head. He was barefoot. The rifle in his arms was shiny and new and his eyes caught some of the luster from the barrel.

He ran right into Jules's arms and seemed to be handing the rifle to him. He clutched at Jules's waist and thighs, falling, and only now did Jules see that he was bleeding from a wound in the back. He fell. Jules lifted the gun clear. The boy clawed at Jules's ankles and Jules cried, "Where did they get you? Somebody call an ambulance!" The boy lay still. Jules stepped aside, looking down at him. Women ran over. "How'd he get himself shot in the back, this little boy?" a woman cried. Jules inched away from them. The boy did not move. Jules liked the feel of this gun, this gift.

"Somebody call an ambulance, an ambulance!" the women cried, taking up Jules's cry, pushing him aside.

Jules escaped. He had been hearing rifle fire for some time without knowing exactly what it was, and now he heard it everywhere. It was getting dark. Someone had shot out the street lights. A car approached him with its head-lights on and Jules ducked into a doorway, clutching the gun. Not a police cruiser, an ordinary car. The headlights jerked over him and someone yelled, "It's a white man! Hey! You want a lift!"

"I could use a lift, great," Jules said.

"Then get in! Get in!"

It was a carload of Kentucky boys, drunk and very friendly. They all had rifles like Jules's. A girl was in the back, complaining about something. "Take the John Lodge, you bastards! I want to go to Saks Fifth Avenue!" she cried. Jules squeezed into the back seat. They made room for him. He sat beside a boy of about nineteen with a fair, hollow face. The boy smelled of whisky. "How do you get there?" the driver cried.

"Take the next street to the right," said Jules, glad to be helpful, using this to wedge himself in.

Everyone was pleased. They passed him a bottle. "First we stop at Saks, then we go right down to Hudson's!" cried the girl.

"The hell, we're going out to Metro. Gonna hijack our-selves a plane!"

"You hijackin' what? You never flew no plane!"

"You get the pilots to fly them, stupid! Hijackin' a plane means taking' the whole load, pilots and passengers and all that."

"What the hell you gonna do with all them?"

"I got my plans."

Rushing out toward the expressway . . . the streets were dark, street lights shot out . . . broken glass on the streets. The boys fired at random into houses. Block after block of houses were darkened. The lights of one house were still on, and three boys shot the windows out. "That'll show that smart-aleck!" they cried.

There was a police barricade by the hospital, so they

made a wild U-turn in the street, heading somewhere else now, just as fast. Jules heard machine-gun fire. He had only heard it before in movies and it did not seem to him very real or dangerous. The girl slapped the neck of the driver, screaming at him. She was very young, with a streaked, puffy face and no lipstick; her lipstick had been smeared off onto her face. She was very drunk. Something struck one of the car windows and a sliver of glass flew into Jules's cheek. Surprised, he took it out at once, drawing it out. He tossed it out the window. The boy beside him laughed. Jules sucked at his cheek as if trying to suck the rushing blood back in, to stop it.

The car was going too fast. It began to shake. One of their lights was out, shot out or smashed. Jules raised his rifle and sighted it on windows along the street. What if his gun failed him? Where would he get another gun for the night? If it failed he would fall back into his lethargy of many months, of a lifetime. The boys in the car were very noisy and excited. Jules felt drawn to them; the swerving and jostling of the car actually threw him against them.

The girl shrieked. "Look at that! Look! Some soldiers!" she cried.

"What the hell!"

A troop carrier was crossing an intersection up ahead, its lights off. Jules could see soldiers with bayonets fixed to their rifles standing on the carrier, looking right down the street toward this car. "You better turn off your light," Jules said.

The driver switched off his light.

"Jesus, they got the Army out! I'm goin' in the Army myself!" one of the boys cried.

The driver did not slow down. Curious and wild, he bore on toward the intersection, and Jules, dazed with their jokes, did not even think to duck. But the carrier continued up the street.

Now they were approaching some fires—sirens and gun-fire and small muffled explosions. "The Fourth of July!" said the girl. One of the boys fired at a burning building. Farther up the block, police and soldiers were standing in a ring around a firetruck.

"Noel, you hadn't better take them all on!" someone said.

The driver turned off. "I'm just tryin' to find that goddam expressway in the dark, that's all I'm tryin' to do, with every goddam light in the city shot out," he said. A series of bullets struck the car, like rain.

No serious damage.

"Is that niggers or police shooting?" someone asked.

The boys fired out into the street, at burning buildings or at buildings not burning but clearly deserted. A Negro ducked into an alleyway. They all fired. "Got that one!" they cried. But it was too late to be sure, the car was going too fast. It ran over something in the street and the jolting knocked most of the window out, next to Jules. A jagged strip of glass remained. Jules kept getting thrown against it, his elbow going into it. He felt a sharp stinging pain that disappeared and came back again, again and again. The bouncing of the car restored his good humor. The boys were talking now about a friend who was in jail at Dehoco. They were talking about breaking him out, their voices explosive, ringing, intoxicated.

Jules felt blood running down his face. Blood. He thought of blood. He thought of two girls in his childhood, twins, who had been stabbed to death along a city block, one of them struck down in front of her house and the other chased and stabbed, so that blood ran in thin streams along the sidewalk, and the next morning everyone had come out to look at the blood . . . the Hecht twins . . . blood. Jules's own blood, pounding in his ears. In the frenzied pounding of his blood he felt something heavy emerging, a solid, violent certainty. He felt obliterated by it. The car rushed along in a hot, smoky darkness, heading toward more darkness, and Jules felt now only a stonelike certainty in its rocking motions and the shouts of the boys and his own ripeness.

"Jesus, look out!"

They swerved to avoid something in the street—a man lying on his back, a body. A bass fiddle lay beside him.

They swerved onto another street: ahead a knot of firefighters and police . . . a barricade set up in the street. . . . "Jesus, I ain't turnin' off any more times! I had it for the night!" the driver said.

They shouted at him, "Noel! You dumb bastard! You turn off here!"

But he did not turn off, he shook his head angrily and headed right for the barricade, limping on one flattening tire. Jules saw a policeman raise a rifle. He ducked. Someone in the car shot . . . a series of shots. . . . Jules was blinded by flying glass.

"Noel, you bastard! Now look!" someone cried.

The car jumped sideways. Brakes screeched. They were on the sidewalk now—now they had crashed into something. A tremendous thud. Jules's hands flat over his head, his body out of control. He was knocked against the front seat. His chest seemed to cave in. Then, breathing again, he fell against a car door and it opened—Jules outside now, safe on the sidewalk?—the rifle fell out with him. A rifle. Still falling he got himself right, he made his legs work, he grabbed the rifle and ran like hell. He heard gunshots.

The wild ride had given him strength. He ran nearly doubled over, his hands raised, the gun raised in front of him. He was in an alley . . . down a street somewhere, an unknown street . . . lights from fires glowed against the walls. . . . Running, he could not stop running! Was this Jules after all, running like this, sprung out of a smashed car and on his own, like a soldier with his rifle? A bullet whined past him. He jumped to the side, then smashed out what remained of a store window and climbed inside, stumbling. "My God!" he cried aloud.

A florist's shop. Skidding on broken glass, Jules with a gun. Smashed flowers, a smashed refrigerating unit, stinking up the flowers, everything broken and ground underfoot. The cash register had been knocked over. Jules ducked and behind him, through the broken window, came the man who had shot at him. He was a policeman, a stranger, yelling at Jules. Why did he yell? Why that strange hopping anger to him, his big face twisted with an emotion Jules could not understand?—he was a man of middle-age, ordinary, a stranger yelling so personally at Jules, raising the butt of his rifle to smash Jules on the head. Jules jumped sideways. He brought his own rifle around and hit the man on the shoulder, a glancing blow, and then managed to hit him again, in the face. Yelling, the policeman seemed to fall upon him, clinging to him, and Jules scrambled backward in the broken glass, panting, crying out, "My God, give me a chance— Let me get out the back door, will you?" The policeman's rifle was tangled in Jules's legs. Jules kicked it aside. With a sudden explosion of strength he grabbed the man's neck and wrenched him around; the man slid on the glass and fell heavily. Jules snatched up his own gun again. The man would not stop yelling. Now he was lunging for Jules's legs, and Jules had no choice but to smash him in the face . . . and this time he felt the gristle of the man's nose breaking. . . .

Having done this he had done everything. It was over. His blood ran wild, he was not to blame for anything, why should he stop? He aimed the rifle into the man's face and pulled the trigger.

8

On the second day of the looting, after watching television with a friend—her own set had broken down long ago—Loretta dared everything and went out. She had watched television until she could stand it no longer. The Mayor's report, the Governor's report, the President's report, the newsreels, the constant, excited pulsebeat of news, pictures, words—were too much for her. She could stand it no longer. She went a few blocks to a smashed store and looked around, and in the rubble at the back she found a portable television set. A few Negroes were milling around. A Negro man asked her politely if she wanted help carrying the television set to her car, but she told him she hadn't any car. She lived right nearby.

As soon as she got the set home she began to worry. It did not work. She read a small shiny piece of cardboard, shaped in a sunburst pattern, that said GUARANTEE on it but it did not say how to get rid of the violent zigzagging lines on the screen. So she sat staring at the useless screen, feeling sick. That night her own building caught fire. Someone threw a firebomb into it, into the front hall. In the commotion Loretta was knocked down and her leg bruised, but she managed to get out. The television set and everything she owned were burned up.

With a weak, sobbing crowd of people she was herded up to the Fisher YMCA. They fed her, they gave her a blanket. She sat in silence for a while, thinking of the television set and of how she had been punished for stealing it, then the memory faded as her interest in this place grew. She fell into conversation with a fat Negro woman, both of them anxious to be friendly, to prove something. The woman wept and moaned over her seven kids. Where were those kids in all this mess? Those brats—always running around, always getting into trouble! "And what we need with a blanket, with this weather? Jesus God, but it near to ninety again, ninety-five!" The woman wept.

Loretta fell into conversation with a kindly, bald, amazed man who said he worked in the Post Office, sorting mail. His name was Harold. His house had been burned down on the first day, the first house in his block. Why had they singled him out? Was it on purpose? "I was always nice to colored. Lots of colored boys work at the Post Office, I was always real nice to them," he told Loretta earnestly. He had owned that house clear but about three years, he told Loretta; he'd been paying a mortgage on it for fifteen years. His wife had died in that house. In the back bedroom. Loretta asked him gently if he had any children. "Yes, four children, gone in all directions," he said mournfully. This touched her oddly.

"What about you, do you have any children?" he said.

"They're gone in all directions too," she said. She hadn't any idea where Ran was even. He could take care of himself.

Loretta sat back and watched. She observed keenly that certain people did not break down but appeared, instead, as if they were only waiting somewhere. They might have been in a train station, certain of their destination. Some whites, some Negroes, had this dignity. She decided that she would have dignity: she was fed up with her life. She talked to the man from the Post Office, Harold, with cheerful dignity. "The important thing is you weren't killed or hurt. I look at it that way," she told him. He considered her words, as if they were profound. As time went on Loretta began to feel restored, curious. She was sorry she hadn't been wearing a better dress when the bomb had been thrown in the front hall.

This place had the air of a carnival that had gotten stuck. Too long in one place. What were so many strangers doing together, so patiently together? Loretta helped a young white girl with a baby, changing its filthy clothes. She followed one of the nurses around and helped. Maybe she should become a nurse herself—go to school somewhere, get training, and become a nurse herself? Nurses were respected, they had dignity and value. She helped with some of the smaller children, though their bawling annoyed her. The children were very jumpy here; some of them were hysterical; they couldn't be quieted but had to cry themselves limp. Then they slept, limp. Loretta was reminded of her own babies. She thought with a rush of warmth of Jules and

Maureen and Betty and Ran, as babies, helpless infants. She had loved them most at that time in their lives. It had been possible to love them deeply then. Now, run off in all directions, stubborn and lost, they did not seem to be her children really. It was a peculiar thing to have children, almost a riddle. Maybe her mistake had been that she had failed to have the right children. Maybe, between Jules and Maureen, there was to have been a wonderful son, Jules's brains and Maureen's sweetness, but she had failed, it hadn't come off. Or the long wait between Betty and Ran, maybe that was a mistake, maybe the right child had been meant for that time, and she hadn't had it, she had failed, the time was past and she would never have another child again in her life.

"Children are hell but it makes you sad to think you can't have any more," she told Harold.

He nodded painfully.

"It makes me feel more alone to think I had kids, and they went off," she said. She spoke with dignity, slowly, choosing her words. All the television broadcasts had made her conscious of words; she might have been speaking on television. "But I think, what the hell, everybody is alone. That's the secret, everybody is alone and can't help it, like right here and now, in this place, everybody is alone and they'd all get up and walk out if they could and never see each other again. We're all like that."

"Is that really true?" the man asked in anguish.

He raised his head to stare at her. Behind his glasses his eyes were watery and perplexed, without dignity. There were creases of dirt on his neck.

They were both sent to the same house, on the far northwest side of the city. A family had opened its home to five "riot victims." Loretta was shy and gracious, feeling herself singled out, a guest. She helped to serve food and to clean up afterward. She talked with everyone, remembering to talk slowly. Nobody believed she was almost a grandmother—but it was true, it was true, she was almost a grandmother. "It won't be long for my daughter now," she said. Then, anticipating their questions, she said, "No, she's real safe in Dearborn. Lucky for her." So she couldn't complain about losing her apartment and things, it was all she wanted to stay alive and see that grandchild; she thanked God she had been allowed to live for *that*.

The house in which they stayed for three days was a large

brick home with a front hallway and two fireplaces. Loretta admired it covertly. She thought the lady of the house—an angular, thin, nervous woman involved in church work—was very elegant even when she wore slacks, always a lady, never condescending. She wore a large diamond on her finger. In fact, the lady seemed shy and hopeful when she talked with her "guests," especially her colored guests, as if opening herself to judgment by them. She spoke repeatedly of the "spirit of the times." She spoke of the tragedy of the ghetto, of the crime of the slumlords; she wore her hair cut short, she shook her head often, agreeing or disagreeing, making herself heard. Her husband wore glasses and was said to be a dental surgeon. Loretta had never heard this term before. She thought the two of them were a wonderful couple, living in so wonderful a home, eager to whip up batter for thirty pancakes at a minute's notice, and very generous with towels.

This far out, it was safe to go for walks. She and Harold walked out often, in no hurry, taking in the sights. Police cars were always passing on Seven Mile Road. Carriers with troops in them were parked at the curb, and National Guardsmen, looking like boys, watched Loretta and Harold pass solemnly, sadly—were they thinking of their own parents, in other parts of the state? Some Guardsmen were assigned to guard buildings. They had to stand for hours, with their rifles out, and Loretta felt very sorry for them. Everywhere she looked there were police, police cars, soldiers, but the activity was slowed down, unexcited. The excitement was in another part of the city.

On Thursday evening everyone watched television, a local show on WDET-TV, broadcast by Wayne State University. They sat in a room off the living-room, with paneled walls. Loretta had never seen walls like this before. The program dealt with the riot. Loretta was sitting beside her friend from the Post Office, who always gravitated toward her, with his sweet, amazed, kindly look, and the lady of the house sat on the floor, with her bony wrists crossed at her knees, wearing slacks. Loretta was very happy just to be here, in this room, this lovely room, with all these people! Everyone tried so hard to be kind. The two Negro women in the group tried especially hard to be kind; they hardly spoke, and when they spoke it was only in very soft, apologetic voices. Loretta was so pleased with her new life that for a few minutes she did not pay much attention to the program. It had no real interest for her—newsreels of the riot, the smoke-filled streets, the broken shops, the carriers of soldiers, and the monotonous shots of tanks and Army paratroopers had been run and rerun, constantly, and these had wearied her; but programs that were all talk wearied her more.

There had been many discussion programs since the beginning of the riot, as soon as it was decided that it was a "riot." And a priest, a handsome, graying man, a friend of the family, had led them all in after-dinner discussions here at the house, his coffee cup in his hand, very eloquent and earnest. The television program was all talk, jerky and unrehearsed. A man was asking other men their opinions. On and on went the opinions! *A grave and tragic time for white America . . . The sins of the fathers . . . oppression . . . evil . . . discrimination . . .*

"And now, let us turn to Dr. Piercy," the moderator said. "Dr. Piercy, many of us are familiar with your stand on race relations here in Detroit, but would you care to explain to our audience once more. Dr. Piercy is the new head of the United Action Against Poverty Program in Detroit, a very high-voltage, well-financed adjunct of the Federal Poverty Program, and an Assistant Professor of Sociology at Wayne State University . . ."

Dr. Piercy had the look of a man whose glasses had been snatched off his face. His eyes were pale and hollow, his face was fixed in a squint. "Everything is going to have to be leveled," he said in a wild and yet polite manner, and the moderator smiled blandly at him and at the television audience. "I'm sorry to say this, but the truth must be told." Loretta could tell, though she wasn't paying much attention to his words, that he was from a good family. He kept reaching up with one hand to steady his glasses, though he was wearing no glasses. Loretta wondered if they had been broken in the riot. "I have been in rat-infested buildings, in filthy rooms where fifteen or more people live and sleep, and I *know*," he said, his eyes jumping about, "I *know* that our society must be leveled before a new, beautiful, peaceful society can be erected. This means the end of the world as we have known it, we middle-class whites, but it must be realized, it must be acknowledged, and we ourselves must work to attain it—or go down in history on the side of the Hitlers and Stalins, the oppressors of mankind, involved at this very moment in a bloody war to put down a revolution in Vietnam—"

"Excuse me, Dr. Piercy, and do your co-workers feel the same way? May we hear from your co-workers?"

The camera moved to show a young Negro dressed in a suit, but this must have been a mistake—the Negro shook his head, frightened, to indicate that he wasn't one of the co-workers. The camera turned onto another man, a white man, dark-haired and pale, leaner and sharper than Dr. Piercy.

Loretta stared. This man was her own son, Jules! "My God," she whispered.

Jules was wearing a dark shirt and no tie, no coat. Why couldn't he have borrowed a coat? Loretta's face went hot with blood, ashamed. She dug her nails into her flesh.

"Yes, I'm new on this committee," Jules said in response to a question, clearing his throat, speaking too loud. "Dr. Piercy has just appointed me . . ."

Why was he speaking so loud? And there was something on the side of his face—a long scratch. It looked absurd. Loretta wanted to jump up and turn off the television set.

"Mr. Wendall, your view of the immediate future? What does this spell for America?"

"Everything in America is coming alive. It's breaking out and coming alive," Jules said eagerly. He had a pleasant face, a handsome though battered face, but there was something unfocused about it. His rapid, hoarse voice ran on with the urgency of someone speaking in a strong wind. Loretta closed her eyes. Her heart was hammering in misery.

"I would like to explain to everyone how necessary the fires are, and people in the streets, not as Mort says here—Dr. Piercy—so that things can be built up again, black and white living together, no, or black living by itself, by themselves—no, that has no importance, that is something for the newspapers or the insurance companies. It is only necessary to understand that fire burns and does its duty, perpetually, and the fires will never be put out—"

"Excuse me, Mr. Wentwell, are you saying—did you say —*fire burns and does its duty?*"

Loretta opened her eyes, she couldn't help it. Her son was leaning forward toward the camera. Beside him Dr. Piercy sat, uncomfortable in his chair, wiping his face nervously and glancing sideways at Jules.

"Violence can't be singled out from an ordinary day!"

Jules cried. "Everyone must live through it again and again, there's no end to it, no land to get to, no clearing in the midst of the cities—who wants parks in the midst of the cities!—parks won't burn!"

"Thank you, Mr. Wentwell," the moderator said, "and now . . ."

Though the camera moved away Jules kept talking. "It won't hurt," his voice was saying earnestly. "The rapist and his victim rise up from rubble, eventually, at dawn, and brush themselves off and go down the street to a diner. Believe me, passion can't endure! It will come back again and again but it can't endure!"

The camera moved on jerkily. The moderator singled out another man, an older man with a turned-around collar. Loretta sat in a hot daze, unable to move. Where was her son? Even his voice had been cut off, someone else was talking now, someone else had taken over. What had happened to Jules? Why had he said such crazy things? She was ashamed of him. She remembered him burning down a barn, as a child. She remembered him pushing through a crowd to stare at a burning plane. *Why, he's a murderer!* She thought clearly, *He is a murderer,* and she had given birth to a murderer. A man with the turned-around collar, an Anglican priest, was speaking in a solemn, clear voice. ". . . the misfortunes of history we must not give in to, nor must we, dare we, give in to despair. I cannot agree with our young friend here that this is on its way and will change us all, or whatever he meant. I must admit that I cannot understand him. I'm of an older generation. My total commitment is for education, enormously enlarged funds for education and the cleaning-up of slums, in order to bring about a new America for all our children . . ."

Loretta began to weep. Everyone turned to her, surprised. She put her hands to her face, weeping. The lady of the house scrambled to her feet and cried, "What's wrong? Please don't cry, what's wrong? Let us help you . . ."

Loretta stood. She wept but with dignity; she was conscious of herself being watched, stared at. Why was she crying? What good did it do? *Jesus Christ, this is a waste,* she thought. *Why should I cry over him?* The lady led her out of the room, into a hallway bathroom. But still she could not stop crying.

9

Maureen answered the doorbell one evening in early August and there he stood, Jules himself. She was carrying a magazine she'd been reading; she tried to put the magazine down somewhere but couldn't think where to put it. She stood staring at Jules and could think of nothing to say.

"Well, what's wrong? Are you surprised I found out your address?" he said.

"Jules, my God—"

"Can't I come in? Just for a minute?"

She stared at him. Now that she was married and living out of the city, in an apartment building, she rarely thought of her family and never expected to see them. Even Jules. Her husband had asked her, seeing this name *Jules Wendall* in the newspaper, whether that was her brother Jules, and she had said no, that wasn't her brother, not him. And now, seeing Jules, she felt a little sick.

"Is your husband home?"

"No, he's teaching night school."

"Why are you looking at me like that?"

"It's such a surprise to see you."

"Do I look bad?"

"No, you don't look bad."

But she felt really sickened, not by his face or his presence but by her own presence, so close to him, her own existence so closely tied to his; she stepped out into the hall and closed the door behind her. "We can talk out here. Please. What . . . what did you want?"

"Can't I stay around and meet your husband?"

"He won't be home for a long time."

"Maureen, you look so pale, you look terrible. Is this because of me? You don't want to see me? Why not?"

"I . . . I . . . I want to see you . . ." she stammered and was silent.

Jules reached over to look at the cover of her magazine, as if it might be a clue to her silence: it was a glossy picture of a pie topped with whipped cream.

"What's wrong?" he said.

"Nothing."

"Your marriage is very secret, huh? I was over to say good-by to Ma—I'm going away—and she was complaining about you, you not calling, she's worried about you and all that. Why didn't you call her, Maureen? She went through an awful lot, being burned out. Even Betty stopped around to see if she could help. Ma's staying with some friend of hers, named Ethel, she's doing all right—she's maybe going to get married again, did she tell you?"

"I heard something about it," Maureen said with distaste.

"But aren't you interested?"

She looked sideways at her brother. He wore a dark pullover shirt and dark slacks. He had the air of a successful thief. His very being, so close to her, was a terrible burden.

"Aren't you interested?" he asked.

"I love Ma and all of them, you know that, Jules, but I have my own life to live now and I've got to . . . I've got to live it. . . ."

"Even Betty came by and gave her a few dollars! It's the least you could do, give her some money or telephone her—"

"I have my own life to live."

"What's so hard about living?"

"Don't talk to me like that! You know! You know everything I know! Jules, please, could you leave now? I don't feel well. I feel sort of sick. We don't have any money, he has to pay child support and . . . and all that. We don't have enough money for ourselves—"

"All right."

"We're going to have a baby, we can't afford to give any money away—"

"All right, I'm leaving." Jules reached over and stroked her head.

Like a cat, sulky and slow, Maureen inclined her head toward him. They stood for a few seconds in silence. Then Jules said, "Mort got transferred to Los Angeles and he's taking me along with him. We've got a hundred-thousand-dollar budget to take care of. Outside is my car—I've already bought a car for the trip, with air-conditioning. And once I get on my feet out there I'm going to go into business of some kind. I can make good contacts, through the government. I might go into real estate, something solid."

"But in the paper it sounded like you were a Communist. Didn't somebody say you were a Communist and want you fired?"

"A Communist! So what? I don't know what a Communist is!" Jules laughed. "I'm not anything. I'm just trying to get along. My boss, Mort, Dr. Piercy, is really crazy, he's out of his mind. Some black kids beat him up last Tuesday—he was out with a police patrol and asking questions, and the police wouldn't do a thing to stop it. The funniest thing, *funny* . . . his glasses got broken for the second time, and he only got the job because the head of the committee had a nervous breakdown. He got me on the committee because he likes me. He has a certain idea about me, about my life. He say he'd like to write my life up, as a case history, but I said *What the hell?* Everything that happened to me before this is nothing—it doesn't exist! —my life is only beginning now. So I'm on my way to California and I don't mean to upset you, I just came over to say good-by. I understand that you might not want your husband to meet me, though really, kid, I'm not as bad as some of our family."

"Jules, I didn't mean that!" Maureen said. "You're a wonderful man, you were a wonderful brother to me, and I love you. I will always remember you—taking care of me, your letters when I was sick, all of that, what we had to live through together, but . . . but I want it over with, I'm through with it, all I have to remember of it is nightmares once in a while. I can take that, bad dreams. If that's the worst it is I can take it."

"I understand."

"And we don't have enough money now for ourselves. I . . . I'd give her some money if we had it, but . . . Jules, I don't want to remember any of it! A few bad dreams, that's all, nothing more . . . please. I wake up sweating and next to *this man*, a man I don't know, I mean I don't remember if it's my husband or not or some other man, someone who picked me up. I can't go through it any more, Jules, I'm finished. I'm going to forget everything and everybody. I'm going to have a baby. I'm a different person."

"Do you love your husband?"

"I'm going to have a baby, I'm a different person."

"What about Ma and the others?"

"What others?"

"Oh, you know, all of them—Ma and her brother, if he ever shows up, and Betty, and Connie, and Ma's crazy friends—"

"I guess I'm not going to see them any more."

Jules gave the back of her neck an affectionate squeeze. He seemed really quite joyful, a Jules she recalled from years ago, light on his feet and filled with surprises.

"But, honey, aren't you one of *them* yourself?"

She did not answer.

She had led him to the stairway, back to the stairway. Why didn't he leave! With one hand he reached out to touch the railing of the stairwell—it was plastic—and she saw how wobbly it was, ready to fall off if someone bumped against it. Thoughtfully, Jules drew his hand away. He said in a low, murmurous, almost ardent voice, "Sweetheart, I understand. I love you too. I'll always think of you, and maybe when I've done better, gotten on my feet, when I come back here and get married—I want to marry her anyway, that woman, the one who tried to kill me, I still love her and I'll make some money and come back and marry her, wait and see—when I come back, a little better off, we can see each other. All right? I love you for being such a sweet sister and suffering so much and getting out of it, using your head, but don't forget that this place here can burn down too. Men can come back in your life, Maureen, they can beat you up again and force your knees apart, why not? There's so much of it in the world, so much semen, so many men! Can't it happen? Won't it happen? Wouldn't you really want it to happen?"

"No!"

"Maureen, really? Tell me."

"No, never. Never."

He stood looking down at her. She pressed her hands against her ears. She was going to have a baby, she was heavy with pregnancy, but sure-footed, pretty, clean, married. She did not look at him.

"Well, I don't want to make life harder than it should be," Jules said.

He took his sister's hand and kissed it and said good-by, making an ironic, affectionate bow over her with his head: it was the Jules she had always loved, and now she loved him for going away, saying good-by, leaving her forever.